HEATHER AND HEATH

For Betty - Mum's long-time friend.
Best wishes from Sally.

HEATHER AND HEATH

SALLY ODGERS

Sally Odgers.

Mum read this in manuscript. It was her favourite.

SATALYTE PUBLISHING

VICTORIA, AUSTRALIA

First published in Australia in 2015
This edition published in 2015
By Satalyte Publishing
ABN 50 145 650 577
satalyte.com.au

ISBN: 978-0-9925580-9-3 (Paperback)
978-0-9942285-0-5 (eBook)

Editor : Alyssa Wickramasinghe

Satalyte Publishing

6 Reserve Street, Foster VIC 3960, Australia

To the settlers without whom this book would never have been written.

Contents

Part One: NESS - 1837-1839

PART TWO: ISOBEL - 1860-1885

PART THREE: ALICE - 1913-1920

PART ONE: NESS - 1837-1839

CHAPTER 1

It had been late summer when the *May Queen* left the dock and now, a bare seventeen weeks later, it was summer again; a summer in December, while the loch-side at home would soon be mantled with snow. The herds would be keeping their sheep close, while the heather grew dim in the glens and up the brae.

Ness McCleod tamped homesickness as her father had tamped tobacco in his pipe. No more Scottish winters for her, and it was just as well. Loch Haven was no longer home; not with Phemie wed again to Lachie Douglas. The thought was distressing, and Ness spared a thought for Phemie's son Donal, whose mother had turned against him to flatter the Douglas. Donal was no blood kin to Ness, but, living under Phemie's tawse-enforced rule had made them closer than kin in their misfortunes. Phemie scorned her son and stepdaughter impartially for weakness and punished them impartially for rebellion, and after Lachie came calling, Donal had seen the future and left the loch at the beginning of the brief Scottish summer.

Ness would have gone with him, had he asked, but Donal left in a rage and took a berth on a brigantine bound for New Zealand, where he hoped to join a deep sea whaler in the Bay of Islands.

The romance of it enchanted Ness, and she pored over a book she had borrowed from the dominie in the village, picturing splendours of sand and sun, palm trees with clusters of nuts and fruit hanging down for the gathering, and smiling dusky natives with strange patterns on their skin. And the whales! Would they come close to the shore, blowing their spumes of air and foam high up like a waterspout? Would they gape their jaws and swallow up their hunters as the whale had swallowed up Jonah in the old story? When she returned the book to the dominie, Ness met the minister's sister at the door. Jean Leslie was a person of indeterminate age between thirty and forty, and she greeted Ness with pleasure and invited her to take a glass of milk in the manse.

'It's bonnie to have this chance of seeing you, hen,' said Jean, as they sat crumbling their oat cakes, 'for I shall soon be awa' on the ship.'

Everyone was leaving her, thought Ness with sudden desolation. First her father had died of the coughing sickness, then Donal had gone to be a whaler. And now Jean was going who knew where… 'But why?' Ness asked, dazed.

Jean laughed. 'My brother is taking a wife,' she said simply. 'She's a bonnie wee jo, but aye soft in her words and none too steady in her opinions. If I stay on there will be trouble and it will not be of her making. It is best I leave for it is daft to have two women in the one kitchen when one o' them's twice the age o' the other.'

Ness had to admit the sense of that. 'Where will you go, Jean?'

'I have a fancy to sail to New South Wales, hen. Free women of education and respectable manners are welcome there, and they offer money for passages to the colony.'

Ness was silent, shaken. It was such a long way for Jean: as far as Donal had gone.

'Yon Phemie is to wed Lachie Douglas, then?' said Jean, as if it were a natural turn to the conversation.

'Aye, it seems so,' said Ness with a sigh.

Jean sighed too, but there was a humorous glint in her small grey eyes. 'It is the way of the world, is it no? One wifie marries three men one after 'tother and another can no find a one to take her?'

'Is that why—' Ness caught herself up, flushing with confusion.

'Aye,' said Jean, reflectively. 'I am thinking if I can no find a braw man in New South Wales, I may well die wondering.'

Ness laughed, amused at Jean's frankness, but after her return to Loch Haven she found her mind often on her friend's plans. With Phemie set to wed Lachie Douglas in the autumn, and queening it at home, Ness was soon so unhappy that she stole away back to the manse.

Jean seemed unsurprised at the visit. 'I was looking to see you again before I leave, hen,' she said.

'Might I come with you, mysel'?' Ness was aghast at her own daring, but she knew her alternatives were limited. She could stay at Loch Haven as a drudge, she could go into service, she could marry a local laddie (if he would overlook her lack of portion) or she could cast in her lot with Jean and travel to a new land. A new land… oh, she loved her Scotland, but it had not been kind to her. The world beckoned with unknown promise. She would never have gone alone. It was not, she told herself, that she lacked courage. It was just that she lacked funds and worldliness. If she went with Jean, she would have a friend at least.

'I would serve you as a maid,' she said hesitantly, for she knew it would be her friend's charity that must pay her fare to the docks.

'Aye, that you could,' agreed Jean, 'and gi' me a great conceit o' mysel'!' She looked steadily at Ness. 'Mind, hen, I canna promise anything but hard work, but there's payment for your passage. It will aye be an adventure, and summer's the time for beginnings.'

'Aye!' Ness held out her small work-hardened hands and grasped Jean's bony ones. 'Aye! That it will!'

'Then be off wi' ye to pack your bundle,' said Jean, smiling as she let go of Ness' hands. 'Stow it safely and be ready. I'll send word as soon as I'm able.'

'But what o' Phemie?' faltered Ness. 'She might take the message.'

'Ye must tell yon Phemie where you're bound,' said Jean. 'She'll no' cut up but it would be unkind to leave her to wonder.'

'Aye,' said Ness. She cared little for Phemie but quite a deal for Jean, so she set off for Loch Haven with a determined step.

The future, once drab and narrow, suddenly opened up.

Phemie seemed glad enough to have her stepdaughter leave the glen. Her only concern was what folk might think with Ness following so close on Donal's heels. 'Ye'll have no joy o' him, lassie,' she'd said. 'He couldna bid his ain mother goodbye.' She frowned. 'At least ye've the wit to go o' your own choosing. I tell ye plain, I'd not want ye in the house when I'm wed.'

'I'll no be seeing Donal,' Ness assured her. 'I'm to be awa' with Jean Leslie as her maid, and so you may tell any who ask. I'll work hard and she'll be good to me.'

Phemie shrugged. 'Go, then. I trust ye'll no' be disappointed in Mistress Leslie. You behave, mind. I willna have you back if you disgrace yoursel'.'

Two weeks later the longed-for word was brought round by the minister's stableman. After a joyless parting with Phemie, Ness travelled with Jean to London to board the assisted immigrant ship *May Queen*.

Ness did not look back, in case she should see the loch shining reproach in the sun. Along with her modest bundle, she carried two reminders of home; the silver brooch fashioned long ago for Granny McCleod in the likeness of white heather and her father's old plaid, stored in the kist since his passing. Callum had no need for it now, and Ness had no wish to leave it for Douglas.

Her first sight of the city did not please Ness. The stink in the streets and the unsavoury sights and sounds at the wharf sickened her, and she hid in her shawl to shut them out. As for the folk who hung about the port! Sailors, hawkers, fishmongers, pickpockets, thieves - Ness was thankful she had followed Jean's advice and pinned Granny McCleod's brooch out of sight on her stays, but the constant din of flat English voices and the appraising stares of gentlemen made her huddle into her summer shawl and keep her head low so her bonnet hid her face. Jean surmounted difficulties with the same firm decision she had employed with her brother's parishioners, and Ness followed as a lamb follows the ewe.

Now, on the brink of departure, she wished she had never left home. But what had there been for her at home? Phemie's grudging company and the prospect of watching Douglas benefit from Callum McCleod's hard work? Loch Haven was prospering finely - aye, Phemie had done a braw job, inheriting money from her first husband and land from her second to live in comfort with her third. Phemie had said she was not welcome there, so Ness could not look back with longing as she boarded the square-rigged barque and left her old world behind with the end of the northern summer. The *May Queen* filled her sails, pregnant with wind and hope.

And now it was summer again, and the hopeful voyage had turned into disaster. Jean was dead of the virulent fever, which had taken several of the passengers and crew at the last port, and now Ness faced the future, alone.

If she'd had the fare, she might have sailed home again. But there was no money for the fare, and no home in Scotland any more. She must remember that.

Phemie would never have her back, disgraced or not, and so there was nothing for it but to take whatever life might offer her here.

Following her pilot, the *May Queen* manoeuvred to the wharf. Wrapped in the old brown and yellow plaid, perspiring with heat and the uncertainty of the future, Ness huddled into a corner, keeping clear of the press of passengers and the scurry of crew as the ship settled at the dock. The *May Queen* was like some great bird that had finally come to land. Jean, a student of poetry and legends, had told Ness of the wandering albatross and how it flew forever over the ocean, sleeping on the wing, riding the winds as the ship rode the waves, and falling only into death.

Ness shivered, despite the prickle of heat.

The *May Queen* had come to rest, and she had made few friends among the passengers. Most were English, coming to take up life in the new world. What had they to do with a young Scotswoman whose reserve had led her to shun their company? In the rush to leave the ship, they swept past her, drawing children close, lugging bundles and straining towards the descending gangplank, anxious to set their feet on dry land once more.

Below decks the cargo of swine shuffled and squealed. Piglets born early in the voyage were now porkers - those that had survived. Some had been slaughtered and served to the passengers as slabs of boiled bacon, while others had died of a fever, like poor Jean.

The passengers were eager to set on the next stage of their journey. For some it would be a short jaunt into the ramshackle sprawl of Sydney Town, for others a much longer journey by bullock wagon or dray to the new land which lay around Port Phillip to the south, land that had been declared open for settlers by Governor Bourke only the previous year. Some were joining husbands and fathers already in the colony, and these women, tired and pink-faced, peered anxiously over the rail in search of familiar faces. Four months was a long time, and most of them had been effectively out of touch with their men for over a year. In a year much could happen; indifference could grow, or disease could strike, and some new arrivals would hear the stark news that the ones they had come to meet were ill or dead.

What of me? thought Ness distractedly. Jean is gone, poor wifie, but I am alive and what shall I do now?

As she waited to disembark, she hung back, hoping ridiculously that someone - anyone - would ask how she was situated, and might perhaps be compassionate enough to offer her work. She could sell the white heather brooch, but she knew it was old-fashioned in setting and form and might bring no more than a few coins. Cries of welcome rose from the docks, but none of the welcome was for her. She supposed she could send word back to Phemie. In any case,

Reverend Leslie must be told that his sister was gone, but a message would take half a year to be delivered, and another half year before she could hope for any response. Dear God, in a year she could be dead! And what would Phemie do, but say she had made her bed and must lie on it? If only she *had* followed Donal to New Zealand, she thought distractedly. He might have welcomed her, but Jean had been set on New South Wales.

Ness gave up her place by the gangplank repeatedly, and drew the plaid around her shoulders, still shivering in spite of the heat of this alien second summer. She had no plans at all.

CHAPTER 2

Hector Campbell was also wearing a plaid at the docks that day, but not for reasons of sentiment or security. At well over forty years of age, Hector had plenty of security, if it was counted in pecuniary terms. He had lived in New South Wales now for longer than he had graced his native Scotland, but he saw no reason to abandon the outward badge of his heritage any more than he saw reason to modify his thick brogue. Hector's acquaintances thought him strange; a man whose Highland name and archaic mode of dress ill-accorded with his position in the new society. Hector did not enlighten them. In his heart he *was* a Highlander, despite his father's insistence on plying a dull and worthy trade in Glasgow and his own myriad occupations in New South Wales.

He'd left Scotland in 1810, a discontented and vigorous young man who quarrelled with his father and brothers just as he was destined to quarrel with almost everyone else he met in life. Vowing he would never work for the tailor whom his father had paid to teach him a trade, he left Scotland with a defiant sovereign in his pocket and worked his passage to New South Wales as cook on a convict ship. He was no more suited to cooking than to cutting cloth for gentlemen, but the sailors, a tough bunch themselves, soon learnt not to tangle with the fiery Scots lad who was as quick to offer a dirk or a punch as he was to empty soaked hardtack over the heads of the plaintiffs. The convicts, poor devils, were grateful for anything they could get.

Perhaps Ewan Campbell was glad to be rid of his changeling son. Certainly the tailor pronounced him a laddie in need of a good skelping, but, since the "laddie" was his own height and almost his own breadth, he declined to deliver it himself.

Hector's mother might have wept at his going if she had not died of exhaustion before the boy was two years old. She might also have imbued him with much-needed softness of nature, and might perhaps have recognised something of herself in his restless search for the ideal. The chance of softening was lost, and so, raised by his dour, clutch-fisted father and ignored by his brothers, Hector grew thrawn as heather roots and hard as nails. His handsome aquiline face and flint-grey eyes attracted would-be friends, but his bitter scathing tongue and volcanic temper drove as many away. The dominie who set him to his lessons failed to gain his respect, just as the tailor did later. Without respect, Hector could not be brought to obey, and so, like a bad business debt, he was deemed better written off and forgotten. If his father thought of him at all in later years it was to praise the lord that his unruly youngest son had passed beyond his circle of concern.

On his arrival at the infant colony of New South Wales, Hector left the ship and joined a company of explorers and surveyors to press along the coast in search of harbours and fertile lands. He had a good eye and a steady hand and soon carved a niche for himself as a draftsman. Though his insistence on wearing the bold green Campbell plaid caused comment, he proved himself the equal of the other men. Clad in duck trousers, or in the tight breeches, coats and beaver hats that had constituted their riding costumes at home in England, his companions carried heavy blankets against the unexpectedly chill nights. Hector, splendidly unburdened, simply unbelted his plaid and rolled himself in its folds, striding on ahead in the mornings as rested as if he newly risen from a good feather bed. His habit of snatching sleep whenever the chance presented itself, and of eating whatever came to hand, made him the envy of the older men. "Trying it on the Highlander" became something of a game whenever they snared some new and curious animal for the pot.

Hector's hearty appetite for new sights and experiences remained unquenched. By the time he was twenty-five, he had gone through a dozen occupations, made few lasting friendships and several enemies. Having achieved each goal, he moved on restlessly to the next novelty. He then claimed a piece of good land, worked it with his own strength and sweat and cannily sold it to a new arrival at a handsome profit. He used the proceeds to buy more land, which he developed and sold once more. The cut timber he had cured and stacked for building, and by the end of 1827, he had taken delivery of some of the new Hereford cattle, which he fattened and bred, doubling his money again. Next, he started a tannery, where he produced good leather from the hides of slaughtered beasts as well as from the strange creatures familiarly known as kangaroos.

By then, the wayward lad had changed so much that his own

father would have been hard-put to recognise him. His tall, rather gangling figure had toughened and broadened, the handsome face had hardened, and, with the addition of a broken nose, no longer attracted admiring glances, except from the half-bred sheepdog he acquired in part payment for a debt.

Since he scorned to wear a hat, his fair Scottish skin tanned to the colour of old parchment and his hair, cut infrequently, grew over his collar and down his cheeks in exuberant waves. Beneath his heavy brows the grey eyes still looked out with vivid enquiry, but now their impact was even greater when contrasted to the stillness of the rest of his face; a visage which his enemies claimed could have been carved from a tombstone and would have been better under one. At something over thirty, he could have passed for forty-five, except when something fired either his temper or his interest, at which time he blazed with youthful ardour.

As he had in boyhood, Hector as a young man attracted friends and alienated them in the same breath. Many who mistook his flaring enthusiasms for generous volatility were shocked and surprised to find him closing a deal with a snap as final and almost as painful as the closure of a gin trap. An acquaintance that tried to cheat him woke next morning with a blinding headache and no memory of the rock-like fist that knocked him to the ground. A drunken convict servant found himself back in irons and professed himself glad to be safely out of the reach of the wild Scot.

For ten more years, Hector bought and traded goods, and built and sold businesses. It was then, in his forties, that it suddenly dawned on him that he was lonely. A vague feeling of discontent had hung round for years, but always before he shrugged it off as the natural frustration of a man surrounded by others whose vision fell short of his own. The culmination of a successful deal still brought a flush of achievement, but there was something missing. After some consideration, Hector knew what it was. He needed a companion.

He had lost his old dog to snakebite the winter before. Rather than see it suffer, Hector shot it cleanly through the head. At the time, he performed this service with the same cold precision he brought to any other necessary slaughter, but afterwards he was struck by a strange feeling of regret. He found he missed the old dog badly. He missed its unobtrusive company, he missed hurling his meat bones into the brush for it to discover, and he missed the excited whines and snuffles as it chased the odd little marsupials through its dreams. Most of all, he missed its adoration. With something of a start, he realised that he wanted to be liked. Not by the common run of settlers and convicts, but by someone who would be on hand in his quieter moments. He wanted someone who would appreciate his efforts. Someone like his dog, but possessed of a greater lifespan and fewer fleas.

The answer was obvious. He must find himself a wife.

The idea seemed so right that he felt some surprise that it had not occurred to him sooner. There had always been women, from the start. Even when males outnumbered females in the colony by four to one, Hector never had trouble finding a willing girl. He scoured his memory, but he recalled none whose charms had not soured with time. They were good for the moment, for the week, or, rarely, for a few months, but always his interest cooled. Most women were well enough under a blanket, but more than once he was tempted to gag one. It was not for fear of screams (for he had never taken the unwilling), but because of their never-failing fund of *talk*. Endearments or curses, pleas or commonplaces or praise were all the same to him. The perky Cockney voices, the rough profanity of the drabs, the insipid tones of the few ladies he had filched from dilatory swains or absent husbands; all palled quickly into active irritation. He felt like stuffing his ears with tufts of wool to shut out their incessant clack of tongues. Why, he often thought in baffled annoyance, could not the women be and let be? Why could they not be like his old dog Rob Roy, affectionate and dutiful and *quiet*?

Despite this drawback, Hector was quite determined to take a wife. Having determined on this course, he discovered something else to desire. He wanted bairns. He wanted a settled home. He had the money, and he had his health and strength. Now all he needed was a suitable property to buy and a suitable lassie to wed. The land would be easy enough. There were good tracts up for the purchase in Port Phillip and Van Diemen's Land. The lassie proved unexpectedly elusive. The young daughters of the settlers were dewy and unfinished, raw as unbaked dough and with no more flavour. Besides, the clever ones were afraid of him and the others were bland as buns. If he took a wife she need not bore him rigid.

Hector attended subscription balls in Sydney Town, but though he could dance reels and polkas with the best of them, he remained dissatisfied. The few ladies he found attractive were either wed already or would have nothing to do with him. Too many had brothers or fathers whom he had crossed or bettered in business. There were older women, friendly widows with children at foot already or spinsters on their last prayers. They were all civil to him, but Hector wanted a family from his own blood. He did not want other men's bairns at his table. He was also vain enough not to want a woman unsought by other men. Besides, he reasoned, for a woman to be single in a colony so short of eligible females argued some defect of form, face, health or temper. When acquiring livestock, land or a wife, it paid to take the very best quality one could afford.

Most of his dancing partners he found unsatisfactory. Some were silly, some were boring and some were so unnerved by his face and reputation that they eyed him as a rabbit eyes a stoat. When their hands met his in the dance, he found them unpleasantly soft, perspiration-damp or brittle as bundles of bone. His own hands, scarred and toughened as seasoned timber, quite swallowed those of his reluctant partners. He found himself opposed to the notion of proposing marriage to any of them.

It was a chance remark made by a brewer with whom he had some business that made Hector change his plans. There seemed no suitable women in Sydney Town, and he had too many enemies to settle comfortably there in any case. The year was uncommonly dry, and drought threatened, so it seemed sensible to move on. He toyed with the notion of immigrating to New Zealand, but he had little knowledge of that colony. There was always the Port Philip district, but that was surely over-run with settlers by now. Instead, he decided to take up land in the island colony of Van Diemen's Land, some six or seven hundred miles to the south. He wished he'd thought of it before, when there were still land grants to be had, but he refused to repine over things that could not be helped. He looked forward to a cooler, damper climate, where he could make his choice, develop a property, build a home at his leisure, and look about him for a suitable woman. There was little time to waste, so, late in 1837, Hector set about realising his assets. With the drought, his land brought less than he hoped, but as he had interests in the brewing trade and several others, he called in some mortgages. He emerged from this voluntary liquidating as a tolerably rich man. He secured property in the north of Van Diemen's Land, then, his portable possessions whittled down to a single set of clothes, a dirk, a double barrelled gun, a pistol, a cut-throat razor and a well-stuffed money pouch, he headed to the harbour to arrange his passage south. At the same time, he intended to inspect the latest cargoes brought in from Britain. If anything appealed, he might buy up goods on the docks and outfit a vessel of his own instead of buying a passage on someone else's. The goods could be traded in Launceston and with luck might turn a moderate profit. Then he could sell the vessel or keep it, put on a clever but unambitious captain and crew, and run some imports up and down the coast.

Scowling with thought, Hector tramped the wharf in his heavy boots, forging through the crowd as thoughtlessly as a Clydesdale might forge through a field of corn. He never shouldered folk aside, but they fell back with automatic courtesy as he passed. Not only did he dwarf them, but the swirl of his distinctive clothing made him look even larger and less civilised. The plaid he brought from Scotland as a young man had disintegrated long ago, but Hector, with typical determination, managed to secure another of similar pattern. The local weaver was stupefied at his demand for a Campbell tartan, but equal measures of bullying and money brought about the desired result. The cloth was not of the same quality, but it was the best that could be had until he could arrange the delivery of another from Scotland. Better yet, he would invest in some good wool sheep and have another created from his own fleece. Fine quality wool, he reflected, would never go out of style. It held rain, turned wind, and protected a man from frost.

An immigrant ship was in; the *May Queen* out of London. Assisted immigrants, he thought with a snort; folk whose passage was funded so they could come to take up work in New South Wales. To be sure the labour shortage was much discussed in the colony, but he had never had trouble finding servants, or of disposing of them either, if they proved unsuitable. The response to the immigrant scheme was less than the government hoped. Apparently few folk had the courage and vision to leave an old country and chance their arms in a new one. Hector paused with faint unconscious scorn as this new batch of Sassenachs came shambling down the gangplank. Innocent as new-hatched pigeons, he thought, aye ripe for plucking by any one shrewd enough to make the effort. He was not in the position to pluck them himself today, and he had other matters to settle, so he turned away from the ship.

On the verge of moving on, Hector stopped and sniffed the air. Above the usual stench of fish, salt and unwashed flesh, he detected another odour, warm and pungent and familiar. Swine. The ship was carrying swine, and these, if healthy and well-conditioned, might serve as his new venture in Van Diemen's Land. Swine and sheep might share a property, and bacon would bring in profit while the flock built up by natural means. Swine were entirely useful animals, if one discounted the squeal. Hector looked for the person in charge of the pigs, then, realising the livestock would not be unloaded until the passengers were all disembarked, he leaned against a bollard to wait.

Idly, he watched the female passengers descend. Some were alone, while others greeted husbands, some stoically, some with ill-concealed dismay, and a few with a light in their faces that transfigured plain features and made Hector blink with sudden envy. He wanted that light for himself. He had no wish for complaisance or tolerance, such as he saw on the faces of squatters' wives. He wanted this transfiguration, this warmth. A lassie whose eyes shone for him, whose arms reached for him by day as well as in the night and ... Och, get awa'! he thought impatiently. Wanting was of no account and what sweet lassie would smile for him without a guinea to sweeten the embrace? What he *needed* was a sensible body of good breeding, who would do as she was bid and produce healthy bairns.

Hector's thoughts broke off, for his gaze, in sweeping the passengers awaiting their turn to disembark, touched on something familiar. It could not be a face, for these settlers were strangers to him, and he had left Scotland before many of them were born. Scowling with surprise, Hector raked the crowded decks again and again, patiently, until he saw her.

She was a small, straight figure wrapped in a plaid. He could not see her face, for she wore a deep-crowned bonnet. The oval brim should have permitted a view of her features, but she seemed to stare rigidly down at the rough surface of the dock. The bonnet was untrimmed, and the ribbons that fastened it disappeared into the folds of the plaid. Hector's eyes burned as he strained to bring the figure into focus. Repeatedly, she was lost from view as others pushed past her. He had an impression of youth and stillness, but that was all.

The plaid that attracted his attention was not the green of the Campbells, but some earthy mixture of brown and yellow. Hector could not call the tartan's origin to mind, but he hardly cared. It was enough that its wearer was so obviously a fellow Scot. No Englishwoman would wear such a garment.

The possibilities of pigs were forgotten. Hector left the bollard and stepped up to the flank of the ship, and directed his gaze at the woman. 'Will you no be coming away down to me, lassie?' he called.

***

Ness remained at the rail, unwilling to take the final steps, which would land her irrevocably in a strange country. Beneath the encompassing folds of the plaid, she clutched her bundle in an old cloak bag containing all she had in the world. A spare sark, shawl and stockings, a calico apron, a dark woollen gown cut down from one of Phemie's, a limp little Bible, and a small money pouch, a brush and her grandmother's brooch comprised every last scrap of her baggage. Jean Leslie had packed a trunk of clothes, and Ness knew she would not have grudged them to Ness, but the ship's surgeon had been adamant. The belongings of the fever-dead must be tossed overboard in the wake of the shrouded bodies. He had not said why, and Ness suspected that a few items, including the sovereigns her patron carried, had not followed her body into the depths. She was nearly sure she had seen Jean's Sunday bonnet on the head of Miss Smithers. And her so rich already!

There was some stramash down below on the dock. A great voice roared out a greeting or curse; doubtless, thought Ness, the man was drink-taken. She was reminded of Alexander the boatman who had shamed her by baying under her window like a hound, until she emptied the dishpan over his ears. After that, he found that Loch Haven was willed to Phemie and never bothered her again. Ness blinked. Why should Alexander come to mind now? Doubtfully, she looked down, and among the crowd she saw something that turned her knees to porridge - a Scotsman in the green plaid of the Campbells! He was quite old, forty or more, for his shaggy black hair was touched with grey. He had a bent, high-bridged nose and remarkable eyes that burned like the flints beneath heavy brows. He was standing foursquare, staring up at the ship, with his arms lifted in welcome. Almost, she made a gesture to answer him, but she knew beyond doubt that he could not be calling *her*. Donal was the only man who would give *her* such welcome, and Donal was a small, sandy man, quite unlike this inky-haired giant who stood on the docks as unconcerned with the crowd as if they were trout in the loch.

She looked about to see who he could be hailing, but there seemed no one to answer him. How could that be? With such a man to call her, what woman would not reply?

'Lassie? Can you no come down?' The Scotsman was calling again. His voice was strong and resonant, but the accent was not like hers. The words were familiar, but the intonation was thicker and flatter, though it still fell with warmth on Ness' ears. She had heard no Scots voice since Jean sank into her final stupor. And finally, as the bright gaze caught and held hers, she accepted that the incredible had happened. He was hailing *her*. Someone in this place was pleased to welcome her.

Ness took a deep breath, her despair lifting. Leaning over the rail she looked down at the Scotsman and called an answer as strongly as she could; 'Aye, Campbell, that I can.'

He nodded, and she stood away from the rail and shuffled determinedly back into the queue. She lost sight of the Scotsman behind a plumed bonnet and several large bandboxes. Though she hurried as much as she could, it took almost half an hour before she made her way down the gangplank. It was quite long enough for her to recover from the madness and to reflect that, after all, the man was a stranger. Barring the fact that he came from the same country and harboured the same outmoded affection for the plaid, she knew nothing of him. He could be laird or ghillie, cotter or dominie, shipwright or thief. He could be wed with a dozen bairns and a sonsy wife, or he could be a widower on the lookout for a nursemaid. She knew nothing of him - but yes; she knew his name. As sure as her name was McCleod, his must surely be Campbell. The colour and pattern of a tartan was by no means a definite identification, for many Scotsmen could and did wear a mix of such tartans as pleased them, but for a man of his stature to wear a single garment of this nature, oh, his name *must* be Campbell, and it could do no harm to ask him advice as she would have asked it of the minister or the dominie back home. He must be a person of consequence.

As she hastened down the gangplank, Ness glanced at the place where the man had stood. It was empty, and she felt a huge pang of disappointment. He had not waited the half hour, after all. It must have been nothing but a whim that made him call.

Tears flooded her eyes, and she tottered blindly for the last few steps. Then, for the first time in many months, she set her foot on solid ground. The dock pitched sickeningly under her feet and Ness, whose stomach had remained staunch through the worst the ocean had to offer, felt ill. She gulped and swayed, catching a waft of ammonia as the pigs were brought up out of the hold. She coughed and doubled up, perspiration standing on her forehead and upper lip. The heat beat up from the docks and the smell of pigs was unbearable. She swayed again, and a hand the size of a griddle touched her shoulder in support. It was a curiously tentative touch. 'Lassie? Are you ill?'

'No' ill,' gasped Ness. 'Just-' She took another step away from the gangplank and again the ground heaved alarmingly. She thought she might faint, but that was ridiculous. Healthy Scotswomen did not faint. That was for the English in their over-tight whalebones and stays. She looked up to assure the Campbell that she was perfectly well, but he seemed to decide otherwise. He picked her up as if she was a bairn or a stricken ewe and carried her away back from the ship, plaid, cloak bag and all.

Hector was aware of an odd feeling of satisfaction as he bore the lassie away. Just what a Scotswoman was doing arriving unescorted in a strange country bothered him little. He accepted her fortuitous arrival just as he accepted other lucky incidents in his life. He wanted a woman and a woman arrived. That, for the present, was enough for him. It occurred to him fleetingly that she might be the property of someone else, but unless she was married already, he would soon persuade any other fellow to relinquish his claims. He would offer threats or gold, or whatever it took. Maybe he should know the lay of the land, though. Accordingly, he stopped short some distance from the shipside and looked enquiringly at his prize. 'Is someone meeting you, lassie?'

'No,' she said faintly.

'Are you a wife?'

'No. I travelled wi' my friend. She is dead. The pigs had a fever and some of the passengers had it as well.'

'Then I'll no be buying the pigs,' said Hector.

'No,' she agreed with the ghost of a smile. 'I doubt you will.'

'A bad risk, with some o' them sickly, and with a fever that passes to folk.'

'Aye.'

There was a dray standing nearby. The nag in the harness was half asleep with its hind hoof resting on its tip and its lower lip hanging open like a wallet. Hector set his burden down on the tailboard and looked down appraisingly. 'Take off the plaid, lassie, and let me look at you,' he ordered.

She looked a little askance, but unwrapped it from her shoulders to reveal a light-coloured gown, well worn, and stained with salt. The cloak bag she still clutched showed rubbed patches and the corners were threadbare. Her cloth boots were mended and the bonnet, as he noted while she was still on the ship, was unfashionably plain.

'You have no man o' your own to claim you, lassie?' he asked.

'I have no one,' she said.

She was not a beauty, but well enough formed. She had a neat little figure now it was freed from the enveloping plaid, and her face was heart-shaped with an appealingly wide brow and a milky, lightly freckled skin so pale he could see the blue veins in her temples. She had straight brows and a fine nose and cool grey eyes. He could see little of her hair under the bonnet, but it appeared to be a light brown, tending a little to red. Her mouth was firm in repose, but he thought it might be generous if she smiled.

'Your father hasna come with you?' he said abruptly.

'My father is dead,' she answered. 'This is his plaid. His - his wife had no need o' it now, since she's taken up wi' Lachie Douglas.'

Hector nodded, well pleased. This woman, and her circumstances, might have been made to order. 'It would be as well if we take a ship to Van Diemen's Land, the day,' he said. 'You'll like it fine; there's no so many people.' He waved his hand at the crowded docks, then turned and sat beside her on the dray. The wheels creaked, the shafts dipped and the nag turned and yawned, showing orange-pink gums and long yellow teeth. 'We'll build a house on a brae,' added Hector. 'A braw house o' stone.'

The lass watched him doubtfully. She looked better now, and there was a faint flush of colour in her cheeks, which Hector noted with approval. He had no wish for a peelie-wally wife. 'Can you cook, lassie?' he enquired.

A doubtful cough made him turn about to frown at one of the Sassenach soldiers that cluttered up the colony. This one was enquiring officiously about the ownership of the dray. Whether he objected to its presence here or whether he suspected Hector of larcenous intentions was beside the point. A man ought not to be interrupted when settling on a wife.

'It isna my vehicle,' snapped Hector irritably. 'I'd be shamed to own it, or the nag.'

'Have you the permission of the owner to occupy said vehicle?' pursued the soldier.

'Please,' broke in the girl, 'I was feeling a little faint, sir, and this gentleman set me here to rest a wee while. I am better now, so we shall move on.'

The soldier hesitated, and then nodded curtly. 'See that you do,' he said, and stood watching until the girl slid down from the dray.

Hector was forced to rise also, for she was still unsteady on her feet, and it was poor manners to sit while a lassie stood. 'What ships are set for Van Diemen's Land the day?' he asked.

'The *Lithgow* is to sail this afternoon,' said the soldier, holding his ground.

Hector nodded. 'We take passage on that.' He dismissed the soldier from his mind and the man, as folk often did when dismissed by Hector Campbell, found himself recalling urgent business at the other end of the docks.

'What if they ha' no room?' ventured the girl.

'They'll ha' room for *me*, lassie, and for you, if I gi'e the word.'

'And - and why should I come wi' you, Campbell?'

Hector was taken aback. Somehow, he'd thought it all settled. If she hesitated now, there were plenty of settlers who would take her in. Non-convict labour was very short and there was a push to prevent the assignation of convicts to private parties. He wanted this lassie for himself. Ah! He thought he saw the problem. 'I'm no' looking for a slavie, lassie,' he said, 'nor yet a loose woman. We'll be decently wed when we get to Van Diemen's Land.'

'Oh.' The girl laughed, a little hysterically. 'Shall we indeed, Campbell?'

'Unless you've other plans?'

'No,' she admitted. 'I have no plans but...'

'But what?' asked Hector, frowning.

The girl shrugged, and handed him the cloak bag. 'My name is Agnes McCleod,' she said, 'but folk call me Ness. I am from Loch Haven.' She dropped a small, unsteady curtsy and held out her hand.

'Hector Campbell.' He shook the hand gingerly. It was small, but not, he was glad to note, overly soft or brittle. He had a slight sense of anti-climax, as if some momentous decision had been taken too lightly. Shaking the hand of a lassie felt wrong. He wanted to embrace her, and bring the light of joy to her expression.

Agnes McCleod regarded him with wide grey eyes. She was very young, he thought, perhaps no more than seventeen, or perhaps as much as twenty. 'It pleases you to wed me?' he asked with a touch of anxiety.

She laughed a little bitterly. 'Whether it does or no makes no matter. I ken nothing else to do.' Maybe she saw the disappointment he tried to hide, for she smiled, showing even white teeth. "I do thank you for the offer, Hector Campbell, for I ha' little more than a bawbee to my name.'

CHAPTER 3

The trading ketch *Lithgow* had a berthing weight of less than seventy tons. It carried imported livestock and implements, foodstuffs, and goods produced in New South Wales. It also carried three passengers bound for Van Diemen's Land, and the master was reluctant to make it five. 'It's not comfortable you'll be, indeed,' he said anxiously. 'You and your lady should wait for the *Bluebell*, or the *Lady Jane*. It's more cabins they have.'

'Do they sail today?' demanded Hector, and the *Lithgow*'s master had to admit that they did not. And so Hector prevailed.

Ness, still numb from Jean's passing and the bewilderment of the events since, had been in a haze of misery. Now, in a moment of frightened clarity, she wondered what she had done. Had she *really* agreed to marry this Hector Campbell? Hearing his voice raised in debate with one of the sailors, she turned to look at him. He had a way of standing with his feet well apart, heels dug in, plaid bunched about his waist with a strong leather tawse. It might have seemed a clumsy costume on a man of lesser stature. Certainly it was archaic, but already Ness could imagine Hector in nothing else. He balanced easily as the ketch passed through the Sydney Heads, the keel biting into the waves as she heeled and began the long haul down the coast to Van Diemen's Land, over six hundred nautical miles to the south. A simple adjustment of his weight or a slight turn of his shoulders sufficed when the ship pitched, she noted. He made no sudden move to grasp the rail. Perhaps he was a sailor, then? But if that was so, why had he paid for passage on another man's ketch?

The argument was growing heated. Campbell was gesturing at the deck, or perhaps at something in the hold, with his chin jutted forward and his free hand clenched into a fist. Ness strained to catch his words. She'd been mad to trust herself to this man! Wed him? She'd as soon wed a wolf or an eagle! She must have been *mad*!

But… what else was there for her to do?

Her mind twisted in a flurry. What else could she do?

And that brought another question. Why would he wed her? He could have anyone, lady or maid, by force of personality. He was a braw looking man, and he had rescued her as the knights rescued the maidens in poor Jean's romances.

'Six *days*?' exploded Campbell. 'You canna tell me it'll take six *days* to run to Van Diemen's Land! Man, the wind's fair to the south and there's no a sign of bad weather ... aye, I could walk the miles on my ain feet and never break into a sweat!'

'Six days,' repeated the crewman. 'Or seven. And if you try to walk off this deck you'll have more than a sweat to break into. You're not the master of this ship, Mr Campbell.'

'I paid good money for my passage!'

'And you are getting what you paid for, Mr Campbell.'

'Och!' exclaimed Hector in obvious disgust. He turned away, dismissing the sailor as he had dismissed the trooper back on the docks. His glittering angry gaze fell on Ness. Apparently recalling her existence (for he had left her without a word when he went to harangue the crewman), he strode across the tilting deck to loom over her. He smiled in a quick baring of teeth, and ducked his head in a possible effort to look less terrifying. 'Will you step down to the cabin, Agnes McCleod?'

'No,' said Ness with haste. There were three lady passengers on the *Lithgow*, all very fine in dress and manner. She was sure they despised her drab gown and plain bonnet. 'I prefer to stay on deck and breathe some fresh air,' she added. 'The deck seems a natural place to be.'

Hector nodded and his teeth flashed in amusement. 'Aye, it would! Stay, then, but wrap yoursel' in yon plaid, lassie, for the wind is unco fresh. I'd not have my wee bride take a chill.'

He took the cloak bag and set it dangerously near the rail, then spread the plaid as if to wrap it about her. Ness made an instinctive dart for her belongings, but was brought up short by Hector's arm. 'Lassie! You'll no be throwing yoursel' overboard, forby!'

'I want my bag,' she gasped, as he enveloped her in the folds. 'I've nothing else in the world.'

Hector looked puzzled. 'No need to fash yoursel', lassie. I'll see to it you've all you need,' he said. That grin came again, glinting like the sun on a tarn. 'Besides, you have me! I'm no' to be counted as nothing.'

Ness met his gaze. 'Mr Campbell,' she said. 'This is madness. I canna wed you.'

Hector's brows came down in a fashion she was already beginning to recognise as a signal of gathering storm clouds. 'You will, when we reach Van Diemen's Land,' he said. 'I've paid your passage to yon sleekit Welshman and what else would you do wi' yoursel', as you said?'

Ness sighed. Hector's regard embarrassed her, and his arm, lying along her shoulder, felt like a spar of pure bog oak. 'I could be a nursemaid,' she said. 'I'm unco' good wi' the bairns.'

'You can be nurse to my bairns, Agnes,' said Hector. 'It will be bonnie to see it.'

'You have bairns?' asked Ness faintly.

'No' the while. But we will have, you and I.'

'Oh!' She stamped her foot. 'I can cook,' she said defiantly. 'I can sew, a little. I know my letters and I can do figuring, some.'

Hector nodded. 'Well. I'd no be wanting an idle or ignorant wife.'

'I could go into service in some great house,' said Ness.

Hector looked puzzled. 'Why would you do that, forby?'

'To live,' said Ness with a snap.

'Live wi' me, Agnes,' said Hector. 'I'll build a braw house in Van Diemen's Land for the both of us. Cook and sew, mind our bairns and warm my—'

'Mr Campbell!'

'Call me Hector,' he said impatiently. 'I've no patience wi' this Mister this and Mister that. I told you I'd not make a slavie o' you. I work hard and so will you, but we'll work together for our family. Think o' that, Agnes McCleod!'

She thought of that. Perhaps he was right. She would have to work hard in any case. Why *not* work for her own place in life rather than slave for someone else?'

'Yon bag's safe enough, and you can have all the bags you want when we reach Van Diemen's Land, Agnes,' added Hector. 'Aye, and gowns as well. Can you make oatcake, now?'

Oatcake! Gowns! It couldn't happen. One did *not* step off a ship and into marriage with a giant. How could she persuade him his plans were impossible? And why had she ever agreed to this madness? Even as she wondered, she knew the die was cast. Her fate had been sealed on the deck of the *May Queen* when Hector Campbell called and she answered. And, as he said, what else could she do? Jean had expected a position, and perhaps a husband, in Sydney Town, but Jean had education and experience. Ness was used to taking herself at Phemie's valuation, which made her lower than Dairy Jennie. This Hector Campbell was offering her work, a position, a home and a husband… oh, she was lucky! 'Ness,' she reminded abruptly. 'They call me Ness. Agnes is my Sunday name, forby.'

Hector nodded, apparently satisfied. And why should he not be wondered Ness giddily. It was clear that he had never doubted the outcome of her little rebellion. And it would be fine to give her problems into his keeping. He looked extremely stalwart, and it was sensible to take such chances as offered themselves in life. She adjusted the plaid around her shoulders, and allowed herself to lean against the warm, solid body at her side. Her head came somewhere below his shoulder, and his dimensions outclassed hers in every direction. Och well, she mused, as Hector's large arm came down to anchor her into position. He wants me, so he'll value me. And if nothing else he'll keep the wind awa'.

***

Despite Hector's disgust at its lack of speed, the ketch made harbour at noon on the sixth day. Shouldering passengers aside as if they were cattle, and swearing in Gaelic at the protesting crewmen who were attempting to steady the gangplank, Hector sprang ashore, then held out his arms. 'Jump, lassie. I'll catch you.' After six days in his company, Ness had still not come to any conclusions about her future husband's occupation or inner motives, but she had developed a complete faith in his practical judgement. If Hector believed she could jump safely across the gap, then she could. If Hector said he would catch her, then he would. Drawing her skirts clear of her ankles, she followed him ashore in a leap such as she would have feared to make near the loch when following Donal from stone to stone. Hector caught her deftly, gave her a huge hug, and swung her down. 'Hold fast to me, Ness, you've no your land-legs the while.'

The ground heaved underfoot, but having Hector to cling to made all the difference. Ness "held fast" as directed, quite without embarrassment, for by now she had come to regard Hector in something of the light of an oak tree, or perhaps a Clydesdale, or a mountain crag. He was something solid and largely immovable, and fine when she needed support. After a time, she relaxed her grip and cautiously tested her legs. The ground still seemed unsteady, so she concentrated on placing her feet where her eyes told her the ground *was* instead of where her muscles *expected* it to be.

Hector retrieved her shabby cloak bag, and tucked it unconcernedly under one arm, before offering the other to Ness. 'We'll be away to the Kirk now,' he said.

Ness gaped at him. 'But, Hector, where is *your* baggage?'

Hector shrugged his massive shoulders. 'I have none, forby.'

He had been sleeping up on deck, whether from preference or from some sense of propriety, Ness did not know. She had assumed he had baggage of some kind stowed in the hold, though now she came to think on it, she had seen him take nothing aboard the *Lithgow.* She knew he could not be destitute, for he had paid for their passages with a banker's draft.

'Is there something you were wanting?' he asked.

'I should like to purchase some soap,' said Ness firmly. She felt grubby, stiff with salt, and if she were to be wed today she would like to tidy herself first.

Hector raised his brows. 'Aye?'

Ness nodded. 'Soap, and perhaps another sark if one can be had.'

'Then you purchase your soap the while I go to the land office,' said Hector.

It was cooler in Van Diemen's Land than in New South Wales. Hector said it was because Van Diemen's Land was nearer the southland where the ice lay forever unmelted, and Ness believed him, although this was the first she had heard of eternal ice. Apart from the softness of the sunlight, and the brisk breeze blowing in off the sea, the surroundings seemed much like Sydney Town. The dock was smaller, and a little less busy, but its environs swarmed with the same rag-tag collection of humanity. London had not the monopoly on grime, but the buildings and fittings of Launceston were less than fifty years old, and had not yet achieved the centuries of complication that had grown up in London. This was a young settlement, although she supposed the sea and the land here were as old as time, and she gazed with eyes that drank in the strangeness.

Struck by her intent regard, Hector glanced about, but there seemed nothing to explain her wonderment in a dock, smelling of salt and fish, and flocked with way too many Sassenachs. Puzzled, he glanced at Ness, and found his gaze held by that quality of interest. She glanced up and smiled at him. His heart jumped in his chest, but he realised the light was not for him. She was inviting him to share in her delight of this place. He looked back, at a loss, and after a moment the light died out of her eyes.

***

Hector was not the only man to be struck by that quality in Ness McCleod. James Galbraith should have been painting a wealthy patron or deputizing in architectural matters for Tobias Scott-Blakeney that day, but he had broken a lens in his spectacles the week before, and had just now fetched a replacement from the glazier. He was adjusting the spectacles on his nose, noting that the purity of the newly ground lens put the other to shame and wishing he had thought to break both, when he caught sight of the young woman. She wore a shabby gown and a clumsy woollen wrap in a yellow brown mix, but something in her face took his attention. Perhaps because it was the first thing he had seen clearly in days, or perhaps it was her expression of child-like wonder, but he stared hungrily until she turned away. His right hand itched for a stick of charcoal and he glanced at it in surprise. The old habits died very hard.

Squinting back through the mists of thirteen years, Galbraith saw a sandy-haired lad with freckles flecking the pale skin of the habitually malnourished. He had worn a permanent frowning squint then, and his forehead had been prematurely lined with the effort of seeing more than a few feet. He had stolen bread and oatcakes and once a basket of salt herrings, but it was the theft of a knife that brought him half across the world. Lying on the ironmonger's stall it beckoned brightly, hissing of charcoal sharpened to a fine point instead of left scratchy and rough. Young Jamie always had charcoal in his hand, even then. He went through life drawing on every available surface, his nose almost touching the pictures in an effort to bring them into proper focus. He longed for paints and paper, but to "Charcoal Jamie" Galbraith these things were as far beyond his reach as the stars were beyond the reach of his short-sighted eyes. Even charcoal was difficult to procure, and he had often been threatened with a skelping as he snatched a prize from the embers. But charcoal, though satisfyingly black, had drawbacks. It would not hold a fine point, and so Jamie lusted after the ironmonger's knife. The temptation was too much. He grabbed it in full view of the ironmonger and his customers. He was caught, of course. No one believed he wanted the knife for charcoal, and only the lack of an obvious victim saved him from trial for attempted murder. Instead, he was charged with simple theft, and transported to Van

Diemen's Land for seven years.

There, he became a scullery boy for Tobias Scott-Blakeney, who had his own reasons for quitting London society and hiding himself in Van Diemen's Land. Tobias found his servant drawing pictures on the hearth and, instead of having him beaten, he gave the boy paper and bade him draw on that instead. Soon, scullery work was interspersed with delicious periods spent in the company of paper, pencils and inks. Random education was thrown his way, and though it left him perpetually short of sleep and sunlight, it satisfied the hunger of his soul. At nineteen, supplied with thick-lensed spectacles and seeing the world clearly for the first time, he was formally granted his freedom, but he chose to continue in the service of Tobias Scott-Blakeney, first as an assistant and then an associate. It was a relationship of benefit to both men, for Galbraith's equable temperament made him able to deal with difficult clients without fuss and offence, something that Scott-Blakeney found more difficult as he grew older. As for Galbraith, he sincerely hoped the vengeful ironmonger would find reward in Heaven.

A week without his spectacles had been an unwelcome reminder of the bad times, and now, seeing a lovely face, he wanted to paint it, in celebration and in thanks. He might have approached and offered his card, but the woman was being led away by her companion.

He lost his chance, but her face stayed with him far into the night, and he began to wonder seriously if he should not follow Tobias' suggestion and take a wife. Tobias had no such inclinations for himself, but having established that James was unrelentingly heterosexual, he gave him every opportunity of meeting suitable young women. It wasn't his fault James was so in love with a beautiful ideal that he could never face up to the reality of marriage with an ordinary girl.

'You'll not meet Aphrodite in Van Diemen's Land, boy,' Scott-Blakeney said often, but James' only reply was that he would never be satisfied with less.

This made it all the more odd that he should have been drawn to the girl on the docks. She was no Aphrodite, but perhaps - perhaps, she might have been an Eve.

***

While Ness took stock of her surroundings, Hector found a coach and persuaded the driver to take them up into the main part of Launceston. There, he descended, lifted down Ness and her cloak bag, and indicated a mercer and haberdasher and a chemist sharing premises across the road. The bell jangled as Hector flung the door open, and a clerk with a yard measure about his neck glanced up in annoyance at the interruption.

'Mistress McCleod is wishfu' to buy some soap,' announced Hector. 'Sell her all she needs, forby, and any other trifles, and have them kept ready.' He dropped a small leather bag in Ness' palm and stalked out. The bag was heavy, and Ness' doubts about Hector's solvency vanished abruptly. Even if it were filled with coppers it would hold a goodly sum, and she had the suspicion that Hector probably used coppers to mend his boot heels.

When the customers already in the shop concluded their purchases, Ness bought lavender soap, rosewater (which was shockingly dear), two linen sarks and some ells of printed cotton and calico. Needles, thread and shears were procured, and other necessities, for each item led to the need for two or three others. It seemed foolish to buy scissors for cutting one garment, so Ness bought a piece of spotted voile and some ribbons.

After the first few purchases were chosen, the clerk ceased to sneer at Ness' outmoded costume and unworldly appearance and began to make helpful suggestions. She had scarcely finished making her selections when the bell jangled again with such vigour that she knew, without turning about, that Hector had returned. She wondered if he might object to the magnitude of her spending, but his gaze slid over the piled goods without a blink.

'Hold the bundles awhile,' said Hector to the clerk, and then, to Ness, 'Come, lassie, we're awa' to the Kirk.'

This canna be happening, thought Ness, but Hector took her arm and hurried her out of the haberdasher's and along the street to a kirk without even the chance to change her soiled costume.

The parson who married them was not of the Presbyterian persuasion. Ness perceived that he was a Sassenach, and also that he had met Hector before, for he shied like a nervous horse as they approached.

He seemed very reluctant to marry them, but Hector had a licence, and in a pungent altercation that brought several passers-by gaping into the kirkyard, he set out the alternatives to an immediate wedding ceremony. Ness, blushing hotly to her hairline, wished the ground would swallow her out of sight. Hector was using terms she understood but vaguely, and that was worse than not understanding at all. She glanced at him surreptitiously. If, as he seemed to be telling the parson, he would cheerfully ravish her unwed, he'd had plenty of opportunity during the voyage on the *Lithgow*. The below-deck quarters might have been cramped and the deck public, but Ness had an impression this would not have worried Hector in the slightest if he decided to lie with her out of wedlock. And to declare himself a sinful man, driven by base desires beyond his control - that was outside of enough. Ness knew very well that Hector could control anything and anyone, if he really wanted to, and surely that included himself.

The old parson had spirit too. Turning his back on Hector's bluster, he came to stand by Ness. 'My child,' he said, looking compassionately at her dusty, salt-marked costume, 'you need not go with this man if you do not wish it. There are other possibilities for you; work that you could do. I could recommend you to several good persons in need of a pleasant maidservant.'

'Och, sir, Mr Campbell has been gey kind to me,' she said uncomfortably. 'He's no the braggart he likes to pretend, forby. I have none other to care for me. My parents are dead, and so is my companion, also.' The thought of kind Jean Leslie brought tears to her eyes, and, not for the first time, she wondered what Jean would have made of Hector Campbell. 'I wish to wed Mr Campbell,' she said, as much to convince herself as to ease the parson's apprehensions. 'He…' She hesitated. *He loves me* was not what she could say, and *he wants me* would not do either. 'He needs me,' she said, having hit on that very truth. 'He needs me to bring him to his dream.'

'Marriage is no dream,' said the parson.

'No, but it is a beginning,' said Ness.

The old man sighed, and advised them to remain in Launceston for some weeks so that the banns might be properly called and so Miss McCleod would have a chance, as he put it, *to prayerfully consider.*

Hector would not hear of that. With or without a wedding, he and Ness would be leaving that night for the Great Western Tiers, the mountainous land where his new property awaited their coming.

This was the first Ness had heard of a specific property, *or* of Hector's plans for immediate departure, but having committed herself to her course, she made no move to protest. The parson held out valiantly, even quoting Scripture in an effort to sway his adversary, but Hector quoted it back, with a gleam in his eye as he announced his intention to *cleave* unto his wife and *to become one flesh in the eyes of God,* so that in the end he capitulated. He summoned his wife and maidservant to act as the requisite witnesses to the wedding.

The service was short and curt. As the strangely familiar words rolled out, Ness was again swept away by unreality. Barely a week ago she was a destitute nobody, with none to care what happened to her. Now, in a few moments more, she would be Mistress Agnes Campbell, with a man of her own, a position in society and a new home awaiting her presence. Incredible. True.

Hector made the required responses with scowling precision, his large cold hand swallowing Ness' small one. *Cold?* Ness thought distractedly. Could Hector Campbell be *nervous?* She glanced up in disbelief, but Hector's granite features gave nothing away. The parson droned on, reluctance in every pore.

Ness was touched when Hector produced a gold ring and pushed it onto her finger. It was not that she'd thought he would have forgotten, exactly, but it would have been more Hector's style to have used a man's signet ring or - or a brass curtain ring. Or even, she thought crazily, a horse's bridle ring, since he seemed to believe in using what came to hand. This gold was fashioned for a lady's hand.

Ness repeated her own responses, and then, abruptly, the parson's droning ceased. The old man coughed, dryly.

Hector bent and brushed a brief kiss across her upturned face; so brief that Ness hardly felt it. She blinked in surprise. It was unlike Hector to be tentative, but then, it was unlike Hector to kiss her. After that impulsive hug when he lifted her from the ketch, he had not been demonstrative. He put his arm over her shoulders occasionally, but that was more in the nature of a restraint or a support than a hug. He patted her shoulder or back now and then, but it had been the sort of caress he might have bestowed on a horse, or perhaps on a dog. Now he looked at their joined hands in a kind of astonishment, then let go and turned away.

She glanced down at the ring on her finger as if wondering how it had got there. It was a dainty ring, and she wondered where he had come by it. She supposed he might have bought it from a merchant that afternoon, but it was just as likely he had carried it in his pouch for weeks or months for use whenever his fancy lit on a suitable bride.

The parson's wife touched her shoulder, with a smile on her wrinkled face. 'Good luck, dearie,' she said, handing Ness the glove she had removed to allow Hector to put on the ring.

'Thank you,' said Ness. She smoothed on the glove, much darned and mended. Now she was married, she might have new ones. The haberdasher had some beneath the counter and she had been about to peruse them when Hector spirited her away.

She looked at her husband, who was again haranguing the parson. His feet were braced apart, and his chin thrust out like the prow of a Viking ship.

Her husband. Ness paused to savour the thought, but it was oddly incomplete. They were just words, without any settled feelings behind them. She was grateful to Hector Campbell for coming to her rescue, but just now he seemed more interested in annoying the old man than in tending to her. He was her knight, but this was nothing like love as Jean's ballads had it. Och well, thought Ness with a mental shrug, he never said it was.

CHAPTER 4

They signed the parish register, Hector with a fierce aggressive squiggle, and Ness with her slow and careful script. She must learn to write her new name soon. Mistress Agnes Campbell. It hardly seemed like Ness McCleod, but another person altogether. And perhaps I am another person, thought Ness. Things still seemed oddly unreal.

Hector accepted a paper from the parson, and dropped a careless guinea into the old man's hand. 'Come, Ness, we must be awa',' he said, just as if she'd been the one delaying them. But she was his wife and so she followed him obediently. 'I see you can write, lassie,' he added as they walked up the street.

'Aye, a little,' said Ness. 'I told you I have my letters. Donal taught me when we were bairns. I can read also, but the dear kens when I'll-'

'Donal?'

'Aye, Donal Kirkbride. My brother.'

Hector stopped, jerking Ness to a halt. 'Donal Kirkbride is your brother? And your name was McCleod?'

'Aye,' said Ness, puzzled at his interest. 'Phemie Kirkbride wed my father, forby.'

'This Donal, then. He is your half-brother?'

Ness nodded dazedly. Hector's grasp was hurting her arm, and after all, it was very nearly true. Donal *felt* like a brother. He had been much kinder to her than Mungo Duncan had ever been to his sister Elspie. And what was there in a blood tie? Phemie was harsh enough to poor Donal and her father, much as she'd loved him, made no real move to save her from Phemie's spite.

Hector's grip relaxed, and he turned and walked on as if nothing had happened. Ness bit her lip anxiously, stepping out in an effort to keep up. 'You'll be needing stouter boots than those, forby,' said Hector.

He bought a pair at the bootmaker's, a few shops down from the haberdasher's. The bootmaker protested that the pair in question had been made for another lady, and were to be delivered the next day, but Hector over-rode his scruples with a generous handful of coins. 'Make her more,' he said curtly. 'My wee wife needs these tonight.' The sum he offered clinched the deal, and Ness' eyes widened, but she was coming to discover that Hector had little regard for money. He saw it merely as a tool for obtaining the things and circumstances he wanted, and considered a successful conclusion the justification for money well spent.

Outside the haberdasher's establishment was a stout wagon drawn by a couple of heavy-limbed but well-conformed horses. Hector gave the servant holding the horses a coin, and Ness saw without great surprise that the packages she'd purchased were already stowed under the seats. And that was not all. Around and about them were great bundles and bolts and barrels of stuffs. She saw canvas and wire, an axe and a saw, a plough, a sack of oats and another of seed, a Dutch oven, cook pots, a side of bacon, a sack of vegetables, and a coil of stiff new rope. There were items of leather and metal, cloth and tools, a smith's hammer, bellows, a cask of flour, a parcel of linen towels and more calico, some coarse wool blankets, a sack of grain, two lanterns and some oil. And she had been troubled over a few trifles from the mercer! Hector added the boots to the pile then took Ness and swung her aboard. As if I were another sack of meal, she thought. It occurred to her that perhaps, in Hector's eyes, that was what she was.

But then... *I will bring him to his dream,* she thought. She would hold fast to that.

It was already quite late in the afternoon as the wagon left Launceston, but Ness did not protest. The road they travelled was no more than a swathe hacked through the thickly wooded land. Underfoot the surface was rough, and Ness doubted the road was wide enough for two wagons to pass if they met head-on. The horses stepped out sturdily, but the wagon clanged and jolted over the stones. The seat was hard and, had she not been packed about with provisions and wedged close to Hector's bulk, she would have had trouble keeping upright. As it was her shoulders soon ached from bracing herself against the jolts. She wondered how far they had to go. If it was a long way, she supposed they would be putting up for the night at some hostelry along the way. She didn't like to ask, and after a while she tried to forget her discomforts by absorbing herself in the sights of the alien countryside.

No heather grew here, no oak, no ash, or rowan. Instead, she saw tough, dark undergrowth and strange tall trees whose bark appeared to be sloughing off in sheets, as Donal's skin had done once when he caught over much sun in the hay field. There was an odd smell in the air, as well. It was a strange, medicinal smell that reminded her of the wintergreen Granny McCleod had used to ease joints twisted with the rheumatics.

'They call them gum trees,' said Hector when she ventured to ask. 'Good timber for building, men say, but to my mind stone's better.'

The sun was setting, and a haze of dust hung above the road. Hector appeared to know where he was going, and Ness asked if he had been in Van Diemen's Land before.

'Once or twice,' he said. He did not elaborate on that, and it came to her that when not actively engaged in doing business or harassing some person who had raised his ire, Hector had very little to say. What did go on in that head of his? The horses plodded on, the wagon pitched and swayed and the sun slid down in the west.

'It is a strange place,' said Ness, to break the silence, but Hector just grunted.

After a time, she began to wonder if they'd ever stop. She was aching all over, the dust made breathing difficult, and besides, she had a call of nature to answer. Her chance came as they approached a river Hector informed her curtly was called the South Esk.

'Hector,' she said, blushing a little in the twilight, 'I need to get down.'

Hector flicked her a sideways glance, and drew the horses to a halt. Encouraged by this prompt response to her request, Ness would have scrambled down, but he looped back the reins and descended to lift her out of the wagon.

Cramped conditions on the *May Queen* and the *Lithgow* made normal modesty difficult to uphold, but there she had shared her discomforts with the other women, not with men. Now, here in the open spaces of her new home, Ness was at a loss. Surely, Hector was not planning to stand guard over her while she did her business!

'It's a braw night,' said Hector, putting his bog-oak arm around her.

Ness knew he had a right. They were man and wife, but she had other matters on her mind right now. 'I'll no be long,' she said firmly, and shrugged away from his grasp.

'Take care where you set yousel', forby,' said Hector. 'An adder put paid to auld Rob Roy, and I'd not ha' you bitten on the backside.'

He moved away to the other side of the wagon, and Ness sighed.

Presumably he had similar matters to take care of himself. It was strange, the way men went about it, standing, as horses did, adding their mites to the burns which trickled down to the loch. She had once seen Donal and Mungo Duncan and had cried out at them not to sully the water so. Mungo reddened angrily, and went whistling away up the brae, kicking at the heather as he went. Even Donal was angry, not because she saw them, but that she made such a daft protest. At least the kindly twilight hid her now.

Ness set her clothing to rights and returned to the wagon where Hector presently replaced her among the packages. His *other* packages, thought Ness ruefully.

Hector girded up his plaid and led the horses across the ford. The wagon lurched and swayed, and Ness closed her eyes and clung to the seat and prayed for deliverance. The horses splashed safely across, and gained the opposite bank. They were a fine pair, and sturdy and Ness thought they would not have been slow-footed had it not been for the wretched terrain. She ventured a remark on the state of the road and Hector laughed.

'Och, haivers. If we'd come down in the winter, we might ha' had a worry or two.'

Ness thought of the fords bursting with water instead of flowing sedately, and closed her eyes again; giving thanks that she had not come to Van Diemen's Land in winter.

The wagon had no carriage lamps, but there was a fine full moon to light the way. They had travelled some twelve miles and it had been full dark for hours when Ness saw a pair of lamps lit in the distance.

'We'll lie the night in yon inn,' said Hector. 'The horses are gey tired.'

So was Ness. And she had long since ceased to appreciate the coolness of the air. Even wrapped in her plaid she felt she was set in a permanently seated position, just as auld Tammas Magill had set when they found him dead in his chair back home in the village.

Hector drove the horses into the inn-yard. He had heard of the hostelry newly opened in Carrick, but had he been alone he would have pressed on through the night while the horses would travel, then hobbled them with tawses and rolled himself in his plaid to sleep on the nearest level ground. It occurred to him, however, that his new wife might expect a softer place to sleep the night. Also, if he bedded the horses in a stable and had the wagon shut in the inn-yard, he stood better chance of arriving at his property with his purchases intact. Lawless men tramped the forests of Van Diemen's Land, and the crime rate was still many times that of the old country. Some convicts ended their sentences and became solid members of the new society; others, resentful of their forcible transplanting, continued to offend, escaping the chain gangs and prisons to "go bush", and emerging to prey on travellers and settlers.

Hector would have backed himself against any one of these marauders, but the curs had the uncouth habit of working in packs. Thus two might engage him in battle while a third made off with the goods. A fourth might abduct Ness, and since he had acquired a wife, he felt obligated to ensure that she, too, arrived safely at her new home. Glancing at the small dim figure beside him, Hector frowned. The lassie was gey young and perhaps had little idea of what being a wife entailed. She must learn, and the lesson might as well begin now as later.

'Hold the horses, Ness,' he said. 'I'm awa' to rouse up the landlord.'

It was well after midnight, but Hector was widely awake. New ventures always enhanced his already formidable energies, and now he had begun on what was to be the best venture of them all. When he reached that land on the Western Tiers, and looked about the acres that were his, he would build himself a home and he and Ness would produce a family to fill it. Away from the drought conditions that were beginning to afflict New South Wales, he would raise fine sheep, and produce better wool than any. There was much to be done before this dream could be realised, but Hector was confident of success.

Pulling a stray fold of his plaid close, (for the night was chill) Hector strode between the lighted lamps that capped the posts of the inn yard and climbed the steps. The hostelry was small, boasting no more than a few rooms, but someone should be awake to welcome travellers and supply them with warmth and sustenance. That was what inns were for.

Scorning the knocker mounted on the door, Hector doubled his fists and knocked for admittance. He continued his barrage for some while until a light rose within and a mumble of complaint could be heard moving closer until the door was opened a cautious crack.

'What?' Evidently, the landlord was not one to waste words.

'My wee wife and I require a bed for the night,' said Hector.

The man surveyed him narrowly through the gap in the door.

Evidently he was not encouraged by Hector's appearance, for he said; 'We're closed.'

Hector's right hand shot out to seize the landlord by the shoulder. 'Haivers! Now, listen to me, you thrawn Sassenach! Is it an inn you're running here or a hen-house? My wife and I require a bed, and we have two horses to be bedded besides. Aye, and a wagon of goods to be stowed in safety for the morning.'

'It's halfway through the night!' said the innkeeper resentfully.

'Aye,' said Hector with ironic humour. 'No doubt you'll be charging us for only half the night, forby! We need supper and plenty of hot water, and a place to sleep, and shelter for the horses and goods. Aside from that, we'll give you no bother.'

'I'll not have you rousing up the house,' said the landlord.

'Then we'll bed in the byre.'

Seeing Hector's determination, and perhaps feeling there would be an even bigger disturbance if this late-come guest were refused admittance, the man capitulated. 'Put the horses in the stable and the wagon in the barn, and then come in,' he said.

Hector frowned. 'That's your business, no mine,' he said. 'Have you no ostler?'

'Drink-taken,' said the man, and followed Hector back to the wagon. When he saw the quality of equipage and goods, he became more obliging. 'Go in,' he said, as Hector lifted Ness and her bag down. 'The woman will show you a room.'

Hector hesitated. Every instinct told him to see the horses made secure. He had owned them for only a few hours, but they were braw beasts and he wanted to be sure they were safe for the night. However, he had had Ness for a short time also, and a newly wedded wife could scarcely be told to run along as if she were a tavern wench. He compromised by giving the horses a pat and the landlord a hard stare before leading Ness into the inn.

***

Marthie the inn wife, a stout old body in a wrinkled wrapper and cap, had already been roused up by the noise. More pragmatic than her man, she squinted at her guests and decided she had seldom seen a more ill matched couple than this gigantic Scotsman, over forty if he were a day, and the girl who looked no more than seventeen. Both wore heathenish Scotch clothes, so perhaps they were father and daughter. They would then require two rooms, which would be more work, but would also bring in more money. The giant soon disabused her of that idea.

'A room for my wife and mysel', supper and hot water,' he ordered. 'Hot, mind. My wife is a cleanly body.'

Marthie looked at the pair mistrustfully. They were travel-stained and the girl, at least, was drawn with exhaustion. Husband and wife! They were a runaway couple, more likely, and runaways were notoriously short of money. Why else would the marriage be forbidden?

'Hot water's two shillun extra after midnight,' she said warningly. Marthie's maxim was simple; charge what the traffic can bear and add a little extra for good will.

'Here's your money, you auld besom,' said the giant coldly, and delved in a pouch. 'Now, have you a room or have you no?'

Marthie peered short-sightedly at the coins he dropped into her hand. They appeared genuine, and the bag from which the giant had withdrawn them still clanked encouragingly. 'Right up the stairs, your honour,' she said.

'We'll have supper first, while the hot water is brought,' said the giant.

Marthie found herself setting up a great loaf she had baked ready for the next day, augmenting it with a wheel of strong yellow cheese and some preserves, and serving the couple with pannikins of stewed tea from the kettle at the back of the hearth. Tea was an expensive luxury, and she hoped the giant would appreciate it.

In the light of the great kitchen, she perceived that the young woman was almost transparent with exhaustion, and decided to set out the new goose-feather pillows she'd bought from the poulterer and put by for just such an occasion.

'Perhaps you'd care for more tea, your honour?' she said winningly.

The Scotsman scowled over the bitter stuff and shook his head as if he knew it had been eked out with the dried leaves of a local shrub. 'The hot water?' he reminded.

Marthie's man staggered up the stairs with the cans of water. She followed, ostensibly to oversee the filling of ewer and basin, but actually to report, in lowered tones, on her discoveries. 'The man's well to do, and will pay us well,' she said importantly, plumping down the pillows.

'I know,' said her husband. 'He has a fine pair, and goods to stock an emporium.'

'Maybe he's a hawker,' said Marthie, but her husband shook his head.

'No, he's a squatter from New South Wales, come to settle in the tiers.'

'Then he'll not be staying more than the one night,' decided Marthie. She wondered whether to repossess the pillows, but the girl looked so exhausted that she left them be.

***

Ness was grateful to find the bed made up with clean linen sheets and pillows. She washed her face and hands in the cooling water from the ewer, and then, as there was still no sign of Hector, she stepped behind the screen and removed her clothes. She sponged herself quickly, regretting the newly purchased soap, still in the wagon. It was such a relief to feel clean once more, for washing in seawater had never been effective.

She dried herself on a linen towel, slipped on her clean sark and scrambled into the bed. The horsehair mattress was hard and lumpy, but Ness was accustomed to worse. The pillows, at least, were deliciously soft and she thought muzzily that it was very generous of Hector to provide all this for her. Surely it augured well for her future. He *did* care for her, even if it was as a new possession. After all, she would bring him to his dream.

She felt rather less in charity with him when he came into the room some time later, flinging back the door with the same vigour he employed in the haberdasher's shop. It hit the jamb and rebounded, and Ness, almost asleep, jerked up with a gasp of shock. She had left the candle alight, and Hector now lit another, and sat down on the bed to remove his boots. The horsehair mattress was a solid piece of equipment, but it dented alarmingly under Hector's weight and Ness found herself rolling into the middle. Before her startled gaze, Hector divested himself of his plaid, shaking it out before draping it over the back of the chair. Clad in a sark and trews, he retreated behind the screen where she heard him spluttering and splashing as if he had fallen in the loch. Had he upended the ewer over his head? She wouldn't put it past him…

He dried himself as she had on the linen towel, and flung it over the back of the screen before stepping back into view.

Ness stared, paralysed, for her husband was mother-naked. With a gasp, she flung herself over onto her stomach, burrowing her face into the pillows to shut out the sight.

Hector, about to climb into bed beside his wife, found himself faced with an excellent view of the back of her head, half screened by her upflung arms. 'What's wrong, lassie?' he asked. 'Have you a colic?' He had come from the stable where the horses were settled with hay and water. He could deal with colic in a horse, but how did one treat it in a woman?

The head moved slightly from side to side and Hector leaned forward, planting his hands on the mattress. It was as lumpy as any he had tried, but it smelled wholesome enough, and the linen sheets were unmarked by specks of blood or dirt. That was as well, for Hector had a strong dislike of vermin and some inns were crawling with the creatures.

Could Ness have seen a rat? He frowned, but could hear no tell-tale gnawing or scrabbling in the wainscot.

'Ness?' he said. She rolled a fraction sideways and opened one eye, then closed it again with a shudder. Abruptly, Hector understood. She was a virtuous lassie who had never seen a naked man before, and the sight caused her embarrassment. Well, she'd soon accustom herself to that. He might have replaced his sark, but it was sweat-stained and sour, and why put on a garment if he meant to remove it almost immediately? Shrugging, Hector turned back the quilt and the sheet and sprang into bed. His gaze fell on his wife's rump, temptingly displayed in outline beneath the calico sark. His eyes narrowed. There were plenty of nights ahead, but after the strenuous work to come, he might have less energy than he had tonight. Ness was tired, but for the once she need not bestir herself unduly.

By way of announcing his intentions, Hector gave his wife a playful slap on the buttocks, an action which brought about another spasm of movement as she rolled away and reared half out of bed. To his surprise, she stammered; 'You have no call to beat me!'

'Beat you, lassie?' he said, bewildered. 'I'd never do that! No wi'out cause!'

'Why did you strike me then?' she asked.

'That was no blow, it was a- a pat.' Hector felt himself in the wrong, and disliked it. 'I am your husband, Ness, and I'll do no more than claim my rights,' he added. 'I will never harm you… why would I?'

'You've no the right to strike me,' she persisted, 'no' wi'out cause. I'll no be treated like poor wee Maggie Graham!'

Hector sighed. He enjoyed a good debate as well as the next man, but there was a time and a place for it, and he had never liked contentious women. He turned his attention to the matter in hand, although he had lost some of his enthusiasm for it now. 'I'll kiss you then - if you've no objection?' he said. He did so quite gently, for he had no wish to alarm her any more. He had never had a virgin before, and his usual lusty tactics would not do.

She made no objection this time, which was as well, for his patience would have been sorely tried if she screamed or tried to push him away when he was engaged in an activity he had every right to enjoy. The thought tickled him, and he shook with laughter.

'What is it?' She sounded agitated now, so Hector put his arms round her and patted her soothingly, then kissed the top of her head.

'I'm thinking this is as new to me as it is to you, lassie.'

'But, surely you've lain with women before?'

'Aye, plenty,' agreed Hector carelessly, 'but never before with the benefit o' the Kirk.'

'Oh.' She relaxed a little as she digested this. 'Then you'll know well enough what to do.'

'Aye,' he agreed.

'Why have you never married, Hector?'

'I have,' he reminded, with another, lighter, pat. Her buttocks were as nicely rounded to the touch as to the eye, and fitted sweetly in his palms. Her sark had become a little rucked up, so he inched his hands beneath the edge, still gently.

'I mean, before now,' persisted Ness. He fancied she had relaxed a little more again. And had she shifted a little to fit better against him? 'Did you never find a suitable lassie?'

'I never thought to look, before,' said Hector frankly. 'I'm no getting younger, and I ken fine it's time to build a home and family.'

'And were there no lassies in Sydney Town?'

'Aye,' he agreed, 'lassies a'plenty, but the best were wed already and the others had fathers.'

'Why should that matter?' asked Ness. 'Every lassie has a father, forby.'

'I'd run against the most o' these fathers in business.' Hector tired of the subject and tugged the sark up a little more. 'Take it off, lassie,' he said. She made no move, so he sat up and hauled the garment over her head. Then he subsided and took her back into his arms.

As couplings went, Hector had known many better, but allowing for his wife's inexperience and travel-weariness, he decided she might do very well. She made no further charges of brutality (which was only right, since he had been very gentle), and neither did she chatter afterwards, or demand fulsome assurances of his love and devotion.

So far as he could recall, Hector had never loved anyone. The most he had ever achieved had been a mild liking, and that had been rare. Most often, Hector was irritated by his fellow man. Those of his own economic class despised him as an uncouth barbarian. The masses disliked him for his unusual success in making and multiplying money. Servants feared his ready fist and bitter tongue, and employers complained of his highhanded manner. Some women had professed to fondness until he decided to move on; their recriminations then rang more true than their previous sentiments. His dog had loved him, and he had been fond of it, that was all.

As Ness lay sleeping at his side, Hector hoped she would continue to be reasonable. He would make no flowery protestations and wanted none in return, and if they continued as they had begun, they would deal well enough together. She was, after all, precious to him for what she offered and for what they would build, together. He rolled over and drew her close to him once more. It was a chill night after the climate of New South Wales, and the inn wife's quilt was hardly the equal of his plaid. His wife was pleasantly warm to hold. He had already discovered how well she fitted into his arms. He raised his head to kiss her temple, and found his lips lingering on skin as soft to the touch as petals on a settler's rose. The urge to do so surprised him, for he had always felt that spending caresses on a sleeping woman was a great waste of time. *This is my wife,* he reminded himself. *My wife, my Ness, my…blessing.*

The last thought came on the cusp of sleep and later he was astonished to remember thinking it at all.

CHAPTER 5

Ness woke alone in the big bed. It was clear outside, but the curtains obscured most of the sunlight. There was a scratch on the door, and a maid entered, lugging cans of hot water. Ness made to sit up, then, recalling her nakedness, subsided.

'Morning, Missus,' said the girl. 'I'll open the curtings for y'.'

Ness blinked in the sudden rush of light, and lay watching the dance of dust motes until the maid had gone. Then she sat up and draped herself in a sheet before taking stock of the room. Hector's plaid was gone from the chair. His boots were gone also, and her cloak bag sat forlornly by the door. Ness had a sudden fantasy that perhaps last night had never happened, that she was not wed, and was still Ness McCleod, the orphan of Loch Haven. But that was haivers. She was naked in the bed, with a gold ring on her finger and her hair spread in lank strands instead of being properly braided away. Wherever Hector Campbell had gone, he would soon return, and he would doubtless expect her to be ready to travel. Unless, she thought suddenly, he expected something first.

It was her duty to do as he wished, but perhaps she should be up and dressed when he returned. Ness sprang out of the bed, wincing from the pain in her muscles. She was sure she was bruised from neck to knee from the journey, and Hector's marital attentions had not helped. He had probably been gentle by his standards, but it had been a strange and uncomfortable experience to her.

With one eye on the door, she retreated to the screen and washed herself thoroughly in the hot water. Next time she bathed, she promised herself, she would have the new soap to use and she would perfume herself with rosewater. She wondered if Hector would like that. She had woken once or twice in the night and been startled to find the heavy weight of his hand on her hip or an arm snugly under her breasts. Any attempt to move away made him gather her closely against him, so in the end she had relaxed and let it be. He was warm and after all, he had the right.

She was drying herself when Hector arrived, carrying her new boots in one hand. Ness stiffened behind the screen. He would see her head and bare shoulders, and although she had been naked the night before she had made him blow out the candle. Hector seemed to find nothing amiss in her unclothed state.

'Dress yoursel', lassie,' he said. 'It's a braw day and we've a way to go.'

'I'll no be long,' said Ness. She laced on her stays, then bundled her sark over her head. Hector waited, eyes glinting, as if he enjoyed her embarrassment. Ness lifted her chin, determined to outface him. If he thought he had married a timorous wife he was wrong. She left the screen and laced herself into her gown, blushing as she encountered Hector's gaze.

'Ye're a bonnie wee lass, Ness McCleod,' he said, and reached out to run his hand over her cloth-covered thigh as if testing the condition of a horse.

'I'm no' Ness McCleod, but Ness Campbell,' she corrected.

He grinned, and swept a bow. 'Aye, Mistress Campbell is right bonnie.' He stood up and looked at her expectantly.

'And Hector Campbell is a braw man,' she said. She put out a hand and rested it against his chest for a moment. If he had the right to touch her as he wished, then she had the right as well.

She moved back and brushed her hair, and looped it back into a roll at the back of her head. The three ladies she had seen on the *Lithgow* had worn their hair in bunched ringlets, augmented with quantities of false curl, but Ness had been doing hers in the same simple way since the days when Phemie threatened to crop it short if she allowed it to hang about her face. Similar threats had resulted in Ness lacing herself into a corset when she was thirteen, although she never pulled it as tight as Phemie wished. A body needed all her breath when walking up and down the brae and around the loch to the village. Now, she put on her bonnet and, on a whim, took out her granny's brooch and pinned it to the bosom of her gown. The ladies on the *Lithgow* had worn dark travelling dress, but their sleeves had been puffed and their bodices boned. Ness felt dowdy in her ill-fitting gown, but the brooch shone out fine from the plain background. Sharply aware of Hector's regard, she turned to put on the boots he had set by the bed. Her husband rose and stopped her with a hand on her shoulder. Ness looked up with a queer little catch of excitement, but Hector's attention was on the brooch.

'Where did you get the pin?' he asked.

'My granny had it from her man, who was a braw hand at the smithy,' said Ness. 'It's white heather, see, the kind that grows up the brae. Granny gave it to me not long before she passed to her reward.'

'Bonnie white heather,' said Hector, as he admired the delicate piece of work. 'I doubt I remember it well. I've been awa' from Scotland a long stretch.'

'It grows up the brae side and in the glens,' said Ness, remembering. 'The stems are aye tough and cut your hands if you pick it wi'out care, but the bells are bonnie. Folk say it brings braw luck and so my grandfather made this for my granny. To bloom for aye, he said.'

'Aye.' Hector let her go and seemed to lose interest in the subject.

Ness was conscious of a small stirring of disappointment as she put on her boots. They fitted well enough, but felt stiff and unwieldy, and Ness stepped out with care as she followed Hector down to the parlour where the inn wife had laid out breakfast. The remains of the loaf appeared, so did cheese and preserves and a can of new milk. Hector purchased food for the journey, and then it was time for Ness to take her place in the wagon.

Hector had overseen the harnessing of the horses by a sullen ostler, and offered to break the man's head if he showed so little regard for horseflesh. 'Yon sleekit, ill-favoured wretch put it on so they'd gall wi'in a mile,' he fumed to Ness while the ostler, cowed, readjusted the harness. He told the landlord to hire a better man, but the landlord turned up his palms and swore there was little good labour to be got from one end of the island to the other.

'What will you be doing, Mr Campbell? Are you bringing in workers from the ships?'

'Och, I'll find plenty hereabouts,' said Hector. He lifted Ness into the wagon and swung up beside her. Ness wondered if he might put his arm about her, but he fell into one of his silences, frowning at the ruts ahead.

Ness found herself watching the horses, half entranced by the whisking of their tails, and the way their shining rumps moved rhythmically and occasionally dipped and trembled as one or the other made a miss-step on the rough surface or paused to snatch at the rough vegetation. One beast was a flea-bitten grey, and the other was a chestnut with a hide as bright as the rowanberries she used to find up the brae.

'Hector, are you displeased wi' me?' she ventured.

Hector turned his frowning face in her direction. 'No, lassie. Wha' makes you say that?'

'You've said nothing since we left the inn.'

'I ha' things to mind,' said Hector.

'You dinna regret being wed?'

'O' course not, you daft lassie,' said Hector. 'It was time and enough I took the step.' He said very little more until they halted by a little burn for luncheon. Even then, he only exhorted Ness to take care where she set herself. 'The snakes are gey bad,' he explained, gesturing with a hunk of bread.

'Where are we going, Hector?' she asked, after inspecting the ground for reptiles.

Her husband chewed, scowling, but by now Ness had realised that Hector's scowls did not necessarily imply displeasure. After a few seconds, he wiped his hand on his plaid and picked up a fallen green stick. He removed a murderous-looking dirk from his belt, carved a point to the stick, and then drew swiftly in a patch of sand.

'Van Diemen's Land is shaped like an apple, with a point to it,' he explained. 'It's no so rounded, but this is close enough. Launceston is here.' He dropped a pebble on the map. 'Hobarton is down near Risdon Cove. The inn was *here* and we should make Westbury *here,* by night, then Shepherd Town, *here,* tomorrow. Another day on, and our land is *here*, on the flank o' the Western Tiers.'

Ness stared, appalled at the thought of so many more days of travel, but Hector was engaged in scoring lines for rivers and arranging ridges of bark for mountains.

'There are settlers here already,' he went on, pointing with the stick. 'Gardiner and Reeve ha' land, and so do MacDonald and auld Jarvis and others beside. There are settlements called Mole Creek and Chudleigh, and a village name o' Mersey.'

'Then we shall be having neighbours!' said Ness.

Hector grunted. 'None too near. My land is on the slope o' the mountain, and lies well back frae the Sassenachs in the flatlands.' He sank his teeth into another piece of bread. 'We ha' some flats as well, and the whole area is well watered by burns and rivers, they say. There is a paper outlining boundaries on the mountain. I have it safe in the wagon.'

Ness watched him eat, and then saw him fall suddenly asleep, laid out on the coarse prickly grass beside her as if it was the finest feather bed. She examined his sleeping face, half-turned and pillowed on one massive arm, then pored over the map in the sand.

The 'land' as Hector called it, seemed unreal, as if they would never reach it. She thought of the inn they might sleep in tonight. There might be a hip-bath, and she would use lavender soap and rosewater to sweeten her hair.

Her thoughts darted randomly as the small brown fish in the burn. If Donal had been with her he'd have been flat with his arms in the burn, seeking to tickle a trout. Ness had copied him a time or two, and she wondered if she could do it still. The grey horse nodded at the flies and rubbed his muzzle against an out-thrust foreleg. The harness rings jangled a little.

Ness looked down at the ring on her wedding finger. She was aware of it all the time. It was gold, and wrought into a true-lovers' knot. She turned it gently between finger and thumb. Like the new boots, it was a good fit, and she must accustom herself to the feel of it. A bird twittered in the tree above, and she peered through the leaves to see. A small twig spun down and landed in Hector's luxuriant hair. Ness picked it out, her fingers lingering a little. Hector turned his head impatiently, trapping her fingers against the ground. Her hand cupped around his cheek, and, unbidden, the memory rose of his hands cupping her in the night. She bent to kiss his cheek, something she would not have ventured when he was awake.

Then she eased away from him and knelt by the burn to watch the fish.

***

By late afternoon on the fifth day out of Launceston, they reached mountainous country. Lumps of limestone stuck up through the ground, and Ness heard the distant roar of water. The mountain ridges cut fantastic shapes, and secret burns purred all about. The trees crowded thickly about the track, but here and there were patches of cleared ground with slab houses and livestock. Ness saw a fine brick house, and her eyes widened.

'Och, Hector, look!' she said.

Hector nodded unconcernedly. 'That will be old Walter Jarvis' holding. Scarborough, he calls it.'

'But the house! It's bonnie!' And so it was, with the imposing brickwork an elegant change from the slab huts and wattle and daub cottages she had seen before.

'Our house will be bonnier,' said Hector. 'And I hear York Hall, back up the road a guid way, is a braw fine dwelling.'

Around a bend in the road, they came suddenly on a flock of sheep, driven by a shepherd on a small dun horse. The shepherd's master watched from the side of the road, idly flicking the loop of his bridle reins. His horse was a black, untouched by brown, unrelieved by white socks or a blaze, and it gleamed with breeding and care. Ness stared in open admiration, and Hector's eyes narrowed. He knew some would beggar themselves for possession of such a horse, but the man in the saddle was no pauper. His tight pale trousers buttoned below the knee, with sleek black boots pulled over them. The tops of the boots were pale, the shirt had upstanding points and the waistcoat was tightly buttoned. The dark coat on top was cut away severely, and the layers of cloth at the collar must have made it difficult for the wearer to turn his head.

Hector's regard held plenty of scorn for the expensive gentleman, but a twinge of envy too. This squatter had wealth and breeding as well. He was as exclusive as his mount. Not for a hundred pounds would Hector have subjected himself to that rigidly correct costume. In any case, no costume would have made him the squatter's equal in the eyes of the world any more than an expensive English saddle would have turned his sturdy horses into thoroughbreds.

The sheep, face to face with Hector's equipage, milled more than ever, baaing mindlessly, tongues protruding as they panted in the sunlight. Hector drew rein and adjured the shepherd to move along so he could pass.

It seemed obvious to Ness that the sheep would never pass unless Hector drove onto the shoulder of the track. It was even more obvious that he had no intention of doing do.

'Take the beasts ba' the way you came!' he demanded.

The shepherd glanced at his master. 'Mr Whitaker- Mr Jarvis, I mean? What would ye have me be doing?'

Jarvis of Scarborough! thought Ness. That explained the man's arrogant stance. Any man who owned a house of that order had good reason for his consequence.

'Hector, can we no move aside?' she asked. It seemed wrong that this lordly person should be put to inconvenience, but Hector thrust out his jaw. It was covered with stubble, for he had not troubled to shave for the past two days.

'We canna,' he said stubbornly.

Ness sighed a little. They had met other obstacles in the road, and at one of the fords they'd waited three hours while the bullock wagon ahead of them had been heaved and forced out of the mud into which it sank when one of the bullocks foundered. Hector reacted to each hold-up as if it had been purposely laid in his path, and had almost come to blows with the bullocky who paused in his labours to light a pipe and relieve himself in the ditch by the ford. Despite this, he had never reacted quite so badly as he did now. But then, none of the other delays had been authored by such an elegant figure as the gentleman on the black thoroughbred. Hector was coming to the boil with rage, but Jarvis was looking bored. His gaze flickered once over the wagon, stayed briefly on Hector's figure as if he scarcely believed his eyes, and passed even more swiftly over Ness. Ness was bowed with weariness and stiff with apprehension over what Hector might do, but she straightened unconsciously at the insult. To be sure she was not looking her best after five days on the road. Her skirts were stiff with mud after the last ford and her hair was lank under her bonnet. Nevertheless, it would have been courteous if Jarvis had touched his hat, nodded, or otherwise acknowledged her existence. Her admiration waned, and she turned slightly to see what Hector would do.

Jarvis turned to the shepherd. 'Have them move aside,' he said.

The shepherd looked doubtful. 'The sheep might go back, I'm thinking,' he said.

Jarvis flicked his boot with a riding whip. 'The sheep are valuable,' he said. 'I'll not have them unsettled. Take the harness of that ugly grey brute and lead it aside.'

The shepherd dismounted from his dun and moved apologetically over to the wagon. 'If ye'd just be letting me have your horses' heads I'll be getting ye safely up the bank, sir,' he said. His gaze flickered to Ness. 'Ma'am.'

'You'll no touch that harness it you wish to keep your health,' said Hector. 'Move the sheep and gi' way, for we're on our way to our spread on the brae.'

The shepherd hesitated, but Hector raised his whip and looked at it significantly. As the man backed away, Hector thrust the reins at Ness and climbed heavily out of the wagon. For a moment, Ness feared he would attack the shepherd as he had tried to attack the bullocky, but instead Hector strode through the panting sheep, wading thigh-deep through woolly bodies as he had waded the fords. Before Ness' apprehensive eyes, he looked over the sheep for a moment. The sheep milled more than ever, but one fat ewe paused to take his measure, staring at him with resentful eyes and stamping her forefoot in the dust.

'Still your haivers, you woolly bitch,' said Hector. He stepped up to the defiant ewe and seized her by the wool on her shoulders. Wrestling her fore-hooves off the ground, he forced her forward through the rest of the flock and manhandled her past the wagon. He took another and another, until the rest of the flock overcame its fear and forged past the wagon, their sides scraping the horses' legs, the wheels and the brush on either side of the track.

Looking at the flooding sheep, Ness felt the wagon was caught in a fast-flowing tide. The equipage rocked and the horses, phlegmatic though they were, shifted uneasily. As the last ewe scrambled past, Hector turned to Jarvis.

'Yon's a lesson in the management of sheep, forby,' he remarked. 'I see you ha' no come by sense since last we met!'

Jarvis looked at him coldly. 'If one beast has come to harm, I'll have you in irons.'

'Aye, or hanged,' remarked Hector. 'You sleekit creature, you're no fit to take charge o' a pot o' gruel, let alone these fine sheep. I dinna ken what auld Jarvis means by it!'

The squatter smiled grimly. 'My father is dead. As for you, you unwashed savage, the sooner you return to the gutter the better. We don't want your sort hereabouts in your hovels.'

'I like it fine,' said Hector, looking up at the mountain. Without further words, he turned his back on Jarvis and swung up beside Ness in the wagon. Touching the horses with the whip he drove the wagon straight past the gaping shepherd.

Ness let out her breath in a shaky sigh. 'Have you met Mr Jarvis before, then?'

'Aye, I ken the bastard well enough,' said Hector. 'I thought him gone back to London, the sleekit creature, but instead he's come to Van Diemen's Land.'

'I see,' said Ness. 'But what if I had no been able to hold the horses?' she added. She was angry now it was all over, a puzzled, frustrated anger with Jarvis for his discourtesy, the shepherd for his impotence and with Hector for pushing the confrontation. Whatever might have happened in the two men's pasts, she had no wish to have it dragged into her present.

'You're a braw lassie. I knew fine you'd come to it,' said Hector.

Ness supposed it was a compliment, of sorts, and aside from occasional approving words on her health and form, it seemed to be the only sort she was going to get at present.

Beyond the Jarvis spread, the road became even worse, and it petered out altogether some three miles farther on. Hector got down from the wagon and led the horses, sometimes having Ness hold them while he strode ahead and cast round like a hound for the best trail. At one point, he had even to back the wagon over the uneven ground, for a huge stand of trees provided an impenetrable barrier directly ahead. Finally, as night fell, Hector paused once more and lit a lantern. Leaving Ness with the horses, he moved out in a wide circle, holding the lantern high. At intervals, Ness heard him stumbling and swearing, but by now she was used to Hector's ready stream of profanity. Most of it was in Gaelic, anyway, and she understood it imperfectly. A few minutes later, she heard an exclamation of satisfaction.

'Here it is, lassie!' he cried jubilantly. 'The blaze- a bit o' bark sliced awa' wi' a dirk!'

'What's to do wi' that?' asked Ness, cold and tired.

'Lassie -' Hector loomed out of the night and caught her out of the wagon in a giant's hug. He gave her a smacking kiss and swung her in a circle until the stars wheeled and the world contracted about her. 'Lassie, it means we're home!'

They spent that first night under the wagon. Hector hobbled the horses and spread a bolt of canvas to keep out the night air. He lit a fire and fetched water, and Ness, stiff with exhaustion, set a pot to the flames and boiled oatmeal for gruel. The bread was hard and dry, but Hector dipped it in the gruel and ate heartily, exhorting Ness to do the same.

'I want no peelie wally wife,' he reminded her, 'and you know wha' they say of those who cook and willna' eat.'

Ness did not, but she ate her gruel. It was less trouble than quarrelling with Hector.

Afterwards, he kicked out the fire, and spread blankets on the ground beneath the wagon. He stripped to sark and trews, and then lay down.

'Come, lassie - you'll see all you need in the morning.' He held up one edge of his plaid so Ness, tired beyond embarrassment, removed her muddy gown and laid herself beside him. Hector tucked the plaid about them both, and slept immediately, but Ness lay awake, feeling the tiredness as an ache in her bones. The ground was hard, and no matter how she rolled about her hipbone pained her. She settled at last on her back, and stared sightlessly at the floor of the wagon. The wind sighed through the trees, a night bird chirred, and somewhere was the whine of a mosquito. There were rustles and squeaks from forest animals, and now and again one of the horses would stamp and snort. It reminded Ness of the Jarvis ewe, which stamped and snorted at Hector, only to lose its dignity as Hector forced it past the wagon. She had a vivid mental picture of Hector treating the stamping horse likewise, and smiled in the dark. And then the horse melted inexplicably into the figure of Jarvis, mounted on his black thoroughbred, and Jarvis became Jean Leslie, who became Donal Kirkbride.

'Donal, I canna come wi' you,' muttered Ness, and slept.

The birds woke her with their singing. For a moment she blinked at the low ceiling above her, registering that Hector's hand lay possessively on her hip. She wondered what the day had in store. Not more travel, for surely they had reached their destination? Ness burrowed out from under the plaid and edged sideways until she could roll away from the wagon. The grey horse was browsing and the chestnut slept in the early sunlight, its lower lip dropped, and one hind hoof resting on its tip. Ness heard the chuckle of a burn nearby.

She hesitated a moment, but there were no dwellings and no roads, so she was unlikely to meet anyone who would care if she walked to the burn in her sark. She glanced back at Hector's feet, protruding from beneath the wagon. He was deeply asleep. Quietly, she rummaged in the wagon for her soap and a linen towel. She took a small new cooking pot, her soiled gown and her plaid, then walked softly away across the bark-littered floor of the forest, pausing to greet Grey Falcon, her favourite of the two horses, with a slap on the shoulder and a soft kissing noise which he seemed to like. There was a wild smell of honey and gum.

She could not find the burn. She heard it, bubbling and purring, but she could not see it at all. Vexed, she moved on up the brae, pausing often to listen to the elusive sound. The trees grew so high and close that the light had a greenish cast and Ness felt she might easily meet Tam Lin, fresh woken from his long sojourn with the people under the hill. Or perhaps the Lady of the Hill herself, come to carry off Hector to the fairy court.

'And muckle joy you'd have o' him, my lady, for he's my ain!' she said aloud. She laughed at her air picture of Hector, arms folded and stubborn heels planted, telling the Lady he had no time for her, as he had chosen a wife already.

As she stood, she realised what had happened to the burn. It was flowing underground! No wonder the forest seemed so lush and green. There was water aplenty, even in this dry season, but it lay hidden under the earth. Ness picked her way up the brae. At last, as she scrambled over a moss-covered tree trunk, her foot splashed down in water. She gasped with the cold of it, and there was the burn diving, canny as a burrowing rabbit, under the log. Away upstream it slid darkly between the ferns. Ness splashed up the burn. Her feet were soon numb, and then her knees as the water rose. Shivering, she scrambled up onto the bank, laid out her soap and towel, and bent to dip the gown in the water. The dirty wool resisted soaking, but she forced it down, then scrubbed it hard, working soap into the muddied patches, before rinsing it clean and hanging it over a bush. Rough laundering could do no harm, she thought, as the gown had already been wet so often at fords and soaked with dew. Hector had said often enough that wool was no good if it couldna' stand the weather.

Next, shaking with cold and her own audacity, she stripped her sark over her head. She had not been wearing her stays since a strip of whalebone worked loose and made a painful reddened patch at her waist. Hector had noticed it two days before, seized the stays and flung them out the inn wife's window, vowing that when he put his hands on his woman he wanted to feel bonnie flesh, and not whalebone and flannel. Besides, he'd added, out the window was the place for anything that dared to ill-mark his woman.

Ness glanced down at her pale body, faintly green in the forest light. Anyone who saw her now would take her for a kelpie's bride! Kneeling, she scooped water into the cook pot and wet herself down, dipping her head and massaging her scalp vigorously. The water was achingly cold and her hair, like her woollen gown, resisted the soaking. Still kneeling, she flung back her hair and wet the lavender soap in the pot, then lathered her body and head. It took some time to remove the slippery scum of soap, and Ness was more blue than green as she finally rubbed herself dry on the towel. The linen was dripping, so she wrung it out and folded it around her head. Her sark was wet and her gown still soaked, so she wrapped herself in her plaid and, gathering her belongings with purple fumbling fingers, returned down the brae to the wagon.

CHAPTER 6

Hector was awake and furious. He had opened his eyes some time before and groped instinctively for Ness, but encountered only rumpled blankets where she should be. Thinking she had gone to answer a call of nature, he lay and scratched his chest pleasurably, waiting for her return. This morning there was no need for early rising, and he looked forward to embracing her without the distraction of other folks a thin wall's breadth away. Last night she had been tired, but this morning she might show some enthusiasm for his attentions.

So far, his notion of choosing a wife had worked well. Ness was still inexperienced, and the gruel she had compounded had had lumps through it, but she proved as hardy as he hoped to the rigours of travel. Hector, a man of iron constitution, never understood why a trek across country should discommode anyone. It pleased him that Ness had not complained, save over the Jarvis incident the day before. Bloody Jarvis! Who would have thought the man would leave the Government House set in Sydney Town for the wilds of Van Diemen's Land! And living on Hector's own doorstep and all.

Ness was taking an unconscionable time, and he hoped the lassie was well. It crossed his mind that she might be breeding, but it was too early for that and he was sure she was pure when he'd wed her. Hector rolled out from under the wagon.

'Ness? Ness, lass?' His voice was swallowed up in the great forest. Hector whistled twice on the shrill double note he had always used to summon his old dog, but, apart from the stirrings of the wind and the birds, the forest was still.

Hector looked about, his first daylight sight of his new acquisition putting Ness out of his mind. He had not been misled about the quality of the timber hereabouts, but much should be conserved, so as not to degrade the mountain land. The soil was a little scanty, but when he grubbed up a handful and sniffed it smelled sweet enough. The soils of these colonies tended to be sharp, but the natural limestone in the water and just under the ground in this area should go a long way to combating that.

Hector went to examine the blaze he saw first the night before. According to the land agent who gave him directions, this blaze marked the middle of his eastern boundary. The property ran up the shoulder of the mountain and down an apron of land that spilled over the flats, ending abruptly at high cliffs falling to the Second Western River, and just yards from a wide burn, which flowed down at right angles to intercept it. This circumstance was one against which Hector had fought long and hard, but the land agent was adamant; the cliffs were high and dangerous and the eastern boundary was well to the side of the burn.

'But no doubt you'll be able to come to some mutually acceptable agreement as to access,' the agent added with more hope than certainty.

'Nae doubt,' Hector said grimly, and he repeated his sarcastic remark now.

In his experience wealthy squatters did not become wealthy through generosity. This applied equally to himself, so he scarcely blamed them, but he had loathed Whitaker Jarvis ever since their first encounter years ago and would never go to him cap in hand. He'd thought Jarvis safely in England; how had he missed hearing of the old man's death?

For now, he shelved the water problem, planning instead to walk the boundaries of the new property, pausing to blaze the trees. This should give him a good idea of the places to clear, those best left wooded, alternative water sources and the site to build a house. It would not yet be the braw house he had promised Ness, but a slab hut to shelter them while he made a start with the land. Hector eyed a fine stand of eucalypts and reached out to touch the wood. Straight and tall, he thought, and nodded approval.

Suddenly he itched to take up his axe and make a beginning, but there was his business with Ness first... and where *was* Ness? Had she wandered away and lost herself in the trees? He saw her boots set by the wagon and frowned. He had flung her old ones in the baggage for later repair, and he could see a worn out sole protruding from beneath a bag of grain. So the silly wee besom had gone off barefoot and likely trodden on a snake.

Or maybe she had met Jarvis out for a constitutional on that twig-legged black. Hector swelled indignantly at the thought. In his mind's eye he saw Ness being eyed by the Jarvis as if she were a prime filly, or a fine-bred ewe. No man had the right to look at Hector Campbell's woman with lust, or with indifference either. And Ness' own admiration when she first laid eyes on the Sassenach had not escaped him. He stamped into his boots and tossed the end of his plaid across his shoulder. The land could wait; he was away to find his wife.

He had gone less than a hundred yards when he saw her coming down the brae. She was barefoot, as expected, wrapped in her plaid, but carelessly, so he could see she was naked underneath. She carried a dripping bundle and her hair was damp down her back. Her feet were flecked with leaf mould and a thin trail of blood trickled down her bare leg from a place where she must have scratched it on a twig. For a moment Hector felt strangely moved at the sight of her, then his anger welled. Bracing himself, feet apart, arms folded across his chest, he waited to confront her. She was still thirty feet off when she saw him. Her eyes flickered and she seemed uncertain, and he thought she was feeling guilty. As well she might. Then, incredibly, she smiled at him shyly and held up a twig of dull grey, fine-cut leaves.

'Look, Hector,' she said, 'I've found some heather in the glen!'

Hector barely glanced at it. 'Where in the name of hell ha' you been, woman?' he bellowed, striding forward to seize her by the shoulders.

She dropped the bundle with a soggy sound and staggered with surprise, but raised her chin and looked him in the eye. He saw she was frightened, but also that she was not to be cowed. The lassie had spirit all right.

'I've been up the brae, Hector,' she said steadily. 'I went to look for the burn to wash mysel'. It buries itsel' down under the ground, so I ha' to go a long way.'

Her wet hair and still damp body upheld her explanation, but Hector was too angry to let it pass.

'You met no one?' he snapped. She seemed honestly perplexed, and Hector forced himself to let her go. He had struck down plenty of men in his time, but he had never harmed a woman without more cause than this. 'You should no be off by yoursel',' he muttered. 'You could ha' been lost in the forest.'

'Och, I marked my way, as I went.' She tilted her head. 'Would you ha' looked for me had I no come back again?'

'Aye, and found you too,' said Hector. 'You're shaking,' he added, as her teeth chattered.

'The water in the burn was verra cold.'

Hector touched her neck. The skin was damp and chill, still beaded randomly with water, and he could see the blue tracing of veins and even the beat of the pulse in her throat.

'Lay the plaid down in the sun, there,' he ordered, indicating a place where the falling of two trees had left an open place through the canopy overhead. A streak of pale sunlight touched the ground like a pool of thin honey, warming it.

Ness looked at him, and compressed her lips. 'I'm gey cold,' she reminded him, 'and the plaid's no so wet.'

Hector unbuckled his belt and saw she was eyeing him uneasily. Surely the silly lassie could not be thinking he would beat her now his anger had cooled! Ostentatiously, he laid aside the tawse, and spread the plaid on the ferns. He removed his sark and trews, and watched understanding dawn in her eyes. She still seemed to find it hard to look at him unclad, for she kept her gaze on his face.

'It's the light o' day,' she said uncertainly.

Hector shrugged. He had no great conceit of his appearance, but he knew his body was a good one, for his years. He was a little heavier than he had been in his youth, but what would a lassie be wanting with a man like a stick? He reached out and tugged the plaid free from her shoulders to pool around her feet, then drew her against him. She was cold, and for a moment he was repulsed, as if he were embracing a drowned woman, or a selkie of the ocean. But they were far from the ocean, and the cold was only that of the burn, so he put the fancies back where they belonged. He smelled the lavender soap she had bought in Launceston. It was a sweet smell, but not sickly like so many of the pomades and dressings other women used in their hair. She was shivering against him, and he wondered if it was entirely with cold. He kissed her, and was sure he felt the beginning of some response other than passive acceptance.

'There, that's bonnie,' he murmured. 'Lay yoursel' down on the plaid.'

Obediently, she laid herself down, hunching over on her side to screen herself from his gaze. Hector settled beside her and stroked her hip and side. The angry mark made by the foul whalebone contraption she had worn was fading, and he ran his fingers over the roughened skin and kissed it. She shivered, so he bent to kiss her again, and then buried his face against her breasts. They were cold but soft; smaller than others he had fondled, but appealing for all that. 'How old are you, lassie?' he asked.

'Eighteen, Hector,' she said with a small catch in her voice. 'Nineteen soon, I think.'

'Eighteen. Then you've grown all you will.' He cupped her breasts in his hands and kissed them one by one. He supposed they would sag after she had a bairn, but time brought changes to all, and not all change was bad. A wife could not look like a lassie forever, and why should she? He nudged her knees apart, and stroked her thighs. If she would relax a little, it would be better for both of them. They had been wed close to a week; he thought she should not have been shy of him now. He eased himself over her body, and she bit her lip. It was the first time he had taken her by daylight, and he saw faint marks that suggested she did this often.

'Now what, lassie?' said Hector, displeased. He had taken the time to caress her first, and not all men would have bothered at that. Surely she did not expect lying soft words as payment when he was taking only what was due?

'The ground is hard,' said Ness politely. 'And...'

Her voice trailed away, and it occurred to Hector that he was close to twice her weight. He eased a hand beneath her hip and felt the pressure of their combined bodies grinding his knuckles into the ground. No wonder the lassie protested! Letting her go, he rolled over on his back and held out his arms. She looked at him doubtfully, but then eased herself over to lie on top of him and even, tentatively, stroked his shoulder. Hector was used to sleeping where he could, and her weight was slight, so the hardness of the ground bothered him not at all, and he was gratified to find his young wife responding to him more than she had before, her cold hair falling over his face and neck. He felt her lips on his shoulder, which was a great improvement on her previous habit of biting her lip as if to keep from crying out. He brought his hand to her buttocks and stroked the soft roundness, then coaxed her thighs apart and slid inside.

'Well, lassie?' he said later. The patch of sun had moved away, and she was sitting up, pulling her plaid around her shoulders where her hair still lay loose and damp.

'It's good to be let to breathe,' she said prosaically. She rose to her feet and turned away to the wagon. A horse snorted and she glanced at Hector in consternation. 'Och, Hector, they saw!'

Hector laughed, and slapped her buttocks lightly, making her squeak with surprise. 'They'll see more than that, lassie, before we're auld and grey.'

He used a handful of fern to clean himself and dressed. 'I'll take a wee look at the burn,' he decided. 'You say it goes down under the ground?'

'Aye, in the place where I found the heather.' Ness spread her gown and sark to dry, and carefully transferred the diminishing block of soap to a broad leaf to harden in the air.

Hector bent and picked up the sprig of leaves she had dropped. It was small and prickly, and he rubbed it between his fingers. 'Aye, I've seen this before,' he said. 'The leaf's a little different, but it has bells in the winter - bonnie pink and white bells.'

'It's heather,' said Ness. 'Heather from the glen. It's like being home, Hector!'

'You are home, lassie,' he corrected. 'Home in your place and mine, but it needs a name, forby. What would you call it?'

Ness thought for a moment, and then reached out to take the spiny sprig of leaves from Hector. For a moment, their hands clasped together over the sprig, and then Ness smiled, despite the small pain she must feel from her pricked fingers. 'Why should we no call it "Glen Heather"?'

CHAPTER 7

For a few days the goods were stacked beneath the wagon while Hector and Ness slept under the dark canopy of trees. Hector cut ferns and dried scrub to make a mattress, and Ness learned to shake up the bedding each morning to dislodge insects. She also learned to cook and wash under the primitive conditions, and became adept at making stews from vegetables, oatmeal and the game Hector shot.

She was disconcerted when presented with her first kangaroo. It was a pretty beast, smaller than a sheep, with long, bent hind legs and an enormously muscular tail. Hector carried it into the glen on his shoulder and dumped it by the hearth; a simple fire-hole ringed with stones. He skinned it, scraped the hide and pegged it out to dry in the sun, then handed his dirk to Ness. Recognising a challenge when she saw it, Ness sawed off joints of meat to add to the evening meal. The meat was dark and lean and very tough, but it made a change from vegetables and gruel. Later, Hector brought other meat; a brightly coloured bird with a hooked, heavy beak, a small climbing creature that reminded Ness of a shaggy cat, and once, a snake. It became a point of honour that Ness would never recoil, no matter how strange the addition to the menu. Some of the larger beasts had to be hung (shrouded in muslin to keep insects away) in the trees for two or three days to render the tough flesh fit to eat.

Meanwhile, Hector decided to build the slab hut deep among the trees. When Ness suggested it might be better to build up the brae, Hector informed her curtly it was his decision, so she apologised and returned to her work. He had every right to chide her, she thought, and wondered what would have become of her had Hector not been on the wharf that day.

Hector began his conquest of Glen Heather by marking and cutting trees for timber. Ness watched in awe as her husband swung his axe, teeth bared with the effort, a frown of concentration in his grey eyes. He was allowing his beard to grow, dark, but streaked with grey, and she thought of the old Scots heroes she had seen in books. The jarring as the axe bit into the wood made the tree tremble, but Hector's shoulders were braced and his forearms seemed hard as the iron. When the tree crashed through the lesser trees about it, Hector lopped the branches, trimmed them, and hauled them aside in a pile.

'I can do that,' offered Ness, but he told her to tend to the blankets. Ness had done so already, but she had learned not to argue with Hector, so she took the goods from the haberdasher and set to fashioning herself a new skirt. It would soon be Hogmanay. There would be no celebrations, but was it not said a Hogmanay in rags meant rags for the following twelvemonth?

The Campbells had not long to spend alone, for on the third day after their arrival, six men arrived at Glen Heather. One was on horseback, but the other five were ragged and dusty, and had obviously tramped for miles. They had greyish bundles on their backs and carried axes and a rusty crosscut saw. Ness could not restrain a gasp of shock when they appeared, but Hector greeted them curtly, gesturing to them to lay aside their bundles and begin work. He spoke briefly to the sixth man, who nodded, and rode away.

Ness stared as the sound of axes and saw began to ring out. She knew Hector was capable, but now she wondered if he were not a wizard. How had he summoned five working men from the forest? Finally, she ventured to ask.

'What business is it o' yours, Ness?' He sounded curt rather than angry, but she felt herself blush.

'We canna feed them all!' she said lamely.

Hector showed his teeth in a grin. 'Nae need, lassie. They've brought their rations wi' them in their swags.'

'Where - where will they sleep, Hector?'

'Och, I ha' them frae Dick Bruning, the carrier at Mersey. He's little to do till harvest, so they work for me and I pay Dick for their services. The overseer will be back at sunset to see them back again.'

'Oh,' said Ness again, faintly. She remembered that Hector had stopped off briefly at the inn at Mersey, but surely he could not have arranged this in half an hour? 'Dinna the men mind being sold off like this?' she ventured.

'They ha' no choice, Ness. They are convicts, sent frae England for all manner o' crimes.'

'But one is only a bairn!'

Hector shrugged. 'Bairns can be bad as men. But ha' no fear - these will no harm you.'

Ness had scarcely thought of that. She had seen some of the chain gangs on their journey from Launceston, lines of hopeless wretches breaking stones with great hammers and carting it in barrows to mend and make the roads. Some of the men had sore eyes, and some were lame. They wore ragged clothes, with dirt everywhere. Even the bairns seemed prematurely greyed and their red-rimmed eyes peered out from dust-laden sockets. She looked again at the five who now worked at Glen Heather. The work was hard, but surely better than stone breaking. Perhaps they were grateful for a change. She caught the eye of the youngest, and smiled in sympathy. He dropped his gaze and Ness sighed.

Hector looked at her sternly. "Ha' nothing to do wi' them, Ness. They're here to work and a'.' He took up his own axe and Ness went back to her scissors and thread.

When midday came, the convicts went into the trees to eat their rations. Ness could not see what it was, but Hector told her it was probably beef and rough bread compounded from their weekly rations of twelve pounds of wheat and seven of meat. Ness had made a thick broth from kangaroo meat, barley and some onions, and baked flour and water into a kind of flat bread in the hot coals, but Hector paused for scarcely ten minutes to eat. It seemed the convicts worked very hard, and they had a long walk at the end of the day. Hector was older than any of them and he worked hard too. But Hector worked for his own land and gain, which surely made a difference. And Glen Heather was hers as well! Ness wished there was something she could do to help, but Hector told her curtly to tend to her cooking and washing and making do.

Even after the hut was built, Hector continued to be preoccupied, clearing land through the long, mild summer of 1837 and 1838. Fencing would have taken valuable time, so Hector had large tree trunks and branches dragged into windrows by a bullock team from Mersey. Small branches and roots were heaped and burned, and the ashes scattered with dung to fertilise the soil. At first Ness shuddered at the gashes and blisters the workers suffered, but she soon became hardened, and found herself using her sewing kit quite often to extract the long, fierce splinters that pierced Hector's hands. It was more difficult to harden to the mess and destruction of the green, lovely forest and she mourned Glen Heather as she first saw it. The blows of the axes and the curses of the men made her head ache, and after a time she would tidy her sewing, put on her boots and set off to explore, away from the smell of smoke and of raw, torn earth.

She did this a good deal during those first weeks at Glen Heather. It was comfort to discover the extent of the forest that climbed the flanks of the range; wild, strange country, both like and curiously unlike her homeland. The stony soil and tough stemmed heather-like plants were familiar, but the stone was limestone, pocked and dimpled with holes like honeycomb or foreign cheese. Some hollows passed as small caves, not narrow wee caves, but caverns worn by the action of water. And water was everywhere. The ground was stony, but leaf-mould made it spongy underfoot. Often, as she climbed the brae, Ness heard the murmur of a burn as it slid secretly underground. Was it the one from which she drew water for cooking and washing? She might have asked Hector, but he was preoccupied with his work on the flats. Ness felt like a ghost, for Hector scarcely reacted to her presence any more. He ate meals she provided, and washed in water she heated in the iron kettle. Sometimes she woke in the night to find him sleeping beside her, but he was out far into the darkness and gone in the morning when she woke. It seemed their moment of accord when she named Glen Heather had never been. She had meant to bring him his dream, but it seemed to her he was following it alone.

Look at me! she longed to say, grasping his arms and turning him to face her. *See me, see your wife, need me, want me...love me.*

Hector was indifferent rather than unkind, so Ness wandered where she would, becoming adept at telling from the angle of sun and shadow when it was time to prepare or serve his meals. She thought Hector might as well have hired her as a maidservant as a wife. But she *was* his wife, and she knew her duty, so she made sure food was always ready when he was hungry and answered politely whenever he spoke to her. He would surely come to think more of her when the house was built and the land open for stocking. And when she had his child... his son... then he would see her. It *would* be a son, she was sure. She could not imagine Hector fathering a lassie.

But the month after her wedding brought her bleeding as usual. She was bewildered; having taken it for granted that Hector's attentions would have resulted in a child by now. He had lain with her several times, and from her observations of her father's bitch she thought one such union should suffice. She hesitated to mention the matter, thinking he would not notice unless he chose to lie with her that night. She suffered cramping pains, but she was used to it, and tore some calico for the necessary rags. As usual, she felt out of sorts, so she left camp early and climbed the brae. Perhaps she was preoccupied, or perhaps her disappointment made her careless, but when she put her foot on a patch of rough grass by the burn she did not test her weight before taking another step. The ground gave way beneath her.

Ness pitched forward, grasping instinctively at the ground ahead. The rough vegetation stung her hands, and her knee struck something sharp. Later, she found she had torn her skirt, but now she was afraid for herself, afraid of lying injured on the hillside for hours. How long would it be before Hector missed her?

"*Would you have looked for me had I no come back again?*' she'd asked that first morning at Glen Heather. And he said he would, and that he'd find her. But he would be so angry...

'Och, stop haivering, Ness Campbell,' she told herself sternly. 'You're no so badly hurt.'

Carefully, she pulled herself forward on hands and knees. Her knee bled, one ankle was wrenched; her hands stung, but that was all. Ness rubbed her ankle, then pulled off her boot and dangled her foot in the burn. The cold soon soothed the pain away, and she turned with belated curiosity to see what tripped her. It was a hole, a veritable hole in the hillside, a little bigger than her boot, with the edges torn and clotted with earth and leaf-mould. Ness leaned to put her hand down. The cold was almost palpable, and she shivered and withdrew. There was no use in peering down, for it was dark as Hades down there.

There seemed nothing further to be learned so she dried her foot, put on her boot and made her way back to the camp. She intended to tell Hector of her discovery, but his abstraction made it difficult to broach the subject. And what was there to say? She had found a hole deeper than her arm was long and had lost her footing. In the end, Ness said nothing, for fear he might forbid her wanderings. Her ankle swelled and turned grey with bruising, but by staying close to home she was able to carry on her work as usual. It seemed likely to her that Hector never noticed at all.

***

Hector Campbell noticed more than Ness realised, but just now his formidable energies were bent to the creation of Glen Heather. The slab hut was quickly built. First, logs were rolled and pegged with wooden stakes, with slabs of timber added progressively. The roof was made of bark peeled from the fallen trees. Each sheet was over an inch thick, smooth and woody on the inside and rough and fibrous on the outer. Like British thatch, it had the advantage of being waterproof and readily renewable. The floor was beaten earth, and Hector trimmed wild cherry branches to make a tolerable bed.

He made the hut big enough to accommodate himself and his wife, as well as the stores and such furnishings as he might obtain. Cost was no problem, for he could readily have bought the contents of a furnishing emporium. What he lacked was the time and the adequate means to transport unwieldy articles through the bush. It would be time to trouble himself about the elegancies of life when the road was made. For now, the hut would do. They might have a bairn or two soon, but the "braw house" would be built before the family grew large.

Hector expected Ness to fall pregnant soon after their wedding. He was a lusty man, and she was bonnie and healthy, so a bairn should follow inevitably, and he had no doubt it would arrive with as little fuss as a lamb.

Once the hut was built, he spent longer days falling timber and readying a field for sowing with grass seed fetched from Westbury by Bullocky George. Plenty of burns started out from the shoulder of the tiers, but most of them disappeared long before they reached the flats, surfacing only occasionally on the way. The one large watercourse was a burn which flowed down a natural gully, and that was on Scarborough land. Water must be provided to every part of the run, for Hector hoped to stock the flats within a year. He was already wealthy, but his investment was centred on this property. It was curiously intriguing to develop a property for his personal use instead of for a swift and profitable resale.

With his energies and thoughts directed to Glen Heather, Hector noticed his wife only as a calm, industrious figure in the background. It was pleasant, but not essential, to return to a hot meal and water drawn ready to wash away charcoal and grime. It was pleasant, but not essential, to have a woman to accommodate him when he felt the urge to lie with her. In the back of his mind, it pleased him that she was comely, and Scottish, and young. It pleased him that she was there, but just at present he hadn't time to spare from his main concerns. A woman could know nothing of clearing and fertilising land, and nothing of the problems that beset him from all sides as he tried to force two years of work into the span of one.

While Hector was absorbed in the future aspect of Glen Heather, Ness learned to love the face it had. The loneliness was part of this face, so she was astonished when she met a horsewoman on a faintly marked path on the mountain. The horse was a sturdy bay mare, the woman looked a half-dozen years older than Ness. Ness was consumed with envy. She had occasionally scrambled on the broad back of Hector's Grey Falcon, but she had only a rudimentary knowledge of riding. Falcon was a patient animal, and well-disposed towards Ness, and she thought she would have felt more secure had she sat astride as the men did, but her long skirts would hamper her terribly and she hesitated to display her ankles to anyone but Hector. Hector told her occasionally that they were right bonnie, and she treasured the rare warmth of the compliment. Ankles, she thought, were an odd thing for him to admire, but she was pleased when the injury faded, leaving hers unmarked.

The strange rider was dressed more finely than the ladies on the *Lithgow*, with flounced skirts, a mannish coat and plumed hat. Ness felt dowdy and abashed in her draggled skirts, but it was the other woman who seemed most disconcerted. Her gloved hands tightened on the reins and the mare came to an ungraceful halt. Wide blue eyes peered out in consternation at Ness, and Ness flushed, convinced the other woman thought her some drab gypsy from the forest - or, worse, a wandering convict. That would reflect poorly on Hector as well as on herself. Drawing herself up, she extended a hand, aware it was bare and scratched.

'Good morning,' she said politely, 'it is a braw fine day, is it no?'

'Indeed,' said the other woman faintly.

'I am Mistress Campbell,' said Ness, her new name still tasting strange on her tongue.

'Campbell!' The stranger's hand flew to her lips in an obvious gesture of dismay. 'Oh, Mrs Campbell, pray do not think ill of me, but if Mr Jarvis should find you on Scarborough land he will not be pleased. He and your - your husband have had a rare falling out, you know. They knew one another in Sydney Town, and I believe your husband has threatened mischief because Mr Jarvis would not sell him some land.'

'This isna Scarborough land, it's Glen Heather!' protested Ness. 'It's yoursel' who is trespassing, if you wish to name it that. I've no objection, forby.'

'Glen Heather? Really? I would swear I had not crossed the stream, but perhaps I chanced on one of the underground fords and so crossed without noticing. Pray forgive me, Mrs Campbell.' The stranger pursed her lips. 'But how remiss of me! I am Mrs Jarvis. Eliza Jarvis.'

'Aye, I thought as much,' said Ness. The flurry of words had washed over her, and she was sure this Eliza Jarvis had said more civil words in a breath than Hector managed in a day.

Eliza Jarvis gathered the reins to turn her mare about, but Ness put out an appealing hand. 'Can you no stop and talk a little?' she said wistfully. 'It's gey long since I had a lassie's company.'

Mrs Jarvis laughed. 'Perhaps I could stay for just a little,' she allowed. 'I have company all the time, alas, tho' not from a *lassie*.' She pulled a wry face. 'Mr Jarvis' mother resides with us at Scarborough and sometimes I yearn for peace from her clacking tongue. She always knows what is best to be done, and never allows me an opinion. She has been mistress of the house for years and finds it impossible to step to the rear. She has a lapdog - the most odious creature! She calls it her dear Kitty.'

'Then you'll no be wanting to talk wi' me,' said Ness, disappointed. By now she had time to look past the elegant clothes and see that Eliza Jarvis had a sweet and open face. Fair ringlets fell forward from her hat and she had a dimple in one cheek. Only by her pallor and a small, primmed together mouth detracted from her beauty.

'I would be glad to converse with you, Mrs Campbell. But - will you husband not be angry if you are late home?'

'He'll never notice,' said Ness. 'He is busy wi' making our dream.'

Eliza relaxed in the saddle. 'I would come down if I could,' she said, 'but I cannot remount without a block. Perhaps you have one nearby?'

'Only a tree stump,' said Ness, 'and those are all at home.'

Eliza laughed. 'Perhaps you could help me back on?' she suggested. 'I would try not to soil your gown.'

Ness spread her hands. 'Och, this is not my best by a long space,' she said. 'I wear it when I ramble.' She took the bridle ring and looked politely away.

Eliza unhooked her leg from the curving pommel, and slid from the saddle. She stood breathing heavily for a moment, then looped her mount's reins about a branch and subsided on a convenient fallen log, arranging her dark blue skirts.

'Have you been married long?' she asked as Ness sat beside her. 'You came from Scotland, I can tell, but how long ago was that? Was it a hard journey? Were you married there? Have you children? I have a son, a sweet boy, but he fatigues me to death; Nannie Goodridge has the care of him today. She is the third nurse I have employed, and has a strong dislike of spirits. One maid I employed managed to drink half a hogshead of good brandy before I sent her away!'

Questions and comment pattered on as limpidly as the water of a burn, and, it seemed, as meaninglessly too, but Ness answered that she had been married over three months ago in Launceston, and had been at Glen Heather since then.

'What, has your husband not taken you to town for a visit, even?' exclaimed Eliza. 'I should fall into a green melancholy if Mr Jarvis did not take me to town each month. We spend weeks at a time there, since Mr Jarvis has an overseer for Scarborough.'

'Hector has been gey busy wi' the work,' said Ness defensively. 'He kens fine I understand. Glen Heather is for the both of us, you see. Do you ride out often, Mistress Jarvis?'

'Oh, do call me Eliza,' said the other woman. 'And then I may call you ...?'

'Ness.'

'What a pretty name! Is it Scotch?'

'It is for Agnes, but I was always Ness to Donal and my da.'

'Donal is your husband's name? I thought you said—'

'Och, no, my husband is Hector. Donal was my brother, back home.'

There was a tiny pause, and then Eliza recalled and answered Ness' question. 'I ride out when Mother Jarvis has fretted me quite to flinders, and also on days like this. Mr Jarvis is having one of the convicts lashed at the whipping post, and I do not like to hear it.'

Ness had thought Hector cold and indifferent to the dusty men who worked for him, but certainly he had never lashed them. He had knocked one down for insolence, but the man had not seemed to resent it overmuch. 'Can you no stop him?' she asked.

'Not at all,' said Eliza. 'The man was insolent, and must be punished. I do not care to be nearby while it is done, that is all.' She smiled ruefully at Ness' horror. 'Mr Jarvis is not a cruel master, Ness. The man will be given seven lashes and have his rations docked for the day. He will not be sent to the chain gang, which is what the poor wretches dread most. And what could I do to prevent it?'

Ness quite saw Eliza's point. A wife could not go against her husband.

'Let us speak of more pleasant subjects,' suggested Eliza. 'Have you a flower garden, Ness? And are you to attend the May Day Subscription Ball at York Hall?'

Ness shook her head. 'I have no garden yet, but there are flowers a'plenty up the brae. Hector has built us a wee house. He has planted onions and other kitchen things by the burn pool.'

'The *burn pool*?' said Eliza.

'Aye, it is where the water comes up to the air. If we could have a good stream o' water instead o' just the pool, Hector would be less troubled.'

Eliza nodded wisely. 'Mr Jarvis talks always of water, and of soil and of his everlasting sheep. Not to speak of horses! I am fond of my Gillyflower, but with Mr Jarvis they amount to a veritable passion! But gentlemen are forever prosing on about such subjects; I know little about it. How big is your house, Ness? Is it brick, like Scarborough?'

'It is a wee house Hector made himself o' logs and caulk. We shall have a better one soon, forby.'

'Oh, I am sorry, I had not realised you were ... were ...'

Ness felt herself redden. Eliza Jarvis obviously thought her a pauper. 'We're no short o' funds,' she protested. 'Hector will build a braw house soon, but the land comes first.'

'I am sure he will, Ness, and I am sorry if I have caused you discomfort with my loose tongue. I had forgotten how short a time you and Mr Campbell have been here. Why, Mr Jarvis' father (rest his soul) had owned Scarborough for fifteen years or more and Mr Jarvis has had it a year and still the grounds at the rear are a veritable wasteland! It puts me to the blush whenever I have callers and I try to contrive that they do not see it.' She rose, brushing twigs and bark off her fine skirt.

'Must you be going?' asked Ness, disappointed.

'Indeed I must. But Ness, could you not prevail upon your husband to take you to the Subscription Ball at York Hall? It is on May Day, and I shall be attending this year, for we are out of mourning for Mr Jarvis' papa.'

'Perhaps,' said Ness, but with Hector working all day and far into the night to clear trees, she could scarcely hope he would find time to take her to balls. Forgetting that Eliza had asked her help in remounting the mare, Ness turned and walked back towards the distant ring of axes.

CHAPTER 8

Eliza knew she had offended the Scotch girl, but really, how could one avoid it? If Agnes Campbell were truly a person of wealth and position, why was she rambling the mountain dressed in a gown which Milly the kitchen maid would scorn to wear? With that strong Scotch accent, she sounded more like a maid than a lady; indeed, her voice was distinctly reminiscent of the late unlamented Kirsty who had had such a passion for brandy... And yet, there was something curiously taking about this girl. She was not coarse featured, and certainly not blowsy or pert. She was...collected.

Eliza shrugged, and put Agnes Campbell out of her mind. She had still to remount her mare Gillyflower. After a little thought, she used the log on which she had been sitting to good effect. It was a sad scramble, and her leg was surely bruised from rough contact with the pommel, but at least she could ride home instead of having to arrive ignominiously on foot, and probably green-slobbered over her habit shoulder from Gillyflower's affectionate nudges.

She made her way slowly home, thinking with pleasure of the coming ball. York Hall was the oldest and finest of all the local establishments. Larger than Scarborough, it had been built twenty years before by an English gentleman, and already it boasted splendid grounds with mature magnolia trees, a rose arbour and a lily pond tastefully lit by lanterns in the boughs that sheltered it. The ball was held annually, and Eliza intended to visit Launceston in plenty of time for the modiste to make her a new gown. Her thoughts strayed to Ness Campbell again. She scarcely believed the girl would come to the ball; and perhaps it would be better if she did not; likely she had no suitable gowns and it would be an unkindness to allow her to make a figure of herself in homespun.

It seemed a long way home, and Eliza was faint with hunger as Gillyflower trotted along the track to the Scarborough stables. She noticed with relief that the wooden triangle was deserted. It would have been most discomforting if she had returned while the overseer was lashing the man Jenkins. He was young, and might have cried out.

Really, thought Eliza, the man should learn to curb his tongue. Did he not know how lucky he was to be employed at Scarborough instead of breaking his body along with the stones on the chain gang? A lashing from the overseer was nothing compared with the horrible injuries road makers suffered. Her stomach turned as she thought of the putrefying wounds she had seen, and smelled, as they passed a chain gang on the road to Launceston. It was said the surgeon had nothing but water and salts at his disposal, so washing and purging were the only possible treatments for ills. Dirty bandages and oozing wounds had given testimony that water and purgatives were not enough.

There was blood on the stones by the whipping post and Eliza averted her gaze, sickened. Worse, a shriek rose from the stable block as she passed, shrill as the cry of a kicked dog. No doubt the overseer was salting Jenkins' stripes, a proceeding which must hurt more than the original lashing, but which was held up as a sovereign remedy against infection. Eliza urged Gillyflower to the mounting block and waited, tapping her crop against her boot, until Soames came strolling out of the stable to take charge of the mare. She would wash and change her habit, and have Nannie Goodridge fetch little Winston to her for a visit before tea. By then, she might feel well enough disposed to talk to Mother Jarvis in the parlour. She would not mention her meeting with young Mrs Campbell. Mother Jarvis would be bound to tell her son and that would lead to tiresome explanations, and even more tiresome animadversions about Campbell and his uncouth manners and low breeding, a subject of which Eliza had already heard quite enough.

***

Ness, too, kept quiet about her meeting with Eliza Jarvis. A ball would have been exciting, but some joys were not to be looked for. Worse, Hector might be angry that she had stopped to talk with his enemy's wife. She bit her lip in thought. One piece of intelligence she had gleaned from Eliza was that Hector had apparently tried to buy some Scarborough land. She wondered when he had done so, and on what terms. And *why*, since he apparently hated Jarvis so? To ask would bring a curt reply or none, so she set herself to forget it, and the ball. She *did* feel, however, that it would be agreeable to meet Eliza Jarvis, or indeed, any amiable lady, again. There were a few questions which sorely troubled her and which she could not quite bring herself to discuss with Hector.

Hector was not in the habit of observing Sundays in the traditional fashion. He chafed all through those days of rest, working alone, and bemoaning the fact that custom decreed convicts must attend Divine Service.

'And little good it will do the rascals,' he complained.

Ness did her best to soothe him on this particular day, reading aloud from her Bible, and dressing in the new gown she fancied Hector liked, but he was restless and even more taciturn than usual. From his few remarks Ness gathered that the continuing fair weather was a trial to him. Not only had it led Dick Bruning to reclaim four of his men for the corn harvest, but Hector had sown grass seed which needed rain to bring it to life.

'If that sleekit wretch Jarvis would but sell me the stretch o' land by the burn, all would be well,' he complained, and Ness bit her lip hard to keep from retorting that if Hector had not provoked Jarvis in the encounter with the sheep, perhaps the man might not have been so thrawn.

'Did you ask him to sell, Hector?' she said instead.

'Aye. He said I should sell up instead, but I'll ha' water yet, will he sell or will he no.'

Ness felt a definite qualm. If Hector riled Jarvis, she would never make Eliza's further acquaintance. She was about to question him when a pair of saddle horses entered the clearing. Hector stood watchfully in his usual braced position, but Ness gazed at the riders in growing delight. One was a man, small and slight-looking (but most men *were* insignificant, when compared with her Hector) but the other was a woman, a comfortable, middle-aged body to whom Ness warmed at once.

'Dick Bruning,' said Hector shortly in answer to her hopeful enquiry. 'And the good lady is his wife.'

Ness smiled. If Bruning had fetched along his wife, the call must be a social one. She shook out the skirts of her new gown, and stepped forwards, extending her hands in welcome.

'Mistress Bruning, how very nice to make your acquaintance,' she began.

'And yours, my child,' said the woman, dismounting from her mare with a puff. She smiled, her weathered skin wrinkling into good-tempered lines. 'Do call me Theodora.'

Hector and Bruning hitched the horses in the shade, then went off among the trees to make arrangements for the return of the convicts when the harvest was done. Ness, left alone with Theodora Bruning, diffidently offered tea, for Hector had had a small chest of the expensive stuff fetched from Launceston with extra grass seed and more flour and salt.

Life with Hector was a bewildering mixture of plenty and poverty. He never stinted on things he considered necessary, but items Ness would have liked were rarely considered. Just occasionally he surprised her with a small gift. When her supply of lavender soap diminished to a sliver a fresh box of it appeared in the delivery along with some that smelled entrancingly of violets. When she tried to make it last, he laughed and told her not to fash herself.

'I ken you like to smell fresh, lassie!' he said and in welcoming guests Ness was pleased to think the woman, at least, might notice the effects of his gift.

'We have only tin pannikins to drink from, Mistress Bruning,' she apologised now. 'Hector says there will be time enough for china cups when our big house is built.'

Theodora sat down on one of the sawn stumps with a sigh. She was stout, and red-cheeked, and the cut of her serviceable grey riding habit was conservative rather than fashionable, but she had a kind face, and assured Ness that the cups did not matter a whit.

'Personally, I hold my breath whenever Mr Bruning touches my good cups. Men and china are sadly matched, and no wonder, when you consider their days are spent holding an axe or a cow.' She smiled. 'The men, I mean, not the cups. One could hardly see a cup holding an axe *or* a cow. I see you can brew tea without turning it to dishwater, which is an admirable trait in a bride, and in her husband!'

'Hector likes it strong, Mistress Bruning,' said Ness. 'And he is no' a mean man.'

'Call me Theodora!' insisted her guest. 'And I shall call you—?'

'Agnes. Ness, if you like.'

'Ness. A pretty name, like Bess, which was my mother's.' Theodora looked about at the neat small hut, at the beginnings of a garden and the hearth where Ness was simmering meat and vegetables for the midday meal. 'So you came here straight from Scotland, Ness,' she said abruptly. 'I expect it all seems very strange to you. And from what Mr Bruning says, Mr Campbell is not one to settle easily into his place in society.' Faced with a direct observation like this, Ness was speechless. 'He is considerably older than you, my dear,' went on Theodora, 'and perhaps overlooks that fact that you need female companionship.'

'Mistress Bruning, I mean, Theodora!' said Ness, abruptly recovering her tongue. 'I doubt you should speak o' Hector in this manner.'

'Bless you, I wasn't reproaching you, or your man,' said Theodora. 'You would scarcely look so blooming if he did not treat you well enough. I just meant that if you ever need to talk to another woman for any reason, you may send word by Dick's overseer. You send word and I come. There. That's what I came to say, and I said it.' She looked shrewdly at Ness. 'You think me a meddlesome old woman.'

'I dinna think that,' said Ness hastily. 'It's gey kind o' you to offer.'

'Have you met anyone since you came from Launceston?'

Ness divined she was not referring to the inn wife, or convict servants, and hesitated. 'I did meet Mistress Jarvis some time ago, but that is all. There are no so many folk about, and Hector works gey hard.'

'Eliza Jarvis is a nice girl,' said Theodora. 'Did she not invite you to take tea?'

'No, but I didna invite her,' said Ness defensively. 'I think she thought me unco shabby and drearsome...' She gestured helplessly at the raw surroundings, and added; 'She lives in a braw big house.'

'Lord, that would never trouble Eliza,' said Theodora with a laugh. 'She has not a particle of snobbery in her make-up and would have no reason to feel herself above you, my dear, but perhaps just at present she is not taking callers. I think the best way to widen your acquaintance is for you to attend a small tea-party at my house.'

'I wouldna put you to the trouble.'

'It would be no trouble, my dear. Believe me, we women have little enough entertainment in Van Diemen's Land. Shall we say three Sundays hence? If your husband cannot escort you, send word. Our groom and his wife will fetch you and bring you safe back again.'

The men returned then, and, shortly afterwards, the Brunings left.

'Until we meet again,' said Theodora in parting. She smiled at Ness, then turned to Hector; 'Mr Campbell, I have asked your wife to take tea with me one a day quite soon. I trust you have no objection?'

Hector nodded curtly. 'Thank you, Mistress Bruning; Agnes will be pleased to accept.'

Ness thought of the coming tea party a lot, but took care not to burden Hector with her speculations. She was sure he would have no interest in any society gathering.

***

It was true that Hector never troubled with society in New South Wales, but with his removal to Van Diemen's Land and his acquisition of a wife and property, he began to see himself in a new light. From holding interests in several ventures, he now devoted himself to just two. Glen Heather must become the foremost wool property of the colony, and his family must be established. By paying his bills promptly, and often in cash, he had already set himself up as a man of substantial means in Launceston, and he made it his business to deal honestly with Dick Bruning. If Ness were to be taken up by Bruning's wife and accepted in the small local community, it would go some way towards establishing the Campbell family credibility. He looked at his wife with calculating eyes as she went quietly about her work, and it occurred to him with a shock that she was looking down at heel. Her Sunday gown was tolerable enough - he thought it was one she had recently made herself - but it lacked a certain flair and dash. The colour was too quiet, and it had deficiencies in style. He thought of the ladies whom he had partnered in New South Wales no more than five months before, and decided their gowns had been fuller about the skirt and tighter about the breast than the one Ness wore. Ness was bonnie, and worth the best he could offer. With typical efficiency, he set out to solve this problem.

He had no time to take Ness to Launceston, so he sent word by Dick Bruning to the mercer she had patronised before. Hector's credit was excellent, and resulted in bolts of cloth, packs of thread, ribbons and more arriving at Glen Heather a week before the proposed tea-party.

'Are these all for *me*, Hector?' Ness asked in amazement.

Hector nodded dourly. 'You need a guid gown for your tea party wi' Mistress Bruning.'

'Och, there's enough for twenty gowns, here!' said Ness.

Hector waved his hand expansively. 'Make yoursel' fine, lassie. The lady o' Glen Heather is the match o' any in the district.' Ness nodded dazedly. 'You'll want to set to right away,' said Hector, patting her bottom. 'Aye, you'll look right bonnie, Ness, when you're dressed up fine. Mind, you look bonnie always to me, but in a new gown you'll overshine them all.'

She flushed with pleasure, but when Hector had taken his axe and gone, she stood staring at the bolts of cloth. There was a soft blue merino, nuns' veiling in dotted yellow, and a green cut velvet. Any of these would make a fine gown, but Ness found her eyes straying to the final choice; a bolt of changeable silk taffeta in crimson. Reverently, Ness fingered the cloth, lifting an edge and holding it to the light. It was lovely, glowing stuff. How bonnie would Hector think her if she wore it? Would the ladies at Theodora's tea party be amazed? Fine feathers made fine birds, but a duck in pheasants' finery was still a duck, and the silk would be utterly ruined by inexperienced cutting. With a sigh, Ness laid the crimson by and picked up the pale blue merino. Even that was finer by far than anything she'd worn before. After spreading some cut sacks on the ground and using her Sunday gown as a pattern, she snapped her shears and began to cut.

When Hector returned that evening, she was fitting the pinned-together result, and he surprised her with a burst of rage.

'I had you fetched the cloth to make a fine gown!' he snapped.

'And so I made one! As fine as any I ever had!'

Hector's face was stony as always, but his grey eyes glinted with exasperation. 'You silly wee besom, you'll look like a kitchen maid besides the ladies o' Jarvis and Reeve and a' that!'

Ness felt herself grow red, then white. 'So that's what you think o' me, Hector Campbell! A kitchen maid! Well and so I might ha' been a kitchen maid, but for you! But no, you'd be wedding me, and bringing me here and now you want me to act the fine lady and wi' *what*? Aye, you fetched me cloth, and I'm thanking you kindly, but I canna cut a gown wi'out a pattern!'

'Nonsense, woman! Make the skirt bigger round, and the breast tighter, aye, and tie up your hair the way the ladies do!'

'I canna!' cried Ness.

'Whisht, woman, get on wi' it!'

He stalked into the slab hut where Ness could hear him noisily preparing for bed. A few tears of rage and misery gathered. 'Och, the man's thrawn and impossible,' she muttered, raking the coals so vigorously that the fire flared in a burst of sparks. She stayed out until the cold and the increasing whine of mosquitoes drove her into the hut. Even then, she would have slept elsewhere, in protest, but the bedding was the only tolerably comfortable place in the hut. Muttering under her breath, she wrapped herself in her shawl and slid under the blankets.

'You're cauld as ice, lassie,' said Hector, as if the spat had never been. Ness stiffened as he drew her closer and thrust his hand down the loose neck of her sark to find her breast.

'You'll tear the cloth,' she said stiffly, tugging away.

'Then you'd best take it off, had you no?' Hector sounded indulgent, and she had no real wish to anger him again, so she obeyed. 'Aye, that's bonnie,' he said as she stripped and lay down. He ran an appreciative hand over her breasts and then down to her stomach. Ness stirred uneasily as familiar sensations began to awaken. Sometimes when Hector caressed her she wanted to stretch and purr like a contented cat, at others she would allow her own hands to explore the surprising differences of his body, tasting the salt of his sweat and smelling the familiar scent of healthy flesh mingling with the ever-present tang of wood smoke and the faint sweet odour of the ferns and wild cherry which made up their bedding. Tonight, she felt taut and twitchy, angry with herself and with him. Hector's hand, calloused and roughened from healed blisters and the drying effect of the sun, ran over her stomach again, spanning her almost from hip to hip with the broad splay of his fingers. The pressure was uncomfortable, and Ness squirmed.

'Are you expecting a bairn, lassie?' asked Hector. 'You feel different.' He pushed his palm against her stomach and then touched her breasts. 'Fuller, here.'

Ness felt the blood rushing to her cheeks. She knew now why she had felt so nervous, and why she had wept with frustrated rage. Her bleeding was due, but how was she to explain to Hector? The first time she bled she had feared the worst and wept by herself in the byre, then gone to Jean Leslie who smiled and allayed her terrors. But Jean was gone, and... she bit her lip. 'My bleeding will be soon,' she said reluctantly.

'Then you'd likely not fall tonight,' responded Hector.

Ness half raised her head. 'But I thought- I thought-'

'If you plant seed in the winter you willna raise a crop,' said Hector simply. 'Nor bairns, at the wrong season.'

'Then you'll no plant seed tonight!' snapped Ness, and turned away. To her chagrin, Hector merely patted her hip then did the same, and was soon asleep.

The half-awakened sensations faded gradually, but Ness lay wondering. There were still too many things she did not understand.

CHAPTER 9

Morning brought cramps and the easing of her tensions. The arrival of Bruning's overseer with the labourers reminded Ness of Theodora's offer, so she sent a message as directed, and the next morning Theodora rode into the clearing. Within hours, she had cut panels of blue merino and left them with Ness to stitch while she sewed ruffles for trimming.

'Perhaps you'd have done better to bespeak Eliza, my dear,' she said comfortably, squinting to thread a needle. 'She is a fashion plate as I am not, but she's not feeling quite the thing just now.'

'Is she ill then?' asked Ness.

'Her health is always delicate, and she is in an interesting condition.'

Ness suppressed a small cry as she ran the needle into her thumb.

'That should come as no surprise,' said Theodora. 'Babes usually follow weddings, you know, and Eliza has a boy already.'

'Och, I ken that, Mistress Bruning but- but how do you ken a bairn is on the way? Some ladies wear lacings so tight nothing may be seen.'

Theodora laughed. 'My dear, they have a way of announcing themselves quite soon. How long have you been married?'

'We were wed before Hogmanay,' said Ness.

'Then you've plenty of time,' said Theodora. 'There's many a lady falls whenever her man hangs his nether garments on the bed post, others take a little while - perhaps six months or more. You've no cause to fret.'

***

When the appointed Sunday came, Ness washed carefully, scrubbing her hair to a lather with her precious soap and drying it in the sun. The scent of violets hung about her, lifting her spirits, and the new merino, when she put it on, felt soft against her arms. At eleven, Hector harnessed the horses to the wagon and helped her to the seat. He made no comment, so she was driven to ask directly; 'Am I lady enough for you today, Hector?' She lifted her skirts as if to arrange them, and stretched her legs so her legs were visible to the turn of her calf.

'Aye, you look right bonnie,' said Hector. That was all he said, but she saw his gaze drift down in what was surely appreciation.

The Brunings lived in a stout timbered house in the infant settlement of Mersey. Hector lifted Ness down and escorted her past three other equipages and two saddle horses to the arched porch, where he touched her cheek and handed her over to a manservant. Ness shivered, knowing herself to be on trial before the ladies of the Northeast. If she passed their scrutiny, then she would take her rightful place in the local scene of society; if not, she would be an outsider.

At first, her eyes blurred with terror as she entered the comfortable parlour, but soon she realised that, far from the censorious crowd she had visualised, she was facing no more than seven ladies, two of whom she knew already. She greeted Eliza Jarvis, now wearing a gown of tussore silk, and saw a gleam of surprised respect in her eyes. So I am no such a shabby wee creature at that, she thought, smiling and holding out her hand to her hostess and then to Eliza. Never by the flicker of an eyebrow did Theodora show that she had seen the blue gown before, let alone that she had lent Ness a suitable small down-padded bustle to wear underneath.

'You look charming, Ness,' said Eliza. 'Did you bring your gown from Scotland?'

Ness shook her head. 'I had it made in the colony,' she said, which was only the truth. 'Hector had some fine cloth sent for me to choose.'

'Mr Campbell has good taste in some matters, it seems,' said Theodora in a dry tone.

The other women were introduced as Mrs and Miss Reeve of York Hall, Mrs O'Hara from Shannon, Mrs Williams of Llanhow, and her companion, Miss Margaret Young. All seemed friendly, yet Ness was aware of the undercurrents as they assessed her appearance, adding Hector's growing reputation and reputed wealth and subtracting her decided Scots accent and her youth. They had plenty of questions, and Ness answered some, turning aside any that seemed too intrusive. By the end of the afternoon, she was able to bid the ladies goodbye with more confidence, accepting Mrs Williams' invitation to visit her at Llanhow the next month.

'But we shall expect to see you at the ball before then,' said stately Mrs Reeve.

'Do come,' urged Eliza Jarvis and Ness said a little stiffly that she would if she could.

Hector watched as she took her leave of the other ladies. She did look bonnie; worth two or three of the others beside her, and seemed quite self-possessed besides. 'It's a braw fine house,' she said as he helped her into the wagon.

The other ladies were leaving too, and Hector noted that most were escorted by grooms and maidservants, and not by their husbands. 'We must ha' servants,' he said, half to himself.

Ness laughed. 'To sleep beneath the wagon?'

'There will be room in our fine house, and I'll hire guid men and maids to serve us.'

'Aye, that will be bonnie,' said Ness. Her smile lingered. 'Theodora did say you had fine taste… for a man.'

Hector nodded. 'I hae' and all. See what a wife I chose!' He slapped the reins and drove away, followed by the curious looks of the other women. They had heard of Hector Campbell, but this was the first any but Theodora had seen of him, and most were taken aback at his eccentric appearance.

'I wonder how Mrs Campbell came to meet a man like that?' mused Harriet Williams.

Her companion gave her a speaking look. 'He is a trifle odd, my dear.'

'Odd, yes, but very well to do,' said Mrs Williams. 'We should offer Mrs Campbell any assistance in our power to make her feel at home in the colony. She is a pretty little thing, and may develop more countenance by and by.'

'Eliza Jarvis claims she lives in a hovel,' said Miss Young doubtfully.

'Oh - Eliza!' said Mrs Williams. 'She is ever prone to exaggerate, but there is not a particle of harm in her. As to the hovel; it is likely a perfectly respectable timbered house. A man who dresses his wife in gowns of that quality will surely not have stinted in his dwelling. And odd or not, did you see how he looked at her?' She sighed as the carriage bumped over the poorly surfaced track. 'Yes, Margaret, I think we may safely say that the Campbells will *do*.'

Miss Young murmured appropriately, but her thoughts were not sanguine.

***

Over the next six weeks, Ness attended other gatherings, for the women of the colony were willing to travel miles to pay calls. The May Day Ball was mentioned often, but she never led anyone to expect she would attend, so she was surprised when Hector brought up the subject on the way home from Shannon. 'But what about a gown?' she gasped. 'There's so little time to make one, Hector!'

'You managed well enough wi' the one you have on,' pointed out Hector. He climbed down and led the horses past a particularly bad bit of track.

'Aye, but only wi' the help o' Mistress Bruning! And Hector, a gown like this isna fit for a ball!'

Hector glanced back at her. 'You look bonnie,' he said.

'Aye, but no for a ball.'

Hector wanted to know precisely why the gown would not do, and Ness, who had been to no balls, could scarcely answer him. She simply knew that it would not.

'We must have a tailor to help,' said Hector.

Ness was appalled. 'Not a tailor, Hector, we need a modiste. And the cost! Ladies pay as much for a ball gown as I'd spend in a year o' gowns- and besides, it is much too late to be setting off for Launceston now.'

Two days later a modiste appeared at Glen Heather. By now Ness was sufficiently accustomed to Hector's ways to accept this development, but it seemed the modiste could not accept Glen Heather. The woman's hauteur did diminish slightly when she saw the crimson silk, but she vowed that no money on earth would make her cut and sew in the open air, or in a dirt-floored hut. Ness dreaded a scene from Hector, but a compromise was reached; Theodora Bruning offered her sewing room and Ness travelled back and forth for the requisite measurements and fittings.

Thus, somewhat in the manner of Cinderella in the fairy tale, Ness found herself dancing at the May Day Ball. Hector had, for once, laid aside his plaid, and Ness scarcely recognised him in breeches and a cut-away coat over a high-collared cambric shirt. He had even had her barber his hair into a semblance of order. It came as no surprise that Hector entered the elegant brick York Hall as if he owned it, and exchanged bows and nods with the gentry as if he were their social equal. And why, thought Ness with a warm rush of pride, should less be thought of a man because he came from Scotland rather than England, or because his wealth came from work and not inheritance? And why should she be considered any less a lady than saucy Mary Reeve, who was dancing with a young man whose impossibly tight coat and high collar prevented his turning his head more than two or three inches to either side? Her Hector was twice the figure of these fashion plates. Perhaps the system of placing folk in their classes by birth and privilege would soon break down.

The subscription ball was a much larger affair than Ness had expected. Some folk had travelled for several days to attend, and she saw not only the ladies she had met already, but others from as far as Launceston and even Hobarton. She was introduced by Theodora as 'Mrs Campbell, of Glen Heather', and wondered what some of the grand ladies would think if they knew Glen Heather consisted, at present, of a few clear acres, much virgin bush, and a slab hut. But perhaps they would see the future of Glen Heather in its beginnings, as Hector did. It was so beautiful, after all.

Hector turned out to be a capable dancer, and Ness enjoyed two decorous circuits of the room, if "enjoyed" could be the word with a partner almost wholly silent. After this, Hector delivered her into Theodora's care, and fell into conversation with various distinguished-looking men, discussing wool prices and corn with all the authority of an expert until supper time. Ness had, in the meanwhile, danced twice with other partners, both young, inoffensive men whom Theodora introduced as her nephews. The supper was plentiful, but Hector seemed indisposed to linger and said it was time to leave the ball. Obediently, Ness put on her wrap, but Dick Bruning appeared at the door and beckoned Hector back into the conversation.

'Now what ails the man?' muttered Hector, but he released Ness' arm and went to see. Ness waited, but Hector did not return to the hallway. Folk began to cast pitying looks, so she raised her chin, slipped her light shawl from her shoulders and walked slowly back to Theodora.

'What Ness, I thought you were leaving us just now?'

'Aye, so I thought mysel',' said Ness with a meaning glance at the room beyond.

Theodora's gaze followed hers. 'Our menfolk have found something new to discuss,' she said dryly. 'It is an old story, Ness. Let two men gather together and they will talk until the cows come home.' Then, perhaps remembering that Ness had not long been married, she added; 'I confess I find it a relief. If Mr Bruning discusses sheep, corn and bullocks with Mr Campbell, he will not discuss them with me and I shall not feel constrained to pretend an interest I have not.'

Ness smiled a little. She wished Hector *would* discuss such subjects with her more frequently. He spoke sometimes of his plans for their future, but just as often he was silent. It was clear he had several weighty matters on his mind.

Theodora was claimed by one of her nephews, bent on a duty dance, and Ness was left alone. She was a little surprised when someone coughed delicately to attract her attention. Ness thought she had met the woman at Theodora's tea party, but she could not remember her name. 'Good evening, Miss...' she said, and let the surname remain as a murmur.

'Miss Young,' said the woman crisply. 'I am Mrs Williams' companion.'

'Och, of course,' said Ness. 'That is, how do you do, Miss Young?'

'Well enough.' The companion was a curious-looking person, with mousy hair, dark bright eyes and a sharp little nose which reminded Ness very much of a mouse. She smiled at the thought, and Miss Young gave her a penetrating look. 'Something amuses you, Mrs Campbell?'

'Och, it's no great thing,' said Ness uncomfortably. 'I was thinking it odd that these folks have all chosen to come across the world.'

'As you did yourself.'

'Aye,' said Ness. It occurred to her suddenly that Miss Williams might think her a convict freed and wed to a settler, so she lifted her chin. 'I came o' my own free will on the *May Queen*. And you hae' come from the auld country?'

'Indeed. Have you ever regretted it, Mrs Campbell? You are very young. Did you make the journey with your family, perhaps?'

'I ha' no kin but Hector,' said Ness, realising it was true.

Miss Young's nose quivered. 'I thought you were wed to the man?'

'So I am,' said Ness. 'Which makes him my kin, forby. We are *one flesh* an' so he told the minister.' She smiled at the memory, then sighed. 'My father is gone, and my mother, years ago. I ha' no one else.'

'So you travelled from Scotland under Mr Campbell's protection?'

Ness glanced about, wishing Hector would come back, or that Theodora would rescue her from this inquisition. 'Och, there is Eliza!' she said. 'Does she no look bonnie?'

Miss Young permitted herself a tiny sniff. 'It is unseemly for ladies in her condition to attend public gatherings.'

Ness looked her full in the eye. 'Bairns follow weddings, you know,' she said, echoing Theodora. 'It is nothing unnatural, forby. I hope to have a bairn mysel', soon.'

'Well, really!' For a moment, Miss Young's carefully cultivated accent slipped, but in a blink she had recovered. 'You travelled from Scotland under Mr Campbell's protection?' she repeated, her gaze openly unfriendly.

'I met wi' Hector in New South Wales,' corrected Ness. 'I travelled frae Scotland as companion to Miss Leslie, the reverend's sister from back home.'

'Whose employment you appear to have left quite soon!' said Miss Young.

Ness could feel ill will emanating from the woman, but she had no idea what she had done to earn such animosity. Perhaps Miss Young realised she had gone too far for propriety, for she added hastily; 'But then- I quite understand how it might have been. We freewomen can take our pick of situations, can we not? I myself have been offered more places than I care to name, but I could never leave Mrs Williams. We are cousins, you understand, and poor Harriet does depend on me so much.'

'What kind o' positions ha' you been offered?' asked Ness. Something was stirring uneasily in the back of her mind. It was something Hector had said. She frowned, trying to recapture it.

Miss Young waved a deprecating hand. 'I could have been a housekeeper, or a governess, although that is a little beneath my touch! Only last month a lady from New South Wales tried to prevail upon me to accompany her to Sydney Town as her companion. Naturally, I explained that I would never leave my cousin ... but I am sure you understand how it is. I imagine you turned aside several similar offers yourself before you accepted Mr Campbell?'

'I met wi' Hector when I had no been long off the ship,' said Ness.

'But my dear!' Miss Young's eyes were round. 'Surely you knew folk are queuing up to employ women of good character! Of course, for those with no taste for independence perhaps a wedding to a gentleman - any gentleman - is a better course than gainful employment.'

'Aye, perhaps it is and a',' agreed Ness, looking at her steadily. 'For those who ha' the chance. But my Hector is no just any gentleman. He could have had his pick o' the ladies of Sydney Town.'

'I must admit,' added Miss Young, 'that I have never yet met a gentleman for whom I felt it worth relinquishing my freedom.'

'How unfortunate for you.' Ness gave a slight, pitying smile, and rose to her feet, smoothing her crimson skirts ostentatiously. 'If you'll excuse me, I must speak wi' Eliza before we leave.' Shaking with an emotion she dared not examine too closely, Ness walked away. She knew she had been rude- perhaps fatally rude- to Miss Young, but what else could she have done? To have sat meekly by and allowed the woman to continue with her insinuations would have been tantamount to accepting an insult to Hector and perhaps to herself. Had Miss Young been accusing her of opportunism or merely of faint-heartedness? Ness could not quite decide. Had she remained, Miss Young's intentions might have become clear to her.

'Och, but if I'd stayed by the auld besom I'd ha' said something worse, and a',' she muttered.

Eliza Jarvis welcomed her with an uncomplicated smile. 'Hello, Ness! So you did prevail upon Mr Campbell to bring you after all?'

'Och, it was Hector's idea we should come,' said Ness.

'And an excellent one,' said Eliza warmly. 'You are not dancing?'

'We were on our way out, but Mr Bruning called to Hector and he hasna come back.'

'It is ever the way. When one is enjoying oneself, one's husband is forever wanting to be gone, but when one feels ill, and is in a fret to be home, he will talk the night away. No doubt he is prosing on about horses, again. Think Ness, Mr Jarvis has paid a great sum to have horses sent from his Uncle Wharton in England. I cannot conceive of why he cannot buy some here and save the ruinous shipping costs.' Then she brightened. 'But I am glad you did *not* go, since we arrived a little late. Come and sit by me. Mr Jarvis is engaged with Mr Reeve and will not be looking for me yet. We are to continue to Launceston tomorrow and spend the rest of the month in town, you know, for Mother Jarvis wishes to see the sights and Nannie Goodridge will see to little Winston until we are home.'

Under cover of Eliza's flow of chatter, Ness began to recover her equilibrium. Perhaps Miss Young had not meant to be unpleasant, for what could she have against Ness? She could not be a disappointed pretender to Hector's hand. Hector had no use for what he called "scrawndy women" and there was no doubt that Miss Young was scrawndy. The thought of Hector was both warm and painful, and Ness realised Eliza was looking at her strangely. 'Are you well, Ness? You seem a little distrait.'

'Aye, well enough. I ha' been talking wi' Mistress Young.'

Eliza's mouth seemed to purse to nothing. 'I own I cannot like the woman. And not only because she apes her betters and speaks as if every word were forced through a wringer.'

'Theodora invited her to the tea party,' said Ness.

'Ye-es-' said Eliza doubtfully. 'You may as well know, Ness, that Theodora invited Harriet, that is, Mrs Williams, to the tea-party. Miss Young invited herself, which was shockingly forward of her, but Theodora could scarcely have her refused admittance. After all, she *is* Mrs Williams' companion.'

'And her kin, forby,' said Ness.

'To some distant degree.' Eliza shook her head. 'Ness, you will be thinking me horridly ill-natured and uppish. Indeed it is not the woman's station that repels me, but her character.'

Ness was glad to hear that, for she suspected her own station was (or had been, before her marriage) much closer to Margaret Young's than to Eliza's.

'She is a spoiler,' pronounced Eliza at length. 'She is envious and full of little pinpricks. How shall I put it? Hmmm. When she knew Mr Jarvis and I were to have another child she smiled so sweetly, but suggested that it was a little *soon* after young Winston's birth. Had it been otherwise she would have said it were a pity to leave it so late! Today she has told me my cheeks quite glow with health, and in another breath wondered if I am not, perhaps, *too* flushed. But there it is. Pay no regard to anything she may have said to you. I think she feels somehow…' She paused. 'Passed by,' she added. 'If she had a household to run and a gentleman's attention then she would, I suppose, be more amiable. As it is she might wed a groom or an innkeeper, but that would not please her consequence.'

So, thought Ness, Miss Young's spite had been habitual envy rather than aimed at her especially.

'I trust she said nothing to trouble you over much?' said Eliza a little too quickly.

'None but haivers,' said Ness. She made a show of watching the dancers. 'Maybe Hector and I shall have a bairn of our own soon.' And because her husband had entered her thoughts again, she added, without premeditation, 'Eliza, is it true there is work and plenty for freewomen frae the ships?'

'I believe so,' said Eliza vaguely. 'Yes indeed, Nannie Goodridge has had several offers since she came to us. Fortunately, she is devoted to little Winston and will not leave us easily. We are lucky to have such a good nurse for Winston. Convict nursemaids seldom answer as they ought. Some are shockingly coarse in their speech and ... and loose in their ways. Respectable maids and housekeepers also are difficult to procure. But why do you ask, Ness? Are you in the way of needing a nursemaid?'

'Och, Hector has said we may soon hire servants,' said Ness mechanically, but her heart, which had been light when Hector brought her to the ball, was as cold and heavy as river clay. Hector had deceived her that first day, or, at the very least, had allowed her to deceive herself.

CHAPTER 10

If Ness was quiet as they left York Hall, so too was Hector. In some ways, he'd enjoyed a most satisfactory evening. Dancing with his wife had been far more of a pleasure than he expected. He thought she looked very bonnie in the crimson gown, very much the lady, and he looked forward to taking her to bed that night. Then he remembered inn walls were notoriously thin, and decided to wait until their return to Glen Heather. That thought brought him full circle to his major concern; the remaking of Glen Heather from a rough tract of mountain to a legend. He had spent much time that evening with other landowners, investigating sources and consolidating ideas. He had already decided to buy sheep in New South Wales rather than locally. The cost of shipping them to Van Diemen's Land would be more than repaid by the fact that the continuing drought had made it necessary for many graziers to sell their stock quickly and cheaply. That was unfortunate for them, but lucky for him, and it would save him the indignity of dealing with Jarvis and his like.

Hector scowled in the darkness. Jarvis' presence had rendered the evening rather less satisfactory, and he realised it had been a mistake to antagonise the man. The master of Scarborough had snubbed him that evening, had utterly refused to discuss Hector's offer (made in good faith) to buy a stretch of well-watered ground or, failing that, the rights to divert water from the big burn to Glen Heather land. Jarvis had laughed with scorn, opining that the sooner the drought led Campbell to leave Van Diemen's Land and return to his native wilds, the better it would be for the colony. Only Dick Bruning's intervention had prevented Hector from demanding satisfaction. His antagonist stalked off to the ballroom and Hector did not follow. He scowled over the bitter memory.

'Ness, did you see that sleekit Jarvis tonight?' he asked abruptly.

'I did so.' He thought she sounded distant, but perhaps she was tired, or breeding after all. 'Did you no see him yoursel', Hector? He's awa' this week, and next. Mistress Jarvis said they were heading to

Launceston.'

'They'll be gone frae Scarborough a week or more?' said Hector.

'Aye, near a month, so she said.'

Hector had no opinion of landowners who spent more time in town than attending to their spreads, but Jarvis' movements were nothing to him, so he transferred his thoughts to York Hall. He had taken the time to learn from Godfrey Reeve the name and direction of the architect who had designed the place; it was Tobias Scott-Blakeney. Hector planned to hire this same man himself. There would be none but the best for Glen Heather.

He continued to plan far into the night. He noticed his wife's silence, but was thankful he had had the sense to choose a woman who was not only capable and decorative, but who could hold her tongue. He remembered again the clacking of the women he'd known in Sydney Town. Aye, he'd chosen well when he'd selected his Ness.

***

Ness held silence that night out of hurt and a cold, shamed fear of what she might say if she loosed it. She was used to thinking of Hector as her saviour, so it had come as a shock to discover that he had been nothing of the kind. She had married him because she believed she had little alternative. She thought herself destitute without his intervention, and saw her man as a hero, a wild hero who swept her from poverty into a new life. She submitted to his demands, was silent when he wished, had held her peace so often, simply because she thought he had a right to her total obedience. She allowed him to treat her as he might have treated a dog, or a horse, or any useful animal adopted on a whim and discarded or disregarded as easily. He was her husband, and she had believed he saved her from poverty.

But now she knew he had not.

'*Folk are queueing up to employ women of good character*!' Miss Young had said, while Eliza Jarvis admitted that respectable servants were difficult to procure.

Now Ness knew she could have been a housekeeper, or a governess or nursemaid, just as she had planned with Jean. She could have been respectably employed as a valued servant or companion, and perhaps might by and by have wed a gentleman closer to her own age and tastes. It might have been a gentleman who would have conversed with her, brought her flowers, perhaps, and paid heed to her desires. Instead, she had leapt headlong from the deck of the *May Queen* into the keeping of

Hector Campbell who, for all his vainglory, was nothing but a shabby Scot with more money than manners; well-breeched, but ill-bred withal.

Ness, uncomfortable on a horsehair mattress in the inn, and horrified at her bitter thoughts, glanced sideways as if her eyes could pierce the dark. She could not see her husband, but she could hear his quiet breathing, and feel his hard, callused hand resting possessively on her hip. He'd looked so fine in his breeches tonight, and she'd felt such pride in him…until the scene with Miss Young changed her point of view.

'Och, get awa' wi' you!' she said savagely. It was as well for Hector Campbell he had not tried to assert his rights to her favours tonight! They were his rights by Church and law, but he had gained them by a trick, by trading on her ignorance, and wedding her without chance or choice. Knowing the truth, she might have wed him, for he had attracted her immediately as a reminder of home, and she still thought him a fine-looking man, but she should have been given that choice and she had not.

A tear lapped her cheek, and she blotted it angrily. It was so unfair. He had taken her chance, her choice, her body and her trust and had given-

He had given her Glen Heather.

He had given her green, lovely Glen Heather, her home. He had given a position in society as his wife and the future mother of his family. He had given her a few precious compliments and some rare moments of accord. He was someone to care for, and that gave her life direction and hope. The tears ran thicker, and Ness wept silently in the night for her own uncertainty. She loved Glen Heather, and Hector treated her well enough. He had wed her lawfully, when he might have taken her as a servant girl and bedmate. He made some push to put her in the way of society.

Aye, but that was for Glen Heather, and not for her sake, she reminded herself angrily. He wanted bairns to bear his name, and so he needed a woman. Any woman who was young, healthy and biddable, would have done for Hector Campbell. Ness laid a hand on her stomach. There was no bairn yet, and they had been wed over four months. What if a year went by? Or two? Or three? Would Hector discard her for another breeding ewe? She shivered, and wondered why. Surely she should hope for just that conclusion! If Hector turned her loose she would be free to take up a good position. But then, she would not be the lady of Glen Heather. And, having been the lady of Glen Heather, and Hector Campbell's wife, could she ever dwindle to being less?

But that was all haivers. Perhaps there would soon be a bairn. And Hector's periods of abstraction could be put to good account, for they left her free to wander the glens and braes as she liked. As long as she provided food and bodily comforts, she could do as she wished with her life. She could think as she wished. She could even love as she wished. And Hector would never know, nor even care, what went on in her private world.

Fortified by this, Ness slept.

She saw little of Hector during the next week, and they exchanged barely a hundred words in a day. Ness knew Hector had some project underway up the mountain, for he, Bullocky George and several strangers took the bullock cart high up the brae. George and his team remained away all night, for Hector returned late and alone to the hut, too tired to do anything but eat and fling himself down to sleep. Ness tried to be grateful for an interlude during which she could come to terms with her new knowledge and consolidate her plans for the future, but she found it very trying to be alone.

Dick Bruning's man no longer came with the convicts, for Hector hired men of his own, independent free men who planned to settle in Mole Creek and Mersey until workmen's cottages were built on Glen Heather. Hector had forgotten, or neglected, to tell Dick Bruning his men were no longer required, for there was some stir when the freemen arrived and found that Bruning's men had come as well. The foreman objected to his unnecessary journey, and Bruning himself arrived next day for a short sharp exchange with Hector. Ness wanted to send her greetings to Theodora, but the normally good-natured Bruning ignored her and rode away.

'Ha' you and Mr Bruning quarrelled, Hector?' she asked that evening, but Hector merely growled that the man was too quick to take offence.

'Have I not paid him well for his men's services, forby?' he demanded.

'No doubt,' said Ness. She wondered if he considered *her* well paid for her services.

'Then why does he make this stramash over the lack o' notice?

Och, there's no understanding the man,' said Hector in disgust. 'I paid the extra day so he's lost nothing.'

'He'll come round, perhaps,' said Ness, but Hector said he would have no more dealings with Bruning.

'And you stay awa' frae that meddling wife o' his!' he added as an afterthought, and swept away, leaving Ness open-mouthed with outrage and astonishment.

The Brunings had never been other than kind to her, and what had Theodora, or Ness herself, to do with any quarrel between their husbands?

Hector was away all day, and Ness heard the ring of axes high on the mountain. His return late at night brought no satisfaction, and he was off again before sunrise. The rough strong windrow fences had been finished around part of the clearing, extending to enclose a goodly patch of forested land as well. Ness was still wondering why Hector had not cleared it all when two wagons arrived at Glen Heather.

'Wool!' she exclaimed, staring at the first of the wagons, but the wool proved to be attached to the backs of ten indignant ewes and a haughty ram. Behind the wagon straggled wild-eyed cattle, white-faced, white-shouldered beasts with hind-parts darker than a chestnut horse. Their legs and bellies were crusted with mud and Ness knew they had been driven hard, through fords and along the rutted track from the coast. Despite their exhaustion, they had plenty of fight, and the bull swung his head and glared about him as if seeking an enemy to destroy.

'The first of our livestock,' said Hector briefly.

'But Hector, we havena the fields to keep them in, nor even the water!'

'These are gey hardy stock, for all they're finely bred. They will do well enough in the enclosure,' said Hector. He looked at her, inviting her to share his satisfaction, but before she could speak his attention was back on the beasts.

The sheep seemed dazed and dull, with only the ram fighting back as he was manhandled out of the wagon. The cattle charged through in a body, almost knocking one another down in their haste. Hector closed the gap with a lacing of heavy branches, spoke briefly to the carriers, then turned back to Ness.

'I'll be away up the mountain,' he said. 'The men will unload the stores into the wee house. Go about your business, lassie; they willna be concerned wi' you.'

Remounting the surefooted Rowan, he rode away, and Ness watched from a distance as more sacks of grain and flour, kegs and casks and barrels, were unloaded from the second wagon. Hector seemed to have bought provisions enough to feed an army, but winter was coming on, and perhaps deliveries would be difficult in the wetter months.

After the men had gone, Ness stared at the sheep and cattle for a little time, but they departed in separate huddles to the far reaches of the enclosure, so she returned to the little garden by the burn. The new stores were stowed away; and she thought that perhaps meals might have a little more savour from now on.

With the new livestock dispersed, the only living creature in sight was the horse Grey Falcon. She talked to him sometimes, and smiled wryly at the thought. Mistress Campbell of Glen Heather, driven to conversation with a beast! She took him to water at the burn at midday, and disturbed a kangaroo from almost beneath his hooves, and that was the only excitement. At least the Falcon was thankful for the drink, which was more than she could say for Hector's cabbages, which had almost ceased to grow in the cool of the autumn.

'Cows!' she said aloud, 'and sheep forby! And not a word o' their coming did he gi' to me.'

It would have served Hector right had they arrived in his absence. She could have refused to take delivery of the beasts, have justly claimed to know nothing. But the men would have over-ridden her objections and left them anyway; carriers would never heed a wife if they'd had firm dealings with her man.

Evening fell with a strange cool hush, and Ness was uneasy. It was too quiet, for the birds were not singing their sleepy vespers and even the murmur of wind had died away. The sky was a strange, bruised green, and Ness shivered and drew her thin shawl closer. For once, she felt no desire to linger on the brae, but lit a lantern and blew up the cooking fire, which had smouldered gently all day. As the flames began to take hold of fresh tinder, the first stirrings of breeze made themselves felt, coming in from the northwest.

'Och, would you then!' said Ness disgustedly. She raised her shawl to keep stinging smoke from her eyes and set the Dutch oven in place. It would take two hours or more to render the kangaroo tender enough to eat, and even then it would take some chewing.

The breeze blew up rapidly, and soon the treetops were swaying with a vigour she had not seen before at Glen Heather. Twigs blew across the ground, and skittered into the fire, blowing away again lit like tiny beacons. Ness watched uneasily. They blew themselves out on the wind, and she thought there was not much danger of fire in the green of Glen Heather. But the gum leaves sometimes flared, and if Glen Heather burnt and through her fault ... if the cattle and sheep were panicked by fire ... Ness removed the oven, then muffled the flames with ashes from the pile. Hector would not be pleased with a cold supper, but he would be less pleased with a burnt-out hut and flaming trees.

This danger averted, Ness tucked her hands under her shawl and turned her face into the wind. The scent of gum and honey was strong, and behind it the smell of smoke stung her nose and eyes. Autumn chill was in the air although the strange trees of Van Diemen's Land neither changed colour, nor shed their leaves. May was half over and the ball a memory.

There was a rattling snort behind her. Grey Falcon was unsettled and Ness remembered that high winds did affect animals badly. She had seen highland cattle running wild before the wind, and even Loch Haven's staid ponies would toss their manes and whisk their tails as if the wind restored their youth, or blew the scent of a mare to their distended nostrils.

Ness wondered if perhaps the wind were affecting her as well. She felt a sudden desire to cast aside her dignity and her boots, to put on her crimson gown and flee the glen with shawl and hair streaming, to be caught up on a saddle-bow by Young Lochinvar and spirited away.

'And verra uncomfortable you'd be, forby,' Ness told herself sternly. She thought if Grey Falcon had not been so resty she might have removed his hobbles and ridden him up the brae to find Hector and the men, but that was haivers. Hector would not have been pleased to see her. He would have stared frankly and told her to go home. And if she fell from Falcon the horse might run off, which would anger Hector more.

A pistol shot crack made her jump as a branch peeled from the fork of a tall gum and tumbled to land across the remains of the fire. Another branch fell, trailing loose bark in a tattered ribbon behind it. It hit the ground some distance away, but the grey horse was abruptly terrified, trying to rear, staggering, with the hobbles biting into his offside legs. Ness made an instinctive move to calm him, but his shoulder hit her with a buffet that sent her stumbling away, half winded. Until then, she had not considered danger to herself from placid Grey Falcon. She stared at him in pained astonishment, which turned rapidly to fear. The horse was in danger too, for if he fell, he could break a leg or his back. Either injury would bring his death, immediately or as soon as Hector returned. Ness bit her lip. She was fond of the horse, and Grey Falcon liked her, but the bond was not strong enough for her to be able to soothe him now. Perhaps it would be best if she left him be, but the falling branches were a danger to her as well as to Falcon.

As she hesitated, another peeled free and struck the horse across the quarters. Snorting with terror, he bounded forward, snapping the hobbles as if they had been brown paper instead of leather. The snaking ends frightened him further, and he made another prodigious leap, which brought him almost on top of Ness.

She flung her shawl over his head, hoping a sudden darkness would calm him. Grey Falcon tossed her off as if she had been a fly, knocking her sideways with a lunge that brought him into noisy contact with the Dutch oven and sent Ness sprawling to the ground with the uncooked supper spilling around her. Falcon bolted, scrambling away up the brae.

Ness could do nothing, but hope the horse would stop when he reached Hector and Rowan. And what of them? Was there danger on the mountain as well?

As these thoughts battered her mind, a small tree fell, toppling to strike the roof of the hut and cave in one side. Driven by self-preservation, Ness snatched her old plaid, picked up her skirts and fled away from the trees to the safety of the enclosure.

Branches were breaking everywhere, with some tumbling end over end as if possessed of independent life. Ness scrambled over Hector's stockade, and ran to the centre of the cleared ground, where she crouched in the tussocky bareness with her plaid over her head and her eyes wide with fear. The cattle had stampeded, and the sheep were out of sight. There was nothing she could do, but try to keep herself from harm, and hope Hector was doing likewise.

CHAPTER 11

Hector accepted rising wind as he accepted other dangers. High on the crest of the tiers, at the upper boundary of Glen Heather, his line of sight was still fifty feet below the tops of the gums that reached for the sky. Nevertheless, it was possible to see the wind riffling visibly up the mountain as breeze riffles a field of rye. At best, a thickly wooded ridge was a bad place to weather a windstorm, but there was no safety closer than the enclosure at the foot of the tier. Hector therefore chose a cleft in the ridge where the long-ago falling of two huge trees had left a clear way to the sky. The resulting flood of sunshine had encouraged the growth of seedlings, which began and often ended their lives in the green twilight below the canopy. Among these tall, slender saplings Hector settled with the men.

'If one o' these comes down we'll no be killed,' he said, quelling a rising mutter from the men who wished to leave for the valley at once.

The fierce buffets of wind lasted a full three hours, roaring and swelling like an ocean of trees. Branches tore and blew like spume, with constant pistol-snaps of breaking wood. By the time the storm blew itself out, full dark had come, and the tier was littered with branches and trunks sheared off like broken carrots.

Hector's chestnut Rowan had been hobbled and fastened head and heel to a pair of flexible saplings, a proceeding he had protested with snorts and plunges, and even the phlegmatic bullocks had had to be yoked two and two so that the ten year old "bosses" could settle their younger brethren by sheer bulk. Bullocky George had crouched by his leaders' heads, withdrawing into his bluey and somehow lighting his pipe against the wind. Bitter smoke ripped from the bowl, giving the impression of a small volcano trapped within the folds of woollen cloth.

Coldly, Hector watched the destruction until it was too dark to see. His first livestock had arrived at Glen Heather, and to have a high wind on the same day could be nothing but a coincidence. He knew the high country had worse gales and more in store before it allowed itself to be tamed. But he knew it never would be truly tamed. A man must fight the elements, assess the odds, and never relax his vigilance for an hour. He must work with the land, never rest in content, and never trust in fortune, for the land that gave could also take away.

And by God, thought Hector, baring his teeth to the wind, he'd have it no other way.

He remembered Ness, but spent little time repining. The lassie had braw good sense, and he could not help her by rushing down the mountain and bringing disaster to himself. The footing on the brae was treacherous, and it would be suicidal to plunge among the snapping trees. If he were injured, work on his grand design would falter and it might take weeks or months to regain momentum. Anyway, he considered Ness to be safer than himself, for she could move into cleared ground. So long as she had sense to keep clear of the trees and hut she would be all right. Surely she would have the sense to do that? If not, he had chosen badly when he picked out a wife. He hoped she would realise there was nothing she could do for the newly arrived sheep and cattle. They might be replaced, but it came to him that she could not.

When night and the wind had fallen with equal finality, it was still unsafe to leave the mountain, so Hector made camp instead. Bullocky George had spent nights below the ridge already, and had constructed a sturdy lean-to. This was easily extended to house the workforce.

Hector ate his ration of hard damper and jerky without noticing the taste, rolled into his plaid and settled to sleep. He was equally untroubled by complaints from some of the men and the chill in the air. If the winds rose in the night, he would wake and return to the cleft in the rocks. If all remained calm, he would sleep until morning, and then go home to see what damage had been wrought. He thought of Ness again, regretting he must leave the lassie alone at night, but what could not be mended must be worn. Perhaps she would even welcome a night alone! Lately she had shown no appetite for his embraces, and little for his company. He hoped that meant she was breeding, for it was time and past time for that since their wedding.

***

The morning dawned clear and cold, and Ness, who had slept poorly with only her fears for company, opened her eyes and groaned. The wind had dropped, and she got stiffly to her feet, wavering as her cramped legs complained at the sudden movement.

The cattle and sheep were not in sight, so, after a few moments, Ness scrambled back over the windrow fence and went to inspect the hut. The roof was down, and a splintered branch had pinned the remains of the bark sheets to the tumble of goods and furnishings below. Perhaps it was as well it had done so, thought Ness, assessing the mess with gloomy eyes. Without the heavy bark for protection, the wind could have scattered their belongings wide and far, or whirled them clear across to New South Wales.

She ate a sketchy breakfast, and then tidied herself as best she could. The Dutch oven lay dented and greasy against the bole of a tree. Mechanically she replaced it on the blackened fire pit. Then she stood by the ruins of the hut and wondered what to do next. She was as lonely in the silent leaf-strewn morning as she had been on the decks of the *May Queen* in the harbour, before she answered Hector's hail. Again she had no one to turn to for advice or support, so she set off up the slope.

On the brae some trees had fallen. A few had smashed their length along the ground. Others had been prevented from reaching the ground by their remaining neighbours. Broken trunks rested in the forks of upright trees, and here and there two would lean together, propped like drunken men. Take an axe to one and the other would fall as well, thought Ness, and she wondered crazily if the wind had conspired to help Hector with his clearing and if these new logs would be employed to make new fences. Why not? It seemed most of the world flocked to do her husband's bidding, so why should he not command the elements?

A way up the brae Ness found again the small hole in which she had stumbled back in the summer. It was clearly visible now, a pockmark grown long as her forearm, dark and secret, and running with the sound of another hidden burn. And why should that surprise her in this upside down place? What alarmed her was the damage around the lip of the hole. She tried to tell herself the enlargement had not been made by hooves, that the grey and red on the limestone lip could have come from a floundering kangaroo, but the coldness persisted in her chest. She was fatalistically prepared when she clambered higher and found Grey Falcon, injured and trembling on the brae.

Ness took hold of his collar and gentled him as well as she could. She feared to look at the dangling hind leg, but at last she forced herself to edge down his belly, smoothing her hand on the unmarred rump.

She could see hairless grooves that the hobbles had cut before parting, but the quivering, distorted off-hind leg gave its own account of the horse's pain. The swelling was considerable, and although there were oozing gashes and scrapes down the length of the hock, the worst injury seemed to be high in the tendons.

Grey Falcon was dead lame when she tried to urge him forward. The only hope seemed that the leg was not actually broken, but Ness could see the horse would not be fit to work again for many months, if ever. And he was a gelding, and could never cover a mare and earn his keep by siring sturdy foals. With a sob of distress she saw that Falcon's probable future was very brief.

If she had only told Hector when she had discovered the hole! It could have been stopped up, covered, fenced off, walled in, and Falcon would not be injured now. Miserably, Ness pondered. If the horse had few hours to live, would it be better to wait with him until Hector came? Or should she try to urge him down to the clearing? Grey Falcon suddenly raised his hanging head to rub his muzzle against her shoulder. Ness began to cry, and then to coax and cajole, a halting step at a time, until, over an hour later, she and the horse reached the broken hut. She fetched him water and some grain, and then she waited.

When he arrived some time later, Hector was obviously annoyed at the ruin of his rough-built home. He seemed fatalistic at the state of his second horse.

'He broke the tawse, Hector, and I couldna keep him back,' she said.

'I hope you didna try,' growled Hector. 'He'd ha' ripped the skin frae your hands, or knocked you in the brush.' He peered at the Falcon's injuries, passed his hand down the horse's neck and sighed. Then he took up his rifle. 'Bring a tether and tie him tight up to the tree,' he told Ness. 'Then stand back, or take yoursel' off up the brae.'

'I can hold him quiet,' she said, but Hector shook his head.

'He'll go down in a heap and you may be hurt.'

'Canna you shoot frae the side, so he'll ken nothing?'

'It must be at this point here, close by the brain.' He touched a spot above and between the Falcon's eyes.

Ness saw his hand linger to brush aside the forelock and took a little heart. 'Hector, canna we save him?' she said in a rush. 'The bone isna broken.'

Hector glanced at her, then made a closer inspection of the horse's wounds. 'It's no the cuts and grazes, but the harm underneath. The strings of the leg are gone and he canna use it.'

'He's touching it to the ground,' pleaded Ness. 'Och, please, Hector!'

Hector hesitated. 'Well, he'd be tough to eat, forby,' he muttered, as if to himself, and abruptly, he put up his rifle. 'He may no recover at a',' he warned. 'If the wounds go bad he'll die, or I'll have to shoot him.'

'I ken fine how to make a poultice,' said Ness eagerly. 'You soak old bread in hot water and mash the whole in a linen rag.'

Hector cut her off with a gesture. 'Do as you will,' he said. 'If he isna on the mend in a wee while I'll put the poor beastie out of his misery.'

'Och-' Ness was cold with relief, and turned towards Hector with her hands outstretched in thanks. Then she collected herself and went instead to the quivering horse. 'Thank you, Hector,' she said quietly, and leaned her face against the Falcon's neck.

Hector watched her expressionlessly for a moment, and then turned away. 'I was gey glad to find you well, lassie. I would no want to lose you.'

'The wee house is gone,' said Ness, still muffled.

'Aye,' said Hector, 'and there's a mess, forby, so we ha' some work to do. Still, we'll set our hands to it, you and I.'

Ness glanced round at him, but he was gazing up the brae. 'Hector, the horse caught his hoof in a hole, a wee cave in the rocks. I ha' seen it before,' she said. 'Shall I show you the place?'

'Whisht, you daft lassie, I ken plenty o' them well enough,' said Hector. 'The whole mountain's riddled wi' the holes as foreign cheese is. You canna avoid the things. All I wished for you was your safety. Now, see to the beast if you've a mind. I must be awa'.' He patted her shoulder, then let his hand drift to her cheek, but as Ness leaned into the caress he turned and strode off.

***

The hut was not so very badly damaged. The bark roof had caved in, and one of the walls was down, but the force of a falling branch had merely smashed away the supporting pegs. The logs had scattered, but they were whole, and a few hours' work and a few strong men would see the place restored with the help of Bullocky George. Nevertheless, the ruin made Hector reassess his plans for the future. He had intended to live in the hut for two or three years while he built the substance of

Glen Heather, but the lesson learnt the night before, coupled with talk at the May Day Ball, made him decide to build a house immediately. A braw stone house such as the one he had in mind would withstand wind and storm, snow, sun and sleet. Such a house would make a haven for Ness when he was away, and it would make it possible to hire and house servants, and add to his consequence so that folk would speak of "Campbell of Glen Heather" as they now spoke of "Jarvis of Scarborough" and "Reeve of York Hall."

He had already chosen a site for his house, and also an architect fit to design it and to oversee the work, for he knew he could not handle everything himself. He must have more men. It scarcely mattered to him if they were convicts, ticket-of-leave, or free. He must have more men, and more horses, and he must build fences and stock Glen Heather with more sheep and cattle. He must bring to fruition his scheme to water the glen and the flats, and he must find a foreman to act as his right hand, his third eye and to make decisions in his absence. All this he must do in half the time it might have taken, for life was short, and Hector was aware of the grey that sprinkled his hair. Strong as he was, he couldn't hope to last forever, and he wanted to see Glen Heather and his family well established while he had his full health and strength. And so, methodically, he turned to the matter of the house.

Having quarrelled with Dick Bruning, he knew he must find a new courier to send his summons to Scott-Blakeney, but there were still more urgent matters to attend to. First, he had Bullocky George help him build a lean-to so he and Ness should have shelter. He then set about his many tasks with a grim face that belied his inward satisfactions. He drove his men hard, and though they respected him he failed to gain their liking. And in the back room of his mind, behind thoughts of weather, sheep, water and plans for the future, was a fugitive fear that perhaps he had somehow failed with Ness. For if all was well with the lassie, why was there no news of a coming bairn? Was the lassie barren? If so, what was he to do? It could not be that Hector Campbell was less than a man. The thought was unendurable, so it never crossed even the back of his mind.

***

It was close to the end of May when Whitaker Jarvis and his wife Eliza returned to Scarborough. Jarvis was angered to find his overseer had been idle in his absence. Ewes should have been tupped, and trees had come down and done damage to the fences. Many remained to be lopped and burnt, the fences lay awry, and livestock strayed at will about Scarborough land and beyond. Eliza was in delicate health with her pregnancy and was now distressed as well, for her mare had panicked in the windstorm and had a hot fetlock, which should have been fomented. Even Scarborough House had a faintly unkempt air; early frosts had blackened herbaceous borders, and the grounds were littered by branches and twigs and shattered ornamentals. The only matter which had been tended as it ought was Winston Jarvis, a little over a year old and as sturdy as his parents could wish. And it was axiomatic that Winston Jarvis had been in the control of the devoted and autocratic Nannie Goodridge, who hated Soames and went to enormous lengths to pretend the man did not exist. Winston would thrive, though ewes might stray and water disappear.

Perhaps Nannie Goodridge had a point, thought Jarvis, as he eyed the results of close to a month of neglect. He was angry with Soames, for he paid the man good wages. The discovery that the water in the lower sheep pasture had been cut off had angered him more, and he told Soames in a few crisp sentences that, if he valued his position, he would be well advised to look to his actions and work as if his master were always at his shoulder. The overseer had the sauce to smirk a little.

'I have been a mite busy, Mr Jarvis,' he began, 'looking out for your interests, as you bade me. There's something more you should know before you bluster any more at me. There's fences down and sheep gone and not through the winds and all. Lay the blame where it belongs, and not on my shoulders.'

Swift action was needed, so coolly, Jarvis gave Soames his notice.

'You will never find a man to watch after your interests as I have!' said Soames resentfully, and Jarvis reflected that he might be right. But sometimes one paid too high a price for such service. Soames might watch, but he reported what he saw only on occasion, and Jarvis suspected that well-waged as he was, the man often earned more in bribes paid by his colleagues to ensure his silence.

'The trouble is, Soames,' he said dispassionately, 'that you look after my interests only when I am present to look after them myself. When I need you to act in my stead, you let me down. This windstorm occurred more than a week ago. Time enough for you to have begun *some* restoration of the fences! Now be off before I have you thrown off. I'll not have you on Scarborough land again.'

'Your father would not have treated me so,' said Soames resentfully.

'My father, God rest him, was a good deal too lenient. Be off.'

Shocked, Soames went. Work was plentiful in the colony, but he was known as a Scarborough man and once word got about that Jarvis had given him notice, he might find it difficult to find other employment. His best option was to offer his services elsewhere, quickly, before rumours could fly. Yes, he must go far from Scarborough and Jarvis' sphere of influence.

Soames sighed. He had no wish to head south for Hobarton, but it seemed he had little choice. He was packing his saddlebags when the thought struck that he might yet buy his way back into his ex-master's favours. Accordingly, he presented himself, cap in hand, and requested an interview.

'Yes?' It was a curt greeting, and Soames knew he'd have to say his piece in a hurry.

'It's about that mad Scotchman, Mr Jarvis,' he said. 'He is up to something, up in the mountains, and I think you should know he has some fine Merino ewe-'

Jarvis cut him off with a brusque gesture. 'I need know nothing you can tell me, Soames. You will find the money owed you in the stable, but I find myself unable to offer a recommendation for any future employment.'

Jarvis was not pleased to find himself in need of a new overseer at close to the end of autumn. Whether the rains came late or whether Van Diemen's Land was following New South Wales into drought, they were due for a cold winter. Jarvis had lived years in the colonies, and he knew the snows of the south could be as fierce as in his native England. In New South Wales sheep were shorn in winter, but in the high country of Van Diemen's Land it was necessary to leave it until the warmer weather came. Even so, early lambs would die in the cold. The hay crop had been poor, and Soames had failed to shield the turnips from the ravages of kangaroos. There was plenty of native vegetation for the creatures; why must they encroach on Scarborough land? To cap all his wife was unwell and his mother openly scornful of her daughter-in-law's indifferent health. Twice in Launceston Eliza had been driven to tears by his mother's acid tongue, and his attempt at mediation had set both women against him.

Yes, Jarvis had enough problems, occupational and domestic, to regret the necessity of dispensing with Soames. He must return to

Launceston for an experienced man immediately, unless he sent word from the unofficial mail depot at Dick Bruning's Mersey home. No, it was better to go himself, he decided, for though Bruning was a good man he might not be scrupulous in holding his tongue. Had he not befriended crazy Hector Campbell? In the meantime he would appoint a temporary overseer and rely on Fahey to handle the remaining sheep.

Gloomily, Jarvis wondered just how many head of sheep he was down since the storm. With fences fallen the ewes could have strayed anywhere on the flats, and some could have wandered up the mountain. There was danger in the pockmarked limestone, in the wild native carnivores, and perhaps from human thieves. With Scarborough the only major wool-growing property in the district it had never been necessary to mark the sheep for identity. If a ewe was found straying, it would generally be returned to Fahey as a matter of course. Naturally, the occasional spring lamb or two-tooth went missing, and Jarvis suspected some had probably been hung in someone's meat-safe, but on the whole he considered his sheep as safe from human depredations as they would have been in England.

Now, with Soames' parting words, he wondered if this were still true. So Hector Campbell had "fine Merino ewes"? To Jarvis' mind there was only one source from which those ewes could have come. And if Campbell had Scarborough ewes in his possession, he must be made return them immediately. Scarborough could not afford the loss. As for the lack of water in the lower pasture, perhaps Campbell had something to do with that as well. The man had been persistent in his requests to buy the strip of land bordering Glen Heather, and it was on this strip the problem had occurred.

Jarvis' mind raced as he weighed two immediate courses of action. He could employ a new overseer and put the matter in *his* hands, or he could pay a visit to Glen Heather himself. The former course was more prudent, but it would take more time. Perhaps he would need a week or ten days to install a new man, and by then Campbell might have spirited the ewes away into the wilds of his mountain property. Jarvis knew of no commerce between Scarborough and Glen Heather, and his men had no time for idle chatter, but who was to say he was truly secure? Eliza had seemed friendly with the Scotsman's wife at the May Day Ball, and had met her at the Brunings' affair, and some times since. Jarvis' mouth tightened. Eliza was much too liberal in the company she kept. He would speak to her again, but not while she remained in delicate health. They already had a son, but Jarvis knew sons could die. He had not become his father's heir until adulthood, when two of his brothers had been carried off by affections of the lung. He must have more children to ensure heirs for Scarborough, and as for Eliza's peculiar democratic leanings, he could rely on Nannie Goodridge as an antidote. Winston and his putative brothers would grow up with a proper sense of their social consequence.

Jarvis dismissed his current and future family from his mind. He *must* replace Soames, and see what money could be spared for fencing. On the face of it, Scarborough was prospering, but the banker's draft sent to his Uncle Wharton had left him financially stretched. The horses would amply repay the outlay once they arrived, but it would be two years or more before he would see substantial returns. Meanwhile, he must play a holding game, and hope wool prices were good enough to ease the strain on his purse strings. And he must demand the return of such ewes as had strayed (or been driven) onto Glen Heather. And before that, he must broach Fahey and try to discover the number of ewes Campbell might have acquired. He'd look a fool if he ordered the return of a round dozen and Campbell had only two, or even none at all. Likewise, he did not want Campbell laughing up his ragged sleeve at a demand for the return of two sheep when he had appropriated fifty.

***

Dismissed and fuming, it occurred to Soames that there was someone else whose favours he might buy with information and insinuations. Soames had nothing against Hector Campbell; indeed, he scarcely knew the man, but if Campbell and Jarvis were at odds, it could do no harm to drive the wedge in farther. No real harm could come to Campbell, and perhaps much good might come to Soames. If Campbell harboured a grudge, he might be induced to trade favours for information.

CHAPTER 12

The track to Glen Heather had widened in recent months. The windstorm had blown large branches across it, but Hector had told Bullocky George to drag them away to do service as windrow fencing. Such fencing wasted pastureland, but formed convenient barriers. These were cheap, renewable and almost indestructible, and land was one thing Hector had in plenty.

Hector was riding to Chudleigh to despatch a summons to the architect, Tobias Scott-Blakeney, whose direction he had extracted from Godfrey Reeve. Rowan had neither the build nor the speed of a fine saddle horse, but a man of Hector's size could not ride a spindle-leg. Besides, with the Falcon still dead lame it made sense to use Rowan for riding rather than to team him with a strange harness-mate. Hector was still on Glen Heather land, plaid hitched above his trews, when another horseman hailed him. He drew rein, recognised Jarvis' man, Soames, and made to ride on.

'Out o' my way, bootlicker,' he growled, when the man refused to give ground.

'Wait, Campbell. There's something I want to say.'

'Nae doubt. But it isna something I wish to hear,' said Hector. The Scarborough man could be up to nothing good, or he'd not have turned a soft answer to an insult. Did Sassenachs have no more backbone than a kipper?

'I think you might want to hear this,' persisted Soames.

'Aye? And *I* think that sounds a wee bit like a threat,' drawled Hector. His mood lightened, and he began to look forward to a lively exchange before the Sassenach returned to his master with a flea in each ear and perhaps a boot to the buttocks as well.

'Take it as you will,' said Soames. He shrugged, but there was a certain smugness about him that made Hector narrow his eyes.

Hector dismounted and tied his horse to a tree. He bestowed on it an absent-minded pat, something Soames noted with interest. Weaknesses could sometimes be exploited.

'Mr Campbell, I think you should listen to me.' Soames removed his hat and dismounted also, a movement nicely calculated to express respect without submission.

'Aye?' Hector Campbell was standing before him with boot heels planted well apart, chest thrust forward above his folded arms. The fellow looked immovable as the Pennines, and almost as big. 'And you will then remove your carcase frae my property?' he suggested.

'If you still ask it,' said Soames. He smiled a little, deprecatingly. His own lack of physical presence allowed him to hear and see things forever denied to men such as Jarvis and Campbell; things that had led to his receiving a glowing reference and a ticket to Van Diemen's Land from his English employer rather than a gaol sentence or a swift dismissal. Yes, unobtrusiveness was often an asset, but there were times when more inches would have been welcome. He sought in Hector Campbell's flinty grey eyes for graft or greed. Either emotion would be profitable to Soames. He was sure Campbell had breached the law somewhere in his dealings with Scarborough. Even if the man had not actively stolen Scarborough sheep, he had made no move to return them, and had almost certainly diverted a stream so Scarborough water might irrigate Glen Heather land.

'Say your say, Soames, and be gone,' said Campbell. His voice was deep and redolent of the lochs and crags, and sent an atavistic thrill of dislike through Soames. To be sure, the crowns of England and Scotland had been one for scores of years, but folk memories were long and everyone knew the Scots were tight fisted bastards who would sell their mothers for a groat.

'You know my name, but not my business?' he said.

'Aye, I do ken your name. Your business is no my concern. Go home, Sassenach.'

'It is your concern, for I wish to talk to you of water.'

'Do you so?'

'And of sheep. Merino ewes, to be exact.'

Not by a flicker did Campbell react. 'Do you so?' he said again.

'It is well known you were a trifle put out when you found you'd been cheated into a property with neither sizeable streams nor easy access to the river,' said Soames.

'Is that so?' asked Campbell, affecting wonderment.

'It is no secret that you tried to buy a certain stretch of Scarborough land from Whitaker Jarvis,' said Soames doggedly. 'Nor that Jarvis turned you down flat.'

Campbell's expression hardened. 'My dealings wi' Jarvis ha' been open enough. And if that is all you want frae me, you can go back to your master. Thank him for his concern, and tell him Glen Heather will ha' all the water it needs, and then more.'

'You admit you have taken what you could not buy?'

'That is the size o' it,' said Campbell, 'but I took nothing that wasna my own by right.'

'And the sheep?' pressed Soames. 'You do not deny you have acquired some Scarborough ewes?'

'Och! Your Sassenach blood has turned your brain,' said Campbell contemptuously. 'You waste my time and stink up my air and I've had my fill o' your presence. Get out before I kick you back to your master on the toe o' my boot.'

'Oh, I'll go back,' said Soames. 'Along with a round tale for Mr Jarvis, if I've a mind to tell it...'

He trailed off suggestively, and sure enough, Campbell touched on the bait.

'You have it in mind that I ha' stolen frae your master, yet perhaps you willna spill your guts?' he suggested.

'I dislike making trouble, Mr Campbell,' lied Soames. 'And yet my duty lies to my master.'

'Your duty lies to yoursel',' said Campbell flatly.

'Or sometimes to justice,' said Soames. For the first time he felt that he and the wild Scot were speaking the same language. The man was neither so uncultured nor so inflexible as he appeared. The grey eyes were narrowed to flinty slits as Campbell visibly considered, before suggesting that blind justice might sometimes need a little more blinding to be fair.

'You might put it that way,' said Soames.

'And if I were to make it worthwhile, you might do the blinding yoursel'?'

Soames nodded slightly and Campbell grinned. The effect was oddly frightening, as if a granite cliff face had split to reveal a ray from the earth's molten heart. He unfolded his arms and crooked a finger to beckon. Soames, convinced the fish had struck, prepared to reel it in.

'And what would you consider a proper price for this blinding o' justice?' asked Campbell.

'I would set no price, but perhaps I might accept a small favour in return.'

'A small favour?' marvelled Campbell. 'And how will you go about it? Is it to be a wisp o' cheesecloth trailed across her vision, like, or a dirk thrust in while the lady sleeps? One eye or two to be gouged, when I gi'e the word?' His expression was suddenly cold as frost, and Soames rejoiced. Campbell was quite unhinged, and his hatred for Jarvis must verge on obsession for him to react so strongly to an allusive suggestion.

'I could tell Jarvis his suspicions are wrong,' he said. 'Or I could tell him nothing. I have no need to return to Scarborough, but if you want a good man I can give you the information you require to stay one step ahead. And more to come, for I've still friends at Scarborough.'

Campbell was silent so long after that, that Soames was forced to prompt him.

'Come, man, what's your answer? You will not have an offer like this again.'

'Aye,' said Campbell, 'that's a thing I believe.'

His expression never altered, but the strong fingers of one hand seized Soames by the scruff of the collar while those of the other took up the negligible slack in the back of Soames' duck trousers. Soames twisted in astonished discomfort and gave a squawk of outrage as he was lifted off his feet.

'Whisht, man, shut your neck,' said Campbell, 'or I'll change my grasp to round the front.'

Soames thought of his throat and private parts held in that clamp-like grip and moaned.

'I told you to *whisht*,' said Campbell. Without apparent effort he swung Soames back and forth a couple of times and let him fall, hauling him upright again with a one-handed grasp to the collar. His free hand moved purposefully downwards, and Soames clapped his own hands protectively over his crotch.

'Aye,' said Campbell, 'you need it for pissing, do you no? Be sure you'd never ha' any other use for the wee pitifu' bit o' haggis. Call yoursel' a *man*?' With a final contemptuous shake he dropped Soames, spat on his palms and bent to wipe them ostentatiously on a tussock. 'I may be hard, but I ha' never been crooked,' he observed.

Shaking with rage and humiliation, Soames looked longingly at the tartan-covered buttocks so displayed, but he knew Campbell was alert, and kept his boots on the ground. The Scot straightened, and smiled grimly. 'Aye, you ken fine no to try that one. Good day, Mr Soames.' He remounted his thick-legged chestnut, twitching the reins free of their branch with one practised tug.

Soames glowered. His attempt to do Jarvis an ill turn and himself a good one had misfired, and now all that remained were the options of revenge and retreat. He knew (for Fahey had told him) that Campbell had a comely young wife. Perhaps that might offer an avenue for revenge? In a rare moment of self-perception Soames knew he'd never have the courage to use it.

***

Hector rode on into Chudleigh, dismissing Soames before the man was out of sight. It had proved poor sport, after all, for the sleekit wretch had caved in without a fight and so Hector felt vaguely dissatisfied. It was a long time since he had faced a worthy opponent, and what had become of the braw men he had known in his youth? Their spines had been steel and their skins proper leather, and some of them had caustic tongues to match his own. They'd tramped the unexplored country, and though they'd carried blankets, they had not been soft. This Soames spoke like a common clerk, and was probably afraid of the dark. With a snort, Hector turned to thoughts of his future house, and to the solution he had found to the water problem. So Jarvis was lacking water and sheep? Let him blame Hector Campbell if he chose - he would prove nothing on either count.

Dwelling pleasurably on Jarvis' total lack of proof, Hector rode on. As he entered the raw settlement of Chudleigh, he saw men at work and hoped Soames was not a fair sample of the foremen/ overseers available for hire. If *so*, Hector would have none of them. If *not*, Jarvis must be even more of a gruel-livered haggis-dick than he'd remembered. But no, Jarvis was no haggis-dick. That was an insult to the haggis.

Hector soon found a carrier who professed himself willing to deliver a note to Tobias Scott-Blakeney. Unfortunately, he would not swear to delivery by any particular date, claiming that a swollen river between Chudleigh and Launceston could delay him indefinitely.

'And who's to say the river will be swelled?' demanded Hector. 'You ken fine there's been no rain this side o' Easter.'

'Not to say there will *be* none,' said the carrier. Since he added that if Mr Campbell was dissatisfied he could take the letter to Bruning instead, Hector was forced to back down.

'I wouldna deal wi' Bruning if he were the last man to walk this earth,' he muttered.

'I hear Bruning's not the only man you've crossed,' said the carrier, safely in possession of his fee. Hector damned his impudence and turned Rowan's nose for home.

It had taken time to find the carrier's direction, so he stopped off at the inn for a dram of whisky before riding home. The spirit proved honest, so the dram became two or three. It might have been more, but it was late, and he had no wish to be too long away from home, in case he had misread Soames and the wretch had it in mind to make mischief at Glen Heather. It was one thing to face storm damage with equanimity, but another to support deliberate vandalism. Hector knew he could cow the man a second time, or call in the constable, but he did not want Ness annoyed. The lassie was distant enough with him as it was. Regretfully, he passed up a final libation and rode towards home, pausing to spit on the trampled ground where he had flung Soames. His shoulder blades pricked, but he doubted Soames had the spirit to attack alone, and he was not a man who would attract accomplices, nor trust them if he did. Hector was no such man either, but he would have dismissed any hint of similarity as contemptuously as he had dismissed Soames that afternoon.

He passed his own workmen on the road with barely a nod. Bullocky George was not with them, which meant he had elected to stay on the mountain again. The man had a positive craving for solitude, and he loved his bullocks a good deal more than most men loved their wives.

His own wife would be alone, and perhaps, for once, he would have the leisure to eat a proper meal and lie with her again. Her slight but shapely body came to mind, along with the softness of her hair. She showed no enthusiasm for bed games, but Hector hesitated to think her cold or barren. The more he thought of his wife the more he wanted her. His multitudinous projects had kept him busy, but every man was due some relaxation. And he *must* get an heir. If not on Ness then on some other wench. He would not repudiate Ness and marry another lassie, but he could offer money to the wench, and give the bairn to Ness to raise. But before resorting to this expedience (which Ness would probably not appreciate) he must spare some energy towards getting a bairn on his own wife. He had heard some women had strange cycles, but if he took her each day for several weeks perhaps sheer persistence would remove whatever impediment there was to his planting a babe in her womb.

It came as a surprise to him, as well as a shock, to find Ness conversing with another man. In the fading light he could not identify the wretch, but he guessed it was likely Soames. It had never occurred to him that the sleekit bastard would seduce Ness as revenge, but now the thought, inflamed by whisky fumes, took root in his mind. Uttering a wild Gaelic yell, Hector dug his heels into the ambling Rowan and covered the last three hundred yards at a gallop.

'Isna one threat to your wee whistle enough for you?' he demanded while still a hundred yards distant. 'Have I to remove it frae its stalk wi' my dirk?'

Ness and the intruder swung round, their faces twilit blurs, and the man's mount, held by a loop of rein, danced skittishly. Rowan pulled up with a snort, and Hector's gaze sharpened. It was the twig-legged black belonging to Jarvis, and by God it *was* Jarvis, staring with cold distaste.

'Get the hell off my land!' said Hector.

'Gladly, Campbell, when you have answered two questions to my satisfaction - and agreed to make suitable restitution.'

Lord, the man spoke like a constipated dominie. Or perhaps like a lawyer. 'If you've come to talk about water or sheep, you can save yoursel' a heap o' trouble,' said Hector. 'I've thrown one man off Glen Heather today, and I'd like fine to make it two.'

'Save *yourself* a spell on Devil's Island,' said Jarvis coldly. 'Return my ewes forthwith.'

'I ha' laid no hand on your ewes, man,' said Hector. 'Not since I was forced to gi'e you a lesson in their management, forby. You ken the occasion I ha' in mind?'

'You deny possession of something up to a dozen Scarborough ewes?' said Jarvis crisply.

'Aye, I do so. Do *you* deny you ha' come onto my land wi'out my word and wi' the connivance o' that piece o' swill you ken as Soames?'

Jarvis ignored that, and of course he would, thought Hector. The man knew he was in the wrong.

'Tell your man Soames, if he sets foot on Glen Heather land again I'll ha' less to say and more to do.'

'That sounds like a threat, Campbell.'

'Och, so a peelie-wally Sassenach like yoursel' has the wit to ken tha'!' marvelled Hector. 'It was no threat, Jarvis, but the honest truth. I willna be spoken to on my own land the way that Soames was set to speak. And so now he's failed you, you come to insult me yoursel'!'

'Soames is no longer my employee,' said Jarvis distantly. He put on his hat and mounted his horse. 'Since you will give me no satisfaction, Campbell, I shall take my leave.'

'Dinna come back!' said Hector.

'Rest assured I will not. You will, however, receive a visit from the constable.'

'But Mr Jarvis!' broke in Ness, 'you have it wrong! I tried to tell you we didna take any a one o' your sheep! Hector wouldna steal frae anybody!'

'Perhaps you are correct, Mrs Campbell. Perhaps your husband did not steal sheep. However, he neglected to return those that strayed onto his land, and prevented my men from conducting a search. That, to my mind, amounts to theft.'

Hector blinked. 'So you're wishful to take the ewes I have in the enclosure, forby?'

'If they are Scarborough ewes.'

'Nae doubt they'll be marked wi' your brand?'

Jarvis made an impatient gesture. 'Unfortunately they are not. It has never been necessary to prove ownership until, shall we say? some six months ago. It is well known, however, that I own the only such sheep south of Mersey.'

'Hay is scarce this year,' said Hector. 'The rains havena come, and there's little fodder.'

'What are you getting at, man?'

'If you're wanting to take awa' the ewes frae my enclosure, you can do so,' said Hector. 'But you will pay me the price of the fodder they ha' eaten.'

Jarvis must have tightened his hands on the reins, for his black shied suddenly.

'Have a care,' said Hector judiciously. 'If that peelie-wally beastie catches its leg in a hole, I'll ha' to shoot it for you.'

'And charge me, I have no doubt, for the bullet!' said Jarvis.

'Aye, and a guinea over for my trouble.'

'So now we know where we stand,' said Jarvis.

'We do so.'

'Keep the ewes then, Campbell! Shear them, eat them, use them as steppingstones across the stream. But let any beast of yours set foot on Scarborough land, now or ever, and be sure I shall shoot it down and send the bill to you. Good day, Campbell!'

'Get off my land, Sassenach, before I knock your bloody chin up through the top o' your head,' said Hector.

Jarvis tipped his hat courteously to Ness. 'Mrs Campbell. Pray accept my sincerest pity for your plight. If ever you wish to better your position, I believe my wife may have an opening for a scullery maid.'

Hector kicked Rowan forward with a roar, but the chestnut was no match for the spirited black, and Jarvis was away towards Scarborough, riding at a pace which was nothing short of reckless.

CHAPTER 13

Ness backed away as Hector slid down and began to remove Rowan's harness. 'If I could get my hands o' that- that-' He dropped into Gaelic, and as weird syllables hissed from his throat, Ness wondered if he were going mad with rage and the drink she could smell.

She watched from a prudent distance as he saw to Rowan and decided he was not so crazed as he seemed. A man in the extremity of passion would have vented it on the nearest victim, and Rowan, although flickering his ears in protest at the volume of his master's opinions, seemed unafraid of his hands. Neither was Ness afraid of physical repercussions. Hector had never yet lifted a hand to her in anger. To be sure, she had not provoked him, but that meant little; Maggie Graham had been the meekest of women, yet her man had been so free with his fists that poor Maggie had seldom appeared at Kirk without a muffling shawl to hide a swollen jaw or bruised cheek.

Ness waited until the storm passed. She might not fear a beating, but she did not want Hector's scathing tongue turned on her. It was bad enough to listen to his opinion of Jarvis. Sadly, she thought her husband had just spewed out as many words of hate and disgust on Jarvis as he had expended in normal conversation with her in the whole of their wedded life. To be sure, she was not feeling kindly towards Mr Jarvis either. He had arrived shortly before Hector's return, and had spoken in a lordly fashion that made her long to argue. Unfortunately, she had been unable to do so, for she could not be sure which statements she should contradict. And that parting slap- she was not sure whether the insult had been aimed at herself or at Hector, but she thought it would have been very satisfactory to fire the contents of a chamber pot at Jarvis' supercilious head. If the man must look on her as if she were a bad odour, it seemed only fitting that he should have some of the real thing for the purposes of comparison.

'It's unco strange,' she remarked at last, 'for Eliza says her man isna a cruel master to his convicts. He had one lashed, but the man wasna sent to the chain gang. Eliza says-'

'A pox upon Eliza,' said Hector. 'The sleekit bitch ha' been making trouble. You'll ha' no more to do wi' her, Ness!'

'But Hector-'

'Be still, woman!'

'Och Hector, I willna be still,' said Ness angrily. 'You ha' forbidden me to speak wi' Mistress Bruning, Mistress Williams and now wi' Eliza. You called the modiste a sleekit auld bitch in her hearing and now she willna co' near to me, and Mistress Young hates me anyway. More, and I will ha' nae friend to my name!'

Slowly, Hector raised his hand. 'One more word out o' you, Ness, and I'll close your mouth for you! Now get yoursel' to the cook-fire and gi' me something to eat. I'm as empty as the balls o' a prize ram.'

'You're as thick in the heid as a prize ram also!' snapped Ness, and departed at speed to the cook-fire. She did not believe Hector would strike her, but if you thrust your hand into the briar patch you can scarcely complain if your skin comes out in a maze of scratches.

In tight-lipped silence, she ladled meat and onions onto a platter and set it on a smooth stump. She tipped warm water into a pail, and set out soap and a linen towel. Not for the first time, she reflected how odd it was that Hector should buy fine soap and towels, yet wash in a broken pail.

To her surprise, Hector washed not only his face and hands, but stripped off plaid and sark to wash his chest before giving her the soap, and presenting his broad back to her. Annoyed but obedient, Ness soaped and rinsed his back and neck, and passed him the towel. He dried himself without comment, replaced his clothes and sat down to eat the congealing stew.

'Are you no eating, Ness?' he asked, cleaning the plate with a hunk of damper.

'I had mine before,' she said distantly, 'and wi' your skelping tongue I ha' no appetite.'

Hector nodded, and swallowed a pannikin of strong, scalding tea in three measured gulps. 'I'll have a wee cow for you soon, Ness,' he said abruptly.

Ness was unappeased. She had wanted a milking cow since summer, and Hector could have provided it any time these last six months. The red cattle were beef bred, and so wild she could never approach them. Any milk they produced was sufficient only to their calves. She bit her lip, reminded of Jarvis' accusations.

'The sheep in the enclosure,' she said, 'are no frae Scarborough.'

Hector gave a faint, ironic smile. 'They are not.'

'Then why did you no *tell* Jarvis so, you daft man?'

'Had he paid my price he would ha' been welcome to them,' said Hector.

'Had you told him the truth when he came, there would ha' been no quarrel.'

'He never did ask if they were frae Scarborough or no,' objected Hector. 'The neep-headed bastard decided they were his own, and I hope it chokes him.'

Ness knew there was a flaw in his reasoning, but she knew also that he was too thrawn to see it. She bent to take Hector's plate.

'Leave the crocks,' said Hector abruptly. 'It's gey cauld and time we were abed.'

Ness had never felt less like indulging Hector in his marital rights. 'I am gey tired tonight, Hector,' she ventured.

'And gey angry, too,' said Hector dryly. 'What ails you, Ness? You ken fine I'd no strike at you wi'out cause.'

Ness shook her head, but Hector took her by the shoulders. 'Are you ill, lassie?' She shook her head again. 'Then come to bed,' said Hector, and propelled her into the re-built hut. He stripped, and Ness noticed resentfully that he had not even the grace to shiver.

She looked askance at the lantern Hector had lit. 'Turn it out,' she said, but Hector did not.

'I like fine to look at you, lassie. Take off the shawl, now, and the gown.'

Shivering, and almost in tears with unspoken resentment, she removed gown and sark and laid herself on the sweet bedding. She would have done better to have become a servant, she thought bitterly. She could then have resented her master or mistress with a clear conscience. From the corner of her eye, she could see Hector's powerful body, already in a state of readiness for what he would do to her. He reached out and Ness sighed, and sucked in her lip. She knew it was going to hurt again. It usually did, when Hector took her, particularly when he decided to dispense with the preliminaries. It was in no way unbearable, but the uncomfortable chafing would be replaced by another pain, deep inside her body, and sometimes the soreness persisted for hours.

'I dinna ken why you bother,' she said resentfully, and quite without premeditation. 'You ha' me over and over, and there's no been a bairnie yet.'

Hector, about to make his first thrust, became suddenly still.

Appalled at what she had said, Ness tried to breathe deeply and failed. As usual, Hector's weight left little room for her lungs to expand, but the pressure lessened as Hector heaved up on his elbows.

'Och, go on,' said Ness, sighing. 'I didna mean it.' A tear rolled out of one eye, and she turned her face away.

Hector's face remained its unexpressive self, but he rolled off to lie beside her. 'Why are you greeting, Ness? Because the bairns dinna come?'

'What you said o' planting in the wrong season,' muttered Ness, 'is as true if you plant in barren ground.'

'Och- I doubt you're barren, lassie.' Hector ran appreciative hands over her thigh and breasts. 'I need to plant more often, perhaps. I ha' been busy wi' the land.'

'H-how often?' asked Ness faintly.

'Each day, to be certain,' said Hector.

He ran his hands around again, and Ness sighed. Such fondling happened rarely; with Hector up on the mountain all the short winter days, his attentions to her were usually swift and workmanlike. Hopefully, she wriggled closer.

'Hector,' she said, hoping to distract him from immediate action, 'you didna lie to Mr Jarvis, but you didna set him right about the sheep.'

'The supercilious bastard had no right to accuse me o' theft,' growled Hector.

'You do that often,' said Ness thoughtfully. 'You tell no lies, but you let folk think a thing true when it isna so.'

Hector's hands tightened on her buttocks, and the unexpected pleasure of the sensation almost made her lose the thread of conversation. 'You do that often,' she repeated, flexing her muscles a little to encourage him.

'Do I so?' said Hector thoughtfully, squeezing again.

'No *that*,' said Ness, with a spurt of laughter. 'I mean the other. Let folk believe what they will when you could ha' set them right. To Mr Jarvis, you did it, and to Mr Bruning.'

'They ha' no right-'

'Did *I* ha' nae right to the truth, Hector?' she asked softly.

'Sheep are no concern o' yours, Ness, and I ha' never lied to you.'

'About the sheep, no,' said Ness, 'but on the docks, the day we met- you let me believe there was no a chance for me but to wed wi' you.'

'Aye, and you agreed.' Hector sounded impatient.

'I could ha' found work in the colony, could I no? Instead o' your wife I could ha' been a servant, or companion, or nursed bairns for a wealthy lady like Mistress Reeve.'

'And why would you do tha'?' asked Hector, in echo of what he had said before. It was obvious to Ness that he could not or would not see her point at all.

'I could ha' been a servant,' she said again. 'I could ha' had a fine place in Sydney Town.'

'There's work enough for you here, wi'out slaving for some high-nosed auld besom.'

'I ken that fine. And perhaps I'd have wed you anyway, had I the choice, but do you no see- I thought I *had* no choice! And you- you let me think it.'

Hector was silent, and after a few moments Ness knew he was not going to answer her. And having said her piece she began to wonder if she had been unfair. She had made no great effort, all her life, but had been content to leave the ordering of her destiny first to Phemie and Donal, then to Jean Leslie and, failing Jean, to Hector. Perhaps she had been as much at fault as he. Hector had moved away, and she shivered.

'It's gey cold,' she said, and touched his shoulder. 'You said then I could nurse your bairns. Had we no best get one planted?' She paused, and because she had already gone so far and had little else to lose, she added; 'After all, you wed me to get bairns for Glen Heather.'

Hector moved at last, putting a hand on her thigh. 'I doubt I ha' the push for it now. Go to sleep, lassie. It wi' keep.'

Perversely, now Hector had lost interest, Ness found her own desires rising. 'Och, Hector, dinna heed my haivers,' she said. She shifted closer, rolling so her breast touched his arm, and brought up one hand to stroke his chest. 'Tell me about the burn,' she said abruptly, and touched her tongue to the skin of his shoulder.

'The burn now?' said Hector, apparently taken by surprise at the turn of subject.

'Aye. I ken fine the sheep we ha' dinna belong to Scarborough, but what o' the water? How should you be blamed if a burn dry up?'

Hector laughed a little, putting his arm around her, tucking her against his side. 'Jarvis thinks I diverted the burn across frae

Scarborough for Glen Heather land,' he said.

'You didna!' said Ness. 'We've no more water than ever we had.'

'We'll ha' water enough by summer,' said Hector with satisfaction.

'But how? You'll no take the burn frae Scarborough.'

'Will I no?' Hector sounded amused. 'It wouldna be so difficult. A new bed dug for the burn, a tree felled or a heap o' rock tumbled in place.'

'Och no,' said Ness scornfully. 'You'd scorn to act so craven, Hector Campbell. You might knock a man down, or call him a peelie-wally auld Sassenach, but you'd never act so shabby as to take what wasna yours.'

'Yet I took you, lassie,' reminded Hector.

'Aye,' said Ness, 'but I didna belong to any but mysel'. Whatever I said in anger just now, I did come to you. And you have told me nothing o' the water. If you've no diverted the Scarborough burn, what ha' you in mind?'

Hector chuckled. 'We've burns of our own, Ness. They burrow under the rock, and disappear, but if we can stop the dive, the water will flow above instead o' below. We hollow logs and wedge them in the burn. The water will run as if in a pipe, down to Glen Heather instead o' under the brae.'

Such a simple solution! thought Ness, in awe. 'And the Scarborough burn?' she ventured. 'What o' that?'

'Perhaps it has taken a dive in its turn,' said Hector. 'Or a tree might ha' fallen across the bed. Jarvis may find out soon enough. But that's enough o' Jarvis.' He had been rubbing Ness' back idly while he spoke, and now rolled over, pulling her on top of him, kissing her in a way that was almost playful. Whether it was the change of position, or the fact that they were in better accord Ness did not know, but there was no pain for her this time. Instead there was pleasure, and afterwards she found she could face Hector's plan for repeated "plantings" with much less reluctance. She even hoped, as Hector patted her absentmindedly and gathered her against him for sleep, that perhaps he would take her with him next day to show her the work on the mountain.

When morning came, however, he was away with the men again, leaving her alone with the chill and the silence and with only lame Grey Falcon for company. The horse's injury was bad, and although Ness' poultices and water from the burn had taken the heat from the wounds, the healing was slow.

Hector had told her brusquely it was as well the season was winter, for a summer injury could not have escaped fly-strike and infection. The torn gashes were crusting, but Ness wondered if they should have been stitched. Hector had declined the task and she knew she would have had neither the strength nor the resolution to do it herself. The hurt leg could not be hobbled, but there was no need. Grey Falcon hopped and limped about the half acre of ground nearest the hut, pausing often to whicker companionably to Ness. She had always been fond of the beast, but now she came to respect him as well. Her attentions with poultice and water must have pained the great creature, but he bore no malice. He was a good friend to her, was Grey Falcon, but even the most affectionate of horses could not make up for the fact that, apart from Hector and the men, she saw no other soul for weeks at a time.

Whether Jarvis or Soames had been blackening Hector's name, or whether Hector's own pugnacity had turned folk against them, she did not know, but she found the total neglect by the local ladies bewildering. She had hoped Hector would relax his prohibitions against Theodora and Eliza, but when she suggested she would like fine to see Mistress Bruning again, her husband reacted with a curt refusal.

'But Hector, I must see another woman sometimes!' said Ness. 'If I canna see Mistress Bruning, may I visit wi' Mistress Williams?'

But it seemed Williams of Llanhow had cut Hector dead in Mersey after the altercation with Jarvis, and so Harriet Williams was not to be visited either.

'You mind your work, Ness, and let me mind mine,' said Hector when she asked if she might have Bullocky George's wife to drink tea. 'What use ha' we for chattering auld biddies?'

'I thought we were to be a part o' society,' said Ness. 'I thought you wished it so.' But Hector turned away, growling there would be time enough when the braw house was built. 'Aye, time enough when I am auld and grey,' murmured Ness under her breath. Once more she cooled toward Hector. No matter how often she told herself he had his good and bad like anyone, no matter how often she remembered poor beaten Maggie Graham, she found herself, in her lowest moments, wondering if life were worth more than a farthing. Love was a fine thing, even the odd love she felt for Hector, but it needed fertile ground to grow and her man was uncommonly stony. To be sure, she had Grey Falcon's company and the everlasting, ever-changing beauty of Glen

Heather, but that beauty would have been more satisfying had she been able to share her delight.

On one of her rambles she found that the prickly heather-like plants had put out flowering spikes of pink and white. Real heather could be white, but was usually of a purple hue, so this pink came as a surprise. She gathered some sprigs and tucked them in the bosom of her gown, but they had lost their beauty by the time Hector returned to the clearing.

***

Ness was not the only one to be disappointed with life. Hector was both angry and baffled at the constant petty hold-ups baulking his plans. He had left New South Wales in a bid for a fresh start, among folk unprejudiced against him for his bluntness and uncanny luck with business. He had thought the procuring of Ness and the purchase of Glen Heather heralded a bright beginning, but, now, some eight months later, the frustrations had begun to crowd him again.

The water problem was solved, but the architect he had summoned had not arrived, the second delivery of sheep from New South Wales had not been made and even the wee cow he had brought in for Ness proved unsuitable; a dry old beast whose sagging udder and blistered teats would have yielded little wholesome milk. After he forced the carrier to return it and bill the owner for its transportation, Hector tried to find another, but few squatters had milking cows to sell, at least, to him. At length he was forced to settle on a virgin heifer, which he fetched to be serviced by the red and white bull. It would be a weary wait until she came in milk, but at least she was not a broken-down old creature fit for the knackers.

The bull, though wild as a stag in the glen, went to his task with a will, and Hector, seeing the resignation in the eyes of the young heifer, was reminded uncomfortably of his own relations with his wife. If only there was more time… he'd never be a sentimental man but he did love Ness and it troubled him that he could never quite tell her so.

***

The winter had set in early that year, cold and sometimes snowing. Ness would wake to a still white world and marvel at the beauty while she shook with the cold. Her old plaid saw much service during June and July, and she was grateful when Hector built another room to the hut. It was provided with a simple chimney so Ness could light a fire when the wind blew up or the snow began to drift. There were no more wild storms, but enough wind for Hector to be constantly caulking or adding another layer of bark to the roof.

During the dark evenings he spent much time plaiting rawhide and whipleather for harness. He was a fine hand with it, lashing the supple leather into intricate patterns and scarcely needing lamplight to do so.

'Come spring we should have our braw great house begun,' he said abruptly one day, 'if the fool man I sent to comes where he's bid.'

'What fool of a man is that, Hector?' asked Ness.

'Och, I'm meaning the man Scott-Blakeney. Him who planned out York Hall and Scarborough. Bloody Reeve must ha' gi'en me the wrong direction, or else that sleekit carrier threw awa' the letter.'

'Perhaps Mr Scott-Blakeney is busy elsewhere, Hector, and canna come,' suggested Ness, but Hector was unappeased.

'The rogue should ha' sent word when he's to come, then,' he said curtly, and after a while Ness nodded. Busy, Mr Scott-Blakeney surely was, but it was only courteous to respond when one was sent a letter of invitation.

'The braw house will come,' she said. 'You will make it happen.'

'Aye…it will be a fine setting for you.' He looked at her hard. 'It will be warmer and you will wear a lighter gown. And we'll hae' a fine wooden bed and goose-feather quilt.'

'Aye,' said Ness. 'Next year, perhaps.' She smiled. 'But for now we hae' shelter and food and violet soap.'

Hector's face relaxed. 'Soap!' he said. 'Was there ever a lassie set such store by soap?'

***

Tobias Scott-Blakeney had taken the invitation from Hector Campbell for a blunt command. Tobias had never been humble, and to be so ordered sat very ill with him. Left to himself, he would have tossed Campbell's letter into the grate, but he chanced to open it in the company of his young associate, James Galbraith.

'Good Lord!' he exclaimed, between amusement and disgust. 'Here we have three eminent gentlemen of Launceston awaiting our pleasure and this man Campbell calmly informs me that I am to present myself at his spread at my earliest convenience. And the place is even beyond Scarborough!'

'With what purpose?' asked Galbraith, idly adding a line or two to the portrait he was drawing before dusting it off and holding it up for his patron's inspection.

Reluctantly, Tobias chuckled. 'Lord, Jamie, you will be the death of me, one day!'

'I do hope not,' said Galbraith gently.

'If not, be sure the lumbago will finish me,' grumbled Scott-Blakeney. 'As for Mr Campbell, he may wait for my convenience until Hell freezes over.'

Galbraith reached for the crumpled letter, adjusting his spectacles to read the vigorous scrawl. 'The man wants a fine house designed and built, and he wants it done soon. Why should that distress you? It sounds a reasonable desire to me, and you might see the charming Eliza! You know she always does you good.'

Scott-Blakeney glowered at him then gave a short laugh. 'Leave it, Jamie, do. I am too old and too bad-tempered to be bothered with such matters now.'

CHAPTER 14

Unaware that his missive had received a cold welcome, Hector chafed more and more as winter progressed. He sent a second letter, in case the first had gone astray, but his pride would allow him to do no more.

With spring, the rains came at last, making the ground around the hut unpleasantly greasy. Ness had to scrape mud from her boots each day and rub them with mutton fat to keep the wet out. She would not complain, for she knew Hector was making all the effort he could. Through late August and September she was enchanted to find some of the sombre green trees blazing with golden blossom made in fluffy balls like the down on baby chicks. The sweetness of the blossom had a peppery smell behind it that set Ness sneezing, but she was delighted all the same.

The pink and white heather plant was still in flower, and some of the great gums had wreaths of cream coloured blossom. Again, she longed to share her pleasure, but flowers meant as little to Hector as the puffy wisps of cloud in the sky. Even when a great flight of white birds wheeled over the hut, shrieking and squawking like demons, Ness could only stare in silent admiration. When Hector returned that night she described the birds, but he merely grunted and informed her they were cockatoos, and a plague to growing crops.

The work on the watercourses was concluded, and Ness was delighted to see a burn where no burn had run before. At first the water trickled through green ferns and over coarse grasses, but after Hector had forced a new bed the length of the mountain it flowed obediently, carried over the holes in the limestone by miniature aqueducts. It seemed a marvel of engineering, and Ness was almost dumb with admiration, but Hector moved on to a new round of tree-felling and clearing, hacking another enclosure out of the virgin forest of the flats.

The second shipment of sheep arrived in October, half-starved and miserable, hipbones jutting beneath their scraggy fleeces. Hector was half-convinced the beasts would die, but with the spring growth and plentiful browsing they began to gain condition. And then, one

November morning, a ram with a curling horn trotted into the clearing, and fought the resident and still starveling ram to his knees.

'One o' the Scarborough flock,' growled Hector, wrestling the creature away from his own ram. 'Randy auld bugger! That sleekit Jarvis had best look to his fences if he doesna want the whole flock away into the forest.'

'What will you do with it, Hector?'

'He can service the new young ewes,' said Hector. 'He might as well have a job o' work or so to earn his keep. No doubt Jarvis will be along to collect him soon enough, aye, and likely the fool will try to lay this one at my door as well.'

Ness wished Hector would return the beast and avoid further trouble, but there was no use expecting that. Hector had never forgiven Jarvis his insinuations of theft, *or* for his insults. The best she could hope was that Jarvis would come quickly, apologise, and retrieve his ram, but the days went on, and Jarvis did not come. Finally, Hector tired of waiting.

'Where are you going?' asked Ness anxiously as he mounted Rowan.

'To Scarborough, to ha' Jarvis come and fetch his ram.'

Hector's words were mild enough, but Ness put a hand on Rowan's rein. 'Canna you send a message wi' one o' the men?'

'The men are paid to work on the land, no to gossip wi' Jarvis' shepherd.'

'Hector - you willna begin a stramash wi' Mr Jarvis?'

'I'll begin nothing,' said Hector. 'I'm awa' to have Jarvis fetch his ram.'

***

Jarvis had soon discovered his mistake in accusing Hector of outright theft of sheep and water. The real culprit in both cases proved to be the windstorm, which had blown down fences and heeled over a giant gum tree on the bank of the stream. The uprooting of this patriarch had torn a gape in the earth, and the broken soil had washed away, exposing a rift in the limestone. Into this rift the stream had poured away.

The climb to the source of the stream was a long one, and Jarvis cursed when he had made it. Had the indolent Soames attended his duties, he could have rectified the trouble, saving Jarvis loss of stock *and* the embarrassment of the interview with Hector Campbell. Yet-Campbell might not have diverted the stream, but he had almost certainly helped himself to the straying ewes. There must be some guilt in the man, or else why had he not protested his innocence? Jarvis tried to dismiss it from his mind, but Eliza mentioned Campbell's wife.

'Their hut can be no more than a hovel, for the modiste from Launceston would not work there at all,' she said to Jarvis. 'I know you and Mr Campbell have had your differences, but Agnes is a sweet girl and I hope she does not suffer.'

'Campbell's wife is not your concern,' said Jarvis coldly. 'You should save your worries for yourself, Eliza. Mother informs me you are not taking your milk as you ought.'

'I dislike milk, and Mother Jarvis knows it. She is making trouble for me, as always.'

Jarvis flushed. 'My mother is trying to preserve your health and that of the child. The least you could do is to benefit from her experience. She has borne five children, after all.'

'I am very grateful,' said Eliza, 'but I wish she would be a little less busy. A word to me would have been sufficient. May I not invite Agnes to visit?'

'You may not. Campbell is an upstart of the very worst type, and he threatened to throw me off his property.'

'None of that has to do with Agnes, and a visit from her would serve to break the monotony,' said Eliza. 'Oh, I have never been so bored in all my life! Cannot we go to Launceston for a visit? I quite long to go to the theatre.'

'Mother believes, and I agree, that you should avoid exertion and strive for a tranquil mind.' Having delivered this advice, Jarvis strode off to his study. He dealt easily with servants and the gentlemen of his acquaintance, and he wondered why his wife must be so contentious. He consulted the almanac, and decided the brig *Almira*, which was bringing his fine horses from England, should now be nearing land. His frown smoothed as he contemplated his future, when fine horseflesh replaced the foolish, wandering sheep.

While her husband contemplated the future with such satisfaction, Eliza Jarvis was sighing heavily. With just weeks before her baby's birth, she was feeling tired and unwell. She could no longer ride out on Gillyflower, and with the weather continuing cold she avoided walking in her garden. The new overseer was a married man, but she could hardly cultivate a friendship with Polly Garth, even had that young woman been willing. Polly was respectably connected to the Brunings, but she had married beneath her. Mother Jarvis would have felt bound to complain to Whitaker of any such friendship, and Eliza would have been lectured again.

She had believed herself finished with lectures when she left her mama, but marriage with Whitaker had not lessened their number. In fact, with Mother Jarvis' influence firmly upon her son, the lectures had become more frequent and more severe. Listlessly, Eliza took up her needle to embroider a smock for Winston, but she had little enthusiasm for the task. Her back ached, she was short of breath, and she found she could settle to nothing. She hated the cold, and wished herself back in Sydney Town.

Hearing sounds in the yard, her interest quickened. If callers had come, she would see them, whatever Mother Jarvis said. Green would have opened the door by now, and would automatically send cards for Mother Jarvis to examine, though it was Eliza's right to make decisions of that nature. It would be like Whitaker's mama to deny Eliza on the grounds of her condition, either receiving the callers herself, or, if in a particularly bad humour, having Green send them away.

Eliza thrust her needle into the cambric and rose, grimacing as she lifted her heavy body. She had hardly taken three steps towards the door when Mother Jarvis bustled through, followed by her lapdog, a small creature with bulging moist eyes and a whip tail, which moved with rat-like speed and went by the unlikely name of Kitty.

'Sit down, Eliza, you should not bestir yourself at this time,' said Mother Jarvis.

'Surely,' said Eliza swiftly, 'it was only this morning you advised me to take a little more exercise, Mother Jarvis! It does not do to put on too much flesh.'

'A turn about the garden is healthful, the nervous exertion of conversing with unbidden callers is to be avoided at all costs.'

Eliza's rosebud lips shaped a word that, had she heard it, would have driven the Widow Jarvis hotfoot to complain to her son. Fortunately, that lady had sailed onwards towards the front door, her massive skirts almost blocking the doorway.

'Old crow,' remarked Eliza, still in an undertone. 'Old *witch*.'

The lapdog squatted suddenly, lifting a leg to scratch vigorously at its ear. It then bit at the base of its tail and, as a finishing touch, sat down abruptly and began to scoot along the floor.

'Ugh, you filthy little beast!' said Eliza and, bent on relieving her irritation with its mistress, she darted forward to kick the slithering Kitty. Her foot failed to connect, and she staggered, and fell, striking her head against the solid chair.

She didn't hear the altercation on the doorstep as Hector Campbell demanded Jarvis, while Green and the Widow Jarvis sought simultaneously to deny him.

Whitaker Jarvis *did* hear the commotion, and went to investigate, to find his uncouth neighbour on the doorstep, clad in the ridiculous garment he affected and shouting obscenities at Green. The usually imperturbable butler was red-faced and angry, and his own mother was clasping her chest in outrage at Campbell's language.

'What is the object of this - this unseemly intrusion?' asked Jarvis.

Campbell looked at him impassively. 'You may remember words we had about yon sheep some weeks ago? Aye, and some crazed talk o' the burn that died?'

'I remember. What of it?'

'You recall on that occasion you threatened to shoot any animal o' Glen Heather you found on your land?'

'I may have said something of that nature,' said Jarvis stiffly. He glanced at the gawping Green. 'Get to the point, Campbell- if you have one.'

'One o' your rams has strayed onto Glen Heather a week since,' said Campbell. 'A gey big creature wi' a horn curled inwards.'

Jarvis frowned. What was Fahey at? 'If you have harmed that animal...'

'Och, I havena touched the beast,' said Campbell. 'Send your man to collect it before sunset and you may have it back, unharmed, but leave it at Glen Heather longer and I'll no answer for the consequences.'

'You may be sure I shall reclaim my property.'

'Aye. That leaves just the wee matter o' his keep.' Campbell offered a slip of paper.

Jarvis read the total incredulously, sure the man knew of his current straitened circumstances and was taunting him. 'You cannot be serious!' he snapped.

'Can I no? Then perhaps you'd care to save your money and leave the beast wi' me?'

'Listen, you bastard,' said Jarvis, cracking at last, 'I shall send Fahey for my ram and you will not get a groat! And if you ever try any more of this- this extortion, I shall have you put in charge for theft. Now get off my land or-'

'Or what?' asked Campbell with interest. 'Or you will insult my wee wife again?' His expression became malevolent. 'So Mistress Jarvis could be doing with a new scullery maid,' he said softly. 'And why's that? Ha' you been playing her false wi' the auld one?'

Mother Jarvis clapped her hands again to her breast, and the butler gaped. Polly Garth, who had heard the commotion, stared avidly. Jarvis, recalling long-ago lessons in fisticuffs, attempted to knock Hector Campbell to the ground. The blow was returned with interest, resulting in an unseemly brawl on the doorstep. Jarvis swung out, bruising his own knuckles on the Scotsman's granite face. A blow to his chin rocked him on his heels, and his vision fogged, but he swung again and felt his battered fist connect.

After that, he found his punches landing wide, and Campbell's fist took him under the ribs in a wheezing jab. Jarvis staggered, sucking in his breath, and drove a fist forward to connect with the Scot's cheekbone.

He punched again, and in the back of his mind he was astonished to find himself hard pressed. Campbell was many years his senior and could never have had the benefit of a first-class coach, but what he lacked in science he made up in reach and strength. Jarvis felt his head snap back on his neck, and a cut opened above his eye. He blinked, for blood was crawling stickily above his eyebrow, and the itch was almost worse than the pain of the cut. Campbell drove his fist into the brow, splattering the blood, and Jarvis delivered a numbing punch to his opponent's upper arm.

The outcome of the match was still uncertain when Eliza's maid, Lucy, came flying out with her hands to her mouth crying that Madam must have been alarmed by the altercation for she had fallen against the chair. 'An' she's moaning something awful!' she reported.

Jarvis delivered one last blow, then turned his back on Campbell and demanded an explanation, while his mother, followed by Nannie Goodridge, hurried to Eliza. Usually these two agreed as well as oil and water, but having helped Eliza to bed and made a cursory examination they turned in unison and told Jarvis to send for the midwife at once.

Cold with rage, still splotched with his own blood, Jarvis left the house. He called for his horse, pausing only to tell Campbell curtly that if the child were to die, he would hold him directly responsible for alarming Eliza.

'Now get off my land!' he finished. 'And if that ram is not returned today, I shall have you charged with theft and extortion!'

***

Even before he dismounted from Rowan, Ness knew Hector had been fighting with Jarvis. She could scarcely avoid the knowledge, for he had ridden to Scarborough in a strangely buoyant mood and now, returning, he had a cut cheek and a reddening bruise below his eye, while his knuckles looked pink and shiny.

'What ha' you been doing?' she gasped.

'It is no great harm and no concern o' yours, Ness,' said Hector, sliding down from Rowan's back.

'But your face, Hector! Ha' you been fighting? Is Mr Jarvis to fetch his ram? And shall I make a compress for yon eye?'

'Whisht, woman- awa' wi' you,' said Hector. 'Keep your doctoring for the horse.'

There was a blackness about him that unnerved her, and his mood worsened when the Scarborough shepherd arrived two hours later and asked respectfully for his master's ram. Hector gave Fahey an ironic good day, handed over the beast and sent a verbal message that next time he caught a Scarborough beast he would shoot it on the spot. He did not, however, hasten Fahey with a kick or a personal threat; the Irishman was scarcely taller than Ness and he would have deemed it a shame to have hit out at such a timorous laddie.

Fahey's departure left Hector obviously dissatisfied, and the veiled menace of the situation had Ness close to tears. Hector proffered no explanation, but went straight up the mountain, so Ness put on her plaid for comfort and made a pad of dry fern for grooming Grey Falcon. The horse was still sadly lame, and Ness had a small fear that Hector would shoot him anyway. She was leaning against the Falcon's comforting shoulder and weeping a few tears into his hide when the thud of hooves made her look up.

In the seconds before the horseman came into view Ness had time for a great many fears and longings, but they died as a strange skewbald cob picked its way along the track. It had a crooked white blaze down its muzzle, one white leg, a walleye and a roughly hogged parti-coloured mane. Ness had never seen such an ill-favoured horse, and a sudden smile lit her eyes, the first for some days. The creature was so very ugly that the effect was somehow endearing.

The rider wore a heavy riding coat and wide brimmed hat, and led a packhorse loaded down with canvas. Grey Falcon, usually phlegmatic in the presence of other horses, whinnied a welcome, and trotted forward in a halting parody of his once confident gait. The skewbald's rider drew rein, peered through heavy spectacles at Grey Falcon and then leaned down to soothe his ugly mount.

'Quiet, the Bruce, good laddie then...' He glanced up and Ness realised he had seen her. Hector had said nothing about hiring any new man, but was it likely he would have done, to Ness? Perhaps he was expecting the rider, or perhaps the man was seeking work. Or he might have missed his way to Mersey or Mole Creek. Ness pulled her plaid around her shoulders and moved forward to wish him a nervous good day.

He was staring at her. And no wonder, she thought with irony. She was wearing her old grey gown, and the unbecoming plaid. She stepped into the sunlight and looked up. 'Good day, sir, who were you wishfu' to see?'

Escorted by the eager Grey Falcon, the stranger dismounted and led his horses forward, then removed his broad-brimmed hat and offered a hand to Ness.

'Have I the honour of addressing Mistress Campbell?'

'Aye, my name is Agnes Campbell,' said Ness, puzzled, touching his fingertips and dropping her hand to her side. 'Ha' you come to see Hector, sir?'

'I wish to see Hector Campbell of Glen Heather, yes.' From the pocket of his riding coat, the stranger brought forth two documents. 'I have here a letter from Mr Campbell dated in May of this year, and a certificate of recommendation from Mr Scott-Blakeney of Launceston.'

'Aye,' said Ness, still puzzled. 'I ken Mr Scott-Blakeney is the gentleman Hector is hiring to make us a house. Ha' you come frae him? Is he to follow on?' She peered past down the track, hoping to see another horseman. Or would a gentleman of Mr Scott-Blakeney's eminence arrive by carriage?

The young man smiled a little. 'Well, Mistress Campbell, I fear Mr Scott-Blakeney could not come at all. He has much to do, and so many clamouring for his services, and he is no longer young, you know.'

Ness' hand flew to her mouth. 'Och, Hector will be most displeased! He is so set on building a braw house here at Glen Heather!'

The stranger looked about the muddy clearing, and Ness saw through his eyes the paucity of her surroundings. When she looked at Glen Heather she saw flowers and trees and the sparkling new burn Hector had harnessed and brought splashing down from the mountain. Now she saw it as a stranger must, marked by roughly hewn stumps, a mean slab hut, a smoking cook-fire and the feeble attempt at a garden by the burn. The onions had been eaten long ago, and the green kale and carrots had suffered the depredations of the wildlife. Hector had had some hens fetched in, but they constantly escaped their coop and scratched about the clearing, clucking and squawking and generally adding to the vagabond air of the place.

'Is Mr Scott-Blakeney so verra grand then?' she asked uneasily.

'Aye, grand enough. But allow me to introduce myself, Mistress Campbell. I am James Galbraith, associate to Mr Scott-Blakeney and very much at your, and your husband's, service.'

'I see,' said Ness faintly. 'You ha' brought a message for Hector to tell him Mr Scott-Blakeney canna do the task he was offered.'

'I have come to offer my own services in substitution,' said Galbraith.

Ness frowned at him. He was, she judged, some several years short of thirty, of respectable height and pleasant demeanour. He had light sandy brown hair, which reminded her of her stepbrother Donal's thatch, and regular, rather finely cut features marred only by the weakness of his eyes. The wire spectacle frames were unobtrusive, but the lenses must have been ground very thick, for they magnified his light blue eyes grotesquely. Aside from this, she found nothing remarkable in his appearance, and knew that Hector would be thoroughly unimpressed.

'Well?' said Galbraith mildly. 'I trust this will be of satisfaction to Mr Campbell?'

Ness suspected it would not satisfy Hector at all. He had meant to secure the best architect in Van Diemen's Land for Glen Heather, and to be fobbed off with an assistant would make him very angry.

Galbraith's eyes were weak, but they were also apparently perceptive. 'From the expression on your face I apprehend this will *not* be satisfactory, Mistress Campbell?'

'Mr Galbraith, I am sure you are verra good at your work,' she said hastily, 'but the fact is that Hector has it i' mind to build a braw house - a grand house - to rival York Hall and Scarborough. I would be content with a wee cottage, with a good roof and strong walls to keep out the weather, but Hector means Glen Heather to be the best i' the land. He works gey hard, but the folk hereabouts dinna respect him as they might. I hope you are not offended.'

'I am not at all offended, Mistress Campbell. I agree with your husband. Too many are satisfied with much too little.'

'Hector likes things to be fit and right,' said Ness. 'He wants the best.' Oddly, she was remembering the crimson silk gown, and that memory made her acutely conscious of her current dress. She must appear a peasant; a poor wee drab of a thing, and it said little for this Galbraith's consequence that he treated her with respect. 'It isna for vanity, that Hector wants a great house,' she said, troubled, 'but he is building for the future. He is a strong man, and hopes for a fine family o' bairns. It is his dream, you see… and mine also.'

'I understand entirely,' said Galbraith. 'However, I cannot see why we should not come to some agreement. I have not the white hairs of my associate, but I *can* design and oversee the construction of just such a residence as your husband desires. I have been taught by a master, and I have his confidence in all matters.'

Ness had no answer. If she sent James Galbraith away, Hector might be angered, but how could she let the man to think he had the commission? 'Ha' you been in Van Diemen's Land long, Mr Galbraith?' she asked at random.

'Long enough,' he said absently. 'Mistress Campbell, would you be so good as to show me where I might set up camp?'

'Will you no put up in the village, Mr Galbraith?'

'I think not,' he said cheerfully. 'It is over an hour's journey each way, and why waste good working hours? You need not fear I'll intrude upon you or your husband, Mistress Campbell. Indeed, you will scarcely know I am here.'

Ness could believe that, for he looked a self-effacing young man, but what would Hector say? 'I really canna say where you should camp, Mr Galbraith,' she said coolly. 'That is for Hector to decide. He should be here in a wee while.' She indicated Bullocky George, who was working in the new enclosure. 'Perhaps we should step over and ask where Hector might be,' she suggested. 'Tie your horses to the rail. Grey Falcon willna harm them.'

'I see he will not,' said Galbraith gravely. 'Poor fellow, has he a torn tendon?' He attended to his horses, and then accompanied Ness across the new enclosure towards the distant bullock team.

CHAPTER 15

The going was damp and squelching underfoot, but there was a wild sweet smell in the air, and Galbraith noted with approval that the enclosure had not been clear-felled, but left with stands of blackwood and gum. There were fringed of blossom on the gum trees, and the strange Antipodean spring was well advanced. And how strange that *he* should find it strange, he thought wryly, for he had spent a bare eleven years in the grimy springs of Glasgow.

The bullocky glanced in their direction. He could not be Hector Campbell, for Campbell had been described as a wild, uncouth Scotsman with an accent that could be cut with a knife and used to butter bread. The phrase had amused Galbraith, for he had managed to soften his own original thick glottal tones only by making a sustained and permanent effort. Tobias Scott-Blakeney had impressed on him early in their acquaintance that a regional accent of any kind would be a handicap in either of his chosen professions, so he had done his best to adopt the unaccented mode of English used by his mentor. Sometimes he felt half-ashamed of himself for his pretence, but had he reverted to the strong Glaswegian tones of Charcoal Jamie it would have been as artificial as if he had put aside his respectable dress for the rags of his youth. Tobias had taught his acolyte well, and the urchin of the Glasgow streets had become James Galbraith Esq, portrait painter and architect. There was no way back, and it was all because he had stolen a knife to sharpen charcoal.

Galbraith marvelled again at the perversity of life as he accompanied Mrs Campbell across the clearing. He had spent almost a year with the memory of a sweet face and eyes that had seemed to see the world new-minted. He had never expected to see the girl again, but here she was, and she was no girl and no newborn Eve, but the wife of a man who was reputed to be "difficult" and so would be better served by Galbraith than by the volatile Tobias. And there was nothing of new-minted joy left in her quiet face.

***

Bullocky George was a man of so few words that Ness was not even aware of his surname, but he removed his pipe from his mouth, offered a horny hand and introduced himself to Galbraith as George Ward.

'Mr Ward,' said Ness gratefully, 'do you know where Hector is working today?'

Bullocky George replaced his pipe, and spoke around it. 'Hector be up the fold, Mam.'

Ness nodded, recognising the appellation. The mountain had many folds and gullies, but *the* fold could only be an exaggerated crease in the foothills, some thirty minutes' walk from the enclosures, which Hector had cleared to make what he termed a "dry run" for the cattle. 'He'm sowing it down,' added Bullocky George.

Ness winced. She knew from observation that ploughing and sowing the shallow, rocky soil of Glen Heather was a hard and backbreaking job. Both Rowan and Hector would be likely to return covered in sweat and mud. Today was a poor time for James Galbraith's news. Galbraith must have reached the same conclusion, for he nodded thoughtfully and half smiled at her.

'Perhaps I should return tomorrow,' he said.

Ness knew Hector might not be home until after dark, and would likely be gone again at daybreak. 'I think you should make camp down by the burn, Mr Galbraith,' she said at length. 'You will be on hand when Hector returns.'

Galbraith nodded. 'An excellent suggestion, Mrs Campbell.'

They returned towards the hut, which looked the more meagre and roughhewn to Ness now that she knew who he was, and then Galbraith touched his hat and led his horses away towards the burn.

Ness found it difficult to settle after Galbraith had left, and when Hector returned, mud-splashed and tired, she did not know whether to be glad or sorry.

'Where is the Falcon?' he asked, nodding thanks for the hot water she had set ready for him.

Ness gulped. 'Maybe gone down to the burn wi' Mr Galbraith and his horses. He has come frae Mr Scott-Blakeney, Hector, about the house.'

'Och, so the man is coming at last!'

'You had better talk wi' him yoursel'.' She stayed in the hut, slowly slicing damper, and waited for the explosion, but there was none. Half an hour passed, and then Hector reappeared, with Galbraith beside him. Hector was scowling, but he had his temper under control, which meant, thought Ness wryly, that he thought it was in his best interest to deal with Galbraith politely. Her husband could always control his feelings when he chose.

'Make a cup o' tea for our guest, Ness,' he said. 'He is come to talk wi' me about the house. It seems he is to undertake the work himsel', for Scott-Blakeney isna up to the job. He's an auld man, gey good wi' the plans, but of no use wi' the stone anymore.'

Not by a shadow of a glance did Galbraith reveal that he had already discussed the matter with Ness. Instead, he thanked her gravely for the pannikin of tea and allowed Hector to explain, inserting words as necessary. Ness noticed his faint Scots accent had deepened to a definite burr. She wondered if this were deliberate, for having witnessed Hector's gracious acceptance of the changed plan she was inclined to credit the architect with more than usual guile.

Galbraith accepted Hector's brusque invitation to dinner, and ate as heartily as his host, answering questions, nodding from time to time, and occasionally suggesting alternative courses of action. After the meal, Hector agreed to inspect preliminary drawings in two days' time. If these met with his approval, he said, the deal would be struck. He then strode away, leaving Ness to deal with the crocks and to eye Galbraith with something like awe.

She said nothing, from loyalty to Hector, but the questions must have trembled in her eyes. Galbraith, on the point of returning to his camp, smiled and remarked that Mr Campbell agreed that his own services, available immediately, were a better proposition than those of his senior partner, which might not be had for two years and more.

'If ever,' he added seriously, 'for Tobias is not in the best of health, and does not care to attend to the actual building. The design will be one approved by him, and all the labour will be carried out by guildsmen.'

'Aye, it will be good to ha' it done,' said Ness.

Galbraith nodded sympathetically. 'Mistress Campbell, I would not return to the old country if I could, but sometimes life in the colonies is difficult for ladies.'

'Aye,' said Ness, 'but Glen Heather is verra bonnie. Ha' you a wife, Mr Galbraith?'

'I have yet to find the right lass.'

'Perhaps,' said Ness, 'you should spend some time on the docks. That is where Hector found me.' She smiled at the memory, and was somewhat surprised at that.

***

James Galbraith spent the two days Hector granted in examining the site, drawing plans and making lightning sketches. On the second day, he asked for charcoal from the fire. Ness thought such a fine gentleman would have as much ink as he wanted, and again, it seemed, he read her thoughts.

'I have plenty of materials, Mistress Campbell, but for some purposes I prefer to work with the medium I know best. Can you conceive I once was known as "Charcoal Jamie"?'

Ness smiled at that, for the name conjured up a picture of a bairn playing in the ashes. Galbraith perceived the smile as the shadow of the luminous look that had so drawn him on the dock that day. 'Do you sketch, Mistress Campbell? It seems a fashionable pastime among some of the ladies of the colony.'

'Och, I ha' no turn for such things,' said Ness uncomfortably. 'Take what you need, Mr Galbraith.' She gestured to the outside fire-hole, for it would have been quite improper to invite him into the hut while Hector was away. She went to the garden, leaving Galbraith to sort through the blackened cinders like a boy. When she returned, he was drawing swiftly, frowning with total concentration.

'Is that the house?' she asked in awe. 'I didna ken it would be so big!'

Galbraith blew the coal-dust away from his drawing. 'Does it please you, Mistress Campbell?'

Ness looked at the picture doubtfully. She had seen old prints and engravings, and Phemie had a painting of a stag hung up in the parlour. The dominie at home had shown her woodcuts, but there were few other opportunities to examine pictures, and none to watch an artist at work. She was reminded of the map Hector once modelled on the banks of the burn while they were travelling towards Glen Heather. That was formed of sand and bark and pebbles, while this representation was of charcoal lines. Each, in its way, was a thing of beauty, but now she looked past the artistry to the building itself. It was two storeys high, of stalwart but gracious proportions, with a high vaulted doorway, an attic, and two small arches apparently set in under the roof. Four stout stone chimneys stood at the corners of the house, set flush with the walls, but rising a foot or so free of the roof.

'It looks like a castle!' Her voice was admiring, but there was a small spark of fear in her mind.

Galbraith noted both the admiration and the fear. Young Mrs Campbell would never be comfortable in her husband's "braw house", he thought. She should have a cottage, sweet and cosy, and not a great stone castle. But Hector Campbell's money was paying for his time, and Hector Campbell would have no use for a cottage, save as a refuge for his workers. Taking back the sketch, he added a few curving lines, swirls and fat puffy shapes like a child's representation of clouds.

'You could plant gillyflowers and roses, and have fish in a pond,' he said quite gently, 'and perhaps an apple tree for shade.'

The girl sighed. 'That would be bonnie,' she said, 'but my husband will not be wanting a posy garden. There are flowers on the mountain, though. Have you seen them Mr Galbraith?'

He shook his head. 'What flowers are these?'

'Och, there is bonnie pink heather, and some that is white. There are flowers like butterflies on tall green stems that are verra pretty.'

Flag irises, thought Galbraith. 'Have you the heather here?' he asked. 'The heath, rather, for as I recall it is not quite like that we have in Scotland.'

'No quite the same,' she agreed wistfully, 'but it bloomed i' the winter. It was bonnie.'

Galbraith added more touches to the picture. Glen Heather House would look well when built; with the warmth of the sandstone it would be beautiful as well as fine. It would make an elegant setting for a stately lady; a lady such as those wedded to Reeve and MacDonald, but it would not do for the Scottish wren before him. She would have been happy in a cottage, but even as she turned away back to the miserable slab hut, Galbraith was struck by the premonition that Agnes Campbell would never be mistress of Glen Heather. She had belonged to Hector Campbell for less than a year, and already she seemed to be fading, as if, he thought, a pink rose had been blanched by the frost. But a rose was not a good image, unless it was of a sweet and thorny briar... No! he thought. She was no rose, but a sprig of white heather, transplanted to a rough and foreign land. He wondered if she knew it.

***

The plans found favour with Hector. No mean draftsman himself, he was able to appreciate the skill of the work, and, more than Ness, to see how the house would look when built. He insisted on eschewing the usual brick and timber of the district for blocks of sandstone, honeycomb-coloured and warm with the sunlight they absorbed. Sandstone was a common building material in Sydney Town, and also in the south of Van Diemen's Land, but the natural stone of the Western Tiers was limestone. Hector demanded sandstone and, after brief opposition from Galbraith, who thought the cost prohibitive, he had his way. Hector, frugal in small matters, was lavish in the large, and he ordered vast quantities of the desired material.

'We shall never need the half of that, Mr Campbell!' said Galbraith, but Hector rejoined that his braw house would require outbuildings, stables and dairies, a shearing shed and a washhouse, and that all could all be built of the same material. The initial cost would be great, but his braw house would stand for centuries; perhaps for as long as the Campbells owned Glen Heather.

It was typical of Hector that, having hired a man to raise his house, he wasted no time in hanging over that man's shoulder. Just as he trusted Bullocky George to manage a team and Ness to manage domestic affairs, so Hector left Galbraith to act as midwife to Glen Heather House. He never considered at that time that his wife might soon be in need of a midwife herself. Since Ness failed to catch a bairn in almost a year, he put the problem out of his mind until he had the leisure to decide what he should do.

***

While Glen Heather House had its beginnings, Eliza Jarvis was confined to her bed. The child had not after all been born prematurely, but the triple alliance of Bertha Ward the midwife, Nannie Goodridge and Mother Jarvis, combined to keep Eliza to her room. The curtains were drawn close lest the faintest breath of unwholesome night air should intrude, so Eliza sometimes felt near to asphyxiation. She was also near to hysteria from boredom and discomfort.

Had anyone ever questioned her about her fall she would unhesitatingly have admitted her own fault. Whitaker would not have blamed her overmuch, for he too, was none too fond of his mother's pet. However, the three imposing ladies in charge of Eliza's health had vetoed any mention of the accident, and so the fiction was maintained that she had risen too quickly and been overcome by a fainting fit. Eliza was disgusted. There had been no bleeding, and the baby continued to kick and tumble in her womb as before. After a while, the effects of a bland diet and lack of exercise began to tell. The virtues of senna pods and castor oil were discussed, patent aperients and syrups of figs proposed, but in the end possible dangers were deemed to outweigh the advantages. Eliza longed for company, and when the first clenching pain of labour arrived, a week before the expected date, she almost welcomed the change from the monotony.

Enforced idleness had robbed her of muscle tone and breath, and it was an agonising thirty-six hours later that her second child was born. By then Eliza was in such a poor way that the midwife told Whitaker Jarvis another such labour would probably kill his wife.

'Her heart is not as strong as I would like, and neither are her lungs,' said Mrs Ward. 'I would suggest a prolonged sea voyage as the thing to brace her up.'

Whether or not it would have helped, Jarvis could not afford such a thing at present. Eliza's recovery was slow, and she was once more compelled to remain in bed. And the disasters had not ended yet. By the end of a month it became obvious that the wet nurse procured for baby Isobel was addicted to spirits. The woman was dismissed and the child weaned onto pap, but even that did not answer and the delicate little creature continued to fail.

'Troubles come in threes,' warned Mother Jarvis, and Nannie Goodridge, whose stern exterior hid a superstitious soul, crossed herself furtively and dosed young Winston with a tonic of her own invention. She prayed nightly, and gave thanks when Eliza began to eat a little gruel and when baby Isobel rallied, but the troubles of Scarborough were not over.

The third disaster struck shortly after the New Year of 1839, in a newspaper report regretting the loss of the brig *Almira*, with all hands, to the north of New South Wales.

For over two weeks Whitaker Jarvis had been expecting momentarily to hear good news of the brig, which had sailed out of Plymouth bearing the prime colts and mares despatched by his Uncle Wharton. As a second son Wharton Jarvis had taken over the family property when his elder brother chose to emigrate, thankfully selling off the cattle and stocking the green acres instead with prime horseflesh. His nephew remembered him as a wiry man some years younger than Walter, a man who spent much time on racecourses and in stables. Whitaker often thought that, had he been older, and had his brothers been alive, he would have returned to help his uncle instead of re-joining his father at Scarborough when the latter's health began to fail.

He was shocked at that time to find the property in poor heart; and dismayed at the deterioration his five years in New South Wales had wrought to his father's mental powers. Walter Jarvis had been only fifty, but his memory had failed and he made several unwise investments. Whitaker was forced to take over, while still maintaining the polite fiction that his father was in charge. And then, barely weeks later, a fall on the mountain broke Walter's neck, and Scarborough came to Whitaker in law as well as in fact. The death duties were crippling, so Whitaker risked all on a venture to bring Scarborough back to prosperity. With Uncle Wharton's assistance, he vowed to make Scarborough horses as well-known and respected in Van Diemen's Land as their counterparts were in England. Once an agreement was reached, he consolidated his small capital and took out a mortgage on the property to cover running costs while he awaited the realisation of his dream.

By now, the *Almira* should have been leaving Sydney Town on the last leg of her voyage to Van Diemen's Land, bringing not only Scarborough's fortune and future, but solid confirmation of Jarvis' ability to repay the debt to his banker, Oakes, but here, in one small smudged column of print, he saw his hopes destroyed.

Pale beneath his summer tan, Jarvis mounted his black and went to Launceston to make enquiries. Any hope that the lost brig might not have been the *Almira* was quickly dispelled; she was gone, along with her captain, any number of sailors, a cargo of ironmongery, and the bright future of Scarborough. As he stepped into the inn to calm himself with whisky, Jarvis mourned not only his situation, but for the horses themselves. When he thought of the beautiful animals, worth more than jewels, as shark bait in the ocean, he was ready to weep more tears than he had shed over his baby daughter. Better if she had not survived, he thought morbidly, if her parents were to be beggared.

He drank a second glass of whisky, and a third, but he didn't feel any better. After a while he paid his shot and went to see Oakes. Destitution was relative. He was dressed in the finest of materials, and he had the price of a meal in his pocket, but with the load of debt facing him now he felt poorer than a shabby tramp that passed him in the street.

***

As Whitaker Jarvis' dream died, Hector Campbell's began to take shape. The foundations of the new house were marked with ropes and trenches, and the first great blocks of sandstone arrived from the quarries in the south. The warm weather brought a flush of growth to the newly laid grasses and the hum of industry suggested prosperity. Hector's lucky touch was working well.

Apart from all this, Hector was enjoying the society of young James Galbraith. The laddie was a Scot through and through, with a shrewd sense of business, a keen wit and the ability to keep a close tongue when needed. He might dress like a gentleman, but his thin artist's hands were capable and he was not above applying a tool or steadying a wavering stone block into position when necessary. The men seemed to like him well enough, but he held himself a little aloof from all but Hector and Bullocky George. The bullock team was always to hand, with George loving every minute. He was always silent, but his seamed old face wrinkled into a veritable smile when he saw a sketch Galbraith had made of him during a brief smoke-o. Hector was interested too. He examined the sketch and turned speculative eyes on Galbraith. 'You draw gey fine, Jamie,' he said. 'Perhaps you paint as well?'

'Aye, portraits for wealthy Sassenachs,' said Galbraith ironically. 'Saving your reverence, George, but most of them have faces like griddle cakes.' He paused for effect and added; 'I have come to the conclusion that the bonnie are not wealthy and the wealthy are not bonnie.'

George snorted, and was understood to say that he was neither wealthy nor bonnie.

'Aye,' said Galbraith swiftly, 'but perhaps you have a handsome soul.'

'Do a portrait o' my wee wife,' said Hector with rare humour, 'and you'll no need to make that remark again!'

Galbraith agreed carelessly, gave the sketch to George as a gift, and went back to work.

Ness had brought the tea and damper, and after the men had gone, she removed the crocks to the hut. Now its time of usefulness was ending, she felt oddly attached to the little dwelling. It was cramped, and awkward, but it felt like home. She wondered if Hector would keep it standing after the big house was complete, but that seemed unlikely. Her own status seemed more solid now, for she was almost certain she was pregnant. She felt ill, sometimes, and her appetite suffered, but her bleeding did not come. She knew she should inform Hector of their good fortune, but the opportunity did not arise. Or so she told herself. Besides, she knew bairns did not always carry to term. Her mother had lost three six-month babes, and Ness had been her only living child.

As she struggled to maintain her usual standards and disguise her condition, she found herself resenting Hector. While he worked alone, she had forgiven his abstractions and his silence, but seeing his camaraderie with James Galbraith, she felt left out. He had so little to say to her, but plenty, it seemed, to say to the young Scot. The plans *she* should have heard were discussed with Galbraith or Bullocky George, the decisions *she* should have had a hand in, were made by Hector alone. She felt herself growing bitter as the stewed tea she made over the fire, but despite her envy of his rapport with Hector she could not dislike James Galbraith.

He was so unfailingly pleasant when he *did* have cause to speak to her, thanking her for meals, smiling and greeting her as he passed on the way to his camp. She had thought him deceitful, but after a time she concluded that he was unaware of his chameleon quality. And after that, she saw many more things to like.

She was fetching water one day when she saw Galbraith kneeling in the grass.

'What ha' you lost, Mr Galbraith?' she asked.

'Nothing at all, Mistress Campbell,' he said politely. 'I have found this. I believe they call it flannel flower; it is of no use that I can tell, but it is a lovely thing, is it not?'

'Hector wouldna see it,' said Ness pensively. 'A thing must be of use to please him at all.'

'I spent many years seeing the world as a blur,' said Galbraith. 'No doubt that is why I appreciate the small beauties as I do. Shall I help you with the water?'

Ness shook her head and hurried on, leaving Galbraith to stare after her with much the same expression as he had had while admiring the flower. Perhaps, he thought wryly, all men should be compelled to spend a year or more with blurred eyes. They could then be fitted with spectacles to see and newly appreciate the world's beauty. He had done just that on the wharf a year ago. He knew it was foolish - and dangerous- to desire Campbell's wife. Hector might appear take his bride for granted, but Galbraith saw the way his gaze followed her, with pride and even affection. Besides, the man clearly had a strong sense of territory and any move to attach Agnes Campbell would be savagely put down. Galbraith would be mad to try, and he knew it.

'*Perhaps*,' she had said, on the day of his arrival, '*you should spend some time on the docks. That is where Hector found me.'* And then had dawned that faint delightful smile.

He wondered then what she had meant, and he wondered still. Had she been a convict servant assigned to Campbell in the same fashion as the young Galbraith had been assigned to Tobias? Could she have been a harlot plying her trade on the docks? No, that was impossible. That quality of innocence, of joy new-minted, had not belonged to a harlot, but to a maiden on the verge of life. And there it was. Suddenly, Galbraith realised she *had* been a maiden when he had seen her then. She had a glow of innocence, and now that glow was muted, as if she had tasted life and found it less sweet than she expected. Was it possible she met Campbell only *that day*? Was it possible that, had he come by earlier, she might have been *his* woman instead of Campbell's? The thought brought an uneasy stir of desire, but even if that *had* been so, the chance was past, and there was nothing he could do about it if he would. He should wait for a woman of his own and put Agnes Campbell from his mind.

CHAPTER 16

This he did successfully for a time, but one Sunday in February Hector repeated his request that Galbraith should paint a portrait of Ness. By now, he knew Hector well enough not to be astounded at his gall in setting another task before the first was half done, and said equably that he had his equipment along and could spare an hour each evening. He named a price, and Hector damned his eyes and asked if he were not paying enough for his services as it was. Galbraith pointed out that Hector hired the architect, and not the portrait painter, and sat back to await Hector's reaction. For a moment it appeared the man would fly into a rage, but a rueful twinkle lit his flinty eyes and he gave Galbraith a buffet on the shoulder that almost knocked him down.

'Be damned to you then, laddie! I can meet your price, but be sure you make a job o' it! Who knows, I may even set you to paint another o' mysel'! A matching pair above the mantel; aye, I would like that fine.'

Galbraith was well pleased with the proposal. He knew Agnes Campbell would be a pleasure to paint, and as for her husband; he would make a subject in a thousand!

Hector wanted Ness displayed to best advantage, and insisted she should wear her crimson gown and heather brooch for the portrait. He gave orders to Galbraith and Ness in the same breath, informed Bullocky George that his wife Bertha would be required to attend the sittings as chaperon, and dismissed the matter, apparently sure his instructions would be carried out.

The next evening, Galbraith set up his easel and, lacking a model's throne, draped a blanket over a sawn stump. The sun was setting, so he fixed a lantern where it would cast the best light and waited until Campbell's wife and her chaperon appeared. Mrs Bullocky George was a grim-looking, elderly dame dressed in black, as if mourning the demise of her youth. As befitted one who was a midwife and person of importance, the lady arrived seated side-saddle on a fine, fast horse, which sneered at Galbraith's ugly skewbald and Grey Falcon. Galbraith assisted her to alight, and she gave him a sharp look quite at variance with her faded features.

'Keep your charms for the flighty gals, young man,' she said tartly, and settled down to knit.

Galbraith would have chosen to paint Ness as he first saw her, clad in an old gown and plaid. His first impression when he saw her arrayed in her best was of a child dressed up. His next was that whoever had chosen that crimson cloth had a rare eye for colour; most ladies were satisfied to wear pale blue or green. In subdued hues Ness Campbell would have been pretty enough, but in crimson, she was beautiful. His next thoughts were nebulous, for he had begun to make his preliminary sketches and, as always when he was working seriously, the outer world fell away.

"Charcoal Jamie" always had a wicked way with a caricature and the mature Galbraith retained something of the same quality. He had never been able to put a name to it, and sometimes he wished it did not exist, for it led to a few of his paintings being rejected by those who commissioned them. The quality, as nearly as Galbraith could define it, was truth. Thus, on his better days, he caught something of the character of his sitters, and at other times he found himself painting lights and shadows and undercurrents he never consciously noticed-*could not* have consciously noticed. It was as if hands and eyes worked independently, at some level other than the everyday.

Painting a portrait by lantern light was a recipe for disaster, especially when the subject was she with whose image he had been half in love for months, but James Galbraith was aware of the danger and was determined to keep his head. He set out to portray Ness as a young lady of fashion instead of a Scottish Eve, but as the work proceeded he realised resignedly that he was painting with too much truth.

He talked to her sometimes as he worked. He knew long periods of silence rendered his sitters passive, and the resulting portraits were inclined to be lifeless and trite. After the original sketches were done, he could operate nicely on two levels; conversing while he focussed the bulk of his concentration on his work. He did try to include Bertha Ward in the conversation, not only from courtesy, but because she regarded him with suspicion. It was uphill work, for Bertha said nothing and saw everything. That was an uncomfortable combination.

Galbraith found that Ness knew little of the world at large, and had no liking for gossip, so he focussed the conversations on Glen Heather. Her features would always become animated as she described the work Hector had done on the burn, the small caves she found in the rocks, and the flowers on the mountain, but sometimes the talk took an unexpected turn, as when a sitting was interrupted by Galbraith's horse, the Bruce.

'Why name such a pawky fellow for a hero?' she asked, watching Galbraith push the enquiring white muzzle aside.

Galbraith shrugged. 'I bought him as a curiosity and gave him the name so he'd have a pride in himself. What of your Grey Falcon? He seems taken with the Bruce.'

'Och, he belongs to Hector. He was hurt during a windstorm. I dinna ken if he will ever be fit for work, but he is a friend for Rowan, forby. And for mysel'.' For a moment the glow of youth reappeared on her face, but it faded, leaving her pale and shadowed. 'I am gey tired, Mr Galbraith,' she said apologetically, and lapsed into silence.

***

Bertha Ward was pleased to act as chaperon for young Mrs Campbell. Most of the colony ladies had need of her services at some time, and she wondered when she would be called to attend to this one. As soon as she saw the way the artist looked at his subject, her eyes narrowed. There was something insidious afoot. She watched the pair closely and as the days passed, her attention was rewarded. There was nothing so blatant as a blush or a meeting of eyes, never a word that could not have been heard by the lady's husband, but still there was an indefinable feeling of attraction between the two. And no wonder, thought Bertha with some resignation. A young girl married to a man like that! Campbell was asking for trouble.

Bertha did not consider herself a gossip, but she told her granddaughter Lucy she had been watching an artistic gentleman at work over at Glen Heather. 'And no better than he ought to be, either,' she added darkly. 'Mr Galbraith is a man to charm the birds from the trees and Mr Campbell ought to know better than to let him near his wife. Mind, I do not say there has been any wrongdoing, but I have seen their mien and you cannot fly in the face of nature.'

Naturally, Lucy felt no compunction about repeating her grandmother's words to her mistress, Eliza. She thought it a rare piece of justice if the uncouth Scotchman who had brought about Madam's fall should be in danger of losing his wife to another man. Eliza told her curtly to stop spreading lies, which convinced the maid that her grandmother had been overnice in her speculations. There was no smoke without flame, and since her mistress refused to discuss the titbit, she offered it to Polly Garth, implying that if nothing had happened *yet* it soon would.

'My granny says Mrs Campbell does not wear *stays*!' she pointed out. 'And Mr Galbraith is very charming. When he painted Madam's portrait he had always a kind word for me.'

Polly was shocked. She was well connected to the gentry herself and several cuts above Lucy socially, but she was young, she was human, and she had observed the fight between the master and Campbell, so she was willing to believe mischief was afoot. Had not the information come from an irreproachable source in the local midwife? Nevertheless, she could not lower herself to gossip with servants, so she told Lucy sharply to mind her tongue. In her turn she told just two people; her own husband and her Aunt Theodora Bruning. There the tale might have stopped, had Theodora not been entertaining Harriet Williams and her companion that day. Miss Young, adept at listening while not appearing to do so, pricked up her ears and tucked the morsel away for further embroidery. And so, running the telegraph lines of gossip, the improper relationship between Campbell's wife and the portrait painter became widely known.

While the Scarborough servants gossiped, their master was deeply troubled. He could not redeem the mortgage, and though Oakes had initially agreed to wait another year before recovering the principal, he inexplicably changed his mind. When pressed, he said he had information of run-down fences and poorly restrained livestock at Scarborough.

'I am informed that in one instance the loss of a valuable ram remained undetected for over a week, and that at another several sheep died of thirst,' he said sternly. 'You must see Mr Jarvis that I cannot allow my investment to run down in this manner. Some part of the property may have to be sold. Would one of your neighbours care to buy some acreage?'

Hector Campbell's offers loomed in Jarvis' mind, but he pushed the memory away. 'No,' he snapped. 'I have only one close neighbour and it is out of the question that I would sell to him.'

'Then perhaps you should sell the property entire. Unless-'

'Well?' Jarvis was as sore in spirit as he had been in boyhood after an unmerited beating.

'You must sell the property unless either you can raise some capital or I can sell the mortgage.'

'Do so,' said Jarvis bitterly, and stalked out of the office. He started home to Scarborough with great bitterness in his soul and, had he been less deep in his problems, he might have observed Hector Campbell riding his chestnut in the opposite direction.

Hector *did* see Jarvis, but made no greeting. He had nothing to say to his neighbour, and besides; he was in a hurry. He had scarcely left the Mersey district since his arrival with Ness, but business in Launceston beckoned, so he left Galbraith in charge of the building, Bullocky George in charge of the stock, and Bertha Ward in charge of his wife and her reputation. Ness protested, but Hector was adamant; his wife could not remain alone at Glen Heather without another woman to lend her countenance. Ness must sleep in Mersey until his return. The alternative was for Mrs Ward to sleep at Glen Heather, and that was untenable, because a midwife must be on hand for any calls that might come in. She might have to ride many miles at any time of the day or night, and the extra distance from Glen Heather could make the difference between a live child and a dead one.

***

It was soon after Hector's return to Glen Heather that James Galbraith decided to pay a courtesy call on Scarborough. He had met the Jarvises in Launceston, and painted their portraits there. He knew there was bad blood between Jarvis and Hector, but he hardly thought it bad enough to preclude his visiting one property while in the employment of the other. It was unfortunate for everyone that the day he chose for his call happened to be the same day Whitaker Jarvis received a very unwelcome communication through the mail.

'What is it?' asked Eliza, as her husband crumpled the crossed sheet into a wad and tossed it into the empty grate.

Jarvis stared at her, hollow-eyed. 'We are ruined,' he said, and Mother Jarvis broke into lamentations. 'Be quiet, Mama, for the love of God!' snapped Jarvis.

This was so unusual that Mother Jarvis gaped at him and Eliza, who had been cooling her perspiring face, laid aside her fan and focussed on her husband. 'What in the world is the matter, Whitaker? How can we be ruined?'

'We are ruined!' repeated her husband in despair. His face was a blotchy mixture of red and white and he looked ill, as if he, too, suffered from the heat.

'We suffered a reverse when the horses were lost,' said Eliza slowly, 'but surely *ruin* is putting too strong a case on it? Mother Jarvis, would you ring for brandy? I think Whitaker has need of some. He has suffered a severe shock.'

Green brought the brandy, and Jarvis tossed it down in a fashion which harrowed the butler extremely. Trouble for the Jarvises might mean trouble for Green and all his minions, and it paid to be in touch with the current situation, so he lingered by the sideboard. It was a further mark of Jarvis' mental anguish that he made no attempt to send Green about his business. Instead, he ordered a refill, gulped it almost as quickly as the first, and then slumped in his chair.

'Whitaker,' said Eliza carefully, 'do you think you might explain what is the trouble?'

'That bloody Campbell!' said Jarvis in a low voice. 'He has taken my ewes, had the services of my top ram, he is a thorn in my side and a blot on the colony and now he means to take my land.'

Eliza's heart beat uncomfortably fast. She'd had frequent spells of pain and palpitations since before Isobel's birth, and now she breathed deeply as the midwife instructed her. 'I know you dislike Mr Campbell,' she said, pressing the heel of her hand to her chest, 'but what, pray, has he to do with our— our financial state?'

Her husband turned to her savagely. 'Oakes has sold him the mortgage on Scarborough, that's what he has to do!'

This was the first Eliza had heard of any mortgage. 'But— has Mr Campbell the means to furnish a mortgage on a property such as Scarborough?' she asked faintly.

'It would appear so,' said Jarvis, between his teeth. 'In any event, he seems to have found the money to furnish himself with mine. Had I known that Scotch bastard would get his hands on it I would never have let Oakes sell. I would have seen us beggared, first, I swear!'

Eliza hardly knew what dismayed her more; the news that the deeds of Scarborough belonged to their neighbour, or the sick look of rage on her husband's face. 'What will you do?' she asked.

'Do? What *can* I do?' he demanded. 'I must raise the money somehow.'

'I could practise a little more economy in the house,' suggested Eliza without much hope, but her husband laughed bitterly.

'You would as well try to stem a flood with a silver spoon.'

Mother Jarvis chose that moment to begin lamenting again, wailing that had her dear Walter lived, he would never have allowed matters to come to such a pass.

'Your dear Walter, Mama, is at the root of our present troubles,' snapped Jarvis. 'It is his senile blunders which have brought us to this pass. Dear God, why could he not have sent for me sooner?'

Eliza bit her lip. She felt faint, and she wished she could be away, riding Gillyflower through the trees. Suddenly, she smelled the scent of the eucalypts, and the damp earthiness of the stream. What had Ness Campbell called it? The burn? What an odd name, to be sure, for everyone knew water could not burn…

'Whitaker,' she said suddenly, 'would you send for Mrs Ward? I feel a little unwell.'

'Damn it, Eliza! Here we face ruin and the end of all I have worked for and you say you feel a little unwell!'

'I—' Eliza raised her hand doubtfully to her chest, where a great stony heaviness was settling. The uneasy pain she'd felt off and on since Isobel's birth struck like a monstrous fist and she cried out and closed her eyes. If she could hold on for a moment perhaps she could ring for Lucy to help her to her room. She was aware of Mother Jarvis still lamenting and of Whitaker's voice, suddenly urgent as he took her by the shoulders.

'Oh dear,' said Eliza faintly, and slumped sideways in her husband's grasp.

CHAPTER 17

Grey Falcon had become attached to the Bruce, so it was not so surprising that he followed the harlequin horse around. Usually his lameness kept him close to home, but since James Galbraith was deep in thought as he headed for Scarborough, he allowed the Bruce to idle, and Grey Falcon was able to keep up. By the time Galbraith noticed this, he had ridden some distance and was disinclined to turn back. Falcon would stay with the Bruce, he reasoned, and there was no danger of his running amok in pasture or crop as a sound horse might do.

Galbraith had much on his mind. His portrait of Ness Campbell was almost finished, yet still he lingered over sittings, finding every excuse to apply finishing touches, to add to the background, to bring out highlights in the crimson gown. Already he had spent almost twice as long as was usual for a painting of this size. Already he was afraid to look too closely in case he found the swift sure lines marred and made heavy by over painting, and as he rode slowly along the track towards Scarborough House, he forced himself to face the truth.

He did not want to give up the painting.

Not only did the portrait of Agnes Campbell reveal too much of her soul for comfort, but it revealed too much of his own. Appraising it with an artist's eye, Galbraith saw the essence of a wistful woman on the brink of some momentous epoch. The shadows under her grey eyes could have attested to ill health, but he did not think she was ill. It seemed more likely that she was troubled, as he was, by the depth of accord between them. He dreaded the day when the sittings must be declared at an end and felt a marked distaste at the idea of handing the portrait to Hector Campbell. Hector had the original model in his keeping, but the girl in the painting was a different person; one Galbraith had coaxed to life during the sittings. She belonged to him, and when the portrait was finished, the fine thread binding it to the real Agnes Campbell would be snapped, and it would cease to be a living, growing thing and become instead a quiescent moment in time; the moment of completion.

Galbraith sighed, and smiled at his own absurdity. 'Gi' me but a single glass o' brandy and I shall be off piping a lament for my luve,' he said aloud, but even as he allowed his old burr to take over his voice he knew it was inappropriate. Charcoal Jamie would never have piped a lament for a lover; he would have been more likely to sell the pipe and spend the proceeds on ink. 'My luve is like a red, red, rose,' he added, and laughed aloud. He had already decided there was nothing of the rose about Agnes Campbell. A lily? No, and not a mountain daisy. Nor was she really white heather; she had too much colour for that. 'Heath,' said Galbraith, 'bonnie crimson heath.'

He tossed away the thought and turned the Bruce into the stable yard of Scarborough. He had heard rumours of debt and disaster for the Jarvises, but the gracious house looked solidly prosperous.

Galbraith tied the Bruce to the hitching rail and tapped at the door. There was a long silence, and then a harried-looking Irish maid appeared. Her cap was askew and her mouth agape, and Galbraith had scarcely spoken before she burst into voluble explanations and apologies.

'Oh sir, you must go— 'tis a bad time to come callin', it is!' she gasped. 'The mistress is gone and the master's creatin' somethin' awful!'

'Gone?' said Galbraith involuntarily. 'Surely not!'

'Gone, sir, dropped dead only an hour since! I thought you were the doctor! Madam is in hysterics, and we have no time for callers.'

Galbraith backed away. 'Then I had best be on my way,' he said, and, making all haste back to the Bruce, he mounted and rode away.

Grey Falcon, grazing around the back of the buildings, perceived his friend had left. He neighed a protest and began to trot unevenly across the stable yard just as Jarvis, stunned and disbelieving at the double blow Scarborough had suffered, stormed to the door. 'Biddy, is it the doctor?'

'No, sir, 'tis the gentleman from Glen Heather I think...'

Glen Heather! Jarvis was flooded with rage against the place and all its inhabitants. He seized the loaded rifle that rested above the hall table, thrust aside the staring Biddy and strode into the stable yard. If he found Hector Campbell in his sights he might have fired anyway, but the only visible intruder was an ugly flea bitten grey, trotting unevenly about the yard. Jarvis lifted the rifle to his shoulder and fired twice. The grey faltered, and toppled over, to lie threshing and screaming on the beaten earth. For a moment, Jarvis stared coldly at what he had done. Then he flung aside the rifle and, letting out a cry scarcely less dreadful than the horse's, ran back into the house.

It was left to Tom Garth, alerted by the shots, to fetch his own pistol and kill the crippled animal with a single shot to the brain. The gunfire brought Galbraith back, dreading some new disaster. His hands tightened on the reins as he saw Grey Falcon stretched on the ground, with blood still oozing from his wounds. He swore under his breath, but there was nothing to be gained from confronting the people of Scarborough— not on such a day. Riding away again, Galbraith wondered unhappily which Mrs Jarvis had died. The Irish maid had said; '*The mistress is gone*' and '*Madam is creating something awful.*' Whichever lady was no more, a human death must take precedence over that of a lame horse... oh, it could not be Eliza, he thought, not sweet-faced Eliza with her eager flow of words and her childlike delight in the portrait he had done...

Shaken, he rode back to Glen Heather. He wished he had never visited Scarborough, and he wished he need not inform Hector of the fate of his horse. And Ness! If only he had brought Grey Falcon back as soon as he had noticed the horse was following! His spirits were dragged low with useless regrets.

As he entered the clearing, he saw Ness ahead. In deference to the heat, she was wearing a gown of light-coloured stuff and a shady bonnet, and she was walking slowly up the hill, calling for the grey horse. Seeing Galbraith, she smiled and changed direction a little to come towards him.

'Mr Galbraith! Ha' you seen the Falcon? I canna find him.'

He could not allow her to hope, and perhaps after all she would not take it so very painfully. The tendon had not healed, so she must have known the grey was living on borrowed time. 'Your Falcon has come by a sad fate, Mistress Campbell,' he said.

'No—' she said in protest. 'Och, no, Jamie—dinna tell me the Grey Falcon is gone!'

'*The mistress is gone*', said the Irish maid's voice in his memory.

'The Falcon is gone,' he said, confirming it.

He saw a glisten of tears before she dropped her face in her hands and turned to lean against a tree for support. Galbraith had a sudden poignant memory of the first time he had seen her, alight and alive, and of the second time, when she had been weeping into the grey horse's shoulder. He dismounted from the Bruce and put his arm around her shoulders. She drew away immediately, wiping her eyes with the heel of her hand.

'Jamie—it wasna Hector who did it? He would not.'

'No,' said Galbraith. 'He was shot on Scarborough land.' He wondered if he should mention the trouble that had come to Scarborough, but he had no certain news. On sober reflection he thought it had probably been the Widow Jarvis who had died; Mrs Eliza was in delicate health, but she was much too young to die so suddenly. It could *not* be Eliza.

Agnes was weeping still, and Galbraith patted her shoulder. He had never cared for snivelling women, but he *did* know, as did any man, that a woman in an emotional state was ripe for comfort, and comfort, if correctly applied, could develop into something warmer.

'Surely,' he said slowly, 'your husband would have warned you if he intended to put the horse down.'

'Hector willna tell me such things. It is none o' my concern, he says.'

Grey Falcon was not her concern? Yet, according to Bullocky George, Hector Campbell would have shot the grey the day after the windstorm. It had been his wife who had applied poultices and nursed the creature back to a semblance of health.

'It was not Hector,' he said again. 'Come, Mistress Campbell; there is nothing for you to do here.'

He offered his arm, but she shrank away, shaking her head, and rubbing again at her cheeks. 'I will come in a wee while,' she said, and he left her to her desolation.

Ness mourned Grey Falcon deeply. For months he had been a friendly presence, a confidante who would never breathe a word of anything she whispered in his ears. And now he was gone, shot, if James Galbraith were correct, by someone from Scarborough.

It must have been Whitaker Jarvis. The thought stuck in her mind like a burr in a stocking, for had not Jarvis threatened to kill any animal of Glen Heather that trespassed on his land? Ness felt a surge of rage at Jarvis, and another, scarcely less bitter, at Hector, who had provoked so many confrontations and allowed the feud to fester. She had not seen Jarvis since he had insulted her months ago, and by now her memory had made him over into a monster. To be sure, Eliza thought him a good man, and a just one, but Ness had not seen Eliza, either. Bertha had mentioned that Eliza had given birth to a daughter, but in the face of the bad blood between their husbands Ness had felt unable to do more than send a note of congratulation via Bertha. There had never been a reply, and she had not liked to ask if the note had been delivered.

She sighed deeply, scrubbed her hands over her face for one final time, and started down the hill towards the new house.

***

Hector had been up the mountain that day, checking the wooden flumes that carried the burn from the heights. He expected autumn rains soon, and if the sultry weather heralded a deluge, he must be certain the flumes were fit to handle a greatly increased rush of water.

Back on the flats, he paused to admire the facade of his new house. Work proceeded swiftly through the dry days of summer, and the building grew like a golden mushroom. Houses could take years to build, but Hector had Galbraith employ sufficient men to cut the time to the minimum. It was costly, but to Hector's mind Glen Heather House was worth every guinea.

The first calves of the wild red cattle were growing apace, and he had been recently to Launceston to arrange for their sale. He had also been alert for fresh investment opportunity, for his wealth was not infinite, and even with the economies he used in the fencing he knew it would be some time before Glen Heather began to turn a healthy profit. Hector was a hearty believer in the adage that one must spend money to make it, but a balance must be struck.

It was in Launceston that he met Soames, formerly of Scarborough. The wretch was drinking ale at an inn, and had the audacity to hail him. The man looked out of reason pleased with himself, and Hector wondered why. 'Aye?' he said curtly. 'I hope you ha' no forgotten our last meeting?'

Soames raised his tankard and took a swallow. 'I have not.'

'No more ha' I. Wha' do you want frae me?'

'To do you a favour,' said Soames.

Hector snorted and turned away. 'I want no favours frae a sleekit wretch like yoursel'.'

'You'd not be interested in sending Whitaker Jarvis to the wall?'

'I wouldna,' said Hector curtly, and left the inn. Soames was incredulous that the Scot would turn aside so excellent an opportunity to make their common enemy squirm, but what could he do? He spat on the floor and left the inn. Oakes proved as hard headed as Campbell about paying for information, so this time, he was leaving the north for good.

Hector rode on down the streets of Launceston. He was no longer on sociable terms with most local landowners, but tradesmen and innkeepers liked him well enough and several asked after the progress of Glen Heather House. Strangely, several asked also after the respective healths of Ness and Galbraith, or commented on the troubles of Scarborough.

'Aye?' said Hector, each time this happened. 'What ha' gone amiss wi' that sleekit Sassenach the now?'

Some informants spoke of the wrecking of the *Almira*, others of the situation that had arisen with Oakes. 'He is to offer the mortgage for private purchase, since Jarvis cannot redeem it immediately,' said a young solicitor who condescended to share a jug of beer with Hector in another inn. Knowing the state of affairs between Glen Heather and Scarborough, he waited avidly for a response, but Hector simply drained his tankard and left the inn. He did not know Oakes personally, but Launceston was not so large that the man could not be found. He located the house, announced his business and was shown into a well-appointed office.

The two men shook hands, eyeing one another keenly. Oakes saw a powerful man who might have graced the pages of Sir Walter Scott; Hector saw a Sassenach with a fussy manner, small dark eyes. To be sure, he was a moneylender, but he had nothing against the breed, having frequently been one of their number himself.

'I hear you have an interest in a property that marches wi' my own,' he said bluntly, accepting a seat. 'I hear also you are willing to part wi' that interest if a man o' substance should offer to take it off your hands.'

'Perhaps,' said Oakes. 'I do, however, have two more options to consider.'

'Aye?'

'I could wait until Mr—until the owner of the property—has funds to pay the mortgage.'

'Aye, you could a' that,' said Hector.

'Or,' said Oakes, 'the property could be put up for sale at a public auction.'

'Aye, so it could.'

Oakes steepled his fingers. 'Of course, the man who bought said property would then own it free and clear, with no legal encumbrances. I would retain such moneys as are owed to me, and the balance would be paid to the current owner.' He paused. 'Would you be interested in buying the property under these terms, Mr Campbell?'

'I canna commit so much capital to the one venture,' said Hector. 'If the mortgage is not for sale, I ha' no business here today.' He stood up. 'Good day, Oakes.'

'Do not be so hasty, Mr Campbell. I did not say the mortgage was not for sale. I thought merely that it would be less vexatious for you if you owned the property free and clear.'

'Aye, so it would,' said Hector frankly. 'But I wouldna spend so rashly.' He paused. 'You'll no be getting your hands o' the mortgage o' Glen Heather.'

Oakes smiled, sourly acknowledging a hit, and when Hector left town later that day he held the mortgage to Scarborough. It did not occur to him to tell Ness what he had done, nor did he approach Whitaker Jarvis. He disliked the man heartily, but he had not bought the mortgage for spite; rather, he hoped to benefit from Scarborough profits for several years to come. He knew Jarvis was too proud to let the property decline further while still its legal owner.

But it was Glen Heather and not Scarborough on his mind when he came down the mountain on the day of Eliza Jarvis' death. He was surprised to find Ness at the new house, for she should have been at the hut, preparing his meal. 'What now, lassie?' he asked.

'Och, Hector, Grey Falcon is dead,' she said.

Hector turned. 'Aye? What happened?'

'He was shot, over at Scarborough.'

'Aye,' said Hector grimly.

'You dinna seem surprised,' ventured Ness.

'I am not,' said Hector. 'I ken fine Jarvis will no be so pleased wi' the way things stand right now.' He put his hand briefly on her shoulder. Ness half turned to him, but he was already looking away. 'How do you know o' the Falcon?' he asked.

'Och—Jamie said. I was talking wi' him a while since.'

Ness flushed a little, and Hector glanced at her, this time with narrowed eyes. 'What ha' you to say wi' him?'

'He told me o' the Falcon.'

Hector nodded, and turned to the house. 'Is it no bonnie?' he said.

'Verra bonnie, Hector,' she said obediently. 'Hector—'

'Aye?' he said impatiently. She shrugged, and followed him to the hut.

It was only a small incident, but when Hector put his wife's uneasiness together with the knowing looks and odd questions that had met him in Launceston, he felt the vague stirring of suspicion. Galbraith, he thought, could bear watching. The laddie was an artist, but he was also a man. And she had called him "Jamie". He said nothing then, to Ness or to Galbraith, but others were not so restrained. The illicit relationship between Campbell's wife and the architect was, if not the talk of the district, at least an accepted piece of gossip. General opinion held that it served Campbell right, but that hardly excused the wife's conduct, or the architect's, and they waited gleefully for an explosion.

The news of Eliza Jarvis' death, coming hard on the heels of Hector's acquisition of the Scarborough mortgage, provided more fodder, but the one was not suitably juicy to eclipse the other, and although the ladies of the colony were sincerely sorry to hear of Eliza's passing, they still found time to talk about Ness and Galbraith.

Galbraith became aware of the gossip when Tobias wrote to ask him if it was true.

"*... I know I have urged you to take a wife,*" wrote Tobias, *'but I had in mind a wife who had not been taken already. I realise young women can be very persistent (having suffered their overtures myself), but I beg of you, my dear James, to consider well what you are about. As well as being unwise to become involved in one's own back yard, so to speak, I find it also to be in poor taste; something in which no artist should indulge.*"

James Galbraith crumpled the letter with an angry laugh, but there was a prickle of guilt beneath his indignation. He was not having an affair with Agnes Campbell, but he knew that if she were ever to make the slightest overture he would not repulse her.

It took only a day for the news of Eliza's death to filter officially to Glen Heather, for Bertha Ward, having failed to arrive to take up her duties as chaperon, sent a note with her husband to explain the necessity of her visiting Scarborough instead, to attend to the laying out. Ness wept for her friend, sobbing out her regret and sorrow as she had wept for Grey Falcon. They had spent little time together, but she had truly liked Eliza.

'I must go to her funeral,' she told Hector and felt numb gratitude when he said curtly that he would take her himself.

The funeral was held in the new slab church in Mersey. There was no regular priest in the district, but the Reverend John Ende rode through once a month from Shepherd Town to hold services. He came also as required for funerals and weddings. St Peter's was packed with mourners, for Eliza had been well liked. The ladies cried over the motherless babies, and agreed that the widower seemed as eaten up with grief as any they had seen. Spinsters yearned over his misery, and many resolved to offer pledges of support along with their condolences, but the parents of marriageable daughters decided to hold off until the affairs of Scarborough were made plain. It would not do to marry Amelia or Edith or Josephine to a bankrupt.

There was no music, but the minister had a fine tenor voice and led the congregation in singing *Abide with Me*, before delivering a eulogy that brought Ness to fresh tears. Hector glanced down at her impatiently, and it was Galbraith, sharing the Campbell pew through necessity, who offered a square of cambric. Ness buried her face in its folds, her tremulous smile fuelling the flames of gossip. The final hymn was sung, and the men went alone to the graveside in Mersey, leaving the women to return to Scarborough where Mother Jarvis had laid aside her black-bordered handkerchief to command a handsome funeral repast.

It was at the graveside that Hector came face-to-face with Jarvis for the first time since the confrontation over the ram. Jarvis, already wild with worry and grief, stared at his neighbour with hollow eyes. He then moved forward with such purpose that two of the pallbearers hurriedly grasped his arms. A third, quite unnecessarily, moved to restrain Hector.

'Bastard!' cried Jarvis, white and sick. 'Have you come to gloat? My wife is not cold in her grave and you have not even the decency to stay away while I lay her to rest! Have you not done enough to us at Scarborough? Have you eviction orders in your pocket?'

'Come, man,' said Hector awkwardly, 'you ken fine I wouldna do that. As for gloating—my wee wife and I were gey sorry to hear...'

'Sorry!' rasped Jarvis. 'My wife is dead, and you are *sorry*! It was shock that killed her, you know—the shock of finding our destinies in *your* hands. Believe me, Campbell, if it were you lying in the grave and not my Eliza I'd drink a toast to Heaven in thankfulness—I would have shot you, you know, the day you came to call. As it was, you were too quick to run. I could only shoot your bloody horse...' His face crumpled and he began to sob silently.

Hector watched for a moment, his own face like granite, and then he turned and walked away from the little graveyard, leaving Galbraith to follow when he would. He went directly to Scarborough, and on enquiring at the crepe draped door for his wife, he was annoyed to see a sly exchange of glances.

'Well?' he said impatiently, 'is Mistress Campbell here or is she no?'

The butler, hurriedly summoned by the maids, considered briefly. Hector Campbell was an unwelcome visitor, but he held the mortgage of Scarborough, and so perhaps he had a legal right to enter. Green made up his mind, and stood aside. If the Jarvises left Scarborough, there was no guarantee they would retain his services. If Mr Campbell was to be the new owner, it would not do to treat him with less than common courtesy.

The parlour was crowded with women and children. Crepe hung everywhere, draining the women's complexions of colour, making them appear as a covey of crones. Hector glanced at them in distaste.

Ness was sitting apart, hands clasped in the lap of her hurriedly stitched black gown. She was not conversing with the others and it appeared the women were slighting her deliberately. Hector was touched to see her unguarded delight at his arrival, but her smile faded, and he wondered cynically if she had expected Galbraith as well.

'Come, lassie, we must be awa',' he said abruptly. 'Jarvis doesna want our company today.'

'I should think not!' shrilled the Widow Jarvis indignantly. 'It was wicked, wicked of you to come! When I think it was your cold blooded ways that put poor Eliza in her grave I wonder you can sleep at nights!'

'It wasna my cold bloodedness, you auld besom,' said Hector unemotionally. 'It was your son's neglect o' business—or maybe the blame o' your own auld man. And I hear she wasna strong. Good day, Mrs Jarvis. Ladies.' He bowed ironically, strode out of Scarborough House and lifted his wife into the light jinker he had purchased for Rowan to draw.

'Hector, what did she mean?' asked Ness. 'What did they all mean? All those women in there blame us for poor Eliza's passing. How can that be? We ha' no seen her for months and I liked her so well!'

'Och, nothing but haivers,' said Hector scornfully. 'I bought the mortgage o' Scarborough a wee while back and Jarvis took it gey hard. If it had not been mysel', it would ha' been another.'

Ness was silent, digesting this latest development. 'Where is Mr Galbraith?' she asked finally. 'Is he no to come home wi' us?'

'Jamie can do as he pleases,' said Hector heavily.

On their return to Glen Heather, he went straight to the fold to inspect his cattle.

Left alone, Ness lingered by the new house, but there was no activity that day. She had lost the Falcon, and now she had lost Eliza. She wished she had made some push to see her friend, and to explain the estrangement was not her wish. And yet—the women at the funeral had been so unfriendly. Even Theodora Bruning had turned aside her greeting with a cool enquiry as to how she did. Surely Theodora did not blame Hector for Eliza's death!

Suddenly, Ness felt a slight flutter in her abdomen. She placed a doubtful hand over the place, frowning. It was neither indigestion nor palpitations; she had never felt anything quite like it before.

The flutter came again, the beating of butterfly wings against her palm. And suddenly, she knew what it was, and sat down on the rough grass to take in the implications of that knowledge.

***

As Galbraith returned to Glen Heather, he was still shaken from the scene at the funeral, still wrestling with the fact that warm-hearted Eliza Jarvis lay in her grave. He had liked Eliza, and had flirted decorously with her, secure that she would not take it amiss. He would have liked to have the chance to say goodbye. And now here he found Agnes Campbell, alone and seeming just as unhappy as he. Without premeditation, he slid from the Bruce to take her in his arms.

'Oh, Ness, what can I do for you?'

She shook her head against his shoulder. 'Nothing, Jamie, you can do nothing.'

'Oh, but I could,' said Galbraith softly. 'I could, if you wanted. I could build you a wee cottage and tell you all I do...'

He closed his eyes, ignoring the reproachful face of Tobias as it rose up in his imagination. Good taste be damned, he thought. His Eve was too desirable to be wasted on a cold man like Hector Campbell. If Tobias were correct, the gossip was rife already; society believed what it would, so why should he not have reality as well as reputation?

'Oh, Ness,' he said again, kissing her wet face. 'Why not come to me and be happy?'

In his mind he could already see the cottage he would build, and foresee the simple, pleasant life they could lead. He ignored the fact that life would have to be lived in some place away from Van Diemen's Land.

'No,' she said, pulling away. 'It canna be, Jamie; I am Hector's wife, and I belong with him.' The thought did not seem to bring her much satisfaction, and she fumbled for the handkerchief he had given her before.

Galbraith would have taken her in his arms again, but the Bruce neighed a greeting and they turned to see Hector riding down the brae.

James Galbraith felt the blood rise in his cheeks, for he had wronged Hector much in thought and a little in deed, but though Hector looked grim, he was no more so than usual.

'You came back to us, Jamie,' he said. 'So you dinna believe I hounded Mistress Jarvis to her death?'

'Of course not,' said Galbraith. 'The funeral is over and I did not go back to the house.'

'Verra wise,' said Hector. 'Come, Ness—you look gey tired.' He dismounted from Rowan and lifted his wife into the saddle in his stead, then led the horse away.

Galbraith watched them enter the hut, and when they did not come out, he clenched his hands. He had no doubt that Hector was even now enjoying the legal favours of his wife. His imagination supplied the scene his eyes could not; Ness Campbell naked in the arms of her husband, held fast and uncomplaining. Or was she weeping, still? And would Hector pause to soothe her and kiss away her tears? Or would he be at his task with the same practical energy that he turned to whatever else he tackled?

Galbraith felt his guts twist with jealousy. Any woman would have done for Hector Campbell, any healthy woman who was capable of breeding him an heir. He had not the wit to appreciate the treasure he so lightly collected on the docks.

***

Ness was wakeful. Hector's possessive hand lay as usual on her hip, but he was so deeply asleep he might have been on the other side of the world. The fluttering of the new life within her became more pronounced each day, and still she had not told Hector. The alteration in her figure was scarcely visible yet, but very soon Hector must guess her condition. What would happen then? Would he treat her with more affection now she had done her duty? If only this happened months ago, she thought mournfully, in the first flush of their time at Glen Heather, when Hector had still made hopeful and regular enquiries about her health. That was before she had learnt of his deception; before she met James Galbraith.

She knew Galbraith was in love with her, and it troubled her deeply. She had turned him aside, but she could not bring herself to treat him harshly, for the fault was not entirely his. She accepted his friendship with gratitude from the beginning, and turned to him for comfort after the funeral. She had offered gratitude and taken comfort. She felt no more than that for Hector when she agreed to become his wife.

Ness had not much experience of love. She'd held her father in dutiful affection, had felt warmth for Donal, Jean, Theodora and Eliza and even Grey Falcon. All had left her or let her down, so what price love at that? And then—there was the strange love she had for Hector, which was not a single sentiment but a tangled mass of confusion. Hector had not left her, but it seemed he would always close her out, and would never have time when he thought of her, alone. And yet she was still convinced he needed her. Or am I deluded still? she thought. Is it me who needs him?

What she felt for Jamie Galbraith was different. There was something very warming about being wanted. It was pleasant to be loved for herself instead of for what she might provide. Would Jamie leave her if she went away with him? Would Hector bother to follow if she left? Love was a snare after all, and she was better without it.

Having made this decision, she felt calmer and went to sleep.

She had uneasy dreams, but woke resigned in the morning. She was wed to Hector, and she was having his child, and the rest of it was haivers. It was far better to live with Hector's generous indifference than with Phemie's disapproval. It was far better to live with a quiet conscience than to follow a course she knew to be wrong. Duty was a kind of love, and there was joy in holding to what was just and right.

The decision seemed so right that she forgot it was hers alone, and when Galbraith brought the finished painting to the hut the next day, she greeted him with composure.

'Och, Jamie, it's bonnie!' she exclaimed.

'Not so bonnie as yourself,' said Galbraith. It was a response he might have made to any of his lady subjects, but his eyes were warm.

'It will need a good frame,' he continued.

'Aye. Hector will be verra pleased.'

'I am not concerned with pleasing *Hector*,' he said, no longer smiling, and added, 'If only you knew how I have agonised over this portrait! If only you knew how I have longed to keep it, because I thought I could not have you.'

'Och, haivers,' said Ness uneasily.

'Och, *haivers*!' he echoed. 'Ness, I meant what I said. I want you to come to me.'

'I canna do that, Jamie. I would not. I am wed to Hector.'

'Any woman would do for Hector. He wants a breeding ewe.'

'Do you think I dinna ken *that*?' snapped Ness.

'You are worth so much more,' said Galbraith awkwardly. It was the first time in years he had found himself at a loss for a smooth phrase. 'So much more, my Eve.'

'I would be worth nothing if I turned awa' frae my duty,' said Ness.

CHAPTER 18

Hector had not gone up the mountain that Sunday. He had felt uneasy since the day of Eliza's funeral, and it was an unease that had little to do with Jarvis' rage against him. His conscience in that matter was clear, for he acquired the mortgage as no more than a business investment. He must soon meet Jarvis and thrash out the terms of the arrangement, but even Hector realised it would be tactless to approach the man now. The unease had nothing to do with Scarborough or with Glen Heather; it had to do with Ness.

The weather was cooling gently into autumn, and bodily contact was welcome. The night before he'd reached for Ness, smoothing his hands over her breasts. He had noted that this caress seemed to make her more receptive to his attentions, and had been about to make his wishes more plain when he realised her breasts were fuller, even through the coarse linen sark she wore as a nightgown. For a moment, he thought nothing of it, except that her bleeding might be due, but he had noted with a stockman's eye that her cycle seemed to run with the moon, and if so, she was out of step. Or perhaps at last they were going to have a bairn.

'Ness—Ness lass?' he said, shaking her a little. She sighed and stirred, but did not wake, so Hector let her be. Lying back with his head pillowed on his folded arms he thought about the future. And then he slept.

It was not until that Sunday morning, when making his habitual rounds of the stock, that he began to have doubts. Surely, if the lassie was pregnant she would have told him. Surely she would have told him, unless she had some pressing reason for keeping the news to herself. The thought nagged so he cut short his tour and returned to interview his wife. She was sleeping when he left, but she should be about by now, setting out his breakfast and airing the bedding.

Ness was by the fire hole, and so was James Galbraith. Hector's eyes narrowed and he paused in the shelter of one of the great blackwood trees. Ness was examining a painting; the painting *he* had commissioned. As he watched, he saw how she turned a glowing face to the artist, and then looked back at the portrait. And he saw the way Galbraith looked at her.

'By God, so *that's* wha' the sleekit auld besoms were at!' said Hector aloud.

He continued to watch, saw Galbraith ask a question, saw the decisive shake of his wife's head, saw the graceful and wholly unconscious way her hand came to rest on her belly. And, in the early sunshine his eyes took in what his hands had told him in the night. His wife was indeed pregnant and, if he were any judge, three or four months along. And there she was, conversing with Galbraith, a young man of easy charm, a Scot who could talk like a Sassenach. There she was, looking up at him with appeal in her eyes, and he was looking down at her.

His wife was pregnant, after more than a year of marriage, and she had not told him, her lawful husband. Instead, she was close in conversation with another man. It pointed in one damning direction. The child could not be his.

Watching the unconscious couple by the hut, Hector turned over the evidence in his mind. Young Galbraith had been with them some months. All those days Hector had worked on the mountain, leaving Galbraith and Ness in the glen, with none but the casual company of Bullocky George and the workmen. And in the beginning, Galbraith had worked alone on the sketches. Had it happened then? Had his wife run, like a bitch in heat, to the nearest dog? He could not believe it of either of them, but against this he had to set the evidence before him.

Hector blinked, aware he had not done so for some time. No wonder his eyes burned so. He rubbed them, and saw Ness shake her head again, then smile tenderly at Galbraith. She lifted her hand as if to touch his shoulder, then turned away. Galbraith looked unhappy. Had Ness just told him his child must be credited to Hector?

Rage boiled in Hector, rage at the two who had deceived him, rage at those sly folk who had hinted and gossiped while he had been blind. Well—he'd not be played for a cuckold. He would repudiate Ness and turn off Galbraith—aye, and give the wretch something to remember him by! His hand went instinctively to his dirk, and then he turned on his heel and stalked off to the old wagon, disused since the Grey Falcon was lamed. In the bed, wrapped in canvas and supple and gleaming with oil, was the driving whip he braided during the winter.

Hector took it out and drew it thoughtfully through his hand. It was cool and tactile as a living snake. 'Aye,' said Hector. 'I have a use for yoursel'.'

He drew the whip through his fingers again, eyes half closed as he listened to its gentle hiss. The plaited handle was a fine fit in his palm.

Coiling the whip Hector strode back towards the slab hut.

***

Galbraith felt like a foolish lad being scolded by his nursemaid. He offered his all to Ness, and she gently handed it back.

'Come on, Jamie,' she said with a smile, when he tried to protest. 'Why dinna you find a lassie free to love you?'

'I have never found one yet,' said Galbraith.

'Then perhaps,' said Ness tartly, 'you havena been looking! Now awa' wi' you and let me get on wi' Hector's breakfast.'

Galbraith sighed, wondering if, after all, he had not made himself ridiculous. He had been seeing Agnes Campbell as a victim, the disregarded treasure of an uncouth Scot, but it seemed she was well enough suited with the situation. She might have been his Eve, but Eve, he remembered now, had been a dangerous lady to know, leading her man into sin in the morning of the world. He looked at the portrait, and at the woman herself. The shadows had gone from her eyes.

'Ness, you know I do love you,' he said carefully, 'but perhaps you are right.'

'O' course!' said Ness. 'Now be off, before Hector comes. I need to talk wi' him.'

Galbraith's eyes widened. 'You'll not tell him—'

'Och, no that.' Ness smiled and gestured for him to leave. 'It will come out fine, Jamie.'

'Aye, it wi' at that!' said a deep voice, and, whip in hand, Hector stepped dangerously into the clearing.

Ness watched, aghast, as her husband released the coiled thong, lifted the handle and gave the whip a preliminary crack. Pace by pace he approached, eyes narrowed to slits and fixed on James Galbraith. The blood drained from Ness' face as she saw her husband's aspect. Expressionless as always, he still managed to look savage and menacing.

'Hector—' she began, but Hector brushed past her as if she had been a shadow.

'You sleekit, weaselling, sneaking, *cur*!' said Hector between his teeth, advancing on Galbraith. He cracked the whip again.

'Run, Jamie!' said Ness tensely. 'He's gone mad!'

Hector continued in the same deadly voice; 'I gi' you work,

welcome you to my house, ha' you eat at my table—' Each phrase was punctuated with another crack of the whip until its wicked tip was snapping inches from Galbraith's face.

'Run, Jamie!' said Ness again. Her world spun around her, and all she could think was that Jamie must get away, right away, before Hector half killed him. 'Run!' she said again, but it came out as the merest breath.

Hector turned on her savagely. 'Whisht, woman!' he snapped, and thrust her hard with his hand. Ness staggered back until brought up by the trunk of a tree. Eyes starting with horror, she put her hand to her cheek. She was shaking so she could hardly stand, and leaned against the tree for support. Hector turned his back contemptuously and resumed his stalking of Galbraith, who had not retreated.

'So you have a wee backbone, you slimy bastard!' he remarked, snapping the whip an inch from Galbraith's ear. 'Aye, you ha' the guts to stand there and face the man you wronged!'

'Jamie, tell him it's all haivers!' gasped Ness. 'You didna wrong him!'

Galbraith shook his head stubbornly, eyes fixed on Hector. 'Hector, you have no cause for this,' he said steadily.

'Have I no? And do you deny you ha' the fire i' yon balls for my wee wife?' The whip touched the front of Galbraith's tight duck trousers, and he took an involuntary step backwards.

'I cannot deny I feel something for Mistress Campbell,' he said.

'Aye,' said Hector with satisfaction. 'Maybe after all you think yoursel' a man!' He flicked the whip so that it snapped against Galbraith's cheek and his victim cried out in pain. A second flick laid the cheek open in a long, red welt. Galbraith touched the place with a shaking hand and examined his bloody fingertips with astonishment.

Hector's arm drew back again. 'So, you may be man enough to cheat on me wi' my wee wife, but are you knave enough to foist your bastard on me as well?'

'Hector—Hector, you canna!' Ness stumbled forward and grasped Hector's arm, dragging it down with all her strength. He put her roughly aside and she fell in the ferns.

Galbraith's face was drained of colour, but now it flushed red around the welling cut as he moved to help Ness to her feet. 'Hector, you must believe me when I assure you there has never been wrongdoing. You have no reason to use Mistress Campbell so cruelly!'

Hector tossed aside the whip. 'Shut your mouth, you wee wretch,' he said in disgust. 'I treat my wee wife as I think guid—and *you* think it well you ha' got weak eyes. If you were half the man you think yoursel', I would ha' knocked you down until you'd no get up again. Since you choose to hide behind a lassie's skirts, I canna gi' you the thrashing you deserve! Now, get your traps and be off. And be thankfu' you can still sit your horse!' He turned to Ness, snapping the whip suggestively. 'And as for you, woman, you get to the hut before I thrash you as well.'

Galbraith blotted his bleeding cheek with one of his cambric handkerchiefs. He could see there was no reasoning with Hector in this mood; the best course seemed to be to do as he was told. Perhaps later the man would be more receptive to reason. And perhaps, thought Galbraith with a trace of his usual wry humour, he would not.

Only one circumstance prevented him from leaving Glen Heather immediately, and that was fear for Ness. A man of Hector's stamp undoubtedly looked upon his wife as his property, so she might soon be in much worse case than Galbraith. Faithless wives had been killed on occasion, and Hector seemed to believe the worst. He looked entreatingly at Ness, but she averted her face, making an unmistakable gesture with her hand.

'Go, Jamie,' she said listlessly. 'It wi' be better if you leave.'

'Aye,' said Hector jeeringly. 'Be off, *Jamie*, and dinna let me see yon face again.'

Galbraith walked stiffly down to his camp where he saddled the Bruce and began to load his belongings on the packhorse. He strained to hear what was happening by the hut, but the burble of the water was too loud. Ruefully, he thought of Tobias and his warning letter.

'By God, Toby,' he said to the trees, 'I should have taken a leaf from *your* book and never come to Glen Heather! I have made a pretty jumble of it all, and put Ness in danger. And the dear knows if ever I shall get paid!'

CHAPTER 19

Ness made just one attempt to explain the situation to Hector. She was hampered by the same consideration that had troubled Galbraith. Although the child she carried was undoubtedly Hector's get, she was not quite innocent in the matter. She should have told Hector her news immediately, and she should never have accepted Galbraith's sympathy.

After Galbraith had left the clearing, she tried to collect herself, pulling her shawl about her with shaking hands. Her movement brought Hector out of his brown study and he swung to face her so abruptly she shied and lifted her arm to ward off an expected blow.

'Och, dinna be a fool, woman!' said Hector. 'Just answer me this; are you breeding?'

'Aye,' said Ness faintly. Her hands moved protectively to her belly, where the flutter of life was touching her again.

'And the bairn—' The words seemed dragged from Hector, as if against his will. 'The bairn—is it o' mysel'?'

'Aye,' said Ness. She found herself breathing more easily. She had only half understood Hector's madness, but now his reasoning seemed clear. 'It could be no one else's. Hector, you didna think I would take another man to my bed—'

'Would you no?' he said heavily. 'Wi' your *Jamie* this and your *Jamie* that beside?'

'Mr Galbraith is a friend o' yours!' said Ness.

'Aye, but that didna keep his thieving hands off my wife! And it didna keep yoursel' frae smiling on him. I saw. Och—get awa' wi' you.'

'Hector,' said Ness, 'the child is your own.'

'Aye,' said Hector very dryly. 'After so many months is it so likely?' He turned on his heel and went to saddle Rowan.

'Where are you going?' cried Ness.

'Awa' frae you,' said Hector, and pulled himself clumsily into the saddle.

***

The next few weeks were the worst Ness had ever spent. Hector did not come home until the Monday morning when he appeared at the new house and curtly bade the workers to go.

'And dinna come back until I send,' he snapped.

He looked unshaven and almost old, and Ness's heart went out to him, but he ignored her tentative overtures as if they had not been made. He left the meal she offered and stalked away up the brae.

This set the pattern for the days that followed. Hector dealt faithfully with the livestock, but the development of Glen Heather was at a standstill, and he never spoke to his wife. Ness wept alone in the nights and spent the days wandering aimlessly on the brae. The half built house mocked her as the ghost of what could have been. At first, she hoped Hector would come to realise the truth, but as the third week came to a close she began to fear the rift was permanent. Truth or not, it seemed Hector could not forgive her for smiling on another man.

Now well into her fifth month of pregnancy, her abdomen was beginning to distend. Her breasts were as swollen and tender as her eyelids, raw from weeping, as the child who should have brought such joy began to feel a burden. She walked by the burn and up the brae, wishing Grey Falcon still limped beside her. She remembered the flowers Galbraith showed her, and the day she had met Eliza, who had thought herself on Scarborough land.

She was standing on the bank of the burn where the crushed ferns of Galbraith's camp had already risen thick and lush, when Hector rode up.

'Och, Hector, will you never forgive me?' she said sadly.

Hector's hands tightened on Rowan's reins. 'I dinna ken why you dinna follow your Jamie,' he said coldly.

'Would you no mind if I did?'

'Do as you will, woman.' Hector jerked the rein savagely so Rowan tossed his head in protest.

'I will then,' said Ness. She watched sickly as Hector rode away. She knew she could not stay at Glen Heather now.

Autumn was well underway, and Ness realised that if she was to make the break it must be now. The child would not completely preclude her from taking up a position as a servant, but it would make it much more difficult, so she must find a place before her pregnancy became too evident. But where could she go? Eliza, who might have helped her secure a position, was dead, and the lady of Glen Heather could hardly go to Mrs Williams or Mrs Reeve and beg for work. She had not seen James Galbraith since Hector slashed him across the face, and in any case she did not consider him a suitable refuge. She was Hector's wife, and she carried Hector's child, so she could no more go to Galbraith now than she could have left with him in the first place.

The thought of Donal Kirkbride crossed her mind, but Donal was away across the sea, and she had not the fare to New Zealand any more than the fare home to Scotland. Phemie would never have her back, and Jean Leslie was dead. There was no going home, or away. Her future must lie in the colonies.

Ness went back to the hut, tied her belongings into a bundle and set off along the track from Glen Heather. On the way, she saw a tuft of the crimson heath. She bent awkwardly to pick it, but its tough stem cut into her fingers so she left it to bloom on the brae.

She went to Theodora Bruning in Mersey. There was not a great deal of choice, for in her current condition she could not walk far. Theodora had been cold to her at Eliza's funeral, but she was a kind woman and Ness did not think she would turn her away.

***

The altercation at Glen Heather had not passed unnoticed. Dick Bruning heard of it, and told Theodora, who had also heard the news from Bertha Ward.

It was Bertha who doctored the slash on Galbraith's face, and she told Theodora without much sympathy that the young man would never be quite so pretty again. Unfortunately, Bertha chose to stop up the wide cut with melted candle wax. Deprived of air, the cut festered and Galbraith was very ill with the resulting fever; so ill that Tobias Scott-Blakeney got wind of it, travelled to Mole Creek and removed Galbraith from his lodgings there.

Tobias disapproved of Galbraith's job at Glen Heather, but he was very fond of his young friend, and it hurt him to see him brought so low.

'I told you to have a care for your reputation, Jamie!' he said reproachfully, touching the barely healing scar.

Galbraith winced. 'At least *my* scar was made by a wronged husband and not by a vengeful mother,' he said with gentle irony.

Tobias glowered at him from beneath bushy white eyebrows. 'My boy, that was unworthy of you.'

'I know,' said Galbraith. 'The husband was not so very much wronged, Tobias. And she is—is—'

'Artemis?' suggested Tobias with the twitch of a brow. 'Aphrodite?'

'No,' said Galbraith. 'She is Eve.'

***

Theodora Bruning was disconcerted to see Ness, and not very pleased, but she said grudgingly that she supposed she had better come in.

'I'll no come in if I am unwelcome,' said Ness.

'You are a silly girl,' said Theodora severely, 'but have I not said you could always turn to me?'

'Aye, but—'

'Of course, I do not condone your behaviour,' said Theodora. 'I suppose you are looking for news of Mr Galbraith?'

Ness frowned and pulled her shawl tighter. Did everyone believe her a whore? 'I am not interested i' Jamie, and I ha' lain wi' no man but Hector,' she said firmly, so startling Theodora's man-servant that he dropped the silver card-tray on the floor.

There was a pause, and then Theodora blushed and bustled Ness into her parlour. They looked doubtfully at one another, then Ness' lips twitched and she began to laugh. 'Oh Theodora, it is all such a mishmash!' Her laughter caught in a sob.

Theodora patted her shoulder, and then had her drink a small measure of brandy. 'I do not hold with spirits,' she explained shamefacedly, 'but sometimes they can be a comfort.'

'Aye,' agreed Ness ruefully, 'but I canna find answers i' the bottom o' the bottle.'

'No,' agreed Theodora. 'But what brings you here today, Ness, if not Mr Galbraith? Has Mr Campbell mistreated you?'

'He hasna beaten me,' said Ness slowly. 'But he is so thrawn he'll no believe the bairnie is his.'

'And is it?'

'Aye, there has been no other, nor ever will be.'

'Your husband is a difficult man,' said Theodora, 'and thoughtless, too. He treated Mr Bruning very shabbily.'

'He didna mean it,' said Ness tiredly. 'Hector is—' She paused, trying to think of words to describe the complex man she had married. 'He has a thought in his head,' she said at last, 'and he canna be brought to ken others might see it in a different light.'

Theodora's lips tightened. 'He has made no friends in the district.

Not only did he treat Mr Bruning without consideration, but he has turned off the men he hired and as for the trick he played Whitaker Jarvis over Scarborough! Oh, that was ill-done of him.'

'If Hector hadna bought the mortgage it would ha' gone to another.'

'Yes, and Mr Jarvis would not now be drinking himself into an early grave,' said Theodora dryly.

'Och, Eliza wouldna like that!' said Ness. She bit her lip. 'Theodora,' she said with difficulty, 'why did Eliza die? It was none o' Hector's doing.'

'I think we may absolve your husband of that,' said Theodora. 'We were sad to lose Eliza, Ness, but it would have come sooner or later. She had a weakness of the heart, and the strain of little Isobel's birth was too much for her. Eliza should never have married.'

'No,' said Ness, depressed. 'Nor should I, forby.'

Theodora said briskly; 'Now, do not begin fancying yourself in the same case as Eliza, Ness! You are perfectly well and strong, and you will have a fine child. If it is like its father it will come roaring into the world.' She paused, possibly to consider the thought of a second edition of Hector Campbell rampaging about the district. 'You should drink beef tea and eat plenty,' she continued. 'You are eating for two, you know.'

Ness nodded. 'But I canna stay wi' you, Theodora,' she said. 'It would anger Hector.'

Theodora must have thought of a maddened Hector Campbell descending on the Bruning household in search of his wife, for she actually shuddered.

Ness smiled a little. 'He willna come,' she said wanly. 'He said I might do as I wished.'

'He turned you out?'

'He said I might go,' corrected Ness. 'He must have thought I would go to Jamie, but I willna do that.'

Theodora raised her eyebrows. 'It would seem Mr Galbraith has not behaved well in this,' she said. 'He has trifled with your affections, and enticed you to leave your husband.'

'Och, Jamie meant no harm,' said Ness uncomfortably. 'He made up a lassie in his mind and for a wee while he thought I could be that lassie. He didna take it much to heart when I turned him down, I trust.'

'Mr Galbraith was lucky not to lose his eye,' said Theodora

reprovingly.

'It was *Hector* took it to heart!' said Ness.

Theodora looked at her guest sharply, but said nothing more on the subject. If Agnes Campbell was in love with young Galbraith she was doing a remarkable job of hiding it. She was quite at a loss as to the advice she should give the girl. A good Christian woman should always advise an erring wife to return to her husband, but what if such a return should lead to violence and endanger an innocent unborn child? She knew Campbell could be violent; her niece Polly had witnessed a savage fight with Whitaker Jarvis (a fight in which Campbell had undoubtedly been the aggressor) and she had seen with her own eyes the damage he did to Galbraith. And over an affair which had probably amounted to no more than sighs and kisses!

Fortunately for Theodora's peace of mind, Ness did not ask for any advice. Indeed, after a day's rest she said a grateful goodbye to her hostess and bespoke a place in Dick Bruning's wagon when the latter took his next load of mail and sundries to Launceston. She gave Bruning the silver heather brooch in payment, and Theodora told him sharply to put it aside in case Ness should wish to redeem it. She sent one of her daughters to lend countenance on the journey, but afterwards she wondered if she should have done more.

***

Tobias Scott-Blakeney never usually interfered in his young friend's affairs. He had tried to tell himself his interest in James Galbraith was fatherly, and to prove it he had urged James to marry. To find the boy in love with a flesh-and-blood woman gave him such a pang that Tobias was disgusted with himself. He thought himself past the age to be lovelorn, and he knew James had no interest in any relationship other than the casual friendship they enjoyed. It was an indignity to find himself antagonistic to a girl who, if Galbraith were to be believed, was guilty of no more than an appealing face and nature and an unfortunate choice of husband. He was not so far removed from magnanimity that he could not appreciate the appeal of Ness Campbell's expressive face, which Galbraith had obligingly drawn for him, several times.

'Here she is as I saw her first,' Galbraith had said quietly, offering sketches for comparison, 'and when I saw her again, she had come to this.'

Tobias studied the two sketches of the girl's face: the child-like wonder of the first, and the resignation of the second. 'Was she ill?' he asked abruptly, tapping the second sketch.

'Ill?' For a moment Galbraith did not understand.

'Remember Eliza Jarvis,' said Tobias.

Galbraith winced. Eliza had been delighted with her portrait, but in hindsight he could see that the translucent pallor he captured on canvas had been the stamp of ill health, evident to his artist's eyes before it was apparent to the gaze of everyday.

'Mistress Campbell was expecting a child,' he said.

'Ah. That explains the look.' Tobias glowered at Galbraith. 'Yours?' he asked abruptly.

'Good God no! I told you there was no affaire!'

'Her husband's, then.' Tobias brooded for a few minutes then asked with frank curiosity; 'Jamie, if she had agreed to come to you, would you have accepted the child? Disliking the father as you do?'

'I was not aware of the child at that time,' said Galbraith stiffly.

'But you painted her with the Madonna look.'

'Damn you, Tobias!' Galbraith glared at his friend for a moment then said reflectively; 'I cannot say. I do not dislike Hector Campbell, Toby. I admire him. I just think him the wrong man for my Eve.'

After this conversation, it was hardly surprising that Tobias Scott-Blakeney, driving his sedate jinker, should recognise the grey-shawled young woman dismounting from the carrier's wagon. He watched curiously as Agnes Campbell thanked the driver and looked about the bustling scene as if waking from a dream. Something about the determined lift of her chin made him feel guilty about resenting her. The lady had character, and integrity too, unless she had come to Launceston in search of Jamie after all.

Tobias manoeuvred his jinker until he was alongside her, and cleared his throat. 'Mrs Campbell, I presume?'

'Aye?' Her response was guarded, her voice soft and heavily accented.

'Allow me to introduce myself, Madam. Tobias Scott-Blakeney at your service.'

He saw her lips silently shaping the words and then recognition dawned and she nodded. 'Aye, you are the man Hector sent for, only Jamie came instead.'

'I am he,' he said, liking her directness. 'And I fear my dereliction of duty has caused you a great deal of trouble.'

'That it has.'

'Then,' said Tobias gallantly, leaning down to offer his hand, 'I must see what I can do to mend what I have been instrumental in breaking. Come along then,' he added as she hesitated, 'there can be no impropriety in riding with me, Mrs Campbell. Not only am I old enough to be your grandfather, but you are probably aware that I have the reputation for preferring the Adonis to the Venus.' He looked at her closely. 'Although, had I been fortunate enough to have met your grandmother in my youth, who is to say what might have happened? We would have been friends, at least.' The young woman smiled doubtfully and mounted the jinker. 'Good,' said Tobias encouragingly as she settled her skirts, 'now the burning question is this. If your husband could be brought to see reason, would you be willing to return to him?'

Tobias did not tell James Galbraith he met Ness on the road. Altruism could go only so far, and he was willing to risk damage to his personal reputation, but not to invite another complication.

Instead, he arranged for Ness to work as housekeeper to a respectable elderly widow while he composed a letter to Hector Campbell. He judged it best to allow the man time to reflect on the situation, and made arrangements for Dick Bruning to carry his offering to Mersey some time later.

CHAPTER 20

As Tobias hoped, Hector was having second thoughts about his treatment of Ness. His rage largely dissipated with his thrashing of Galbraith, but the furious hurt remained. The lassie was *his* wife, and she had no right to look so tenderly on a wee bit of a man who needed spectacles to see more than a yard in front of him. As for lying with him, and allowing him to get her with child when he, her lawful husband, had failed over the many months of trying ... the thought made Hector feel ill. It gave him a coldness in his belly as if he would never be whole again. How *could* Ness have been so faithless? Had he not rescued her from penury? Given her everything she could have desired? Built her a grand house? And all he had ever asked in return had been loyalty, obedience, peace and a family of heirs.

The hurt remained, and as her pregnancy became more evident, he could hardly bear to look at her. On the one hand, he wanted her badly. He wanted to lose himself in her softness, to explore the new contours of her body, and to caress her into wanting him as she had done on the night he had told her about his triumph with the burn. On the other hand, he knew that to touch her would have brought the image of James Galbraith before his eyes. The four-eyed picture-painting laddie who had dared to enjoy the favours of his wife, he thought furiously. And whose favours his wife had enjoyed also?

At the thought that Ness might have responded more to Galbraith than to himself, Hector's gorge rose until he feared he would vomit.

In the end he could not bear to think of her *or* look at her, and if she drifted like a ghost about Glen Heather, so did he; an angry and vengeful ghost who could not help driving away the thing he had wanted most. Finally, he had come on her unawares down by the burn, had seen her grieving over the site of Galbraith's camp. And she had the temerity to ask his forgiveness! Standing there, bulging with Galbraith's child, she asked him to forgive. He responded bitterly, she answered in kind, and when he had returned the next morning, he found she had taken him at his word and gone.

Well, he was well rid of the faithless lassie. Hector tried to consider what he should do next. He had lost his enthusiasm for the whole venture, but he owned the deeds to Glen Heather and the mortgage to Scarborough, and with the worsening drought in New South Wales it was a poor time to try to sell land. He could not marry again at present, but there was no reason why he should not find a willing woman and get an heir. The Kirk and society and the law might frown on adultery, but a wee Campbell laddie would do fine to cleanse the taste of failure.

Hector made a trip to Mole Creek, but the only single women he encountered were Miss Reeve and Miss Margaret Young, and the one was too flighty and the other too ugly and feline to appeal to him in any way. Besides, he had fallen out with Reeve over the Scarborough mortgage and Miss Young was a companion to the Williams woman of Llanhow, whose man had ignored Hector's existence since the affair of the Scarborough ram.

Scarborough, thought Hector bleakly, was at the seat of most of his troubles. He should never have bought that mortgage. It was an unlucky place, too; one master had been senile at forty-five and dead at fifty, and the second was a young widower drunk and maudlin with grief. Hector shook his head. There must be bad luck in the Jarvis family somewhere, yet Whitaker Jarvis had two bairns and he had none.

With Ness gone, his plans collapsed about him. The wee cow was in calf to the red and white bull, the sheep were flourishing, the grass had grown and the turnips were ready to pull. Glen Heather was coming to life, but its braw house remained a shell and its lady had gone away.

With mounting alarm, Hector realised he was growing as maudlin as Jarvis, and, on an impulse, he mounted Rowan and rode over to Scarborough. The place seemed unkempt, as if Scarborough's master, too, had lost interest and heart. Hector looked about with a proprietary air. A manservant and the sonsy wife of the overseer stared at him in trepidation, so he bowed ironically and wished them good day.

'I want to see Jarvis,' he said baldly when they enquired his business.

'Mr Jarvis is indisposed,' said the butler.

'Drink taken, frae what I hear,' grunted Hector. 'Fetch him out, man, and tell him it's time he saw to business.' He paused. 'Tell him Scarborough's a braw place,' he said quietly. 'Tell him I'd like fine to see it do well under its master, because if he lets it lie, I shall ha' to take over mysel' and just now I have no such inclination.'

Having delivered his sarcastic message to Jarvis, Hector rode home again. It was May by now, and he found himself thinking of the May Day Ball a year ago, and seeing his Ness as a thing of beauty in a crimson gown. He had meant to have her in an inn that night, he recalled, but it hadn't come about. A flash of colour attracted his eye. Scowling, Hector bent from Rowan's saddle and caught at it. He found himself holding a tuft of flowers and hurled it away into the burn. He was done with crimson heath.

Bullocky George awaited him at Glen Heather.

'Geordie,' said Hector by way of greeting. Bullocky George had never quite seemed to understand his presence was not needed, or more likely he disliked the company of his vinegar-tongued woman and came to Glen Heather to avoid it. He was leaning contentedly against his lead bullock's shoulder, and scratching it behind the ear. Hector was reminded of the way Ness used to lean against Grey Falcon. He spat violently into the ferns. Must *everything* remind him of the lassie?

'Letter for you, Hector,' said Bullocky George. 'Bruning give it me.'

Hector frowned at the grimy paper, faintly damp and tobacco stained from contact with the interior of Bullocky George's pocket. Then he broke the seal. He noted that the letter bore the signature of Tobias Scott-Blakeney, and would have thrown it away, had it not struck him that the man might have had the temerity to send a bill. He had forwarded sufficient funds to pay for Galbraith's weeks at Glen Heather (though it stung him to do it) but possibly Scott-Blakeney might think more was owing in the way of damages.

Hector smiled grimly. If the sleekit bastard thought his young associate was due any moneys for the slash across the face, he could think again. The young rooster was lucky the slash hadn't been made with a dirk, and positioned a good deal lower on his anatomy.

He read the missive, frowned incredulously, and read it again. Then he whistled gently through his teeth. Scott-Blakeney, far from demanding money or apologising for his own lack of courtesy in refusing the work, had written a righteously indignant letter in which the words *abuse of trust* and *refined tastes* and *boon companion* appeared. What it boiled down to was a simple accusation that Hector had encouraged Galbraith to associate with *youths of a certain persuasion* ... and from this it took no leap of intelligence to understand that not only was Scott-Blakeney a man of 'certain persuasions', but that James Galbraith was as well. No wonder the laddie was gey good at making pictures!

Hector read the letter a third time, and laughed long and bitterly.

The words put another complexion on Galbraith's relationship with Ness, and he saw now why the lassie had found her Jamie a good companion. No doubt they had talked very happily of flowers and pictures, birds and gowns and baby lambs! He had thought Ness faithless, but if Scott-Blakeney were to be believed, Ness might just as well have taken up with another lassie.

Bullocky George rasped his throat and asked if there was any word from Mrs Campbell. Was she still holidaying in Hobarton and would she soon be home again?

Hector damned his eyes loudly. 'Geordie, you rogue, you ken fine she went to Launceston wi' Bruning. And aye, I hope to see her gey soon. I need to talk wi' her.'

As if conjured up by his words, his wife stepped out of the hut. Hector goggled and made a hasty step forward, then pulled himself together. 'Lassie, are you well?'

'Aye, well enough, Hector. I shall ha' your dinner in a wee while.'

Hector nodded, then turned to glower at Bullocky George. 'I ken fine you fetched her home from Mersey, Geordie. I thank you for the courtesy, and now I suggest you be off before I recall you lied to me.'

Bullocky George grinned and took the hint.

***

Ness had returned to Glen Heather, but Hector found her distant and cool. The rush of pleasure when he saw her frightened him, but he felt he could have welcomed it if she had only looked at him with equal warmth.

She never spoke much of her time in Launceston, save to mention that she had worked for Widow Barton, and met Tobias Scott-Blakeney. She cooked Hector's meals, washed his trews and sark, soaped his back and lay down beside him at night, but she took no more rambles about the property and little joy in the early snows, and she never mentioned the lack of progress at Glen Heather.

Spring came at last, and with it another windstorm. This time Hector was down on the flats and he took Ness and Rowan to shelter in the half built walls of the stone house. Ness was quite near her time, and he would have shielded her from the buffets as they walked, but she dragged her plaid about her and moved away from his arm.

After the storm was over, Glen Heather was littered with fallen trees and branches, and one great hollow gum had crashed across the new burn, knocking aside the flumes. It took two days of hard work to restore the course of the burn and return the water to the sheep, and since Bullocky George had not returned, Hector chopped the branches himself. While clearing the fallen wood he was disconcerted to hear an angry shriek.

At first he thought it was Ness, but the cry was repeated and from among the crushed branches of the hollow tree emerged one of the crested birds that wrought so much havoc to young crops. This one was parrot-like, pure white with a few grey feathers and a tuft of yellow like a plume at the back of its head. It had a heavy grey beak, and was hissing angrily, stabbing at his hands and trailing an injured wing.

About to put the thing out of its misery, Hector suddenly realised that the bird was not miserable at all, but merely hurt, frightened, and very, very angry. He took hold of it carefully, one large hand securing the wings, another clamped to the back of its head so it could not peck. Then he carried it to the hut.

Ness was wearily collecting the scattered kitchen implements when she heard the shriek, followed by voluble swearing from Hector. She smiled a little wryly. Her husband had been unusually mild-mannered since her return, so mild that she missed the old Hector. Now, it seemed, he was back. She looked up to see him approach, and saw he was scowling and carrying something wrapped in a jumble of his plaid.

'What ha' you there?' she asked, overcome with curiosity.

'A wee bird.' He parted the plaid and a tufted head reared up, twisting snakelike on a long neck and hissing snakelike as well. Hector's hands were bleeding from shallow gashes, and Ness exclaimed in surprise. 'It has a hurt to the wing,' he added. 'Bind it up, lassie, while I hold the head awa'.'

Bemused, Ness did as she was told, splinting the wing and wrapping it in layers of linen. Hector then calmed the creature by the simple method of upending a tea chest over it.

From initial wildness, the bird became quickly and surprisingly tame. Ness named it McCleod, and by the time her baby was due to be born, the creature had made it plain it intended to stay at Glen Heather. It had learned to say a few simple words as any parrot might, and Ness was contented in its company.

Hector sometimes wondered if he had been wise in his impulse to give McCleod to Ness. The bird had little time for him, and Hector saw with dismay that Ness conversed more with his feathered rival than with himself. He watched with envious eyes as she offered it choice seeds and grasses, crooning to it, and holding it in her vanishing lap while he often ate alone. He thought she feared him sometimes, for he would look up to find her gazing at him with huge eyes like pools in a burn.

'When the bairn is born, perhaps you might come up the brae wi' me,' he said tentatively. He thought she would be pleased, but after a moment she dropped her eyes and said she would be too busy.

This unsatisfactory state of affairs continued until Hector, noticing that Ness seemed to be in discomfort, asked if she needed the attentions of Bertha Ward.

'Och no, not that auld besom!' exclaimed Ness. 'It was her clacking tongue set the ladies against me!'

'And wha' has set you against me?' asked Hector bluntly.

'None but yoursel', Hector. You had no cause to beat Jamie so. And to think I'd play you false!'

Hector grunted. 'If you dinna wish Mistress Ward, would you want Mistress Bruning to attend to you?'

'Did you no call her a meddling auld wifie?'

'Aye, but Bruning has done me a gey good turn in bringing you back to Mersey.'

Ness dropped her gaze. 'Then thank you, Hector,' she said. 'I would like fine to see Mistress Bruning, and could it be quite soon?'

Hector bearded a protesting Theodora and demanded her help in bringing his child safely to birth. Theodora threw up her hands, but having heard that Ness was asking for her particularly she gathered some linens and put on an old gown. By the time they reached Glen Heather, Ness was in full labour, and Hector found himself abruptly dismissed from his own hut. He saw McCleod similarly ejected from his perch and approached the bird to offer sympathy. McCleod cocked his head on one side, and surveyed Hector through calculating reptilian eyes.

'Sleekit!' it remarked, and bit him on the thumb.

'Aye,' jeered Hector, inspecting the slight damage, 'so the lassie has you tamed as well, my feathered friend. Time was you'd ha' had the thumb off me!'

He moped about the clearing for some time, stoked up the fire under the kettle, and then, hearing a cry from the hut, strode over to find out how things were going with his wife.

'Out, Mr Campbell,' said Theodora. 'You have no place here.'

Hector bristled. 'Och, you auld besom, how dare you try to keep me frae my wee wife and bairn?'

'Mr Campbell, I think you have caused your wife enough distress. Now go and occupy yourself elsewhere. Make some tea.'

Hector thrust out his chin. 'I want to see my wife.'

'Och, let him in, Theodora,' said Ness resignedly. 'It is his bairnie and a'. He has the right and—and—I want him here.'

Theodora was outraged, but after some hours in the hut she welcomed the chance for a breath of fresh air. She was reluctant to leave the strange couple together, but what could Hector Campbell do? Surely he would hardly begin accusing his wife of wrongdoing again at a time like this! She made the required tea, and drank it, then returned with a pannikin of the cooling liquid for Ness. She expected Hector to look pale and uneasy, as men usually did when forced to contemplate feminine mysteries, but his face was unreadable as ever. He was holding his wife's hand and she was clinging to his. This seemed a good sign, and Theodora softened a little. Perhaps after all Hector Campbell was not so black as he was painted. Or perhaps, she reflected, as he growled at her when asked to leave, he was.

Evicted from the hut, Hector wandered the clearing again. There had been frost in the morning of the sparkling spring day, and from the snap in the air he thought there would be frost again that night. The bush was green and still and the scent of the wattles wild and fresh. It was far sweeter than the air in the fusty hut.

Hector walked restlessly up and along the brae to the clearing where the new house stood unfinished and neglected in the cold. The stones were mild to the touch, and the rooms were wide and airy. The second floor was begun, and served as a roof for the lower rooms, and it occurred to Hector that he and Ness would be much more comfortable living in Glen Heather House, despite its unfinished state, than in the hut. And why should they not live there? This house was their future, now that it appeared they had one.

Hector's knuckles still ached from the way Ness had gripped him in the hut. His wife's fingers seemed imprinted on his hand and he felt closer to her than he ever had before.

She had wanted him there. She wanted *him*.

Seized with an idea, Hector threw back his head. His eyes narrowed, his chest expanded and, tossing a fold of plaid over his shoulder, he left the silent house and stripped branches from a wild cherry. He arranged the feathery boughs in a pile on the bare floor of his braw house.

He strode up the brae and gathered sprigs of heath, pink, white and crimson, which he jammed into a pannikin as he had seen Ness do in happier times. Then he took off his plaid and laid it over the springy couch.

In his sark and trews he returned to the hut, and flung open the creaking hide-hinged door. His wife was panting on the bed, tears of pain and exhaustion running down her face, and Theodora Bruning was soaking linen in clean water to bathe them away.

'I told you to stay *out* Mr Campbell!' she snapped.

'Och, get awa' you auld besom!' said Hector.

'Hector!' wailed Ness. 'Dinna speak so cauld to Theodora!'

'Och, lassie, you ken fine I mean nothing by it!' protested Hector. 'She is a guid woman, but I am your man. Can you stand?'

Ness shook her head, crying out as another contraction seized her.

'Mr Campbell!' cried Theodora. 'Have you lost your mind?'

'Begging your pardon, Mistress,' said Hector with a sly glance at Ness, 'but I have a fancy for my son to be born i' the braw house.'

'I would like that fine, Hector,' said Ness, 'but you see I canna come.'

Hector knelt beside her and held out his arms. 'Lassie?' he said, and his voice broke just a little, 'Lassie, can you no come up?'

Ness caught her breath on a sob, but her voice came out strong and clear as she struggled up into Hector's supporting arms. 'Aye, Campbell, that I can.'

PART TWO: ISOBEL - 1860-1885

CHAPTER 21

Isobel Jarvis stood calmly as Nannie Goodridge helped her into her wedding gown. It was a lovely thing of ivory-figured satin over a modest crinoline, and Margaret, Nannie and Isobel had sewn for weeks to have it ready.

'All that work for a wearing of three hours!' thought Isobel with wondering amusement. Of course, the gown could serve later as an evening gown, but to Isobel such conversions were seldom successful; a wedding gown *looked* like a wedding gown until the end of its useful life. Perhaps she should retire it honourably in muslin wrappings for her daughters? It was forward of her, to be thinking of future daughters when she was not yet married, but who could fail to think of daughters and sons, when one was marrying for such a reason, and when one had had such an unpleasant experience a month ago with the medical man in Launceston?

'Your papa merely wishes to ensure your health is fit for your future duties, Issa,' Margaret had said kindly, but what future duties could be worth the pokings and proddings she had endured, the cold instruments and embarrassing questions she had been made to answer? Only when the medical man had put his ear to her breast and counted the beats of her heart had she understood. Her mama had died of heart failure soon after Isobel's birth, and perhaps Papa feared the same weakness in her own constitution. The medical man had explained that her body was made up half from Mama's family and half from Papa's, but Isobel had barely attended to that. She knew she looked nothing like her mama at all.

According to those who had known her, and to the portrait in the parlour, Eliza Jarvis had been a beauty with yellow curls, blue eyes, a dimpled cheek and a fashionable rosebud mouth. Isobel knew she was considered handsome, but she had none of Eliza's melting looks. Her hair was a strange shade of light brown, with ash-coloured streaks, her eyes were deep set and dark as strongly brewed tea, and she had olive skin, like her papa's. She was a good deal taller than her mama had been. She had told this to the medical man, but he had continued to prose on, explaining that outward appearance had little bearing on the matter. At last he had been forced to pronounce her perfectly fit. He then dismissed Isobel, whose constitution it was after all, and spoken seriously to Margaret for some time. The nature of this conversation had never been referred to, so Isobel supposed that it pertained to Margaret's own health.

And now Nannie was lacing Isobel into her wedding gown. 'To think of you wedding That Woman's son!' she said.

'Are you referring to Mr Campbell's mama, Nannie?' Isobel asked coolly.

'Who else?' muttered the old woman. 'Oh, she may sit in church in her weeds, but *I* remember when she was the speak of the neighbourhood, she and that painter man.'

'Which painter man, Nannie?' Isobel knew one should not encourage servants to gossip, but Nannie was hardly a servant, and she always had a fund of long ago scandals to recount.

'Galbraith, who else?' Nannie fastened the small pearl buttons on Isobel's sleeve. 'Painting her portrait, they *said.* Alone for hours at a time! Oh, old Mrs Ward was there, but who's to say when she was called off to a birthing or a laying out?'

'Nannie, you have an idle tongue,' said Isobel crossly. 'You make stories from nothing.'

'You cannot argue with plain fact, Miss Isobel. And plain fact is that that man Galbraith was to paint Mr Campbell and his wife, but only the one portrait was ever finished. Fled away, he did, after a quarrel with Mr Campbell, and scarred forever after, they say.'

'Mr Galbraith is a distinguished gentleman and lives in Sydney Town,' said Isobel.

'Hmmm,' added Nannie meaningly. 'Times change, turn strange, and often not for the better.'

Isobel sucked in her bottom lip, a habit when thinking. 'Times are changing for me, Nannie,' she said. 'I have lived at Scarborough always and after today I shall live at Glen Heather. I shall be Mrs John Campbell. Think of that.'

The old woman set a circlet of silk flowers on her charge's hair. 'I never thought I would see this day- never,' she muttered. 'If Mr Whitaker had not married That Woman- and since when was *she* a friend of the Campbells?' Divining that Nannie referred to Margaret this time, Isobel shook her head. For as long as she could recall Margaret had been there at Scarborough, older and plainer than her father, but a helpmeet to him withal. The gossip went that Margaret Young had been on her last prayers and Whitaker Jarvis deeply in debt when they married, but the prophets of gloom were wrong and it was a very successful union.

After ten years of Margaret's capable management the Scarborough mortgage was half paid off despite the universal hard times, and Hector Campbell had ceased to make his regular visits of inspection. Isobel remembered that she had been sorry about that, for Hector always brought his boy John when he came to visit. Officially, John came to play with Winston, but Winston pronounced him a snivelling little milksop and so Isobel had been the beneficiary of his company. Winston never wanted to play with her, either, and it was pleasant to find someone who did. To be sure, John was a few months her junior, but what did that matter? She had liked his slow smile and pleasant manners.

She saw Hector Campbell sporadically through her childhood, and had always been in awe of him. He spoke so loudly and used such strange words that she didn't always understand him. He told her she was a bonnie wee lassie and informed Winston that he was a sleekit, scrawndy haggis and needed a "guid skelping". Isobel had not understood that at all, but the words pleased her so she repeated them to Margaret. Papa had taken offence and told Mr Campbell his children were his own concern. Mr Campbell ceased to visit Scarborough so often after that, and Isobel lost John Campbell's company. She had rarely seen Hector since then, and she had never seen John to talk to until the occasion of his father's funeral, a little over a year ago.

The funeral was a large affair. It seemed that Hector Campbell when dead had more friends than he had ever had alive, and for the first time in her life, Isobel visited Glen Heather House. Mrs Campbell was composed but somehow extinguished, and Isobel felt awkward approaching her. She felt awkward with John, too, but it would have seemed wrong to have gone home with Margaret and not said something to her old playfellow.

John was dressed in black, with mourning bands on his crisp white shirtsleeves, and Isobel was struck by how grown up he looked. At nineteen, he had not achieved the height and breadth of his father, and never would. He had the dark Campbell colouring, with black silky hair, and narrow grey eyes, but his features and expression were his mother's. Agnes Campbell was a lovely woman in a fine-drawn fashion, and John was very like her. His younger brothers, Hector, Edward and Jamie, were more like their father; big boys with still faces and pugnacious jaws.

John and his mother received mourners for the funeral meal, and Isobel felt the touch of his gloved hand long after she had passed by and begun to sip tea and try to eat a sponge finger. She looked up from this exercise to see John approaching her. Isobel murmured correct regrets, but John cut her off with a gesture.

'It was good of you to come, Miss Jarvis.'

Isobel felt her heart twisting painfully and was suddenly near tears. It was not that she had been so very fond of Hector Campbell, but funerals were tragic and poor John looked drawn and exhausted.

'Oh Johnny,' she said, the childhood name slipping out unguarded, 'I am so very sorry. Your father was so... so...' Words failed her and after a moment she muttered; 'I can scarcely imagine him gone.'

John smiled very slightly. 'My father had that effect on people, Issa. I keep thinking even now I'll feel his hand on my shoulder or his boot on my backside – I do beg your pardon!' Poor John had flushed hotly, his very ears glowing red. He had been turning away when the Campbell solicitor cleared his throat and informed the gathering in suitably funereal tones that it was time to read the will. Most of the guests took their leave then, and Isobel went home with Margaret and Winston, leaving her father to enter the office at Glen Heather.

Hector Campbell's will was the beginning of it all, thought Isobel as she adjusted her veil. It had been a highly individual document. Even knowing Hector as little as she had she could imagine the way he would have browbeaten the eldest Mr Bertram into drawing it up exactly as he ordered. There were a number of strange or eccentric bequests. He bequeathed to his wife Ness the crimson heath (whatever that had meant) and the portrait that hung in the hall of Glen Heather as well as enough money to keep her for the rest of her life. To his son John he left the property of Glen Heather, free and unencumbered, with the proviso that the land itself must never be sold but held in trust for the male heirs of the Campbells in perpetuity. The other proviso was that John must marry and that his wedding must take place before John's twenty-fifth birthday and result in an heir within five years after that.

Otherwise, the property would pass to John's brother Hector Campbell and *his* male heirs. Failing Hector, it would go to Edward and his heirs and, finally, to James.

The other Campbell children were provided for, and a few small and rather ironic bequests had been made to sundry folk of the district, including Mrs Theodora Bruning, old George Ward and Dick Bruning, for unspecified services. A sprig of crimson heath and a rawhide whip had been left to one James Galbraith of Sydney Town, but the greatest bombshell in Hector Campbell's armoury was reserved for Isobel's father. The balance of the mortgage owing on Scarborough was to be waived, on the condition that a wedding took place between Isobel Whitaker Jarvis and John McCleod Campbell.

What an uproar that had caused! Isobel's father almost tied himself in knots, fighting indignation and temptation in equal parts. It had taken a visit from Ness Campbell and a pale, embarrassed, John to calm him sufficiently for the question to be discussed at all. Isobel had been excluded from the gathering, but Winston was present, and provided a caustic account to her afterwards, which had been softened and supplemented by John.

'But why, *why*?' Margaret had demanded. 'Did he not despise us all at Scarborough?'

'Hector didna despise you, Mistress Jarvis,' Ness Campbell had said in her soft Scottish voice. 'Didna he tell you he liked it fine for Scarborough to continue under its master? And he always did say yon Isobel was a lassie after his own heart.'

'And how do *you* feel about this, Mrs Campbell?' Whitaker Jarvis had asked. 'Do you think Isobel a suitable match for your son?'

'If she is the lassie her mother was, I couldna look for better,' said Ness warmly. 'O' course, she is your daughter also, forby...'

Whitaker had flushed angrily at that, but it was left to John to make the final suggestion. 'Why not consult Miss Jarvis?' he said, and his mother had turned to him with a warm smile.

'Aye, Jock, we should leave i' to the two o' you. You are the ones who must bed together.'

There had been an outcry from Margaret at this speech, but it was finally settled that as soon as a suitable period of time had passed, John should pay his addresses to Isobel.

This conversation Winston had obediently repeated to his sister, assuring her of his own support for the match.

'Why should it matter to you whether or not I marry John Campbell?' Isobel had asked curiously, and Winston blinked at her as if the answer were self-evident. A chance to see Scarborough unencumbered? How could she be so selfish as to pass it by? Her father had added his persuasions, and to her astonishment Margaret suggested she'd not get a better offer.

'Margaret, I thought you did not like Mrs Campbell?' Isobel had said curiously.

Margaret's thin face had flushed. 'Oh, as to that- we have never been intimate, I confess, but there is no real harm in her.'

'John is very like her,' Isobel said, 'and nothing like his father.'

'Hmm,' Margaret had said and turned the conversation to other things.

Such friends as Isobel consulted had been frankly envious. To marry a young gentleman of impeccable manners and great wealth, and to be mistress of Glen Heather! How could Isobel contemplate turning down such a chance?

'And Mr Campbell is an excellent dancer, Issy,' her friend Gwynneth O'Hara had opined. 'He stood up with me at the May Day Ball last year and I declare, if I were not devoted to Winston I would have been half in love with him for weeks!'

'Then perhaps you should marry him instead of my brother!' Isobel said tartly, but Gwynneth shrugged and said she was promised to Winston. 'Of course, John is a little young...' she had added thoughtfully. Isobel, conscious that she had passed her twentieth birthday while John was still nineteen, sucked in her lip. 'At any rate,' Gwynnie said lightly, 'if you marry John, you will not be left a young widow, unlike his poor mama.'

And so, by degrees, it had become an accepted thing. John came while still in half-mourning to pay his addresses, and was very formal and correct. It had been out of the question that they should attend balls or parties, but John took her driving, and they drank tea together in the parlour of Glen Heather. During these occasions they were chaperoned by Ness Campbell. Isobel had been nervous, aware that Mrs Campbell was assessing her character at these times. The white bird they called McCleod was usually perched on a stand by the window. This bird made her nervous as well, for it always erected its crest and hissed at her with an open beak until John gave it a slice of apple to devour. Even then it kept one beady eye trained on her. She had been mildly alarmed on one occasion when John had been called away by the Glen Heather foreman, Mr Harkins, leaving her to converse with Ness.

John's mother was still in blacks, but she seemed to have regained her serenity, and after a few moments she smiled at Isobel.

'Mistress Jarvis, you need not fear I shall be underfoot when you are wed to Jock,' she said softly. 'I recall gey well how your mother hated living wi' auld Mistress Jarvis.'

'But Mrs Campbell, this is your home before mine.'

'Aye, so I would feel. And so I shall go to my brother in New Zealand for a wee while. He has written years ago to ask, but I never would go wi' Hector alive.'

'But – you love Glen Heather!' Isobel had protested.

'Aye,' Ness had said sadly. 'That I do. And I ken fine I couldna stand by while you ha' the ordering o' things. And so I shall go, and take the bairns wi' me.' She sighed and moved restlessly over to the window. 'I canna go on here. Wi'out Hector, I canna go on. My Jock is a good laddie, Mistress Jarvis, but Hector was aye hard on him. He must learn to stand tall on his own account, wi'out Jamie and Edward and young Hector forever behind his heels. There! I ha' said my piece, and I hope you dinna take it amiss that I must go.'

John had come back then, and Ness Campbell relapsed into silence.

And now it was Isobel's wedding day.

She dismissed Nannie Goodridge and spent a few minutes in contemplation. She should have been dwelling sentimentally on the union to come, or thinking of her mother, or saying her prayers, but nothing came to mind. Sighing, Isobel drew on her gloves, examined her reflection one last time in the pier glass, and moved onto the landing. For the last time she walked down the stairs of Scarborough. But that was foolishness, for she was sure she would come back often. John would not be a harsh husband, and so far as she could see her life would not change a great deal. She would still see her papa and Winston, Nannie and Margaret, and her maid Emma would accompany her to Glen Heather. Of course the wedding need not have been yet. John was only twenty, but Isobel herself was twenty-one. The mortgage repayments could cease from the day of the wedding, the betrothal had been formally announced, and the banns called in Mersey, so there seemed little sense in waiting.

***

The wedding took place in the drawing room at Scarborough. Since the Campbells were only just out of mourning, it was a quiet affair, with fewer than forty people present. It seemed odd to Ness that old Reverend Ende, who had buried Hector, should be solemnising the marriage of his son. Before the ceremony could proceed, she handed her white heather brooch to Isobel.

'My Granny McCleod's man had this made for her when they were wed,' she said. 'I'd like fine for you to wear it for your wedding.'

Ness wondered if the girl would be embarrassed, for the brooch had been old-fashioned when Ness was young, but instead Isobel smiled and pinned it to the breast of her gown.

'Aye, that's bonnie,' said Ness, nodding. She took Isobel's hands and reached up to kiss her on the cheek. 'I hope you will be as happy wi' Jock as I was wi' my Hector,' she said quietly. 'But if things seem gey hard to you – remember – the crimson heath still grows on the brae.'

The thought of the heath brought the tears that were never far away, but she was determined to smile for her son's wedding day. Hector would have been delighted, she thought, that folk had gathered to do his bidding one more time. Now it remained only for Isobel to produce a son and the future the Campbells of Glen Heather would be assured.

***

Isobel often tried to remember her wedding in after years, but all she could ever recall was snatches. Her father's face as he saw her wearing Eliza's wedding veil. Ness Campbell's luminous eyes. The younger Campbell boys, like as a row of peas in their pod. The impressive side-whiskers worn by the minister. John's cold hands as he slid the ring into place on her finger.

Absurdly, one of Nannie Goodridge's maxims chattered in her mind as the ring was eased into place. *Cold hand, warm heart, gold ring, never part.* And then, she supposed, they were man and wife. And she still felt as detached as she had before.

There was a wedding cake to cut, advice to be listened to, and finally they were away. It would have been inappropriate if they had taken a wedding tour, so it had been decided they would go straight home to Glen Heather.

Decided by whom? Nobody asked *Isobel's* opinion. She thought it would have been more of an occasion if they could have seen the sights of Launceston, or even paid a visit to Hobart Town and had their images made at one of the new photographic studios. And surely a wedding *ought* to be an occasion? The gown, the ring, the flowers and the cake, were all simply symbols of the change wrought in her life. She put on the wedding gown as Isobel Jarvis, and she was helped out of it as Isobel Campbell. Isobel Jarvis arranged the flowers in the parlour, while Isobel Campbell cut the cake. It was all very odd, to be sure.

The wedding night was very odd as well. John was quiet as they drove back to Glen Heather, alone except for a silent groom. Isobel, still struck by the ordinariness of it all, attempted to converse, but her husband seemed abstracted. He smiled at her once or twice, but that was all.

'Johnny-' began Isobel at last, and then stopped in confusion. 'Oh dear, I never thought. Would you rather I called you "Jock" as your mama does?'

John roused himself. 'Whatever you please, Issy. Isobel? Or is it Bel?'

'Issy and Johnny,' said Isobel slowly. 'No, we cannot. We are not children any more. It must be Isobel and John, I think, unless you prefer that I address you at all times as "Mr Campbell"?'

'Good lord no!' said John hastily. '"Mr Campbell" was my father.'

'"John", then.'

'And "Isobel".'

With this settled, they arrived at Glen Heather House. The lamps were lit in welcome, but it seemed very quiet.

'Mother and the laddies are staying in Mersey for a time with Mrs Bruning,' said John, and blushed. 'They thought- I thought you would prefer it.' He helped Isobel out of the carriage. The groom drove away to the stables and they looked at one another uneasily. 'Have you ever been in a situation when you dinna ken what to do?' asked John finally.

'Yes,' said Isobel. 'Especially now.' She saw John's lips twitch in the moonlight, and smiled in response.

'I think I should carry you over the threshold,' said John, but Isobel did not want to go into the house. Not just like that.

'Could we walk a little first?' she asked. 'It is not so cold, tonight.'

'Why not?' John sounded relieved, and Isobel wondered why. It was a bride's right to be nervous, but the bridegroom should have been champing at the bit to do whatever bridegrooms did do with their brides. Margaret had tried to explain it, but her explanation had been so elliptical that Isobel remained confused. It sounded embarrassing and very odd and John did not seem to be champing, so perhaps he was confused as well. She didn't know him well enough to be sure. And that seemed odd too, because they had been very good friends when they were children.

'Do you remember the dog, John?' she said slowly as he took her arm and they began to walk up the hill.

'Auld Jasper.' She could hear the smile in his voice, and his accent had broadened as it did when he forgot to guard his words.

'Yes. Poor old Jasper. He belonged to Fahey. You do recall Fahey?'

'My father used to call him that "sleekit Irishman". But then, he used to call *your* father a "bloody Sassenach".'

'Well,' said Isobel fairly, 'my father used to call *yours* a- er- "a deranged Scotchman".'

'Aye, well, he was not so far wrong at that,' said John pensively. 'But aye, I recall Fahey. He kept auld Jasper tied in the byre and you let him loose and cried when you couldna catch him again.'

'You helped me and my father thought it was you who let him loose.'

'Aye. I got a good skelping for that when I got home.'

'I never knew that.'

'No, I doubt you did.'

His smile was still slow, and suddenly the ordinariness fell away. Her heart gave an odd thud of excitement. 'Perhaps I owe you something for that,' she said.

'Aye, perhaps you do.' John put his arms around her and kissed her gently. 'I think I shall like being married to you,' he observed, 'even if it was the auld man's idea.'

'Yes. We only did do it to please other people.'

'Did we now?' said John. 'I canna quite agree wi' that.'

Isobel counted that moment on the hill overlooking Glen Heather as the true beginning of her married life. It cheered her wonderfully to know that John had not been coerced into the wedding, and she found his grave exterior concealed a good deal of playfulness. He was subdued in the company of gentry or servants, but when they reached their bedchamber at night, he took off solemnity with his outer garments.

***

That first night, John left Isobel with Emma to undress while he took a turn outside. He returned to find her in the unfamiliar bed with the coverlet pulled up to her chin. They eyed one another warily in the candlelight, and then Isobel said; 'I am to sleep in here, John? You did not expect me to go to the guest chamber?' Her voice sounded tart in her ears, and to her relief, John smiled.

'Aye, in here is fine. This is new to me too, Isobel.'

'So I should hope!'

'No, no' that. Well, it is, but I meant the room itself. I'm no' used to sleeping in the master bedroom, but my mother says it is mine by right.'

He went into the small dressing room next door, and emerged clad in a nightshirt. Isobel scarcely knew where to look, but John turned back the coverlet and climbed in beside her. He blew out the candle and lay down.

Isobel held her breath as the mattress settled. She had not shared a bed since childhood. She could hear John moving about, and could not restrain a squeak of shock as his elbow encountered her arm.

'I'm sorry- did I hurt you?'

'No,' she said.

'I willna if I can help it,' he said.

'No.' Isobel swallowed. 'Of course not.' The John she had known as a child had always been gentle.

'We could just sleep the night, if you prefer,' said John.

After Margaret's fumbled explanations, Isobel thought she probably would prefer it, but the mystery could not be put off forever. 'No,' she said again. She raised one hand and put it timidly on his arm. 'John?'

'Aye?'

'I'm not sure what is supposed to happen, but- but I'm willing to try.'

She thought at first that he wasn't going to answer, but he moved again, putting his arm over her body and gently gathering her towards him. Isobel accepted an embrace that seemed familiar enough from dancing, but John pulled her closer still, and kissed her. His lips brushed her mouth and then her jaw, and trailed off down to the side of her neck. Isobel stiffened as his hands slid lower and stroked her lower back, but then John pursed his lips and blew heartily against her throat. It was so unexpected that Isobel found herself lapsing into giggles.

'Oh, that tickles!' she gasped.

John chuckled, and did it again, then hugged her. 'I've been wanting to do that so long,' he murmured, 'but was never sure you wouldna slap me for my trouble!'

'Oh.' Isobel squirmed. Her interview with Margaret had not covered anything like this. Still, if this was the way things should be-

She had tucked her chin down to preserve her throat, but now she turned her lips to John. She meant to blow at him, but instead her mouth brushed his. His arms tightened, and he kissed her again, much less gently than before. Isobel felt her heartbeat pick up, but she was not afraid. Even when John's hands closed hard on her hips and his legs tangled with hers in a confusion of cloth she was aware only of the unexpected pleasure his caresses were giving her. She found herself gasping against his mouth, and heard him gasp as well before he gently touched her tongue with his.

'John… please-' she found she was shaking, but when he drew away she moved closer. 'Please-' She wasn't sure quite what she was asking, but John pulled at the tangle of cloth so their bare limbs were able to meet. After that, things became stranger still.

'I willna hurt you if I can help,' whispered John, but Isobel was scarcely aware of what he was saying. Her body seemed to have taken over from both mind and modesty, and she heard herself gasping as if she had run a long way.

He did hurt her a little, but the pain, brief and burning, soon faded. John, too, seemed overtaken by events, and after a few moments he cried out and slumped against her.

They lay in silence for a few seconds more, and then John disentangled them. He set the bedclothes to rights and drew Isobel back into his arms. His face, when he leaned it to hers, was damp with exertion.

'Aye,' he said rather gloomily. 'I made a great mull o' that, did I no?'

'How would I know?' said Isobel.

'Aye well- there is that. Did I hurt you?'

'Not much. And it doesn't hurt now. Only-' She winced, feeling uneasy. She wanted, no *needed*, to be closer to him. 'John?'

'Hmm?' Incredibly, he sounded sleepy.

Isobel sighed. 'Goodnight,' she ventured.

'Goodnight.' John yawned, and his arms slackened for a moment. 'It will be better next time,' he murmured. Then he kissed her cheek and settled beside her to sleep.

Isobel lay wakeful for a while, trying to sort out exactly what had happened. Had that been the mysterious congress that would result in an heir? She felt oddly hollow, but John had been kind, and she could not expect protestations of love and devotion. Sighing, she closed her eyes.

***

She woke while it was still dark, unable for a moment to remember where she was. Then she became aware of the warmth from another body in the bed, and of the faint, regular sound of breathing.

That was it, then. She was married. This was her husband, and this was the way she would be waking from now on. She listened to the soft breaths and realised, suddenly, that the tempo had changed and that John was awake. She reached out a tentative hand and touched his shoulder, and he pulled her close, pressing his face against her breast.

'Oh, Isobel.' His breath came warmly through the thin cambric, and she felt the uneasy excitement building again. She put her arms about his shoulders, holding his face against her, but he moved away and she felt his fingers brushing the ribbons at the neck of her gown.

'Och, you're wrapped up like a parcel, Mistress Campbell,' he complained, and then murmured with satisfaction as the ribbons came loose. Isobel might have protested, but then she felt his warm lips on her skin and swallowed a gasp instead.

'Is this- next time?' she asked with difficulty.

'Aye,' said John. 'Aye, it is. Let me feel you.' His hands slid under the nightgown and he stroked her thighs. Isobel went still with shock, and then, gradually, her body took over again.

***

After the first few nights, he asked her shyly if she would object if he dispensed with his nightshirt.

Isobel, who was brushing her hair before the glass, put aside the brush and thought about it. 'Not if you wish to do so,' she said.

John pulled the voluminous garment over his head and dropped it on the floor with obvious relief. Then he lay looking up at her. 'O' course if you were wishfu' to do the same I wouldna forbid it,' he said.

Isobel wavered. She knew Margaret would be very much shocked. She knew Nannie Goodridge would fear a chill or an inflammation of the lungs. Then she shrugged. After all, Margaret and Nannie were not there, and John was. And he had touched her all over already, so what difference could a layer of cambric make? She blew out the candle, slid off her nightgown and dived under the blankets where John gathered her against him.

'I like this fine!' he said gleefully, and tickled her until she almost fell out of the bed.

At such times she remembered how young he really was, despite the outward trappings of maturity. They fell asleep curled up together with her head on his shoulder, and in the morning it was a scramble to make themselves decent before Emma brought in the hot water. There were quite a few such disconcerting moments, but on the whole Isobel decided she liked being married very much.

CHAPTER 22

Ness Campbell and her sons came home a week after the wedding, and spent a few days at Glen Heather before embarking on the voyage to New Zealand. Isobel greeted them warmly, but she was still a little awkward at the thought that she was dispossessing John's mother as lady of the house. She suggested that Ness might change her mind and stay on, but was relieved when the offer was refused. It was not that Ness was a difficult person to live with- in fact, she was so like her son that Isobel was disposed to love her- but the rivalry between John and his brother Hector was palpable. There was no active contention, but young Hector was bigger and stronger than John, and at eighteen he made it obvious that he envied his brother not only his position in the family and his ownership of Glen Heather, but also his bride. It made Isobel uncomfortable to find Hector's gaze upon her. He had grey eyes, like John's, but while John's were lit with an inner warmth his brother's were opaque as slate.

The younger brothers, Edward and Jamie, were less alarming. At sixteen and fourteen they were already big lads, both as tall as John. Isobel thought she might have become fond of Jamie in time, for he had a warm smile and a merry whistle, but he dropped his gaze whenever she spoke to him. It was very difficult. Isobel tried to remember the house had been the Campbells' home long before her own, but it was a relief when Ness and her sons left on the long journey to New Zealand.

'I canna say how long we will be,' said Ness. 'Much depends on Donal. He may have changed a deal since I knew him at home. The dear knows how he ever had my direction to write, unless he mended his bridges wi' Phemie. I wrote home when Jock was born, but she never did reply.' She lifted her chin as if at some bitter memory. 'And now Donal is a man o' property near Dunedin and he bids us to stay wi' himself and his wife- they ha' no bairns o' themselves.'

John wanted to escort his mother and brothers to the port, but this Ness declined in favour of a simple leave-taking at Glen Heather. Isobel stood awkwardly by, clasping hands with the three boys in turn. She was touched when young Jamie, blushing vividly, reached over and kissed her cheek before vaulting into the carriage beside Edward and the scowling Hector. Isobel wondered if his stony face hid resentment or sharp unhappiness, but surely young Hector must have accepted his secondary place in the family long ago...

Ness had put off her blacks for half-mourning of grey, and in her bonnet she wore an unexpected touch of crimson ribbon. Seeing Isobel's surprise, she smiled slightly and raised her hand to touch the trim. 'Och, Hector liked fine to see me in crimson, so I wear it to please him still.' She kissed Isobel on the cheek and turned to her son. 'Goodbye, Jock, lad,' she said with a smile. 'Keep Glen Heather in good heart, and write to me in Dunedin if you ha' news to tell.' She hugged John and allowed him to help her into the carriage. Young Hector snapped the reins and the horses trotted down the drive and out of sight.

'Well, John,' said Isobel uncertainly, 'it is sad to see your mama leave.'

'Aye, but Glen Heather has a new mistress now and Mother kens fine where her duty lies. Hector and the others canna stay now, working ground that canna be theirs- unless...'

'Hush!' said Isobel superstitiously.

John looked shaken himself. 'They need a place for themselves,' he amended. 'Hector is a man grown and Eddie and Jamie are big lads. One o' them should have been my father's heir, you know. They would have been better suited, and so would he.'

'Nonsense,' said Isobel robustly. 'You will manage perfectly well, John. You may even win over some of the folk your father- well, he was not the most amiable of men.'

'Perhaps I may,' said John wearily. He took her hand. 'Well, Mistress Campbell, we ha' the place to ourselves again.'

'Except for Emma, Fanny, Mrs Baker and Perry,' said Isobel wryly. 'Not to speak of McCleod.'

John had ostensibly been brought up to hold the reins of Glen Heather, but while his flamboyant father was alive, he had little chance to try his authority. In later years Hector had hired an overseer whose ways he could support, a man as meek as his master had been pugnacious. John retained Harkins' services, but Isobel knew it was a thorn in his side.

'The man seems incapable of making a decision without changing his mind half a dozen times,' he told Isobel one evening as spring came on. 'The sheep should have fetched in for lambing by now.'

'Can they not have their lambs where they are?' asked Isobel. She could not recall her father taking much interest in where his sheep were at any given time; his prime horses had consumed his attention for the past ten years. These had not brought quite such a profit as he hoped, but he had sold some of the timber from the slopes of Scarborough and that brought in some extra funds.

'Father had the fold made for a dry run, but I think it ideal for lambing,' said John. 'It's sheltered and smaller than the enclosure.'

'Then why not have Harkins take the sheep there?' asked Isobel.

'He willna,' said John. 'He says today was too windy, tomorrow will rain, the auld dog is too idle, the new dog too sharp; och! the job will never be done unless I do it myself.'

'Then do it now,' said Isobel.

'Harkins has gone home. I couldna stand his haivering, and it is a job for two men.'

'Why not a man and a woman?' said Isobel. 'You have a pony your mama used to ride, have you not?'

'Aye- the Heron.'

'Then I shall be your shepherd,' said Isobel. 'Come John, it will be an adventure.'

'Aye.' John sounded dubious, but the temptation of presenting the finished task to Harkins in the morning was great. Almost like mischievous children the master and mistress of Glen Heather left the house by the back entrance, and John saddled his Thunder and his mother's Grey Heron. He released both dogs from the kennels and helped Isobel into the saddle. She arranged the skirts of her habit and nudged the pony forward.

'Shall us go to work, master?' she asked, touching an imaginary forelock.

'Aye,' said John with a grin.

The ewes resented the moonlit disturbance, but were too heavily in lamb to make effective protest. With the help of the dogs, Isobel and John were able to flank the flock and keep it headed right, and John rode ahead to guide it in through the gap leading to the fold.

'Do I make a good shepherd, John?' asked Isobel a little archly as he closed the gap with a hurdle.

'Aye- the best. Did you ride round the sheep often wi' your father?'

'No, Margaret and Papa did not consider it a fitting occupation for a lady,' said Isobel. 'It was seemly for me to learn to bake and brew and sew a seam, but I know little of sheep, although they formed the foundation of Scarborough.'

'We depend too greatly on sheep in the colonies,' said John. 'There was a great downturn in the wool trade some years ago, and another may come at any time. Had Glen Heather depended on wool sheep alone we might have been ruined, but my father had cattle and other interests besides, and he had begun outcrosses of the Merino wi' the Leicester- they are better suited to the cold and give better mutton besides.' He sighed. 'Father had a lucky touch. I doubt I have the same, but perhaps we can make our own luck.'

'Why not?' said Isobel, buoyed with success. 'If I can move sheep, why should I not learn how to do other things as well? John, you could dismiss Harkins and work with me instead.'

'All this from two hours of moving sheep forby!' marvelled John. 'What a verra masterful woman I ha' wed!'

'And what a wonderfully flexible man I have wed!' said Isobel slyly. 'Will you have me work with you, John?'

'Aye, until you ha' other calls on your time.'

Isobel sucked in her lip. She was not often embarrassed in John's company, but "other calls" could mean only one thing; an heir for Glen Heather.

John did not dismiss Harkins, but gradually reduced the man's duties while taking all the major decisions himself. Isobel fought down any resistance by simply saddling Grey Heron and following him to the fold when lambing began. To Harkins' horror, she helped with difficult births and took cold limp lambs home on the front of her saddle to be warmed and fed with milk wrung from soaked flannel. When a flume was washed away in a spring flush and the water in the lower enclosure failed, she put on her oldest riding habit, hacked off the train with Emma's shears and borrowed Jamie's discarded boots to climb the mountain with John. She was so enchanted with the experience and with the view from the top that John promised to build a slab hut at a halfway point so they could spend a night on the mountain in summer.

'My father could build a hut in a day or two,' he said. 'I cannot match his strength, but it need only be a wee hut.'

'Oh yes, John!' cried Isobel. 'I would so love to have our own place, away from Emma- and McCleod.'

'Och, McCleod is well enough,' said John.

'Perhaps,' said Isobel with dignity, 'but he has a coarse tongue. Why, he called me a sleekit besom today!'

John built the hut soon after, and Isobel helped. It took much longer than they expected and dark was closing in before John finished pegging bark for a roof.

'Aye, I'm not the man my father was,' he said, kicking the structure suspiciously. Isobel was a little tired, so they decided to return home in the morning. It was a cool night, but John made them a couch of branches and they covered themselves with his riding coat and Isobel's cloak. John looked a little thoughtful in the morning and opined that cherry branches would never replace goose-feathers or even horsehair or straw for a mattress and Isobel did not feel like arguing. She blinked, groaned and sat up cautiously.

'Bel – are you faint?' asked John putting his arm around her protectively.

'No,' said Isobel, tight-lipped. 'Let me up John- I am going to be ill.'

She was extremely ill, cold and sweating, and unable to drink the tea John brewed from their few supplies, but as the morning brightened the malaise wore off and she was able to descend from the mountain with equanimity. She was inclined to pass off the faintness as the result of a night spent unprepared on the mountain, but Emma exclaimed over her heavy eyes and lack of appetite at dinnertime, and the next morning she woke again to illness and misery. When it happened a third time, she realised she was going to have a child.

So soon! She had been married barely three months, and there was so much to do, and so many places left to explore in John's company. As soon as she felt able to face a teacup and a slice of dry bread, she had Emma help her dress. At lunchtime, she informed John of her condition and watched his slow smile dawn.

'Aye, that's bonnie!' he said, and she laughed at his delight before hurrying to the privy to part abruptly with the tea and bread.

Fortunately, the nausea and faintness did not last long, and within a few weeks Isobel felt as well as ever. They planned a journey to Launceston, and went to two dances in Mersey, and Isobel took tea with some of the other ladies of the district. She also resumed her treks about Glen Heather with John, and, when she grew too cumbersome to ride and walk far, she exercised her acute brain by taking over the household accounts from Mrs Baker.

John, seeing her acumen at the task, asked diffidently if she felt equal to facing the general accounts as well.

'Of course!' said Isobel warmly. 'If you think you could trust them to me.'

John smiled at her. 'Och, you need not be careful o' my consequence, Isobel. 'You know fu' well you ken better than me how it goes on.'

'Margaret taught me about figures and accounts,' she said quickly. 'She used to see to such things for the lady whose companion she was before she married Papa.'

'Aye, and I am gey glad she did. But do not tire yourself or the babe.'

'The babe is not tired,' said Isobel precisely. She took his hand and held it against her abdomen. 'You see how he kicks?' John was enchanted, and did not trouble to remove his hand even when Mrs Baker came to discuss the day's menu.

After her marriage, Isobel had intended to make regular visits to Scarborough, but she found herself much too busy at Glen Heather. After she became pregnant, her condition was an excuse to remain at home. When Margaret came to call she seemed shocked at Isobel's lack of tight lacing and haphazard preparations for the child.

'Will you not redecorate the nursery, Issa?'

Isobel looked vaguely at the room where Ness Campbell had cradled her sons. The sandstone was panelled over with timber, and the floor made of polished slate. To be sure it was not a cosy room, but there was a great fireplace and the curtains at the window were a glowing crimson.

'I like it the way it is,' she said decidedly. 'What was good for John is good for his son.'

'Your John was born before this house was even completed!' snapped Margaret. 'He was born in the slab hut over the way where the workman's cottage is now.'

Isobel opened her eyes at her stepmother. 'No. John was born here in Glen Heather House,' she said with certainty. 'His father carried Mistress Campbell here to make it so.'

There had been a slight coolness between the two women after that, and when Whitaker Jarvis arrived to see the young couple a week later, his wife stayed behind at Scarborough. Isobel wondered if she should visit Margaret to make amends, but she had plenty of other things to occupy her mind. There was John, and the account books, the fact that her maid Emma was walking out with the Glen Heather groom, and of course there were always preparations for the coming child. She had time and plenty to heal the slight rift over the cradle of her baby when it arrived.

Then, early in March, one of the Scarborough horses trotted down the drive.

'If that is Papa,' said Isobel, 'tell him I shall come as soon as I change my gown. Oh, why cannot he and Margaret send word of their coming? I feel so ugly just at present.' John laughed and kissed her, and then went to intercept the caller, but when he returned, the laughter was quite wiped away.

'John, what is it?' asked Isobel quickly. Her heart gave a painful lurch and she sat down. 'Tell me, quickly. Is it bad news?'

'Bad news, Bel!' John's voice broke. 'Aye, that it is. The worst.'

'Your mama- the boys?' faltered Isobel.

'No.' John swallowed. 'It was a carriage accident. Your brother has come to see you- shall I have him come in?'

'Yes- yes,' said Isobel wildly. 'Oh is it Margaret? Papa? Oh- not- not both of them?'

John's face gave her the answer even before Winston entered the room.

***

Since their wedding, John had come to love Isobel dearly, and to respect her for the qualities he felt he lacked himself. It seemed strange that a lassie should be so strong, and he felt her the equal of anything. Even when racked with morning sickness she had managed to turn aside her discomfort with a flippant comment and a sigh of regret that her social position would hardly allow the use of rouge to ease her sallow complexion. Now, for the first time, he saw her crushed and diminished and was powerless to help.

At least, he thought wryly as Isobel sobbed in his arms after the funeral at Scarborough, his wife could mourn her parents without guilt. When his own father passed on he'd been unable to balance a sense of relief that he need no longer tread warily along with a great regret that he had not, somehow, achieved a closer relationship with Hector. But Isobel could have no such regrets! In supposing this, he soon found himself wrong, for his wife blamed herself for being inhospitable when Margaret came to visit.

'Oh, if I had been kinder! If I had made it up to her!' she wept and

John, at a loss, could only beg her not to cry so much that she injured the child. It seemed a lame enough thing to say, but he had by accident hit upon the very subject needed to give her thoughts a more positive turn. 'Our child will love us, will he not?' she said pleadingly. 'We will never push him to be something he is not... we will never force our ideals on him...'

'Amen to that,' said John feelingly.

'Nor leave him to the servants to raise...'

She fell asleep abruptly, and John lay beside her and watched the candle burn down. The melting wax made fantastic shapes and he shivered. Hector Campbell and Whitaker Jarvis had been rivals-enemies, almost. Whitaker had been distantly civil since the wedding, but how would Scarborough and Glen Heather go on now it was John and Winston in control? They had never been friends, but perhaps the new era would be better than the old. Perhaps after Winston was married to Gwynneth O'Hara he would be softer, less willing to take offence.

The candle guttered out, and John tucked his wife more closely against him. Her body bulged beneath the nightgown and he treasured the feeling of holding wife and child together in his arms. His old family had broken when Hector died, but a new one was underway, and when the child was born he and Isobel would ride around the sheep again, climb the mountain again, and spend stolen nights in the half-way hut. I *must* take bedding up the mountain, thought John, and slept.

CHAPTER 23

The maid was new and inexperienced, or else she would have known to say correctly that the mistress was not at home. Unfortunately, it was a Saturday evening, the master had gone to Mersey and most of the servants had been given leave to attend the wedding of Emma and her man Sim Perry. It was a wedding of necessity, though a happy one withal, but it left Jennie Comfrey with no one to ask for advice. And the gentleman requesting an interview with Mistress Campbell was nicely spoken, distinguished, and quite old, and claimed to be a family friend besides, so surely (she thought) there could be no harm in letting him in.

Smiling nervously, Jennie led the gentleman into the parlour, where Isobel was working over accounts. With her baby's birth quite imminent, she was wrapped for comfort in Ness' old plaid over a loose mourning gown, and looked up enquiringly at the sound of voices. She thought the visitor must be Winston, for who else would arrive unannounced at this time? *Surely* the girl Jennie would have had the sense to deny her to any stranger. She knew she and John were considered unconventional by their peers, but to greet guests in her condition, still in mourning and dressed as she was- no, that was impossible, and Jennie must know that.

She half rose to greet her brother, but the person who entered in Jennie's wake was a stranger. And such a stranger! Instead of awaiting Jennie's announcement, as was proper, he was coming forward into the room, with a flat package tucked under one arm.

'Oh, my dear, I cannot say how sorry I was to hear of your husband's passing!' he exclaimed.

There was a hint of Scotland in his voice, and Isobel, shocked and annoyed, wondered who he could be. It could not be John's step-uncle Donal Kirkbride, for Ness and the boys gone to *him*. And as for regretting her husband's passing, that was ridiculous. She had seen John an hour before.

'Sir, you are mistaken,' she said with hauteur.

At the sound of her voice he halted, groping in the pocket of his driving coat. Isobel started, but he removed nothing more alarming than a pair of spectacles, which he hooked on awkwardly with his free hand.

'Oh dear, I *do* beg your pardon, ma'am,' he said with obvious chagrin. 'I have come to pay my respects to Mistress Campbell upon the passing of her husband, but I see I am addressing quite the wrong lady.'

'I am Mrs Campbell,' said Isobel. 'And my husband is very much alive, thank you.'

'I was looking for Mistress Agnes Campbell,' said the gentleman.

'Ma'am, should I show the gentleman out?' asked the flustered Jennie.

'It is a little too late for that,' said Isobel tartly. 'Mr...'

'Galbraith,' said her unwelcome guest. 'James Galbraith at your service.'

Isobel's eyes opened a little wider at that, but she answered composedly. 'I am Mrs John Campbell, Mr Galbraith. It is my husband's mother you wished to see, but you are too late.'

Galbraith's myopic gaze took in Isobel's black gown and he looked stricken. 'No,' he said softly. 'Not Ness gone as well-'

'Mrs Campbell has gone to New Zealand to visit her brother,' said Isobel. 'She was well enough when we last heard from her.'

'Thank God for that! I quite thought-'

'I know what you thought, sir,' said Isobel. 'Since you cannot speak with Mr Campbell's mother, may I be of assistance?'

'Perhaps,' said Galbraith. 'May I sit down?'

'Of course, if you will excuse my...' She waved her hand dismissively. 'Jennie, have the goodness to fetch us some tea.'

Galbraith seated himself in one of the upright chairs, propped the package carefully against the arm of it and crossed one booted foot over another. Isobel thought he looked around forty-five, and he had brown, lightly greying hair, and blue eyes magnified enormously by his spectacles. His voice was soft and cultured, and with his faint accent he sounded a little like her husband. So this was the James Galbraith who had painted the portrait of Ness Campbell, and who had fallen out with her husband to such a degree that he had been whipped off the property. And there, on his left cheek, she saw what must be the very scar of that whipping. A shocking and very unwelcome thought intruded, and though she shook it away, it took possession of her mind so she could scarcely bring her attention to what Galbraith was saying. Polite regrets about Hector's death, she thought, and something about a painting, better made late than not at all.

'I beg your pardon,' she said, 'but I cannot quite understand what you mean. When were you last at Glen Heather, Mr Galbraith?'

'Many years ago, Mrs Campbell, perhaps before you were born.' He paused. 'I had the honour to work on the plans of this house.'

'That was less than a year before my husband was born,' she observed. Her mind worked furiously, putting together Nannie's gossip and Margaret's cryptic remarks. Galbraith looked puzzled so she added hurriedly; 'You knew my parents, Mr Galbraith. They were Whitaker and Eliza Jarvis of Scarborough. You painted their portraits as well.'

Understanding dawned in his eyes. 'So, you are Eliza's daughter! She was a lovely lady and we all felt her loss so much. But you would not remember her at all?'

'Through your portrait I feel I know her very well indeed. I thank you for that, Mr Galbraith. You also painted this portrait of my husband's mother, did you not?'

Galbraith glanced up to the portrait above the mantel and smiled reminiscently. 'Aye, that I did.'

'I have often wondered,' said Isobel, 'why there is no comparable portrait of Mr Campbell, and why you never returned to finish the work on Glen Heather.'

'Have you indeed?' said Galbraith. His pleasant expression did not change, but there was a definite edge to his voice. He rose casually to his feet. 'Mrs Campbell, since the lady I have come to visit is not at home, perhaps it would be better if I were to leave you now.' He paused, then added gently; 'It would never do for gossip to begin, would it?'

His mild gaze never left her face, but Isobel blushed furiously. 'Mr Galbraith- I...'

'I think we should leave it at that, do you not, Mrs Campbell?' He stepped forward so Isobel, perforce, had to rise and offer her hand. He held it for a moment in a cool clasp and looked at her closely. 'Dear old Tobias was perfectly correct,' he said inconsequently. 'Reputations are hard to make, easy to break, and gossip never forgets. Good day, Mrs Campbell. I shall see myself out. Give your husband this package with my regards. Since I admired Hector so greatly it seemed the least I could do for his wife and his son.'

He bowed and left her.

A little later Jennie Comfrey came in, carrying a heavy tea tray. 'Here you are, ma'am,' she said.

'Oh, take it away,' said Isobel with something of a snap.

When John returned he found her in a fluster of self-disgust. 'What now, Bel?' he asked, putting his arm around her and patting her bulge. 'Have you detected an error in the accounts? To be sure I made a great many and we have never run aground yet.'

'John, I have been quite hideously rude to Mr Galbraith,' said Isobel, almost weeping.

'Galbraith?' John was at a loss. 'You canna mean the Galbraith who painted my mother?'

'*And* your father,' said Isobel.

'No he dinna. They had some stramash, and to be sure there were few who did not, with my father, and Galbraith left before Glen Heather was ever finished.'

'He did though- oh, *John*! And he brought the portrait for your mama. Look!'

John gave her a last pat and went slowly over to take the portrait and tilt it to the light. 'By God, it's him to a life, the auld bugger!' he said admiringly. 'But this must have been done years ago, Isobel- his hair is still quite black.'

Isobel shivered. 'Mr Galbraith last saw him years ago,' she reminded. 'And oh John, I was so *rude* to him...'

'What did you say?' asked John, fascinated.

'I said- I implied- oh John, you do know there was some- talk- about your mama and Mr Galbraith years ago?'

'Aye, but my father wouldna hear a word against her, ever ... so I have come to the sad conclusion the auld bugger really *was* my father.'

'John!'

John smiled ruefully. 'Had there been any doubt of that- any doubt at *all* in my father's mind, do you think he would ever have made me heir to Glen Heather?'

And that, thought Isobel, eyeing the scowling arrogant face in the portrait as John hung it on the wall next to its mate, was the best argument of all.

***

That winter was a hard one, and it would have dragged interminably for Isobel had it not been for John. He kept her company, talking of his childhood and hers, of the tales of Glen Heather as he had heard them from Ness and, especially, of his plans for the future.

'If we clear the land we must keep it in good heart,' he said once. 'If we cut awa' the trees, we must keep good grass in their place, aye and tend the sheep well. And we must leave trees on the mountain. If we canna do that, we ha' no business to hold this land at all.'

'Would you never chop down trees then, John? Winston plans to clear the rest of Scarborough as soon as he can.'

'I would cut out only those we need for timber, or those that are dangerous on the brae. Too many trees down in this land, Bel, and the water will wash away the soil. Then we'll have nothing but the bare rock and we canna use that. Remember how it is on the brae, where the hut is? The heath and the ferns, the wee trees and the big ones- all grown together like a family. Cut awa' all the fathers and how will the others survive?'

'You are one of the fathers now, John,' said Isobel.

'Aye.' John looked contemplatively at the portrait above the hearth. 'And I can thank the auld bugger with a good will for that! Left to myself I might not have had the sense to wed you!'

Isobel was uneasy all that week and one evening, in the middle of July, eleven months after their winter wedding, she told John apologetically that he would need to fetch the midwife. Emma was feeling ill, so when John returned from Mersey two hours later, it was Jennie Comfrey and Mrs Baker who were doing their best to comfort Isobel. She was crying for John, but the midwife, a stern-visaged woman called Mrs Pullen, thrust him bodily from the room.

'If you must do something, pick some flowers for your wife,' she told him, and closed the door. 'There,' she added in an aside to Mrs Baker, 'that will keep the man from our hair. There are no flowers to be had this time of year. Brace up, Mrs Campbell!' she added as Isobel cried out, 'you have a long night ahead of you so you might as well rest while you can.'

It was a very long night. Long for John, pacing around in the frosty dark, long for Jennie Comfrey, boiling endless hot water and brewing tea no one ever drank, long for Emma, who wanted to help but whose face was so blanched with sickness and the terror of her own coming ordeal that Mrs Pullen sent her off again. It seemed longest of all to Isobel, for Mrs Pullen did not believe in dosing mothers-to-be with laudanum or spirits, and reacted to screams of pain with the unfeeling suggestion that the breath was better kept for pushing when the time came.

The pain was something Isobel had never imagined, a grinding, tearing horror, which screwed itself into her bones and ran white-hot along her lower limbs. Her cries were of despair as well as agony, for she could not see how she was to endure the night.

McCleod the cockatoo was disturbed by the sounds, and reacted by shrieking and raising his yellow crest, beating the air with his wings and creating such a draught in the parlour that Isobel's accounts went swirling across the floor.

'What in the name of God is *that*?' asked Mrs Pullen sternly as Isobel rested between contractions.

'McCleod,' said Isobel, as more shrieks rent the air.

'The master's pet bird, ma'am,' said Mrs Baker.

Mrs Pullen looked outraged and Isobel laughed weakly, but she felt her body gathering itself for another onslaught and the laugh changed to a choked scream.

'Mrs Campbell!' said Mrs Pullen. 'You must show *some* fortitude.'

'You- old- bitch!' gasped Isobel indignantly. 'You wicked old *bitch*!' She sat up and vomited into the basin fetched by Mrs Baker.

'That's more the spirit,' said Mrs Pullen. 'Now use some of that anger to push!'

The pains came quicker, swift as running feet, and Isobel was caught up like a leaf on a flooding river. She lost her sense of time and swirled dangerously, biting her lips and clenching her hands, struggling with the agony that racked her. And then, with a final push that seemed to burst her apart, there was a long wet slither, and the child had arrived.

'My word!' said the midwife admiringly, slapping the minute bottom, 'what a fine big fellow- I declare, this is the biggest baby I have ever birthed!'

Isobel uttered another cry, this time of indignation, and reached out blindly. 'Give him to me!' she demanded, but Mrs Pullen said the child must be cleaned first.

After what she had gone through, it seemed unfair to Isobel that others should enjoy the sight of the child before herself.

Two hours later, Mrs Pullen was drinking tea in the kitchen with Mrs Baker and Jennie. Isobel leaned stealthily out of bed and reached for the swaddled baby. He was hers, after all, and she was burning with a desire to unwrap the shawls and examine him from head to heel. The door opened with equal stealth as she parted the cloths and she looked up defensively, and then burst into tears at the sight of her husband.

'Oh, John- I have had such a *horrid* time!'

John was holding a bunch of flowers, pink, white and crimson heath, and he offered them mutely.

'Oh!' wailed Isobel, 'you must have walked miles to find so much!'

'I couldna do anything else,' said John. 'Oh, Bel, I am so sorry.' He laid the flowers on the night table, looking with interest at the partly unswaddled baby. 'Is this the wee man then?'

'*Wee*!' scolded Isobel. 'Why, Mrs Pullen says he is the biggest babe she has ever seen!'

John opened the curtains. The sun was rising, and light gushed through the window like melted honey. The baby opened slaty blue eyes, yawned crookedly, and sneezed. John took him from Isobel and carried him into the light.

'By God, he's a proper wee Campbell laddie!' he said, and she could hear the jubilation in his voice. 'Bel- he's- he's-'

'He is a wonder, is he not?' said Isobel. She wiped away her tears and lay back, looking lovingly at her husband, as he stood in the sunlight holding his child. The light sparkled and blurred, and she found herself very weary.

'How strange,' she said, 'it is morning and I want to go to sleep. But Mrs Pullen says I am perfectly well.'

John sat down in the chair beside the bed, wrapped the baby securely and held it against his shoulder. 'Bel, you dinna know what this means to me,' he said quietly.

'It means that you keep Glen Heather.'

John looked hurt. 'I never thought o' that!' he protested. 'But you and I and wee Robert- oh, we have such a future, Bel, so much to look forward to-'

'Oh? And who said we were to call him Robert?'

'Had you a better plan?'

Isobel hesitated. Part of her wanted to name the child for her own father, but Whitaker Jarvis was gone, and would never know he had been honoured, and besides, she could leave it to Winston and Gwynneth to keep his name alive in their own family. It seemed unfair to name the child for Hector, given John's ambivalent feelings for his father. And then, why should the baby *not* be Robert? It was a fine name, the name of a great Scots hero, and John wanted it so.

'Robert Campbell is a splendid name,' she said, and smiled.

Afterwards, in the midst of her pain and sorrow, she held on to that memory as to a lifeline. She knew she had given John his heart's desire.

***

August brought heavy rain that year, and the mountainside was greasy with mud. John had been into Mersey to despatch a letter to his mother and brothers. He would not have been human if he had not felt very much the man, for he had just passed his twenty-first birthday, and was not only master of Glen Heather but the father of a fine, legitimate son.

'*The wee laddie looks much as Jamie did as a babe,*' he had written affectionately. '*He is a braw Campbell, and I think Father would have been gey pleased. You know Father and I did not always deal well together, but every morning I thank God he had the thought of wedding me to Isobel. Mother, you have no notion how happy we are, and how the laddie delights us. We would be gey pleased to see you home again whenever you wish- and Mother, it is good to hear Hector settled with Uncle Donal ... Isobel sends love, and so do I – and you will be pleased to know McCleod is prospering finely, thrawn as always.*

Ever your devoted son, Jock.

John was thinking of the letter as he rode Thunder toward the burn. He knew it grieved Ness that he had had such a poor relationship with Hector; and hoped his words would ease her mind. 'And it's true,' he said aloud to the horse. 'I *do* thank the auld bugger.' He thought about Isobel, and realised pleasurably that it was over a month since young Robert's birth. Soon he could return to the master bedroom with his wife. Custom decreed they must sleep apart until the mother recovered from the birth, but John had left his dressing room to spend many illicit hours with Isobel. A fine thing when a pack of women decreed he could not sleep with his own wife!

Smiling at the thought of the small subterfuge they had practised in defiance of Mrs Pullen, Mrs Baker and Nannie Goodridge, John was struck by a desire to be home again. Isobel had abruptly tired of wrappers and shawls and had informed him she expected to be up and formally dressed to greet him that evening.

'I shall put on the amber gown you like so well, and the white heather brooch,' she had said. John scarcely liked to tell her he liked her best when clad in nothing at all, but perhaps if he could reach home a little before she expected him… He glanced at the sky, saw rain was coming on again, and nudged Thunder with his heel.

'Run, laddie,' he urged. 'My lady is waiting!'

Thunder launched himself into a canter through the thickening twilight. As they approached the creek, a native hen dashed squawking from beneath Thunder's hooves. Thunder shied violently, sought vainly to regain his footing on the greasy ground, and fell. John was thrown from the saddle, his head striking one of the sharp knobs of limestone by the creek. Thunder heaved to his feet with a great rattling snort, and, dripping mud and water from belly and side, bolted back towards the stables.

CHAPTER 24

Isobel was out of bed, dressed in the amber silk gown from her trousseau. She felt excited as a girl as she bade the pale Emma to brush her hair up into a new style.

'You see, Emma, I have my waist quite back,' she said, patting the tightly swathed cloth into place. 'I thought it would never come!'

Emma nodded, tight-lipped. She thought it very odd of her mistress to insist upon nursing baby Robert herself, but perhaps after all such activities paid off. Ladies who employed a wet nurse were often plagued with excess flesh for months after delivery. And the child himself, doted upon by both parents and old Nannie Goodridge, was a taking little thing, roaring for sustenance, but otherwise quiet as a pudding. For the first time Emma looked forward to her own child as a person rather than an inconvenient burden.

Her preparations finished, Isobel twirled to admire herself in the glass. She had pressed some of the flowers John brought between two heavy volumes from the library, and now pinned some sprigs of the crimson heath to her breast along with the white heather brooch Ness gave her on her wedding day.

'Do I look fine?' she asked Robert, bending over the crib. 'Does Mama look fine?'

She spun away from crib and mirror and went to the parlour, seating herself so that light from a branch of candles fell becomingly across her face and hair. She knew she had never looked better in her life. Twilight was well advanced, but when Jennie Comfrey came to draw the heavy crimson curtains, Isobel held up her hand.

'Leave them, Jennie, I like to watch the sunset.'

The rain clouds were so low Jennie doubted the sunset would be visible, but it was well known that the mistress liked to watch the master home, so she simply smiled and dipped a curtsey.

'Yes ma'am - and ma'am, shall I have Mrs Baker hold dinner back?'

'That should not be necessary,' said Isobel. 'Mr Campbell will be home before dark.'

She waited for some time, occasionally walking to the window. Her own eyes reflected darkly in the glass, and she wondered what was keeping John. Had old Mr Bruning lured him into the house for a dram to wet the baby's head? She rang for Jennie and said perhaps after all Mrs Baker should be told to keep the dinner.

'Mr Campbell must have been held up in Mersey.'

Jennie vanished and Isobel took up her position at the window once more. Her breasts were beginning to feel uncomfortably full, and if John did not come soon she would have to nurse Robert again. To be sure John always seemed to enjoy watching this exercise, but tonight she wanted to put off the mother and be seen as wife and lover. The thought of suckling the baby brought, as usual, a flush of milk, so she pressed her forearm to her bosom to stem the tide. If she did not take care, the bodice of the amber gown would be stained. She was sucking her lip, wondering what could possibly be keeping John, when she heard the rapid beat of hooves. The horse sped past the house towards the stable yard and Isobel smiled with relief. John was coming home, and she would chide him for riding so fast in the dark. He should have taken the carriage with the lights if he meant to be home so late. Now she must wait until he had given his horse into Perry's hands, and removed the worst of the mud from his breeches.

Once more she summoned Jennie. 'Tell Mrs Baker we shall want dinner in twenty minutes. I hope it has not been spoiled.'

Jennie, who had been privy to Mrs Baker's complaints about the feckless ways of the gentry who ordered intricate dishes and then did not arrive in time to consume them, smiled uneasily. She was on her way back to the kitchen when there was a knock at the front door.

'Pish and tush!' said Jennie, which was what her mother always said when vexed. Since Mr Galbraith's visit she had been very wary about opening the door and preferred to leave it to one of the others, but no one came.

The knocker rapped again, and Jennie hastened to answer. Perhaps after all it was the master- though why he should knock for admittance on his own front door she could not imagine. She smoothed her apron and unlatched the door, schooling her face into the proper blankness required.

'The Mis...' she began and then stared, incensed, at Perry. 'Lawks, Mr Perry, what are you doing here? Emma is still-'

'Never mind Emma, girl,' said Perry urgently. 'I need to see the missus. The master's horse has come back alone, and he's had a fall,

Thunder has.'

Jennie gasped. 'You better go and find him then, Mr Perry.'

'The missus will want to know,' said Perry stubbornly.

'The missus is not to be upset,' hissed Jennie. 'Get Mr Ward and Mr Harkins.'

'Harkins!' Perry went to spit, then thought better of it. 'Mr Harkins will-'

'What is going on here?' Isobel had heard the knocking, and when no one came to tell her who had called so late, she had emerged to find out. Seeing Perry arguing with Jennie on the doorstep she at once came to the conclusion that the groom was looking for his wife, but the apprehensive glances the two servants exchanged told her the matter was more serious than that.

'Well?' she said quickly. 'Can you not tell me? If something is amiss in the yard, you would do better to apply to Mr Campbell. I heard him come home a few minutes ago.'

Perry shuffled his boots. The Campbells had been remarkably forgiving to himself and his Emma, allowing them to marry and to keep their places, and even promising Emma her position after the child was born, but he could still not face Mrs Campbell without feeling as if his boots were too big and his hair full of straw.

'Mr Campbell has not come home,' he blurted.

'But surely I heard his horse?'

'Thunder is back, but not the master. And Thunder's had a fall, he has.'

'Then you must look for him immediately. No, wait, Perry- saddle the Heron. I shall ride out as well. Jennie- you must help me into my riding habit.'

She panted up the stairs with Jennie whimpering in her wake. If anything happened to the mistress as a result of this mad start, Jennie knew who would be blamed.

Divested of her amber gown Isobel dropped it carelessly on the bed. She considered her habit with its myriad tiny buttons and shook her head.

'Jennie, go into the master's dressing room and fetch me a pair of his breeches.' When Jennie did not move immediately, she stamped her foot. 'Hurry, girl! Do not stand gaping like a lackwit!'

She and John were much of a height, but the breeches were too loose around the waist. She dragged a belt around them and put on a

Garibaldi jacket and her boots then ran down the stairs with Nannie Goodridge expostulating behind. She felt shaky after so long in bed, but what else could she do? If John was hurt, she could not endure to wait while others searched.

Grey Heron was fresh after so long a rest, but Isobel curbed him fiercely. She took a small lantern from Perry and set out at a cautious trot along the road towards Mersey. Every instinct urged her to gallop, but if she risked a fall herself it would not help John. She kept the Heron to a steady pace, holding the lantern aloft and scanning the road ahead. At first she expected every moment to see John coming towards her, perhaps limping, cursing himself for letting go of the reins when he fell. Folk fell from horses every day- she had had several tumbles herself- and the vast majority of them were not badly hurt. Bumps and bruises, grazes and the occasional cracked rib or broken collarbone were common enough, and even a severely wrenched ankle might have kept John from hurrying home.

'John!' she called, and her voice was swallowed by the gums and blackwoods. 'John! Cooee!' Every so often, she reined in the Heron and listened intently, but all she ever heard was the sound of the swollen creeks, the occasional shouts of Perry and the other men and the sound of night creatures going about their business.

A tiger passed, a black devil yarred ahead. There was no wind, and the peppery scent of wattle was sharp in the damp air.

'John!' cried Isobel again.

The rain began to patter on the leaves and on Isobel's hair. She had never ridden out bareheaded before, and the drops were cold on her scalp. The going became progressively worse as she approached the creek, and in the light of the lantern she could see the ground poached with hoof prints. There were some long skids and a churned area in the muddy bank, and there, lying a little downhill, sprawled on his side with one arm flung out, lay her husband.

Isobel slid from Grey Heron's back, retaining just enough presence of mind to loop the reins about a branch. It would never do to have Heron bolting back to the stable as well. Slithering and sliding through the mud, she set the lantern on a knob of rock and fell to her knees.

'John – John!' She stripped off her gloves and touched his face with trembling fingers. His flesh was cold as the rain. In a passion of fear she flung herself down to listen for his heartbeat, a faint thud beneath her ear. And he was so cold! Isobel gathered him against her breast and kissed his chilled face. 'Oh John, John-' But there was no use wailing there, so she raised her head and called ringingly for help.

Perry's voice answered from behind, and in a moment he arrived. 'You found him then.'

Isobel could have hit him, but she needed Perry's good offices if she were to get John home. 'Perry, could you take the master on your horse?'

'Should rightly get a litter, Missus. His leg could be broke.'

'I know- I know,' cried Isobel, 'but he's so cold. I think we must get him home as soon as we can. Take his legs, Perry- oh- I suppose we shall have to lay him on his front.'

Between them, they managed to lift John onto Perry's fat cob. Isobel loosed Heron to follow as he would and while Perry led the cob she walked alongside, supporting her husband's head. It was a nightmare journey, for the wind blew up and the rain drove against their faces. Isobel's jacket was dark with water and blood, and later she found rivulets of red had run down her borrowed breeches. Her feet slipped in her boots, and more than once the cob staggered.

At last the lights of Glen Heather shone out of the murk. 'There, my love, we shall soon make you comfortable,' said Isobel through numb lips. 'Hurry, Perry, he is slipping.'

Perry hurried, reaching the stable and Mr Harkins' ineffectual help just in time to support John as he slid from the saddle. They laid him flat in the straw, and Isobel began to wipe the blood and mud from the white face. Perry cast a practised eye over his master and glanced at Harkins over Isobel's head. He very slightly shook his head, but commanded the older man to fetch blankets from the tack room. Isobel was crouched by her husband, holding his hands, watching his still face as if by sheer force of her gaze she could make him open his eyes.

'Ma'am,' said Harkins apologetically, 'you will have to leave, ma'am. We gotta strip those wet duds off him.'

Isobel rounded on the older man with exasperation. 'Oh, do you think I have never seen my husband unclothed?'

'Ma'am!' Harkins looked shocked, but hovered indecisively and Isobel thought; I can see why John cannot abide working with him.

'Get on with it,' she said curtly. 'And Perry, fetch hot water from Mrs Baker- no, we shall take him into the house first- into the parlour, I think, to avoid the stairs, and then Perry must go for Mrs Pullen. She will know what to do.' She knew it was no use sending for the doctor. He was far away in Shepherd Town.

The men stripped John and wrapped him in blankets, then improvised a stretcher from brooms and a horse rug to carry him into the house. They made up a bed in the parlour, and Isobel sat by, sponging John's face and holding his hands until Nannie Goodridge, fetched by a terrified Jennie Comfrey, came and forcibly changed the scandalous breeches for a wrapper. She brewed a hot posset, which she forced upon Isobel, overriding protests with the same ease with which she had dealt with childish tantrums.

'Drink this, Miss Isobel, or you will be ill, and what use will you be to your man like that? For the cost of a posset, a lady was lost, so they say. Come, drink up and then I shall fetch Master Robert. He's been roaring this past half hour.'

Isobel drank the nauseous brew but shook her head. 'I cannot tend the baby now, Nannie. Feed him some pap. It was good enough for me, was it not?'

Nannie Goodridge bridled. 'You chose to feed the child yourself, Miss Isobel, and it is your duty to continue,' she said. 'Duty calls, and the godly answer. No, not another word!' And away she bustled to fetch down the child.

Shivering and burning, numb with fear, Isobel held her child to her breast with one hand while clinging to John's hand with the other. She had a superstitious fear that if she let go for an instant he would slide so far from her that she would never have him back. Besides, if she let go, she would miss the instant when John would wake, and would surely tighten his lax fingers around her own. His hand always turned responsively to clasp hers, even when he was deeply asleep.

His breathing was shallow and difficult, and she tried to tell herself it was the cold he had been fighting off for the past week or more. He had told her it was quite gone, and when he woke she would be wearing her amber gown and would smile and he would reach out for her and take her in his arms and never let her go and- but she was not wearing the amber gown, she was wearing muddied breeches.

Isobel blinked. Baby Robert had drained one breast and was making anxious faces as he sought the other. Isobel looked round helplessly, but she had to release John's hand to move the child. He resumed his suckling and the rhythm of the sound blended with the sigh of John's breath and the hiss of the hastily lighted fire and the ruffle of

McCleod's feathers as the bird stirred, shook himself and went back to sleep.

Nannie Goodridge returned and took Robert away, and Isobel closed her wrapper and slid from the chair to kneel by John's side. If she could hold his head against her breast, surely, surely he would wake. She bent awkwardly and lifted his head, but something was wrong. The bleeding had stopped, but there was a faint depression where no depression should have been.

Horrified, Isobel looked at her fingers as if doubting their message, but she could feel the phantom wrongness still. She drew in her breath to scream for someone to help, but of course the men had seen the trouble, and of course they could do nothing. She must wait for Mrs Pullen and pray while she waited.

Still kneeling, she slid sideways and rested her cheek against her husband's cold one. Nannie Goodridge looked in once, Jennie brought tea, and Mrs Baker stood in the doorway with tears running down her plump cheeks.

The night wore on.

Isobel slipped into an exhausted doze, woke to deal with Robert's demands, and took up her agonised vigil again. She talked to John softly, rehearsing their plans for the future, reminding him of all he had to live for, as if she could bring him back to consciousness.

'Remember the hut, John, the hut on the mountain? As soon as you are well we shall go there and look down over Glen Heather, *your* Glen Heather, and your mama will come home to see Robert, and we shall make Glen Heather great as we planned- and I promise you John, it will happen. I shall look after things until- until-'

John's hand never moved in her grasp, and his cheek had warmed against her own, but Isobel knew when something changed. The difficult breathing had stopped.

In a panic, she shook his shoulders, but there was nothing left, only a beloved shell with all the life drained away.

CHAPTER 25

It took a long time for Isobel to recover from John's death. The shock and misery coupled with the chill she had received brought her close to delirium at times, but she forced herself from her bed to attend the funeral.

Winston came over from Scarborough with Gwynneth to lend support, and at first Isobel, numb with the horror that had overtaken her, was glad to leave matters in their hands. She and Winston had never been close, but apart from little Robert he was the only family she had now, so she clung to his presence. She clung also to Reverend Ende, and the old man tried hard to give her comfort. There were two faint lights in her darkness. She had given John his son, and his death had been so swift.

Mrs Pullen had explained (gently, for her) that unconsciousness would have been instant and total, and that John would never have felt more than an instant's pain. She had also explained that if she and all the physicians in Tasmania had been present when the accident occurred, they could have done nothing to help him.

Mrs Pullen was not quite certain of that, but she believed her duty lay more in upholding the widow than in telling the absolute truth. And, with a depressed skull fracture of that kind, what *could* have been done? No suitable surgeon could have been within a hundred miles at the time. It was better to believe it had been hopeless from the start.

Isobel reflected bitterly through the days and dreaded the nights, for she knew the hour would come when her hands would grope in the emptiness and she would wake to the nightmare again. John had been so warm, so loving, and so alive. It seemed impossible that he was gone. And she had still to tell his mother.

She had not yet faced up that task when a letter came from Ness herself, brief and carefully penned as if the writer were unpractised in forming words.

The substance was delight in the birth of a son for Glen Heather, approval of the baby's name and an earnest hope that they should not be offended that she chose to remain a while in New Zealand. Her stepbrother and his wife had made her welcome, and she was happily occupied with a newfound talent for sketching.

Can you conceive of me making pictures of the bonnie flowers? she wrote. *A gentleman suggested it to me long ago, but I never did try before... Donal believes I should chance my work in a wee book...*

Faced with this, and with the fact that Ness had neglected to write her own direction on the epistle, Isobel could not tell her what had happened. There would be time enough when Ness wrote again, she thought drearily, but Ness did not write for many months and when she did, it was on another subject entirely.

***

While Isobel was prostrated with grief, it was her brother Winston who consulted with Bertram, the Glen Heather solicitor, and saw to it that the death duties were paid. The duties for Hector had been handled with comparative ease, for Hector had had several sources of income, but with John's death coming so soon after his father's, it was a greater drain on the estate. Fortunately the property had recovered from the economic downturn of the 1840s, but Winston looked a little thoughtful when he returned from his interview with Mr Bertram. He went directly to Scarborough and perused ledgers and accounts for some hours before making a decision that would benefit himself and Gwynneth as well as his unfortunate sister. He then waited until he considered the time ripe to approach Isobel, some two months after John's death.

His sister looked pale and ill, and black became her not at all, but she was eating again and really, thought Winston, she could not mourn forever. John Campbell had certainly been more likable than his brute of a father, but he had been a solemn stick and so self-effacing it seemed unlikely she had developed any great attachment. It also seemed likely she would be driven by the cares of Glen Heather to marry again soon, perhaps unwisely. And it was Winston's duty to indicate the other alternative open to her.

It was a good offer he meant to make; generous, even. To be sure the property had been left to Robert Campbell, but he was a baby and Isobel would be forced to hand the care of the estate to someone. Why should she not sell (or lease) it to her own brother? The money could be put in trust for the child's future and in any case, there seemed a slight chance that the child would...

Winston glanced apologetically at the heavens. He wished no

further grief on his unfortunate sister, and he had better hope the child *did* survive, for surely the estate passed to John's next brother in the event of the death of his heir. If young Hector Campbell took over it would benefit neither Winston and Gwynneth *or* Isobel.

As he entered the Glen Heather parlour, a bird hissed from the back of a chair. Winston was not fond of pets, and could not see why the bird had not been banished to the stables, or at the very least to a cage in the kitchen. He glanced irritably at his sister, but she was holding her child in her lap and made no move to chide the bird even when it gave a piercing squawk.

'My dear,' began Winston, with one eye on the feathered menace on the chair, 'this has been a sad time for us all, and you will not wish to be troubled with business at a time like this.' She looked at him dully, and he cleared his throat. 'However, you must give some thought to the future.'

'I have thought,' said Isobel. 'Hush, McCleod, do.' She took a small biscuit from the bowl beside her and held it out. The bird gave a shrill whistle, clambered down from the chair to receive the treat and then returned to its perch.

'Of course you have!' said Winston heartily, averting his gaze from the business-like beak as it worked on the biscuit. 'And you have no doubt reached the sensible conclusion that you must sell the property, or lease the land to a good manager who will keep it in good heart.'

'No,' said Isobel.

'This being so, I have decided-'

'I said, *no*, Winston,' said Isobel coolly. 'I know what you are about to say and I thank you for the offer but *no*, I will not sell Glen Heather to you. You could never afford the asking price, and I doubt you wish to beggar Scarborough again? Besides, John did not like your habits of management and no more do I.'

'But surely we could come to some suitable arrangement?'

'Suitable for whom, Winston?'

'I would never try to cheat you, Issa!' he said helplessly.

'I know that,' she assured him with a fractional smile. She looked down at the child for a moment, and stroked his cheek with a fingertip. 'Tell me, Winston,' she said in a softer voice, 'if you *did* have the management of Glen Heather, what would you do?'

'Why, I would fell the timber and sell it, for there is a great call for timber in Victoria at the moment. To be sure, transportation would raise a small problem, but I am confident that could be easily overcome. As the owner of Scarborough I have certain resources.'

'Aye, I thought as much,' said Isobel reflectively. Since John's death she had begun to use the occasional Scottishisms as he had done. It was disconcerting to Winston, but he did not quite like to chide her. She was smiling wanly, and after a moment she continued. 'In any case, the question is academic, Winston. I cannot sell Glen Heather because it does not belong to me. It belongs to Robert.'

'A sum of money, wisely invested, would be of more use to a fatherless boy than land let go to ruin and neglect for twenty years,' said Winston.

'No, Winston,' said Isobel, still softly. 'It is impossible.'

Winston sighed, making his moustache ruffle with the wind of it. 'Then I shall take over the management of the property myself until I can find a suitable man to take the let. It will be a great charge on me, but I cannot let you suffer.'

'No, Winston,' said Isobel again. She raised her dark eyes and looked at him steadily. 'Thank you so much for the offer, and thank Gwynnie too, but it is enough that Robert must have Mr Bertram as his guardian instead of myself. I shall manage Glen Heather in my own way, just as I promised- as I promised John. Now, if you will excuse me, Robert needs to be fed.'

'Then ring for Nannie Goodridge!' snapped Winston. He was a little aggrieved that his old nurse had turned aside his offer of a handsome pension to go to Isobel.

'There is no need for Nannie to come. I attend to the matter myself.' Isobel raised a hand and began to unclasp her bodice. Winston stared in disbelief, then flushed, made his farewells and left.

Isobel stared after him. A tear rolled down her cheek and she rubbed it away with an absent fist. It was not her brother's fault he had made such crass assumptions. It was hers. She had allowed him to believe she would turn to him, and in fact, she *had* turned to him in the extremity of her grief, but Winston Jarvis had nothing to say to the management of Glen Heather. That was for Robert, and until he came of age, it was for his mother.

***

Over the time that followed, Isobel found no reason to change her mind. As soon as Robert was old enough to be weaned onto pap, she handed his daily management to Nannie Goodridge and took up the reins of Glen Heather.

The crinoline gowns in her wardrobe were utterly unsuited to her new role, so she exchanged them for severe riding habits and then, in a burst of impatience, for John's breeches, which were still folded away in lavender as he had left them. She knew the wearing of them made her appear ridiculous (if not downright immodest) in the eyes of society, but in some small way it brought her closer to him.

She rode daily around the sheep, made the decisions Harkins could not, and finally finished what John had begun by asking the old man to take over the neglected gardens of Glen Heather. He could hardly do any harm there, she thought, for she had no interest in the domesticity of the grounds- not while the crimson heath bloomed on the mountain. After some thought, she appointed Perry as her general overseer. She left it to him to employ a new groom, and approved his choice of a young man named Elijah Ward, great grandson of Bullocky George.

Three times in the winter of 1862 she climbed the mountain to clear flumes that had become blocked with leaves and bark. If she suspected a section was washed away rather than blocked, she sent Perry to attend to it instead. She even spent a night in the hut on the mountain, and though she wept in the gum-scented dark of the little shelter John had built, she comforted herself that no one would ever know it but herself.

It was a hard road she had chosen, and she was constantly exhausted, but she welcomed the creeping tiredness, for it kept her from thinking too much. When summer came she had been a widow longer than she had been a wife, and still the coldness had not lifted from her heart.

***

Nannie Goodridge was shocked at the change in her nurseling. She could have understood a sustained emotional collapse, for she had seen that in Whitaker Jarvis when Eliza died. She could have understood prolonged tears and moping, or refuge taken in delicate health, but Isobel had become so hard, so cold, so *masculine*. It did not seem right that a young woman (and a mother at that) should turn from the softness of femininity. Nannie fairly shuddered when she looked down from the nursery window and beheld the trim figure of Glen Heather's lady dressed in breeches and jacket and riding astride on Grey Heron or even, sometimes, on John's Thunder. Nannie would have understood if Isobel had ordered the horse shot, or sold off, but to ride it herself! There was no understanding Isobel any more.

Isobel, too, felt herself a different person. At twenty-three she felt drawn and tired and old. Had it not been for Robert and the promise she had made John, she could have given in to melancholy. As it was, the only refuge was to become hard as ironbark and prickly as the heath that grew up the mountain. She clung to John's memory, but as she grew older in years and knowledge, she felt she was leaving him behind, just as he had left her when he stepped forward into death.

A letter came from Ness in the winter of 1863. This time she wrote that young Hector was betrothed to a lass from a good Scottish family.

'*It is amazing to see the change in the laddie,*' she wrote. '*Edwina is a dear lassie, and they are to be wed in the spring. It seems strange that my Hector stayed unwed so long and here his sons are aye in a rush to take a wife. Young Hector was a wee bit fashed to leave Glen Heather, but he says you could not pay him gold enough to return, not with Edwina and his work with Donal. Eddie is to be a dominie in the village here- and he so much against books as a bairn! As for Jamie, nothing will please the laddie but to try his fortune on the goldfields - unless it be to follow in the footsteps of poor Mr Burke and Mr Wills. I own I am pleased to have him go - there is trouble with the Maoris here and I would not have Jamie going to fight. Perhaps he may return to you at Glen Heather for a spell? I know you and Isobel will make the laddie welcome. I pray he will come back again with news of you and wee Robert.*

Ever your loving mother.

It gave Isobel a terrible pang to read this letter, and she sat down at once to write a reply. It seemed cruel to give the news to John's mother, but it would be more cruel to allow her to return to find him gone, or to believe him neglectful of her.

The letter reached Ness in good time, but was too late for her son Jamie. He had already sailed for Victoria on the *Kirsty B.*

***

At seventeen, Jamie Campbell was an engaging mixture of his parents. He looked very like Hector, with black hair, narrow grey eyes and a determined jaw, and he had Hector's sudden enthusiasms and adventurous spirit. He was less volatile than his father, and, like Ness, he appreciated beauty whenever he found it. He had heard of gold in Bendigo and, having known from childhood that Glen Heather would never be his, he decided to search out a fortune. He gave Ness no peace until she permitted him to buy a passage on the packet to Victoria; after all, he was fully as old as she had been when she left Loch Haven to travel across the world.

Ness saw him off at the port, and he hugged her carelessly and went aboard, his eyes alight, his agile mind already leaping to the goldfields and beyond. He had with him a money belt, his father's old dirk and a boundless appetite for life and experience.

Having disembarked at Port Phillip, he made his way north by various means, riding when he could, walking when he could not. He bought a handsome bay horse for a song just outside Melbourne, but had hardly ridden ten miles before he discovered a number of vices, including the habit of dashing under trees in an attempt to dislodge its rider. Having narrowly escaped braining on a low branch, he could neither bring himself to abandon it on the road nor to sell it to another unsuspecting buyer. His problem was solved when he chanced on a bushranger in the act of robbing a private coach. He offered the horse in exchange for the occupants' freedom and continued his journey with less elegance but more safety.

The grateful owner of the coach took him many miles along his way, and set him down with good wishes and a bank draft for the price of another, more reliable, horse.

Instead, Jamie chose to purchase a small handcart and a whistle, which he presently taught himself to play. For a while he amused himself by playing pedlar, buying goods in one centre and trading them in the next, piping for his supper like a bard. This soon palled, and he set off again for the goldfields of New South Wales.

His luck was in, and he made a strike, but the foul water on the diggings made him ill, so he turned to shearing, and then joined a cattle drive. The rush for gold had left the properties sorely short of labour, so Jamie enjoyed two years of varied agricultural occupation and scarcely missed a meal.

By the time he was nineteen, he had made money and lost it, gambled, brawled and piped his way back to Victoria where he rode the rail from Echuca to Melbourne. Recalling the family at Glen Heather, he then spent a week singing sentimental ditties in a tavern to earn his passage to Launceston. Then, just as he left for the port, he was accosted by an elegant gentleman, who stared in disbelief before asking if he would spare a moment to talk.

'Aye?' he said affably, shaking back his mane of uncut hair and smiling down into bespectacled blue eyes.

'Young man,' said the gentleman slowly. 'I will bet you the price of a drink that your name is Campbell!'

'Aye, so it is,' said Jamie. 'I am Jamie Campbell. What is it to you?'

The gentleman smiled faintly and held out a thin but surprisingly strong hand. 'Jamie Campbell indeed! Then we share a name, or part of it.'

Jamie cocked an eyebrow and waited, still smiling, for enlightenment.

'I am James Galbraith,' said the stranger, 'and although I seem to have won the stake, I would be honoured to buy you a drink.'

Jamie took the offered hand. 'And I would bet that *you* are the fine gentleman who built Glen Heather and painted the picture of my mother!' he said mockingly. 'Aye, I shall drink wi' you, Mr Galbraith, but make it quick. I sail tonight and I'm off home.'

His benefactor left and returned with two glasses and a jug of beer. It amused him to be served by a fine gentleman, and he wondered what Galbraith expected in return. Having no bent for subtlety, he put the question directly.

'I want information,' said Galbraith.

Jamie took a long swallow and wiped his mouth with the back of his hand. 'What would an ignorant laddie like me know that would be of use to a fine gentleman like yourself?'

Galbraith leaned forward. 'Perhaps nothing, Jamie Campbell, but that is the risk I take. Tell me, are there many others in your family? And did your father put his stamp on every one of them as he has on you?'

'Hector, Eddie and me, aye, we look like him. John isna such a fine big laddie as I recall.'

'It is John who is at Glen Heather?'

'Aye, with Isobel and their bairn, maybe more than one, by now.'

'So there is to be a dynasty of Campbells for Glen Heather: just as your father planned. Is your mother well?'

'Last time I saw her she was in bonnie health,' said Jamie, surprised.

'And when was that?'

'It was two or three years ago. I left her in New Zealand, forby.'

'Thank you. So now you are off to Glen Heather. And after that?'

'Who knows?' said Jamie with a grin. 'Sydney Town again? Perhaps Dunedin?'

'Next time you see your mother, tell her I am still searching the docks,' said Galbraith, and rose to his feet.

'Is that it then?' asked Jamie, a little disconcerted.

'Aye, that is it. Tell Ness that Charcoal Jamie is still searching the docks for her equal. And give her my direction, if ever she is in the mind to contact me.'

Galbraith wrote on a paper, folded it, and laid it on the table, leaving Jamie to finish his drink and ponder the cryptic message. He could make little of it, so after a while he shrugged philosophically, tucked the paper in his shirt, and headed for the docks.

He meant to go directly to Glen Heather, but Bass Strait was its usual turbulent self and Jamie, having lost his beer and his supper to the waves, set off in search of sustenance. He ate at an inn, paid his shot and was on the point of leaving when a young lady entered the coffee room on the arm of a plump gentleman with immense side-whiskers. She had glossy dark hair under a tilted hat and there seemed to be a lighter streak at the front. Her face was round and her figure diminutive inside the modest hoop of her crinoline.

Jamie stared, fascinated, as her companion seated her. He had known several women in New South Wales, but none had appealed to him so. Like his father, Jamie was a man of sudden decision and decided taste. He found himself staring at the lady like a dog at a bone. He looked away, but his eyes kept returning and as if feeling the force of his regard, the lady looked up. Her cheeks flushed, and she raised gloved hands to cool them, but her bright blue eyes signalled interest. Jamie moved in reply to this silent invitation, but the lady dropped her gaze demurely and made a show of examining the bill of fare.

Recklessly, Jamie sat down again and ordered a second breakfast. The object of his interest ate daintily, and glanced occasionally his way. He had still not introduced himself when the plump gentleman paid his bill and ushered his charge out into the street. Jamie flung down a sovereign and followed, cursing himself for not bespeaking the couple's coachman while they were engaged in the inn. Instead, he asked information of the ostler, and the price of a drink brought the information he sought.

The lady's name was Miss George, and she had been recently released from a select seminary in Launceston. The gentleman was Frederick Lambert, her uncle and guardian, a well-to-do merchant who lived near Longford.

Jamie was charmed, and, after a little thought, he obtained a horse and covered cart and persuaded a haberdasher to sell him ribbons and laces, jet beads and other trinkets, and a chandler to provide rope and nails, wire and twine and wax. He then acquired a respectable suit and drove off, grave as a judge, to sell his wares.

He turned a small profit in the countryside, brightening the days of his customers with his cheerful piping and enquiring wherever he went for Miss George. His likeness to old Hector Campbell was remarked on by a few, and probably saved him from being thrown ignominiously from many doorsteps. The Campbells were respectable and if one of their number chose to make a figure of himself by playing hawker, no doubt he had a good reason.

However, with some vague feeling that perhaps John might not quite like to hear of his activities, Jamie re-christened himself as James McCleod.

In due course, he arrived at the Lambert house. He waited until the uncle had gone out, and then presented himself at the door, asking if the ladies would care to view his wares. Miss George came out with her maid, and while she turned over ribbons and laces and matched cottons and silks, Jamie had the leisure to examine her closely. His steady regard its effect, and Miss George glanced up several times. Blue eyes met grey, and she blushed and smiled.

The maid, a severe-looking person with beady eyes, was squinting closely at the silks, and Miss George moved casually to Jamie's side of the cart.

'It *is* you,' she said in an undertone. 'I saw you in Launceston on my way home from Thornleigh Grange, did I not?'

'Aye, so you did,' said Jamie. Just as casually, he offered her a bunch of flowers he had collected from the roadside. 'Do you ever walk down by the river hereabouts, Miss George?'

Miss George pursed her lips. 'I walk every day at eleven with my maid. I may go to the river on occasion, perhaps.'

Jamie eyed the maid with disfavour.

'Martha is very deaf, you know,' said Miss George, 'but she is a good creature, despite her looks.'

'Then I might be seeing you again, Miss George.'

'Perhaps, Mr...'

'McCleod,' said Jamie. 'James McCleod, late of Dunedin.'

Miss George smiled and said loudly; 'I do not believe we need buy anything today, Martha.' Her eyelid fluttered in a wink and Jamie, well pleased, touched his forehead and clucked up his horse.

Charlotte George was not a naturally defiant girl, but she had been cooped up in Thornleigh Grange for some two years and was ripe for a little freedom. Her uncle, a single man who had had guardianship thrust upon him when Charlotte's parents died, took little notice of his niece save to see that she was nicely dressed. He was thankful that she enjoyed healthful outdoor pursuits, which allowed his ears surcease from her constant chatter.

Martha the maid was short sighted as well as deaf, and quite welcomed the chance to sit in the shade by the river while her charge strolled with a young gentleman whom Miss claimed, with truth, to have encountered in Launceston while in the company of her uncle.

Jamie enjoyed his summer greatly. He spent his mornings courting Charlotte under the trees and his afternoons hawking his silks and laces, ropes and nails about the surrounding countryside. The weather remaining fair, he slept under the cart, washed in the river and spent his evenings playing his whistle and carving trinkets from pieces of nicely figured wood. He had not forgotten Glen Heather, exactly, but like his father he was inclined to focus on one object at a time, and in that summer of late 1866, his object was the winning of Charlotte George.

CHAPTER 26

Meanwhile, Glen Heather was blooming. To the chagrin of her brother and the astonishment of the other landowners around Mersey, Isobel Campbell proved herself an able manager.

Glen Heather sheep were well husbanded, fed and watered, and the survival rate of their lambs was little short of miraculous. Mindful of John's views on over-grazing, Isobel kept the numbers to a moderate level, and moved the flocks regularly to new pasture, avoiding many troubles that plagued less careful shepherds. The natural bush provided shade and varied additions to the ewes' diet, and the cleared flats were regularly harrowed and harvested for hay. The red cattle installed by Hector thrived and multiplied, and there was a good demand for beef and hides.

Isobel often considered buying more cattle of a breed that would be suitable for the production of milk and cheese, but isolation continued to be a problem when it came to marketing Glen Heather produce.

After hearing of John's death, Ness Campbell wrote less often, and although she still mentioned her eventual return, it was always couched in vague terms. It seemed that for the foreseeable future, Ness was content to remain where she was, with two of her surviving sons at hand, the society of her stepbrother and his wife and her "wee books" of sketches, which were having a modest success.

Sometimes Isobel wished Ness *would* return, for she was sorely in need of company. Perry had no conversation beyond the health of the sheep and land and besides, he was married to Emma. They had three daughters already, and a fourth child on the way. It humbled Isobel to see how happy they were in the sandstone cottage: five people dwelling in two rooms while she and Robert occupied the vast empty space that was Glen Heather House. Nannie Goodridge spoke of nothing but Robert's small doings, and Mrs Baker was wholly concerned with dough and pastry in the kitchen.

Now that Emma had so much to do with caring for her children,

Isobel had taken Jennie Comfrey as her maid, for the job entailed so little that Jennie was able to combine it easily with her household duties. Jennie was a sweet child, and intelligent, but even an acknowledged eccentric like Isobel Campbell could not be friends with a housemaid.

The only folk of her own class whom Isobel saw were her brother and Gwynnie, and the businessmen she met on infrequent trips to Mersey or Launceston. Relations between Glen Heather and Scarborough were cool and distant, for Gwynneth had taken her husband's side in the disagreement and had never been particularly cordial to Isobel since.

Yes, Isobel was lonely, in the midst of a hard working day and a dozen or more folk who depended on her in some way or another for their livelihoods. She was more pleased than not when Gwynnie's brother Niall O'Hara, a widower with three small daughters, began calling regularly to see how she did. Upon arrival at Glen Heather, Niall would hand the children thankfully to Nannie Goodridge and he and Isobel would spend a pleasant hour drinking tea or sherry and discussing the world beyond. Niall was an avid student of world events, so there were several spirited discussions on the rights and wrongs of the American Civil War, the capture and demise of Ben Hall and Mad Dog Morgan and the sinking of the *SS London*, a ship which was to have brought a renowned Shakespearian actor to perform in Melbourne. And sometimes, inevitably, conversation would turn to sheep and timber, cattle and corn and rain.

Isobel enjoyed these visits, and was even grateful that Gwynnie's brother seemed willing to overlook her inappropriate behaviour and mode of dress. She was surprised, however, on the day when O'Hara asked to inspect the account books.

He must have sensed her withdrawal, for he put a hand companionably over hers. 'Come Isobel,' he said, smiling, 'surely such a request is quite in order from an old friend such as myself?'

'Indeed, Mr O'Hara?' said Isobel, 'and would you feel the same way if I were to request similar entree into the accounts of Shannon?'

'Shannon is my father's property, Mrs Campbell,' said O'Hara, withdrawing his hand.

'Aye, and perhaps you have had enough of playing the underling there,' said Isobel shrewdly.

O'Hara stiffened a little. 'Mrs Campbell, just what are you implying?'

'I could ask the same of you,' countered Isobel. 'Entree into account books of a property to which you have no right usually implies an interest of some sort in acquiring that property, and you must know Glen Heather in not for sale.'

'I understand that,' said O'Hara, 'but I thought perhaps you might be interested in- oh, how shall I put this? We are comfortable together, are we not? We are good friends?'

'I have thought so,' said Isobel coolly.

'Then why not marry me?'

When she did not answer, he tried to take her in his arms. Since she was seated in an armchair and made no effort to rise, he had to bend and the resulting kiss landed unsatisfactorily on her temple.

Isobel pushed him backwards with considerable energy.

'Why *not* marry you?' she said as he sat down once more, red to his hairline. 'Surely the question here is, rather, *why*?'

O'Hara spread his hands. 'This cannot have come as a surprise to you. We enjoy one another's company, you need a man to support you and my children need a mother's touch. Why, we have been courting this past six months!'

'Courting?' marvelled Isobel. 'Is *that* what you call it? Why, Mr O'Hara, I have always understood that courtship was carried on at balls and parties, with the couple concerned arrayed in their finery and their best manners! You, on the other hand, have never troubled to invite *me* to any of the concerts and plays you describe so well. Instead, you take your mother!'

'I- I did not think you would be interested!' stammered O'Hara.

'Instead,' pursued Isobel, 'you sit in my parlour and ask to see for the accounts of Glen Heather. For shame Mr O'Hara! Is it I you wish to marry or my son's inheritance?'

'But Isobel,' he stammered, 'are you never lonely? Do you never miss a man's company? Even, to put no fine point on it, a man's touch?'

'Often,' said Isobel frankly, 'but I would never buy either at the expense of my son and my independence. If you wish to continue to visit, and enjoy conversation as we have done, you are most welcome, but if your interest is solely in wedding a person with property, and in finding a keeper for your daughters, then you should go elsewhere.'

Niall O'Hara flushed vividly again and took his leave, replacing his hat with such force that McCleod squawked and flapped on his perch. 'Sleekit! Sleekit!' he remarked.

'Yes indeed,' said Isobel, and gave him a biscuit.

Afterwards, she regretted treating Niall so harshly. Her real objection was not to his motives, which were no worse than her own brother's, but to his assumption that he could step into John's shoes, and John's bed, so easily. She tried to summon her husband's beloved face, and wept a few tears before going to visit Robert in the nursery. Deliberately, she took McCleod with her, for she knew Nannie Goodridge would refuse to receive him and Robert would object and the resulting argument would give her something to think about.

Niall O'Hara was not the only suitor to approach Isobel over the years, for the local bachelors and widowers and younger sons could scarcely be expected to overlook such a temptation as Glen Heather and its lady. The property was flourishing; the lady was attractive (if uncomfortably blunt) so it was clearly the will of God that some altruistic gentleman should enjoy the fruits of both.

Isobel was sorry to refuse them all, not because she had the slightest desire to marry again, but because refusal inevitably brought about the loss of their company. As for the womenfolk; she made no friends with them either. The spinsters and mothers of marriageable daughters watched Isobel Campbell turn down proposals that never came their way, and even married ladies could not talk to her. The gulf between their interests and hers was too wide.

They managed households, while she managed a property. They dressed in the new draped gowns with the fullness gathered at the rear, while she wore breeches and striped Crimean shirts. Even when she did wear a gown, it was frequently an antiquated model with a hoop. She had a child, but seemed disinclined to report his small sayings and as for the iniquities of servants (always a promising topic of conversation), she always proclaimed herself completely satisfied.

***

Jamie Campbell's courtship of his Charlotte was proceeding merrily. Jamie partnered her at several balls, retiring to an inn beforehand and sprucing himself up to a degree that other dancers, if they chanced to recognise him as the musical hawker who had plied his trade in the district all summer, blinked and shook their heads. Miss George's partner must be another young man, they decided. No hawker could be so neatly clad and gravely spoken, and old Frederick Lambert would never allow his ward to associate with a person of such lowly occupation.

They would have been astonished had they realised how little

Frederick knew of his niece's activities. Her chaperon was Lambert's sister, an indolent lady who asked only that Charlotte should conduct herself in a seemly manner and not take the wind out of her own Hester's and Elizabeth's eyes. She was happy to see Charlotte partnered by a young stranger, and when he was introduced as "James McCleod of Dunedin" she thought her niece had a good matrimonial prospect and regretted that her own daughters had not seen him first.

A native of Melbourne, she had no way of recognising the mysterious "Mr McCleod" as a Campbell of Glen Heather.

Thus the courtship continued happily, and, as autumn approached, Jamie proposed marriage and was joyfully accepted. His plan for taking her to Glen Heather after their wedding and then travelling on to Sydney and Dunedin seemed a little unusual, but Charlotte had seen for herself that Jamie was well breeched, and he was a charming companion. She had realised long ago that his hawker's cart had been an expedience for finding her and remaining in the district and, since her aunt accepted him and he spoke easily of a handsome yearly allowance (which he had not bothered to collect for some time), she assumed him to be a perfectly suitable candidate for her hand. Besides, she enjoyed the kisses they shared by the river and behind the greenery in supper rooms, and looked forward to the delights Jamie assured her were still to come.

As for Jamie, he was blissfully happy. He had won his lady, and having had no trouble providing for himself over the past three years, he saw no trouble in a future in providing for two, especially as his wife-to-be was an heiress in her own right. He looked forward to showing his prize to Ness, Eddie and Hector, but first of all, he determined to tie the knot and then go and visit his brother John.

He knew that at some point he would be forced to explain his deception over his name, but if his Charlotte loved "James McCleod of Dunedin", why should she not love Jamie Campbell of Glen Heather just as well?

The idyll came to an abrupt end when Jamie asked Frederick Lambert for his niece's hand in marriage. Being a Campbell, he phrased his request as a demand, which annoyed Frederick no end. A lax guardian he was, but he cared for his niece's wellbeing, and his own consequence, so he eyed the young suitor narrowly and questioned his occupation and prospects. Jamie listed the more respectable occupations he had held, mentioned the inheritance from his father and the investments that yielded his yearly allowance.

'And what of your background?' asked Lambert, frowning. 'I do not know the name McCleod.'

A vision of his mother's cockatoo brought a smile to Jamie's face. This was a mistake, for although Lambert was not privy to the joke, he did feel that the young man was unaware of the dignity of the occasion.

'I do not know the name McCleod,' he repeated stubbornly.

'I have come from Dunedin,' reminded Jamie, 'but have you heard of Glen Heather?'

Lambert frowned. 'That's the Campbell place near Mersey. What has that to say to anything?'

'Aye,' said Jamie, pleased. 'You know it, then. John Campbell, who owns it, is my brother.'

'Indeed,' said Lambert coldly.

'Aye. My mother's name was McCleod before she wed my father and so I have adopted it.'

'And why would you do that?' asked Lambert.

This interview was not going to Jamie's liking, and he realised it would be foolish to explain his motives. This pompous fool had never played a joke in his life, and would never believe him, anyway.

'May I have Charlotte or may I not?' he asked impatiently. 'With my income and her own, we shall be able to live in comfort.'

Lambert folded his arms. 'You may not.'

This was not the end of it, of course. Jamie objected, argued and finally yelled, and Lambert, tight-lipped and disgusted, called for his manservant to see the young man out. Jamie refused to leave, and in the end he was ejected forcibly, propelled from the front door by two husky footmen. Lambert retired to his book room to drink a glass of port and to brood, for although he had disposed of the dubious young man, he still had to deal with Charlotte. He was not cruel, nor even severe, but he would be failing in his duty if he allowed an obvious fortune hunter to marry his niece. The young man was not only shiftless, but a liar as well; his mother's name might well have been McCleod, but as for his brother being Campbell of Glen Heather, why, even a retiring gentleman such as himself knew that John Campbell had been dead and gone these five years and that the owner of Glen Heather was a child.

Charlotte was devastated when her uncle told her she could not marry

James McCleod. She cried and pleaded and stamped her foot, so he locked her in her bedchamber and gave orders for her to be let severely alone. She was sobbing on her bed, flushed and sodden, when she heard a sweet piping whistle outside. It might have been a butcherbird or a magpie, but it sounded very familiar. Holding her breath, Charlotte listened acutely. The sound came again, a snatch of an old Scottish air Jamie often played. Charlotte rolled off the bed and raised the window sash. In the dusk, she could just make out the figure of a man.

'Jamie?' she called softly.

'Aye,' came the beloved voice, full of laughter. 'Can you come down, Charlotte?'

'No.' She bit her lip. 'I am locked in.'

'Then I shall come up to you.' There was a small pause. 'Catch the rope I throw and fasten it to your door latch.'

Charlotte was about to protest that she could never climb down a rope, but already the coil was singing through the air. On the second attempt she managed to catch it, abrading her fingertips somewhat, and drew it in through the window. With difficulty, she fastened the rope to her door-latch as she had been bidden, and, following Jamie's low-voiced instructions, took the rope a turn or two about the legs of the iron bedstead. She then realised that the lower part of the rope was not merely a rope, but a ladder, cunningly made from wooden spacers fastened to rope sides.

The whole contraption swayed alarmingly as Jamie climbed up, but within five minutes she was held fast in his arms. To her indignant surprise he was shaking with laughter.

'I have always wanted to do this again,' he said in explanation. 'My brothers and I were forever making ladders o' this kind when we were bairns on the mountain!'

'Jamie, you should not be here!' she said belatedly. 'If Uncle finds you he will- oh, I do not know what he will do!'

'Whist,' said Jamie, giving her a smacking kiss. 'Do you want to marry me or no?'

'Of *course* I do, but Uncle says we may not!'

'I have a plan to change his mind,' said Jamie. 'Come away with me now. Tonight.'

'Uncle says you are a liar,' faltered Charlotte, 'and a fortune-hunter and a great many other horrid things!'

'Aye, so I am a liar,' said Jamie calmly, 'but only in so far as my name. You were willing to marry James McCleod, so will you still marry Jamie Campbell? Come with me to Glen Heather- now- tonight. My brother and his lady will make you welcome!'

'Uncle says Mr Campbell of Glen Heather is dead,' said Charlotte.

'Aye, my father is dead, but my brother John is not so much older than I.' Jamie was tiring of the conversation. 'Come along, Charlotte,' he said sternly, giving her a little shake. 'Will you come, or will you no? Be sure I'll not ask you a second time!'

'*Yes*!' said Charlotte.

The climb from the window was hair-raising, even with Jamie's arms below to steady her down. The ladder had to be left hanging, but Jamie had a fine fleet horse waiting below that would carry both of them. He mounted and turned to hoist Charlotte up behind him. The horse, startled by the flurry of skirts and petticoats that slapped down on its rump, uttered a snort and leapt forward. Charlotte squeaked with terror, Jamie laughed exultantly, and then they were away.

CHAPTER 27

Isobel was riding wearily back from the fold when she saw a horse coming up the drive. It was a fine animal, and it carried two riders, a man and a woman. Isobel waited resignedly, expecting to greet her brother and Gwynnie, though surely their parsimony did not yet extend to sharing a mount!

As the couple neared the house, she realised the man was one of the Campbells. She was stabbed with grief that John's brothers were alive while he was gone, but the question was, which brother had returned? She knew already that the lady could not be Ness; she was much too young, and had dark hair with a light streak at the front. The younger Campbell boys had always looked alike, but she reckoned young Hector would be twenty-five, Eddie twenty-three and Jamie just about twenty. *As old as John when they had married.* But which one *was* it? Then the young man smiled, and she recognised him without doubt.

'Jamie dear!' she said in welcome, but he seemed oddly uncertain about greeting her.

'*Isobel?*'

'Aye, have I changed so much?'

Jamie Campbell looked at her with quizzical eyes. 'What is Jock doing, to dress you like a laddie? Not that it doesna become you- you were always bonnie, Isobel.'

'John,' she said numbly.

'Aye, where is Jock? I wish to introduce you both to *my* lady. Isobel, this is Charlotte. Charlotte, the lady in the breeches is wed to my brother John.'

The young woman stared at Isobel, but Jamie had already dismounted and was assisting her to do likewise. On the ground, she appeared to be a very young lady, perhaps no more than eighteen, with a pert pretty face, a tip-tilted nose and rumpled dark curls rioting under her hat. And that strange streak at the front! Isobel had never seen anything like it.

'Oh, Jamie!' said Isobel, and reached out to hug him in greeting and dismay.

He returned the hug and kissed her on the cheek, then turned to the girl. 'Charlotte, this is Glen Heather!'

The girl seemed impressed, and even oddly relieved, and Isobel wondered why. The whole situation seemed crazed, and she was still trying to understand when Elijah Ward came to take charge of Thunder and the other horse.

'Elijah!' exclaimed Jamie, and slapped the groom on the shoulder. 'How do you come to be here? Where is Perry? And Harkins?'

Isobel shook herself and touched Jamie's arm. 'Come along in, my dears.' She was so taken up with the terrible news she must give to Jamie, that it never occurred to her to question the presence of Charlotte. She would have supposed (had she thought of it at all) that the couple must be man and wife, for no lady would ever travel unattended with a young man, and Charlotte, despite her travel-stained garments and dust-marked person, was clearly a lady. To be sure they were young to be married, but she and John had been little older, and Ness had written in her last letter that young Hector and his wife had a daughter. Jamie had always been the nicest of the younger Campbells, so why should he not have won this enchantingly pretty girl for a wife?

Isobel had Jennie Comfrey ready a guest room, and left her to help Charlotte change her gown while she spoke with Jamie in the parlour.

Jamie heard her out quietly, stroking McCleod with a fingertip. He nodded once or twice, and sighed, but showed no outward sign of grief. It had been six years since he left Glen Heather, and the lanky boy was now a man.

'Where is he laid, Isobel?' he asked at last.

'In Mersey, next to your father.'

'Aye.' Jamie grimaced. 'I hope they deal better in Paradise than they did at Glen Heather! But Isobel, how have you managed? Surely old Harkins isna running things?'

'No,' said Isobel steadily, 'I am running things. Glen Heather belongs to Robert now, and I must keep it in heart until he comes of age. Mr Bertram is Robert's guardian since the law will not allow me the position, but I am the guardian of Glen Heather.'

'Robert- aye, my nephew! I'd like fine to see him. Does he favour Jock?'

'No,' said Isobel sadly, 'he looks like you.'

'What a calamity,' said Jamie.

'I didn't mean it like that,' said Isobel, 'but oh, I wish he could have looked like John.'

Jamie held out his arms and hugged her again, but she soon moved away. If she closed her eyes he was very like John, and the ghostliness of that made her feel uneasy.

Robert was enchanted with his newfound uncle and aunt, especially when Jamie played him tunes on the whistle. Isobel was pleased to see it, for apart from occasional visits from Winston, her son had lacked a man's company since she turned off the last of her suitors.

Jamie introduced Charlotte to McCleod, and after that they had dinner and talked long into the night. Isobel saw them off to bed with a touch of envy (for they were obviously much in love) but no scruple.

It seemed much too early the next morning that the household was roused by a thunderous knocking on the door. A flustered Jennie ran to answer it, and came back quaking and stammering that two gentlemen were demanding admittance. Isobel was annoyed at the intrusion, and went to deal with it herself.

'We have reason to believe you are sheltering a miscreant calling himself James McCleod,' said one man, when she asked their business.

'There is no one of that name here,' said Isobel. 'I am Mrs John Campbell, and this is Glen Heather. What is this person supposed to have done?'

The men exchanged glances. 'I think it best if we speak with the owner,' said one.

'It will do you no good,' said Isobel, but the men insisted, and in the end she sent for her son. 'This is the owner of Glen Heather,' she said, her hands on Robert's small shoulders. 'Now ask your questions and then leave us in peace.'

The larger young man cleared his throat. 'We have reason to believe that the said James McCleod has unlawfully abducted the niece of Mr Frederick Lambert and carried her off for- ahem- lewd and immoral purposes.'

'Have you indeed?' said Isobel. 'And what makes you think this Mr McCleod is here?'

'We have had information that there is a person of that name residing in this house.'

'Aye, so there is,' said Isobel dryly. 'Our pet bird is called McCleod. He has much to say for himself, so I believe someone has been indulging in a prank at your expense.'

One of the strangers began to bluster, but Isobel held up her hand.

'Had this person you seek been here indeed, what would you expect me to do about it?'

'It would be your Christian duty to hand over the miscreant to be dealt with according to the law of the land,' droned the constable.

'No doubt,' said Isobel. 'However, I cannot help you. The only folk here apart from myself, my son and the servants are my son's uncle and aunt who are visiting from Dunedin.'

'You decline to assist us, madam?'

'I *cannot* assist you,' said Isobel firmly. 'However, I can promise you that if a Mr McCleod and an abducted heiress should arrive at Glen Heather, I shall send you a message to that effect. Good day, gentlemen.'

The constables went grumbling away, and Isobel called for Nannie Goodridge to take Robert back to the nursery. Then she sat down in the parlour and quaked.

'My *wretched* tongue!' she said aloud. 'It is forever bringing me to grief.'

She sighed, and stood up, then went away to tell Jamie and his sweetheart that they had better leave Glen Heather before the law returned with a warrant.

'And please do *not* tell me where you mean to go,' she added with a wry smile. 'I have come very close to lying today already, and I do not wish to come closer.'

She looked hard at the young couple. Jamie and Charlotte were now holding hands, and looking the picture of guilt.

'I suppose-' she began slowly, and then shook her head. 'No. I do not wish to know. Just tell me one thing. *Did* you abduct her, Jamie?'

'Aye,' said Jamie.

'No!' said Charlotte.

They smiled sheepishly at one another, and Isobel shook her head. 'Oh, be off with the pair of you!' she said. 'Jamie, you recall your brother's horse Thunder?'

'Aye?' Jamie looked a little surprised at the change of subject.

'He is stabled in the end stall, and he needs exercise,' said Isobel distinctly. She turned and walked away.

'Where are Uncle Jamie and Auntie Lotta?' asked an aggrieved Robert that afternoon.

Isobel shrugged. 'I do not know, my son.'

'Oh.' Robert digested this and pouted. 'I liked them.'

'So did I,' said Isobel.

'Will we see them again, Mama?'

'I hope so, one day,' said Isobel, 'but who can say?'

***

Over the next two years Isobel expected to hear news of the runaways from Ness, but the infrequent letters from Dunedin mentioned only young Hector and his family and Eddie, now a schoolmaster in a nearby village.

Isobel was disinclined to ask locally for news, for fear of drawing unwelcome attention to herself and the family. And so the time went on.

1868 brought many excitements to the colonies, but life at Glen Heather continued in its steady rhythm. The routine of a working property brought seasonal variation, but to Isobel one year was very like the next. The ewes lambed and were dipped, shorn and tupped in season, the numbers of cattle waxed and waned. The hay crops varied with the vagaries of the weather, and the turnips grew and were taken to market.

Old Grey Heron became stiff and lame in the mornings, and sometimes Isobel regretted the impulse that had led her to give John's Thunder to Jamie. But she reflected that Thunder had not been so very young either. She purchased a new riding mare from a farmer at Chudleigh, and wondered if she had ever been young herself.

Robert was seven years old now, an unmistakable Campbell in looks, but curiously mild in character. Sometimes Isobel wondered if he were not *too* biddable, for surely young boys were meant to be rambunctious?

She had long ago had Nannie Goodridge put him into breeches, and sometimes she took him out with her to work, seated before her on the new mare. She tried to be his friend, but it was always Nanny Goodridge to whom he ran if hurt or afraid. He was a quiet child, always trying to please, and Isobel wondered at her own impatience.

His placidity reminded her of his father and she wondered with a pang if John's sweetness might not have eventually begun to grate on her too. But if John had lived, she would not have become the tough-shelled person she was today. If John had lived, she would never have had to grow hard and cold and incisive. She would never have developed the caustic tongue that Nannie Goodridge detested and Robert feared. Instead, she would have been the contented mother of a large family of black-headed, fighting, thrawn Campbell children. She would have drunk tea with other ladies and discussed silks and servants instead of sheep and straw. She would have been dressed in fine gowns and would perhaps have grown a little plump by now.

And John would have laughed and hugged her and claimed that he loved every ounce of the extra flesh.

If John had lived she would have had other sons and daughters. Robert would have had company and would have learned to be assertive and noisy, like other children. And John would have been nearing thirty by now, and would have-

No, thought Isobel bleakly, she must not imagine John as he would have been now. She must think of him in Paradise and try to keep Glen Heather as he would have done.

***

It was in the spring of 1868 that James Galbraith returned to Glen Heather. He had kept in contact with Tobias Scott-Blakeney after his move to New South Wales, but as demand for his services had risen, he found himself tied increasingly to his new home. His old friend and mentor had died during the summer of 1862, and since then Galbraith had had no pressing reason to cross the strait to Tasmania. Tasmania! Even the name was new.

Young Charcoal Jamie had arrived in Van Diemen's Land, but now both Van Diemen's Land and the convict ships were fading into history. Just so had his youth faded into middle age, thought Galbraith with rueful whimsy.

He hardly liked to see himself in the mirror any more. His sandy hair was heavily flecked with grey and his scarred face was growing lined and seamed. Only his blue eyes, forever magnified behind the thick lenses, remained young and aware. He thought he had been lucky. He had found a generous measure of fame, and he had friends and sufficient money to last till the end of his days. What he did not have was a family, and for this he blamed himself. He had tried to explain it to Tobias, the year before the old man died.

'Toby, I did try, but I just could not bring myself to settle for second best,' he said. 'If you had only known her... then you would have understood.'

Tobias had looked at him with derision, but there had been compassion too. 'Jamie, I *did* know her,' he said dryly. 'No-' (as Galbraith tried to interrupt) '- you hear me out! I met your Eve when she came up to town, oh, many years ago it is now.'

'Why did you never tell me?' Galbraith had asked, as much puzzled as incensed.

'I thought it better not to. No, do *not* interrupt me, Jamie. You know I detest it when you interrupt me! Let me see, it was - yes, it was just a few weeks after I fetched you back to recover from your fever. Mrs Campbell had left her husband and had come up to town with the carrier.'

'*What*!'

'She had come up to town,' Tobias continued inexorably, 'to find a situation. Her husband had been put about over your affair and she thought it best to leave. And this despite the fact that she was in a certain condition.'

'I would have helped her! I would have taken her in, and the child as well!'

'Of course you would. However, you would also have troubled the poor girl with protestations of love and devotion. You would have proposed to her on bended knee and taken her burdens on your own shoulders, and loved her child as your own.'

'Of course I would,' Galbraith agreed warmly. 'That was what I wanted; what I *always* wanted. I loved her so much.'

'It was not what *she* wanted,' the old man said austerely. 'Your Eve was a lovely woman, Jamie, but she was truly in love with her husband. You would never have been better than second best, for her.'

'It would have been enough.'

'For you, perhaps, it would have been enough. But it would have never done for her. I could see misery ahead for both of you, so I- er- I made it possible for her to return to her husband without a stain on her character or on his honour.' Tobias had the grace to look a little guilty when he said that and continued briskly; 'There now! They say confession is good for the immortal soul and I must admit I have been forced to consider the state of my own soul quite frequently of late.'

'You should not have done it,' Galbraith said. 'You should not have interfered.'

'I had to, my boy. I wanted you both to have the best.'

'And now I am too old.'

Tobias had smiled suddenly, and almost angelically, his gaunt old face almost skull-like against the richly upholstered armchair in which he spent his final days. 'Believe me, my dear boy,' he had said, 'you are never too old to love. *Never.*'

Perhaps Tobias had been right, but Galbraith was very much aware of the passing years. He had hoped, when he heard of Hector Campbell's death and received the mocking legacy, that Ness would contact him. When she did not, he had gone to Glen Heather, only to find himself too late. Ness was in New Zealand, and in her place had been the decided young woman who had married Ness' son. That had given him a bad jolt, for the son in question was an unborn baby when he loved and lost his Eve.

He had taken offence at the young woman's insinuations, had dumped the gift he'd brought for Ness, and walked out, deciding once and for all to put Glen Heather and its lady out of his mind forever.

And so he might have done had he not chanced to meet young Jamie Campbell in Melbourne.

As his fame had grown, Galbraith found himself increasingly in demand as a portrait painter to the wealthy, but he had never quite lost his taste for the lower level of society, the busy brawling folk who made the colonies such a colourful place to be. He had been in Melbourne for the Intercolonial Exhibition, and had also stolen some time to frequent inns and theatres and watch the world go by. And there he found Ness' youngest son.

He recognised him immediately, although he had never met the lad and had not been aware of his existence. But there he was, singing a mournful ditty with a twinkle in his eyes, then shouldering his way out of the crowd with exactly the same unconscious arrogance Hector Campbell had always shown.

The lad had been wearing breeches and a spotted Crimean shirt in place of a green plaid, and the arrogant, stone-cut features had been less rigid, but nevertheless he was unmistakable. He *had* to be Hector Campbell's son, and during the conversation that followed it had become clear that he was Ness' son as well. Jamie Campbell seemed a pleasant lad, if unpolished, but Galbraith searched his features in vain for a trace of the girl he had loved. And this lad was older than Ness had been then, and time was passing on, so, mindful of Tobias's words, Galbraith decided to send a message to Ness. He had written his name and direction on the paper and asked the lad to act as courier.

And nothing happened.

In two years, nothing at all had come of his unspoken plea. And so, at the age of almost fifty-four, with his youth far behind him and the words of his oldest friend echoing in his mind, James Galbraith was riding back to Glen Heather.

He could have written, but he knew from experience that letters were easily ignored, and besides, he had a yen to see the place again. The Bruce was long dead, but something of his pawky spirit seemed to linger as Galbraith trotted his hired nag along the road from Mersey.

It had been new and raw when he first rode that way, and scarcely better when he left ignominiously, with blood still wet on his face. Galbraith touched the mark on his cheek. It looked like a duelling scar and had attracted welcome attention in his younger days, but he never thought of it without realising how very, very lucky he had been that day. He had no doubts at all that, had Hector chosen, he could have been effectively blinded. The man had been a virtuoso with the whip. He could have scourged Galbraith until no skin remained on his back. He could have thrashed him like a convict.

A shudder went up Galbraith's spine at the thought. Having experienced one flick from Hector's whip he knew he could never have borne a lashing.

The road had changed since his last visit too. With a start, he realised that had been seven years before. Was it really so long since he faced Eliza Jarvis' daughter, dressed in heavy mourning and asking impertinent questions about the past? Galbraith shook the thought away and kicked the horse into a canter. He was not so old he couldn't put that young woman in her place if she tried it again! But better to deal with John Campbell himself. The man would be-how old? Galbraith calculated years and winced at the total. If Ness' son was nearing thirty, Ness herself must be closing on to fifty. Oh, that was impossible. To him, Ness was forever his Eve, and Eve was eternal.

CHAPTER 28

McCleod was being impossible. That was not so surprising, because he was a recalcitrant bird by nature, but today he had the wind in his head. Ever since lunchtime, he had been perched in the apple tree by the kitchen door, methodically picking off blossom and dropping it on the ground.

Mrs Baker had called him a blamed bird and he had responded to the scolding by dropping to hang upside down like a bat, flapping his wings and shrieking at the top of his lungs. Mrs Baker flapped her apron at him, and he scrambled back onto his perch and glowered, then set out purposefully to destroy some more of the blossom. He was still engaged in this pursuit when James Galbraith rode up to the house. As he had been seven years before, Galbraith was filled with admiration for Hector's vision and with pride in his own work. These days he produced portraits only, so it was many years since he had designed and overseen the building of a fine house.

Yes, he thought nostalgically, Glen Heather had been his first major project and his best, even if he had not been able to see it through to the end. He wondered who completed the work and when, then noticed with delight that someone, probably Ness, had taken his advice and planted an apple tree by the door. It was a fine specimen, some thirty years old, and covered in blossom like a virgin bride.

Galbraith had a sudden whim to paint the tree as a maiden, or a maiden as a tree, but there was little call for dryads in this cold age of reason.

Something moved in an upper branch, and he peered at it short-sightedly, straining to see through the maze of blossoming branches. A white head twisted snake-wise to peer down at him, with wicked black eyes taking in his every move. Galbraith blinked as the bird snapped off a fine twig of blossom and dropped it contemptuously on the ground.

'And who are you?' he enquired whimsically. 'The serpent in the Tree of Knowledge?'

'No, that is McCleod,' said a voice behind him.

Galbraith twisted in the saddle to see a small boy in knickerbockers and a loose, striped shirt regarding him solemnly from his seat on a sawn stump. The child had a fair, freckled face, thick black hair, grey eyes and a firm chin. He was a Campbell, without a doubt.

'Good morning, Master Campbell,' said Galbraith. 'Is your papa at home?'

The child shook his head. 'My papa is in Paradise,' he said. 'I have been helping Mr Harkins in the garden. We have been planting daffy-down-dillies, but Mr Perry says we should have planted them in the autumn.' He held out grubby hands for inspection.

'I see,' said Galbraith rather faintly. 'Is your mama at home?'

'Aye. She is in the stable with Daisy, who is having a foal. If it is a colt, Mama says I may have him as my own.'

Galbraith nodded. 'And McCleod, is he your own?' he asked, watching the white bird in the apple tree.

'McCleod belongs to my Grannie Ness.'

'Your Grannie Ness is here then, at Glen Heather?'

The child shook his head. 'I have never seen Grannie Ness, but her picture is in the parlour. It was painted by a clever gentleman whose name is James... James...'

'James Galbraith?'

'Aye. There is a picture of Auld Hector as well. Mama says I look like him.'

'You do,' said Galbraith.

The child accepted this with equanimity. 'My name is Robert,' he said. 'I am Robert John Campbell. My papa named me that before he went to live in Paradise.' He paused. 'My papa fell from a horse, and struck his head.'

'My name is James Galbraith,' said Galbraith.

'Like the clever gentleman who paints pictures?'

'The very same. Robert, I wish to see your mama, but first I need to tie up this horse. Could you show me where to go?'

The lad nodded. 'It is not a very good horse,' he said dubiously. 'Is it your own?'

Galbraith reassured the boy on this point and disposed of the hired nag, then looked about the yard for inspiration. Having made young Robert's acquaintance, it seemed a little late to knock on the door, and besides, if the child was correct, Mrs Campbell would not be within. A little nervously, he wondered when John Campbell had died. It could not have been long ago, for had not young Jamie been coming to visit his brother a bare two years before? Yet the child seemed to feel no more distress for his father than he felt for his grandfather's passing, which had been before his birth.

Robert tugged his sleeve. 'Do you wish to see my mama in the stable? Mama said I was not to go in until she called, but you could go in. That is the stable over there.'

Galbraith thanked him gravely, and entered the sandstone building. At first he thought the child had been wrong, for there seemed to be no lady in the stable. Instead, he saw two men and a lad, attending a labouring mare. The lad, a tall, slight figure in breeches and a striped shirt, was holding the mare's head and soothing her. Unlike the other two, the lad was not wearing the ubiquitous mutton-chop whiskers, nor had he a hat.

The two men had each gripped a foreleg of the emerging foal and were drawing it into the world, while the lad's hands were white-knuckled on the halter. Galbraith watched in silence until the foal arrived with a long wet slither and fell in the straw. One of the men bent to clear its nostrils, and the other lifted one of the gangling hind legs.

'A fine colt, ma'am,' he said cheerfully. 'Master Robert will be pleased.'

Ma'am? Startled, Galbraith raised his eyes from the new foal and focussed on the lad who held the mare. And of course it was no lad at all, but Isobel Campbell. Now he knew the truth, he could scarcely see how he could have been deceived- except that one hardly expected the lady of the house to be dressed in breeches, assisting with the delivery of a foal. Even Ness, who had been unconventional in her way, had always worn a gown.

Galbraith waited until Isobel Campbell looked up and saw him.

'May I help you?'

Her voice had not changed at all. It was cool and decisive and clipped as her father's had been. She looked like her father as well, with the haughty Jarvis carriage and the dark, guarded eyes that went oddly with her mass of soft hair. And how could he have thought her a lad with *that*? He saw she was thinner than she had been, and that her brow was marked with lines that had no business there for ten years to come. To be sure, she had been a little older than her husband.

'Mrs Campbell?' He took the offered hand. 'I am James Galbraith. We met some years ago...'

'Aye, so we did.' Her eyes were steady, but he thought she was embarrassed. As well she might be, remembering the conversation they had had then.

'I was very sorry to hear of your husband's passing,' he said carefully. 'I collect it was fairly recent?' (It could not be *very* recent, however, since she wore no mourning.)

Isobel Campbell blinked. 'My husband died seven years ago,' she said calmly.

'But young Jamie was coming to visit him just two years ago... I do beg your pardon!'

'I think,' she said warily, 'we should perhaps continue this conversation in the house. Come in, Mr Galbraith, and do not hesitate to make yourself at home.'

Wondering what he had done to vex her this time, Galbraith followed her trim figure across the yard. She paused only to tell young Robert that his new foal had arrived.

'You may go and help Mr Ward and Mr Perry make him fit to be seen,' she said, 'and then go in to Nannie and tell her about it. You must think of a good name for him, too.'

'Mr Ward?' said Galbraith, as the boy ran off. 'Is he a connection of old Bullocky George Ward?'

'I believe so.' Isobel Campbell paused by the blossoming apple tree and looked up. 'McCleod, that is quite enough,' she said firmly. 'Come along!' She held out a slim arm and to Galbraith's surprise the cockatoo sidled down the branch and stepped down onto her fist.

'Hello, McCleod!' it said clearly.

'Hello McCleod indeed,' said Isobel.

Carrying the bird on her wrist, she ushered Galbraith into the parlour he had visited before. The portrait of Hector Campbell hung beside the one of Ness and he nodded ironically at the man who had bested him.

Isobel saw his glance and said abruptly; 'I have written to John's mother to tell her of the portrait. She was very pleased to hear of it, and directed we should hang it in Glen Heather. Sit down, Mr Galbraith, and tell me about Jamie. I have often wished for news of him and Charlotte. Are they well?'

'I met him only once, two years ago in Melbourne,' said Galbraith. 'I have never heard of anyone called Charlotte.'

'Then you have not come with a message from them for me.'

'No.' He found himself nettled at her tone. 'I have come, rather, to see if you could send a message for *me*.'

'Oh? If it is to Jamie Campbell, I have not seen him for two years either.'

Galbraith brushed this aside. 'I have no messages for Jamie Campbell, engaging youngster though he is. No, Mrs Campbell, I would like you to send a message to Agnes.'

'To *Ness*?'

'Aye. I see she has not yet returned from New Zealand, and perhaps may never return. May I speak bluntly, Mrs Campbell?'

'Of course,' said Isobel, adding, with a grimace, 'as I recall you spoke bluntly enough on the occasion of our last meeting. And pray do not think that I blame you for that. It was my own unwarranted impertinence that was at fault. I had no right to accuse you of- of-'

'Of fathering your husband?' suggested Galbraith. 'Come Mrs Campbell; a lady who dresses like a gentleman should not recoil from plain talk.'

'I deserved that,' she said dryly, 'but have a care Mr Galbraith. I may be a widow but I am not quite without protection.'

Galbraith thought of the men in the stable. 'Of course you are not,' he said. 'I merely reminded you of the facts. Since you have not fainted away, I collect you are able to stomach plain words?' She nodded. 'Then I have some for you.

'As you remarked before, I was working at Glen Heather in the months before your late husband's birth. I did not know at the time that Mistress Campbell was expecting a child, and it seemed to me that her husband, although an estimable man, did not always treat her with concern.'

'Hector Campbell was an auld bugger,' said Isobel. 'Or so John used to say. But go on.'

Galbraith's jaw dropped, but he hid a smile and went on. 'To put it bluntly, I fell in love with Ness. I was young and romantic and I wanted us to elope, but she was unwilling. She gave me to understand that her duty lay with her husband, and that there was no hope for me. Unfortunately, Hector thought otherwise.' He touched his cheek reflectively. 'Ness told me to find a lassie of my own, and I said I would, but I have never found one to compare with her, and I would not take second best.'

He thought Isobel might sneer at him for that, but there was a luminous glow of sympathy in her eyes. It was gone almost at once, but she nodded, as if she understood his sentiments.

'When Hector died,' said Galbraith, 'I hoped Ness would turn to me, but instead she left for New Zealand without a word.'

'Aye, she went to stay with her brother,' said Isobel.

'When I met young Jamie on the docks, I gave him a message for Ness. She has never replied. I am a fool to hope, but perhaps he never delivered it.'

'Jamie is not in New Zealand, and I think he has not been back,' said Isobel slowly. 'His mother never mentions him.'

'Then presumably that message *was* never delivered.' Galbraith took off his spectacles and rubbed his eyes wearily. 'I doubt young Jamie is much of a hand with a pen. Mrs Campbell, I like rejection no more than any man, but I am not getting younger and neither is she and so I have just a small hope that we might still be together, as friends, if nothing else. And so I am asking you if, by your charity, you would send my direction to her, and tell her how I feel. If she feels anything for me at all, or if she would like to greet me for old time's sake, she might send me word.'

Isobel sat silently for so long that Galbraith was certain she would refuse. Eventually, however, she turned to open the roll-top desk. Galbraith, seeing her buttocks outlined against the breeches, was surprised with a sudden twinge of desire. He pushed it down, shocked and disgusted with himself. The lady was dressed as a gentleman, and was young enough to be his daughter. To cap it all, she was the widowed daughter-in-law of his long-time love! That was a tale fit for the music halls, he thought wryly, but he knew that lust had little to do with love.

'I will not send any message for you, Mr Galbraith,' she said distantly, 'but here is Mrs Campbell's direction so you may send her a letter yourself.'

Galbraith looked down at the letter she offered. He supposed it was in Ness' own hand, but since he could not remember ever having seen her writing, he could not be sure.

'Read it, Mr Galbraith,' said Isobel. 'It is in no way private, and may reassure you that Mrs Campbell takes considerable pleasure from life, even without you.'

With a word of apology, Galbraith smoothed and read the letter. In Ness' careful phrasing he heard the rhythm of her voice, saw the tilt of her head as she bade him visit the docks. His eyes were damp when he had finished, and he glanced up at his hostess.

'It was I who suggested she should try sketching, you know,' he said slowly, 'but perhaps I have no right to interfere in her life again.'

Isobel turned away. 'Mr Galbraith,' she said harshly, 'you should never turn away from hope, not if you have a chance. Write to her, please. Perhaps you may yet be happy together.'

Galbraith folded the letter and put it in his pocket, then looked at his companion's bent head. She was not at all like Ness, but the two women must have had *something* in common, for they had both loved and married Campbell men. He had achieved the purpose of his visit. Ordinarily, colonial hospitality would have seen him invited to put up at Glen Heather for the night, but Isobel Campbell was no ordinary colonial hostess and, for the first time in years, he felt unsure of his welcome.

'Thank you, Mrs Campbell,' he said at length. 'I am grateful for your assistance in this matter. Now, if you will excuse me, I shall take my leave.'

Isobel roused herself and turned to face him. 'Why not stay to dinner, Mr Galbraith? It is a long way back to Mersey on an empty stomach, and besides, the weather looks unsettled.'

He looked closely at her, not wanting to take advantage of mere politeness, but her eyes were friendly, and even pleading.

'We lack company at Glen Heather,' she said lightly. 'It is good to meet one from the outside world, especially a gentleman as socially distinguished as yourself.'

Was this meant as flattery or barbed sarcasm? With Isobel Campbell it was difficult to tell, but Galbraith decided it hardly mattered. She had issued the invitation and seemed anxious that he should accept it, and besides, an enticing aroma was drifting in from the kitchen.

He thought back to the meals he used to eat at Glen Heather; dried beef jerky and stewed tea by the creek, or game and onions, turnips and damper at the slab hut. He smiled, remembering the happiness he had savoured in those days, and said he would be happy to stay.

Dinner was an unexpectedly pleasant occasion. Isobel had put on a gown of dark green wool, and pinned her hair into a tidy pleat at the back of her head. She looked very much the gracious lady, and seemed to have put away her astringent manner with her breeches.

Galbraith found he was trying to please her, telling stories against himself and other members of Sydney society, and even pausing to sketch the wicked McCleod for Robert's amusement. The child had been allowed to sit up for dinner, which was evidently a rare concession, for an old nursemaid bustled him off to bed as soon as the batter pudding was eaten.

'We rely rather on nursery favourites here, Mr Galbraith,' said Isobel with a hint of apology, but Galbraith smiled and said he enjoyed them himself.

'They are easy on the tongue and on the digestion.'

'And remind you of your childhood?' asked Isobel.

Galbraith shook his head, reflecting that his childhood had been more of the thin porridge and dry bannock variety. And that had been on the days when he was lucky.

They lingered over the meal, and his hostess asked so many eager questions that Galbraith realised she had spoken the truth when she claimed to be starved for companionship. He told her a little of the building of Glen Heather, and something of his own early career.

'If Tobias had not taken me in I do not know what would have happened to me,' he said. 'He was probably the best friend I ever had, but we could scarcely have been less alike.'

'Folk need not be alike to be friends,' said Isobel. Her eyes were shadowed and she was turning her wine glass as if she might find an answer in the depths.

'That's true,' said Galbraith gently. 'But Toby and I were very, very different. He was a great man, an artist, and I was a convict scullery brat.' He saw her eyes flicker, and smiled. 'You did not know I was a convict? I thought it was common knowledge.'

'Perhaps it is, but I do not go about in society.' She hesitated, seemed about to ask a question and then subsided.

'You would like to know what I did, to bring me here in chains,' said Galbraith. He looked at her steadily across the table, and told her.

'It seems little enough,' said Isobel after a moment.

'Aye, little enough to change a life.'

There was a long silence, and he realised that in a spell of bitter reflection she was thinking of a little thing that had changed her own life.

'Tell me,' he said suddenly, 'how did a daughter of Scarborough come to Glen Heather? As I recall Hector Campbell and your father were permanently at cuffs.' He was remembering the ugly scene at Scarborough when Grey Falcon had been shot.

'I think they were at one time,' said Isobel reflectively, 'but Mr Campbell was always kind to me; kinder than he was to John, by all accounts. When he died, he arranged that Papa should be excused the remainder of the mortgage if John and I were married and had a son.'

'Good God!' said Galbraith involuntarily.

'Papa and Margaret, God rest them, did not live long to enjoy the freedom from debt, but John and I- we were- so very happy.'

'Who is at Scarborough now?'

'My brother Winston and his wife Gwynnie and their children.'

'And you are alone at Glen Heather.'

Isobel lifted her chin at that. 'Robert is here. He is the owner of Glen Heather.'

'To be sure.' Galbraith wondered what he had said to offend her.

He was about to make a social thank-you and take his leave, when he realised the threatened rain had blown down from the mountain and was beating against the windows. He looked at Isobel with dismay. He supposed he could always bed down in the stable. He would come to no harm and he had slept in many worse places as a child. He was about to suggest it when Isobel rose to her feet.

'You must stay the night, Mr Galbraith,' she said decisively. 'I will have Jennie show you to the guestroom, but of course you know already where it is?'

***

After James Galbraith retired for the night, Isobel wandered bleakly into the parlour. It had been pleasant to have company at dinner, especially as Galbraith was so much older than she. There was no danger of *his* turning into a suitor, even if he had not been hopelessly in love with Ness.

Isobel sighed. They were quite a pair, she and James Galbraith. He was in love with a woman he had not seen for close to thirty years, and she with a man who had been dead for seven. Fancy's fools, she and Galbraith both. To be sure Ness was alive, but she was no longer the lovely young woman who looked out of the painting above the mantel. But neither was Galbraith the young man who had fallen so foolishly in love. At least, if they met again, they would meet with all the years apart lived equally by both. If she and John could meet again- dear God, thought Isobel painfully, he would be twenty-one and I almost thirty!

She slept poorly, waking often to listen to the distant drum of rain on the roof, and found in the morning that it was raining still. She always disliked the spring, for with it came not only the anniversary of her widowhood, but also the difficulties of mud and water on the mountain. If there was too much rain, the sheep suffered footrot and other disorders, while too little meant the hay crop would be short in the summer. And the lambs were always a concern, whether it rained or not.

Isobel rose early, and dressed in her usual working costume. Rain or no rain, some tasks still were waiting to be done. She would check the new foal in the stable, and inevitably there would be a few bedraggled lambs to succour and warm in the kitchen.

Galbraith was up when she entered the parlour, dressed in his rumpled clothes of the day before, and running a hand over his unshaven chin. He was gazing pensively out the window at McCleod, who was disporting himself under the water pouring from the eaves, flapping and squawking with glee.

Isobel knew the cockatoo would soon tire of the game, and would tap on the glass with his beak until someone let him in. He would then sit like a bedraggled hen, preening the water from his feathers and glowering at anyone who tried to scold him.

'Does he never fly away?' asked Galbraith, eyes still on the screeching bird.

'McCleod cannot fly very well,' said Isobel. 'His wing was damaged in a storm long ago and anyway, he seems content to stay with us here.'

'A willing captive,' murmured Galbraith. He cleared his throat. 'Unfortunately,' he remarked, 'the weather is worse this morning.'

'You are welcome to stay until it clears,' said Isobel, and then, fearing she had been ungracious, she added; 'I shall be truly glad to have your company.'

She went out directly after breakfast, returning at ten o'clock with three soaking lambs.

'The ewe drowned in the burn,' she said briefly, and went away, leaving Jennie Comfrey to feed the lambs on sweetened milk.

She was a little surprised on her next return, to find Galbraith sitting cross-legged on the stone-flagged kitchen floor beside Jennie, holding a steaming lamb in his lap and coaxing it to take some milk.

'Well, so the great artist sits on the floor like a common mortal!' she said, and then regretted it when Galbraith looked hurt. 'Oh, my wretched tongue! I am quite out of practice at playing the hostess!' she said remorsefully. 'Please, Mr Galbraith, accept my apologies and my thanks for your help in what can be a very thankless task. Indeed I did not mean to be so offensive.'

She was relieved when Galbraith forced a smile and remarked that even great artists needed a change of occupation. But really, she thought, she *must* learn to guard her tongue; otherwise she would have no friends left at all.

The rain continued steadily for several days, and as fast as one lamb was revived and returned to the ewe, another would be carried into the kitchen, where Galbraith seemed to have constituted himself to be chief nursemaid. Isobel first became used to his constant presence, and then to enjoy it. It was very pleasant to be greeted with a literary quotation or an elliptical comment instead of with domestic news or a complaint from Nannie Goodridge. It was when she realised how much she was looking forward to the evenings they spent conversing over dinner that she realised the danger ahead. She was becoming much too fond of her guest, much too dependent on his gentle humour, and much too comfortable with the sound of his voice. She was even overlooking the weird effect of the magnifying lenses, and had begun to appreciate the mild good humour in his blue eyes.

On the second day she had lent him a razor Jamie Campbell left behind in his flight from Glen Heather, on the third day, Perry had diffidently offered the loan of his Sunday set of clothes. Galbraith declined this offer with grace, but had gratefully accepted a shirt and an old pair of breeches that Emma Perry had put by to mend. He looked comfortable in this shabby costume, but Isobel wondered if she should have offered something of John's. Apart from the breeches and shirts she had commandeered for herself, her husband's belongings were still laid away in lavender.

And to what purpose had she kept them? she asked herself. Even in childhood, Robert set fair to be a bigger man than his father had ever been, and by the time he was of an age to use such things, they would be sadly out of style.

It was when she found herself consciously saving up little incidents to tell Galbraith over dinner that she realised their friendship had gone far enough. She could not allow herself to become dependent on anyone, and she decided that, as soon as ever the weather allowed, James Galbraith would have to leave Glen Heather.

CHAPTER 29

Secure in his long-time devotion to Ness, Galbraith failed to notice the warning signs. He was comfortable at Glen Heather. For many years, he had been despised for his background or fawned over for his talent, and he had found that even in New South Wales his history was widely known.

Here at Glen Heather, he was able to be himself. Isobel Campbell seemed to have dropped most of her barbed comments, and spoke to him as she might have done to an old friend, or even, he thought whimsically, to a favourite uncle. He had grown accustomed to her breeches, (although he felt more comfortable seeing her in gowns) and had come to admire her for the task she had undertaken and for the uncomplaining way she carried it out. It could not have been easy for her to step away from the life of an adored young wife and mother to become the master of Glen Heather. He thought most women in her position would have hired an overseer and retired to live in Launceston or married again, but then, would any husband wish to take on responsibility for a property which could never belong to him?

During the ten days of heavy rain Galbraith saw a lot of young Robert, and took to amusing the boy with whimsical sketches. He drew Jennie Comfrey in the guise of a mouse, Mrs Baker as a cottage loaf, Harkins as an amiable turnip and bustling Emma Perry as a comely ewe. These sketches he gave to Robert with the instructions that they were not to be shown to their subjects. This was more to give the child the pleasure of a secret than because he thought the kindly caricatures would cause any discomfort or offence. On Robert's request, he even drew the child himself, grown to manhood in his knickerbockers, but he hesitated over drawing Isobel, unable to think of an appropriate guise.

To exaggerate her masculine dress would have seemed a cheap jibe, and to have shown her as an apple-tree bride would have been cruel in her widowed state. In the end he decided to draw her exactly as she was, as a gracious lady with decided views and a certain imperious strength. The first sketch did not satisfy him, and neither did the second. The third was better, and the fourth was an improvement on that. In all he had done some half dozen representations of his hostess before he recognised, with chagrin, what was happening. His strange talent had taken over and he was drawing her with love.

It was a sobering thing, to find himself in love again after so many years of immunity to women. It was not that he had ceased to care for Ness, but more that she had finally taken her place as a bittersweet memory of his youth. Isobel Campbell was his present, and if his first love had been impossible, so was his second. He could not have Isobel any more than he could have had Ness.

Isobel was a widow, but he was quite sure she was deeply wedded to her young husband's memory, and she was very young herself. She would easily find a man in his thirties should she wish to marry again.

Galbraith looked at the betraying sketches with pained disgust.

'You are an old fool, Jamie Galbraith,' he said aloud. 'You are a *very* old fool.'

What was it Tobias had said in those final days? '*My dear boy, you are never too old to love. Never.*'

Galbraith sighed resignedly. 'Well, Toby, and so you are proved right yet again,' he said, and wondered what he should do. The answer came easily enough. He should do nothing. If love in his twenties had been painful, love in his fifties was not. His guilt over Ness had led him to face a vengeful Hector and resulted in a permanent scar. He felt no guilt over Isobel, for in loving her he was harming no one, and taking nothing. He would not even trouble her as he had troubled Ness, for of course she would never know of his awakened feelings. But nor would he harrow himself by staying on. He laid aside the latest sketch, and vowed that he would leave Glen Heather next day.

***

Isobel was sorry when Galbraith had gone, but relieved he had come to the decision for himself. It would have been unpleasant for her to send him away.

Robert was bereft for a while, wanting to know why their friend had left so abruptly, but then the ripples of Glen Heather closed as if the interlude had never been. Only sometimes, Isobel found herself looking in the glass in the evenings and wondering why she had bothered to change into a gown. There was no one to care whether she wore breeches or not, no mild blue eyes to smile at her from behind those ridiculous spectacles, and no one to provide her with a window on the wider world.

It was some weeks before she discovered the sketches that Galbraith had done for Robert. She had been searching her desk for a mislaid letter and chanced to see a corner of paper protruding from beneath the sofa, where Robert had evidently considered it concealed. She knelt and drew it out, and found herself holding a portrait of a mouse; a mouse that was also, unmistakably, Jennie Comfrey.

A further search under the sofa yielded more sketches, the likenesses so true that she gasped with admiration. She smiled over the Emma-ewe, and the turnip-Harkins, but when she reached the sketch of Robert her hands grew suddenly still.

Galbraith had drawn a face which was unmistakably her son's, but which was also that of a grown man. The features could have been Hector Campbell's, but the expression was not Hector's. This was an altogether softer face, gentle, mild and kind. Her gaze moved to the portrait of the real Hector Campbell, a portrait completed many years after the fact. It seemed, so far as she could remember, to be a perfect likeness. If Galbraith could paint a person he had not seen for twenty years, and if he could paint a man who as yet existed only as a boy, why should he not paint John?

It was a source of grief to Isobel that she had no picture of John. She had no artistic talent herself, so she had always believed it could never be but now, faced with the evidence of Galbraith's peculiar talents, she began to hope.

Hurriedly, before she could doubt the wisdom of her idea, she sat down to compose a letter of commission.

***

Galbraith's first thought on receiving word from Glen Heather was that Isobel had sent him news of Ness. His second was a shamed and short-lived hope that she had discovered some feeling for him. The third, when he realised what she was asking, was furious distaste. She wanted him to paint the dead.

She pointed out that he had done it once, in painting his memory of Hector, and also that he had drawn her son's future self. She offered to supply a precise description of her husband's features, and claimed herself ready to travel to New South Wales and pay whatever price he considered fair for the work. She wanted him to paint the dead.

His immediate reaction was to refuse. These days, thanks to the success of his work and a generous legacy from Tobias, he could afford to please himself in the commissions he undertook. This being so, why should he do something that filled him with such distaste? But beneath it all he knew he would have to do it, and also that he would be doing it at Glen Heather.

It was late summer when he finally crossed the strait to Tasmania. He spent some time in Launceston attending to business there, and then hired a horse and set out for Glen Heather.

He had purposely given no warning of his coming, hoping to catch Isobel unawares. She was tallying accounts in the parlour, and if he hoped for unguarded joy at the sight of him he was disappointed. Instead, she looked wary, and a little ashamed.

'I had no right to ask you to do this,' she said.

'No,' he agreed. 'No right at all.'

She looked disconcerted at that, and he could see her thinking that it was a very odd artist who would turn down a rich commission. Yet she must have had some doubt, or she would not have said it at all.

'You came, though,' she observed.

'Oh yes, I came,' said Galbraith impatiently. 'I did it once for Ness, and I can do no less for you. I have all my materials in my valise, so let us begin.'

'But- the price-' said Isobel. 'We have not discussed the price! And you have only just arrived; you must be tired.'

'The price is nothing,' said Galbraith. 'I had work to do in Melbourne and Launceston in any case, and there is more to do when I leave here. As for being tired, I may be old, Mrs Campbell, but I am not yet decrepit.'

He had wondered if his feelings for Isobel would have died over the months they spent apart, but he knew immediately that they had not. It was inconvenient, but no doubt if it hadn't been so he would have turned down this commission and the others in town, and stayed where he belonged.

He switched deliberately into his working mode, sat down in an armchair and opened his valise to extract a tablet and a stick of charcoal.

'Tell me,' he said conversationally, 'what did your husband look like?'

Isobel gulped. 'He looked rather like his mother,' she said slowly.

'Then he had reddish hair? And a heart-shaped face?'

'No. His face was longer than hers, and his hair was black, and soft like Robert's. He had grey eyes, quite narrow.'

Sketching busily, Galbraith kept on firing questions. How long had her husband's hair been? Had he worn a moustache? Did his eyebrows arch or meet? Had he a scar or a dimple? And were his ears set high or low?'

Isobel began to stammer and contradict herself, and Galbraith looked up impatiently. 'Come along, Mrs Campbell; do try to concentrate. I cannot do a portrait if I have no face in mind. Think, now. Was the dimple in his left cheek or his right?'

'His... his... oh!' cried Isobel in anguish, 'I cannot remember!'

Galbraith looked at the drawing he had made. Anger and resentment shrieked from every line of it and he did not, no, he *would not* envy the dead. Slowly, he crumpled the ruined sheet and tossed it into the grate, and then looked thoughtfully at the two portraits on the wall. He had done it for Ness, and he could do it for Isobel, but he must do it in his own way. He closed his eyes for a moment, and then began to sketch, creating a masculine version of Ness Campbell's face, a little older, a little thinner than hers had been, but with the same sweet steadfast expression. He used Hector's bold colouring, Ness' slight build, and something of the love he could see reflected in the widow's stricken eyes.

'Here,' he said gently after a while, 'does this look a little like your John?'

Isobel looked at the sketch and burst into a passion of tears.

'Come,' said Galbraith uncomfortably, 'if I have it so wrong we can always begin again.'

'No, no, you have it right! That was John, exactly. But oh, he looks so *young*.'

***

Galbraith worked for three days on the actual portrait, and in all that time Isobel never looked at it once. He finished it very late one night, and set it aside to dry.

As always after an intense period of concentration, he felt wrung out, and afraid to look at his creation for fear his talent had mysteriously deserted him. As always, he cleaned his brushes and palette meticulously, and then found himself drawn to look at it after all.

He looked steadily at the young face he had painted. It was a good face, and it was the face of the man whom Isobel had loved. He wondered, as he had often wondered before, why he had the gift of painting what his eyes could never see. And he wondered, as he had rarely wondered before, if the gift might sometimes be a curse.

The floors of Glen Heather were made of solid slate, and the parlour was covered with oilcloth, but he knew, without even a betraying creak, that someone was standing behind him.

'Well, Isobel?' he said. 'Are you satisfied now?'

She did not ask how he had known she was there. She simply came to his side and looked directly at the portrait.

'I am perfectly satisfied,' she said. 'That is John, to the life.'

'John,' said Galbraith, too tired to be kind, 'is dead.'

Isobel looked at him sadly. 'Do you think I do not *know* that, Mr Galbraith? I go to sleep knowing it, I wake knowing it, and in the night I reach out in my sleep, still knowing it. On the night that we were married I woke up with John beside me, and I thought that this was the way I'd be waking from that time on. And it was true.'

'Do you think he would have wanted you to grieve forever?' asked Galbraith curiously.

'Why, no, Mr Galbraith! John would never have been so foolish, and he had never such a conceit of himself.'

'And yet here you are, still grieving.'

'Here I am. But what about *you*, Mr Galbraith, have *you* not grieved forever? And you had less cause than I, for *your* love is still alive.'

'I would have loved someone else if I had ever found a way.'

'Would you? Are you sure you have not found it convenient, all these years, to think yourself a martyr to love? Hopeless love,' said Isobel, 'is very safe. It saves you the trouble of making an effort with the living. It is clean and romantic, but it does not keep you warm at night.'

Galbraith felt the colour rising in his cheeks, but he looked at her steadily. 'What about you, Isobel? Do you enjoy martyrdom?'

'No, I do not!' she said passionately. 'I want to be free of it, but I promised John I would care for Glen Heather, and how could I do that if I loved another man? He would want to take me away, or else he would want to run Glen Heather.'

'What you need,' said Galbraith, 'is a gentleman who is prepared to compromise, and to accept that he cannot come first in your thoughts.'

'I know that,' said Isobel. She had been staring at the portrait, but now she looked up at him with a challenge in her dark eyes. 'Well, Mr Galbraith? Have you written to your Mistress Campbell yet, and asked her to come home to you?'

'I have not, and I will not.'

'Are you afraid, Mr Galbraith?'

'Not at all,' said Galbraith calmly. 'But I have finally faced what I really knew years ago. If Ness had wanted me then, after Hector died, she would never have gone to New Zealand. If Ness wanted me now, she would have written and let me know. Or she would have come back here, for she knew I brought the portrait.'

'So we both face a hard truth at last,' said Isobel. She turned away, and headed for the door, then came suddenly back to Galbraith. 'Mr Galbraith, I am so *lonely*.'

'I know,' he said.

'If you were a gentleman,' said Isobel reproachfully, 'you would offer to remedy that.'

Galbraith took off his spectacles and watched her tragic figure dissolve into a blur. 'Let me take you to bed.'

He wondered if she would slap his face, but was unsurprised when she did not. Nothing Isobel Campbell did was conventional, so why should she act conventionally now? He waited, but she said nothing for some time.

'It was only a suggestion,' he said dryly. 'If you dislike the idea simply tell me so, if possible *without* a horsewhip in your hand.'

Isobel made a choked sound that could have been a sob, but which he thought was probably a laugh. Encouraged, he put out his hands towards the blur.

'Of course, I am considerably older than you,' he said fairly. 'Your brother would hardly approve of such a proceeding.'

'Why have you taken off your spectacles?' she asked suspiciously.

'To preserve them,' said Galbraith. 'If you had slapped my face as custom decrees, I could have been badly cut with broken glass. One scar is romantic, or so I have been informed, but several begin to suggest carelessness or undue quarrelsomeness on the part of the bearer.'

'Nonsense,' said Isobel sharply. 'You took them off so you would not see my face when you asked me. I am not your Ness, Mr Galbraith.'

'And I am not your John, as you can see perfectly well.'

There was a pause, and Galbraith wondered what was coming next. She could order him from the house, she could laugh at him, she could flay him with words, she could ignore it like a lady- or she could fall in with his suggestion.

'Not in my bedchamber,' she said.

'I beg your pardon?'

'Not in the parlour.'

Galbraith smiled, catching her meaning. 'In the barn, perhaps?'

'We are not horses, Mr Galbraith! I think the guest chamber would be the most suitable place. Shall we go?'

The room Galbraith had occupied for the past three nights was cool and dark. Isobel lit a candle and set it by the bed. She was wearing a wrapper over her nightgown, and he wondered if she had had this in mind all along. She took off the wrapper, and he turned aside politely, but when he looked back she was still standing there, a pale, slender blur. She seemed quite naked in the candlelight.

Galbraith groped for his spectacles, but with a smile that he heard rather than saw, she forestalled him.

'Not this time, Mr Galbraith!' she admonished, and climbed neatly into the bed.

He moved away to strip, grateful that her first sight of him would be softened by dim light and distance. Her husband had been an attractive young man and Galbraith, even in his own youth, had never been reckoned handsome. He had developed a slight paunch with the years of prosperity, and his shoulders were a little stooped. He hoped she would not be repulsed or disappointed.

He laid aside his shirt, trousers and drawers, and then turned diffidently towards her. It would have been ridiculous to have put on his nightwear when she had removed all hers. A modest lady should have snuffed the candle or turned her back at this point, but then no modest lady would have removed her own nightgown.

'I really would prefer to have my spectacles,' he said. He got clumsily into the bed and then reached out for her. Her skin was warm to the touch, and his hands found curves and planes and valleys waiting to be explored. Perhaps clear sight was not necessary after all.

'You are so beautiful,' he said and turned his face to her breast.

Isobel had wondered if she would remember what to do. With John, it had all been quite easy. They had learned together, enjoying the discoveries they made. But they had had so little time for exploration. For much of their year together Isobel had been either ill or cumbersome with pregnancy. She thought she would have to leave it all to Galbraith (who was undoubtedly more experienced), and wondered what it would be like.

She enjoyed his company enormously, but they had never so much as kissed one another before. And why would they? And why should either of them believe that sharing a bed would relieve their loneliness? She wondered if she was making an enormous mistake, but then Galbraith reached out to touch her. His hands were gentle; artist's hands, she thought; and she felt they were drawing her from memory.

And he said she was beautiful. That, coming from a painter, was surely more than a meaningless compliment.

'Mr Galbraith?' she said after a while, 'what am I to call you?'

He laughed, as if she had surprised him. 'You should call me James, of course. Why do you ask?'

She drew in her breath with pleasure at his caress. 'After this I can scarcely address you as "Mr Galbraith".'

'Nor shall I address you again as "Mrs Campbell", except in public.' He kissed her gently and drew her against him. 'I love you, Isobel.'

'You need not say that.'

'Why not? It is perfectly true. I never meant to love you, but it crept up on me while I was here before. I love your soft hair, and your beautiful mouth, and your...' His voice became muffled as he bent to kiss her breasts again. 'And besides,' he said, emerging, rather rumpled, 'I love your- er-'

'Lower back,' said Isobel helpfully as he patted the object of his affection. 'And no, James, you *cannot* kiss that- James! James, that is not *decent.* Come out of there before you suffocate!'

'Aye,' said Galbraith contentedly, 'that *would* take some explaining to little Jennie in the morning!'

Isobel found that, after all, she had not forgotten what to do. Margaret's long ago advice had been that she should lie still and leave everything to the gentleman, but John had not agreed with Margaret, and neither, apparently, did James. She had the feeling that, just as James was not shocked by plain speech, so he would be not shocked by plain actions. She also felt that she would blush when she had to face her reflected self in the morning.

Her body welcomed his with almost embarrassing readiness and she gasped with a half-remembered pleasure that was familiar but utterly new. James' ways were not like John's, and so there were no ghosts to confound her.

She had at first planned to return decorously to her own bedchamber, but when it came to the point, she could not bear to leave him. It had been so very long since she had had someone to hold her, and so long since she had talked with a lover in darkness. With the candle out she could say anything, and there was suddenly a great deal to say.

'I cannot marry you, James,' she said abruptly. 'I could not come to live with you in New South Wales.'

'I know that, my dearest,' he said. 'And you know that I cannot live here.'

Isobel drew his head down onto her bare shoulder, and put her arms around him. 'But you will come back often, won't you?' She tried to keep the wistfulness from her voice. He had made no promises and neither had she.

'Often,' he agreed. 'I love you dearly, but I doubt I'd make a good husband, even for you. No, *especially* for you. You have Glen Heather to manage and I have most of my work in New South Wales. But I will come back *often*,' he said again, 'and I will kiss every inch of your – your lower back. And Isobel, may I give you a piece of advice about that?'

'Of course,' she said, 'but I do not promise to take it.'

'Then take care on whom you turn your back. Those breeches!' He sighed expressively. 'Those breeches do terrible things to a man's...'

There was a little pause and then Isobel laughed. 'Lower front?' she suggested demurely.

'Aye. They do terrible things to a man's lower front.'

***

They intended to keep their new relationship a secret, but it proved impossible from the beginning. Jennie Comfrey knew quite well the mistress had not slept in her own bed that night, and Perry, who enjoyed a cheerfully lusty relationship with his Emma, noticed with approval that his employer had the appearance of having been thoroughly loved. He could scarcely say where the change lay. Perhaps it was in the flush on Mrs Campbell's sallow cheeks, or perhaps in the contented curve of her mouth, but he would have had to have been blind to have missed it. He said nothing, even to Emma, for it was really nobody's business.

CHAPTER 30

Galbraith remained at Glen Heather for some weeks, and then departed reluctantly for Launceston, Melbourne and New South Wales. He felt younger than he had done in years, and even the sight of his own reflection ceased to depress him.

Isobel Campbell thought him worthy of her arms and bed, so who was he to object to the sight of his less-than-perfect body? It seemed unfortunate that she could see him clearly in the candlelight while he saw her only as a blur, but since she stubbornly refused to lie with him if he wore his spectacles, he had to make the most of touch instead of depending on sight. And touch could be wonderfully illuminating.

The autumn in New South Wales passed slowly, and he decided to visit Glen Heather again in the spring. Isobel greeted him with composed delight, and everyone else seemed pleased to see him, and again he spent a month of love and laughter and succouring lambs before turning again for home.

By 1871, he had made three such visits to Glen Heather. Isobel continued her usual daily routine while he was there, so he found himself joining her in all kinds of tasks from clearing flumes to dipping sheep and moving cattle. He had his sketchbook with him always, and over the years he produced a whole range of work, picturing Isobel at every activity and in every guise. Some of his drawings seemed to shock her a little, for he drew her without clothes as well as with them, but she could no more prevent his drawing than he could prevent her from tending sheep. And he drew with such love that the pictures were scarcely offensive. Sometimes they spoke of marriage, but the practicalities always defeated them. They agreed that society would talk if they married and lived apart for much of the year, but managed to remain unaware that society was talking already.

***

It had not escaped the notice of Winston and Gwynneth that Isobel had taken a lover. Winston was appalled, especially when he discovered the man's identity. He and Gwynneth were fully aware of the old gossip linking Galbraith with Ness, and they agreed that this new situation was nothing short of disgraceful.

'You must speak to her, Winston,' said Gwynneth. 'She must be brought to see her behaviour will not do. It is not as if she could marry the man.'

'Good God no!' said Winston. 'I shall visit her tomorrow, and you must accompany me, my dear. There are certain delicate matters which may need a woman's touch.'

Galbraith was in the guestroom when they arrived. Isobel never slept with him in the master bedroom, feeling that to do so would have been a betrayal of her relationship with John. The guestroom was their unofficial love nest, and he was in the habit of keeping clothes there so he need not carry much baggage when he came to Glen Heather.

Whenever he was in residence, he was accepted as a natural part of the household, and came and went as he chose, taking care to behave with circumspection on the rare occasions that outsiders called. He had met the Jarvises only once. He had not taken to Winston, whom he considered a pompous bore, and he had found it difficult to believe that plump Gwynneth was his Isobel's contemporary.

When he looked down and saw their carriage arrive in the yard, he was tempted to remain where he was until they left. It was only the appearance of Jennie Comfrey, who was intent upon making up the bed and cleaning the room, which made him change his mind. He descended the stairs, and was on the point of entering the parlour when Isobel's angry tones brought him to a halt.

Isobel had not been pleased to see her brother and his wife arrive. Superficially, they were on good terms, but Isobel knew she was a source of embarrassment to both of them. They loathed her mode of dress and behaviour, and Gwynnie, once a girl of vivacious good nature, had become more and more critical as she left her twenties behind.

Winston still offered his sister advice, and was offended when she failed to act on his suggestions. Having learned from his father's mistakes, Winston was cautious to the point of miserliness, and Isobel thought that she could have offered *him* some pertinent advice on life, but she never did.

It was a Sunday, and she perceived that her brother and sister-in-law had come straight from an early divine service, for Gwynnie was wearing her best hat and a gown with a fashionable bustle, obviously made over from an old crinoline.

'Good morning,' she said pleasantly. She wondered if this was a social call, but it seemed unlikely, since they had not brought their children. 'Winston,' she said, touching hands with her brother and disliking the plumpness of his fingers. 'Gwynnie.' She moved to press cheeks with Gwynnie in their usual greeting, but her sister-in-law flushed and moved back a little as if, thought Isobel angrily, she feared contamination.

In deference to the Lord's day she had put on a gown herself, so it could not be her attire which was offending Gwynnie. She sighed inaudibly.

'What can I do for you today?'

'We have come to see you on a matter of some concern,' said Winston. He sat down and lifted his left hand to touch his moustache, a nervous habit he had had for some years.

'I hope the children are well?' said Isobel. 'And nothing is wrong at Scarborough?'

'No, we are going on prosperously.'

'Then what is this matter of concern?' asked Isobel.

'The fact is, Issa, that we have heard some disturbing reports of you,' said Winston.

'Matters which impinge upon us as a family,' added Gwynneth.

'Whatever are you talking about?' asked Isobel blankly. Surely news of Jamie Campbell and his abducted heiress had not finally filtered through to Scarborough? And where *had* that young couple gone?

Winston coughed. 'You have been receiving visits from a certain gentleman.'

'A certain Mr Galbraith,' put in Gwynneth.

'Yes? What if I have?' Isobel managed to sound politely puzzled, but her blood was beginning to seethe.

'You do not deny that this man Galbraith has been paying you distinguishing attention?'

'Is that what you call it?' thought Isobel. She wondered if Winston paid Gwynneth distinguishing attention, and whether Gwynneth enjoyed it as much as she did. The thought was oddly obscene.

'I do not deny that Mr Galbraith has visited Glen Heather,' she temporised. 'Why should I? He is, after all, an old friend of the family.'

'Not of our family,' said Winston heavily.

'Oh yes, I think so. Did he not paint the portraits of Mama and Papa? And haven't those portraits increased greatly in value since his reputation was made?'

'That,' said Winston, 'was many years ago.'

'As I said, he is an *old* friend of the family,' murmured Isobel. 'He spent some months here at Glen Heather with John's father in the beginning.'

'*And* with John's mama!' said Gwynnie.

Isobel looked at her steadily. 'I hope you are not harking back to that old tale, Gwynnie,' she said. 'To be sure, some ill-bred folk may have gossiped about Mrs Campbell and Mr Galbraith, but that was nothing but haivers, as John would say.'

Gwynneth leaned forward. 'You cannot know that, Issa. You were the merest babe at the time.'

'While you were an elderly person of two years old! Why, next you will be implying there is some improper relationship between Mr Galbraith and myself!'

'No, oh no, we do not think *that*,' said Winston hastily. 'That would be an accusation of the basest kind.'

'And why is that?' asked Isobel curiously. 'Neither I, nor Mr Galbraith, is married to another person, so such a relationship could be described as fornication at the very most. And I believe there is no commandment against fornication, although adultery is expressly forbidden.' She looked hard at Winston.

Gwynnie turned an ugly shade of purple. 'Winston,' she said dangerously, 'I cannot remain here and be so insulted!'

'But surely it is I who am being insulted,' said Isobel.

Winston made calming gestures with his hands. 'Now Issa,' he said reproachfully, 'I have not accused you of anything other than indiscretion, *yet*. I merely point out, for your own good, that it is unwise for a lady in your situation to entertain a single gentleman in her house. And it is especially improper to entertain this gentleman. Why, did he not fall in love with your husband's mother?'

'Certainly he did,' said Isobel.

'And it appears he is trying the same thing with you! Isobel, you must have a care. Surely you know what this man wants?'

'Oh yes,' said Isobel. 'I believe so.' Some of the things Galbraith wanted would have shocked Gwynnie into a spasm.

Winston stared. 'You *know*? Then how can you be so foolish?

Obviously, the man is after money.'

Isobel smiled with genuine amusement. 'My dear Winston, Mr Galbraith could probably buy and sell Scarborough twice over if he were of a mind. He is not only a much-sought-after painter, but he inherited a good deal of money from an old friend.'

Winston frowned. 'Then what the devil is the man after?'

'Perhaps,' said Isobel coldly, 'you should ask him! No, you are not to say another word, Winston. I am insulted and I do not wish to see you again until I come to terms with the fact that my own brother – my only brother! – believes a man must be bribed to find me worthy of his affections.'

Galbraith, who had been listening with mounting amusement outside the parlour, applauded silently. His love's stick of a brother was expostulating and the sister-in-law was babbling about indecency, so he decided it was time he took a hand. His intervention could scarcely make the situation any worse. He strolled into the parlour, smiling vaguely at the guests.

'Mr Jarvis, Ma'am,' he said, and deliberately offered his hand.

Gwynnie stared as if at a snake, but Winston reluctantly accepted the challenge. Galbraith put aside a desire to squeeze the soft hand until the bones creaked, and shook it briefly. He then turned to Isobel and, smiling into her stormy dark eyes, lifted her hand to his lips. 'Good morning, my love,' he said in a soft but audible voice, 'have you considered whether or not we should go to watch the running of the Melbourne Cup?'

Isobel's eyes, which had been snapping with rage and hurt, softened. 'James, you know I cannot leave Glen Heather for such a frivolous reason.'

'We might make it our wedding trip,' said Galbraith hopefully, but Isobel shook her head.

'Now, James, you know my thoughts on that.'

Winston pushed his chair back so abruptly that McCleod, who had been dozing on his perch in the corner, rose to attention with eyes glaring and gave a startled squawk.

'Come, Gwynneth,' said Winston awfully, 'I can see we are not wanted here.' Coming face to face with McCleod as he turned, he flapped his hand angrily, making McCleod hiss in alarm as Gwynnie flounced out.

Galbraith closed the door gently behind the Jarvises and then offered a finger to the bird. Slowly, McCleod lowered his crest and his eyes half-closed in dreamy anticipation.

'Scratch McCleod?' he said hopefully. 'Scratch?'

***

Galbraith and Isobel did not go to see the Melbourne Cup being run, but, since they had had no success hiding their relationship from the world, they decided it would be better to still the gossip by appearing openly in public. They were careful to address one another in formal terms, and Isobel always introduced Galbraith as an old friend of her husband's family. Galbraith was happier than he had ever been, and only regretted that his happiness had come so late. He spent more and more time at Glen Heather, but kept up his official residence in New South Wales.

In September 1873 he arrived at Glen Heather with a newspaper cutting for Isobel's amusement. His love affair with Isobel had settled to a pattern which brought immense pleasure to them both, and he looked forward eagerly to seeing her again. She was well over thirty now, but he thought her beautiful as ever. He wondered a little regretfully why they had never had a child. They had discussed the possibility of an unplanned pregnancy, and Galbraith had quite determined to marry Isobel in good time if the occasion arose, but for some reason, it never had.

Lacking a child of his own, he took an interest in young Robert who was still a sweet-natured boy with none of his mother's strong character. Isobel had sent him to school in Mersey, but when she contemplated having him further educated in Launceston, the boy begged to remain at home. Thereafter, Isobel taught him arithmetic and Galbraith attended sporadically to his knowledge of the classics and art. Perry and old Harkins had imparted practical knowledge, and so Robert, if not a brilliant scholar, was not so ignorant as he might have been.

Galbraith rode into Glen Heather with a smile of anticipation. As usual, he had sent no word of his coming, for he always preferred to keep it as a surprise. On some occasions he would simply go to find her at work, and on others he would head for the kitchen and wait for her there. Today, seeing her mare Daisy tied at the rail, he stabled his own nag and knocked at the door.

'Hello Jennie, not married yet?' he asked as Jennie Comfrey came to admit him.

It was a well-worn joke, for Jennie had been courting one of the Scarborough grooms for years. They had always intended to marry when it was convenient, but somehow, it never had been and sometimes Galbraith had wondered if his own and Isobel's example had something to do with their procrastination.

This time, however, Jennie smiled shyly and lifted her hand to display a wedding ring. Galbraith felicitated her and wondered what else had changed since his last visit. He was soon to find out, for on entering the parlour, he found Isobel entertaining a guest.

The other woman was small and slender, and wore her grey hair braided in a smooth coil. She had her back to him, but he could see she was dressed quietly but expensively. Galbraith was about to retreat when Isobel raised her eyes. He saw a flash of the pleasure she always showed at such times but almost immediately it vanished, leaving anxiety and regret. His immediate conclusion was that she had met another man, and was entertaining her intended's mother. You always knew it could come, he admonished himself, and you, of all men, could not complain.

'Well, Mrs Campbell?' he said aloud, and managed to smile.

'James- I...' Isobel stopped in obvious confusion, and the other woman turned her head to see who had come in. She gazed at him for a moment and he saw she had fair skin and a straight nose and wide grey eyes with a fine network of wrinkles at the corners. She rose and came towards him, with a smile. In a dream, Galbraith reached out to take her hands.

'*Ness*?' he said.

Her smile widened. 'Aye, Jamie, it is mysel'.'

There was great affection in her eyes, but Galbraith could not help glancing at the portraits over the mantel.

Ness Campbell glanced up also. 'It is a long time ago, Jamie Galbraith, is it no? And you painted my Hector at the last- You did a verra good job o' him- and o' my Jock.' Tears stood suddenly in her eyes as she looked at the portrait of her eldest son.

Galbraith bent and kissed her cheek. It was as soft as it had been on the only other time he had kissed her, soft as a calfskin glove, but now it reminded him of a glove that had seen much service. The scent of lavender-water hung about her, as it had always, and he felt himself swept back to the days of his youth. He looked wonderingly at Isobel, and suddenly and clearly, he saw her misery for what it was. She believed that he was still in love with Ness!

He glanced ruefully from his new love to his old one. If he made a mull of it now... But Ness was smiling again. She squeezed his hands, and retreated to her seat.

'Och, kiss your lady, Jamie,' she said kindly. 'She has been aching for the sight o' you, I know.'

Isobel had not known how to explain matters to Ness. The woman was John's mother, and how would she react to the news that John's widow and her own old admirer were lovers? She had been tempted to avoid the issue, when Ness wrote that she was coming home, by sending a message to Galbraith and telling him to stay away. But that would have been the act of a craven, and Isobel couldn't do it. Instead, she welcomed Ness affectionately and prayed that Galbraith would not come. But Robert had mentioned him several times, and there had been the portrait of John and a matching one of herself to explain away.

Ness was no fool, and had very soon perceived that the subject of Jamie Galbraith made her daughter-in-law uncomfortable. And now, seeing the two together, she realised what was afoot. And why should it not be afoot? James Galbraith had been a romantic laddie, so why should he not have conceived a passion for a young and beautiful widow? That the widow in question had been married to her own son was immaterial; to Ness' way of thinking Isobel would have been a faithful wife if John had lived, but he had been dead a long time.

She saw it was up to her to cut the constraint that bound them all and smiled at them deliberately as they kissed.

'Och, Jamie did always ha' good taste,' she remarked approvingly as they sat down, holding hands. 'You two ha' not been wed?'

'No,' said Isobel slowly. 'It does not seem the right thing to do.'

Ness smiled mischievously. 'So you still like fine to lo' where you shouldna, Jamie!' She reached across to McCleod. 'And this thrawn creature still rules the roost. He hasna changed a bit and I shall make a sketch o' him while I am here and put him in my next wee book. That will gi' him a grand conceit o' himsel'!'

Galbraith found his voice at last. 'Do I not remember a lassie who had no turn for such things?'

'Aye, so I thought then, but my brother Donal liked fine the pictures I made and so now I make them often.'

It was a day of joy and wistfulness for all of them. For Ness,

Glen Heather was haunted by Hector and John, and even by her old Grey Heron, and for Galbraith the past had merged and slipped away. There was some awkwardness as evening approached, for Ness was sleeping in the guest-chamber, but Isobel, having set her hand to the wheel, would not draw back, and welcomed Galbraith into her own bed at last.

CHAPTER 31

Ness stayed on at Glen Heather for a year, and then said regretfully that she must leave. 'I like it fine, the way you ha' looked to the place,' she said, 'but I canna stay here forever. Eddie writes he is to sail for Scotland after Hogmanay, and I think I shall go with him. Phemie and the Douglas are gone now, but I may still find some o' the lassies I used to know by the loch.'

'But why go back, after all this time?' asked Isobel blankly. 'You are most welcome to stay here forever. Robert loves you, and so does McCleod. It is not James and I...?'

'Och, haivers!' said Ness. 'How often must I tell you I like it fine to see you and Jamie together? Take the best chances that come, Isobel, or you may grow auld regretting.'

'Have you never regretted anything?'

'Och, only that Jean and Eliza and my Jock were taken too soon. And I would ha' liked to ha' seen my own Jamie wed. I dinna ken if he is alive or no, for he is no hand wi' the pen. But you say he had found a bonnie lassie, so perhaps he is settled somewhere.' She sighed. 'But think on it, Isobel, I ha' drawn the bonnie flowers o' New Zealand and Van Diemen's Land, and now I shall do the same in Scotland. And you know, I should like to see Loch Haven again before I die.'

Ness sailed in the summer of 1874, fetched from Glen Heather by her bachelor son Edward. Before she left, she hugged Robert warmly, for he was her delight. He was her only grandson so far; young Hector and his wife having produced three girls.

'I ha' hopes the lassies o' Loch Haven may take my Eddie's eye,' she remarked slyly to Isobel. Then her eyes softened. 'Fare you well, lassie,' she said gently, and was gone.

It seemed very quiet after Ness left. It was silent, and somehow flavourless. Ness had never been talkative, but her soft voice, which had never lost its strong Scottish overtones, had been enough to cow McCleod, to soothe Isobel and to sting Robert into activity.

'Och, let the laddie have a time to have his word,' she would say when Isobel became impatient. 'Glen Heather will be his to run in a handfu' o' years, and he canna do that if he willna speak his mind.'

Isobel had thought long and deeply about that. It came as a little shock to realise that Ness was right. Robert was taller and bigger already than his father had been at twenty, and it was time he took a greater interest in Glen Heather. She had taught him what she could of accounting and sheep, but he was a naturally contemplative lad, and it drove her wild when he hesitated over decisions and failed to keep his mind on his work. She often spoke harshly and then regretted it when Robert retired further into his shell. Old Nannie Goodridge had passed on three months before, and Robert, great lad that he was, missed her badly.

Isobel took her doubts to Galbraith, but for the first time ever; he failed her. 'Isobel, I am not the lad's father,' he said apologetically. 'I love you dearly and I would have married you any time these past six years, but I have neither the right nor the inclination to take over the management of your Robert. He is a Campbell.'

'Then who am I to turn to, if not to you?' asked Isobel. 'He has neither father nor grandfather and his uncles, save Winston, are not here. Even if they were, I could not expect them to train the boy who took their places. If John had never had a son, Glen Heather would have come to young Hector.' She grimaced, aware that "young Hector" was only a handful of years younger than herself. 'Even if Jamie had come back, how could I have asked his help when Robert inherits over his head? And Winston could never teach him to be a Campbell.'

'I cannot teach the lad to be a Campbell either,' said Galbraith, 'but he has good blood in his body! Look at his forebears, Isobel! There are Hector and Ness, and you and your John as well.'

'There are also my grandpapa, my papa and mama,' said Isobel dryly, 'not to speak of Winston and his brood. Grandpapa went senile, Papa was nearly bankrupt, and Mama was weak in constitution. Winston is a miser.'

'Then it is up to you to direct him,' said Galbraith. 'Let him take decisions and make mistakes, and see the consequences. In all charity you cannot keep him in knickerbockers and then hand over Glen Heather on the day he comes of age.'

Isobel sucked in her lip. They were lying in bed, but she felt too tense to respond to his caress as she usually did. Now she sat up. Careless of her nakedness, she lit a candle and handed Galbraith his spectacles.

'Put them on, James,' she said harshly, 'and look at me. I am a selfish woman.'

Galbraith blinked as his eyes adjusted to the strong lenses. She looked like a goddess to him. Her long ash-brown hair waved and curled over her shoulders, half-covering her breasts, but her eyes were dark and tormented.

'My dearest, you are the least selfish person I have ever known!' he said. 'You have given up so much to keep your promises. You have given up the life of a lady, and you have given up the chance to be a wife of a young man again. You took pity on an aging man and you light up his last years.'

'Stop it!' gasped Isobel, and actually put her hand over his mouth. 'Stop it James! You are not old at all!'

'I am almost sixty,' said Galbraith calmly. 'Many good men have died in their youth, as you well know. I have been blessed far above any deserving already, so let us not waste the time we have left with this foolish talk of selfishness!'

Isobel lay down and embraced him. 'I am selfish,' she repeated stubbornly. 'I bullied poor John into letting me work at his side. And that's not all, and not the worst of it. James, I resented it when I found we were to have a child. I knew it would take me from John's side and set me back in the parlour. And then, when John died, I had the chance to work again, and I took it! I turned poor Robert over to old Nannie Goodridge just as I turn the orphan lambs over to Jennie, and I took over Glen Heather. I could have married Niall O'Hara or any other of the gentlemen who came asking. I could have hired a good man to act as overseer, but I did neither. Instead, I took it all on myself, as if it belonged to me.'

'But it doesn't,' said Galbraith gently.

'No. It never can. And one day I must begin to hand it all over to Robert, who is the owner, after all, and all I can feel is that he will not do the job as I would! He has not got the resolution, nor has he the ruthlessness he will need. And James, I know now that John did not have it either. Glen Heather has done better under my management than it would have done under John's, and I can see only that it will fade again under Robert's hand. And he is my only son!'

Galbraith was shaken by her vehemence. He was too old for this, he felt. Even had he had the inclination he could not have helped

Isobel now. His mind slipped back to the portrait he had drawn when Robert was a child. He had drawn a Campbell man, with the Campbell face, but the ruthlessness of old Hector had been washed away. And yet, Robert was a pleasant lad, and who could blame him for having an unformed character at fourteen? He had no father, and his mother was so strong that any pleasant boy must seem weak in comparison.

Galbraith had a premonition that unless care was taken to prevent it, Robert would marry young as his father had done, choosing a strong-minded woman and losing himself in the process.

'Robert is a dear good lad,' he said gently. 'He is well-liked and kind, and he has not an ounce of vice in his makeup.'

'He is *too* kind,' said Isobel tensely. 'He has quite ruined Dogwood with his haivering. He would not have him broken as a colt by Perry and now see what has come about! The creature cannot be bridled, will not be saddled and is fit to carry no one.'

'Perhaps the management of a colt was too much for a lad his age.'

'It should not have been,' said Isobel.

Galbraith had no answer to that. At the age of eleven he had been making his own way in Glasgow, a way that brought him to thieving, transportation and then to final prosperity.

'Do not be too hard on the lad, Isobel,' he said sadly. 'He is as he is and he cannot change it any more than you can.'

'No,' said Isobel in a low voice. 'I see that he cannot. And perhaps, after all, he will grow a little stronger. He is only fourteen.'

'And you are beautiful,' said Galbraith. He buried his hands in her thick hair and kissed her hard. It was not until she gave a surprised squeak of pain that he realised he had neglected to remove his spectacles.

***

Isobel tried very hard to include her son in the ordering of his inheritance. She put a curb on her bitter tongue and took Robert with her to work during the day. She gritted her teeth as his horse Dogwood napped and jibbed, swinging his quarters wickedly when asked to ford the burn.

'I shall give you a lead,' said Isobel at last, and the obedient Daisy splashed through the water.

Dogwood fussed a little longer, then crossed in a bound that all but unseated Robert. He was thrown against the pommel of the saddle and Isobel saw tears start in his eyes, but whether they were from pain or humiliation she did not know.

'Come along, we do not have all day!' she said.

'I am sorry, Mama,' said Robert.

'I know that, Robert,' said Isobel, and could not help adding; 'but if you would only show a little more resolution you'd have no need to be sorry! Perhaps you could call me something other than 'Mama'?'

Robert grew rapidly, and by the time he was sixteen, he looked startlingly like Hector. As well as teaching him the work around Glen Heather, Isobel showed him something of society, for she knew he would need to be comfortable with his own class as well as with men like Perry and Elijah.

***

Isobel and Galbraith took Robert to Launceston, and once they went to Melbourne. Here, they had their likenesses taken at a photographic studio. Robert expected an artist like Galbraith to dislike such an idea, but the man smiled and said there was room for photographs in the world, just as there was room for both sketches and paintings. Just as there was room for both roast mutton and apple pie, for that matter.

Robert was ill on the boat and his dread of the return voyage quite coloured the first few days of his holiday. He was grateful for Galbraith's presence, for in his experience his mother was likely to view any weakness with scorn and ill-concealed impatience. Even to himself Robert did not like to admit the relationship between the two. He knew it caused sniggering between his elder cousins Whit and Wesley Jarvis, but when he had asked straight out what they found so amusing, they exchanged silly grins and asked if he did not think it odd that his mama had a suitor so many years her senior.

'Grannie Ness was a great deal younger than Grandpapa Hector,' he had replied austerely, but it did not stop the sniggers.

Finally, he had been driven to take his uncertainties to Galbraith. To his surprise, his friend seemed uncomfortable with the question. He removed his spectacles and rubbed them absently on his sleeve and, instead of replacing them, looked vaguely at Robert through poorly focussed eyes.

'My boy, you know your papa died when you were very young,' he said at last.

Robert nodded impatiently, realised Galbraith could not see him, and replied verbally instead.

'Then perhaps,' said Galbraith carefully, 'you may not think it odd that your mama missed having a man to- to cherish.'

Robert thought about that. As far as he could see, Isobel cherished no one and nothing, except perhaps Glen Heather. 'Oh, I see,' he said obligingly.

'I doubt if you do,' said Galbraith. 'Ladies can be very strong, as your mother is, but still they might feel the need for the attentions of a man. We all need to love someone or something, and to be loved in return is an even greater blessing.' He paused. 'Your mother loved your father very much, but she had him for just a short time, and she was alone for a long time after he died.'

'But now she has you?' said Robert.

'Aye, she has me. I love your mother, Robert, and she loves me. She and I, and the way we are together, are doing no harm to anyone. And so you may tell your foolish cousins.'

'And do you still love Grannie Ness?' asked Robert curiously. 'Wes said you did love her once.'

'Of course I do!' said Galbraith. 'Your Grannie Ness is a lovable person. And so, I believe, was your own father, although I was never lucky enough to meet him. When you are a little older, Robert, you may find a lady of your own to love, and then you will understand all this better.' He smiled a little wryly. 'A word of advice, though- when you choose yourself a lady, do make sure she does not belong to someone else already! It will save you no end of trouble.'

Robert nodded thoughtfully. He was far from sure that Galbraith had answered his question, but he knew the man had done his best. He wondered if *he* was a lovable person. It seemed unlikely. His face in the mirror always seemed to belong to someone else, to a firm-minded, decisive sort of person such as his mother wanted him to be. The strong chin and commanding nose, the narrow, slate-grey eyes and luxuriant black hair seemed a bad mismatch with the person he was inside, and none of it looked remotely lovable to him.

That conversation had taken place two years before, and now he was sixteen and he knew a good deal more than he had known then. He knew ladies and gentlemen lay down together to make children, and he knew his mother and Galbraith often slept in the same bed. He supposed it must be something like tupping sheep, but when he tried to imagine any of the folk he knew engaged in such an occupation it seemed terribly unlikely. His Uncle Winston and his Aunt Gwynneth, for example... in his imagination he dressed Uncle Winston in wool and placed him behind his aunt, but surely the bustle would be in the way? As for Mr and Mrs Perry and Jennie Comfrey and her husband- they were all privy to the mysterious secret as well.

He had noticed that Jennie Comfrey's man seemed to love Jennie a lot, for he had seen him kissing her in the kitchen late at night. Jennie was very kind and pretty, and he wouldn't have minded kissing her himself.

It was while he was in Melbourne that he learned the secret firsthand. His mother and Galbraith wished to see a play and, sensing that they were tired of his company, he elected to stroll down the street to watch a famous contortionist who, if the handbills were to be believed, could tie himself in reef knots. He was hovering by the door, wondering if he had sufficient funds to pay for a ticket, when a lady touched his arm. Thinking she needed assistance, Robert leaned politely towards her and removed his hat.

'Can I help you, ma'am?' he enquired.

'Well, dearie,' she said with a smile, 'I was wondering if I could help you!'

Robert flushed. He had thought he looked quite the man in his town clothes, and now this woman seemed to regard him as a lost lamb. 'I am perfectly all right.' he said. 'I need no help.'

'I could teach you quite a lot, young man,' she said. 'Your lady will thank me for it.'

Robert looked at her uncertainly. Could she have mistaken him for someone else? Her hand was still on his arm, and she was smiling in a very friendly fashion.

'It will be worth your while, and it will not cost you very much,' she said. 'What's your name, dearie?'

'Robert Campbell,' said Robert cautiously.

'Well, Robbie, you can call me Peg- the square peg with the round hole! And how old are you, dearie? Eighteen? Nineteen?'

'Almost,' said Robert.

'Well, that is nice. And a man is never too young to learn his manners, that's my motto.'

A woman who quoted proverbs as Nannie Goodridge had done could hardly be other than respectable. Robert wanted to believe that, and he was curious to see what would happen, so he took the proffered arm and allowed his new acquaintance to lead him into the building.

To his surprise, she did not stop where the seats were already filling for the show, but led him on through a curtain and up some stairs to a bedchamber. She had him take his coat off and offered him a drink, but when she removed her own gown and he saw what she was wearing underneath, he began to have a faint conception of what he was about to learn.

She lay back on the bed and patted the pillow beside her and once Robert overcame his initial feelings of shock she did teach him quite a lot, though why she imagined any lady would want him to know it was quite beyond him.

'There, dearie, you did very well,' she said. 'You've quite worn old Peg out!'

Robert began to apologise, but she laughed at him and told him he was a caution. And then she helped him on with his clothes (although he didn't need help), and straightened his collar for him, and kissed him goodbye.

When he rejoined his mother and Galbraith after their play, he was very quiet and thoughtful, but he supposed they put it down to the fact that he was dreading the voyage home next day. Isobel offered him ginger root to chew, but he was so ill on the ship that he arrived in Launceston more than half convinced that the amazing Peg and the room above the concert hall had been a feverish dream.

***

Galbraith did not return with them to Glen Heather, but took another ship up the coast to New South Wales. Robert spent odd moments trying to piece together Peg's information and Galbraith's talk of cherishing, but he had not much time for reflection for his mother was determined to have him learn some more social graces. To this end he found himself packed off to Scarborough where a master was teaching his cousins and some of the other local young folk the rudiments of dancing. He partnered his cousin Lizzie, or sometimes Annie Llewellyn the doctor's sister or Mary MacDonald. This was interesting, for he found that his experience in Melbourne made him look at young ladies in a new and different light. To be sure they were still in the schoolroom, and Mary and Annie could be no more than fifteen, but the movements of the dance offered an opportunity to try out a few of the more respectable things he had learnt from Peg. It also resulted in Annie's slapping his face, which added one more item to Robert's social experience.

Dancing was all very fine, and he quite enjoyed it, but being able to master the intricacies of the quadrille was of no help when it came to handling sheep. Robert was not fond of sheep; they seemed to him to be ridiculous creatures with very little brain in their heads. Why, for instance, did they insist on crowding together so? And why did they constantly mislay their lambs and drown themselves in the burn, and get cast on hot days? He felt some sympathy with them when it was shearing time and they ended up with bloody nicks and cuts, but he could not see why Perry and his mother could discuss them for hours.

It was one of his daily tasks to ride around the fold and the enclosures and inspect the residents. In summer he must watch for fly-strike, in winter for footrot. In the heat he must assist cast ewes, in the spring he was to watch for scouring lambs. It was impossible to keep an accurate count of the creatures, for as fast as he tallied those in one end of the enclosure, something would panic them and they would stream away to the other. They were totally unpredictable, and supremely boring.

Sometimes he had to help his mother or Perry move flock or herd to another enclosure. It was then his job to ride ahead, and to turn the mob into the correct gap. Often Dogwood would refuse to co-operate, but he had no redress, for his mother had told him plainly that if he could not master his horse it would have to be sold.

Robert hated the idea of that, for although he would have preferred a more biddable mount, he also knew it was largely his own fault Dogwood was difficult. If he had been firmer during the colt's schooling, or if he had allowed Perry to use his usual methods, Dogwood would have learnt to behave. It never occurred to him, when his mother was short or impatient with him, that she had similar feelings of guilt herself about him. If she had been firmer, she thought, and if she had not left the boy so much to Nannie Goodridge, perhaps he would have learnt to be a proper Campbell.

The years passed too quickly for Isobel. Not only was the time coming when she must hand over the reins of Glen Heather to a son who was unready, but she could also see a time when she would be alone again. She loved James Galbraith dearly, but she was haunted by the fact that he was so much older than she. She remembered how diminished Ness had been after Hector's death and had long ago faced the fact that she would almost inevitably be left a widow for a second time- and a widow who, for the lack of a wedding ring, would be accorded no sympathy by society.

She tried to find comfort in the thought that she and Galbraith were together for only two or three months of each year, but it made no difference; even when she was at Glen Heather and he was in New South Wales he was *there*; a warm, loving presence in the back of her mind. And he wrote to her often, sending clippings from the Sydney newspapers, sketches of interesting things he had seen, and occasional invitations to join him in Launceston or Melbourne. And one day she must lose her lover, and a very dear friend besides.

In all her troubled thoughts it never occurred to her that she might be the one to die.

CHAPTER 32

Robert was nineteen, just as John had been when he and Isobel had been betrothed. Isobel tried not to think it, but the memory kept intruding. How mature John had seemed, how grave and certain in his mourning clothes, and how kindly he had put her at ease. Compared with the way John had been, Robert was little more than a well-meaning, pleasant child with no more idea than a yearling colt of conducting himself in life.

Isobel was almost forty, but the years had treated her kindly. She could still have worn her wedding dress, had she had a mind to try, but it had been bundled for years in a camphor chest in the attic, awaiting the daughters who now would never be born.

The ladies of Mersey and the surrounding district often shook their heads and opined that it was unjust that Isobel Campbell, who was undoubtedly a sinner, should look so much more youthful than her virtuous peers, but Isobel was barely aware of her appearance, except during Galbraith's visits, when she luxuriated in the fact that he considered her beautiful.

The accident occurred on the brae, after one of the windstorms that periodically shook the tiers. Isobel had always disliked having trees felled, partly from her own disinclination to see destruction, and partly because Winston had laid Scarborough nearly bare. And John had believed in felling only for necessity.

After the storm had blown itself out, Isobel and Robert rode up the brae to inspect the lower flumes. Along the way Isobel noticed several trees half-uprooted by the wind and rain, and now leaning dangerously. Some of the roots had pulled out to reveal pocks and caves in the limestone. She waited for Robert to comment, but he seemed sunk in a dream.

Of late, Robert had mentioned his ownership of Glen Heather once or twice, but she had never discovered just what he wanted to know, for any probing made him snap shut like a clam. She knew he often rode into Mersey, and had wondered if he was courting. If so, she hoped he had made a sensible choice. Robert Campbell of Glen

Heather, despite his personal diffidence and his mother's eccentric reputation, would be considered an excellent match by many watchful parents. To be sure the Campbells and Jarvises were not quite on a social par with the Reeves, but they were a cut above the O'Haras and the Finlays.

Robert might choose to marry one of his cousins, and such a union would be quite acceptable from a worldly point of view, but Lizzie and May were very young, and reminded Isobel of Gwynnie. She could not imagine enduring the company of either one for an extended period, nor could she see how she could avoid it since she had no intention of following Ness' example and leaving Glen Heather.

She would hand over control of the property when Robert was twenty-one, but she must be available to give advice when he needed it. And surely he would.

Isobel drew rein by one of the dangerously leaning trees, and waited.

'Robert,' she called with ill-concealed impatience, 'what would you suggest we do about this?'

Robert fought a brief battle with Dogwood before circling back to the tree. He looked at the split in the trunk, at the sheared-off branches, and then glanced at his mother as if for inspiration.

'I suppose we shall have to cut it down,' he offered.

'We certainly shall. And then?'

The answer came more slowly still. 'We could have Elijah's father bring in his bullocks or- maybe we could chop it up- or burn it?'

'Would you not think it a trifle foolish to start a fire in the middle of the bush?'

'I suppose so,' said Robert. He smiled at her. 'If we leave it alone it might fall by itself?'

Isobel raised her eyes to the heavens then slapped her reins and rode on up the brae. Had she been concentrating more on her surroundings and less on the inadequacies of her son, she might have seen the warning signs in the sky. Usually, a fierce windstorm was succeeded by a period of calm, but today the lull was brief. Up on the mountain the trees were already beginning to bend and sway, the surf-sound of the leaves swelling above. A few small branches snapped off, and up near the hut another tree, its roots already damaged by the winds of the preceding night, heeled over with a smash that echoed down the brae. The clouds, ripped and heavy, tossed a scatter of hail, and, belatedly,

Isobel realised the danger.

She called curtly to Robert to turn for home, but decided to press on to the next flume. She suspected it was blocked and if the coming storm was a bad one, it might be days before she or anyone else could attend to it.

Daisy was placid, but like most horses she disliked high wind and muddy going. She began to snort in protest, sidling whenever another branch snapped above. Isobel curbed her, and glanced at Dogwood just in time to see him rear up under a tree. She gasped with fear, but Robert had already bent sharply to one side to avoid a blow on the head. He sat down hard and clouted Dogwood with the end of the reins. Dogwood reared again, and with a sharper twinge of fear Isobel remembered how John had died.

'Hit him between the ears- hit him!' she called, trying to keep the panic out of her voice.

Robert leaned forward to strike Dogwood on the poll, but the horse was going up again, and even from her position some fifty yards up the slope, Isobel could hear the dull crunch as Robert's face was struck by the horse's ascending crest. Such a blow could break his nose, or, perhaps more dangerously, knock him dizzy. Robert was a good horseman and very strong, but if he was dazed and Dogwood bolted there would be another tragedy at Glen Heather.

'Hold on,' called Isobel. 'Daisy will calm him!'

She nudged the jittering Daisy with her heels. The mare sat back on her hocks, slithering in the mud and fallen leaves. She was so slow that Isobel vaulted out of the saddle and ran down the slope instead. She seized Dogwood's bit-ring and jerked it hard, and the horse's fore-hooves came abruptly to the ground.

Isobel glanced up at Robert. His nose streamed blood, and his eyes were swimming.

'Get down and lead him,' she snapped, and turned back to Daisy. As she did so, she heard a warning creak above her.

Hail stung her face and she stared in disbelief as the wattle's upper branches drew an arc in the sky. The tree is falling! she thought, but her mind seemed as numb as her face.

'Leave the horse, leave him!' she screamed to Robert.

And then the dark mass of branches, capped with fluffy scented blossom, blotted the light entirely.

Robert's eyes were running with tears from the blow on the nose, but through their blurring he clearly saw the tree come down. It seemed to happen in slow motion, but he was frozen to the spot. His mother was calling something about a horse, and Robert supposed she was telling him, as usual, not to let Dogwood bolt down the track. One of his grandfather's horses had broken a tendon during a windstorm, and had subsequently been shot. Sometimes, in his darkest moments, Robert wished someone would shoot the unruly Dogwood so he could escape the decision of selling him, but he could not wish the creature to be hurt and lamed. Just- not there anymore.

'I have him safe!' he called back, and then had to use all his considerable strength to keep the horse from bolting. His arms were almost lugged from their sockets, and a glancing kick on the knee made him yell out with pain, but through it all he was aware of his mother's mare galloping away down the brae.

'Mama?' he called, yanking Dogwood's reins. 'Isobel? Are you all right?'

He reckoned that for his mother to have let go the reins she must have suffered at least a broken collarbone, or perhaps she, too, had been kicked in the knee or thigh.

Receiving no answer, he dragged Dogwood around to the fallen tree. Sweetness rose on the wind from the crushed blossom, and Robert sneezed, making his bruised nose hurt more.

'Isobel?' he called.

He could not see her up or down the brae, and he was sure she had not been on Daisy's back. He tried to think logically. Isobel had been higher up the brae, but she had run down and forced Dogwood to the ground while he was still groggy. She had turned away to Daisy, then the tree had fallen and Daisy had galloped away.

'Isobel?' cried Robert above the rising wind.

He looked about wildly, for his mind still could not accept what the facts were telling him. His mother must be under the fallen tree.

Afterwards, he thought the heroic thing would have been to have dragged the tree away, picked up Isobel and loaded her onto Dogwood to bring her safely home, but at the time all he could do was stare at the jumble of branches and leaves. More trees were snapping, and Dogwood had reacted to his master's inattention by taking off after Daisy. Robert became aware that his damaged knee was hurting, and then that both legs were trembling with cold and shock. He took a step forward, felt the bad knee buckle, and swore. He seized the main branch of the tree and heaved until his muscles creaked, but he could not shift it.

He wondered numbly if he should stay or run down the mountain for help. Popular wisdom said a person in trouble in the bush should sit tight and light a signal fire, but nineteen years of experience said it was better to get home as quickly as possible and to hope no one had missed him.

'Isobel?' he said aloud. 'Isobel?'

There was no answer, and it was just possible she *had* remounted Daisy before the tree came down. In that case she would be at the bottom of the brae, waiting for Robert. And when a riderless Dogwood arrived, she would recall the night her husband's horse had bolted home alone. Certainly, he must go home. If his mother were there it would relieve her mind, if she were under the tree (and surely, surely, she could not be!) he could raise the alarm and have Mr Perry and Elijah Ward help bring her home.

Robert slithered down the track, limping heavily with the pain in his knee. It hurt a little less after a while, but he thought that was because he was so cold. Snow had begun to drive down on the wind and, for the first time, Robert could understand why sheep sometimes just laid themselves down and died.

***

Sim Perry was not an imaginative man, but when two riderless horses trailed into the stable he went cold. If the mistress had asked *his* advice about riding up the brae today, he would have told her to leave it, but she never asked *his* advice and for him to have offered it unsought would have invited a stinging reprimand.

Not for the first time, Perry wished Mr Galbraith lived at Glen Heather all the time. When her lover was in residence, Madam was softer, and happier, and it reflected in her dealings with those around her. Perry thought about living apart from his Emma for nine months of the year and shook his head. That wouldn't work at all. Not only would he have to do for himself, but he liked to keep Emma under his eye; she was a comely woman and despite having borne four children she still had a figure to draw a man's thoughts away from the how-do-you-do and off to the let's-do-it-now.

He sighed. If there had been an accident up the brae he would be late for his dinner again. He stabled Daisy and Dogwood and went to fetch Elijah and Jennie's husband Luke Christopher from the lower enclosure. It was no use calling old Harkins, for he would dither and dather and go nowhere fast.

The wind was getting up again, and it was starting to snow. Perry alerted Emma to expect trouble and delay, put on his coat, and followed the other two up the brae.

'It will be Mr Robert for a surety,' said Christopher gloomily. 'And Mrs Campbell will have stayed to patch him up. The young fool.'

'Watch your footing, man, and watch your tone,' advised Perry gruffly. He had his own opinions of Mr Robert, but Christopher was a newcomer and must be taught his place. He gave a ringing cooee, and the other men joined in.

***

Isobel woke to a curious green-laced twilight. The smell of blossom was sharp in her nostrils and her head ached dully. One cheek was numb and her chin hurt. She supposed she had fallen off Daisy. Even the best riders fell sometimes and Daisy had been jittering in the storm.

Her arms were outflung, so she flexed each hand in turn. No damage there. She attempted to gather herself into a sitting position, but there was weight on her back and shoulders and she couldn't move. She frowned, and fought for memory. She had not been riding. She had been walking. Robert had been in trouble and a tree had fallen. That explained the green dimness and the smell of blossom. It also explained the weight on her shoulders. She must have been struck a glancing blow by the leafy twigs and fallen under a branch. Her hands began to sting and she realised it was cold. Her legs were numb and she couldn't feel her feet at all.

'Damn!' said Isobel.

She made a supreme effort to curl up, hoping to conserve what warmth she could until someone found her. Then she fainted.

The next time she woke it was darker. She could no longer feel her hands, but her thigh ached. It felt clammy and wet and one eye was swollen closed. Her tongue and lip hurt, as if she had bitten them when she fell. There was a metallic taste of blood in her mouth. She was afraid now, and tried to summon a cry for help, but the effort of inhaling made her sick and dizzy and she fainted again.

She could hear voices, thickly, as if her ears were plugged with fleece. They were calling, and she knew she should answer but she couldn't move her mouth. Her head hurt and she wondered vaguely if she had broken her skull, like John. Perhaps she was dying. She thought that if someone moved her she would die. She had been crushed like a beetle and there was nothing she could do. *They shoot horses*, she thought and then, *I shall see John in Paradise.* But neither thought seemed to make sense. She wondered if John had thought of her in the moment before he hit the ground. She wondered if he had dreamed of her in the slow hours before he died. She thought about James and about Robert. She hoped she would manage to die before they found her, because they might expect her to say something appropriate and her mind was empty of anything but bitter regret.

CHAPTER 33

They found her while she was still alive. It was not yet dark, but the searchers had turned back to fetch lanterns, ropes and bandages when Robert told them about the tree.

'We can never lift it,' Robert kept repeating, but Perry said they would use an axe.

'Brace up, lad, brace up,' he said, forgetting in the stress of the moment that Robert was his employer. 'We need you to show us where she is.'

'But she may not be under it,' said Robert numbly. 'She may be looking for me!'

'Come on, lad,' said Perry with sympathy.

They called out sometimes as they climbed the brae. Robert could not remember precisely where the tree had come down, but he knew it had been a blossoming black wattle so it was a matter of finding one fresh-fallen. The wind had dropped again, but the snow was still sifting in the air. Perry was very worried, for even if the mistress had not been badly hurt, the bleak chill would make her condition much worse. He thought it likely she had been knocked cold, and had since recovered and crawled out from beneath the tree. She could be anywhere, wandering in a daze. If she had staggered off the track she could have fallen in the burn or through a hole in the limestone. At best, she would be difficult to find, and at worst, they would find her dead or not at all.

'The tree is up there,' said Robert.

Perry thought the lad looked ill. His fair Campbell skin was almost translucent. Perry had liked John and had had a hearty respect for the old man, but he felt the blood had thinned in Robert, which was odd, for his mother had the heart of a man.

'Black wattle,' he said. 'We should be able to haul that clear, we should.'

'Will that not hurt my mother, if she is underneath?'

Perry shook his head, less in negation than at the naivety of the question. Such a course *could* further injure anyone who lay under the tree, but how else were they to get her out? Bullocks with chains and pulleys might lift the thing clear, but by the time a team was fetched up the brae the lady of Glen Heather would be dead of cold.

'We may find her under the top branches, we may,' he said. 'With any luck, that is. We can cut the branches and get her out.'

Robert went cold. If it were so easy, he could have done it himself. Suppose he had been straining to lift the great tree and all along his mother had been lying stunned under twigs he could break aside one-handed? When they reached the tree he began to grope feverishly under the smashed twigs and blossom, trying not to let himself remember how disaster had come to Glen Heather before in the spring.

Isobel heard the activity, and held her breath. She was in so much pain now that she felt she could not bear to be touched. If so much as brushed by a twig she would scream with the agony. Reverend Ende said death could be kind, and now she knew what he meant- death was the friend, dying was the enemy.

She could hear Robert's voice, and also the fluff and rustle of leaves and blossom. The breath of snow touched her cheek and she thought it was death and willed it to take her wholly. Something feathered her hand, and cold fingers fumbled at the wrist. She heard a cry from Robert, and the sound of Perry's voice. She liked Perry and she wished she had told him so.

She had heard that folk in the extremity of pain sometimes cried for their mothers. Her mother was not even a memory, but for her there had been Margaret, Nannie and Ness. And there had been James, more tender than any mother.

The cold hand left her wrist, but she heard the snap and rustle of branches, and, incredibly, the staccato bite of an axe. The weight on her shoulders shuddered and she screamed, scrabbling wildly for escape like a lizard under a boot. She screamed her breath away and screamed again with no more breath to give. It was a silent scream because she could not bear it.

The weight was plucked away and the green dark gave to jagged streaks of light. She saw the toe of a riding boot, dark and clotted with leaves. She heard Perry's voice, hoarse with effort and Ward and Christopher together. Robert's face was there, but not his voice; tears ran down his cheeks and splashed on her upturned face. That meant, she supposed, that they had moved her. And then she saw a dazzle of light and heard a choking cry.

'My God- look at her leg!' it rasped and someone vomited in the bushes.

***

They took her home on a stretcher. Perry thought from the first it was no use, but they could not leave her alive on the mountain. As he had done once before, he directed the making of a litter, this time using branches and buttoned coats. He and Elijah and Luke Christopher shuddered with the cold, but he made Robert keep his coat on. The lad looked so shocked that Perry feared he would faint.

Before they moved her, Perry tore an old shirt and used it with two stout branches to form a splint. The shattered thigh was beyond his skill, so he wrapped flesh and jagged bone together out of sight. He bandaged her eyes and bound her to the stretcher, his strong hands shaking as they had never shaken before. She was quiet now, and her face was a mask of mud and blood so he could hardly tell the damage. Only her thick hair, dressed in a knot on the back of her head, had saved her from instant death. Perry reckoned fate had been unkind in that.

There was a doctor in Mersey now, young Floyd Llewellyn. Perry thought it would do no good to call him, but folk would talk if he made no effort, so when they reached the foot of the brae he set Robert to ride to Mersey. His touch on the still figure's wrist told him she lived.

***

Robert rode so fast to town that Dogwood was blown and cowed. Every time the horse tried to drop from a canter, Robert kicked him onward, until his breath whistled shrilly as bagpipes in his lungs. It never occurred to Robert that he was venting his own guilt on the horse, he knew only that if he had not been so soft about Dogwood, the whole ghastly business might never have come about.

He reached the doctor's residence in the dark, and knocked double-fisted on the door until the doctor came.

Llewellyn was used to thunderous summons, for it was harsh country and injuries were rife. Most of the population still relied on tradition and the help of redoubtable midwives for births, deathbeds and the alleviation of childish ills, but a surgeon's assistance was sought in severe cases of disease and broken bones. A surgeon probably lost more patients than the untaught women, but that, thought Llewellyn tiredly, was because most of *his* cases were hopeless to begin with. They were tough, the folk of the tiers, but even the tough can break.

He was surprised to see young Robert Campbell at the door. He had noticed the lad in Mersey, collecting stores, kicking a ball with other lads, and watching young ladies from beneath the brim of his hat.

Llewellyn's sister Annie opined that Robbie Campbell had as much sense as a yearling ram, but he thought there was no harm in the lad. The half-shut eyes seemed to denote heredity rather than stupidity and he was a fine physical specimen. He wondered if Annie's comments indicated an interest in young Campbell. If so, he would not oppose the match, for he had a sweetheart himself and no desire to begin wedded life with an unmarried sister in the household.

'Well, young man, and what do you mean by this uproar?' he asked briskly. He was in his shirtsleeves, still munching a piece of cake made by a grateful patient. He thought guineas were more useful than cake, but he often had to settle for payment in kind. 'Speak up, man!' he added. The boy seemed tongue-tied, or perhaps drunk, for his mouth gaped soundlessly like that of a baby bird begging to be fed. 'Have you come calling on Miss Llewellyn?' he asked. 'She is at her supper.'

'N-not Annie,' stammered the boy. 'Please, Dr Llewellyn, it's Isobel. My mother.'

'What's amiss?'

'Aye, a tree fell on her and her leg is smashed- she's all broken up. We carried her back to Glen Heather but Perry said to come for you.'

Llewellyn swallowed the suddenly tasteless cake. He had seen a man die of a broken back only a month before. If only such a patient could be made to lie stone still, he thought such injuries might heal, but having been dragged down from the mountain on a hurdle, the man had stood no chance at all.

'Is she alive?' he asked.

'Aye-' The boy sounded uncertain. 'Mr Perry thinks-'

'Wait, I shall fetch my bag.' Llewellyn gestured to the boy to wait in the hall while he went to prepare for a journey whose object had probably died by now. He looked at the lad's white face when he returned, and hastily mixed brandy and water. 'Drink this,' he ordered, 'before you get in the gig. Your horse will be safe in the stables and I do not want you fainting on the way.'

To his immense surprise, his patient was still alive when he reached her. His eyebrows rose a fraction when he realised that the lady was wearing the remains of a pair of breeches, but one leg had been cut away with shears.

'Someone had some sense,' he commented, seeing that no attempt had been made to remove her from the makeshift litter. A trim, attractive young woman nodded and smiled slightly. Llewellyn glanced automatically at her left hand, and noted that she was married. The good ones usually were.

'Mrs Campbell- can you hear me?' he asked loudly.

There was no response, but he had not expected one. From the injuries he could see, it appeared the patient was doomed. The body was broken beyond repair but some spark of life was refusing to be snuffed. He held the muddy wrist for a few minutes, counting the pulse. It was weak and erratic- shock, he thought, and probably loss of blood.

'How long was she out in the weather?' he demanded, keeping his eyes on his watch.

'No more than three hours, sir,' said the stolid man who had engineered the rescue.

Exposure might not be such a problem, but if a rib had pierced a lung pneumonia would set in and, in her weakened state, it would be fatal. Llewellyn paused, fingers still on the wrist. He examined the lax hand; it was long-fingered and elegant, but the row of calluses across the base of the fingers told of hard, manual work. The nails were clipped short, the palm broad and deep. Palmistry was bunk, but he saw the strongly incised lines that he had noticed usually betokened forceful character. Perhaps the job was not quite hopeless. This woman was a fighter.

'Bring me warm water and clean cloths,' he said abruptly, 'and you, Mrs-?'

'Jennie Christopher, sir,' put in the pretty woman with a small bob.

'Mrs Christopher, you cut off the rest of these clothes and swab away the mud. Do not be too careful, for she cannot feel a thing.'

This took some time, but when the patient was clean and draped in a sheet she was still breathing, so Llewellyn began his examination, with the capable Mrs Christopher standing by to preserve the decencies. By the time he finished, he was wondering what tenacity of spirit had kept the woman alive. The shattered right thigh alone would probably kill her, for compound fractures were notoriously prone to infection and she had lost a great deal of blood. There were at least two broken ribs, one of which might have damaged a lung, and the spine was so badly bruised he could not tell whether there was a fracture or not. There was a gash on the back of the shoulder where a splintered branch had scored a long, bloody line. There was concussion, certainly, and a badly torn eyelid that required stitching. The lower lip was cut through, probably by the patient's own tooth, but perhaps by a sharp flake of limestone. There was a scalp wound which had bled profusely, but which was not dangerous in itself, and one broken ankle: a simple fracture.

Llewellyn was not a sentimental man, but he was drawn to the character he saw in the bruised and battered face. He had heard mixed reports of Isobel Campbell; that she was a beauty, a tarter, a loose woman and a hard taskmistress. He thought the first two descriptions were probably true, and possibly the last as well. She might work those around her hard but the evidence of her hands suggested that she worked equally hard herself. As for her reported laxity of morals, he could only hope that her lover, whoever he was, had the strength of devotion to see her through the painful months ahead. If she survived. Pragmatist that he was, Llewellyn had noticed that love could sometimes tip the balance between survival and defeat.

***

Isobel woke briefly at midnight to see a dark face looming over her and to feel fingers on her wrist.

'James?' she murmured. Her voice sounded wrong, thick and woolly, and her face felt wrong, too. There was something wrong with one eye and her chin and lip stung fiercely. She lifted a hand, but it was taken in a light, restraining clasp.

'Not just now, Mrs Campbell,' said a voice with a faint accent she recognised as Welsh. 'I am Dr Llewellyn. I was called in to visit you because you have had an accident. Do you recall it?'

It hurt to think and her eyes refused to focus. 'I was on the mountain,' she said at last.

'Very good!' The voice sounded approving as a nursemaid's when a small child had announced that one plus one equalled two.

'I do not like to be patronised.' Her voice was not her own and that frightened her.

Her fear must have shown in her eyes, for the doctor laid her hand gently on the coverlet. 'I shall have Mrs Christopher fetch you a drink of water.'

'Mrs-' Isobel scowled in an effort to remember. It took her some time, but at last she had it. 'You mean Jennie Comfrey, of course. The Jennie mouse.' She closed her eyes, exhausted by her small triumph.

She was burning hot, and shivering, wet and parched with thirst. It was dark, then the sun came up and twilight came again. She coughed and moaned because it hurt her ribs, and saw the doctor by the bedside. She closed her eyes because they hurt, and when she opened them again, the doctor had gone. So had the darkness, and in its place was a rosy glow of sunshine through crimson curtains. She was in her own bedchamber, and from the look of the sun it was high time and away for her to be about her work.

This time there was no groping for memory. She knew well enough she had had an accident on the mountain. The men must have pulled the tree off her, but she was flat as a cast sheep and twice as helpless. Only time would reveal the extent of her injuries and only patience would see her healed enough to venture out.

A fire burnt in the grate and she heard a door opening. It hurt too much to turn her head, so she lay still.

'James?' she said, for no one else would enter without knocking.

It hurt a good deal to talk and when she licked her lips she found one hard and crusted. She wanted James badly, but she did not want him to see her. He would not think her beautiful now.

She rolled her eyes down toward the foot of the bed, but it was not Galbraith who had come in. It was Robert, and he looked so tall and big that she could hardly believe he was her son.

'Robert,' she said, and tried to smile at him.

'Isobel!' There was great relief in his eyes, and dread also, and he came and took her hand then kissed her formally on the cheek. Isobel tried to remember when he had last hugged her spontaneously, but just now she was glad he did not. Nothing was actively hurting, but she knew pain was waiting just beyond the threshold of a touch.

'Well, Robert,' she said, forming the words carefully through stiff lips, 'do you think you could fetch me a drink?'

'Jennie Comfrey-'

'Not Jennie Comfrey. You. It was you who fetched Perry to help me, was it not?'

Robert nodded slowly. 'But if I had not had trouble with Dogwood-'

Isobel could not bear to hear all that. 'Robert,' she said gently, 'I am very thirsty. I do not believe I can sit up, but perhaps you could help me?'

Robert lifted her clumsily and held a glass of liquid to her mouth. Her ribs ached savagely and much of the drink slopped down the neck of her nightgown. It tasted bitter.

'Nannie Goodridge has been making her foul brews again,' said Isobel.

'Nannie Goodridge?' Robert looked a little afraid.

'She will not find you here,' murmured Isobel.

She wondered if there had been laudanum in the drink. She knew Mrs Pullen did not believe in the substance, but sometimes oblivion was blessed, and Nannie had a good supply of noxious substances.

'No,' said Robert after a moment. Isobel had no idea what he meant, so she smiled at him vaguely and went back to sleep.

***

It was three weeks before Isobel really understood what had happened to her, and weeks more before she knew she would never fully recover. By then James Galbraith had arrived, sent for by Jennie Christopher without reference to anyone else. Isobel would have forbidden it had she known, for she had determined that her association with Galbraith must come to an end. He had loved her beauty. Had he not said so repeatedly? She knew he was too loyal to let her down now she was no longer beautiful, but she had too much pride to bear the pity in his eyes. She had had Robert bring her a looking glass, and she knew her face was scarred. Her lip had healed tolerably well, but there was a depression in one cheekbone and an angry red line slanting from eyelid to cheek. Her skin was pallid from illness and lack of fresh air and her hair had been cut close to her scalp for convenience. And that was just the beginning of the damage.

Her ribs and ankle had mended, and she had miraculously escaped pneumonia, but the doctor told her frankly she would never walk without a crutch or cane for support.

'It is your lower limb, Mrs Campbell,' he began briskly, casting a wary glance at McCleod, who had established himself on an upright chair by Isobel's bed. He had patients who treasured mangy cattle dogs or cats, but never one with such a wicked-looking bird.

Isobel sighed. 'Dr Llewellyn, say what you mean. If you wrap it up in clean flannel I shall never know and it is, after all, my body under discussion.'

Llewellyn reflected that perhaps the university was wrong in its refusal to admit females to the study of medicine. Some of the ladies he had met had stronger minds and stomachs than he. His sister, for example: Annie would do very well if only tradition had allowed her to train as a medical man.

'Very well, Mrs Campbell,' he said. 'We shall dispense with the flannel. Your femur, that is the large bone in your upper leg, was splintered, probably by a sharp piece of limestone as well as the weight of the tree. It is my opinion that it will never mend sufficiently to allow normal locomotion.'

'Which means?'

'You will probably be able to walk after a fashion, but you will always need some kind of support. You might prefer to use a bathchair, for comfort's sake.'

'I see,' said Isobel. She gazed blankly at the patch of crimson curtain and watched it shift and waver before her eyes. 'Will I be able to ride?' she asked abruptly.

'It would be extremely unwise. The pressure of a side-saddle could not fail to be extremely painful and might well distort the limb further.'

'Dr Llewellyn,' said Isobel gently, 'I ride astride.'

'It might be possible in that case, but not, I think, without grave discomfort, and not for some time. And if you fell- the human body is a miraculous thing, but we can mend it only so many times.'

'I see,' said Isobel. She was silent again.

'I am sorry, Mrs Campbell,' said Llewellyn. 'I wish I could give you better news but quite frankly I am surprised you survived your injuries at all.'

'So am I,' said Isobel. 'A simple blow to the head killed my husband, Dr Llewellyn, so I find it very strange that I could break so many bones and still survive.'

'You may find yourself prone to rheumatic conditions in the broken bones as the years go on,' said the doctor.

'Yes,' said Isobel bleakly. 'So I may. Well, doctor, I suppose we must take the hands life deals, must we not?'

'That we must,' said Llewellyn. He was relieved to find his patient accepting her disability with such composure. In her place he knew he would have railed against fate, for it seemed to have dealt her a poor hand indeed.

'Do you know Mr Shakespeare's plays, Dr Llewellyn?' she asked suddenly.

'I have seen a few of them presented.'

'Then perhaps you recall the blasted heath in the tale of King Macbeth. There is heath on the mountain here, Dr Llewellyn, white and pink and occasionally crimson. It blooms in the cold weather. Fire or drought can render it dry and barren, but when it rains it comes again.'

Llewellyn wondered if she were rambling in her wits a little. It seemed likely that the shock that had cushioned her initially would have had some blunting effect on her intelligence. He took her hand respectfully and bowed a very little.

'Goodbye, Mrs Campbell,' he said.

***

It was late that evening when Galbraith entered the room. He had arrived the night before, but Isobel refused to see him. Now he came without warning, closed the door behind him and bent to scratch McCleod under the wing.

'Someone is pleased to see me back,' he remarked as the bird cocked its head and made a croodling sound. 'Hello, McCleod.'

'Hello, McCleod,' replied the bird gravely. 'Hello, person. Scrattttch?'

Isobel turned her face to the wall. She was propped in bed, clumsy beneath the quilt. 'Go away, James,' she said tiredly. 'I told you not to come.'

'I love you,' said Galbraith. 'I had to come.'

'You loved me as I was before,' said Isobel. 'It is no use now.'

Galbraith turned away from the bird, absently dusting the white feather-powder from his hand with a handkerchief. 'Why is it no use?' he asked.

'You of all folk should know that, James. You value beauty and you used to find me beautiful. I am not beautiful now and I never will be again. I have scars.'

'So have I,' said Galbraith. 'You have never appeared to find it repulsive.'

'Mine are ugly. My hair is cut short and my leg is the ugliest thing of all. I am not whole.'

Galbraith looked down at her steadily. 'So you are not the girl you were when I first met you,' he said. 'I am not the man I was then either. And I am not the young man I was when I first came to Glen Heather. Life has been cruel to you, Isobel. Is that any reason to be cruel to yourself- and to me?'

'It would be cruel to me to have you love me out of sympathy.'

'Then I will love you out of selfishness. I have always been a romantic, Isobel. I have always loved where I should not. I loved another man's wife. Then I loved a beautiful widow. Why should I not love a lady determined to send me away?'

'I am a cripple,' said Isobel.

'And I am as grey as a rain cloud and twice as ugly. I am also very tired. You have never withheld your favours from me before.'

'Oh James!' Isobel laughed with exasperation. 'I doubt I will have any favours to give.'

Galbraith removed his coat, shirt and trousers and tossed his fashionable bowler so that it landed neatly on the bedpost. 'If you want to look at *ugly*, here it is,' he said, indicating his naked self. He climbed carefully into bed beside Isobel and composed himself for rest. 'I never sleep as well away from you,' he said. 'I should like to share your grave when the time comes.'

'*James!*'

'Surely,' said Galbraith, 'your John would hardly object. I have loved you much longer than he.'

And better, perhaps? wondered Isobel. She prodded him. 'James, you cannot stay here. Jennie will be coming in the morning to see to my needs.'

Galbraith yawned. 'Aye, so she will. I have no doubt she's a verra good nurse. Have you heard that they hanged Moonlight and Kelly? And the judge who sentenced Kelly is dead as well. There is talk of a curse...'

CHAPTER 34

The painful months of convalescence were succeeded by more pain, physical and spiritual, as Isobel learned to walk again. She leaned heavily on James Galbraith, and cried and swore and scolded as she tried to force her badly mangled leg to cooperate with the use of a crutch.

Galbraith had remained longer at Glen Heather than he had ever done before, and when he was forced to leave in the winter of 1881, he spoke seriously of selling up his assets in New South Wales and returning permanently to Glen Heather. This Isobel refused to allow.

'You would not have done so had I been the way I used to be,' she said crossly, 'so why should you change now? Go home, do your business, then come back as you would have done then.'

She was sitting in the parlour with a rug on her legs, working over the accounts and trying to ignore the constant ache in her bad leg. The distortion of the limb was very visible, so she wore gowns made fuller than the prevailing cuirasse fashions as a disguise. The pain was not unbearable, but it nagged all the time and made her bad tempered, and she knew she would never be entirely free of it.

The month's figures were displeasing and she had a sinking feeling that they would continue to be so until she was able to take up her duties again. Perry was a good man, but he could hardly be expected to care for Glen Heather as she would. She wished Robert would take a little more interest, but though he had tried hard in the first few weeks after her accident he seemed to have lost his resolution. He was always finding an excuse to ride off to Mersey, or to go fishing in the river. He spent some time schooling Dogwood which would have pleased Isobel had there not been so many other matters needing his attention.

She wondered again if he was courting, but had no inclination of going into Mersey to find out. If Robert had been visiting one of his cousins so assiduously Winston or Gwynnie would have been on her doorstep by now, so she supposed the young lady, if there was a young lady, must be somebody else.

She had feared that Robert and pretty Jessie Perry would fall in love, but Jessie had her sights set on one of the footmen at Shannon. Her sisters Pris and Ruth were, Isobel trusted, too quiet to attract Robert.

Isobel put aside the account books and wedged her crutch under her arm. Elijah Ward had carved and polished it, and Jennie had padded it with wool and quilting, but despite the care they had taken Isobel hated it as a symbol of her own infirmity. She took one shuffling step with her left leg, swung her right shoulder forward and forced the right leg after it. The effort made her sweat with pain but she would not give up and spend her days in a bathchair.

Letters came sporadically from Ness, who was now comfortably established in Scotland. She had met her old friend Elspie Duncan, she wrote, and had settled to board with her for a while at Loch Haven, which Elspie's son was now farming. She had put out another "wee book", and Eddie had produced some ballads as accompaniment. Ness sent her best love to Robert and Isobel, James and McCleod, which led Galbraith, who had returned with the spring, to speculate on whether she held him in greater or lesser esteem than she held the cockatoo.

Isobel's letters in reply said nothing of her disability. What could Ness do, but worry, and why should she be troubled?

It was almost a year after the accident that the doctor informed her that she had healed all she would. Isobel retired to her bedchamber and closed the door, not wanting company, from Galbraith or anyone else.

'And that goes for you as well, McCleod,' she said, 'so out you go.'

She opened the sash and, with difficulty, persuaded the bird to abandon his perch for her wrist and then thrust him out the window. McCleod squawked with outrage and snapped his beak, and went on clinging to the sill outside even when she had closed the sash, beating his wings like a hurricane.

'You are a wicked old bird,' said Isobel, rapping on the glass.

She wondered suddenly how old McCleod really was. John had said only that the bird had been at Glen Heather for as long as he could recall. If John had lived, he would have been over forty now, so McCleod must be approaching that age as well. Isobel shook her head in fascination, and then readmitted the furious bird. After all, McCleod had had a distorted wing for many years, so perhaps he was an appropriate audience for what she planned to do.

Balancing against the windowsill, Isobel let the crutch slide from beneath her arm. She glanced across to see herself reflected in the long glass against the other wall. Her gown had three deep flounces and a frilled high collar, and the whole was buttoned down tightly to below her waist. Her hair, growing out into a fine fringe, looked unexpectedly fashionable, from the front. She was thinner than she had been, and she wondered detachedly how Gwynnie Jarvis managed to cram herself into the new fashions. She had not seen Gwynnie for an age.

Balanced on one leg and leaning on the wall, she made a supreme effort to take a step. Her bad leg buckled and the good one shook with the strain. The skirts bound and dragged about her legs.

'Damn this!' said Isobel.

She sank ungracefully to the floor and retrieved her crutch, then manoeuvred herself upright again. She limped over to the chest and fetched out her breeches, unworn for over a year, and then sank down on the mattress and, with trembling hands, began to undo the masses of tiny buttons that fastened her gown.

***

Robert was twenty, and looked twenty-five. He had been grateful for his appearance during his encounter with Peg, and had found it useful on occasions since, but usually he regretted the spurious maturity folk perceived when they looked at him. Glen Heather was his, and he wished very much it were not. He had no affinity for sheep, no touch for the land, and no feeling of ownership at all.

Sometimes he wondered what he would have done had he had the choice in life. Would he have studied medicine or law? Painted pictures like James Galbraith or learned to use photographic apparatus? He thought sometimes he would have enjoyed prospecting, or teaching children to read and write. He liked children, and had always been a good hand with the younger ones around Glen Heather. Little Hannah Christopher was never happier than when seated on "Mister Wobert's" shoulders.

He was less at ease with the young ladies he met at dances and parties, for he never seemed in tune with their wishes. If he treated a girl with formal correctness, she seemed disappointed, but if he tried to steal a kiss, he risked a shrill rebuff, or a slap. He remembered the things Peg had taught him, but he felt she had taken him from the middle to the end of the alphabet. What he needed now was another tutor who would take him from the beginning to the middle.

In December he went to a party held at York Hall for one of the Miss Reeves, newly returned from Thornleigh Grange in Launceston. Felicia Reeve was a beauty, and Robert was smitten. He was angling for an introduction when a brisk voice warned him not to bother.

'I beg your pardon?' he said.

'Felicia is betrothed already,' said Annie Llewellyn, 'so why waste your time?'

'There has been no announcement,' said Robert stiffly. Annie was looking very well, but he had been wary of her ever since she slapped him.

Annie snapped shut her fan. 'There will be,' she said confidently. 'She is to marry my brother, you know.'

'Your brother?' Robert could scarcely keep the astonishment from his voice. It seemed a shocking mesalliance for a Miss Reeve of York Hall to marry a doctor.

'Floyd is an excellent physician,' said Annie dispassionately. 'Had it not been for him, Felicia would have succumbed to the typhus.' Her satin-clad toe was tapping gently to the music, and her gaze was on the dancers revolving in the great hall.

'Dr Llewellyn is not even present!' said Robert.

'No,' said Annie distantly. 'He is saving a life. But perhaps you think that unimportant compared with attendance at a ball?'

Robert knew quite well what Glen Heather owed the doctor. 'I do not think that at all!'

'Good,' said Annie. The music ceased and she sighed as the gentlemen led their partners back to the seats and began to ply them with lemonade and punch.

She was not even looking his way, but Robert became aware of a slight tension in the line of her neck. 'Annie,' he began, 'Miss Llewellyn?'

'Mr Campbell?'

'Perhaps you would care to dance? After all, we know our steps fit well enough.'

'Thank you, I should like that,' she said, and then spoiled it by adding that she hated of all things to sit still.

Robert danced often with Annie after that, not only at York Hall but also at the other gatherings they both attended. He found her good company, if a trifle tart-tongued, but after the first time he learned not to pay her pretty compliments. Annie was small and dark and vivacious, but she knew perfectly well her features were too pronounced for her to be considered a beauty.

'What will you do, Annie, when your brother has married Miss Reeve?' Robert asked her once.

'I think perhaps I shall train as a schoolmistress,' she said. 'Floyd will not mind, so long as I find respectable occupation.' Robert drew in his breath with envy. 'Yes, Mr Campbell? Had you another suggestion?' said Annie. In any other young lady he would have taken this as an invitation to a flirtation, but Annie was always direct.

'No,' he said gloomily, 'not really, Annie, unless- would you care to marry me?' He felt himself flushing with the enormity of his suggestion and began to stammer. 'That is- perhaps one day. When I am older. I shall need a wife.'

Annie looked at him, considering; and Robert held his breath. If she accepted him he would be really in a bumble-broth, but perhaps after all it would be pleasant to be married to Annie. She was intelligent and personable and he liked the clean smell of her hair. He remembered Galbraith's advice that he should find someone to love.

'No thank you, Robert,' she said as if he had offered her a second glass of lemonade. 'I like you very well, but my brother says I should never wed a man I can dominate and, dear Robert, I fear I could easily dominate you.'

'I suppose you could,' said Robert, discouraged. Now she had refused him he was disappointed. 'I would like to have been a teacher myself,' he added inconsequently.

Annie laughed. 'Would you have the resolution to beat bad boys?'

'Perhaps not, but some of them would enjoy learning. My mother's friend, Mr Galbraith, taught me all about literature and art.'

Annie looked unconvinced. 'Anyway,' she said, 'why should you be a schoolmaster when you have Glen Heather?'

Robert sighed. 'Aye,' he said, 'I have Glen Heather. Would you care to dance again, Miss Llewellyn?'

'I think not, in the circumstances,' she said. 'Why not ask Mary MacDonald? She thinks you are very handsome and quite a man of style.'

'Does she?' Robert was not used to thinking himself handsome.

'Oh yes,' said Annie. 'To be sure she does. She is over there with her aunt and her mama, who is ailing, as usual. Why not be kind enough to rescue her?' She tapped Robert on the cheek with her fan and went away.

***

Isobel was trembling with fatigue by the time she managed to change her gown for the pair of breeches. It disgusted her, to find herself so weak, and she was reminded, after more than twenty years, of the way she had felt after Robert's birth. She took up her crutch and levered herself to her feet. Freed of the drag of heavily trimmed skirts, she felt more herself than she had done for months. She glanced down at her legs. The left one was straight, if a little thin from lack of muscle tone. The other was bent and twisted. Isobel laid the crutch on the bed and stood, swaying, without support. Then she deliberately allowed herself to fall forwards so that her hands met the warm wooden panelling with a gentle smacking sound. She took a single step with her good leg, then, somehow, dragged the other forward. It ached fiercely, and it was so heavy she wished the doctor had amputated it in the beginning. Perhaps she would have managed better with a wooden leg, but Llewellyn had told her frankly that he doubted she would have survived the operation at that time, and after the healing she had lacked the resolution to suffer more. The leg had healed as much as it would and she must learn to use it all over again.

Sweating and breathing hard, she slid her palms along the wall to the window ledge and, using the sill for balance rather than support, she took another step, and another, until she had dragged herself round the room. Afterwards, she changed back into her gown and rested demurely on the bed as she had been instructed.

***

James Galbraith knew Isobel was up to something. He had known her too long and loved her too well not to know there was something afoot, but he made no attempt to discover what it was. She had never given him the right. He still slept by her side when in residence at Glen Heather, but they had never resumed their physical relationship. He had begun to believe they never would, and though he regretted the loss of what they had shared, he reminded himself that he had reached an age where celibacy was not only acceptable, but expected. At least he could still hold her in the night.

Asleep with her head on his shoulder, Isobel seemed at peace, and when he held her in his arms and told her the news of the colonies he could almost believe she was happy.

One day, he heard squawking in the attic storeroom at the very top of the house. Supposing McCleod was up to devilment, he climbed the stairs and found not only the bird in the attic, but also Isobel. She had her crutch by her side and a sheaf of papers in her hand, and she was going through them, one by one.

With a lurch of surprise, Galbraith saw that they were some of his old drawings. If she had found the original portraits he had made of her- he went cold at the thought. The differences between the serene beauty of health and youth and the pain on her scarred face now would be too cruel.

'Isobel?' he said uncertainly.

She looked up, and he saw a glisten of tears in her eyes.

'James- do you remember the picture you did of Robert?'

It was the last thing he had expected, but he thought back obediently. 'I have drawn Robert many times. He has an arresting face.'

'He was nine years old at the time, but you drew him at twenty-one.'

Galbraith nodded, remembering now. It had been that drawing that led to Isobel's commissioning the painting of John in the parlour, and to their whole relationship.

'You got it right,' she said. 'Look, James. Here is that old picture and it is Robert's very face today.'

Galbraith glanced at the piece of paper, and then took it to the window for a closer look.

'So it is,' he said, fascinated. It was his own work, and he remembered it well enough, but how had he ever managed such a feat?

Isobel was watching him steadily. 'What can you not do, James? You can paint someone twenty years behind or a dozen years ahead. You can picture the dead and those who do not yet exist. Could you paint someone who never existed, I wonder?'

Galbraith was very uneasy. Since the accident Isobel had had occasional spells of forgetfulness, and at times her thoughts seemed all awry.

'Who did you have in mind, my love?' he asked gently. 'And why are you up here alone at the top of the house?'

'I have McCleod with me, and I thought I would sort through the chests,' she said vaguely. 'It is spring, after all, and Jennie and Emma have work to do. Mrs Baker is too old to climb the stairs.'

And you are too lame, thought Galbraith, but he knew he would never say it. It must have taken her an age to reach the attic storeroom, but then it took time to reach her bedchamber, too, and she refused to move to the lower floor.

'I wondered if you would be able to paint our daughter,' said Isobel.

Galbraith stared – and then realised what she meant. She was not adrift in her mind this time; she was simply nursing regrets.

'No, I would not do that,' he said. 'We never had a daughter, Isobel, and now we never shall. It is no use regretting lost chances. Let it go.'

'I have spent my life letting go,' she said passionately. 'But if we had had a child, James, I wonder what she would have been like? Robert is pure Campbell, much more so than John.'

'And he is positive proof that John was Hector's son,' said Galbraith dryly.

He let his mind dwell for a moment on the might-have-been child. If they had had a daughter, she would not have had a drop of Campbell blood in her. She would have had brown or blonde hair, not black, and her face would not have been carved in stone. She would have had an eye for beauty, and a fund of love to give... and by now she could have been ten years old.

Galbraith knew he would have been able to paint the child who did not exist. He had only to let his talent run free. He also knew he would never try. Some regrets were better left in the shadows.

Isobel had sorted other things from the chests before chancing on the sketches, and Galbraith looked at them with interest. There were crinoline hoops and knickerbockers, a horseshoe, a dented Dutch oven, an old coat which must have belonged to John, and two worn plaids, green and brown. He remembered them well and was surprised that Ness had left them behind. But Ness had left Glen Heather and the memories behind. She had even left the portraits of herself and Hector.

There was also a wedding gown, unmistakable in ivory figured satin.

'Mine,' said Isobel, catching the direction of his gaze. 'I was keeping it for my daughters.'

'Perhaps,' said Galbraith carefully, 'your Robert will marry and his bride will wear that gown. It is beautifully worked.'

'Robert must marry,' said Isobel. 'There must be an heir for Glen Heather, but his bride will have her own traditions, and may wear her mother's gown.' She picked up the wedding dress, laid it back in the chest and closed the lid.

Galbraith took Isobel's hand and helped her to stand. She wedged the crutch under her arm and began her slow way to the head of the stairs, and for the first time he realised she was wearing her breeches.

'Where are you going now?' he asked.

Isobel balanced on the crutch and gave him a look at once sly and mischievous. 'James, my love, can you keep a secret?'

'Of course,' said Galbraith, bending to offer his fist to the crossly waddling McCleod. McCleod would accept his assistance on the stairs. Isobel would not.

'Then come with me to the stables. I wish to ride out on Daisy and I doubt if I can manage to saddle her myself.' She swung herself slowly through the door and closed it with an emphatic bang. 'Well, James, have you no protestations? Are you not going to try to stop me?'

'Would it be of any use if I did?'

'Not a bit,' said Isobel.

Galbraith smiled. 'Then I shall not trouble myself to try.'

CHAPTER 35

Isobel decided to hold a ball to mark Robert's coming of age. She knew the time had come for her to relinquish control of Glen Heather, and she also knew her son was quite unready to run it in her stead. There was nothing she could do about that, so she looked the future steadily in the face and planned a celebration.

Glen Heather had no ballroom, but the parlour possessed huge double doors, which could be opened into the sitting room next door to give the effect of one large room. With the oilcloth rolled back and flowers banked all around the walls, the effect was impressive. The crimson curtains added warmth to the room, and Isobel had had the notion of using native vegetation to carry on the theme. Crimson flowers were few, but the two youngest Perry children climbed the brae and brought back all the flowering heath they could find. Wild clematis and ferns, wild cherry boughs and myrtle made a charming background for the flowers, and Isobel framed the four portraits with cherry leaves as well. She wanted them clearly seen, for tonight she had determined to lay to rest any remaining doubts the inhabitants of Mersey might harbour about Robert's lineage. She had also decided to have Galbraith at her side to receive the guests, and to let the gossips make of it what they would.

Old Mrs Baker would have been mortally offended had they hired outside caterers, so Isobel had left it to Jennie and Emma to find sisters and daughters, aunts and nephews ready to help out. She was determined to make the occasion a social splash. She had invited all her local acquaintance, including as many young folk as she could find. The Jarvis cousins were coming, but unfortunately there would be no Campbell relatives, although a friendly letter had come from Edwina Campbell in New Zealand to congratulate the master of Glen Heather upon his coming of age.

There was no word from Jamie, but by now Isobel had ceased to expect it. Jamie Campbell could have walked off the face of the earth and as for his lady –Isobel remembered only her name; Charlotte; and the way she had looked fifteen years before. The couple's stay at Glen

Heather had been so very brief, overshadowed by news of John's death and the arrival of the Law on the doorstep. No one had ever told Isobel where Charlotte had lived, or where her family was, and after so many years it seemed pointless to speculate.

Isobel padded the guest list with folk who had some connection with Glen Heather. There was Mr Bertram, the solicitor who had been Robert's distant but official guardian, Dr Llewellyn, who had undoubtedly saved her life, and some distinguished associates of Galbraith's from Launceston. One did not usually know one's doctor or lawyer socially, but so far as Isobel could see Llewellyn was a worthier man than her brother Winston.

A modiste came from Shepherd Town to fit Isobel with a suitable gown. Isobel declared the suggested colour made her look like a dowager and chose a dark green instead. On the breast she pinned the white heather brooch she had worn as a bride. She was grimly satisfied.

On her instructions, Robert crammed his broad shoulders into a tightly cut suit, and resigned himself to an evening of discomfort and embarrassment.

'Must there be such a to-do, Isobel?' he asked plaintively.

'There must. This birthday marks the end of your minority,' said his mother impatiently. 'You will be accepted as a man of the world after tonight. You are already a man of substantial property.' She paused, and tugged at his lapel. 'Come now, Robert, see if you cannot look a little more gracious. There are many young men who would desire to be in your shoes today.'

'Aye, and they would be most welcome,' said Robert.

To his surprise Isobel flew into a temper. 'How dare you say such a thing! I do not expect you to be grateful for all the effort expended on your behalf, but you might show respect for your heritage. The guests will wish to greet the master of Glen Heather, not a sulky boy.'

'Mama, *you* are the true master of Glen Heather, and have been all my life,' said Robert desperately. 'Can you not continue to be so?'

'While you idle your days with a fishing line or book in your hand?' said Isobel bitingly. 'I think not, Robert! At your age your father was a man of responsibility, a man with a wife and coming child.'

A man who had also no more than months left to live, thought Robert unhappily. Aloud, he said; 'But Mama, Isobel, I am not *ready*!'

'Do you think your father was ready to run Glen Heather when his father passed away? Dear God, do you think I was ready?'

There was a pause. Despite his age and size Robert did feel very much like a sulky boy. 'In a few more years, perhaps,' he mumbled.

'Robert, you must face your responsibilities,' said Isobel more quietly. 'You have known for years that this was coming. In the words of Mr Perry, brace up, lad, and face life as it comes.'

She patted his shoulder and swung away, leaning heavily on her crutch.

Robert stared after her. He had never understood his mother, and he knew he never would. He would have sworn she would welcome the chance to remain in charge, for had she not worked her heart out to learn to ride Daisy again after the accident? To be sure she could no longer handle sheep or cattle, but she rode about Glen Heather just as she always had, and if she occasionally forgot things or suggested something out of season, Galbraith would gently remind her or Perry would set her right.

He thought of approaching Galbraith, as he had in the past when faced with imponderables about his mother, but he was an adult now, as she had astringently reminded him. He could not go running to an old man, good friends though they had always been.

***

Glen Heather was lit from within, with the crimson of the curtains glowing like rubies and lanterns strung in the apple tree. The yard was full of horses, carriages and gigs, and Perry and the other men fully occupied in directing the traffic. Six-year-old Will Perry, sent out by Emma to keep him from her feet, was shrilly excited, vying with Hannah Christopher to spot the greatest number of dappled horses. They had both seen Mr Robert dressed in his finery, and had gravely wished him a happy birthday. Birthdays were lovely occasions, bringing sweetmeats and gaiety, and they could not see why Mr Robert seemed so gloomy.

There was music playing softly, and the wattle blossom was sharp in the air. Robert, who had been standing in the receiving line with his mother and Galbraith, was not enjoying himself. Annie Llewellyn was present, along with her brother and his betrothed, but he could not rely on Annie for comfort any more than he could rely on his own mother. Perhaps the two women were a little alike, he thought, and wondered if that was what drew him to Annie. Annie had claimed she could master him, and his mother certainly could; was that what he wanted from life?

By nine o'clock, the ball had fairly begun, and the big double room was full of whirling couples. The flounced gowns of the young ladies were ruched and draped with lace, and so tightly fitting it was a puzzle to Robert that they could breathe, let alone dance. Whatever they wore underneath seemed surprisingly firm and unyielding. He had a sudden brief fantasy that the ladies were made like yabbies in carapaces, and would require nutcrackers to extract them for consumption. He danced with Annie twice, but she declined to partner him a third time.

'No, Robert- folk will begin to talk.'

'Would you mind?' he asked curiously.

'No doubt you think it would boost my consequence to be seen as the designated property of the master of Glen Heather,' she rejoined with surprising bitterness.

Robert had been thinking along those lines, but he was offended that Annie should say it. He found her often in his mind since she refused him, and had considered proposing to her again, and making a better job of it.

'What have you against Glen Heather?' he asked instead.

'Nothing!' Annie seemed honestly surprised. 'It merely seems wrong to me that all this-' and she waved her hand -'should come to you as of right while my brother has had to work so hard for all he has, and to suffer the snubs of folk who consider him to be beneath them. They call on him fast enough if they have a colic, but there have been sneers in plenty since his betrothal to Felicia. They call him a fortune hunter, but he would marry her if she had nothing.'

'We do not think like that here,' said Robert, nettled. 'Your brother is our guest tonight, is he not?'

'Yes, and no doubt you feel yourself very liberal in consequence,' said Annie.

Robert would have flung away, but this was his birthday ball and he could not behave like an over-indulged child. 'If you feel so badly about us, I wonder you have come,' he muttered.

Annie smiled. 'It is ungracious to say such things to you. I apologise unreservedly.'

'But you take none of it back,' said Robert.

'Well, no. To do so would be to commit a falsehood.'

Robert offered his arm and after a moment she took it. 'I know I do not deserve Glen Heather,' he said, 'and truly, I would prefer to see it go to someone more suited to husband it. However, my grandfather's will laid it down that I must be the one, so there is no avoiding it. You might have approved of him, Miss Llewellyn. He was a wild Scot who earned everything he had. He built Glen Heather from nothing. Are you sure you will not dance with me again?'

'Quite sure,' said Annie.

'Nor marry me either, I suppose.'

'No,' she said quietly, 'for after all I have said and you have said, we would never be sure of the other's motive. I might be marrying for envy and position, you to prove a point. No, Robert Campbell, I will not marry you.' She pulled a little face. 'In fact, I doubt I shall ever marry! A gentleman whose company I could support always could probably not support mine!'

Annie left him then, and Robert gazed after her. He had a strong feeling he had made a mull of things, again. But he had too much pride to make himself ridiculous by proposing to the lady a third time, so he turned away, determined to dance with someone else.

Pretty Mary MacDonald was immured in a corner, wedged between her stout, ailing mama and her equally stout and rather silly Aunt Lavinia. She was a charming girl, soft, light haired and pink-cheeked. She was a little plump, and she had a shy smile and a habit of dropping her eyelids demurely. Robert decided she was just the thing to ease the sting of his encounter with Annie, and presented himself at her side.

'Would you care to dance, Miss MacDonald?' he asked.

Mary's eyes snapped sideways towards her mother. 'Mama, you will not object if I leave you for a little?'

Amelia MacDonald fanned herself languidly. 'To be sure I feel one of my sick headaches coming on, but you need not regard that. Go and enjoy yourself, my dear. Your Aunt Lavinia will tend to me.'

Mary looked a little quenched, but took Robert's offered arm. 'I must not be too long.' she said nervously. 'Poor Mama suffers so.'

Robert nodded sympathetically, his gaze on Isobel, who was conversing with her sister-in-law across the room. He did not know what it cost her to stand so calmly in her green cut-velvet gown, and, as he danced with pretty Mary he saw Galbraith standing by, watching Isobel with pride and devotion in his eyes. The movement of the dance swept him against Mary and she stumbled a little.

'Please accept my apologies, Miss MacDonald,' said Robert.

Mary looked up and smiled. 'It was quite my own fault, Robert. Oh! I suppose I should call you Mr Campbell now, for we are not children any more. What a very fine house this is. I never was in here before.'

'I hope this is the first of many visits,' said Robert warmly.

Isobel was making heavy weather of talking to Gwynnie. It was some time since she had spent time in the company of her sister-in-law, and she was struck anew by her essential shallowness. How could Winston stand her? And those fat giggling girls of hers! Isobel prayed earnestly that Robert would not look too often in their direction. She looked about the room at the other young ladies, trying to see them through a young man's eyes. Which would be Robert's eventual bride? She liked the look of the small dark girl with the vivacious smile, and Robert had danced with her twice already. Maybe that would be a suitable match.

Excusing herself to Gwynneth, she swung herself over to Galbraith. 'James, you are a man.'

'I have always thought so,' said Galbraith. 'Indeed, I have always hoped I was.'

'Fool,' said Isobel impatiently, 'what I am asking is this; if you were choosing a wife from this assembly, who would you select?'

Galbraith did not deliberately misunderstand her, but he did raise a brow. 'A wife for whom, my dear?'

'Why, for Robert, of course. Who else?'

He put his arm around her shoulders and shook his head. 'Isobel, you have been steward of Glen Heather for a long time, but surely you deserve a little freedom now?'

'Freedom?' she said vaguely.

'Aye,' said Galbraith. 'I am a selfish man, my love, and before I die I should like to show you to Sydney Town. And I want to marry you there. I should not care to die a single man.'

'But how could I ever leave Glen Heather? And Robert?'

'Glen Heather and Robert can look after themselves. Come, Isobel, you deserve it, and so do they. And so, perhaps, do I.'

'I am lame,' she said.

'Not so lame that you cannot dance with me.' He gave her a little shake. 'Come now, did you really believe I did not know the progress you have made in walking without support?'

'I wanted it to be a surprise,' said Isobel.

'It is an excellent surprise. Now put down that crutch and grant me the pleasure of this dance.'

Isobel took a halting step and then another. 'I cannot do it,' she said. 'I can walk a little, but I shall never dance again.'

'Nevertheless, we shall try,' said Galbraith, 'and tonight I think we should try something more.' He began to slide his hands down her back in his old caress, and then stopped abruptly. 'Good God what was that?'

A shadow had coasted past the lights, making them flicker.

Isobel looked up. 'That,' she said, 'was McCleod. Drat! I wonder who let him out of the kitchen?'

Still in one another's arms, they turned about, just as Jennie Comfrey opened the door to yet another guest, a grey haired lady. She was elderly, yet did not look incongruous in her crimson gown.

'Grannie Ness!' Robert's voice rang out in glad surprise, and he urged his partner towards the door. 'Mary, here is my grandmother! But I thought you in Scotland, Grandmama!'

'Och, how could I stay awa' wi' the master o' Glen Heather a man at last!' said Ness. Her bright eyes took in the whirling dancers and the flowers and greenery. 'And what a homecoming forby!' she added admiringly.

'Will you stay awhile, Grandmama?' asked Robert.

'Aye, I'll stay as long as you'll be having me, laddie. I'm no so young and I'd like it fine to live out my days at home.'

Isobel watched the glad greeting between her mother-in-law and her son. The two had always dealt well together, far more so than she had dealt with Robert. Perhaps- perhaps, if Ness stayed on at Glen Heather, she could do as Galbraith wanted. Perhaps she could let go? Still supported in his arms, she looked up at the lined face of her lover. His blue eyes were beaming a welcome for Ness, but his hands were holding her.

'James,' she said abruptly, 'do you recall saying once you would like to share a plot with me when we die?'

He looked down and smiled for her alone. 'Aye, that I do, my love.'

'Then so it shall be,' said Isobel firmly. 'So it shall be. And since it is not seemly for a lady to be buried with a single man, I shall have to take you as my husband and come and live with you in New South Wales.'

Ignoring the fascination of some of the guests, Galbraith bent and kissed her mouth with slow appreciation. 'My lady, you have made me a very happy man.'

'And I shall continue to do so for a long, long time!' she said tartly. Then she smiled. 'Oh, James, James, after so long, do you think we shall ever survive the respectability?'

PART THREE: ALICE - 1913-1920

CHAPTER 36

When Alice MacDonald Campbell returned from her year at boarding school, her mother decided to it was time to launch her into society. 'We shall hold a ball,' decreed Mary, 'just as you had for your coming of age, Robert.'

'Will Alice enjoy that?' asked Robert doubtfully.

Mary gave him a reproving look. 'Of course Alice will enjoy it,' she said. 'What girl would not?' She looked appraisingly at their elder daughter.

Alice was very dark, with tea-coloured eyes, wildly curling hair and the still face that characterised all the Campbells but Rosalind, Mary often wished she had a little more animation. Then Alice would smile. It was as if the sun came out then, to play across the surface of one of the mountain lakes and tarns, striking a heart of silver. It was as if the grey drab heath burst into crimson bloom.

Mary glanced sideways at the parlour glass and saw herself reflected. She looked well enough, with her hair, still barely touched with grey, rolled above her brow and her dotted voile blouse showing off the prow of her bosom, but aside from the regal set of her shoulders she saw nothing of herself in her elder daughter. She turned back to pump Alice for information about her former schoolmates. Which girls should be invited to the ball? Which girls had eligible brothers and cousins to swell the numbers of potential partners?

'How would I know that?' asked Alice, perplexed. 'Young gentlemen were not permitted to visit us at Swan House, nor were we encouraged to speak with them in the town.'

'I should think not!' said Mary. 'But it is different now, Alice. You are a young lady and we must make some push to launch you into society, such as it is. We must ask your Uncle Wesley's boys, and of course your Aunt Lizzie's Martin, although he is a little young and of course he cannot dance with his foot the way it is. What a pity your Uncle Whitaker is a bachelor - Scarborough would have been an admirable setting for a ball had he had the forethought to marry. But have you made up your list as I bade you?'

Alice had, and Mary made discreet enquiries, crossed off some names, added others, and wrote invitations for many of her own relatives. Next, she turned her eye to the local landowners and to such professional gentlemen as she deemed suitable company. There were few enough to be found, but Mary invited young Mr Garland, the clerk who had recently joined Mr Bertram the solicitor, personable Dr Michael Blake, and the eldest son of the Jenkins family - not quite top drawer, perhaps, but heir to a flourishing family business. There was one young Mr Reeve, two Misses O'Hara, and a distant connection of Isobel's on her mother's side...

'But Mother,' expostulated Alice when she read the amended list, 'I scarcely know any of these folk! What about my friends? Miss Llewellyn - she has always been good to me - and Hannah and Arthur Pritchard, of course. And dear Jennie Christopher would be company for Granny.'

Mary stared. 'Alice, you cannot be serious! Miss Llewellyn - perhaps. She is received everywhere. But as for Hannah!'

'Hannah is my friend,' said Alice. 'She is almost part of the family. Isn't that what Dad has always said? She grew up at Glen Heather, after all.'

'Your father is a very liberal man, but the fact remains that Hannah Christopher was our housekeeper until she married,' said Mary darkly.

'What has that to say to anything?' asked Alice. Her level dark brows lowered in a manner Mary knew all too well.

'Don't *frown*, Alice!' she snapped. 'I should have thought a year at Swan House would have taught you that a lady should never frown.'

Alice smiled instead, and the effect was oddly disturbing. Mary felt more uneasy than ever. Alice's smile held a quality of danger, and she disliked it very much. 'Have you not reflected, Alice, how cruel it would be to take a simple person such as Hannah into society?' she said hastily. 'She would be gauche, embarrassed - her gown would be shabby - in any case, she cannot come.'

'Why not?'

Mary coughed and glanced over to where Rosalind, put out and neglected in the fuss surrounding her sister's come-out ball, was sulkily sorting cottons on the window seat.

'Hannah is in a Certain Condition and is unable to appear in public,' murmured Mary.

Alice translated the words and tone without difficulty. 'I'm glad! I know Hannah always wanted children. When will it be born?'

Mary flushed angrily and jerked her head towards the window seat, but Alice ignored her. 'I shall go and visit Hannah tomorrow,' she decided. 'Would you care to come too, Rosie?'

'Alice!' wailed Mary.

Alice contemplated her mother's mottled cheeks. 'Do you feel quite the thing, Mother? Perhaps this planning is too much for you. I would gladly forego the ball if it threatens your health. Perhaps if we wait a little Hannah's child will have arrived and she will be able to come.'

'Not… in…front…of…your…sister!' mouthed Mary, her head jerking alarmingly.

Alice stared. 'Rosalind is twelve,' she said quietly. 'Surely she knows …'

'Surely I know what, Alice?' asked Rosalind.

'That we are having a ball dear,' said Mary. 'A ball for Alice.'

'Of course I know!' said Rosalind scornfully. 'And I think it is mean that you will not let me dance too. I am the best in my class at dancing, so Miss Llewellyn says. I can do the polka and the barn dance and the waltz as well. I am sure I dance better than Alice.'

'It does seem a pity to waste such talent,' said Alice, straight-faced. 'Mother, why should we not have a family dance at New Year instead of a ball? Then we could invite all our true friends and Rosalind could come and show me how well she dances. She could have a new party dress - you would enjoy that, wouldn't you Rosie? I would prefer it too.'

Rosalind sprang up and clasped her hands. 'Oh, yes, Mother! Oh Mother - say yes! Could the frock be blue, Mother, with pink scallop lace?'

Mary did say yes. It was not the done thing, of course, for girls of Rosalind's age to attend dances, but there could be no objection if it were an informal occasion in the home. And Rosalind was such a very rewarding child. Fair and blue-eyed, neat and biddable - she could scarcely have been more unlike her sister Alice. Mary sighed a little. If her other three pregnancies had carried to term, she would have had other daughters - and sons - but fate had ruled otherwise. There was no use fretting and at least there was Rosalind, born when she was close to forty, a late and delightful surprise.

Having adopted the idea of a family dance, Mary threw herself into the preparations with enthusiasm, for at the back of her mind was the thought that this was only a beginning, a rehearsal for her real triumph; the future launching of Rosalind.

Annie Llewellyn was surprised but not particularly gratified to receive an invitation to the Glen Heather dance. She and Mary MacDonald had never been friends, and the fact that she had connived with Mary to send Alice to boarding school gave her no more sympathy for the woman. Mary had done it as a last attempt to turn Alice from a lively hoyden to a polished young lady; Annie did it for Alice's sake - and just a little for her own.

After her brother's marriage to Felicia Reeve, Annie went to Launceston and spread her wings, meeting others who shared her quick intelligence and ranging curiosity. Three years she had, but then Floyd's young wife died in childbirth. Annie's promised emancipation ended abruptly, and she returned to Mersey to teach the local school and keep house for her widowed brother. Had Robert Campbell renewed his attentions, Annie might have accepted, but by then, Robert had embarked on his long, long betrothal to Mary MacDonald. Sometimes, Annie felt she had done herself and Robert a great wrong in refusing him, but then - Robert's marriage had resulted in his daughter Alice, so who was to fly against Providence?

Annie had expected Robert Campbell's child to be as sweet-natured and pliable as Robert himself, and perhaps as pretty and vapid as Mary, so she was totally unprepared to be faced with a dour, dark-browed child whose thin arms were a mass of old scrapes and scratches and whose eyes burned with a fierce intelligence. And there had been other anomalies. Alice Campbell could read fluently, yet had little grasp of the alphabet. She was also irremediably left-handed, and there was no help for that. Using her left hand, Alice would work absorbedly for hours, but if forced to use her right, she would do nothing at all. Apart from this obstinate streak, and a reserve which prevented easy friendships, Annie had no complaints about Alice, save for a small, shamed sadness that, had she chosen differently, this odd, brilliant, infuriating child could have been her own daughter. Unfortunately, the brilliance was matched with a stubbornness seldom met in children and almost never in girls. It came as a harsh surprise to Annie when Alice firmly turned aside her advice that she should seek higher education and train as a teacher. 'Would your parents not agree?' Annie had asked. 'Your father, as I recall, always wished he had been free to take teacher training.'

Alice had given her strange slow smile. 'I cannot be a teacher, Miss Llewellyn, although I can see it is a fine occupation for ladies such as yourself.'

Annie felt the old nettles stinging. She had thought better of Alice - and of her father. 'Why not for you?' she said, rather sharply. 'Times are changing, Alice, and teacher training can only be an advantage to a lady, especially if you have children of your own, by and by.'

'You know, Miss Llewellyn, that my father has no son?'

'I know that, Alice, and I understand it is a great disappointment. However, there are many enlightened folk who are beginning to see that the feminine brain is in every way...'

'Never mind my brain for the moment, Miss,' Alice had said seriously. 'I am trying to tell you I have plenty to do at Glen Heather. My grandmother is very lame, you know. She still keeps the accounts, but she finds it difficult to ride, so I help out often with the sheep.'

Annie nodded, understanding that well enough. Isobel Galbraith had moved back to Glen Heather on the death of her second husband in 1894, and had lived there ever since, assisting her son, antagonising Mary and quarrelling with Mary's Aunt Lavinia. It was an uncomfortable situation for everyone involved, and she would hate to see Alice overtaken by the small intrigues that seethed perpetually in the Campbell household. 'Glen Heather is not the only place in the world, Alice,' she said with some desperation.

'It is for me. Besides, Miss - one should do whatsoever thy hand findeth to do with all thy might – is that not what you say yourself? And so I shall, even if it is my left hand that findeth all the work to do.'

Annie smiled reluctantly. 'Take care that all your might does not lead to obsession.'

'Whatsoever thy hand findeth to do with all thy might,' Alice repeated. 'And now, Miss, it is time I took Rosalind home. Do not trouble yourself - I know what I'm doing.'

Yes, Alice Campbell's blind devotion to Glen Heather came as an unwelcome surprise to Annie - particularly in the light of the fact that Robert had so resented the burden. Or had he? Annie thought back. Robert had claimed at his coming of age ball that he did not want Glen Heather, but how much of that had been a young man's wish to look well in the eyes of his lady? Not that she had ever been Robert's lady ... and what a bad turn she had done in thrusting him at Mary

MacDonald! But Mary had been sweet and pretty and devoted to her mama - a devotion which kept her at home through so many years when she might have been married to Robert and bearing his children. Annie put away regrets, dipped her pen in the inkwell and wrote an acceptance for herself and her brother. It would be good to see Alice again. A year at Swan House would have smoothed over some rugged edges and given a polish to her high intelligence, but Annie had no doubt the essential essence of the girl would be unchanged.

The Christmas of 1913 was overshadowed as Mary schemed and planned, ordered provisions and viewed bolts of cloth. Her Aunt Lavinia was a tower of strength and opinion, and of course, Rosalind was thrilled. Alice was not thrilled, but since her father and grandmother approved of this dance, how could she object? And so she smiled steadily when the dressmaker from Shepherd Town pinned her into her gown, and was at pains to listen with at least the appearance of pleasure as Mary detailed the arrangements which had been made on her behalf. Mary had impeccable taste, and she knew it was useless to dress Alice in the frilly creations depicted in the illustrated papers and fashion plates. Instead, she chose for her daughter a plain lemon-coloured gown which fell in graceful narrow folds to the ankles. With flowers in her hair, Alice looked very well, but her manner was one of resignation rather than pleasure.

The preparations involved everyone at Glen Heather with the exception of Isobel. For fifteen years, Isobel had been back at Glen Heather, working accounts, watching impotently as Robert bowed again and again to Mary's whims. She had a year of companionship from Ness, who then passed on peacefully with the redoubtable cockatoo McCleod by her side. After Ness' death, McCleod selected Isobel for his next slave/companion. Nothing would sway him from this and Isobel had been rather glad. Thrawn and disagreeable as he sometimes was, McCleod was better company than Mary and Lavinia. Alice was better company still, but Isobel knew she must not make too much of the girl. At all counts she must avoid the temptation to relive her life in Alice – or to see her as the daughter she and James had never had. She held stolidly to this decision, but still it had come as a pang when Alice went away.

Left to the increasingly burdensome company of Lavinia and Mary, Isobel retired more and more often to her room, where she sat with

McCleod and knitted or read, occasionally giving in to the melancholy pleasure of examining the contents of her deed-box - a box she kept locked against Mary's curiosity. One day, she thought, she would show the contents to Alice - but not until the girl was safely wed.

Since she spent so much of her time out of circulation, it was taken for granted by the household that Isobel would not attend the New Year's Dance. And yet - why not? She was not ill, nor even so very old, but merely tired and crotchety. It seemed a bitter thing to Isobel that all her striving to hold Glen Heather through Robert's minority had been in vain. Robert had taken over as the master, but Robert had no sons. Unless Mary were to die, and Robert remarry ... but Mary was as strong as a horse, and in any case Isobel did not wish her ill. Mary was a good wife and mother, according to her lights. It was not her fault the other three children had not survived to be born. And so it seemed the game was nearly played. It had been a good one while it lasted. And Isobel was tired.

She sat in her chair and listened to the preparations for the dance, distantly appreciating the occasional efforts made to involve her. Dutifully, she inspected the patterns for Alice's lemon gown, for Rosalind's party frock, for Mary's blue and Aunt Lavinia's lavender crepe, and was surprised to feel a stirring of interest. She'd had handsome gowns herself, once. An amber crinoline John had liked, and a green velvet James favoured. She had disposed of the amber gown after John's death, but the green was still in the attic, packed away against the moth with her ivory wedding gown. And, little by little, a plan formed in Isobel's mind.

During her long widowhood there had been no balls at Glen Heather. Her second marriage had been a glad one, but had been spent largely in New South Wales. And now she was home again. And why, thought Isobel, should she not attend the ball? She would not be able to dance, but she could still enjoy the festivities, if only she could ready herself to attend. This time, there was no James Galbraith to lend his support. She and Lavinia had never agreed, and although Mary would help, she would do so with martyrdom. Vainly, Isobel longed for Jennie Comfrey, or even Jennie's daughter Hannah. She longed for Emma Perry, and she longed for James. She swung her bell for the cook/ housekeeper, but only attracted the attention of McCleod - and Alice. McCleod demanded homage, but Alice, bless her, listened quietly to Isobel's request.

'Granny, is it wise to exert yourself so much?'

'Wise? Of course not!' said Isobel tartly. 'I am an old woman, Alice, and I am tired, but I would like to be part of things again. Oh - the guests will see a shrunken old woman of no account, but we shall know better, you and I. So open the trunk in the attic, and fetch me my green gown. And Alice -'

'Yes, Granny?'

Isobel smiled mischievously. 'Not a word to Mary! She will fuss me so!'

On the evening of the dance, Alice helped her grandmother dress, and pinned the white heather brooch to her breast, and then took her arm. Isobel shook her head. 'I can walk alone if I take my time. If I could not, I would stay in my bed.'

In the parlour, Isobel settled into her long-backed, cushioned chair and leaned back contentedly to watch the arrival of the guests. Even if her gaze dwelled more on the portraits above the mantel than on the folk of the present, everyone must agree that the old lady of Glen Heather looked very well indeed. It was a pity, thought Isobel, really a pity that there were so few of her generation left to attend this dance. Her brother Winston was gone, and Gwynnie no longer socialised. Niall O'Hara had come, but he was a bent old man, and his three chattering little daughters had grown into thin, middle-aged women. Really, there was only Lavinia, plump and foolish, but elegantly arrayed in her lilac crepe. Unlike Isobel, Lavinia had had a new gown made, but she sensibly eschewed the narrow, skimpy fashions of the present year. And just as well, for even on the younger ladies they looked almost indecent... Isobel shook her head at her own foolishness. No doubt she had looked even more indecent in her breeches.

She wondered pensively what Galbraith would have made of the new fashions, and decided he would have liked them very much. James had always had an eye for a lady's shape, as the contents of her deed-box could affirm.

Critically, Isobel watched the dancers, and decided that Alice outshone them all. She wasn't beautiful, but she had so much character in her face. She was a far, far more worthy child of Glen Heather than Robert had ever been, and Isobel marvelled that such a girl could have come from such parents. But then - heredity was a strange thing and as yet only half understood.

Alice was a nimble dancer, but she kept her eyes cast down and her lips closed, so few of the young men who partnered her begged a second dance. The general agreement was that Miss Campbell was lacking in conversation and charm. Mary was exasperated. Modesty was a virtue, but Alice was taking it much too far. It was not as if the girl was *shy*. She waylaid Alice and told her to make an effort.

'How?' asked Alice blankly.

'Talk to your partners,' said Mary, tight-lipped, 'or they will think you quite insufferable! And *smile*.'

Alice tried for a little, but her smile felt like the mechanical baring of teeth and none of the young men on whom she turned it seemed enchanted. After a while, she excused herself and went to sit by Annie Llewellyn who greeted her with an approving smile. 'Good evening, my dear. You are looking very well.'

'Am I?' said Alice, pulling a comical face. 'I feel like a crow arrayed as a canary. Now, *you*, Miss Llewellyn truly do look well. You have not changed a bit since I saw you last.'

Annie acknowledged the compliment with a dry little smile. 'Tell me, Alice, was it worth it?' she asked.

'Going to Swan House?' Alice considered. 'I think so,' she said at last. 'It was very hard - gey hard, as Granny would say – to be away from home so long. To be sure, I had Aunt Emily to visit me, but we never have agreed too well. I learned a great deal, though, and not just arithmetic and book-keeping. Miss Swan is a splendid person, isn't she?'

'She is indeed,' said Annie, apparently well pleased. 'Did you find much change when you returned?'

This time Alice hesitated even longer. 'Rosie had grown a good deal, of course, and my dear old Bob dog is older and grey. Mother and Aunt Lavinia are much the same and Granny ...'

'How about your father?'

'Dad seems a little tired,' said Alice briefly. Even to Miss Llewellyn she could not describe the shock when Robert had come to fetch her from Mole Creek Station. The shock of seeing his thick black hair receding and greyed. And the weakness in his face ... had it always been there? Now the memory dimmed her pleasure in Miss Llewellyn's company and she excused herself and went to join an acquaintance of her school days.

Isobel watched the revolving couples with contentment. She thought a lot about the past and a little of the future, but the present seemed clear and calm. At eleven o'clock, she beckoned to Alice to say goodnight.

'Will you not stay to see the new year in, Granny?'

'I have seen too many new years in,' said Isobel with a shrug. She unpinned the silver brooch from her gown and handed it to Alice. 'Put it on, lassie, it will bring you luck, perhaps. I had it from your Grannie Ness on my wedding day, but it seems right to give it to you now.'

'Did it bring *you* luck, Granny?' asked Alice.

Isobel thought over the years since she received the pretty ornament from Ness. John and James were gone, so were Winston and Ness. Gwynnie was old and frail and Isobel lame and tired ... but there were still the Campbells at Glen Heather, and there was still McCleod. He at least had never changed. 'Aye,' she said slowly. 'It brought me luck - but the luck of Glen Heather is thrawn.'

'The luck of Glen Heather is good enough for me,' said Alice contentedly as she helped her grandmother to undress.

Isobel contemplated her for a moment. 'Aye, you were ever one to know your own mind, Alice,' she said. 'A Campbell through and through, and the Campbells always know their own minds. The pity of it is sometimes they know what they want and find they cannot have it. Like my Robert. Some folk are bitter if they cannot have what they want, but Robert has done his best with what he has. Remember that, Alice, if ever you are tempted to despise him.'

Alice bit her lip. She remembered that weakness perceived in her father's face. But she had also seen the pleasure at her return. 'Granny,' she said softly, 'what did Dad want and never have?'

'He wanted Annie,' said Isobel clearly, 'and he wanted to be free of Glen Heather -'

'Miss Llewellyn? Surely not! And surely Father loves Glen Heather, just as you do!'

'Aye, he loves it, I love it, but love can be a curse ...'

With dismay, Alice decided her grandmother was wandering in her mind. 'I have always loved you, Granny, and counted it a privilege,' she said gently.

Isobel laughed. 'Then see to it, Alice, that I am laid where I wish to be,' she said. 'I chose my resting place long ago, between John and James. *Between* them, mark you! There is a space! Mary would have it that James had no right to a Campbell plot, but he loved me as well as any Campbell of them all.'

'Of course, Granny,' said Alice. 'But you'll not be needing that plot for a long time yet.'

'Not for a while,' said Isobel. Her gaze left Alice's face and she stretched out an arm to the bird. 'Give me McCleod.'

Alice offered her wrist, but the bird was already clambering from the bedpost and waddling the length of the bed, to settle in the crook of Isobel's arm. 'Scratttch?' it said hopefully.

'Now whoever would scratch a thrawn creature like yourself?' said Isobel fondly. She smiled at Alice. 'Back to the dance, child, and enjoy yourself.' Alice left the room and Isobel composed herself for sleep. The music was faint, and she waited for dreams to come.

Alice was disinclined to return to the dance after she had seen Isobel to bed, but she knew there would be trouble if she failed to reappear. She was about to re-enter the parlour when she heard the unmistakable sounds of a late arrival at the door. At first, she failed to recognise the dark young man on the doorstep, but then he smiled and removed his hat. 'I trust I am not quite too late for the festivities, Miss Campbell!'

'Not at all,' said Alice stiffly. 'Come in Mr...'

'Blake, Dr Michael Blake,' he said with another engaging smile.

'Of course! You are Dr Llewellyn's assistant.'

'I used to see you sometimes when you came to collect little Miss Rosalind from the schoolhouse,' he said. Alice's slow smile dawned and the doctor blinked, and allowed her to escort him into the parlour. It was close to eleven thirty, but the dancers were still waltzing. 'I expect your programme is quite filled, Miss Campbell?' said Dr Blake wistfully.

'Not at all,' said Alice. 'I have been helping my grandmother to bed, so I did not engage myself for any of the supper dances.'

'Then may I have the pleasure?'

As they danced to the strains of *You Made Me Love You*, Alice realised that the doctor was rather less talkative than her other partners. Recalling Mary's strictures, she sought for some unexceptional topic of conversation. The weather could be fairly dealt with, and then there was the recent rescue of Douglas Mawson - surely a doctor would be interested in that? She was about to make a comment when her partner forestalled her.

'That is a charming ornament you are wearing, Miss Campbell. It looks to me like a sprig of heath. Has it special significance?'

'I believe so,' she said. 'It came from Scotland and once belonged to my great grandmother's grandmother. It is heather, not heath.'

'A family heirloom! And now it belongs to you?'

'My grandmother gave it to me tonight.' She smiled.

'Something amuses you?'

'Well, yes. I was thinking about our other family heirloom - the one that is alive!' She told him about McCleod.

Seeing Alice dancing with the doctor, Mary began to relax. She could not hear the conversation, of course, but she saw Alice talking eagerly, and the young man was laughing and looking quite besotted. Times were changing, and a doctor might not be such a very poor match for Alice. Of course a girl in her position *should* have been able to look much higher, but Alice had not been much sought-after by the social set before her sojourn in Launceston. And why should she have been? A girl who rode astride and *whistled* and had more to say to her old sheepdog than her own mama! But tonight there was no sign of the hoyden of a year before. With her simple gown and high-piled black hair, Alice looked almost elegant.

Midnight struck shortly afterwards, and the company came to a halt and linked arms as the hired musicians broke into the strains of *Old Lang Syne.* Michael Blake sang along in a quite tuneful tenor voice, and when the plaintive music came to a close he bent and gave his partner a decorous kiss on the cheek. Alice started, and blushed, and he smiled down at her cheerfully. 'Happy New Year, Miss Campbell! May 1914 bring you joy.'

'Thank you. I hope so too. And of course I wish the same to you, Dr Blake.'

'I'm sure it shall,' he returned.

Michael Blake paid a courtesy call to Glen Heather less than a week later. Alice was out with her father, but Mary received the doctor graciously and invited him to drink tea with herself, Aunt Lavinia and Isobel. Since the dance, Isobel had alarmed Mary by emerging from seclusion and taking an interest in the day-to-day affairs of Glen Heather again. Fortunately, the doctor appeared to like the old lady, smiling at her astringent comments and turning aside her strictures about Dr Llewellyn, whom he considered sadly out of date.

When Alice finally arrived for her tea, Mary was put out to see that she had troubled neither to change her skirt nor to re-pin her bun. Loose corkscrew curls were rioting about her cheeks and she was a far cry from the dainty figure who had appeared at the dance. Mary expected Dr Blake to lose interest on the spot, but he continued to converse with Isobel and Robert for another half hour before excusing himself on the grounds that he had patients to attend. 'I should like to return, if I may, to continue our discussion,' he said, but although he was apparently addressing Robert, Mary was gratified to see his gaze touch approvingly on Alice.

Mary remonstrated with Alice after he had gone, but Alice merely nodded, promised absently to change her gown after riding in future, and went on talking to Robert about sheep. Sheep! Sometimes Mary was sick of the sound of the word, and occasionally she suspected Robert of feeling much the same way. But sheep or no sheep, she had no doubt they would be seeing the young doctor back at Glen Heather very soon.

Alice was very busy during the first hot months of 1914. Not only did the doctor call frequently to take her driving, but she had persuaded Robert to teach her something of property management to supplement lessons learned at Swan House. To Mary's disgust, most of this teaching took place in the shearing shed or on horseback as she and Bob helped Robert shift the sheep to better pastures.

'Sheep don't need much pasture,' explained Robert as if reciting a lesson got by heart, 'but if they're allowed, they will graze grass into the ground. The wind comes up and away goes your topsoil. In a mountainous place like this you must guard your soil like gold, or the rain simply washes it off into the creeks and river. You have only to look at Scarborough - the land was over-grazed in your Uncle Winston's time, so now your Uncle Whit is selling off the young timber. If it were up to me ...' But Robert shrugged and bit off whatever he had been going to say. 'Your grandmother feels it,' he said, 'but it is Whitaker's land and he has the final say.'

Alice helped move the rams, panting in the February heat, along to the creek. The slow pace suited her old dog Bob, and Alice laughed as he collapsed in the water and grinned at her from the shallows. Nearby was a small stone marker, where her grandfather had fallen on a spring night long ago. Alice sensed the melancholy of the place, but John was long dead, and apart from Isobel and Elijah Ward, no-one at Glen Heather remembered John any more - unless it were McCleod.

Alice helped bring in the hay harvest, riding scratched and dusty on the dray as it rolled slowly towards the barns. Mary wished loudly that the barns had been built a respectable distance from the main house. 'She'll be the talk of the district, if anyone sees what she's at!'

'She's still very young,' soothed Robert. 'One day she'll marry, and settle down.'

'But working with all those rough men!' wailed Mary. 'What if one of them ...' She could not voice the awful words, but closed her eyes and shuddered.

'The men answer to me,' said Robert. 'Every man of them knows he'd feel the toe of my boot if he harmed our Alice. Besides - my mother worked with the men for years.'

'That,' said Mary acidly, 'is no recommendation!'

It was on a hot afternoon in late February, after the flurry of dipping, shearing and harvest was done, that Alice decided to pay a visit to Hannah Pritchard. 'Don't forget,' ordered Mary. 'Dr Blake is dining with us tonight.' Alice liked Michael, but she had no intention of hurrying home on his account. 'I shall be back by six,' she said firmly. Her pony Blackwood was lame, so Alice decided to walk into Mersey. She swung along at a good pace, carrying a basket of ripe apples. McCleod had been picking the blossom again, but the thinning had done the fruit good, and the surviving apples were sound and rosy. It was a long walk, and the cottage was apparently deserted. Alice knocked and listened, knocked again. Surely Hannah would not be out? Ladies in her condition took their exercise in the kind dim light of the evenings.

'Who is it?' called Jennie Christopher's well-remembered tones from the rear of the house. 'Come through, if you will!'

'It's me - Alice Campbell. Is everything well?'

'Miss Alice! Do come in - Hannah's out in the dairy, but she should have come in long ago. I would have gone to her, but I sprained my ankle and I cannot walk just now.'

Alice went out to the dairy. Her friend was milking the cow, and was obviously in some sort of pain, for she raised a pale and sweating face when Alice called. 'Miss Alice? Where did you spring from? I'd like to invite you in, but it's a bit -' She gestured ruefully, then gasped and doubled up.

'Hannah! Is the baby coming?'

Hannah nodded. 'A bit before we expected. You'd best be off home, Miss Alice.'

'Won't you need someone with you?' asked Alice. 'Have you sent for Martha Ward?'

'Plenty of time when Arthur comes,' said Hannah, but her face was beaded with sweat.

Alice put down the basket. 'You go into the house and - and lie down,' she said. 'I can finish the cow, and then I'll come and make you and Jennie a cup of tea.'

'You're a rare one, Miss Alice,' said Hannah, 'but what your ma would say is beyond me!'

Hannah's labour progressed must faster than any of them had anticipated. By the time Alice had released the cow from the bail and gone into the kitchen to make the tea, Hannah was having heel and toe contractions and could scarcely raise herself to drink it. Alice went to Jennie Christopher, who wrung her hands in frustration. 'It's very quick for a first baby,' she said, 'and if I could get up I'd come, but as it is ... would you fetch Martha Ward, Miss Alice? There's no time to wait for Arthur.' Her round, sweet face was creased with concern.

The midwife lived on the far side of town, and when Alice arrived, panting, her cottage was locked and quiet. Alice left a message with the neighbour, but on her way back to Hannah's she was overtaken by Dr Blake in his sulky. 'Miss Campbell! What's the trouble?'

Alice turned, her face lighting up at the sight of him. 'Dr Blake! The very person!'

'Is something wrong at Glen Heather?' he asked quickly. 'Is it Mrs Galbraith?'

'Hannah Pritchard's baby is coming and Martha Ward is away.'

Dr Blake wavered. Hannah was not his patient, but he felt he would like to oblige Alice. 'I'd better come and see to her,' he said, and reached down to help Alice into the sulky.

It took only minutes more to reach Hannah, but her labour was already much more advanced. Dr Blake made a quick examination and then came out to ask for warm water. 'You had better be off home, Miss Campbell,' he said. 'Tell your mother I'm sorry, but I may be a little late for dinner.' He smiled. 'Babies wait upon no man's continences, you understand.'

Alice looked at him steadily. 'Can I not help Hannah? Jennie - Mrs Christopher - is laid up at present as you see. And - perhaps I should tell you I have helped ewes have their lambs on occasion.'

Dr Blake grinned at her. 'Then you know this is not a delicate job! If you faint, I shall leave you where you drop.'

'Do,' said Alice cordially, and followed him into the room.

Mary was horrified when the pair of them arrived at Glen Heather dishevelled, buoyed up with achievement - and very late for dinner. Her first wild suspicions were quickly soothed, but the reality was not much better than her imaginings. 'Such a thing for a well-brought-up girl to witness!' she exclaimed. 'Why, it might scar her for life! These women of the lower classes show so little resolve!'

'Really, Mother, how can you be so foolish?' snapped Alice, but a pleading look from Robert made her run upstairs to change her gown.

'Miss Campbell would make a splendid nurse, ma'am,' said Dr Blake in soothing tones. 'No doubt you think it strange, Mrs Campbell, but some of us really admire the new breed of women. Times are changing - often for the better.'

Mary did not at all agree, but she smiled. Alice had not attracted any other suitors, so this one must be nurtured diligently.

Dr Blake continued to pay frequent calls, and often invited Alice to accompany him on his rounds. She enjoyed his company, for he was intelligent and articulate, and she had grown used to stimulating conversation during her time at Swan House. Custom still dictated that young couples could not be left alone, but they were able to converse freely in the open sulky, or in the Glen Heather parlour under the chaperonage of the increasingly deaf Aunt Lavinia.

It was in winter, just before Alice's nineteenth birthday, that Dr Blake asked her to marry him. It was hardly unexpected, and Alice had wondered often what she should say. On the one hand, she liked him very much, on the other, she felt that duties as the wife of a busy physician and the mother of his eventual children might not leave a great deal of time for her first love.

Understandably, Dr Blake had no doubt of his reception. Alice Campbell might be the daughter of Glen Heather, but she was not to every man's taste. She would require a good deal of the man she married, but she would also give in generous measure. She was so dark and solemn much of the time, but he felt she would be a passionate lover, given the right encouragement. She was held to be a dowdy, but she had good bones and a far-ranging intelligence to match his own. She seemed fond of him already, and he knew her parents approved, so he couched his proposal in hopeful terms. 'I won't be in Mersey all my days,' he said. 'I have plans to practise in Sydney, eventually.' He looked up as he reached for her hands, wanting to see her extraordinary smile break as she promised to be his wife, but to his consternation the light was dying in her eyes. 'Miss Campbell?' he said uncertainly, 'Alice?'

Alice sighed regretfully. 'I am sorry, Michael, but I cannot marry you.'

'But why - why?'

Alice lifted her hands. 'I cannot. You will be practising in Sydney, you say?'

'Why, yes. But what has that to do with it?'

'I had thought you would stay in Mersey with Dr Llewellyn,' said Alice.

Dr Blake rose and moved restlessly around the room. 'That was my original intention, Miss Campbell, but just lately I have been in discord with Dr Llewellyn. He means well, but he resists change.'

Alice looked up. 'Is that such a fault?'

'Sometimes it is. Why, if every doctor from the dawn of time had felt as Floyd does, we would still be little more than witch doctors. Medicine needs a combination of the trusted remedies and a willingness to explore other possibilities... but forgive me if I don't care to enter a philosophical debate with you just now.' He sounded offended, and his smile was consciously rueful. 'I am looking rejection in the face.'

Alice bit her lip. 'That was *not* well done of me, was it? I expect I have hurt your feelings, and I am truly sorry to do it.'

'Then why not accept my offer?'

'Because I cannot.' Alice was regretful but obdurate, and quite soon, Dr Blake went away. He didn't fully understand, but to Alice it was simple. He would have taken her far from Glen Heather.

Naturally, there were recriminations. Michael Blake might have had modern ideas about medicine, but in some ways he was a very traditional young man, and had asked permission from Robert before addressing Alice. Alice had to face a surprised and peevish Mary. 'But Mother, I thought *you* would understand!' she said dejectedly. 'You refused to marry Dad until your mother no longer needed you.'

'That,' said Mary, 'was different. I had a duty, and we married when I was able.'

'*I* have a duty to Glen Heather,' said Alice. 'How could I fulfil that if I lived in Sydney?'

Mary sniffed. 'One day, my girl, you will find there is more to life than sheep and hay harvest. I hope for your sake you don't come to the knowledge too late.'

Aunt Lavinia was even more vocal. 'You'll be sorry, my girl, you'll be sorry! It was a good match you whistled down the wind. Do you think there is a queue to marry a girl like you?'

'No,' said Alice truthfully.

'Are you waiting for a royal prince?'

Alice laughed. 'Maybe I'll settle for single bliss, as you have.'

There was not a lot Aunt Lavinia could say to that, but she said it anyway, and so did Mary. Even Isobel disapproved, and Robert told Alice regretfully that he would have welcomed Michael Blake as a son-in-law.

I don't want to leave Glen Heather, Dad,' said Alice reasonably.

Robert shook his head, but again he defended Alice to Mary. 'She's young yet, my dear. One day she'll be ready to settle.'

So far as Mary could see, Alice was settled already - too much so. The girl should have been dancing, attending parties, driving and meeting her friends, not isolating herself at Glen Heather. And though Mary searched assiduously, she could find no more than a handful of men whose age and station made them acceptable suitors for Alice.

The only person who sympathised with Alice was Annie Llewellyn, but even she ventured a hint of caution. 'I hope you are very sure that you won't regret this,' she said. 'Reject poor Michael if you feel you must, but be certain you do so for the right reasons.'

'But Miss Llewellyn, surely *you* understand!' said Alice. 'Did you never reject any gentleman's proposal yourself?'

'Yes I did,' said Annie abruptly. 'I rejected your father - long before he proposed to Mary. She has never known, and I trust you will never tell her.'

'Of course not,' said Alice. 'But what an extraordinary thought! You might have been my mother!'

'So I have often thought,' said Annie pensively.

'But why - why?' asked Alice. 'My father is a good, kind man.'

'I thought at the time I had right and sufficient reason. I had such plans! Later, when I had to return to Mersey, I knew I might as well have married Robert and been contented.'

'What a pity,' said Alice. 'You rejected a gentleman who would have kept you here, whereas *I* rejected a gentleman who would have taken me away!'

'What a pair we are, my dear!'

'Yes indeed,' said Alice, but although she regretted disappointing Dr Blake and her family, she could not be entirely sorry. She would do whatsoever her hand found to do with all her might - and she knew she could not have brought such devotion to a marriage with Dr Blake.

CHAPTER 37

The dust of disapproval had hardly settled after Alice's rejection of her suitor when disaster hit the family. Robert rose, called for his shaving water - and collapsed across the basin. Maisie screamed, the rest of the staff came running and Mary rushed in to kneel beside her husband and cradle his head against her bosom. Aunt Lavinia recommended burnt feathers, but Isobel, whose lameness brought her to the scene very much later, told Alice to send for the doctor. Her face was blanched with terror, for the sight of her son lying on the couch had brought back his father's death so many years before.

'What is it?' asked Alice tensely. 'The doctor will want to know.'

'Some kind of attack - perhaps an apoplexy,' said Isobel. 'Hurry, child! And send for Reverend Neil as well.'

Alice rushed away and Isobel sat tensely in the low chair, resisting the impulse to rock back and forth in silent pain. Mary was anything but silent, grasping Robert's lax hand and exhorting him to wake, to speak to her - and Rosalind was crying with fright.

Dr Llewellyn arrived two hours later, to find his patient still unconscious. He made a long and careful examination and told Mary that Robert had had a stroke. 'Too early to say how much damage has been done,' he said, 'and there is no point in removing him to hospital now. The journey would surely injure him further. I'll send a nurse.'

Alice clenched her hands in frustration. 'Surely something can be done - are there no new treatments to try?'

Dr Llewellyn shook his head. 'Tried and true methods are best. We shall know more when the patient wakens.'

The patient ... Alice sighed with frustration. She knew Dr Blake would have had helpful suggestions, but Michael had taken her rejection much to heart, and had left for Sydney within the month. Alice glanced wonderingly at Isobel, now quite calm. Perhaps Isobel had faith in Dr Llewellyn, who had attended her after her accident on the mountain. But Isobel's eyes were sorrowful. She knew some vital spark had died in Floyd Llewellyn when his young wife passed away.

The first few days of Robert's illness were confused and frightening for all of them. He became conscious a few hours after his collapse, but he hardly seemed aware of anyone. His speech was slurred and one side of his body stiff and unresponsive. The uniformed nurse was efficient but condescending, and made it clear she would not prepare food or drink, change linen or wash plates. She provided medical care with unsmiling competence, scorning to gossip with the servants yet too stiff to converse with the family. Robert, as he slowly rallied, referred to her as "Sister Starch".

After a time, Dr Llewellyn pronounced himself satisfied that adequate care could be given by family or hired staff, and moved Sister Starch to another case. Alice caught his arm as he was leaving. 'Dr Llewellyn, how long before my father is well again?'

'It is a matter of time and nursing now, Miss Campbell.'

'But he *will* recover?'

Llewellyn was grey and bent, but he could still appreciate intelligence in a woman and he remembered Alice well from her sojourn in Annie's schoolroom. 'It is impossible to predict the extent to which a stroke patient will recover,' he said slowly. 'I have seen two men similarly affected, but while one is almost completely recovered, the other remains an invalid. There was no difference in care, and no difference in the severity of the condition.'

'There must have been *something*.'

'There was a difference in attitude,' said Llewellyn in a curiously dry voice. 'One patient had everything to live for - a loving wife and children, a secure position in society - yet he folded his hands and accepted his lot as the will of God. The other was a volatile man of uncertain temperament. He was a fighter, and he is much improved, and able to move quite freely with the aid of a cane, much as your grandmother does.' He smiled a little. 'And *there*, Miss Campbell, lies your father's best hope of recovery. His own mother is just such a fighter. I consider her a sterling example, for if it had not been for her immense strength of character, she would be in very much worse case than she is today.'

Mary and Rosalind were shocked at Alice's treatment of her father. 'So cruel!' moaned Mary. 'She won't do a thing for him! Just tells him to do it for himself.'

'And she his favourite, too!' said Rosalind indignantly. 'Poor Dad, poor Daddy.'

'He'll never be the man he was, you mark my words, he'll never be the man he was,' said Aunt Lavinia from her chair. Aunt Lavinia was failing visibly, but she retained her sharp eye and sharp opinions. 'Poor Robert reminds me of my own papa,' she added. 'He had a turn one day and was never the same again.'

'Nobody stays the same,' said Isobel tartly. 'Except McCleod. Robert must try harder to be well.'

'We must make him rest,' said Mary, ignoring Isobel.

'Actually, he's reading an auctioneer's report at the moment,' said Alice with a grin. 'Perhaps Granny would care to go and discuss it with him? I promised I'd ride around the sheep in the lower enclosure and check for footrot.'

'The men can do that,' said Mary.

'There's no manure like the farmer's boot.'

'You,' said Mary, 'are not a farmer.'

'Yes I am,' said Alice. 'I haven't been working with Dad all these months for nothing. And Granny can tell me how to go on if I falter, can you not, Granny?'

'Aye, that I can,' said Isobel, but her eyes were on McCleod, who was savagely destroying Rosalind's old summer hat.

'Alice, I cannot understand you,' lamented Mary. 'Your poor father is helpless and all you can do is talk about sheep and their feet! It would be more daughterly if you were to read to him. You know he has trouble turning the pages, and your grandmother's arthritis ....' Mary dropped her voice '...makes her a very unsuitable person to sit with him.'

'Dad can turn pages if he tries hard enough, but he cannot ride around the sheep - yet. If I tell him all's well he'll believe me.'

'Get a report from one of the men,' said Mary.

'If *I* tell him all's well he'll believe *me*,' said Alice softly. 'And that's because he knows that if all's *not* well, I'll tell him the truth just the same.' She tugged on her boots, and left the house, whistling for old Bob.

'That Alice!' said Mary. 'So hard-hearted! Nothing like myself, *or* poor Robert.' Her gaze lingered on Isobel as if she were to blame for Alice's unfortunate character.

That evening, Alice did sit with her father. He looked very ill, and her spirits fell. Perhaps, after all, she was needlessly cruel. 'How do you feel, Dad?' she ventured.

'Useless!' said Robert, hitting the bedcovers with his good hand. 'There's work to do and I'm like a cast ewe.'

'Elijah, Isaac and Jim will do the work,' said Alice.

'But iss no' - no' jus -' Robert's voice slurred and he drew a deep breath and tried again. 'Iss not jus' the work, Alice, you know tha'. The bes' workers skimp sometimes. They don't mean any harm, but I know. I'm tempted sometimes myself tha' way. It's jus' so easy to walk round one mob of sheep and just cast your eye on t'others over the fence. You see an old ewe down - who's to say she's no' jus' having a res? Even the bes' men need overseeing. They expec' it - they have no res-respec' for a boss who lies in bed ... It iss m-my *duty*...'

Alice put her left hand over his stiff one. 'I'll see to it, Dad.'

'You!'

'Why not?' said Alice warmly. 'I've been about the land with you since I was a wee thing and didn't Granny do it for years? I shall be your legs outside and I'll report to you. You make decisions just as you've always done, and I'll pass on the word to the men.'

Robert sighed. 'Ask Elijah an' the boys - step in here 'fore they go home, Alice?'

Alice kept her word. Like Isobel before her, she gloried in the chance to prove herself, though she regretted the means by which it had come about. It was easy, and it was not. It was easy, because she had spent years observing and accompanying and learning farm management from Robert and Isobel. The routine was a seasonal thing, with everything in its due appointed time, subject to the vagaries of weather and the idiocies of sheep. What went for 1913 should go equally for 1914, and it did, at first. The men treated her with condescension which soon warmed to acceptance of the fact that Miss Alice spoke for the boss.

But Alice discovered that sometimes established pattern and observation were not enough. Things that had been second nature to Isobel and Robert were tangled enigmas to Alice, and she could not always return to the house to ask advice. At first, she faithfully reported every query to Robert and Isobel, but as time padded on and the winter deepened she noticed with distress that Robert seemed less and less certain of the answers. And as for Isobel - she was a redoubtable woman, but she was also seventy-five years old, and sometimes vague.

Although most of Australia suffered a drought during 1914, the high country was wet. The burn flooded and burst its banks and the low-lying flats disappeared under a sheet of water. Alice put on oilskins and rode out to move the sheep up the brae, but the mountain seemed bleak and cold and the sheep hung back. Elijah Ward and the other men stayed until every mob had been accounted for, and by then the moon was sailing free and reflecting in a dazzle on the flood. 'What now, Miss Campbell?' asked Isaac as Alice slumped on Blackwood's back.

'You'd best be getting home, Miss Alice,' urged Elijah.

Alice straightened her back. 'Not yet, Mr Ward,' she said. 'I'll need to take some hay up the mountain first. The sheep face the cold and wet better with dry fodder.' Elijah Ward stared at her in the moonlight. 'Well?' said Alice. 'Isn't that what my father would say?'

Elijah nodded slowly. He thought the boss would have left it until morning, but maybe Miss Alice was right. He nodded with more decision. 'Right you are, Miss,' he said.

As the water went down the sheep wandered the flats searching for something better to eat than slimy grass. They found it - or thought they had - in quantities of fodder turnips which had washed from the ground and now lay in inviting heaps. The Glen Heather stock feasted. The turnips, piled, frost-bitten and sodden, began to rot. Two milking cows had died of colic before anyone saw the danger.

'I should have thought!' cried Alice, conscience-stricken, as she and the men tried to drive the beasts away from the dangerous food. 'Why didn't I think?'

'You weren't to know,' said Elijah Ward. 'If anyone should have thought, it was me.'

Alice rounded on him furiously. 'It's my business to know!' she snapped. 'Oh - I'm sorry, Mr Ward, take no notice of me. I'm tired. I suppose - ought we to feed some hay?'

Ward nodded. 'Sounds like a good plan to me, Miss. Only -'

'What, Mr Ward?'

'It'll run us short for next month,' said Elijah, 'and there could be more snow yet.'

'I know,' said Alice, 'but if we don't feed now, there'll be no beasts left to eat next month. Let's feed and pray for an early spring!'

The gamble worked, but before the spring, in the wake of the invasion of Belgium, Britain declared war on Germany. Within hours, Australia had reiterated its pledge of support for the mother country and was at war. And Alice wondered, along with many other stunned

Australians, just how much the welfare of the sheep mattered now. And how much did it matter that old Bob, her companion for so long, had finally succumbed to old age and died in his sleep? If Australia were to be invaded...

But at first the official mood was optimistic, with Prime Minister Cook declaring that Britain had accepted his offer of an expeditionary force of 20,000 men. The war would be over by Christmas... but though the people of Glen Heather carried on as usual, the war news took over from the local gossip as the major source of conversation. And then, while the expeditionary force trained in Broadmeadows, Aunt Lavinia died.

Alice was truly sorry - and apprehensive for herself. How much more demanding would Mary become now her old aunt was gone? Isobel was still available, but Mary and Isobel had never been close... and then there was Rosalind, who had always been Aunt Lavinia's pet. Rosalind had left school over a year before, and although Alice made occasional attempts at companionship she had to admit defeat. She and her sister were as little alike as Isobel and Lavinia had been, and could never be good companions.

Rosalind was a dainty girl, well on her way to fulfilling Mary's hopes of beauty. There was no doubt she was happier in the parlour than in the paddock, and although she rode well, she preferred dancing, stitchery and other lady-like pursuits. In this she had been encouraged by Mary and Aunt Lavinia and now, with Aunt Lavinia dead, Rosalind sobbed herself almost sick.

Dr Llewellyn had come to attend to the necessary formalities of death, and he remained to administer a sedative of laudanum. Rosalind's sobs died away to whimpers and soon she slept. Even tear-swollen and red-eyed, Rosalind was lovely. Alice smoothed her sister's light hair and sighed, then turned to Mary. 'Well, Mother,' she said quite gently, 'Rosalind is sleeping now. You should lie down as well. It has been a hard day.'

Mary lifted her head bravely. 'Someone must sit with dear Auntie.'

'I'll see to it,' promised Alice. 'We shall need mourning, too. Maybe a dark frock of mine will fit Rosalind - she has grown so tall.'

'Dear Alice, so practical. But Rosalind must have new blacks and so must I. Those I had for poor Winston are scarcely in the mode ... would you ask Hannah to come? She is a neat hand with her needle. Oh, and Alice, Auntie wanted to be laid to rest in her lavender crepe.

She said so often. There are so many arrangements to be made.'

'I'll see to it,' said Alice resignedly, and she did. In the late afternoon, Rosalind stirred and awoke. She saw her tall sister dressed in black and fresh tears formed as Alice came swiftly to her bedside. 'Oh Rosie, I'm glad to see you awake,' she said calmly. 'Hannah is in the sewing room making your blacks. I know she will want your help, since Granny's fingers are too stiff to sew much anymore. Hannah has brought her little Sheila along, too - you could play with her a little if she frets.'

Rosalind shook her head. 'I couldn't!' Her voice rose. 'Poor Auntie!'

'Aunt Lavinia was very good and kind to you,' said Alice, 'and we'll all miss her sadly.'

'Not you,' said Rosalind swiftly. 'She always said you were a cold, unfeeling girl.'

'Of course I shall miss Auntie! She loved you best though. I remember how happy she was the day you were born. She said how sweet you were, and what a fine girl you would be. Now it's time for you to begin, for you can be much more to Mother than I.'

'I could tend her in her declining years?' suggested Rosalind.

'Not quite that,' said Alice. 'Mother hopes you may marry in four or five more years, but until then you can be a great comfort. Poor Mother is very unhappy, so if you go and help Hannah I can tell Mother you are being brave and womanly and working hard. She will be so very proud of you.' The idea appealed, and Rosalind went to the sewing room. Alice sat down abruptly and put her face in her hands. Mary would never be proud of her unless she became the daughter Mary wanted, and if she did that, she could not be proud of herself.

After the funeral, Robert left his bed for longer periods and gradually, as the dreadful year wore to its close, he took back the management of Glen Heather from his daughter. He walked now with a heavy limp and his mind, like his mother's, had spells when it refused to make proper connections, but Dr Llewellyn was fully satisfied with his condition.

Late December found the country's optimism wavering as the war news continued to trickle back from overseas. Australia had yet to see active service, although thirty-nine ships had left for Britain in early November, as heavily laden as the immigrant and convict ships had been seventy-five years before. There was no New Year's Eve Dance this year, for Glen Heather was in mourning for Aunt Lavinia, but in any case Alice doubted anyone would have felt like celebrating. What was there to rejoice about in the year just ended? She pondered that as she sat in the Kirk and listened to Reverend Neil's words of hope and courage. A few happy weeks with Dr Blake - which had ended in recriminations! She closed her eyes and tried to remember herself a year before, dressed in her best, dancing with the doctor - the world had been before her then. But now Michael Blake had gone, Aunt Lavinia was dead, and Robert was a shadow of himself. And Australia was at war - wearily, Alice prayed that 1915 would bring a better time to Glen Heather.

As she relinquished the reins of the property to their rightful owner, she found herself forced increasingly to duties about the house. She had never realised how much Aunt Lavinia contributed to the smooth running of Glen Heather. For years she had supplied Mary with company, petted Rosalind and disputed with Isobel in the parlour. With Robert in control again, Alice found herself forced into the role vacated by her great aunt. It was not a role that suited her.

She was nearly twenty years old, a woman grown. Glen Heather was her life, but how was she to shape it? By keeping her mother company for twenty years more?

To her credit, this was not what Mary wanted. She wanted Alice to marry, and quickly. To be single and unsought at almost twenty was serious in Mary's lexicon, although she had married late herself. After her father's death, her mother had declined into invalidism and became heavily dependent on Mary. Had it not been for Robert's steadfastness, she felt she would have dwindled into spinsterhood, as Annie Llewellyn had done. She could never have borne that, and she could not bear to have it happen to Alice. Who knew how the existence of an old maid sister might affect Rosalind's chances? Yes, Alice must marry as soon as possible after Aunt Lavinia's death; certainly before the end of the year. She said as much to Alice, who replied gently that suitors to her hand seemed in short supply.

'And whose fault is *that*?' hissed Mary. 'Miss High and Mighty - if you had accepted that young doctor! If you would make a push to be agreeable to other young gentlemen!'

'There is no shame in being single, Mother,' said Alice. 'More, surely, in wedding a gentleman simply to avoid old maidenhood! Auntie was single, and what could we have done without her?' If Alice had left it at that, Mary might have acquiesced, but Alice did not. 'Miss Llewellyn is a maiden lady, and think of the good she does! Had she married, she might have had children to nurture, but as a schoolmistress, Miss Llewellyn has shaped the lives of a generation of girls and young women! So has Miss Swan!'

'And made them old maids by their example!' said Mary shrewishly. 'The local men weren't good enough for Annie Llewellyn. She must go to town in search of something better!'

'You sent *me* to town,' reminded Alice, keeping her temper with an effort.

'And much good has it done!' Mary's sense of grievance grew. 'Here you are, nearly twenty years old, no prospects in sight, and you make not the slightest push to help yourself. Why, pray, have you not attended the balls to which you have been invited?'

'Dad has been ill, I have been busy - besides, there is a war and we are in mourning.'

Mary raised her eyes heavenwards.

Alice went to her bedroom under the eaves. It had once been a part of the attic store-room, but after Isobel's return to Glen Heather the attic had been divided to make an extra room. Clasping her hands, Alice gazed out of the darkening window, across the apple tree to the grave where Bob, her dear childhood companion, lay. What had gone wrong with her life? She wanted, as she had always wanted, an active role in the running of Glen Heather. She did not want to be a small, exhausted cog in the household, the maiden aunt of Rosalind's children. She was only a little younger than Isobel had been when she had taken over the property, but Isobel had been a widow with a small son. Isobel had a choice in life. She could have remarried as a young woman; she could have left Glen Heather. Instead, she had taken control.

Alice had no such choice. She had no suitors, nowhere to go, and no control of her life if she stayed. Yet Isobel had done it! *How* had Isobel done it?

Alice went to visit Isobel in her chamber. 'Granny? Have you a few minutes to talk to me?'

'Aye,' said Isobel. 'What is it, Alice? Have the lambs the woody tongue?'

'No, no, Dad is with the lambs,' said Alice. 'Do you recall, Granny? Dad is better now.'

'Hmph,' said Isobel. She looked warily at Alice. The gaps in her memory seldom bothered Isobel at all, but she hated to be confronted with evidence that they existed.

'I have a problem.' Alice sat down and lifted McCleod from his perch to her own wrist. She tickled the soft white feathers around the bird's hooked beak and McCleod whistled softly with contentment.

'We all have problems,' remarked Isobel. 'All but McCleod. And his dust-sheet needs cleaning again.'

'I know that Granny, but this is something you could perhaps explain. I have wondered how it is that you were able to order your life as a young woman, and yet I cannot.'

Isobel examined her brown, gnarled hands. 'I ordered my life, as you call it, to preserve my son's inheritance,' she said. 'When Robert came of age, I left Glen Heather with James.' Her dark eyes softened as they always did when she thought of her second husband.

'You chose to stay on when Grandfather John died,' reminded Alice.

Isobel shrugged, her eyes veiled. 'Aye, so I did, but the only escape would have been to hand Glen Heather into the keeping of someone else and marry Niall O'Hara. My father and Margaret were dead, you see, and my brother Winston much under Gwynnie's thumb. He would have stripped Glen Heather as he stripped Scarborough in the end. He and Whitaker ...'

Alice nodded slowly. She saw now the differences in their respective situations. Isobel had been a widow and an orphan with a child of her own, answerable to no-one but her own conscience. Alice was a spinster with living parents.

'I kept Glen Heather on for *Robert*,' said Isobel with peculiar emphasis. 'We women cannot own Glen Heather, Alice, it must go to a Campbell man. If you forget that you lay up trouble for yourself.'

Alice stared. Surely, her redoubtable grandmother did not ascribe to the myth of male superiority! But Isobel was old, her opinions, however eccentric, rooted in the middle of the nineteenth century.

'I would not have stayed if I had not had Robert,' said Isobel. 'I *could* not have stayed if I had not had Robert.'

Alice thanked her, and went away. Isobel had not helped as she'd hoped, but she had given Alice something to think about. For as long as she remained unmarried, and under her parents' domination, she would have little say in the ordering of her life. Yet - what could she do about that? If she *did* marry, her husband would take over. Widowhood was the answer, but she could scarcely scheme for that!

At first, the war made little practical impression on Glen Heather. The news was bad, but removed from everyday life. Sheep were shorn in the summer of 1915 just as they had been shorn in Glen Heather summers for three quarters of a century. The fleece was sent to Launceston, the hay came in ... and then, in the autumn, in the wake of the ANZACs' fearful glory, the trickle of local volunteers turned to a flood. Isaac Ward was the first to leave Glen Heather, and Jimmy Sargent complained he had been left in the lurch. But then, within weeks, Jimmy too had gone, first to the training camp at Claremont and then to Queensland, en route to the trenches of Gallipoli and France.

'At least Elijah won't be leaving us,' said Robert. 'He's too old to fight, and so am I.'

But all around Mersey, the young men were leaving. The Jenkins boys held a great send-off and went away in a body, and with them from Mole Creek station went almost every able-bodied man between the ages of eighteen and forty-five, including a handful who were over and under these ages but who hoped no-one would notice.

In June Robert made a rare trip into Mersey to visit the bank, and to see Mr Bertram, the solicitor and returned with the news that Mersey was half deserted. So were the other towns, and Hannah Pritchard's Arthur had gone with the first wave.

'He said it was his duty,' said Hannah, dry-eyed but strained when Alice went to visit her. 'He said he'd never lift his head again if he left the other boys to defend his wife and kids while he stayed safe at home. I'm going to shut up the cottage and try to find work, if anyone will take me on with Sheila and the babe - not to speak of poor Mum.'

'Why not come home to us at Glen Heather?' suggested Alice.

'No, Miss Alice, I wasn't hinting for that.'

'Hannah, we need you. Jane has gone to do war work and we're so short-handed that I'm back in the paddocks and Mother has problems in the house. And you know your mother and Granny have always dealt well together.'

'I wouldn't mind,' said Hannah. 'Mum could watch the kids and keep them from howling.' She indicated her children, the little girl and the sturdy baby boy. 'I don't reckon I could go on if it weren't for the kids,' said Hannah simply.

Alice felt a strange catch in her chest. Once Hannah had been a single woman, a housekeeper and cook. Now she had a soldier husband

and children to love and plan for. Alice could have had the same ... but it was Glen Heather for Alice, and it had taken the war to renew her chances. Not even Mary could marry off Alice when the war had taken all the young men.

So - in the wake of the volunteers, Alice put on her oldest clothes, pinned up her hair and climbed into the saddle as Robert's left-hand man. The war went on, but so did the sheep. Footrot must be treated, lambs marked and hay reaped in season. Robert groaned when the hay was fetched in by Tim Jenkins and other boys too young for the army, but there was no help for it. Mersey waited and hoped and the war went on.

Alice heard from Annie Llewellyn that Dr Blake had left Sydney and gone to Egypt on a troop ship. And both Uncle Wesley Jarvis's boys had joined up and were now somewhere in France. She dreaded the newspaper reports with their grim lists of the wounded, the missing and those who would never come home. One of the Jenkins boys was gone, dead in the battle of Pozieres. Slowly, the bad news came, as brothers, husbands, fathers and sons fell in the fields and trenches. Hannah worked like a slave, not to please the exacting Mary, but to deaden her own anxiety. Her baby Hughie grew to a sturdy toddler, and all old Jennie Christopher's ingenuity couldn't keep him from mischief. With Jennie back at Glen Heather, Isobel was overjoyed, and they spent much of their time together. Jennie had known Isobel in her youth, Jennie had known James and John. Isobel had known and liked Luke Christopher, who helped to rescue her on the mountain. So Isobel and Jennie sat with Hannah's children and McCleod while Hannah baked and brewed, swept and scrubbed herself to exhaustion.

Then came the news that Arthur was wounded, that he was in hospital and coming home. Hannah wept with gratitude and sorrow, for Arthur's right eye was gone and his lungs were affected. He would never return to the front.

Annie Llewellyn held First Aid classes, which Alice attended with Rosalind until exhaustion forced her to sleep instead. Working with the men was what she wanted; working from first light until moonrise with an ailing Robert and slow-thinking Elijah was almost more than she could stand. Robert did his best, but his heart was not in Glen Heather - it never really had been.

'Miss Alice, you must rest,' said Hannah, when Alice couldn't eat her dried-out meal.

Alice shook her head wearily. 'I can't, Hannah. The work's there to be done, and I'm the only one fit to do it. Mr Ward has the rheumatics and it troubles Dad when things aren't done.'

'And if you knock up with the strain, what will come of Glen Heather then?'

'No-one ever died of a good day's work.'

'It's not the days, it's the nights,' said Hannah. 'You're out half the night and up with the rooster! You'll wear yourself out!'

'Not I,' said Alice. 'The Campbells are tough.'

'The Campbells are human, like anyone else,' said Hannah. 'I'll make some tea to put some colour in your cheeks. You look like skim milk!'

Alice laughed, suddenly. 'Skim milk! That's what Aunt Lavinia used to say! Whey-faced, she called me in winter, sunburned in summer. She never could make up her mind but either way she said I'd never get a husband! And she was right - I'm married to the mountain, and my children are the sheep!' She laughed again, on the edge of hysteria, and Hannah hustled her off to bed as she had hustled the six-year-old Alice fifteen years before.

Rosalind came in soon after, delivered from her First Aid class by her cousin Martin Lester. Martin had volunteered for the army, but had been turned away on account of his club foot. 'Hannah, I'm going to be a nurse!' she said impressively. 'It's a wonderful ambition, Miss Llewellyn says, a hard life given over to selflessness and the helping of the less fortunate.'

'Hard's the word, Miss Rosie,' said Hannah quietly. She made no attempt to talk Rosalind out of her ambition, knowing that could be left to Mary. Besides - Hannah had worries of her own. Who knew whether Arthur would ever be fit to work again?

It was Mary who solved that problem - at least temporarily. Since she was motivated by self-interest rather than altruism, she did it promptly and efficiently. Hearing that Arthur had been invalided out of the army and was returning home, she realised Hannah would leave Glen Heather. Unwilling to lose her a second time, Mary went to Robert.

Robert was aware of his wife's talent for manipulation, and admired it. It was one of the features that had drawn him to Mary in the first place, although he hadn't recognised it at the time. By the time he *did* find out what lay behind Mary's apparent softness, he had also found that her ways frequently helped him to avoid unpleasantness. If he had to dismiss an employee, Mary was bound to supply him with justification. If a deal went sour, she could present the facts in a way which allowed Robert to be seen as unfortunate rather than inefficient. So here was Mary offering him a chance to ease the burden of work and responsibility that had fallen on himself, Alice and Elijah Ward, while seeming to do a favour to someone else. As a bonus, it would keep Hannah at Glen Heather. Since his stroke, Robert had trouble writing, so he called Alice and dictated a letter to Arthur offering a position at Glen Heather.

'We cannot make use of him like this!' objected Alice. 'He won't be well!'

'He will be glad to have a job,' said Robert. 'Write the letter Alice.' He smiled to soften the harshness of his order. His elder daughter was a good girl, and a hard worker. She had been a great help during his illness and he owed her a lot, but the sooner he had good men working for him again, the better. This business with Arthur simply proved his point. It was no good expecting a young woman - however capable - to think like a man. For a moment a vision of Isobel rose before Robert's inner eye - not the old woman she had become, but the Isobel of his youth, straight and strong and efficient. But there had been nothing soft and womanly about Isobel; he thought she might just as well have been a man.

Arthur returned to a hero's welcome. Alice drove Hannah to Mole Creek Station, and stood back while Hannah embraced her gaunt husband. Arthur's head was bandaged and his missing eye covered with a patch, but Hannah was gazing at him as if at a fairytale prince. Alice blinked. She had always assumed Hannah had married for convenience. And it seemed that Robert was right, for a few weeks later Arthur came to work at Glen Heather. He had adjusted well to his disabilities, and proved an asset to the property.

'You can't get away from us, can you Hannah?' said Alice wryly.

Hannah sighed, but her eyes were friendly. 'That's right, Miss Alice. The bad penny, I am. Still, we're glad of the chance.'

'Hannah, will you do something for me?'

'I might,' said Hannah slowly, 'and then again, I might not. Depends what it is. If it's a good frock you're wanting sewn, we'll go straight to the draper, but if it's my husband you want to borrow - well, that depends what you want with him.'

Alice laughed. 'Then stop calling me "Miss Alice". The war's changing things, isn't it?' Hannah nodded soberly. 'It's sending good, ordinary men out to kill one another, and the land's going backwards for want of care, families are breaking up ... we've always been friends, haven't we Hannah?'

'I've always thought so,' said Hannah. 'Even as a bit of a scrap you had an old head on your shoulders. Too old in some ways. You should be having fun. Most girls your age ...'

'*Most* girls my age have been working for years,' put in Alice.

Hannah grinned. 'You've got me there. 'Alice" it is, except in front of your ma, of course! Now out of my kitchen and clean yourself up. Right now the cows would be ashamed to call you cousin.'

Alice smiled, for Hannah didn't change.

The seasons swung round, and it seemed there had always been a war. Rosalind brought home khaki wool from Red Cross meetings and the women at Glen Heather spent their evenings knitting for the troops. Rosalind made the legs of the socks while Alice, Mary and Hannah turned the feet. 'I'll look like a balaclava soon,' complained Rosalind, but she didn't stop knitting.

'I never thought you would stick it so well,' said Alice with more truth than tact.

'I'm getting quicker,' said Rosalind. 'It used to take me a week. But Alice, if you knew how I long to knit in pink or blue - anything but khaki!'

It was a period of harmony at Glen Heather, for Isobel, whose presence had always grated on Mary, had astonished them all by spending some of her inheritance from James Galbraith to buy a newly empty cottage on the road between Glen Heather and Mersey.

Robert opposed this decision, but Isobel refused to listen. 'My dear Robert,' she said, 'I have been under Mary's feet quite long enough. I am, as you know, very fond of you all, but all good things come to an end.'

'But Isobel - why?'

Isobel smiled at her son. 'You know, I really expected to be dead by now,' she said meditatively. 'James is gone, and most of my old friends and acquaintances have passed on, but I seem to go on living - and growing more and more thrawn by the week.'

'We don't mind your ways,' said Robert uncomfortably.

'*I* mind *yours*,' said Isobel. 'Robert - my mind is made up. I can no longer be of any help to you here, for you have Alice to handle the accounts.'

'You cannot live alone,' said Robert rather plaintively. 'Folk will say we turned you out!'

'Then I shall tell them differently. I do not give a snap of my fingers for what folk will say. I never did and I never will. And I shall not live alone - Jennie is coming with me. We deal so well together, and now Arthur is back Hannah no longer needs Jennie so. She is a little younger than I, and I fully expect her to outlive me, so I shall leave her a lifetime interest in the cottage and after that ...'

'I suppose it will go to Hannah and Arthur,' said Robert a little resentfully.

'No, I shall leave it to Alice,' said Isobel, and gave him a very straight look. 'I think you know why, Robert.' Robert nodded. 'Precisely,' said Isobel. 'I must provide for McCleod, and Alice is the only one I would trust to keep him.'

The period of peace that followed Isobel's departure was shattered when Robert had another turn. Nothing serious, said Dr Llewellyn, but Robert must take life more easily. Why not sell his land? Or rent to his cousin at Scarborough?

'You're a croaking old woman, Floyd,' said Robert. 'I'm not in my grave yet. And why should I give Whit Jarvis the chance to do to Glen Heather what he has done to Scarborough? My mother would never forgive me.'

'Because you're not young,' pointed out Llewellyn. 'Neither am I, and it does me no good to be fetched out here to Glen Heather at all hours.' He paused. 'I never give advice, as a general rule, but I'm going to give some now. Sell up! It isn't as if you had a son to follow you here. Move into town and give those girls of yours a chance.'

Alice, waiting to escort Dr Llewellyn to his sulky, felt the blood drain from her face and listened in agony for the answer.

'I cannot sell, Floyd,' said Robert. 'There must be a Campbell at Glen Heather.'

Alice sighed. It was all right. It was all right! She took a deep breath to steady herself, and then another. Then she went briskly into the bedroom. For a moment, her voice refused to work, but it returned with a rush. 'Would you care for a cup of tea, Dr Llewellyn?'

But that was not the end of it, after all. When Alice went to settle

Robert for the night, she found Mary stirring up trouble. 'It was a definite warning, Robert, and you must see that. Give it up now. Put a manager on - or a tenant.'

Robert sounded more curt than Alice had heard him. '*No*, Mary. I cannot give it up. Has it escaped your notice that we are at war? Every able-bodied man can find employment three times over! Have you any idea what we'd have to pay a manager? And as for a tenant ...did my mother put on a tenant when my father died? Glen Heather is Campbell land!'

'Your precious Campbells!' said Mary coldly. 'Has it escaped *your* notice that this is all for nothing? If we'd had a son you might have carried on - but now you must write to Bertram. You always knew it would come to this in the end, so why put it off any longer?'

'I suppose you are right, my dear,' said Robert wearily.

Alice went in then, and Mary, tight-lipped, left the room. Robert said nothing and neither did Alice, but for days she waited tensely for a summons to write a letter for her father. No summons came, so it was a considerable shock, a week later, when Mr Bertram arrived with a very youthful clerk whose hugely magnified eyes peered out from behind spectacles as thick as bottle-glass. 'Good morning, Mr Bertram,' said Alice. 'And ...?'

'This is my nephew,' said Mr Bertram. 'Miss Campbell, Samuel Garland.'

'Of course,' said Alice. 'You came to our New Year's Dance before the war.'

'Yes indeed!' Garland grasped her hand enthusiastically and Alice was startled all over again. The spectacles had led her to expect a limp, lady-like grip. 'Hello, Miss Campbell; it is good to meet such a lovely lady again.'

His voice was deep and pleasant, but Alice eyed him with disfavour. The fellow was a flirt, and she had no time for nonsense. 'Indeed,' she remarked, and turned to Mr Bertram. 'I shall tell my father you are here. Has anyone seen to your horses?' It was a sign of the times - once, there would have been no need for her to ask.

'That will not be necessary,' said Mr Bertram gravely. 'We came in the motor.'

'The reason I have escaped the office,' said Mr Garland cheerfully. 'Uncle cannot drive.'

'Indeed,' said Alice again. She went to her father's office and tapped on the door. 'Mr Bertram and Mr Garland to see you, Dad.'

'Forgive me if I don't get up,' said Robert. His voice was slurring again and Alice looked at him in quick concern.

'Of course, of course!' said Mr Bertram. 'Samuel, lay out the documents and leave us.'

Mr Garland did as he was told, and then followed Alice out of the room. 'Kicked out, by George!' he said as the door closed firmly behind him.

Alice badly wanted to know what was happening, but she could hardly linger under the magnified but intelligent gaze of the clerk. Silently, she led the way towards the parlour. Mary could entertain this upstart young man. His amused manner was making her uncomfortable.

'Just one moment, Miss Campbell,' he said. 'Uncle will be some time with Mr Campbell, so would you care to take a spin in Tin Lizzie?'

Alice blinked. 'I cannot drive a motor.'

'*I* can,' said Mr Garland. 'But well - never mind. I say - who's *that*?'

This sudden change of tack flustered Alice, and she glanced out the window to see Rosalind sauntering by, freshly arrayed in a new dress which almost reached her ankles. She had certainly not been wearing it at breakfast time. 'That,' said Alice a little dryly, 'is my sister, Rosalind.'

'Ah. I see.' Mr Garland had lost his former glibness. 'I won't keep you, Miss Campbell. No doubt you have a great deal to do. A household of this type must keep you extremely busy.'

'Come to the parlour and have a cup of tea?' suggested Alice. 'My mother is there.'

'I think I should see to the old motor,' said Mr Garland. 'Uncle fancied he heard a knocking noise in the rear.' He smile vaguely at Alice and went out, leaving her to worry her original problem. Why had Robert sent for Mr Bertram? Ever since his stroke, she had been dealing with all official correspondence, so why had she not been asked to deal with this? She was twenty-one years old, and understood the day-to-day matters of Glen Heather as well as Robert did. So why had she not been warned about today's meeting with Mr Bertram?

Mary was most displeased that Alice had refused the offered "spin" in Samuel Garland's motor. She was even less pleased to discover that Rosalind had gone instead. 'What were you thinking of?' she asked Alice in a tight, brittle voice. 'Allowing a child of Rosalind's age to go off with a gentleman like that! I just hope that young man is thoroughly ashamed of himself.'

Alice very much doubted that, but she was tired of Mary's recriminations. 'Come Mother, where's the harm?' she asked tartly. 'You always moan about the fact that there is no young company here for Rosalind.'

'But to go off with a young man like that - unattended!'

'Mother, she's a child,' said Alice. 'Mr Garland seems a pleasant young man; no doubt he thought to give Rosie a treat. I think it was rather kind of him.'

'*You* refused to accompany him,' said Mary with one of her baffling switches of focus.

'I am twenty-one years old,' said Alice. 'Much too old to go off joy-riding with young men. There's work to be done.'

'Twenty-one!' said Mary. 'Twenty-one and not an admirer to your name! And when a fine prospect like Mr Garland comes along, what do you do? You greet him dressed like a servant, you neglect the common courtesies, you refuse to make the slightest effort to engage his interest! You have no more notion of what is proper than your grandmother!'

'Leave Granny out of this!' said Alice coldly.

'How can I?' snapped Mary. 'You are just like her! It's Campbell this and Glen Heather that, everything for sheep and nothing for anyone else. She despises me because I could not produce an heir for her precious Glen Heather - do you realise that? She *despises* me! She, whose carryings on made her the speak of Mersey! Do you think I don't know how she indoctrinated your father, forced him to run the place, and tried to mould you into her image? Glen Heather - Glen Heather! I tell you, Alice, I wish I'd never seen the place!' Mary was so angry that the bitterness of twenty years came spilling out. 'You're just like your father! Glen Heather this and that and no time for anything *I* might like. Don't you think I'd have liked to go to town? To attend balls and parties? But no, he'd never leave the place for more than a day or so at most. And why? For fear of what his *mother* would think! And look what it's doing to you - hands rough as bags, feet like a ploughman's, skin like leather. Twenty-one and all your opportunities gone to waste. Not a prospect to your name!'

Alice turned away before she lost her own temper and said bitter things to Mary that could never be taken back. Mary was wrong - Alice had prospects all right, and they were getting clearer all the time. It was so logical now; it had come to her while Mary railed at her. Robert's business with Mr Bertram *must* have to do with Glen Heather. Her own twenty-first birthday was behind her, so it followed that Robert meant to recognise her worth and make her his legal successor. He had had no sons, so why should he not consider his elder daughter his natural heir? No doubt Mary knew and felt hurt and excluded, but she must be brought to see, upon sober reflection, that Alice was the obvious one to take over the property if - when - something happened to Robert. Mary could not; she had no aptitude for such things. Isobel was far too old and Rosalind too young and uninterested besides. Besides - Rosalind was bound to marry well. And Mary need not worry - there would be a home for her at Glen Heather for as long as she wished. A daughter of the Campbells knew her duty.

Alice went about her work with a new serenity, and when young Samuel Garland arrived a week later with papers to be signed, Alice greeted him so graciously that his opinion of himself rose like yeast. He bowed so deeply over her hand that she feared for the security of his spectacles, and beamed at her with warm brown eyes. It struck Alice at that moment that he was a little like Isobel's treasured photograph of James Galbraith; to be sure the costume differed, and Garland was very much younger, but he radiated the same amiable charm. And of course, they both wore spectacles. So she smiled at Garland for Isobel's sake and he smiled back for his own. And, once again, Rosalind appeared mysteriously clad in her most becoming dress, with her hair in a rolled-up halo. This time, Mary was vigilant, and sent her younger daughter to her room. She was only fifteen, after all.

Alice saw young Garland to the door on his departure, a little amused that he seemed greatly interested in the sweep of drive beyond the stables. He was clearly reluctant to leave, so Alice took pity on him. 'It was very kind of you to take my sister for a spin last week,' she told him with a friendly smile. 'Children love novelty, do they not?'

Samuel looked at her shrewdly. 'They do indeed, Miss Campbell - even young ladies such as your sister.'

'Especially *young* ladies such as my sister,' agreed Alice cordially. 'She is six years younger than I.'

She saw Samuel's lips moving as he worked that out, and then he smiled. 'I have a sister who is just fifteen, Miss Campbell. Perhaps she and Miss Rosalind may become acquainted?'

'Perhaps they may,' said Alice gravely.

Mary gave her a look of rare approval when she returned to the parlour. 'So you and Mr Garland found some common ground after all!' she said coyly.

'Oh - yes, we did,' said Alice, 'but pray do not regard him in the light of a suitor for me, Mother. I have little use for young men who admire themselves. And why is he not in France?'

'Mr Garland,' said Mary repressively, 'is severely astigmatic. He volunteered for the army two years ago, but was turned away on medical grounds.'

'Blind as a bat without a doubt,' said Alice cheerfully.

'His misfortune aside, he would have made an admirable soldier,' said Mary.

'You may well be right. I'm sure his nerve is in wonderful shape. He certainly has plenty of it.' She wondered if she should warn Mary about Samuel's interest in Rosalind, but held her tongue. She meant the young man no harm, and today she was at peace with all the world.

'Mr Garland may well wish to call upon you,' said Mary.

'I am sure he will not. And in any case, I have neither the wish nor the need to marry.'

'But what else is there for you to do?' asked Mary in honest exasperation. 'You are scarcely cut out to be a governess-companion. You could do clerical work, I suppose ...'

'I shall continue as I am,' said Alice placidly. 'What else?'

'But when your father and I are gone? He is not well, you know, and neither of us is young. What will you do? Where will you go?'

'I shall keep Glen Heather,' said Alice.

'Alice, you cannot. I have told you that repeatedly and so, I am sure, has your father.'

'Do not *worry* so, Mother,' said Alice. 'Granny managed Glen Heather for twenty years and that is long ago. We live in modern times - ladies are taking up responsible positions in all walks of life.'

'Isobel's case was different,' said Mary.

'Not so very different,' said Alice. 'And now, I must go. I promised Dad I'd see how Arthur was managing the mowing. He still has trouble judging distances.' Alice hurried away, more than usually impatient with her mother. Why was Mary so blind?

CHAPTER 38

It was only later that she began to wonder if there were more to Mary's reaction than prejudice. Rosalind was sulking in the sitting room, and she was very ready to share her grievance with Alice. 'Mother treats me like a child!' she stormed. 'Why should I not wear my good dress if I choose? Why should I not put up my hair?'

'You are only fifteen,' said Alice. 'You have years ahead to put up your hair.'

'Years ahead! And so have you! Years to knit with Mother and listen to Granny's maunderings when you visit the cottage. I want more from life than that.'

'Be patient,' said Alice. 'The war will end and there will be dances again. Look, Rosie - why do you not ask Mother and Dad if you could go away to school as I did? Miss Swan could teach you a very great deal.'

'School!' cried Rosalind. 'I had enough of that with Miss Llewellyn! The old witch was forever telling me I was not as clever as you. Not as clever as you! And look where your famous cleverness has got you!'

'It was only a suggestion,' said Alice mildly.

'Coming from you! That's rich, Alice! You and your Miss Swan - what good has your Swan House ever done you? Do you know what folk call you in Mersey? They call you *Farmer Campbell*, with rocks in your head and dung on your boots!'

Alice laughed. 'Is that all? No doubt they have a similar name for Dad.'

'Yes,' hissed Rosalind, 'and that's not all. They say he had straw for a backbone and chaff for brains and I agree. What else can you say for a man who gives his life to a farm that isn't even his?'

Alice stared and Rosalind's gaze dropped first. "Well, it's true,' she muttered.

'What do you mean - it isn't his?' demanded Alice. 'Of course it's his! Glen Heather has been in the Campbell family for nearly eighty years! Ever since Auld Hector's time!'

'Oh, the Campbell family, yes,' said Rosalind. 'But Glen Heather does not belong to our father and never did, so see what you've been giving your life to!' She lifted her skirts, turned, and ran upstairs.

'Rosalind!' called Alice, 'come down this instant!' Rosalind climbed faster, so Alice followed, detaining her sister just as they reached the landing.

'Let me go,' said Rosalind through her teeth. 'I am going to change my clothes.'

'*After* you explain yourself,' said Alice tautly. She propelled Rosalind into the bedroom and closed the door behind them. 'Well?'

'Well?' mocked Rosalind, rubbing her arms. 'How strong you are, sister dear. You have muscles like a labourer, which is all you can ever be on Glen Heather!'

'Explain yourself.'

'Very well. You asked for this, so don't blame me if you don't care for it! Have you never wondered why our father does not sell Glen Heather? He cannot manage the work anymore. He never enjoyed it anyway, even when he was strong. There are not enough men left to carry his weakness now, and it is not as if he had a son.'

Alice frowned. 'He has us.'

'He has *you*. That is what you mean, is it not?'

'Well - Glen Heather is nothing to you, is it?' said Alice. 'You have never troubled yourself with it.'

'Neither should you have done. You can never have Glen Heather, Alice,' said Rosalind in a hard, mocking voice. 'You are a woman.'

Alice had been very frightened for a moment, but now she laughed. 'Not you as well, Rosie! You must have been listening to Mother. Being a woman doesn't matter a jot. Look at Granny! She managed Glen Heather for twenty years after Grandfather died.'

'You cannot use Granny for an example, Alice. She is not a Campbell.'

'Her name might be Galbraith now, but it *was* Campbell.'

'She was Isobel Jarvis first of all,' said Rosalind.

'I know that, goose! But she married Grandfather and after he died she ran Glen H—'

'Stop! *Stop*!' cried Rosalind. 'Do you think I have not had that tale rammed into my ears all my life? Brave Granny, looking after Glen Heather, *keeping it in heart*, until her little son grew up!' Alice shook her head in bewilderment, and her sister continued with awful patience. 'Listen. Grandfather John died when our father was a baby, did he not?'

Alice nodded. 'Granny was a young widow with a son. Right? So tell me, Alice, *whose property was Glen Heather*?'

'Granny's, of course, after her husband died.'

'It never was, or it would be still. It was left to our father, for his lifetime. He cannot sell it ever, so owning it means nothing. He cannot sell it, and he cannot will it away.' Rosalind tossed her head impatiently. 'You still don't understand, do you Alice? Has our father never told you? Has Granny never told you? Glen Heather cannot be sold. *Entailment* it is called, I believe. That means it has to pass from father to son.'

'But Dad has no sons,' said Alice, 'so in our case it must pass from father to daughter.'

'No, Alice, it must go from father to *son*, or to the next male heir. Since you are a woman, that cannot ever be you. It must go to our eldest male Campbell cousin.'

'But we have none!" objected Alice. 'Dad was an only child, and his uncles are all dead or - or...'

'Or missing,' supplied Rosalind. 'Missing things can be found, Alice, and Samuel says Mr Bertram has a wonderful reputation for finding folk. So that's that, isn't it, Alice, unless ...'

'Unless what?' said Alice numbly.

'Well, unless our father has a grandson. A grandson would be a nearer male relative than a cousin, I believe, and a grandson might have enough sense to make Glen Heather pay! But that offers nothing for you, Alice, since you are an old maid. Now, if you have quite finished,' she added, 'I should like you to leave so I may change.'

Alice climbed to her attic room and stood numbly by the window as everything fell into place. Mary's insistence that Alice could not stay at Glen Heather. Isobel's curious attitude. Robert's silence. Even Mr Bertram's visits made sense now. Robert had not been making arrangements for Alice's eventual take-over; he had been putting in train a search for his closest male relation. Alice clenched her hands. She had never met a single Campbell relation, and neither had Mary. Only Isobel had known Robert's uncles, and Isobel had not kept in touch. Surely - surely such old men, if they were still alive, would have no interest in Glen Heather. But old men could have sons and grandsons. So somewhere in the world was a man, young or old, to whom would eventually descend the right to hold Glen Heather until his death. Alice felt sick with envy.

Strangely, it never occurred to her to doubt Rosalind's story. It explained too many things. It would have seemed logical that Robert or Isobel would have told her beforehand, and now, with painful hindsight, Alice could see that Isobel almost had.

'I kept Glen Heather on for Robert,' Isobel had said once. *'We women cannot own Glen Heather, Alice, it must go to a Campbell man. If you forget that you lay up trouble for yourself.'* And Alice had believed Isobel had meant nothing but outmoded prejudice. And there had been even more - *'I would not have stayed if I had not had Robert,'* Isobel had said. *'I could not have stayed if I had not had Robert.'* Alice had read grief at her widowhood in that, but again Isobel had meant it literally. She *could not* have stayed had she not been the mother of John Campbell's heir. It would have gone to John Campbell's brother.

Yes, Isobel had told her, and Alice had chosen to misunderstand. Yet Robert - surely Robert should have made it clear? But his silence had not been inexplicable - for Robert. He was a kind man, a faithful husband and indulgent father, but he had a weak spot in his character. He hated unpleasantness. He knew - he must have known - that Alice had been counting on a future at Glen Heather, but he had somehow made himself believe it a passing whim. He must have thought Alice would marry and move away, that he would live to be ninety, that no male heir would be found. He must have believed everything but the truth. The truth was that Alice had turned down her only suitor in expectation of a future that had never been more than a chimera. Alice shivered and turned from the window. She could not really blame Robert; for it was not he who had arranged the entailment. But neither could she face him - tonight.

Isobel was knitting in the cottage kitchen with Jennie Christopher. She was contented as she had not been in years, for the companionship of Jennie and McCleod suited her exactly. Jennie was cheerful and kind, McCleod opinionated and impolite - a perfect combination. Now that she had her own cottage, Isobel saw less of her son and grand-daughters and almost nothing of Mary. This suited Isobel, for she had no bent for diplomacy, and no patience with fools.

She had wronged Mary in returning to Glen Heather after James' death, but she had not wished to live alone and she would have dealt far worse with her nephew at Scarborough. Poor Scarborough; it needed urgent attention and a great deal of generosity, but Isobel was far too old to take the task on now, even if her nephew would have allowed it. It was a great pity, she thought, that she had not bought the cottage straight after James had died, but at that point Jennie had still been housekeeper at Glen Heather.

It was growing dark, and the lamps were lit in the kitchen, when Isobel heard a rap at the door. Left to herself she might not have answered it, but Jennie retained the powerful conditioning of her servant days and went to admit the visitor. Isobel knew immediately that something was wrong. Alice was always pale in winter, but tonight she looked like a ghost. Robert, thought Isobel with a pang of grief. Robert is gone!

Jennie, who had also perceived Alice's distress, poured some strong tea and excused herself from the kitchen. 'Don't go, Jennie,' said Alice dully, but Jennie said placidly that she must shut up the cow.

Isobel knew the cow had been shut up two hours before, but she gestured towards Jennie's vacated chair. 'Sit down, Alice, and tell me what has happened to distress you.'

Mechanically, Alice sat down, warming her hands around the cheeks of the teacup. She was shaking, and Isobel saw her hands were chapped and cold. 'You want butter and lard on those hands,' she said abruptly. 'And cotton gloves when you sleep. Is it Robert again?'

'Dad's well enough,' said Alice with an obvious effort.

'Got yourself a lover, have you?' Alice shook her head. 'Then perhaps you should,' said Isobel. 'There's nothing like it, you know.'

'Granny,' said Alice, 'is it true that Glen Heather is - is entailed?'

So that was it. 'I tried to tell you. I did.'

'I know you tried. I didn't want to listen.'

'I should have tried harder,' said Isobel reflectively, 'but it was Robert's job, not mine.'

'Can you tell me how it came about?'

'Auld Hector,' said Isobel. 'He built Glen Heather for his dynasty. He laid it on John - your grandfather - to run the place and pass it on to his son. If John and I had not had a son it would have gone to young Hector or to - to - the next brother or to Jamie. There was Robert, so that did not happen, and I managed the place until Robert was twenty-one.'

'It sounds so simple,' said Alice miserably. 'And I suppose if Dad had had a son, it would have passed on to him. But what will happen now?'

'Your father is only fifty-six,' said Isobel. 'He should have plenty of good years in him yet.' She knew in her heart that wasn't so, but what else could she say to Alice?

'Dad doesn't think so,' said Alice. 'Mother has persuaded him he must give up Glen Heather now.'

'He cannot, while he lives.'

'He could put a tenant on,' said Alice. 'Sell the sheep and sell the timber off. Or he could do what I believe he is trying to do - find the heir instead. But Granny - who could it be?'

Isobel thought back. 'Young Hector had three daughters,' she said. 'The other laddie married in Scotland, but I cannot recall that he had any children. Jamie ... och, I've not thought of dear Jamie in years! I have his portrait somewhere - and some of myself. I will show you when you are wed.'

'Then you cannot help me,' said Alice.

'My dear Alice,' said Isobel crisply, 'no-one can help you but yourself. Perhaps you should marry soon.'

'There is nobody left,' said Alice. 'And I would not if I could. A husband would be a complication in my life.'

Isobel patted her hand. Affection had never been easy for her, but she was very fond of Alice. 'I expect some of this is my doing,' she said ruefully. 'James would say so. It was my example made your father what he is, and my example that gave you false hope. I am sorry, Alice, that it is you who will pay for my mistakes. But now let us talk of happier things. Speak to McCleod. He is feeling neglected.'

Alice drove herself back to Glen Heather is a calmer mood. She could see how she had deluded herself, and she knew she had been as much to blame as Robert. She put away the gig and went to find her father. He was in his office, sitting in his leather chair with his bad leg on a stool and a book held limply in his hand. 'Dad?' she said softly, questioningly.

Robert's head jerked round. 'Oh Alice! Do come in.' His voice was faintly slurred. 'Is it supper time? I have been reading a bit.'

With the light so low? How could he see the print? Alice sat down. 'It isn't supper time yet,' she said. 'I need to talk to you about Glen Heather.' Even without the light she could see the wariness in her father's eyes. 'I know the property is entailed,' she said quickly, 'but - who is the next heir? You have no sons ...'

'I'm not looking to cock up my toes for a few years yet,' said Robert stoutly. 'And by then I'll have grandsons to burn!'

'Their name won't be Campbell,' said Alice.

'The name doesn't matter. A grandson is a closer relative than a cousin or such.'

'Are you sure it works that way?'

Robert waved his good hand. 'Old Bertram can sort it out when the time comes. Or, if he's gone, young Garland gets the job. Right out of my hands, it is.' He looked at her directly for the first time. 'I did check the wording of the entailment quite recently,' he said. 'If it had said "heirs" it would have come to you. It says "heirs male". Sorry, Bonnie Alice.'

It was years since he had called her that, and she had never felt it to be more of a lie. She didn't mention the subject again.

Gradually the war news became more hopeful. The impregnable Hindenberg Line was stormed in May 1917, and the Germans were falling back. Worral Jarvis was wounded at the Somme, and wrote shakily that he was coming home as soon as he could travel. Brigadier-General Grant led two cavalry regiments in a charge at Beersheba, opening Palestine to the Allies, and 400,000 men died at Ypres ... the horrors continued, with blood on every victory as 1917 drew to a close. No more was said of the future of Glen Heather, so Alice continued her usual routine. She drove regularly to visit Isobel, and sometimes went to Mersey for newspapers and essential stores. On one occasion, she went to the sales and bought a heifer calf. The remaining cow was aging, and had never been much good, but typically, Robert had put off replacing her. Now Alice had taken matters into her hands. If she was to milk the cow she would choose one to please herself, so she selected a well-bred young Ayrshire and named her Bluebell.

The Great War ended in November of 1918. Ten million lives had been lost, including almost 60,000 from Australia. Many of those who survived were wounded in body or spirit, and the effects would be felt for many years to come, but for the folk of Glen Heather, as for Australians everywhere, the immediate reaction was relief that the long struggle had ended.

In the winter of 1919, six months after the end of the war, Robert had a second stroke from which he did not recover. 'Look after Mother,' Alice told the bitterly weeping Rosalind. Holding her own distress in check, she made the necessary arrangements - first for Robert, and then for Glen Heather, and, barely a week after the funeral, Mr Bertram arrived with Samuel Garland.

'I cannot tell you how sorry we were to hear of your loss, Miss Campbell,' said Samuel, eyes glowing with sincerity behind his spectacles. 'Er - would it be in order for me to pay my respects to your mother and sister?'

'Mother is not receiving callers at the moment,' said Alice. 'However, my sister is in the parlour, and I know she would welcome a friendly face.'

Young Mr Garland disappeared with alacrity. His uncle looked disapproving, but Alice led the way into the office. It was just as it had been during Robert's and Isobel's tenures, but now Alice sat in the leather chair behind the great blackwood desk. 'I need some information, Mr Bertram,' she said. She was dressed in black, with a silver brooch pinned at her throat and Mr Bertram looked at her compassionately.

'Miss Campbell,' he said, 'I cannot begin to tell you ...' Her expression stopped him and he cleared his throat. 'Is there no-one else who can deal with these matters?'

'No-one,' said Alice. 'My mother knows nothing of the running of the property and my grandmother is - is a little vague. Come, Mr Bertram, you know Glen Heather! Your father stood guardian for mine until he was of age so surely you can spare me a little advice.'

The solicitor nodded, and looked at her with more respect.

There was much to be discussed. Funds which had been automatically frozen when Robert died had to be released. 'Naturally, we cannot countenance any great expenditure,' said Mr Bertram in his dry legal voice.

'Naturally,' agreed Alice, 'but the men's wages must be paid and the bills met.' She cleared her throat. 'Fortunately, it is winter, so there should not be any great outlay for the next month or two unless it freezes hard.' Mr Bertram looked a question. 'If we have a long cold period,' said Alice remotely, 'we may need to buy in extra feed for the livestock.'

'Perhaps we should sell off the stock?'

Alice shook her head. 'It will be spring soon enough and ungrazed pasture grows long and rank and will be a fire hazard in the summer.'

Eventually, they reached the part of the discussion that Alice dreaded. Her voice shaking, she asked when the family must leave Glen Heather.

'This presents a problem. Yes indeed.' Mr Bertram removed his rimless spectacles and polished them nervously. 'This situation is decidedly uncommon and most people in your position would reach suitable agreement with the new owner. In your case, however, the situation is complicated by the fact that the identity of said new owner has not yet been established.'

'My father was an only child,' said Alice, 'but he had uncles, and at least three cousins.'

'Unfortunately,' said Mr Bertram, 'your father could give us no addresses save that of his Uncle Hector in New Zealand. We - er we made an attempt to contact Mr Hector some time ago, but it bore no fruit.'

'Well, the Campbells are no great hands at writing letters,' said Alice.

'Quite so. Do you know any possibilities?'

'I know the names of my father's uncles,' she said. 'They are all entered in the family Bible. Unfortunately my grandmother, who made most of the entries, was most concerned with our own branch of the family and was a little short on details.'

She fetched the heavy Bible from the parlour and they pored over the names. 'There were four possible lines of succession,' said Alice. 'John, my grandfather, died after only a year of marriage and had one child, my father.' She looked up at Mr Bertram. 'I have asked Granny if there is any chance my father could have had half-brothers, but she believes it most unlikely. Grandfather was only twenty-one when he died and he had never been a wild young man.'

'Quite,' said Mr Bertram hastily.

'The next brother (as you know) was Hector, who went to New Zealand,' continued Alice. 'He died a few years ago, Granny says. There were three daughters, at least. And then there is Edward, who married in Scotland. I know nothing further of him, save that he may have lived in a place called Loch Haven where my great grandmother was born.'

Mr Bertram made a note of the name. 'What about Jamie Campbell?' he enquired, peering at the Bible.

Alice shrugged. 'Once again, I have only the information my grandmother could give me. Jamie Campbell left Glen Heather as a child, and to her knowledge returned just once, in 1866.'

Mr Bertram sighed heavily. 'Then the trail is fifty-three years cold,' he said.

'Your nephew tells my sister that you are skilled at finding people.'

'Believe me,' said Mr Bertram frankly, 'in this case I shall need to be.' He gathered his papers and continued more formally. 'Since Hector Campbell was the second eldest son, it seems logical to begin a more diligent search for his descendants.'

'Yes,' agreed Alice, 'and it would seem he may be the simplest to find. Even if there were no sons or grandsons, some member of the family may know something of Edward and Jamie. One of them may still be alive - although even Jamie would be over seventy.'

'Believe me, I know how difficult this must be for you, Miss Campbell,' said Mr Bertram, 'but I fear it may take some little time to find your cousins.'

'I realise that,' said Alice. 'Have no fear, I shall keep Glen Heather in good heart. My father's heir - whoever he is - will have no cause for complaint.' She rang a bell above the desk and Hannah came to show the solicitor out.

Mr Bertram, who had already decided to interview potential farm managers, was taken by surprise and found himself ushered into the yard without having informed Alice of his intention.

'An extraordinary young woman!' he remarked to his nephew.

Mr Garland, who had spent the last hour comforting Rosalind in the parlour, turned startled eyes to his uncle. 'Miss Rosalind?' he faltered. (*How* had the old man known?)

'Miss Campbell's name is Alice, I believe,' said Mr Bertram sedately.

Mr Garland removed his coat and applied himself to the motor, which made obedient raucous noises. Mr Bertram thought again of Alice and shook his head. He prayed he would find the Campbell heirs in New Zealand. Quickly.

Hannah returned to the office after she had seen the solicitor out. Alice was seated behind the great desk with her head on her folded arms. Hannah's heart gave a great thump of pity, and she closed the door silently and knocked. When she opened it, Alice was busily sorting papers. 'Yes, Hannah? Is anything wrong?'

Hannah crossed the room and put her hand on Alice's shoulder. 'Alice, you're skin and bone,' she said, 'but things will come right - you'll see.'

'No Hannah,' said Alice quietly, 'I don't believe things will ever come right for me.'

Life went on at Glen Heather. Alice, at first astonished that it could, found herself forgetting her problems for hours at a time. The spectre of her looming departure from Glen Heather remained, but as the weeks flowed past and became months, it began to take on the unreal quality of a nightmare. The spring of 1919 was late, and cold, and Alice, having considered the quantity of fodder laid in, bought more ewes.

'It's too cold, Miss,' said Elijah Ward. 'We'll never feed 'em. Why do you reckon everyone's selling?'

'The ground will warm up soon,' said Alice. 'The prices will rise. We can hold until then.'

Elijah looked at her sideways and grumbled under his breath, but there was nothing he could do. Miss Campbell was the boss - for the moment. 'And I hope she doesn't damned well ruin the place!' he said to his wife. 'If the new owner comes and finds the place run down, who will be getting the blame - and the sack?'

'Miss Campbell is a fine young woman,' said Mrs Ward.

'Girls,' said Elijah, 'have no right to play at being farmers. It was all right while the boss was alive - he could have seen her right - but now there's only the old lady, and she's close to eighty if she's a day.'

The soldiers had begun to return to Tasmania, coming home as soon as they were demobbed. An air of deep thankfulness rested on Mersey and the surrounding districts, but too many of the young men who had left Mole Creek Station would not be coming home. It was over, and none of them would ever forget. Some had been wounded, some, like Arthur Pritchard, had lost an eye or a limb. All carried something of the horrors they had seen. To live day after day in the shade of death, to see the possibility of death reflected in the eyes of their mates, to wonder hourly if they would ever come home again - how could they fail to be marked by that? More than one man had tales of amazing escapes, of being the only one of a dozen to escape the bursting of a shell. More than one man treasured a slouch hat with a bullet hole, or a piece of shrapnel which, having failed in its mission of death, had been kept as a talisman against its fellows. They were all a little strange.

Perhaps those who had survived the war unmarked were most to be pitied, mainly because they never were. They came home from the fields of horror, from the sand, the mud and the madness, to be reunited with parents, wives, children and sweethearts. Nothing could replace the years they had lost. Nothing could bridge the gulf between those who had gone and those who had waited at home. Mothers, intent on feeding up their reclaimed sons, scarcely recognised the boys who returned. Young men looked at the smooth, unmarked faces of their sweethearts and felt that time had stood still. Many a reunion went sour because it had not. But some were lucky. Some returned to loving arms and the eagerness of wives to show off babies who had grown into little boys and girls. And some, having carried photographs for years, found the originals a thousand times more beautiful.

Joseph McKenzie felt himself to be one of the fortunate. He had survived the war without serious injury, had put in weary months of guard duty, and now he was returning to his sweetheart, and to an attractive position in her father's firm. He whistled as the train swayed towards Park Street station. Her letters were always brief and he had not heard from her at all lately, but mail was often delayed and Dorothy had never been a great writer. Joseph's thin face creased in a reminiscent smile. His little flighty sweetheart - she would not have changed. She had the lightness of heart and the doll-like prettiness that remained sixteen forever, and Joseph, who felt he had never been young, found fascination in that quality. He leaned forward, as if he could make the train speed up by sheer force of will. Soon the door would open to the rest of his life.

The train wheezed into a teeming station and he swung out and looked about eagerly, and then with increasing anxiety. He had written that he would be home on this train, written it twice, in two separate letters, to be sure. The milling crowd was breaking into smaller groups, fragmenting again and again. Couples embraced, tears fell. Children backed away from tall strange figures they barely remembered. A flotilla of hats and frocks brought him hope, for Dorothy always wore clothes of the latest mode, but the eyes met his unrecognisingly, and the ladies passed him by. Mothers and fathers were there, grandparents, frail and joyful. Envious schoolboy brothers, worshipful sisters ... at last there was only a handful of people left on the platform and Joseph had to accept that she had not come. But maybe she was ill? Or perhaps her father's car had refused to start. He wondered if old man O'Riley still had the same Humber; it had never been reliable. Well, he would go to her, and they would laugh over the silly circumstances which had kept her from the station. And perhaps a less public reunion would be more satisfactory, after all.

Joseph shouldered his kit bag and turned towards the exit of the station, but a porter was approaching with a letter in his hand. 'Excuse me, sir, was you expecting a Miss O'Riley?'

Joseph nodded with relief and took the letter. Some silly little circumstance ... He slit the envelope with an impatient thumb and read the single sheet through.

Dear Joey...

He read it again. His hand slowly crumpled the page and he tossed it away into the darkness.

'Mother, would you like to go to stay with Aunt Emily?' asked Alice in December.

Mary dabbed at her eyes and shook her head. It was over six months since Robert died, but his widow still wore unrelieved black. She seemed to have lost interest in life and hardly spoke at all.

Concerned, Alice sent for Dr Llewellyn, but after examining Mary he would not commit himself. 'Talk to her,' he suggested. 'Get her to take an interest in life.'

'It would do no good,' said Alice wryly. 'I was never my mother's favourite person.'

The doctor glared at her. 'Fight a lot, do you?'

'Not anymore. I try not to upset her.'

'That's probably half her trouble,' said Dr Llewellyn gruffly. 'I daresay she's spoiling for a good fight. You don't want her sinking into a decline.'

'Of course not!'

'Then give her something to think about. Invite my sister Annie to visit - that'll stir her up! Open her curtains. Play dance music on the gramophone. If all else fails, run away with the first unsuitable young man you meet. But don't stay away. Come home and fight it out.'

Alice threw back her head and laughed heartily. Then she cried.

'You watch yourself too, young woman,' said Dr Llewellyn. 'Good nourishing diet. Early nights. Get yourself a man.'

'Th-that's what my granny says,' sobbed Alice.

Dr Llewellyn nodded. 'She would,' he said, looking down the long tunnel of memory. 'Isobel Campbell always knew the value of a good man.' He drove himself home, sufficiently concerned to break his long-standing habit of reticence about his patients' affairs. 'Young Alice worries me more than her mother,' he told Annie. 'Mary Campbell is a survivor. She'll bend and come up straight again. Young Alice, now - she'll not bend and those that don't can often break. Go and visit Mary, Annie, and see what you can do for Alice.'

One by one, Mr Bertram's enquires drew blanks. Letters travelled across the Pacific and the Tasman Sea, parish records and shipping lists were scanned and the Commonwealth Roll examined. Hector Campbell's wife had left the Kirkbride farm after his death in 1907, and had remarried, so it was not easy to find her whereabouts. At last, a few months after the war ended, it was established that Edwina was dead, and that Hector's surviving descendants were female. 'Two elderly ladies, both unmarried,' said Mr Bertram. 'The Misses Edith and Janet Campbell. Their sister Ailsa is deceased and they claim to be the last of their line.'

'They should know,' murmured Alice.

Mr Bertram shot her a peculiar look over his spectacles and cleared his throat. 'Quite.'

'No illegitimate children?' asked Alice.

'None.'

Alice leaned forward. 'What if there were?'

'Were ...?'

'An illegitimate child,' said Alice patiently. 'What if an unmarried descendant of old Hector Campbell had fathered a son? Would the son be able to inherit?'

'In the absence of other suitable heirs?' Mr Bertram considered. He consulted his papers and leafed through the pages of a dusty book. 'Surprisingly enough, I think he would. There is no prerequisite for legitimacy. The exact wording is this; *heirs male in perpetuity*. Er - why do you ask, Miss Campbell? Have you perhaps encountered a young man with the Campbell chin?'

Alice gave him a doubtful look. *Was* Mr Bertram making a joke? It seemed unlikely, so she shook her head. 'That seems to dispose of young Hector then,' she said without regret. 'How about Great Uncle Edward?'

Mr Bertram consulted more papers. 'Edward Campbell. Emigrated to Scotland forty-five years ago. Married there in 1890, at the er - somewhat advanced age of forty-six.' He looked up at Alice. 'Since his wife was a lady of even more mature years, it is safe to assume they never had children, and both have - ah - passed on now.'

'And I suppose any earlier children he might have had would be impossible to trace.'

Mr Bertram looked at her reproachfully, obviously picturing a world littered with unacknowledged Campbell heirs.

'I suppose we are down to Jamie then,' she said. 'Have you any news of Jamie?'

But here Mr Bertram had drawn a complete blank. So far as he had been able to discover, no-one had set eyes on Jamie Campbell since he rode away from Glen Heather on that day in 1866. 'A fascinating problem,' he observed. 'I have already explored the fact that Miss Edith, Miss Janet or Mr Edward might have known the whereabouts of Mr Jamie. However, there seems to have been no correspondence.'

"I don't know about it's being so fascinating,' said Alice tartly. 'I want this cleared up. Have you tried the prison records? According to my grandmother, Uncle Jamie did leave Glen Heather in rather a hurry. One step ahead of the Law as it were.'

'This may take some time,' said Mr Bertram, his eyes glinting with zeal. 'In the meantime, we must appoint an interim manager for Glen Heather. This has gone quite far enough.'

'I am the manager of Glen Heather,' said Alice.

'It will not do, Miss Campbell,' said the solicitor. 'You have managed up until now, but it may take years to locate the descendants of Jamie Campbell - if any.'

'On the other hand,' argued Alice, 'it may happen next week. Tomorrow, even. You have advertised for information in the newspapers?'

'That was one avenue, certainly,' said Mr Bertram, 'but I was loath to use it. Such advertisements tend to bring - er - undesirable persons to your doorstep. And in the meantime, I would be failing in my duty as your late father's executor if I failed to appoint a suitable manager.'

'I have held the position in all but name for years.'

'Come, Miss Campbell, without wanting to appear to denigrate your work here ... perhaps Mr Ward would care to take the position?'

'He is much too old, and Arthur is unwell.'

Mr Bertram managed to look as if he had unexpectedly bitten a lemon.

'I have a counter-proposal,' said Alice. 'Appoint me as the official manager. I know more than anyone about the proper management of Glen Heather - except Granny, of course, and she is nearly eighty. You might find a manager who was experienced in New South Wales, perhaps, or even the midlands - but his experience would pertain to conditions very different from those we experience at Glen Heather.'

They argued back and forth for some time, and eventually reached an uneasy compromise. A capable manager would be appointed and given limited power, with any large decisions first having to be cleared with Alice. 'It really is most irregular,' complained Mr Bertram, gathering his papers.

'But not unheard-of, surely,' said Alice. 'Ladies are taking all sorts of authority now.'

She extended her hand and Mr Bertram gripped it gloomily. 'I have a feeling I am going to regret this,' he said. 'I do indeed.'

'There is just one more point,' said Alice, almost apologetically. 'I would like to reserve the right to interview the applicants for this post myself. After all, if I have to work alongside the appointee, it must be someone with whom I may be easy. Good day, Mr Bertram.'

The solicitor was left with the feeling that he had been manoeuvred, and reflected that there might be something of her mother in Alice Campbell after all. He disliked the sensation, but was conscious of an unwilling admiration. If Miss Campbell had been a man she would have made an excellent master for Glen Heather. He said as much to Samuel Garland as the latter finished cranking the starting handle and bounded into the driving seat.

'An admirable woman indeed,' said Samuel, steering expertly between the gateposts. 'She frightens me half to death.'

'Unlike her sister,' said Mr Bertram drily.

'Quite so. I shall have to come to terms with Miss Campbell, I suppose,' said Samuel reflectively, 'since I hope to marry Rosalind.'

'Has it gone so far then?'

'Nothing has been said, as yet,' said Samuel.

'And not too much has been done, either, I trust.'

'Why, Uncle, you shock me!' said Samuel after a moment. His clever face crinkled with amusement. 'I hope you are not implying that anything improper has taken place between Miss Rosalind and myself? I have not proposed because I am by no means sure she will accept.'

Mr Bertram squinted dubiously at his nephew. Despite his heavy spectacles, the young man was handsome and well-made. 'You have a certain amount of personal charm,' he said. 'And she has known you for some years.'

'That may go against me,' said Samuel seriously. 'I could not serve in the army, and as for the other considerations; do they allow me to aspire to a Campbell of Glen Heather?'

'She is only that until we find the heir,' said Mr Bertram astutely.

'I had considered that,' said his nephew. 'If it weren't for that - to be honest, although it seems hard on Miss Campbell, this entailment could work in my favour. I tell you, Uncle, I want nothing of Glen Heather.'

It was a new day in a new year. A bitter young man in a well-worn uniform was reading the newspaper in the north-bound train, simply for something to do. It was not his own newspaper; it had been left on the seat by some passenger who had disembarked at the last station. Joseph McKenzie was not looking for anything in particular, for there was nothing to interest him in Tasmania now. Dorothy O'Riley had found and married a better prospect some months before; married him while her betrothed crouched in a trench in France re-reading her few letters and creasing her photograph a little more each time he removed it from his pack. She hadn't even bothered with the formality of a 'Dear John' letter until he had already returned.

Joseph had spent the first night in a pub, staring blindly at the walls. The next morning, he had visited his ex-love's father at his place of business. The older man had shown pity, but more than that, it had been acute embarrassment. Joseph might have been sorry for him if he'd had any sympathy to spare. 'For my part, you'd be welcome to come back and work for me here,' said O'Riley miserably.

'I don't think that would be a good idea,' said Joseph. 'Besides,' he added without premeditation; 'somehow I've a yen to return to the land. I've seen enough of smoke and walls.'

O'Riley looked relieved. 'Of course, you're right,' he agreed too quickly. 'I can quite see it would be difficult for both of you if you stayed here, Joe. And I won't see you empty handed.'

Joseph couldn't blame the man. It wasn't Tom O'Riley's fault his daughter's veering fancy had deprived a young man neatly of wife, trust and livelihood. 'If she'd written and told me when it happened, I wouldn't have embarrassed you by coming back at all.'

'No - well - we thought - she thought - it would have been cruel to have written to you while you were on the front. She would have met you in person, but - well, she's in a delicate condition, you understand? Besides, her husband is a little -' O'Riley's voice trailed off and he said a shade too heartily; 'You're a sensible man to take it this way, Joe. Dorothy told me about your - um - unfortunate history. Pity you had to spring it on her when you had that last leave. She took it rather hard, you know.'

Joseph felt sick. He could barely bring himself to shake hands with the man as he refused the offer of money and left to get on with his life. What was it they all said? Better a jilt before the wedding than after. He didn't really agree. If it happened *before* the wedding, a man had no option but to take it on the chin, and do the gentlemanly thing by disappearing. If it happened *afterwards*, he would have been fully entitled to have knocked the other fellow to the ground. Not that it would have regained his girl; he would never have taken her back after she'd left him for someone else, but it would have made a more satisfactory conclusion to the affair. *Affair.* That was a joke! His relationship with Dorothy had been a pure as well-water. And, like some well-water, it had held hidden dangers. Brooding on this, he realised there was nothing for him in Hobart at all since his father had died.

Restlessly, he thought he might try his luck in Gippsland or New South Wales. New Zealand, even. Anywhere, so long as it was well away from the orbit of Dorothy, nee O'Riley.

She was having a child. Certainly it could not be his - he had not seen Dorothy for two years now and had never taken her to bed. Some other fellow must have been less reticent, or luckier, perhaps. Now that it didn't matter he wondered what she would have been like. Moist and voluptuous or cold? Had she cried out or had she clung? Joseph felt sick, and concentrated on wishing she hadn't told his story to her father. He had never been ashamed of his background, but he disliked the curious or pitying glances the tale attracted.

He spent no more nights at the pub but left Hobart and the south as if the devil or the Germans were at his back. And so here he was on a train, heading north to board the *Rotomahana.* He looked gloomily out the window, but with nothing but the flat prospect of the midlands before him, his gaze dropped to the newspaper instead. None of the week-old news held much interest, so he turned to the advertisements at the rear, and bent to read with more attention. The train panted on.

Mr Bertram wrote courteously to Alice, suggesting that he should interview applicants and send the two or three most promising on to her. Alice wrote courteously back and refused. 'There won't be many applicants, anyway,' she said to Mary. 'And I won't put up with someone who tries to take over, which is the type Mr Bertram would appoint. Most men of the right calibre wouldn't want a job that could last for a year or a month or end even before it begins.'

'Rubbish,' said Mary. 'Let Bertram deal with it. That's what he's paid for. Have you any idea how many men are looking for work just now, Alice?'

'Plenty, I expect,' said Alice. Mary snorted and Alice rejoiced silently. She had taken at least some of Dr Llewellyn's advice and now spent a regular hour each evening talking - and disagreeing - with Mary.

'You're Robert's daughter, and no mistake,' said Mary when Alice persisted in her plan. 'Pure Campbell, through and through, pig-headed as all get out.'

'But Dad always agreed with you, Mother!' said Alice.

'He had his ways,' said Mary. 'Is that a motor? Rosalind should be back. All this running around is getting her talked about.' But there was satisfaction in her voice. Samuel Garland was not the only man to show an interest in her younger daughter, and the war was over now.

For a week, Alice interviewed men each morning. 'Those who are suitable try to patronise me,' she complained to Hannah. 'One of them even made me a proposal - of a sort.'

'Oh dear,' said Hannah, 'what did you say?'

'I gave him a flea in his ear,' said Alice cheerfully. 'I told him there were plenty of stud rams on Glen Heather already, and that they were all better bred than he was in any case.'

Hannah nodded. 'It was good of you to think of Arthur,' she said, 'but we'll be moving back to Mersey. He isn't strong, you know.'

Alice understood that. 'There are plenty of men,' she said restlessly, 'but it's so difficult. I must employ someone fit and strong for the sake of - of the new owner, when he comes, but I feel bad when I reject the less fortunate. It is hardly *their* fault they are in poor health, and many of them have suffered a great deal.'

'I know,' said Hannah soberly. 'To give up a good position and fight for your country and then to come back wounded and find there are no jobs for you to do - it's downright indecent.'

'I am asking for someone who will stay at Glen Heather and tend it as if it were his own, someone who has initiative yet will take advice from a woman, someone who won't ask any assurance of permanency.'

'You don't know yet that the new owner wouldn't keep your manager on,' argued Hannah. 'Whoever he is, he doesn't know he owns Glen Heather yet. Have you considered, Alice, that he may not wish to live here? He may be middle-aged, and settled wherever he is.'

Alice's eyes widened with hope. 'He might not want Glen Heather at *all*?'

'I wouldn't go that far,' said Hannah. 'Glen Heather brings in a tidy income and I never heard of a man who'd turn his back on a windfall. More likely, he'd put on a tenant or a manager. Your man might be asked to stay on. Even you.'

Alice frowned. 'I hadn't thought of that,' she said slowly. 'How odd. I would have said I'd give my left arm for the chance to stay on at Glen Heather, but to be kept on for someone's convenience, or from pity - no.'

'That's the Campbell pride talking,' said Hannah. 'Where will you go?'

'I should move to the cottage with Granny, if it weren't for Mother,' said Alice. 'I expect she will take a house in Launceston near Aunt Emily. Strange, isn't it Hannah? Rosalind is bound to marry soon, and Granny is so old - of all the family it will soon be down to Mother and me - one who doesn't care and one who cares too much.'

'You might marry. You're only twenty-four, and the men are coming back.'

'I couldn't marry for convenience,' said Alice. 'No man could measure up and I'd make him miserable. A good man deserves better than that.'

'I know you loved your father,' said Hannah, 'but ...'

'Dad?' Alice's voice choked on a laugh. 'I'm not using Dad as a yardstick, Hannah! I loved him, but I never thought him infallible.'

'Then it's Glen Heather,' said Hannah. 'I reckon you're right, Alice. Unless you can say; it's only grass and dirt and there's plenty more where that came from; there's no hope for you.'

'Then there's no hope for me, ever,' said Alice sadly.

She had a bad night, and a bad morning, and by lunch-time her serenity was sorely tried. One applicant had seemed possible, until he made the mistake of patronising her. When he leaned forward and patted her hand, she rose and told him coldly that she would let him know. The next man was too cautious. Alice could see that not a penny would be spent, not a sheep sold until the market was glutted. He wouldn't do, and neither would the third, who was slick and sharp and smooth. His mind was keen and so were his eyes, but Alice didn't trust him. He'd be feathering his nest in no time.

She spent the afternoon with Flip, the apprentice sheepdog, grandson of her own Bob, looking over the sheep for lice. At six, having checked on Bluebell the Ayrshire and her calf, she washed and went to have dinner with Mary and Rosalind.

'Any luck?' asked Rosalind. She smoothed the cuffs of her new summer dress, which swung freely above her pretty ankles. The new style suited her and after war-time austerity, Rosalind revelled in it. She read the answer in Alice's face and added with a dainty yawn; 'In my opinion there never will be. The truth is, for you, nobody is good enough for Glen Heather.'

'It's your home too,' snapped Alice. 'Do you want to see it go to ruin?'

'Now, girls,' chided Mary. 'Sisters should be friends.' Alice and Rosalind exchanged glances, and laughed. 'I shall never, never understand you two,' said Mary.

There was a commotion on the porch as Flip began to bark. 'Someone is coming,' said Rosalind unnecessarily. 'It cannot be Samuel. The dog only barks at strangers.' She sauntered over to the window. 'It's a man,' she said with a faint lilt of interest in her voice.

'Another one?' said Alice wearily. 'I'd better go and see him.'

'I don't know why you don't leave all this to Bertram,' said Mary. 'That's what he's ... oh, all right, be off with you. That dog is giving me the headache.'

Alice left the dining-room and glanced at her reflection in the glass that hung in the hallway. She smoothed a rebellious curl behind her ear, but it bobbed back from her fingers like a corkscrew. It didn't matter. No doubt this man would not do either.

CHAPTER 39

Joseph knocked one last time on the heavy door. It seemed there was no-one there but the barking dog. He clicked his fingers to the pup, scarcely disappointed. It had been a mere whim, after all. He would put up in Mole Creek and leave on the morning train.

The door opened behind him, and a clear voice hushed the dog. So someone *was* at home. The woman on the doorstep was standing under the wide veranda and at first he saw her merely as a shadow. Even when she stepped forward into the golden evening light the impression of darkness remained. Black hair escaped in a spiral to touch one cheek, amd dark brown eyes regarded him beneath heavy level black brows. She wore a dark skirt with a plain blouse, some years behind the fashion. 'Good evening,' she said, and extended her hand. The lady of the house then, not the maid.

'Good evening, Miss ...?'

'Campbell,' she said, 'Alice Campbell. Do come in.'

Campbell! Naturally. He hesitated. 'I don't wish to intrude, Miss Campbell.'

'That's quite all right. I was not expecting anyone at this hour, but since you're here, I shall see you now. How did you come?'

'Train to Mole Creek, bullock wagon to Mersey, and then I walked,' said Joseph. 'Nice country, isn't it?'

'I think so. Come along, I shall interview you in the office.' Pretty highhanded! Joseph opened his mouth to explain himself, but she was already on her way. Between irritation and amusement, he gave an infinitesimal shrug and followed her down the hall to the office.

Alice clasped her hands on the desk, surveying her visitor in silence. She had found this an effective ploy during the past week. Few interviewees could resist rushing in to fill the well of silence, and she'd learned more from what their haste revealed than from a score of conventional questions. This man showed no such discomfort. He folded his own hands and gazed back at her unblinkingly. Alice felt her cheeks growing warm as a blush rose from beneath her sensible collar. Even as she blushed, she registered approvingly that the man had dark blue eyes, tanned skin and hair as dark as her own, though his had a single white streak above one eye.

'A freak of nature,' he observed.

'I beg your pardon?'

'My hair. A freak of nature. My grandmother had it too. The chin, I am reliably informed, was a gift from my paternal grandfather.'

Alice cleared her throat. It was time to take up the reins and steer the conversation in its proper direction. She glanced for inspiration at the pink milkmaids in the vase. In proper season milkmaid would be preceded by wattle and followed by parrot food and crimson heath. 'How much has Mr Bertram told you of this position?' she asked.

'Nothing,' said the man. 'I know no Mr Bertram.'

'Oh - oh dear! I'm afraid when I kidnapped you from the doorstep I assumed you were an applicant for the management position!'

'I am. I was on the train and I glanced through an old newspaper someone had left. Your advertisement took my eye, and as I had no particular plans, I came to Mole Creek for the night. I thought I'd take a chance on coming out to Glen Heather, although I assumed the position would have been filled by now.'

There was a faint question in his voice, and Alice found herself answering it. 'In the ordinary way, it would probably have been taken long since,' she said, 'but the way things stand the position may not be permanent. The right sort of man usually has no interest in a position which might last for ten years - or ten days. And those who do not ask for security ...'

'Do not offer it either,' he said. 'I take it the owner is away?'

'You might say that,' said Alice. 'But I have the power to appoint a manager.' She considered him candidly. 'Would the uncertain nature of the position put you off?'

'No, it rather appeals to me. I was heading for the mainland, but I had no particular goal there. I would be happy to work here for a time.'

'You have no family?'

His face went cold. 'I have no ties, here or anywhere else. I am as free as the wind.'

Alice reflected that freedom seemed to give him very little satisfaction, but his troubles were not her business. 'Have you experience with sheep?'

'My father was an itinerant shearer, and my mother's family had land near Wonthaggi. My grandfather believed in making me work for my keep. I liked it, and after I finished school I stayed on with him for three years. Then he died, and the place was sold off by an aunt. I followed my father to Hobart and worked for a shipping firm, but I always had it in mind to go back on the land. Then the war came. Like a lot of other young fools, I volunteered in 1915.'

'You won't be returning to your old position?'

'No.'

She waited, but he did not elaborate. His face was cold again, and somehow remote, and again he seemed to feel no need to fill the silence.

'If I offered you the position,' she said carefully, 'it would be on the basis of a month's mutual trial. Would that be acceptable to you?'

'Oh yes,' he said, but not as if it mattered to him greatly. 'That would be quite adequate.'

'Well then.' Alice rose to her feet and extended her hand across the desk. 'Welcome to Glen Heather. Can you begin this week?'

It wasn't until the newly appointed manager had left for Mersey that Alice realised she had forgotten to ask his name. It took some time for the implications to sink in; that she had engaged a man who had offered no references, volunteered no name, and who had certainly not applied through the proper channels. She didn't look forward to telling Mr Bertram that. Filled with foreboding, she went out to the sheep, returning in the dark to find that Rosalind had gone out dancing with Samuel.

She lay awake for half the night, wondering what she had done. What she *hadn't* done added up to quite a lot, too. The only sense she had shown in the business had been to insist on a month's trial ...

In the morning, she went to the cottage and told Isobel the news.

Isobel laughed. 'Have a little more faith in your judgement, child,' she said bracingly. 'Do you like the man? Did he make a good impression?'

'He seems very suitable.'

Isobel rapped on the floor with her cane. 'That is not what I asked you, child. Do you *like* the man? Is he attractive?'

Alice smiled reluctantly. It was a long time since she had allowed herself to consider things like that. 'He is attractive in his way,' she said, 'and very self-contained. Not very expressive.'

'Samuel Garland is attractive,' said Isobel. 'He reminds me of James.'

'He *is* very much like your James,' said Alice gently. 'But the new man is nothing like Mr Garland. He is tall and dark, too thin, too quiet. He gives nothing away at all.'

'A very dangerous type,' observed Isobel. 'Eh, McCleod? We know all about the silent ones.'

'Sleekit! Sleekit!' muttered McCleod drowsily.

'Very often they are,' said Isobel. 'Watch your step with this one, Alice. But the name - what's his name? He does have one, I trust?'

'No doubt,' said Alice. 'I shall bring him to meet you and Jennie one day, Granny, and you can ask him his name yourself.'

She took her leave before Isobel could ask any more inconvenient questions, and walked home on the old track that led past Scarborough. At one time, it had apparently been difficult to find the boundary between Scarborough and Glen Heather, but now it was very evident; her Great Uncle Winston and her Uncle Whitaker after him had sold off almost all the timber from Scarborough and the mountainside was bare. The creeks had washed out their banks and formed marshes in the flats, and the heath, which grew white, pink and crimson on Glen Heather, was reduced to dusty-looking clumps which turned dry in the sun.

There was no heath flowering in the summer, so Alice didn't linger on the brae but hurried down to the house. She was not over-pleased to find the Tin Lizzie parked in the yard and Samuel Garland taking his ease in the parlour. 'Good morning, Mr Garland,' she said repressively. 'Have you papers for me to sign?'

'Uncle wondered if you had anything to report concerning the interviews.'

'So he had you come and ask,' said Alice mercilessly.

'Mr Garland knows he is welcome any time,' said Mary.

Well - perhaps he deserved his welcome; he had been nothing if not constant. Alice smiled suddenly. It was not Samuel's fault she had been foolish. 'Of course,' she said cordially.

Rosalind broke in to ask Alice how she had fared with the evening applicant. 'He didn't stay long,' she said gaily. 'Was he quite ineligible? Did he pat your hand?'

'I engaged him,' said Alice briefly. 'Is there any tea left in the pot, Mother?'

The new manager arrived that afternoon. Alice greeted him coolly; he still looked strong and honest. As for sleekit - she had no idea. It was just one of the odd words Isobel and McCleod used occasionally. 'Have you had lunch?' she asked.

'Yes thank you, Miss Campbell.' His voice was rather more educated than she would have expected from his brief description of his background.

'Is that all your kit?'

Her new employee glanced indifferently at the small bundle by his side. 'The army does not encourage a man to lay in worldly goods.'

Alice frowned. The man did not add up. He was standing on the veranda, quite relaxed, his boots light with dust, a soft hat in his hand. Today he was wearing the traditional farm-worker's outfit of light trousers and a flannel shirt, quite aggressively new. But then - he *had* come straight out of the army. 'You'll be over in the cottage,' she said. 'Mr and Mrs Ward lived there until recently. They could have stayed on, but they preferred to go to their daughter in Mole Creek. It's fully furnished. I hope you find it comfortable.' She was babbling, and she knew it, and that was ridiculous. *He* should be the nervous one. *He* was the one on trial.

'May I stow my bag now, Miss Campbell?'

'Of course,' said Alice. 'About your meals - we have two men and a boy on again now and they come in daily and bring their lunch. Perhaps you had better eat with us in the house.'

'No thank you, Miss Campbell. I can cook.'

Alice was relieved. Mary and Rosalind would not have enjoyed eating with an employee. 'By the way,' she said, 'I seem to have forgotten your name.'

She blushed for the lie, and he looked at her oddly, and hesitated. 'I am Joseph McKenzie,' he said, with peculiar emphasis on the name. 'Joe, if you prefer.'

Somehow, Alice thought he was lying. She opened her mouth to challenge him, then gave a mental shrug. She had not been entirely truthful herself and the name would do. 'Come along Joe,' she said, but it sounded wrong. He did not look like a "Joe". 'Joseph,' she amended. He gave an unsmiling nod and followed her past the stables and down the slope to the cottage. His eyebrows rose just a little as he took in the mellow sandstone building, a single-storey replica of Glen Heather House. 'This cottage was built on the site of the first building at Glen Heather,' she told him. 'I am afraid the inside is not as elegant as the outside.' She opened the door, and the inside of the cottage did look rather forlorn now the Wards had gone. 'I'll have Maisie fetch over some linen; I should have done so before, but I have had a great deal on my mind.'

'That explains it.'

'What?' she asked defensively.

'I did think it a trifle odd you didn't ask my name.'

'You could have volunteered it.'

'So I could. But just at this point in my life I see volunteering as a foolhardy option. You may gain very little and lose a great deal. Do you still wish to employ me?'

Alice smiled, with an effort. 'The month has hardly begun. When I make a bargain, it stays made.'

His eyes lit up. 'A woman of her word. I take my hat off to you, Miss Campbell. Or I would if it were still on my head.'

Alice blinked. Joseph McKenzie had gone from cold and stern to open and charming in the space of a few words. She wondered what Isobel would say. Something obscurely Scottish, probably, which was odd, since Isobel had never been to Scotland. 'If you will excuse me, I have some paperwork to deal with,' she said. 'Come to the house when you're ready, and I shall give you the records of the last couple of years. Read them and you will know what to expect of our conditions, which are rather individual here in the high country.'

Joseph nodded politely and turned to unpack his bag. Alice returned to the house with an uneasy feeling of having been dismissed from the cottage - and from his thoughts.

Unpacking took very little time. He had only his personal effects, his new clothes and a studio portrait of his mother. Joseph's face softened. His mother had been a lovely lady, well-read and endlessly kind and patient. She had needed to be, to put up with his father.

Dad, he thought, you were a cross-grained old beggar. Chip on your shoulder the size of Mt Wellington, face like the business end of a bullock - but you must have had something once.

He smiled suddenly, wryly, wondering what the old man would have thought of his son's arrival at Glen Heather. Kicked his backside out of it, most likely. But then, James McKenzie hadn't thought much of the berth at O'Riley's, either. Poor old man - he had spent his life looking for his own place in the world and had never really found it - except in the arms of Joseph's mother.

Joseph sighed and laid his spare shirt away in the drawer, considering his new employer. Miss Campbell was an odd sort of woman. Look at her clothes - skirt hem draggled, blouse washed out - didn't mind how ugly it looked. Lanky piece, too. Joseph liked his women small and trim and neat and a little shallow, like Dorothy. Frowning, he thought of Dorothy as he had last seen her, neatly gloved and hatted, weeping gently as she waved him back to war. He had bought her a ring before he left, and, feeling emotional and uncertain, had told her his history. With his father gone, there would be no-one left to remember the real Joseph McKenzie if he did not come home again. He should have kept his mouth shut, but would it have made any difference if he had? Dorothy had kissed him and cried all over his uniform. He had had a photograph of her, seamed and soft at the corners, which he carried in his pack for years. That had gone out the train window, somewhere north of Hobart, and perhaps, in time, Dorothy would follow it into oblivion.

Wrenching his mind away from the unchangeable past, he contemplated his malleable present instead. The workman's cottage at Glen Heather was not palatial, but it was sturdy and undoubtedly waterproof, and at least it didn't roll around, which was more than you could say for the troopship. He'd do well enough here for a while, and if it turned out sour, or if Miss Campbell proved too much of a harridan, he'd move on. Strange set-up. Fine old property, absentee owner, a dour young woman who seemed to have an unusual amount to say in what went on. Who *was* the owner, anyway? Where was he, and when was he coming back?

He realised that Alice Campbell really hadn't parted with any more information than he had, although she had warned him it wouldn't be a permanent job. He didn't want it to be permanent. He had come to Glen Heather out of idle interest, an interest born of long-ago childhood tales and a current aimlessness. If it hadn't been for the war, he would never have come here. If it hadn't been for the war, he would have been settled in Hobart, married these three years, and probably the father of a hopeful family. He would have been secure in his niche in the O'Riley shipping firm and rising rapidly to directorhood under the aegis of his father-in-law. Or would he? Would Dorothy have left him anyway, once she knew his history?

But there *had* been a war and here he was standing in an austere farm cottage out in the sticks. Life was funny, sometimes. Bloody funny. If a bloke wasn't careful he could die laughing, but he had only to stay a month. He could look on it as a resting place, a platform from which to take decisions and plan a new life. If it were no good at Glen Heather he could be leaving on the *Rotomahana* in four weeks' time. Until then, he could find out more about this odd situation and get to know his forbidding employer, but he wouldn't volunteer information about himself, let her dig as she would. And he would never let her get the upper hand. He had let one woman walk all over him and she had trodden him into the mud.

'Stop it,' said Joseph aloud and wearily. Brooding didn't help, but he was going to keep his mouth shut in future. Perhaps if he worked very hard at it he might find compensations for being jilted. Possibly, if he remained in the wilds of Tasmania, he might avoid the influenza epidemic currently raging in New South Wales. Joseph looked about him. Perhaps, here at Glen Heather, he would find security - for a while.

To Alice's relief, Joseph McKenzie proved an exemplary manager for Glen Heather. He had a wide knowledge of general farming and a natural sympathy with stock. He even appeared to like sheep. Alice didn't know anyone else who actually *liked* sheep. One depended on sheep, bought and sold them, sheared them, crutched, dipped and often kicked them, but *like* them? Nobody liked sheep, except for Joseph. The sheep seemed to sense it, too. Even the most bloody-minded old ewe became civilised when Joseph was there and he oversaw the enormous jobs of shearing and dipping with perfect good humour.

'We can't shear in the winter here,' Alice told him the first week. 'Some farms hereabouts shear in April, but Granny always said that encouraged fly-strike. This way we can dip at the same time.'

Joseph nodded politely. 'You'll need to do it again later, even here.'

'In March,' said Alice. 'The hay has to be in by the end of this month too. I'm afraid we've thrown you into deep water, Joseph, having you start in summer.'

'I can swim,' he said.

Alice glanced at him suspiciously. He was ducking a sheep in the bath of dip as he spoke, and she decided he had rather a strange sense of humour. He had seemed so solemn, glum almost, when he arrived, but now she could never tell if he was laughing at her or inviting her to share the joke. It was unsettling. If he hadn't been such a capable worker, she might have been rather glad to see the back of Mr Joseph

McKenzie. But he *was* capable - even in the matter of the cow.

Alice had always liked cows, and enjoyed milking, but she made a mistake with Bluebell. Handsome and well-bred the Ayrshire might be, but she showed a paranoid lack of trust and had a kick like a kangaroo. Alice always used a leg rope, a heavy bribe of pollard and a lot of discretion when she milked Bluebell, so she was very surprised to enter the cowshed one morning and find her new manager placidly stripping the last few drops from Bluebell's teats. The heifer, moreover, was not objecting.

'I didn't know you could milk,' said Alice in a low voice. It didn't do to speak loudly or suddenly near Bluebell, unless you wanted the morning's milk kicked over.

Joseph looked up at her with a half-smile, the side of his head still pressed against the glossy brown and white flank. 'Grandpa hated milking, so, like it or not, I served my apprenticeship with the bucket and stool.'

'You should have put a leg rope on her,' said Alice. 'This lady can kick you to kingdom come and she puts her foot in the bucket. I reared her from a calf, too, the ungrateful besom.'

'I'll bear that in mind next time,' said Joseph meekly.

'It isn't your job to milk the cow anyway. I do that. It's a restful way to start the morning.'

'I beg your pardon,' he said. 'Will it be putting you out if I carry the milk to the house?'

Alice looked at him narrowly. 'Thank you; I can manage.'

'Then I'll be on my way.' Joseph eased away from the cow and handed the bucket to Alice. 'I like Ayrshires,' he remarked as he left the shed.

'I don't,' she muttered. She was halfway to the house when Flip cast himself against her skirt in a bound of greeting. A wave of warm milk sloshed over the rim of the bucket and streamed down her leg. 'Damn!' said Alice. 'And that, my girl,' she added, squelching uncomfortably to the house, 'is what you get for being ungracious.' Yet what else could she have been? Joseph McKenzie was so self-sufficient that if she gave him an inch he would take two miles and hang her with the slack.

She told her woes to Isobel when she made her weekly visit on her way home from Kirk. 'He's so efficient, Granny,' she complained. 'He makes me feel a neophyte.'

'Aye, but you'd not be contented if he were a muddler,' said Isobel.

'He is too efficient. He is thrawn.'

'Likes his own way, does he? Tries to tell you what to do?'

'No,' said Alice, puzzled. 'He doesn't. But he only ever needs to be shown once, and that just doesn't seem natural. And he likes sheep. And he can milk Bluebell without a leg rope and-'

'He sounds a fine investment, child,' said Isobel.

'Hmm,' said Alice darkly.

'I suppose he knows the position? That you do not own Glen Heather?'

'Yes.'

Isobel nodded. It seemed to her that Alice might have met her match in this Joseph McKenzie, but what *kind* of a match, it remained to be seen. It could be love, it could be war, or it could be utter disaster. Only time would work this out, and perhaps there would be no time - if someone claimed Glen Heather.

Alice found herself treasuring each task in its season, always aware that she might be performing it for the last time. Joseph was efficient, as she told Isobel, but he was uncertain about the peculiarities of the district. He and Alice fell into the way of spending an hour or so each evening comparing notes, looking back over the records of previous years and making short-term plans. They could plan nothing beyond the next season, for by then the management of the property might have passed to other hands. Joseph never asked whose hands these might be, and Alice never volunteered the information. It seemed so ridiculous to say she did not know. She found she liked him very well, but she was always on her guard.

Not everyone liked Joseph. Rosalind, particularly, was inclined to be hostile. 'There's something strange about the new man; he talks like a gentleman, so what is he doing working here? I wonder what he was doing before the war?'

'Something in Hobart, according to Alice.'

'I think we ought to find out.'

Mary was surprised at her persistence. 'The man does his work, that ought to be enough,' she said. 'Alice seems satisfied.'

'Alice! So long as he professed admiration for her precious Glen Heather, Alice would be satisfied with Kaiser Bill! You know and I know she is wasting her time.'

'That will do,' said Mary, but she was hardly attending. Robert had left her quite well-to-do, and she looked forward to moving to a suitable establishment near her sister in Launceston as soon as they were able to leave.

Joseph had been at Glen Heather for nearly a month when Mr Bertram called to see Alice. 'I hear your new employee is an admirable man,' he said.

'I think so,' said Alice. 'Have you any news on the - the other matter?'

'Not as yet,' said Mr Bertram. 'I gather that is not unwelcome?'

'It *is* unwelcome,' said Alice fiercely. 'I want it settled, Mr Bertram.'

'Jamie Campbell,' said Mr Bertram precisely, 'seems to have disappeared. I have examined shipping lists and advertised in the mainland papers. It appears he has not married, committed a crime, nor left these shores. At least not in the past fifty years.' He polished his spectacles. 'It is an enigma. We should probably forget Jamie Campbell and concentrate our search in Scotland. Perhaps your great grandfather had brothers who may yet be traced...'

'Can we not simply break the entailment?' asked Alice miserably.

Mr Bertram looked at her sternly. 'Not until every avenue has been explored could I countenance that. And yet - matters might not be so difficult as they seem.'

He did not elaborate, but late in the January of 1920, Alice found out what he meant. Samuel Garland presented himself at Glen Heather and requested a private interview with Mary. The two emerged from the drawing room, smiling and obviously well pleased with one another. Rosalind, who had been lurking outside, came in on cue and accepted a motherly kiss and some tears from Mary.

'Well, Sister Alice, are you going to congratulate me?' asked Samuel, beaming at her through his spectacles.

'Of course!' said Alice cordially. 'Welcome to the family, Samuel. We are delighted to ... I mean, we hope you and Rosie will be very happy.'

'I'm sure we shall be,' said Samuel with satisfaction.

Alice turned to Rosalind. 'I am very happy for you, my dear,' she said stiltedly.

The pair went off presently to acquaint Samuel's parents with the news and Mary sighed. 'Samuel is a fine young man and a good match, if not a brilliant one,' she told Alice. 'Your father would have been pleased at the way things are turning out.'

'I think you are right,' said Alice thoughtfully. 'It *is* a good match. Samuel must know Rosie by now, but he's fond of her just the same. Maybe he'll be able to joke her out of some of her little ways.' Mary looked at her blankly. 'Was that not what you meant, Mother, about it's being a good match?' teased Alice.

'There is that, of course,' said Mary with a reluctant smile, 'but that was *not* what I meant, and well you know it, Alice Campbell! Fetch me some writing paper, if you would. They wish to be married this year and so I must begin planning at once. Samuel is a reliable young man and I am sure Rosalind will wish to be married from Glen Heather.'

Alice turned away. 'I hope that will be possible.'

'You should not take this so hard, Alice,' scolded Mary. 'If I warned you once, I warned you a thousand times. "Don't get too wrapped up in the place," I said, but no, you would never listen, would you?'

'No, I would never listen,' said Alice wryly. 'But you never told me everything. You never really explained, did you Mother? None of you did. Not you, or Dad or even Granny. So I made myself a world and now it's fallen apart.' She moved to the window and looked out across the stable yard. A single lamp glowed down the hill in the workman's cottage. 'It's the waiting that's so hard to bear,' she said. 'Mother, what if the new owner doesn't care for the land? You have only to look at Scarborough to see what could happen.'

'There's nothing we can do but wait and see,' said Mary.

'So here we stay as caretakers until Mr Bertram finds a Campbell who was lucky enough to be born male. Mother - this could go on for years!'

'So it could,' said Mary brightly, 'but Rosalind is getting married, and no doubt she and Samuel will have a family.'

'No doubt they will,' said Alice listlessly, and bit her lip.

If Rosalind married and had a child, it might be a son. And if no other heir turned up ... such a baby might fulfil the criteria of the entailment. Alice looked at that thought and tried to feel pleased and relieved, but all she could find in her heart was a gathering apprehension.

Mary spent February making plans for Rosalind's wedding. And, with increasing frequency, she reiterated her hopes for a grandchild the following year. This from Mary, who had been so annoyed when Alice had mentioned Hannah's pregnancy! Alice was torn between laughter and dismay. 'Mother, they're not even married yet!' she expostulated.

'These things should not be too long delayed,' said Mary. As I am in a position to know. *This* time, there must be no mistake.'

'Why do you mind now about Glen Heather, Mother? You would prefer to live in Launceston, would you not?'

'But *you* would like to stay, if it could be managed.'

Would she? Alice was afraid to hope. Afraid a Campbell cousin would arrive in the next few months, to take up life-long tenure and pass the property on to his own heir. Conversely, she was also afraid a Campbell cousin would *not* arrive. She knew Rosalind and Samuel would never turn her out, but could she stay on as *their* pensioner? As steward for Rosalind's son? She had an unpleasant feeling that she would dwindle into a maiden aunt, running the household while Rosalind socialised and produced a flourishing family of children. One of them would inherit Glen Heather.

The intensive work of shearing was finished, and late February brought more peaceful concerns. The permanent workforce, now united under the direction of Joseph McKenzie, became occupied with general maintenance work on fences and buildings. Alice worked with the men; not because her presence was needed, but simply to be busy. She no longer enjoyed the morning milking, because even the restless fidgeting of Bluebell, made more irritable than usual by the thronging black flies, gave her too much time for introspection. Over and again, her hands would lose their steady rhythm and the milk flow would become uneven, spurting in tune to her darting thoughts.

'If it could all be finished, over, today, I'd know for sure, she thought. I could hand over the property and go. Away. Anywhere.'

She could move to the cottage with Isobel and Jennie; but Isobel was old, so the refuge would be likely to prove a short one. And how could she bear to live on the edge of things, knowing what went on, yet no longer a part of it? How had Isobel borne it when it had happened to her? But Isobel had not had to bear it. She had married James Galbraith and gone away to a new life in New South Wales.

One early March morning Alice settled on her milking stool as usual. It was a sultry grey day and the flies were bad, drugged and sticky, settling in black sheets on anything warm and damp. Alice blew at them irritably and Bluebell kept up a constant cranky stamping, a quivering of skin, an angry swishing of her tail. Alice swore as the coarse tassel hit her across the face, and raised her arm to blot her stinging eyes. The Ayrshire shuddered again, and kicked out, catching Alice a solid blow on the shoulder.

In seeming slow motion, the stool wavered and tipped, and Alice was sprawled onto the thinly strawed floor of the shed. Furious, she planted both hands in the mucky straw to lever herself upright, and Bluebell, startled by the noise, kicked out at the bucket with one hind hoof and planted the other squarely on Alice's outspread left hand. There was a moment of numbness, and then Alice cried out against the grinding pain. She tried to drag her hand away, and Bluebell twisted, pivoting on the same hoof. Alice screamed, but it seemed an age before the heifer plunged and she was able to roll away and prop herself against the cowshed wall. She cradled her injured left hand in her right and closed her eyes.

'Miss Campbell? Are you there? Miss - oh!' The voice cracked with amazement and Alice looked up into the round blue eyes of Timothy Jenkins. 'You all right, Miss Campbell?'

Do I look all right? When she tried to say it, no words came out.

'Gee!' Timothy took in the pool of spilled milk and muck, the fallen bucket and stool. His mouth opened, and he shot out of the cowshed. Alice bit her lip. Damn the lad! If he couldn't do something practical, why had he come at all? Now everyone would know of her carelessness. Mary would fuss and Rosalind would curl her lip - she must get up immediately. It would never do to be found collapsed like a rag doll against a wall.

A dull, sick ache had replaced the first sharp pain, so Alice got up, annoyed to find herself shaking with reaction and shock. A nice situation! Isobel had stoically borne the pain of a shattered thigh; here was her grand-daughter falling to pieces over a trodden-on hand! Dully, she heard the approaching Timothy's voice, full of importance. 'Looks in a bad way, fair about to pass out! Must o' hit her head, I reckon. Shall we call the doc?'

Alice pulled a face. Too late. Timothy had already run his unwanted errand of mercy.

She composed herself to face Mary or Hannah, but it was Joseph McKenzie whom Timothy had fetched. 'Are you all right, Miss Campbell?' he asked formally.

Still shaking, Alice nodded, gesturing towards the cow.

'Tread on you, did she?'

Again, Alice nodded. Joseph released Bluebell and sent her out of the shed, then pulled up a hay bale. 'Better sit down,' he advised.

Alice sat, feeling the sharpness of the straw through her summer skirt. She nursed her hand and wondered where her voice had gone. In a moment, Joseph would be demanding explanations and she was afraid nothing would come out. And whatever respect he had for her as an employer would be gone, if it wasn't already. Sheer carelessness to have forgotten the leg rope. And to let her mind roam like that - she was lucky she hadn't been kicked in the head. Almost, she wished it *had* been Mary who had come. So much for keeping the upper hand!

Joseph reached out and took her gently by the wrist. 'Is it broken, Miss Campbell?'

It took an enormous effort of will to unclench the right hand from the left, but she managed it and looked down at the mess of dirt and blood that oozed from her crushed knuckles. Her fingertips pulsed, seemingly twice their normal size, and her whole hand felt as if it had been smashed with the back of an axe. But she didn't think it was broken.

'Can you move your fingers at all?' asked Joseph.

I'd rather not try, thought Alice, but she made an obedient effort and the fingers straightened. More blood oozed out, and she drew in a shaky breath.

'Good!' Joseph sounded so fatherly that Alice felt a hysterical giggle bubbling up in her throat, but his next words wiped away a desire to laugh.

'When you feel up to it, I'll take you to the house. You ought to have that cleaned up, Miss Campbell. There could be lockjaw about.'

He would take her to the house? And hear Mary scolding and Rosalind exclaiming her disgust? Alice found her voice. 'No,' she said.

'Come over to the cottage and we can clean it up there, then,' he said equably. 'But first, I'll go and tell young Timothy all's well. He had you at death's door, silly lad.'

Alice nodded. She felt very small indeed. Such a fuss over a minor injury! What must Joseph, who had seen such ghastly wounds during the war, be thinking of her now? The shaking died away, and she leaned wearily against the wall. There was no point in stoicism now.

Joseph dealt unhurriedly with Timothy, and then returned to tidy up. 'Shall I do the milking for a few days, Miss Campbell?' he asked, as he pitchforked away the soggy straw and hung the stool on its nail.

His face was perfectly solemn, so after a moment Alice nodded shamefacedly. 'Thank you, Joseph. It was my own fault, you know. Bluebell hit me in the eye with her tail and I leaned back ... I should sell her I suppose, or use her for a nurse cow. She's a menace.' She rose to her feet and followed him down to the cottage.

She had not been inside since the day he had arrived, and was a little disconcerted to find that it hadn't changed. The only personal touch was a photograph of a sweet-faced, elderly woman; presumably his mother. The sparseness argued a sense of impermanence even greater than her own, which was his own business, of course ... He waved her to a chair and bent to put more wood on the stove, then filled two basins from the still-warm kettle and set it back on the stove. 'I expect you could do with a cup of tea, Miss Campbell?'

'Thank you.' Alice sat primly in the straight-backed chair, feeling like a visitor. She wondered if she should comment on the weather, but instead found herself watching apprehensively as Joseph wet a clean rag, then tipped salt into one of the bowls and pushed it towards her. 'Better put your hand right in, Miss Campbell. Let some of that muck soak off.'

There was no putting it off while he was watching, so Alice slid her hand into the bowl, biting her tongue to hold back an exclamation of renewed pain. She was damned if she'd act the weakling now.

Joseph took her chin in one hand. 'I'll just clean your cheek a bit, if you'll allow me,' he said.

I can't very well stop you, thought Alice indignantly. He was treating her like a child. Aloud, she said brightly; 'A bit mucky, is it? Bluebell's not particular where she puts her tail.'

Joseph grinned appreciatively, and applied the cloth. 'A sort of tiger-striped effect. A big graze, too.'

'I expect that happened when I hit the ground,' said Alice. 'I didn't notice much after she trod on my hand.' Wincing, she lifted her hand from the water and examined it. 'Give me the cloth,' she said.

'Aren't you left handed?'

'Yes, unfortunately,' said Alice. 'My sinister streak, Miss Llewellyn used to say.'

'Then I'll attend to that too.' Joseph grasped her wrist and began to swab the muck away from the undamaged skin, working towards the oozing wounds. Rather than look at the mess Bluebell had made, Alice kept her gaze on Joseph's bent head. The white lock stood out in relief against the black of his hair, and she wondered if the texture felt any different. She had actually drawn breath to ask when the cloth touched a particularly sore spot and she gasped instead.

'Sorry,' said Joseph. 'That's the worst bit.'

I knew that without looking, thought Alice. *Damn* you, Bluebell! She closed her eyes, wondering what had got into her. She never asked personal questions as a rule. Nor did she usually show pain. It was that time of the moon again, and she was always a little edgy.

'Miss Campbell?'

She opened her eyes with a start to find him looking at her apprehensively. 'I'm sorry?'

'So am I. Soak your hand in the other basin while I make the tea. Kettle's boiling.'

'Tea as well as sympathy,' said Alice dryly. 'Thank you very much.' She gave a little laugh to hide her embarrassment.

'Not at all. Weak or strong? Sugar? I suppose it would be tactless to offer milk?'

'Very.' She took the mug awkwardly in her right hand. Some of the tea slopped over her skirt, adding a new stain to the muck and milk and stray bits of straw. 'I suppose I should go and change,' she said, sipping the hot liquid. 'I hope I haven't held you up too much with my foolishness,' she added as she set down the empty cup.

'I did have an appointment with the boss,' he said, 'but in the circumstances she might not mark me tardy.'

Alice smiled uncertainly and went out, leaving Joseph to empty basins and wash two cups. She had no idea what he was thinking, but she was afraid her stock had tumbled to an all-time low.

Joseph was equally uncomfortable about what had happened. He'd had a certain wary respect for Miss Campbell from the day they'd met, but he had been used to seeing her as a sexless figure who happened to be his boss. He still offered her the courtesies on which his mother would have insisted, but it didn't surprise him when she turned them aside. She was Miss Campbell of Glen Heather; he was Joseph McKenzie from nowhere special. No doubt she considered him in something the same light as her sheepdogs - useful but nonessential. She would turn him off without a second thought if it suited her purpose.

It was common compassion for her painful hand which led him to invite her to the cottage, but once there he should have brewed the tea and let her tend to herself. He should *not* have bathed her hand and he should never have touched her face. He would not have done so with another man, and to have done so with her implied a relationship they did not have and an awareness of her gender he had better not develop. If she once suspected he felt anything but mild respect things could become very complicated. If he ever *did* come to feel anything more it would be even more complicated. There was no reason why he should do so, but he felt the uneasiness all the same.

CHAPTER 40

Alice made it up the stairs without hindrance. Undressing was difficult, for one hand was quite useless, already puffed to almost twice its natural size. She'd be awkward for days now, but at least Joseph was around to deal with the milking. Joseph. Struggling with her waistband, Alice shook her head. Joseph was so very efficient in everything he did. It seemed that nothing discommoded him; not a tetchy cow, nor a dramatising boy, or even a trodden-on employer. If only she could be as phlegmatic, she could save herself a lot of grief.

She tidied her hair and wrapped her hand in some muslin, then scooped up the soiled clothes. She was on her way down to the wash-house when Mary met her on the stairs. 'Where have you been, Alice? You missed breakfast!'

'We had a small mishap in the cowshed.'

Mary sniffed pointedly. 'By the smell of those clothes, it was more than a *small* mishap. Alice, have you no sense at all? And what have you done to your hand?'

'Oh - skinned my knuckles,' said Alice.

'Then you ought to be more careful.'

'Don't worry, Mother, I shall be!'

She went out as usual at evening milking time, and leaned on the bail as Joseph milked Bluebell. She felt she ought to say something, to get their relationship back to normal, but in the end it was he who spoke. 'Dipping again soon, Miss Campbell? And shall I carry the milk in now? I'd like to look at those records in the office, if I may.'

She reached for the bucket, but her hand gave a warning throb. 'Thank you Joseph,' she said. 'Please do.'

She found the relevant records and gave them to Joseph, then took herself off to get ready for dinner. She was late, as usual, so she fetched her own meal from the serving hatch. Raised voices from the dining room made her pause. Presumably Mary and Rosalind were disputing some point about the wedding. Alice sighed. She had a sudden extraordinary wish to go and eat her dinner with Joseph instead. She was tired of Rosalind's wedding. Maybe her mother was right and she was an unnatural sister, but she found the details of dress, music and guest list quite uninteresting. To listen to Rosalind and Mary discussing them was bad enough, to hear them quarrelling about them would be insupportable. 'Damn!' said Alice quietly. The door of the dining room was ajar, and she looked in cautiously through the gap.

'I tell you I won't!' Rosalind was crying in a high voice. '*No*, Mother, don't interrupt! Let me say my piece for once! I have gone along with you on everything else, and we have agreed you may make your home with us if you wish, but that home will be where it suits me. And I tell you, we shall *not* be living at Glen Heather! Glen Heather is nothing to me!'

'If you have a son, Glen Heather will be his,' said Mary. 'Like it or not, it will be his inheritance, just as it was your father's.'

'So we'll put a tenant on it!' cried Rosalind. 'Someone with no stupid, outmoded ideas of heritage and all that old slush! Places like Glen Heather are done, played out, finished. Nobody cares any more for this Big House rubbish except for a bunch of country loobies without even the sense to take the straw out of their mouths. If I had *my* way, I'd sell off the timber now, as Uncle Whit has done. Sheep! Who wants sheep? Sheep are a greasy pain!'

'What of Alice?'

'What *about* Alice? That is all I hear! I tell you, I am *sick* of Alice! Dad's little helper, making a martyr of herself for nothing! Look at her now, out there doing something to a sheep or a cow - why doesn't she have the men do it? That's what they're paid for! But no, Miss Wonderful Alice Campbell has to shove it down our necks that we're sitting in here while she's slaving in the heat. That bandage - oh, I'm *so* sorry for her! Hurt her hand, did she? Well if she hadn't been out there pretending to be a man, it would never have happened. I cannot *bear* the way she goes on, smelling of manure, probably rolling in the hay with that precious manager of hers - so much for prim and proper Alice! I've seen the way she looks at him and I tell you, Mother, it makes me *sick*!'

'Rosalind, you do not know what you're saying!' said Mary coldly.

'Of *course* I know what I'm saying!' howled Rosalind. 'I'm talking sense for the first time! Let Alice look after herself. I won't do it.'

The plate began to slide from Alice's numb fingers and she caught it in her bad hand, biting her lip hard to avoid a cry of pain. Mechanically, she returned the plate to the serving hatch, and spread a clean cloth over the food. She turned to go upstairs, but hesitated. She might as well know for sure. Perhaps Rosalind had been talking through her hat.

On lead-weighted feet, she entered the dining room. Rosalind and Mary turned to face her, their recent quarrel visible in both flushed faces. 'Hello Mother, Rosie,' she said. She intended to sound normal, but her voice came out tight and cold.

'Alice,' said Mary. She sounded a little embarrassed and Rosalind, her eyes still stormy, said nothing. Rage became Rosalind, but all it did to Alice was to make her look ill.

The silence was unbearable, and Rosalind was drumming her fingers. 'I suppose you heard that,' she said with a little laugh.

'I could hardly fail to, since you were shouting at the top of your voice.'

Rosalind gave a tiny shrug. 'Then you know where we stand and I, for one, am thankful. I am tired of pretending for you.'

'Then what -' Alice felt her throat closing and she could scarcely speak. She licked her lips and tried again. 'What are your plans for Glen Heather, Rosie, if - if you have a son?'

'You must see, Alice, that I would have to consider the best options,' said Rosalind importantly.

'Then surely - surely the best option would be to live here, and bring up your child as we were brought up?'

'No,' said Rosalind. 'I would sell the timber and have Samuel invest the money. That would be sufficient to give any child a fine start in life. One man could see to the place then, if we kept just a few of the sheep. No need for all these wages.'

'But what about Glen Heather?' asked Alice. 'It would run to ruin.'

'What *about* Glen Heather? It is a piece of land, that's all, and where's the ruin? Cleared, it would be useful for all manner of things.'

'For what?'

'For growing crops, for ...'

'Rosalind, you must know you cannot grow crops on stone!' said Alice, 'and stone is all that would be left if you let them take the trees.'

'Uncle Whitaker—'

'Uncle Whit grows crops on the flats, and has a poorer yield year by year. The mountain is almost bare.'

Rosalind shrugged. 'I wouldn't want any child of mine to be a farmer,' she said. 'Our son - if we have one - will follow Samuel into a profession.'

Alice looked into her sister's face. She had always felt a certain baffled but deeply rooted affection for her younger sister, and had assumed it was reciprocated. Now she saw she was mistaken. Rosalind did not care a bit for her, and probably never had. 'Does Samuel know what you intend to do?' she asked.

For the first time Rosalind's certainty wavered, but then her pink mouth curved into a smile. 'Oh, Samuel will do what I want,' she said gaily. 'He has told me over and over he is in no way interested in farming. In fact - in fact, he would rather we were not troubled with it at all.'

.'I see,' said Alice blindly. She nodded to her mother and went upstairs to her room. The window square was a faint grey and the mountain was a shadow against the sky. Alice took off her shoes and skirt and looked down at herself indifferently. She removed her blouse and, shivering slightly in her chemise, climbed into bed. She couldn't sleep, and she didn't expect to. Her hand throbbed hotly and she tucked it into the other one against her ribs for comfort. Round and round like mice her thoughts skittered, up and down. 'Oh Rosalind, how *could* you?' whispered Alice. She turned her face into the pillow, soft with the feathers of Glen Heather geese, and cried.

After a while she felt calmer. Of course Rosalind didn't really hate her. She had said all those things to Mary because she had been hitting out blindly in a rage. Mary must have been nagging her - and Mary *could* be very provoking. And then later she had stuck to her story to save face before her mother.

'But,' whispered her common sense, 'she didn't know you were listening, at first. You don't say things just to hurt if your target is out of range. There's no point.' So Rosalind *had* meant what she said - and what's more, she had been saying it over and over since childhood, if only Alice had troubled to listen. It was always Alice who rode the brae and tended the sheep with her father, never Rosalind. It was always Alice who listened to Isobel's tales of the past, never Rosalind.

Alice wiped her eyes. She wanted to run like a child to be comforted, but there was no-one to understand. Hannah disapproved of the way she felt about Glen Heather, and Mary was no help. Isobel was half an hour away, and what comfort could Isobel offer, after all? She had lost Glen Heather herself, and left it behind to marry her James. But Alice had no long-time beau, waiting patiently for his lady.

For the first time in years, she longed for old Bob. He had been her friend and companion, her comfort when Mary snapped, when the arrival of the baby Rosalind supplanted her. Bob adored her, and it seemed pitiful that the one love of her life had been a dog. Stop it! thought Alice. Stop wallowing! So Rosalind doesn't like you and Mother pities you. You've known that for years. When Rosalind has a son, he will own Glen Heather, unless someone turns up to claim it first. You knew that too. A child of Rosalind's will be a Campbell, by blood if not by name. A Campbell is the proper heir for Glen Heather.

'*Places like Glen Heather are done, played out*,' mocked Rosalind's voice in her mind.

No son of Rosalind's would be brought up to love and respect the land as she had been, as Robert had been, as Grandfather John had been. A son of Rosalind's would regard Glen Heather as a source of income, to be stripped of its living wealth rather than nurtured in perpetuity. Rosalind would see to that.

Alice lay watching the square of window grow dim. Her hand had swollen more and she had to loosen the bandage with her teeth. It hurt terribly, but in a month or so it would be healed. If only her other problems could be healed as easily!

Towards morning, she slept and dreamed. She sat on the outcrop of the mountain, surrounded by the blooms of crimson heath. Glen Heather spread below her like a tapestry, and in her arms she held a warm bundle, a bundle in which she felt a fierce pride. When she woke in the dark dawn her arms felt empty and her mind was clear. She had the solution to her problem - if only she dared to grasp it. Awed, she went back to sleep until full daylight.

She was late - or she would have been, had she had to do the milking. She dressed clumsily, and went to the veranda to put on her boots. The mountain dithered a little in the early haze. It was going to be very hot. Flip beat a lazy tail in the dust near his kennel and flattened his ears ingratiatingly as she passed. She patted him, and looked up again at the green-mantled mountain. It would be cool up there under the trees, cool and scented with the wildness of the bush. She would like to climb the mountain and leave her life behind.

Perhaps, she thought with a surge of fancy, she could move into Isobel's hut and live the life of a hermit above Glen Heather. Isobel's hut, built for her by Grandfather John - still Isobel's hut, despite the fact that Isobel had not been able to climb the mountain for many years. Robert and Elijah Ward had gone up periodically to inspect and repair the hut, but Alice had not been there for some time. Since her father's death her trips up the mountain had been for necessity, to seek out straying stock, to clear the flumes which carried the water down the mountain of leaves and bark and mud. She had no time for rambling.

She dropped her gaze to the harvested paddocks and enclosures; where the autumn rains would soon make Glen Heather wholly green again. She looked at her wild, untouched mountain and the tamed and tended flats. How she loved it all, how she belonged to it, bone and soul. She couldn't see it go to someone who would regard it as Rosalind did. Her strange, predawn idea had been incredible, but no more incredible than the alternative - that she would let Glen Heather die.

For two weeks Alice went through her routine with outward serenity and inward disquiet. Her hand went from red to purple to yellow as the bruising faded and the lacerations healed. The swelling subsided, and although it still hurt, she was able to write and milk again. She avoided Rosalind and Mary, and all the while her mind was busy, worrying the idea as Flip worried a bullock bone too big to encompass with his jaws. She wanted to consult Isobel, but dared not. Even Isobel would think her mad if she knew what Alice was planning. In her mind she could hear her grandmother's acid tones; *'Child, have you run mad? Sometimes one must simply accept the facts, let go and move on.'*

'And sometimes, Granny,' said Alice in imaginary reply, 'one must simply take the facts and make them match necessity.'

Her solution was obvious, on the surface. Alice must have a son of her own. Why not? If a son of Rosalind could be accepted as heir to Glen Heather, so then could a son of Alice.

Achieving that son was another matter. The route of adoption would not do; to fit the spirit of Great Grandfather Hector's entailment, the heir to Glen Heather must have Campbell blood. She must bear the child herself, but that simply bristled with complications. A child needed a father to exist. She could marry, but with Rosalind's wedding date set for the last week in June there was no time to attract a husband. Even if there were, a husband would be another complication. She had no current admirers, and her only past suitor was Michael Blake, whom she had not seen since before the war. Was it possible that his interest remained? Even if it had not - Michael Blake was a medical man, and sensible. He would not be shocked by her proposition and he might be able to suggest some alternative solution to her dilemma. To find out,

Alice went to visit Annie Llewellyn.

Annie was grey now, thinner and smaller than Mary, but her eyes still held their old expression of restless curiosity. 'How very kind of you to call, my dear!' she said, when Alice arrived. 'Come in, and tell me all the news. So Rosalind is to marry young Mr Garland?'

'Mother is very busy with the preparations,' said Alice mechanically. 'We like Samuel very much. I am sure they will be happy. Miss Llewellyn - I was wondering if it would be possible for me to - to read some of Dr Llewellyn's books? Those pertaining to the internal workings of our bodies?'

Annie's heart went out to her young friend, for the girl looked quenched and pale. Her eyes were red-rimmed and it appeared she had not been sleeping. 'Are you ill, my dear?' she asked abruptly, 'or - or in trouble? Perhaps you should consult the doctor.'

Alice blushed. 'I am not ill, Miss Llewellyn, and not in trouble. At least, not in the accepted sense.'

'Well,' said Annie stoutly. 'I am sure if you had been, you would have borne it with fortitude. But how are things at home?'

'Busy,' said Alice. 'We've been carrying out the maintenance we had to leave undone during the war. So many men went away -'

'Forty per cent of those eligible!' said Annie. 'A remarkable tribute to old England.'

'Yes, all the Jenkins boys but poor Timothy, Arthur Pritchard, at least seven Wards ...'

'The Wards were always a numerous family,' said Annie. She was about to offer another innocuous comment when Alice spoke again. Her voice was carefully casual, but her eyes so anxious it was obvious the answer mattered very much.

'Did - I believe you told me young Dr Blake went to Egypt. Have you heard if he came back?'

'He did indeed,' said Annie gently, 'and he is married to an English lass.'

'Oh. Oh, that is nice.' Alice glanced up and down again, and Annie saw deep, shamed colour staining her cheeks. 'I ought to be going,' said Alice after a moment, and rose to her feet. 'The books?'

Annie led the way into her brother's domain. 'You may find the information you are seeking there,' she said, indicating a shelf of books and periodicals. This is most irregular, and my brother would be displeased ...'

'I shall return everything to its shelf,' Alice assured her. 'And have you not always claimed that ignorance is a thousand times more injurious than knowledge?'

Annie sighed and returned to her work. Trust Alice to turn her own words against her in this fashion!

Alice returned philosophically to Glen Heather. It had been only a faint hope and now it was quite dead. Anyway, she didn't want to marry Dr Blake. He had been a pleasant young man and it would have been ill-done of her to have used him so. Mentally, she cast about the district, but she could not imagine herself approaching any local man. She could have arranged for the servicing of a mare or a bitch without a blush, but this was another matter. Surely there was *some* recourse open to women in her situation?

A lover would be as difficult to acquire at short notice as a husband, and could prove just as much of a complication, so she must handle this in a business-like way. She knew some women were professional whores, and sold their favours for money. Could there be men who did the same? Perhaps, but how did one find such a person? And even if one *did*, the idea was repugnant. She did not want to be pleasured, she wanted a child. A male whore, if such a thing existed, would be willing to accept her money, but would she want the child of such a man? It was now accepted that feeble-mindedness was passed down from father to son, and so, perhaps, was weak moral fibre. It occurred to her that her own moral fibre must be weak as well, or else she would not be considering this idea.

A professional person was not the answer, then. What she needed was an amateur, a pleasant man in need of funds. Not someone she knew, and not a man of her own class, but a person she could trust. In the end, she decided to advertise in the newspaper, just as Mr Bertram had done when appointing a manager, but first she went to visit the solicitor himself and asked for news.

The old man shook his head. 'Part of the problem is that there are many families named Campbell; it is one of the more common names in Scotland. I have followed up information on a number of gentlemen named James or Jamie Campbell, but all have proved to be members of a different family. There is still a faint hope of tracing the family members who remained in Scotland, but I cannot hold out any hope of an early result. The period we are dealing with - prior to your great-grandfather's arrival in New South Wales - is well over a hundred years ago, and the hope of tracing the correct family and finding the nearest remaining relative to Hector Campbell senior is slight. The cost would be great, and the outcome uncertain, so in the circumstances, I believe the answer must lie in a new heir. Since Miss Rosalind is presently embarking on matrimony, we may yet look forward to a happy conclusion.'

Not the one *you* hope for, Mr Bertram. Not if I can help it, thought Alice. For an instant she wondered just how hard Mr Bertram had been searching since the announcement of his nephew's engagement to Rosalind, but she dismissed the suspicion as unworthy. Mr Bertram's integrity was unassailable.

The proper wording for her advertisement was beyond her, but after several attempts she came up with something she hoped would do.

Lady wishes to meet suitable man for confidential proposition. Short term work. Payment negotiable.

It was clumsy, and it was vulgar, but what else could she put? To have couched it in clearer terms might have led to someone trying to sell her a kidnapped child.

Detesting the need for secrecy and stealth, she caught the train to Shepherd Town and posted the advertisement. She used a false name, and arranged to collect replies from the post office there, and then hurried home, feeling ill at the thought of what she had done. Everyone she passed seemed to be watching her slyly, and she felt her wickedness was written in scarlet across her brow. She was tempted to hope there would be no replies at all.

Joseph knew there was something the matter with Alice. Ever since the announcement of her sister's engagement, she had become progressively more tense and silent, and now, in the middle of April, she informed him curtly that she needed to visit Launceston on business and asked if he would drive her to Mole Creek station in the gig. She was drawn and very pale, and he wondered what had happened to make her look so ill. He might have asked, and expressed concern, but she was not very friendly of late. Presumably she had objected to his familiarity when he treated her injured hand. Since then, he had been very careful to offer her nothing but punctilious courtesy, but now, as he watched her walking down the platform to catch the train, he thought she might have been going to her execution.

Alice felt very much as if she were. There just three answers to her advertisement. One was illiterate, another couched in such lurid terms that she shuddered and threw it in the fire. Only the third seemed possible, and she dithered for days before deciding to follow it up. She wrote briefly to the address enclosed, and arranged to meet the gentleman in a teashop in Launceston. She then informed Mary that she was going to Launceston.

'I may be away some time,' she said casually. 'Miss Swan has invited me to visit her, and I may also go to Aunt Emily.' This was a lie, but what was a lie when compared with the enormity of what she planned to do?

Even as she sat in the east-bound train, Alice could scarcely believe what she was doing. She'd had a new suit made for Rosalind's wedding; a narrow skirt that swung some five inches clear of her ankles covered with a hip-length belted jacket to which she had pinned Isobel's white heather brooch. Mary objected strenuously to her wearing this outfit into town, pointing out (with justice) that Alice was bound to pick up smuts and stains, but Alice insisted. Was not Mary forever bemoaning her daughter's old-fashioned skirts and blouses? Now she took off her wide straw hat and set it on the seat beside her and smoothed her hair with both hands. Perhaps she should take Rosalind's advice and wear a shingle; it would undoubtedly be more practical. But what if her wiry, cork-screw hair refused to lie flat? Most likely, thought Alice gloomily, she would look like an unshorn sheep.

As she disembarked at Tamar Street Station, she was greatly tempted to sit down and wait for the next train back to Mole Creek, but it was all for the sake of Glen Heather, so she forced herself to set off along Brisbane Street. She remembered Launceston fairly well from her sojourn at Swan House, but things had changed a good deal since the war. She reached the rendezvous, sat down at a table and ordered tea and scones. Then she gazed out the window, watching bright young women passing on the arms of their escorts. They reminded her of Rosalind, not of herself. A few men passed, but they never glanced her way. It would have been so much easier had she not had to go to the lengths of advertising. So much easier if she had been a woman who attracted admirers. She went to the powder room and re-pinned her hair, eyeing her reflection severely. Her costume was neat and modish; the white heather brooch was as simply elegant as always. She wasn't ugly, or even plain, but she lacked appeal. She wasn't girlish, and she never had been. And yet, Robert had always told her how like Isobel she was, and Isobel had never lacked for suitors. It was very strange. Alice peered into her own deep-set eyes, and saw that they were haunted. And perhaps that was the trouble; she looked too desperate. Women who already had admirers were secure in their own attraction. 'To her who hath, shall be given,' quoted Alice. 'And she who hath not must advertise.' She nodded ironically to her reflection, and returned to her table for more tea.

Every time the bell rang over the teashop door, she glanced up in dread, but those who entered were nearly always ladies or couples. And then the door opened again, and a young man came in. Instead of making his way to a table or the servery, he hesitated, glanced at a pocket watch, and then peered around the teashop as if looking for someone. Alice's heart sank, and she looked down steadily at her hands. If only he would go away ... but instead, he came hesitantly across and paused by her table. 'Miss McCleod?'

Alice jumped nervously and looked up. The young man was dressed in city clothes, somewhat the worse for wear, and his bowler perched rather unsteadily on the back of his head. He wasn't bad-looking, she thought dispassionately, if you discounted the pale, plump hands. He had sandy hair and a moustache, and eyebrows so fair it almost appeared he had none. She stared at him dumbly, and he removed his hat and bowed, holding it to his chest.

It took her three attempts to greet him, and offer her hand, and she felt the tide of blood rising in her cheeks. 'Mr Smith?'

'That's right,' he said. 'Reggie Smith. And you are ...?'

'A - Adelaide,' she said. 'Addie McCleod. Do sit down.' She felt ridiculous, as if she were his hostess.

Reggie sat down, and placed his hat carefully on the table. It was rubbed and shiny and had clearly seen better days, and so, thought Alice, had its owner. He was by no means starved, and nor did he appear to be ill, but he had an air of being down-at-heel, his pale eyes were watery and his hands shook slightly. She could not meet his gaze, so she looked at his hands instead. The nails were bitten and stained with nicotine - but then, her own were not in much better case. She had never joined the new vogue for smoking, but her hands were scratched and the left one still bore shiny pink scars. She cleared her throat. 'I suppose you will be wanting to know what all this is about.'

'You're offering folding money?'

'I am prepared to pay what you require - within reason - if you agree to do as I ask.'

'Then I ain't too particular about the job. What is it you want doing?' He sounded casual, but his hands were shaking more, and he leaned forward suddenly and grasped her wrist. 'Something you don't want known about, I'll be bound.'

'People will know about it, soon enough,' said Alice wryly, removing her hand from his grasp. 'But have no fear; your name will never be mentioned.'

Reggie looked alarmed. 'I ain't killing anyone.'

'I am not asking you to do that,' said Alice. 'Quite the opposite, in fact.' She watched his lips moving as he worked that out. His intelligence did not appear more than moderate, which was probably just as well.

'You want me to make out I'm someone else? Make out I'm your husband, like? Sign some deal for you?'

'Not quite,' said Alice. 'At least, that is almost right. Oh dear.' Her cheeks were burning. 'I need a child.'

'Kidnapping's out.'

'Indeed it *is*.' Alice watched unhappily as understanding dawned in his red-rimmed eyes.

He swallowed and drew in a quick breath, then nodded, twice. 'How much?'

'Ten pounds?' It was all she could afford, without exciting comment at home.

'Well, Miss Addie, looks like you got yourself a deal. You got the money?'

'Yes.'

'You want to do it now?'

She swallowed, but where was the sense in waiting? To make another appointment would involve her in more lies, more deceit and more complication and, most importantly, in more delay. And, from the information she had gleaned from her surreptitious visit to Dr Llewellyn's private library, it appeared that the timing of her cycle was exactly correct. To "do it now" would not guarantee a son, or even a child, but it seemed her best chance. And she could always try again. 'All right,' she said reluctantly. 'Have you a room?'

Reggie laughed. 'You don't want to go there, Miss. It ain't fit for a lady. I daresay you can see I been down on my luck a bit.'

'Nevertheless, it must suffice,' said Alice. 'I cannot go to an hotel without baggage.'

The room, as Reggie had said, was *not* very nice. It was in an insalubrious part of town, and, rather too late, it occurred to Alice that what she was doing was not only wicked but dangerous. Reggie might, if he wished, rob her and leave her for dead.

But of course he would not, she told herself stoutly. It was daylight, and if she screamed there were any number of folk who might hear and come to her aid. She glanced at him as he went to draw the shabby curtains, but there seemed no evil in his face - he merely looked commonplace, tired and rather vapid. She wondered what had brought him to such a case, but did not ask. She had no wish to know more about him than was necessary. She thought his first name was probably the one he had given her, but had doubts that his last name was Smith. Well - her name was not Addie McCleod, either. She wished she liked him better, but she was not here for the pleasure of his company.

Trying not to look around the bleak little room, she took off her hat and laid it on the nearest chair. After that, she stood rigidly, gazing down at the threadbare mat, as Reggie took off his coat and hat. 'Well,' he said uneasily. Alice felt her knees begin to shake, and took a deep breath. The aroma of old cabbage and unwashed linen was making feel ill. Reggie was in his shirt sleeves, and seemed to be waiting impatiently. 'The money?'

'I have it here.' She took out ten pound notes and put them next to her hat. It had seemed little enough to pay for her heart's desire, but now she began to wonder. Reggie picked up the money, counted it and put it away. Then he looked at her uncertainly. Alice waited. She supposed he would kiss her first, but beyond that she had no real expectations. She knew how the thing was done, in theory, but the finer details escaped her. Novels dwelt on warm glances and touching hands, but they were short on kisses, and the doctor's books, although admirably frank, had little to say about what might be called the social conventions of the act.

Reggie stepped forward, and Alice made a huge effort not to retreat. He put his fingers under her chin, and turned her averted face in his direction. His fingers were cold and clammy, and they smelt unpleasantly of stale tobacco. Alice flinched and set her teeth as he put his arm around her, sliding his hand down her side to her hip, and leaned towards her. She felt he was bracing himself; his breathing seemed to be getting faster as if he were excited. Her skin crawled, but that was ridiculous. Kissing was merely a matter of brushing the lips. A formality, really, dutiful or affectionate as one chose. But there was no affection here, and no duty ... merely a shabby affair of ten pounds to pay for the right to hold a piece of land.

'Wait,' she said. Reggie was pulling her closer, so she put her free hand to his chest and pushed. Her knuckles twinged in warning, and instead of falling back as she expected, he was leaning in, grinding her hand back against her own chest. The heather brooch dug into her knuckles and she gasped with pain as his mouth came down on hers. Her exclamation was smothered in the kiss, not a formal brushing of lips but a disgusting sloppy invasion. Appalled, she realised Reggie was putting his tongue, (cold and clammy like his hands) into her mouth. Her gorge rose and she retched, choking. In a minute she would be sick! Reggie seemed to realise dimly that something was wrong, for he let her go and stepped back.

Alice spat into her handkerchief. It was an unthinking gesture, an attempt to rid herself of the disgusting tobacco-and-whisky-flavoured spittle in her mouth, but Reggie took it as a direct insult. His amiable face darkened. 'What's the matter with you?' he asked disagreeably. 'Something you ate? Or are you a tease?'

Alice licked her bruised lips and scrubbed at them with her handkerchief. 'Something *you* ate, or rather, smoked,' she said.

His face flushed an unbecoming crimson, and he jammed his hands in his pockets. 'This was your idea, Miss McCleod. You asked for it, so you've no cause to complain.'

'Do you *have* to kiss me?' asked Alice.

'A fellow needs some encouragement, or else he can't.'

'Not even for ten pounds?' Alice regretted that, as soon as she said it. She *had* asked for this service, and she had paid for it - it was hardly his fault she couldn't face the process itself.

Feeling sick, she knew herself to be utterly in the wrong and was about to beg his pardon when he leaned forward again, put one hand insultingly on her breast, and squeezed. It hurt, quite a lot. 'Well, I can tell you one thing, lady. I reckon you wouldn't have been much fun.'

'You weren't going to do it for *fun*, you were doing it for money!' said Alice tartly. 'Keep it.' She resisted the temptation to rub her maltreated breast, but instead, she picked up her hat and left the room.

Much chastened, and quite unable to face Miss Swan, she spent the night with Aunt Emily and caught the morning train. You are mad, mad! she told herself, swaying in rhythm with the carriage. You have wasted ten pounds on a nightmare. She groaned, putting her face in her hands, grateful she had the carriage to herself. The nightmare could have been so very much worse if she had allowed it to run its course, and she knew now that there were some things she couldn't face, even for Glen Heather.

Perhaps, after all, she would have to leave it to Rosalind, and hope Rosalind would change her mind. Rosalind could not really wish to devastate Glen Heather - Rosalind, who had shared her high country upbringing. But Rosalind had shared everything. Rosalind, too, was descended from lovely Grannie Ness. Rosalind, too, was descended from Auld Hector, the fierce, thrawn Scotsman in the portrait at home. And from Grandfather John and Granny - stalwart folk all, who had loved and moulded Glen Heather. And yet - Rosalind inherited none of that love.

Love can be a curse ... said Isobel's voice in her mind, and Alice sighed. Love *could* be a curse, if it led you to neglect your duty or to commit sins you would otherwise never consider. But what if love were all you had? Then that was just your own bad luck, thought Alice. She had been very, very foolish and now she must give it up.

She had not said when she'd be back, but Joseph decided to meet the morning train, just in case. He might have sent Timothy instead, but he had nothing pressing to do and perhaps she needed company. Alice was disembarking when he arrived, remote and withdrawn.

'Hello Joseph,' she said vaguely.

He offered his hand to help her into the gig, but she ignored it, and settled herself without comment. Her costume was not as fresh as it had been, but as she stretched out her legs he noticed with some surprise that she had an attractively turned ankle. Somehow, since she wore long skirts and boots every day, he would have expected her to have cart-horse legs. She might be rather handsome, he thought, if she was happy. He suppressed that thought quite ruthlessly and clucked to Blackwood.

'Satisfactory trip, Miss Campbell?' he asked politely.

'No,' she said softly. 'Not in the least.' Then she seemed to shake herself. 'Joseph, have you ever done something you shouldn't have done and had it blow up in your face?'

CHAPTER 41

It was three weeks later that a fierce autumn storm tore across the tiers, sluicing the brae with rain and bringing down trees in its wake. Such storms had always been part of Glen Heather, and Alice knew the damage they could cause. One had brought about Isobel's injury, forty years ago, and in the wake of another her grandfather had died. The mountains were beautiful, but danger was never far away. More prosaically, mountain storms caused considerable nuisance. The rain would have done no harm, but Alice was not so sure about the wind. The barn roof was damaged, and what had it done to the fences?

Crutching and drenching was necessary in any case, so Alice decided to have the sheep brought into the yards. She would also have Joseph send some of the men around the boundary fences. There were too many pits in the limestone to allow the sheep free range in the bush, and the rams must soon be joined to the ewes in proper ratio. Alice sighed. The seasons had no business to move on so quickly, when every one might be her last at Glen Heather. She went to fetch Bluebell into the shed and discovered something else. The yard pump was useless. Alice pulled a face as the handle moved too easily in her grasp. The pressure was way down.

'Trouble, Miss Campbell?'

Alice jumped. 'Good morning, Joseph.' She waggled the pump handle in explanation. 'A tree must have come down across our water supply. We'll have to send someone up the mountain after breakfast to get rid of it.'

Joseph raised an eyebrow. 'I don't doubt your word, Miss Campbell, but it'd take a pretty big tree to cut off one of those creeks.'

'Not the creek, the flumes. My great grandfather laid them as a sort of artificial creek bed to act as a gutter in places where the creek would naturally disappear down a hole in the limestone. If one is damaged or dislodged, we have no water in the yard.'

'I'll see to it,' said Joseph.

'Send two of the men. They know where to look, and it's a dangerous job for one man. If a new tree falls on the mountain - well, you've heard what happened to my grandmother.'

'I would prefer to see to the job myself. The others can start on the barn roof.'

Alice felt a stirring of unease. In the depths of her misery, she had hardly noticed Joseph McKenzie, but over the last week or two she had begun to realise that her inattention was a mistake. She looked up, aware that he was considerably taller than she. 'Independence, Joseph?'

Joseph met her gaze steadily. 'If you like to call it that, Miss Campbell. I believe in doing things myself.'

Alice nodded slowly. She felt much the same way, but she was still uncomfortable with this new insubordination. It seemed all of a piece with a certain lack of courtesy she had lately detected. Thinking back, she felt that it dated from her ill-starred trip to Launceston - or perhaps even from her accident in the cowshed. Somehow, she was losing Joseph's respect, and the thought was disturbing.

'On the other hand,' said Joseph suddenly, 'perhaps it isn't independence but simply a desire to see this inventive piece of bush plumbing.'

'Which is it?'

A smile lit Joseph's usually expressionless face. 'Take your pick!' Then the lightness was gone as if it had never been. 'I shall need a guide. I'm not familiar with the mountain, as you say.'

Alice frowned. 'I shall come with you.'

'*You*, Miss Campbell?'

'*Me*, Joseph. I've been climbing this mountain since I was seven years old. I am also quite capable of manual labour when I reach the top.'

'I don't doubt that,' said Joseph, peering up the mountain. 'The question is, shall I be?'

Alice hurried through the milking, then returned to the house to stoke the fire and make tea. While it brewed, she put provisions in her satchel, then dressed in her warmest skirt and took Robert's old oilskin from the boot cupboard under the stairs. She added spare clothes to the bundle; clearing the creeks was cold, wet work and she didn't want a chill. She drank her tea, ate a heel of bread and dripping and left the house before Mary and Rosalind were abroad.

Joseph was by the stables, talking to the men. Despite his recent coolness, Alice still liked and trusted him, but it was not the pleasure of his company that drew her to the mountain today. It was the place itself. She knew it would be beautiful, tinkling and murmuring with tiny waterways and steaming richly in the sun. The light would be refracted from a million raindrops and the dazzle would shine like gems. There would be flowers on the mountain; not the golden blossom of springtime, but the lesser blooms of autumn. And perhaps the heath would be in blow. Alice had always loved the heath. Not only was it a flower of the cold weather, but it seemed to symbolise her life. It might look grey and spiky at times, but the time would come when it would explode into bells of pink and white, and some of it would be crimson.

Crimson heath! Grannie Ness had painted it in her delightful "wee books", Grandfather John had given it to Isobel when their only child was born. It didn't last long when picked; to appreciate its full glory one must climb the mountain to the places where it grew.

She waited by the pump while Joseph took his leave of the men, impatient to be gone. Joseph looked up enquiringly, so she said; 'Bring spare clothes. This is a wet job.'

Joseph fetched a bundle from his cottage and they tramped across the lower paddocks and up the hem of the mountain. 'We could ride up, normally,' said Alice, 'but the brae will be very slippery and the horses don't like it. You can see where the burn ought to be if you look down there. It's worn a deep bed for itself since my grandfather's day - incidentally, a burn is a creek. It's a family habit to call it that - it's a Scottish word, you know.' She could feel her spirits lifting. Whatever happened in the future, nothing could spoil today.

'Och, aye,' said Joseph. 'Ye're no the only ain wi' the Scots ancestry.'

Alice laughed. 'Awa' wi' ye, McKenzie! The track follows the course of the burn wherever possible, but as you go up it gets more difficult. I hope the blockage isn't too high; the track may be in a bad way after the storm.'

Joseph opened the gate which led from the cleared lower slopes to the bush and stood back until Alice preceded him. 'Where did the creek go originally?'

'Underground, somewhere. The mountains are riddled with caves. My grandfather found some when he was a laddie, but most of them were only pits in the limestone, or else full of water. There is one called Scotts Cave which people explore sometimes, and another called Baldocks - there must be plenty still waiting to be discovered. That's one reason the mountain here was never cleared; my great grandfather - and my grandmother - thought the risk hardly worth the trouble. Just as well, for if you want to know what over-clearing can do, you need only look to Scarborough, my grandmother's old home.' She bit her lip, and pushed away the thought of what might happen. She was going to *enjoy* today.

'Have you ever found a cave, Miss Campbell?'

'No, alas,' said Alice wryly. 'It was one of my ambitions when I was a child, but Dad would never allow me to roam far without him and by the time I was older - well, I was away at school, then Dad had his first stroke and I had enough to do without exploring.'

'Glen Heather is quite a charge on you. Have you no brothers?'

'No, there is only Rosalind and myself. My father used to say I was the Campbell and my sister the MacDonald. But I should not be running on like this. Our family matters cannot possibly concern you, and we'd better save our breath for climbing.'

Anger at this snub rose in Joseph, and deliberately he tried to turn it against himself. *Know your place.* That was an excellent adage and one he would do well to remember, but for a little while his employer had been almost friendly. She had seemed very silent lately, and when she *did* speak it was either on a strictly practical subject or to say something odd. Such as the time she asked if he'd ever done something he shouldn't have done and had it blow up in his face. He'd give a mint to know what she'd meant by that, and why she'd looked so beaten.

Another woman, he thought, would have turned off his impertinent query by asking him something of his own life and times, but he was unsurprised that this woman did not. She had always respected his privacy, and as far as he was aware she had never asked any questions about him. Presumably she was fully occupied with her own affairs, but it was more likely that she simply wasn't interested. Joseph had considerable respect for the exigencies of class and rank. He had seen it in the army, and he had seen it at work at O'Rileys. Those in control had no interest in the personal feelings and backgrounds of their underlings, except in so far as such things might affect their performance.

She was climbing ahead of him now, making good time on the slippery track. Joseph looked thoughtfully at her back. She was very straight and upright and rather tall, and the lamentable clothes she wore concealed her silhouette. He had only once seen her wearing anything that gave an indication of her figure. That was on the occasion of her overnight stay in Launceston, and her misery had masked the salubrious effect of her clothes. Today she looked an utter dowdy, yet still she could make it clear that so far as she and the world were concerned, she was very much his social superior.

Just as he reached this conclusion, she stopped and glanced over her shoulder at him. There was nothing remotely coquettish about her expression, but she was smiling suddenly, as if with some rare delight. Her dark-browed face was glowing, and Joseph felt her attraction as a blow in the pit of his stomach. The careful barricades he had erected wavered as if hit by a high wind. Almost, he smiled back at her, but renewed caution brought on his most wooden expression. She had been about to say something, about to share some private enjoyment of her mountain, but her smile died as his had, and she turned back to the track. Joseph wondered what she had intended to share, but all he could see was a small prickly plant of mountain heath with a few bell-shaped crimson flowers ...

Flowers. It was flowers that had brought that glow to her features, and the knowledge brought a further twist to his gut. She tried so hard to quench her femininity, but it was down there, all the same ... he had a foolish desire to probe further, and set himself to catch her up, but by the time he did so, she had retreated into her thoughts.

They climbed in silence. Sassafras and myrtle, blackwood and gum, man-ferns and native clematis, all grew in a luxuriant tangle, reaching greedily for a share of the sun. The track lay in perpetual green twilight, lit by occasional flashes of gold where the canopy had been damaged by storms. Birds flitted through the branches and the wind sighed, and all about was the sound of water, dripping, trickling and gushing.

'Most of these creeks are temporary run-off after the rain,' said Alice presently. 'We need the one we can rely on in the summer, and the major source of the burn comes from right up among the lakes. There are hundreds of them up on the tiers.' Joseph nodded, and there was silence again, except when Alice stopped to remove a mass of fallen branches from the creek. 'Look,' she said after a time. 'There's one of the flumes. They're iron, so they're inclined to rust, but Dad thought anything else was too difficult. The first ones were made from wood, so Granny says. Of course iron is lighter, but that means it's easily knocked aside. It only takes something heavy ...'

'Like a rock,' said Joseph, whose boot had just dislodged one. He paused, then put out a small verbal feeler, searching for the woman he had glimpsed beneath her dark exterior. 'Have you ever wondered, Miss Campbell, what the underground course is like without its water? Are there "haunted caverns measureless to man" down there?'

He almost held his breath as he waited for her response, but she merely gave him an ironic glance. 'Poetry, Joseph? From you?'

To her surprise, he gave her a strange look, as if she had disappointed him. 'I *can* read, Miss.' He kicked the flume back into place and moved on past her to climb at an increased pace.

Alice found she had to hurry to keep up with him. Presently, a stone turned under her boot, and she stumbled, coming down on one hand on the muddy track. 'Oh ...'

'Say it, Miss Campbell,' advised Joseph, looking down from the next loop of the track. 'You'll feel ever so much better.'

'An evil tongue is the refuge of a weak mind,' said Alice primly. 'Somebody should tell McCleod that.'

'McCleod?' Joseph sounded oddly arrested. 'Who is McCleod?'

'McCleod is my grandmother's cockatoo - a white beastie with an evil eye and a very evil tongue. He has the Gaelic, I believe.' Ruefully, she examined her muddied palms.

Joseph came back down and looked at her with a shadow of apology. 'Are you all right, Miss Campbell?'

He offered his hand, but as usual she ignored it and scrambled to her feet with as much dignity as she could manage. 'Please don't feel obliged to help me, Joseph. I am perfectly capable of looking after myself.'

Joseph's face didn't alter, but his eyes turned cold. 'Again I beg your pardon, Miss Campbell,' he said and turned away. 'Believe me, I shall never offer my hand again - unless you ask for it.'

By the time Alice had scraped the worst of the mud from her skirt, he was out of sight. She climbed more carefully after that, wishing she hadn't been so sharp. For a time there, discussing the habits of mountain creeks and caves, she had been happy. It had been the first real conversation she had had with anyone in a long time. But Joseph seemed strange today. Simmering, she climbed on, her pleasure in the day quite dulled. Now each rain-rimmed branch across the track was an irritant, a trap set to slash her face with the force of Bluebell's tail. The gurgling and muttering of underground water seemed like the sly tattling of gossips now, and the pleasant glow of exercise was replaced by the discomforts of a hot sweaty back, wet feet and the clumsy embrace of a damp skirt.

The track went around a giant gum and bent back on itself like an elbow. It had once been wider here, but another cave-in had forced a narrow path. In the wake of the rain it was even more difficult than usual, but Alice bunched her skirts and clambered up. Just past this section of the track was an outcrop of stone which commanded a good view of Glen Heather and formed a natural resting place for those who climbed the mountain. She was not surprised to find Joseph there, gazing over the flats. Chest heaving with exertion and anger, she slid her satchel from her aching shoulders. 'Joseph, there is absolutely no need for you to wait for me,' she said. 'I told you before, I can climb this mountain with ease.'

Joseph swung round, expressionless as ever. 'So you keep saying, Miss Campbell,' he remarked. 'But we both know it isn't true. How you can climb mountains at all in those clothes is beyond me; since you're determined to be a man in all but fact, why have you not gone the whole way and put on breeches? And why have you not acquired a pipe and a whisky bottle and taught yourself to curse? You are a strong woman, Miss Campbell, and the men respect you for it. I respect you for it. Isn't that enough for you? Do you have to try to be a man?' He had not raised his voice, and he was still sitting in a relaxed pose on the rock, but his expression chilled her. 'Well,' he said affably after a moment. 'Are you not going to slap my face, Miss Campbell? Presumably that's too feminine a reaction for you. Shall I stand up so you can knock me down instead?' He rose and stretched elaborately, but he was still watching her, and she thought he was wary now. Did he really think she might do it?

Alice's left hand itched to strike out as he had invited. But would it be a lady's slap or a man's punch? She hardly knew. As in the situation with Reggie, she felt herself to be sorely in the wrong, but this time it hurt far more. She had really not cared for Reggie's opinion, probably because she shared it.

'Well?' said Joseph impatiently, 'why don't you say something?' Alice shook her head. 'You can do better than that, Miss Campbell. Tell me to mind my own damned business. Tell me I'm discharged from my duties. Say something.'

Alice felt a strange tingling beginning in her fingertips. Her head seemed to be floating a long way from her feet - or was it her feet that had retreated? She swayed slightly, and it occurred to her that she was about to faint. Ridiculous. She had never fainted in her life, and certainly not as the result of a few sharp words. 'Of course not!' she said. Or that was what she meant to say, but something was still wrong with her voice. She took a deep breath and another, and her sight began to clear. Oddly, she seemed to be sitting down, with her cheek on the rough damp serge of her skirt. An arm was around her shoulders, holding her in that position. Alice wriggled indignantly.

'Better keep your head down, Miss Campbell,' said Joseph. 'I don't want to have to carry you down the mountain and I'm sure you wouldn't care for it either.'

Frightened, she obeyed. What had come over her? It was almost like the reaction she had when Bluebell trod on her hand, but that time she had put it down to the shock of pain. She was in no pain this time. Shock, then. Joseph had said cruel things - She raised her head, and the view swam and steadied. Her left side felt warm, and that was because Joseph was sitting beside her on the rock. She could feel the breath expanding his chest ... She gave a little shiver and edged away.

'All right now, Miss Campbell?'

She nodded, and his arm dropped. Alice straightened cautiously, and found her voice had returned. 'I am not in the habit of fainting,' she said stiffly.

'I can quite believe it,' said Joseph. She saw that he was twisting his hat in his hands. That made her feel stronger, a little. 'Shall I leave tomorrow?' he asked.

Alice shook herself, pulling her damp skirt away from her legs. 'Not unless you want to,' she said absently. 'I have never yet sacked a man for speaking his honest opinion.'

'Nor for insulting you?'

'Nobody insults me. Except Reggie, of course, and that was my fault too.' She shook her head, aware she was rambling. Joseph could have no idea who Reggie was - and just as well! 'I had no proper breakfast,' she said more positively. 'It made me light-headed for a moment.' She bent to pick up her satchel. 'You can carry this, Joseph. If I weight you down with mutton chops I may be able to keep up with you without straining my poor little female self.'

There was a small pause. 'Is that all you're going to say?' asked Joseph.

'What do you want me to say?' Her voice sounded brittle. 'Would you like me to break down and tell you I tried to be the son my father didn't have? I could always tell you how lonely it feels when I can't let my guard down, even for a moment, because too many people have warned me I'm not up to this job. They're waiting for me to admit it and turn away. And these people aren't enemies, or even competitors; they're family and friends, the very people I should be able to look to for support. Even my grandmother, who ran Glen Heather herself for twenty years - even she believes I should have turned my back. And so I might have done, if I had known the whole story. But by then I was in too deep.

'I have to depend on myself, you know, because I am all I have. And a few weeks ago I let myself down, very very badly. And now - since then - I have tried to accept it. I am due to lose everything that is dear to me for no better reason than that I am a woman, and so I must take whatever is left to me.' She smiled derisively. 'There! I've gone and told you anyway. You're a dangerous person to have around. Granny warned me to watch my step.'

Joseph put on the satchel, adjusting the straps to accommodate his broad shoulders. 'I trust you really do have food in here as well as your entire wardrobe, Miss Campbell, otherwise I shall be the one fainting from hunger.'

So he was not going to discuss her lapse. Good. Very good. A comforting word and she might have run wailing down the mountain. 'Chops and bread and butter, I have. Tea, of course. Where would we be without chops and tea in the bush?'

'Isn't the ground too wet for starting a fire?'

Alice squelched the toe of her boot into the outcrop's thin coating of soil. 'Much too wet,' she said briskly. 'But there should be plenty of wood in Isobel's hut, along with the spare flumes for the creek, and it's not too much farther to walk.'

Joseph extended his hand, looking at her in a way that made it a challenge.

'You said you'd not offer your hand again unless I asked,' she said. 'And I have not.'

'Come on,' he encouraged. 'You're too much of a gentleman to give me a slap in the face.'

'And too much a lady to knock you down. Damn you, Joseph! You put me in the wrong - again.'

She offered her own hand, expecting him to shake it, but instead he held it in a warm clasp. 'Miss Campbell,' he said, looking down at her, 'you are too soft. You should have sent me packing while you had the chance.'

'I still may,' said Alice warningly. 'If I find you idle, shiftless or dishonest I shall have no hesitation in telling you to go.'

'I'll bear that in mind. You can depend on me, for what it's worth.'

'I know that,' she said steadily. 'I always did know that.'

The question was, she thought as they resumed their climb, what was it she could depend upon him to do?

It took another half hour to reach Isobel's hut, squat and sturdy, but weathered to silver-grey. Alice looked at it with great affection. Apart from the posthumous portrait in the parlour and a gravestone in Mersey, it was the only memorial John Campbell had left to his widow. Her private income had come from her second husband, James.

'Was it a snarers' hut?' asked Joseph, 'or was it built to house the flumes?'

'Neither,' said Alice. 'My grandfather built it for Granny, and they spent a night up here during the first year of their marriage.' She sighed. 'The only year they had, as it turned out. Granny used to come here after he died, she said, trying to make sense of things. Then, around the year I was born, my father and some friends stocked the lakes with trout. Dad used the hut when he went early-morning fishing, and he always said I could do the same one day - but - Dad was ill and the war came. I haven't been here since last spring, so I hope everything's all right.'

She opened the door, having to force it a little. The air inside the hut was still and cold.

'It's not so bad,' said Joseph. 'I've slept in many worse places.'

'We're not going to sleep here,' said Alice. 'Just collect the new guttering. And cook.'

There was plenty of wood, cold but dry, so Alice lit the fire and opened a wooden chest in the corner. 'There's a billy-can and a lantern here, and blankets,' she said, shaking them out to air. 'The weather being what it is, people have occasionally had to bide here longer than they intended.' She saw his smile and said a little stiffly; 'I expect it seems odd to you, climbing a mountain to find a burn and fetch it back home. Unless you did it at Wonthaggi too?'

Joseph dropped a fistful of tea-leaves into the billy and swung it gently before pouring it into enamel mugs. 'Grandfather's spread was flat.'

'Have you ever thought of going back?'

'No. I left it behind long ago. Since then I've worked in Hobart - went directly there when my aunt sold the farm. My father had been on the shearing circuit, and he'd settled down south, but he died just before the war and I went into the army.'

'Hobart's an odd place for a shearer to settle,' said Alice.

Joseph laughed shortly. 'Dad was an odd man. He was passing through and saw a place he liked the look of, and just stopped. Is the tea all right, Miss Campbell?'

'Excellent, thank you, Joseph.' She sat down on one of the sawn logs which doubled as seats and firewood and stretched her legs. Her skirt began to steam. The silence stretched. Alice looked thoughtfully over her mug into the fire, sipping and blowing.

Joseph watched her with a smile. 'A penny for them, Miss Campbell?'

'They're worth no more than a farthing. I was thinking I might take your advice.'

'Oh,' said Joseph. He looked mildly disconcerted and Alice waited. The silence became loud - a battle of wits which Joseph presently and deliberately gave away. 'Which piece of advice is that?'

'The breeches, Joseph,' said Alice gently. 'I really should have some. Granny always wore them. Dreadfully mannish, of course, but then I *am* her grand-daughter.'

There wasn't much he could say to that, so Joseph merely lifted a hand to acknowledge a hit. Out on the outcrop, he had spoken to wound, and out of a queer frustration, but he realised, as he raked the fire and fetched in green wood to replace what they had burnt, that there was a kernel of truth in what he had said. There *was* something of the masculine in Alice Campbell's make-up. In his experience no other woman could have accepted his insults so gracefully. Dorothy would have struck back in instinctive revenge, and his aunt would have delivered little pin-pricks of pain for weeks. But apart from the remark about the breeches, Alice Campbell had shown no animosity.

He wondered what she would look like if she *did* put on breeches. Would she be more masculine still, or would the fitted garments reveal alluring curves? It was an intriguing thought, and a dangerous one. Alice was rinsing the billy-can and scouring the pan with a handful of fern, using her left hand as she always did. It must be awkward to be so out of step with most of the population, but then, Alice Campbell was out of step by more than her sinister orientation. Joseph turned his gaze from her once more, but somehow it kept returning. Exasperated, he turned his back and waited while Alice selected a spare gutter and put the satchel and his pack in the corner of the hut, and when they set off he walked ahead.

The track beyond the hut was overgrown, and it was midday before they found the problem. A small tree had wrenched itself out of the ground, heaving up a great mound of pebbles and soil and tipping the flume to the side. On one side of the blockage the water flowed steadily down the mountain. On the other, there was nothing but a muddy trickle. Alongside the shattered tree, the water rolled in a smooth green wave over a lip of rock and disappeared down a long gullet into the dark.

'You were right,' said Alice thoughtfully, nudging the root-ball with her boot. 'All those tunnels down there in the dark - what would you find there?'

'Tempted to go down and see?' asked Joseph.

'No indeed. Unlike Mr Carroll's Alice, I would never get down the hole. And oh yes, Joseph, I too can read.'

Joseph laughed unwillingly. 'Have you no room for visions splendid?'

'Visions splendid do not clear the creek.'

'Maybe someone should mention that to Mr Paterson,' said Joseph.

The only way to correct the damage was for Joseph to chop the crown away from the trunk of the fallen tree so the branches could be hauled away piecemeal from the water. Alice and Joseph got very wet in the process.

'You can reach for the original gutter now,' said Alice, leaning against one of the still-standing trees. She rubbed back her hair with her sleeve, leaving a muddy streak over one cheek, so clearly, she was leaving it up to him. And after all his hard words, how could he complain?

Joseph pushed his wet sleeves up again and climbed back into the water. Chill and clear, it gushed against his arms as he fought to lift the metal trough clear and replace it.

'It would be this one,' said Alice cheerfully. 'It's the heaviest of the lot.'

Joseph heaved, the end of the flume rose and the jet of water kicked it savagely. A tidal wave splashed up and hit him in the face. Without a word, Alice slid down and joined him in the creek bed. 'Together now,' she said, and they heaved. Alice splashed up and sat on one end of the gutter to hold it in place, while Joseph lifted the downstream end into its proper bed and wedged both ends with boulders.

He grinned with primitive satisfaction and clambered out of the creek. 'Miss Campbell?' He offered his hand, and this time she took it without comment and pulled herself up. The weight of her skirt must have been terrific, for she staggered a little as she climbed onto the bank. Joseph's legs were numb, and his teeth were chattering. 'God, that's cold!' he said with a rueful laugh. 'I can barely feel a thing below my waist.'

'I can't feel my hands,' said Alice.

Joseph rubbed them briskly between his own. 'Can you feel that?'

'I w-wish I couldn't.' She turned away and began wringing some of the water out of her skirt. The drag on the waistband was clearly visible and Joseph wondered what she would do if the fastening gave way. Step out of it and proceed down the mountain in her petticoat, most likely, and wouldn't *that* be a sight? She gave up on the skirt and removed her boots. She was wearing heavy khaki socks, and Joseph had a sudden vision of her knitting comforts for the soldiers and prosaically using up the last of the wool after the war ended. Oddly, he found her shabbiness rather endearing now.

'What now?' he asked hurriedly.

'This is w-where that change of clothes comes in,' said Alice. 'Back at Isobel's hut.'

The fire was almost out, but Joseph built it up again and made more tea while Alice removed her dry clothes from the pack. He picked up his own things and went outside to change, stripping naked without a thought. There was no-one to be offended, and Alice Campbell would not be peeping. He spread his wet clothes on a bush, waited a while, then re-entered the hut, whistling tunefully as a warning.

She was fully dressed, and the dry clothes were no more becoming than the others. Her black hair was wet, and as he watched a drop of water slid slowly down one of the cork-screw spirals and ran down her cheek like a tear. She flicked it away with a careless finger, and the gesture was curiously touching. As if aware of his regard, she looked up, drew breath as if to say something, then visibly decided against it.

'What is it, Miss Campbell?' he asked, a little more abruptly than he intended. 'Are you about to give me my notice after all?'

'I was wondering if you would object if I took down my hair.'

'Now why should I object to that?'

She shrugged. 'You shouldn't, of course, but most folk do.' She lifted her hands and removed the pins holding her bun in place. In another woman, the action could have been consciously seductive, but when Alice Campbell took down her hair, she did just that, shaking her head like a dog coming out of the water. The heavy mass tumbled, and a scatter of droplets flew, several of them landing on Joseph, making him blink in surprise. 'Oh - I'm sorry,' said Alice.

'Think nothing of it,' he said, wiping his face. 'What's a little water between friends?'

The innocuous words hung between them, more true than trite. There were a great many reasons why he should not, but he *did* feel friendship for Alice Campbell. She would be a good bloke, if she were a bloke. As it was - friendship with a woman - especially *this* woman - could be difficult and dangerous and he was by no means sure it was possible. He must put today behind him on their return, and he really should avoid being alone with her again.

She seemed unconscious of his reservations, and pulled the curly mass forward over her shoulders to let it dry. She looked younger with her hair down, and he wondered why she had not had it shingled for convenience. It was no business of his, so he drank his tea, and presently she went out to spread her own wet things to dry.

The clothes were still damp when Alice decided it was time to leave the hut. 'There's a lot to be done,' she said with a hint of apology, as she replaced the blankets in the chest, 'and we ought to be at home doing it, not leaving it to the men.'

Joseph nodded, then watched with a half-smile as she pinned up her hair and tried to force her skirt into the satchel. 'Why not leave it here?' he asked.

'I suppose I could - yes, why not?' With obvious relief she shook out the damp garment and draped it over one of the sawn logs. 'I expect it will be dry by next spring,' she said with a hint of irony. 'Will you leave your things, Joseph?'

'No,' said Joseph. 'I may not be here again.'

'None of us may be here again,' said Alice sadly.

The light was going, the barn was mended and the men gone home when they reached the lower enclosure. Alice was conscious of extreme weariness. 'Joseph, would you like to eat with us tonight?' she asked impulsively. 'You won't feel like cooking.'

Joseph looked at her meditatively. 'You still have mud on your face.'

Alice turned away. He had no need to remind her of her lack of charm tonight. 'You would be most welcome,' she persisted.

'No thank you, Miss Campbell, I don't think so,' said Joseph. He turned abruptly and went into the cottage.

Alice paused to deposit her wet blouse and socks in the wash-house. She tidied her hair, removed the mud from her face and went to the dining room, where Mary was eating alone. 'Evening, Mother,' she said.

'So you've finally condescended to come home.'

'The highest gutter had been knocked out by a tree and it took a while to fix.'

'So you were up on the mountain all day. Who was with you?'

'Joseph,' said Alice.

'The other men?'

'Were needed to mend the barn and ride the fences. Mother, what *is* this? Since when have you had any interest in my work?'

'You were up on the mountain all day,' said Mary, tight-lipped. 'Alone, with this Joe. Alice, have you taken leave of your senses? What will people think?'

'We went up to work, we did the work and came home again. Why should people think anything?'

'It took all day to replace one small piece of iron?'

'*Yes*,' said Alice. 'Unless you choose to count the time we spent eating at Isobel's hut. Nobody will know, if that's what's worrying you.'

'The men know.'

'Well, of course! But they have better things to do than gossip - even if there were anything for them to gossip about. For pity's sake, Mother - look at me!' she added with a spurt of anger. 'Who would gossip about *me*?'

'You might think of Rosalind, if you won't think of yourself.'

Alice became still. 'So we're back to Rosalind, are we?' she said slowly. 'Rosalind's been planting her ideas in your mind. Time was, Mother, when you didn't care what I did, so long as I didn't actually greet your guests covered in manure. I am hardly a young girl, Mother, and I have no desire to please Rosalind, just at present.'

'I care if you act like a wanton.'

Alice blushed hotly, but there was no way Mary could have known about the debacle in Launceston. 'Mother - you cannot think there is anything improper between Joseph and myself. He is a decent man.'

'Decent or not,' said Mary, 'he *is* a man. I am concerned for you, Alice. You have always been so heedless, so headstrong. I would hate to see you in an untenable situation for the want of a little thought. People are always ready to talk about this family. Your grandmother saw to that.'

'What do you mean?'

Mary inclined her head. 'You are very like her, Alice. It has been remarked often. Of course most of the people who matter know you are like her only in appearance, but there are always the ill-natured few who are only too willing to say that *blood will tell*.'

'I beg your pardon?'

Mary sighed. 'Alice, I cannot believe you have remained unaware, all these years, that your grandmother is not at all the thing?'

'I *beg* your pardon?' Alice felt the blood rising in her cheeks, although she had no idea why. 'Granny is perfectly respectable - oh come, Mother, surely you are not dragging up that old tale about her *breeches*?'

'No doubt that was part of it,' said Mary, 'but I am referring to her association with James Galbraith.'

'But he was her husband,' said Alice.

'She married him in the end - but Alice, they were lovers for *years* beforehand. The talk was rife.'

'Not while Grandfather John was alive?'

'Not then,' said Mary darkly. 'Although I believe there was some story about Mr Galbraith and old Mrs Campbell ...'

'*Mother*! This is outside of enough!' cried Alice. 'You are tattling. Exactly like those *ill-natured few* to whom you referred!'

'Not at all,' said Mary stoutly. 'I am explaining that you must be *extremely* circumspect, Alice. More so even than any other woman in your position. There will be plenty of folk who will delight in saying you are as loose as your grandmother. But we shall say no more. Sit down and eat your supper.'

'I have lost my appetite,' said Alice between her teeth.

Seething, she went upstairs. She longed for a hot bath, but for now a sponge-down in tepid water must do instead. How dare Mary malign her grandmother in such a fashion - but as Alice undressed, Isobel's own words echoed in her mind. '*Got yourself a lover, have you? ... Then perhaps you should. There's nothing like it, you know.'* Presumably Isobel had been speaking from experience - and perhaps she had not been using the word in a general sense. Alice shook her head impatiently. Whatever Isobel had done or had not done was in the past, and folk must have long memories indeed if they held it against Alice now. If she had been able to carry out her plan for Glen Heather, *then* folk might have talked with a will! Whatever Isobel's peccadilloes had been they could hardly have equalled the deliberate bearing of a bastard. And for Mary to cast aspersions at Joseph ... Alice's hand tightened on the sponge.

Joseph. Why had she never considered Joseph as a father for her child?

True, she had put away the idea since the bungled arrangement with Reggie, but perhaps there was still a chance. She liked Joseph and respected him. He was a fine man, with integrity, strength and good health, all attributes which would stand any child in good stead. He was a fine-looking man too, and best of all, from a practical view-point, she did not cringe from his touch.

She remembered the way he had tended her after the silly accident in the cowshed. And today, he had taken her hand and even put a supporting arm around her - the effect had been warm and pleasant, not distasteful at all. In fact - Alice swallowed and blinked, ashamed to find herself smiling foolishly. She put aside the sponge, dried her face and arms on her towel, and changed her chemise for a nightgown. She brushed her hair until it crackled and considered.

Should she go to the cottage now, tonight, in her nightgown and seduce him? Her face burned with embarrassment at the thought. She was not built for soft words and seduction and to act against her essential nature would bring only an embarrassing failure, as it had with Reggie. She could imagine Joseph's incredulity, his anger even, if she approached him now. Or would he laugh at her? Either way, the idea was insupportable. She must put it to Joseph as a business proposition. She would not offer money, as she had done before, but she must offer *something*, to make it a fair bargain. Yet as she considered, she realised there was nothing she could offer Joseph McKenzie in exchange. He was the most self-sufficient person she knew.

Perhaps she should ask it as a favour. If he disliked the idea, he could always refuse. Alice nodded in the darkness. A dignified request would be the best method for both of them and really, there was no need to be embarrassed at all. He could only say yes or no.

The next morning, she decided she couldn't blame Joseph if he *did* refuse. Her reflection looked most unattractive in the bleak morning light and she had a feeling that a man must at least like the look of a woman before he could lie with her. Reggie had implied as much. He had also said a fellow needed encouragement. Alice put her hands over her hot cheeks. She had not even tried to encourage Reggie.

Maybe she should visit Isobel and ask for some pointers before approaching Joseph ... she gave a slightly hysterical laugh. She could just see her grandmother's reaction to *that*. Even if Isobel *had* had a lover, surely she'd never put the question herself! And it was foolish to involve anyone else. This was between herself and Joseph, and must be settled today in a businesslike fashion.

Two hours later, she sat facing Joseph across the desk. He looked back enquiringly and Alice cleared her throat. 'Joseph -' She stalled.

'Is there a problem, Miss Campell? Have you decided to give me my marching orders after all?' He seemed mildly interested, no more. Damn him! Did he have to be so cool, so uninvolved? Did he not care that tomorrow he might be out of a job? But he had asked a question and he required an answer, so she shook her head.

'Not at all,' she said with difficulty. 'As I told you yesterday, we shall consider the - the incident closed.'

'Then how may I help you, Miss Campbell? You seem a trifle put out.'

'Joseph,' she said desperately, 'why don't you call me Alice?'

Joseph looked wary. 'Is that a question, Miss Campbell, or a request? If it's a question, the answer is that you are my employer, and if it's a request - well, I can't help wondering at the reason behind it. Particularly in the light of yesterday.'

Alice winced.

'If it is your wish, of course, I would have no objection to calling you by your given name,' he said briskly, 'but if I did so, it would have to be all the time. I would never remember to look about to see who might be in earshot, and I wouldn't wish to remember. So perhaps we should stick to Miss Campbell, Miss Campbell.'

'No, I would prefer that you made it Alice. All the time.'

'Alice it is then. Will that be all, Alice?'

Alice gulped and closed her eyes for a moment, praying for strength. It was a foolish thing to do, considering the nature of her intention. But fornication - in a good cause - was surely a lesser sin than, say, adultery. And there was a thought! 'Joseph, are you married?'

Now he really was surprised. 'No, Miss Campbell - Alice. I thought you knew that. Or did you suspect I had deserted a wife in Hobart?'

'I would be surprised if you had,' said Alice honestly. 'I simply thought it better to be certain. You see, Joseph, I have a - a request to make.' She stuck again, clasping her hands together so that the knuckles showed white.

Joseph waited without any sign of impatience, but he was not about to help her, either. She was taken back to the day in summer when she interviewed him in this very office. Just so had they faced one another, just so had she waited for him to fill a silence, just so had he failed to do so. He must have iron control, for she knew he had a temper, and a temper suggested impulsiveness. 'Joseph,' she said at last in a high voice, 'I need a child. A son.'

That shook him. Alice, minutely examining the grain of her father's desk, heard his sharp intake of breath. 'I need a son,' she repeated in a stronger voice. 'And I am asking you to be the father. If you have no objection, of course.'

A very strange expression crossed Joseph's face and he leaned forward. 'I beg your pardon, Alice,' he said carefully, 'but am I to understand - are you by any chance asking me to marry you?'

CHAPTER 42

'M*arry* me!' cried Alice, half rising in her agitation. 'You mustn't think - oh dear, what must you be thinking of me? I would never ask you to do such a thing! All I need is a son to carry on at Glen Heather. And to do that, I need - a child needs a father, as well as a mother.'

'It is customary,' said Joseph, and now there was a definite edge on his voice. 'And so you have hit upon me as a likely prospect for fatherhood.'

'Not only a likely prospect,' said Alice hurriedly, 'but the best! I like you Joseph, and you have many admirable qualities. I should like to see them reflected in my child.'

'I am healthy and my teeth are my own,' said Joseph coldly. 'Care to inspect them?'

'Don't be foolish!'

'I have no spavins, I am sound in wind and limb, I neither bite nor kick and I have never foundered.' There was a very nasty little pause. 'You have it all worked out, have you not?' said Joseph. 'You want to breed yourself a child and I am to be the lucky man.'

'Well, you have no wife to object and I wouldn't take up very much of your time!'

Joseph stood up and planted his hands on the desk. 'And when would this very small piece of my time be given? Today? Tomorrow? Next week? Right now? And how much time is a little? Once might not do the trick, you know. Were you considering repeated servicings to make sure the thing is done properly?'

'Of course not! I have learned to calculate the correct time for the ...'

'The word you are looking for is not used in polite company,' said Joseph distantly, 'but you do not consider me polite company, do you, Miss Campbell? I am a servant.'

'A manager. And afterwards you could forget all about it.'

'And so could you, I suppose! You could face it once, but you don't think you'd have the stomach for more? You'd close your eyes and grit your teeth, no doubt! Then let me tell you something, Miss Campbell; a child should be got with love, not stoicism. If I ever have a child it will be because its mother wants me as I want her. But what had *you* in mind? Something very polite with a screen between us? And a bonus if I perform to expectation?'

'If you so dislike the idea, you have only to refuse. You have no need to be offensive.'

'Have I not?'

'No, you have not. I - I can quite understand if you can't bring yourself to do as I ask, but why are you so angry? No - don't answer that. Just - leave.'

'Can't bring myself to do as you ask ...!' Joseph sounded more stunned than angry. 'You cannot get a child by touching hands.'

'I thought it was easy for men,' said Alice miserably.

'Easy. Oh yes, very easy.' Joseph turned away, pushing his hands into his pockets. 'So very easy many of them do it without intention.'

'You won't consider it,' said Alice flatly. Her own hands were shaking and she clasped them together again.

There was a deadly pause, and then Joseph turned to face her. 'Did I say that?' he said softly. 'Come here.'

Moving like a sleep-walker, Alice came around the desk. Joseph took her hands in a firm grip. 'Why do you want a son, Alice? To prove yourself a woman?'

'A son is male!' spat Alice. 'By reason of my great grandfather's whim, my father's daughters cannot inherit Glen Heather, but a grandson *can*. And Rosalind is to marry soon - oh, you will think me greedy and selfish, but she cares nothing for Glen Heather! She will marry and move away, and put a manager on the property. She will take what profit comes and she will have the timber cut from the mountain - her son will be rich and Glen Heather will be starved. It will remain in our family, for it can never be sold, but it will be empty and dead.'

Joseph stared, and she thought he was about to say something, but he shook his head instead. 'Your sister would really mismanage the place? I thought she had no interest in it at all.'

'She has not - but still she is a Campbell and Campbells are thrawn to the bone.'

'Why have you not married? You are young and attractive - you must have had offers.'

'One offer,' said Alice bitterly. 'The gentleman was a doctor, whose ambition it was to practise in Sydney. And then the war came. But I do not want to marry - I have never wanted to marry. I only want a son.'

'You only want a son.'

'So there is nothing to be gained by this discussion. Since you'll not help me, go away.' She looked up into his dark blue eyes and read compassion beyond the sternness. Her vision blurred and she blinked.

'There is one way I will agree to your request,' said Joseph.

'You would like to be paid?' she said faintly.

'Alice, wash out your mouth with soap!'

'Then what *do* you want?'

'Can't you guess? I want you to marry me.'

Alice dragged her hands away. 'Don't be so ridiculous. I have told you - I do not want a husband. A husband is an inconvenience.'

'So I am good enough to take into your bed, but not into your life. Or was it to be my bed, in the cottage? Or even that traditional spot for sinning, the hayloft?'

'I hadn't thought that far,' said Alice.

'You should have,' he said flatly. 'And you should have thought about the child. What if you bore a girl? Would you set it aside and try again? Or would you bring it up to break its heart as you have broken yours? Even if you achieved your son - bastard is an ugly word. It can turn a man's whole life sour if he thinks himself the result of an accident.'

'*You* are a bastard yourself!' exclaimed Alice. '*That*'s why you're so angry!'

'Not *me*, Alice. My father was a bastard by name and became one by nature, and that's a thing I'll *never* have happen to a child of mine. So it's all or nothing. If you won't take my hand in marriage you'll certainly get nothing of the rest of me! I can see myself out.'

Alice knew that if Joseph left now it would be the end of it. She would never be able to face him again, and in losing him she might lose far more than the chance of a child. 'Wait, Joseph!' she said desperately. 'Come away from that door, please. Do you *want* to marry me?'

Joseph closed the door and came back to the desk. 'I want to marry you. God help me, and God knows why - you're thrawn as all get out. Perhaps you remind me of my dear old dad. He had a chin like yours.'

Alice ignored the insult. 'When you said I was attractive,' she said slowly, 'did you mean attractive to *you*?'

A glint of something showed in the back of his eyes. 'That's right.'

Alice frowned in honest puzzlement. 'But I'm sallow and I have frizzy hair and I am too tall and bony. I am not pretty, or even handsome.'

'Quite true,' said Joseph. 'You may not be to everyone's taste - in fact, until quite recently I would have said you were not to mine. I liked women small and sweet and soft, but then - I'd not met a Campbell woman before.'

'I am not small, or sweet, or soft -'

'A man can change his mind, and this one has. You may not be beautiful, Alice, but there's something about you that draws me - unfortunately. Have you ever had a man?'

'Does that matter?'

'I would like to know.'

'Very well then, I have never had a man. I planned to once, and found I couldn't face it. I could face it with you, I think.'

'Then marry me, Alice, and we'll make some sense of this.'

Alice looked into his eyes and saw baffled anger and something else - sincerity, she supposed. She felt suddenly tired and empty. 'Then I shall marry you, if that's what it takes.'

'You might sound a little more eager.'

'So might you. You would never have thought of it if I hadn't mentioned the other. You would never have thought of me as anything but "Miss Campbell".'

'I would always have thought of you as something more. I *have* always thought of you as something more.'

'As what?' she asked, but he shook his head.

'I'll not tell you now and perhaps I never will. I had some interesting thoughts when you were drying your hair in the hut, however. I had some interesting dreams last night. I wasn't even sleeping.'

'Really.' She sighed. 'I suppose it's the best solution, since you're so thrawn. Glen Heather needs a good master and a son. To get a son I need a man. It might as well be you.'

'Not a man, Alice. A husband.'

'Husband. Man. Either may get a child, but I warn you, if I could do it another way I would. Since I cannot - I must be resigned.'

'How very cool you sound.'

Alice shrugged. 'Perhaps it won't be so bad. We work well together and respect one another - most of the time. No doubt many a marriage has a weaker foundation than that.'

'Be careful,' said Joseph acidly. 'You might get to thinking it a good idea.'

'I might. But what's in it for you?'

He gave her an odd smile. 'More than you might think, Miss Campbell. Perhaps the winning of a dream. A dream that once belonged to someone else.'

'I cannot imagine whose dream I could represent. But I shall marry you.'

She put out her left hand and Joseph took it. 'I believe it is customary to seal these agreements with a kiss.'

Primly, Alice offered her cheek.

'Shame on you!' said Joseph. 'These things should be done properly or not at all.'

'Then you'd better do it properly,' she said.

It was nothing like the distasteful experience she had had with Reggie, but she really hadn't expected it would be. So far as she was aware Joseph neither smoked nor drank to excess and she knew he had pleasant hands. As for that disgusting business with the tongue, and pinching her breast ... he would never be so depraved. She expected him to be brisk and efficient as he was in everything he did, and so he was. What she did *not* expect was that she would feel any enthusiasm for the activity. If enthusiasm was the word for what she felt. It was most peculiar and she had never felt anything like it before. Her reaction certainly seemed to please Joseph, who responded with a much more comprehensive embrace. In fact, it was he who drew away first, looking down at Alice in something like disbelief.

'Alice? I'm sorry if I alarmed you, but you really shouldn't do such things if you expect a man to keep his head.' He shook her a little. 'Say something! Tell me you didn't hate it?'

She shook her head and frowned as if in puzzlement.

'If we are playing charades,' said Joseph, 'I would guess your voice has gone.'

Alice nodded, and he laughed and hugged her. 'Alice, Alice, you are such a fool!' When he let go, she looked at him indignantly. 'You sat there,' said Joseph deliberately, 'and coolly invited me into your bed, but now one little kiss sends you dumb. Well, I shall know how to silence you in future.'

'And why should you want to?' she asked peevishly.

'This is not the last time you'll talk unmitigated rubbish and need to be silenced.'

Alice frowned. Joseph was changing, and she was by no means sure she liked it. She had meant to ask a decent working man a favour. Instead, she had found herself the subject of a strange proposal from a resolute and angry man. The world was turning inside out and who knew where she would find herself once it steadied down? 'And how shall I silence you?' she asked resentfully.

'No doubt you will find a way.' He gave her an ironic half bow and, without waiting for her formal dismissal, left the office and the house. And Alice sat down suddenly and quaked.

Joseph spent much of the following night wondering if he had run mad, for surely not one man in ten would have reacted as he had done to Alice Campbell's proposition. Some might have been flattered, and others would undoubtedly have taken advantage of her offer for the sake of novelty. It was not every day a working man had a chance to lie with a lady - and a virgin at that. And *this* lady - there was no denying that to lie with Alice Campbell would hold a spice of the forbidden - for him. And to be begged for a child instead of being begged to prevent one - that was novelty indeed. But she had chosen him, and he was neither flattered nor about to take advantage. Not in the usual way. Her jibe that he would never have thought of marriage had been close to the truth, but now the subject was raised, he found he did want to marry her - and soon. Because of who she was and what she represented, or in spite of it?

Alice Campbell had it all worked out, but there were some things she didn't know about Joseph McKenzie, and he had no idea how she would react when - and if - he chose to tell her. Perhaps he never would - and not before the wedding. If he told her before the wedding, and she married him anyway, he would never know her motives, and perhaps she wouldn't know herself. Better, far better, to marry her in ignorance, confess his secret and take what came. And hope to God he had judged her right.

He didn't want to think about that. Instead, he lay in bed and wondered just how he would have held onto his principles and his anger if she had approached him by night, in the cottage, instead of in the practical light of day. Not that daylight had helped him much. Kisses such as the one they had shared should have had only one ending - but although the thought had a certain piquancy, he could hardly have had her on her father's desk.

He did not delude himself that anyone would be pleased at their coming union, and he knew some people might be very angry. It remained to be seen if Alice's resolve was firm enough to withstand the anger, but then - she might have changed her mind already. She had certainly avoided him throughout the day.

So Joseph slept poorly, when he slept at all, and was early at the office, wondering if she had changed her mind. And if she *had*, would he find himself confessing his secret in a suicidal attempt to keep her?

His spirits sank when she greeted him with the desk between them. It seemed she was staying out of reach. 'Miss Campbell? Does our engagement stand?'

'It stands,' said Alice. 'I am a woman of my word - remember?'

'Then we should visit the Manse this morning.'

'This morning ...'

'I believe it *is* the customary way to proceed.' He gave her an ironic smile, and went out to hitch up Blackwood.

Alice joined him ten minutes later, and he was gratified to see she had changed into her Sunday best, a severe dark blue with a glossy straw hat.

'I must be mad,' she said, in an echo of his own thoughts, but she joined him in the gig and sat in silence until they arrived in Mersey. Then she turned to him and said in some bewilderment; 'You want us to behave as if this were an ordinary wedding? As if we were an ordinary couple?'

'Why not?' asked Joseph. 'I proposed and you accepted me.' He tied up the pony and offered his hand to help Alice down. This time, she took it. She seemed to have overcome her aversion to his touch. Had she been attracted to him all along? Had she feared her desires would show? Joseph was not a vain man, but neither was he foolish. Alice Campbell claimed to like and respect him, so why should she not desire him as well?

He had thought, as she undid her hair in Isobel's hut, that she was lacking in coquetry, but having held her in his embrace he thought she might be much more passionate than she seemed. The major goal of the modern woman seemed to be to reduce herself to a breastless, hipless parody of a boy, but it was quite evident that his Alice wore no corset, and under her deplorable clothes she was satisfactorily curved and warm. He looked forward to exploring her further, but marriage must come first. And there was an irony as well. Most women, he understood, refused to give themselves to their suitors for fear of being used and cast aside unwed. He rather thought he understood their fear, for he was now in a similar position himself. If he were to lie with Alice Campbell before they had been joined at the Kirk, she might achieve her child and repudiate the wedding. Would she do it? Perhaps. She had said as much when she finally accepted him. On the other hand, she claimed to be a woman of her word.

As he helped her down from the gig he realised her hand was cold. 'What is it, Alice?' he asked briskly. 'Second thoughts already?'

'We were on the mountain,' she said. 'Now we are at the Manse.'

'Fresh air and cold water can make a man look at life in a whole new way,' said Joseph philosophically. 'Especially when followed closely by a - shall we call it a proposal?'

'Please - don't feel you have to make pretty speeches,' said Alice. 'I know I am caught in my own web.'

Reverend Neil was sitting in the porch, and, not surprisingly, he assumed that Alice had come to discuss her sister's wedding. 'Have your man put the pony in the yard and come along in,' he said, rising to greet her. He glanced at Joseph as if expecting him to efface himself as a good servant should, but Joseph stood his ground and waited to see what Alice would do. She had the perfect opportunity to back out if she wished. She had only to give him a repulsive glance and order him to leave and it would be over.

But Alice was actually taking his arm and drawing him forward, her breast soft against his elbow. And was that an accident, or not? 'This is Joseph McKenzie,' she said. 'He is my - the manager out at Glen Heather and we both need to see you today.'

In the office, the Reverend Neil seemed surprisingly mild and kind. 'How may I help you, my children?' He looked at Alice, but when she failed to answer, his eyes sharpened and came to rest on Joseph. 'Young man?'

'We would like you to marry us, sir,' said Joseph.

'Quietly,' put in Alice.

Reverend Neil's eyebrows climbed, but he said calmly that he would put the matter to the Kirk elders. 'A formality, only,' he assured. 'Have you a date in mind for the ceremony?'

'Perhaps next week?' said Alice.

The tone of the interview changed abruptly from the avuncular to the astringent, and they were strongly advised to wait for a while. The banns must be called on two consecutive Sundays, and birth certificates produced by both parties. Three weeks hence was the earliest possible date the parson would countenance, and he thought that much too soon. 'It does not do to rush such matters, my children,' he said. 'One must be very sure.'

'We are very sure,' said Alice.

'Then a longer period of waiting will do no harm at all. I would suggest at least a year.'

'Reverend Neil,' said Alice desperately, 'we cannot wait a year.'

The suspicious gaze came to rest on Joseph. 'Young man, I trust there has been no untoward behaviour?'

'None,' said Joseph. 'Until yesterday, Miss Campbell and I had exchanged no more than conversation. However, such restraint is difficult for both of us - is it not, my love?'

Alice gave him an uncertain glance and he reached out to take her hand, stroking each fingertip in a way that seemed to convince the Reverend Neil and unsettle Alice exceedingly.

The parson advised them to go away and consider prayerfully before coming to any irrevocable decision, and then dismissed them from his office.

Alice was white with temper as Joseph handed her into the gig, and some of the inhabitants of Mersey stared openly at the sight of a clearly furious Miss Campbell out driving with the Glen Heather manager. 'Now what has made you so angry, Alice?' asked Joseph quietly. He raised a friendly hand and waved to Abraham Ward.

'You have,' she said. 'Stroking my hand like that.'

'Did you not enjoy it?'

'You are reprehensible!' she snapped.

'If we must be married quickly, we must be seen to be in love,' said Joseph. 'Your family and friends will all say I am marrying you for your social position and money, and they will suggest that you must have been on your last prayers to accept me. If we display an attachment there will be less for them to prate about, and that's the honest truth.'

'The honest truth is that *I* am marrying *you* to secure Glen Heather,' retorted Alice. 'Your reasons for marrying me are less clear. I suspect it is pure bloody mindedness because I had the temerity to refuse you.'

'*I* refused *you.* And try to look a little less militant, or the good citizens of Mersey - Good morning, Miss Llewellyn! - will be convinced I am carrying you off by force. I shall put my arm around you, so you must try to look gratified.'

'I hate this play-acting,' she said. 'I want to be married so we can - oh, you know what I mean! So we can stop this nonsense. And don't you kiss my hand.'

'A certain amount of nonsense is inevitable. I believe you would dispense with everything except the relevant act, would you not?'

'Wouldn't you?'

'I would dispense with nothing. Except perhaps those lamentable clothes.' She looked shaken, so he said; 'Tell me, did you really think I would agree to your original proposal?'

'Don't,' said Alice wretchedly. Her anger seemed to have burnt out. 'Please, Joseph - I - I didn't think much at all. I was so desperate, you see. And then you offered so much more than I asked.'

'And insisted on so much more than you wanted?'

'I need some time to get used to the idea. That's all.'

And that, thought Joseph as he put away the gig and watched his betrothed trailing into the house, was not an encouraging sign. He went back to the cottage and made a pot of tea. It would have been pleasant if Alice could have shared it, but he doubted that would ever happen - and certainly not today. Most likely she would do as the minister advised and prayerfully reconsider.

Alice broke the news to Mary that evening. She was depressed after the encounter with Reverend Neil and an unsatisfactory parting from Joseph by the stable. Since then, she had seen him only at evening milking and that had been unsatisfactory also. She had been struggling with her thoughts and trying not to think at all when she looked up and saw him leaning on the bail, watching her. Immediately, she became aware that her hair was escaping its pins and that she was sitting ungracefully hunched on the stool. It mattered, and she was so disconcerted that her fingers became thumbs and Bluebell began to shuffle. Biting back a curse, she slapped the cow and nearly knocked over the bucket. Her eyes met Joseph's and she thought he recognised her confusion and was amused by it. She dropped her gaze and when she looked up again, Joseph had gone. In no good humour, she released Bluebell and carried the milk to the kitchen. He might have said something. In the gig on the way home he had said too much, but tonight in the cowshed he might have said *something*.

She washed and changed and then went to share her news with her mother and sister, delivering it flatly and baldly over the vegetable soup.

Rosalind's reaction was entirely predictable. She put down her spoon, blotted her lips with a napkin and turned indignantly to Mary. 'Mother - tell her she can't do this!'

'Don't be foolish, Rosalind,' said Alice wearily. 'Of course I can. I am twenty-four years old and Joseph is even older.'

'You are on your last prayers,' said Rosalind cruelly. 'You can't bear to see me ahead of you, that's what it is!'

Mary was equally predictable. 'You don't know anything about him, Alice!' she said more than once.

'He is dependable and intelligent and a good manager,' said Alice. 'He is single and healthy and he kisses very well. What more do I need to know?'

Mary ignored this piece of blatant provocation. 'Who are his parents, Alice?'

'His father was a shearer and his mother a farmer's daughter from Wonthaggi in Victoria. They are both dead.'

'McKenzie - McKenzie - could be anyone! Could have come from anywhere!'

'They probably came from Scotland, wouldn't you say?' said Alice. 'Just as the Campbells and MacDonalds did. Anyway, I have said my piece. I am going to marry Joseph McKenzie at St Peter's in three weeks' time - unless we can persuade Reverend Neil to an earlier date.'

'Mother!' Rosalind turned appealingly to Mary. 'Make her see she can't do this! Not until after my wedding, anyway!'

'Hush, Rosalind. Alice, have you considered what you are at? Why is this man keen to marry you so quickly?'

'It is I who am in the hurry.'

Rosalind stared, her pretty face suffusing with a plum-coloured blush. 'Alice - you haven't got yourself into trouble?'

Alice licked her lips, tempted to allow Rosalind to believe just that, but it would have been a cheap and short-lived victory. And since, if she had had her way, she *would* have been "in trouble" it was difficult to feel properly indignant. 'There is no possibility of that,' she said clearly. 'And if I marry Joseph when I wish there *will* be no possibility.' She watched that threat bite home and added another touch. 'Not every man has the admirable self-control of your Samuel, Rosie! Some men find it difficult to wait when they are in love.'

She left the dining room and went upstairs, quite disgusted with herself. Perhaps she *was* jealous of Rosalind. Almost, she ran back down the stairs to beg Rosalind's pardon, but she caught herself in time. If she showed any sign of weakness now they would try to talk her out of her decision. She would not change her mind, but the process of convincing them of that would be long and distasteful.

More importantly, she felt that she should go to the cottage to talk to Joseph and regain some of her standing in his eyes. She got as far as putting a shawl around her shoulders and finding her shoes, but shyness overcame her. What if he refused to let her in? Or, worse, what if he thought her visit a renewed attempt at obtaining his services without the formality of a wedding? He had a bitter tongue when roused, and she wanted no more lectures tonight.

Only two people seemed truly pleased with the news of Alice's betrothal, and to her surprise, one of them was Samuel Garland. 'Go to it, Sister Alice!' he said privately after Sunday Service, as Rosalind flounced ahead. '*I've* no brief for Glen Heather! I've said from the start I'd feel better if it were out of Rosie's picture. And don't you worry - I'll talk Rosie round. She's fond of you really, but you've always made her feel of no account.'

This speech convinced Alice that Samuel was both kinder and less intelligent than she had thought, but she was grateful for his support, knowing it would go a long way towards reconciling Mary.

The other person who was pleased was Isobel, whom Alice told of the impending marriage the day after she told Mary. 'I don't really see the need of marriage, Granny,' she said, 'but Joseph does, and it seems a sensible idea.'

Isobel nodded. 'A lover's a fine thing, but not sensible,' she agreed. 'It does no harm to turn them into husbands.'

Alice flushed. 'Joseph is not a lover, Granny, though he insists on being a husband,' she said. 'And - I hope - the father of a son.'

'Then you're marrying to get a son for Glen Heather,' said Isobel.

Alice nodded. 'It seems the sensible thing - it seems the *only* thing.'

'This man McKenzie - does he know what you're at?'

'Of course! Do you think I'd try to deceive him?'

'You might deceive yourself.'

'Well I won't,' said Alice. 'This is a business arrangement, Granny, just as it was when you married Grandfather John. I know it and Joseph knows it. The rest of the world does not, but I wanted you to understand.'

'You had better wear my wedding gown,' said Isobel. 'It is in the chest in the attic, if the moth has not been at it. I never had a daughter and I never offered it to Mary. It won't do for Rosalind, but I would like fine for you to wear it.'

Until then, Alice had planned to marry in her Sunday best. She could not face the costume she had bought for Rosalind's wedding, which seemed soiled by the memory of her visit to Launceston, and she had not wished to try to obtain a wedding gown at such short notice. She was touched at Isobel's thought and when she went home, she tried on the gown in the privacy of her own room.

The ivory of the gown was deepened to cream, and the graceful sweep of the crinoline surrounded the wearer like the wings of a swan. Isobel must have looked like a princess, thought Alice. Hopefully, she turned to examine her reflection in the looking glass, and her eyes darkened with disappointment. Her face was autumn-pale and her eyes red-rimmed from restless nights. Her hair was frizzing in the damp, and she looked like a white-faced witch. Better to wear her dark blue costume. It might be sedate and plain, but at least it did not make her a figure of fun. But then - Isobel would be disappointed.

Alice shrugged philosophically. She would wear the gown and let the folk of Mersey make of it what they would. And, naturally, she would inform Joseph of her decision, so that he could hire or purchase suitable garments for himself.

On the Sunday before the wedding, Joseph drove her to Kirk as usual. The banns had been called for the final time, and the members of the congregation had ceased to crane their necks and exchange amazed glances when Alice and Joseph entered arm in arm and sat in the Glen Heather pew with Mary, Samuel and a rigidly disapproving Rosalind. Alice heard little of the service, and was almost startled when Joseph took her elbow to escort her back to the gig. She smiled and thanked him coolly when he handed her up the step, and settled herself for the customary silence of the drive home.

Beneath her calm, she was very frightened. Already, her hopes for a businesslike relationship had undergone a sea change. Since the day she had accepted him, Joseph had never kissed or hugged her once. All he had done was stroke her hand and draw her to his side in public. On their return from Mersey, he would become quite distant again, as if he regretted their situation. She had been used to giving him orders, but now she felt he was ruling her. Isobel was right - she should have watched her step. She should have stayed cool and superior and she should never, never have asked him for a son. He had so much power over her now - how much more would he have when married? And would he be so distant then?

The night before the wedding, unable to bear the uncertainty for another hour, Alice braced herself, and went to visit Joseph. Mary was lying down with a headache and Rosalind was out dining with Samuel, so there was no-one to see as she knocked on the door and slipped inside the cottage. 'Joseph?' she called softly. 'Are you there?'

Joseph came out of the other room, carrying his shirt in one hand. 'I was just sewing on a button,' he explained, apparently unruffled, although his eyes had widened a little at the sight of her. 'Sit down, Alice. I'll not be long.' He passed the needle through the button a few more times and broke off the thread. 'What is it?' he asked without looking up. 'Have you never seen a man with his shirt off before?'

Alice averted her gaze with some haste. 'No,' she said. 'I have not.'

'Am I such a dreadful sight?'

'No.'

'You will see a lot more of me after tomorrow,' reminded Joseph. 'Are you sure you can face it?'

It had been a mistake to come. The whole thing was a mistake, and the sooner she put a stop to it, the better. She knew now she could rely on Samuel to keep Rosalind in line, so there was no need to continue this charade. Practicality was all very well, but she could not face marriage to a man who seemed intent on needling her. She was about to say so when Joseph spoke again. 'You can look now, Alice. I'm decent.'

'I need to talk to you,' she said.

'Well, go ahead.'

'Joseph,' she blurted. 'Do you have to make it all so difficult?'

'How have I been making things difficult? By insisting on this marriage, do you mean?'

'You've hardly been insisting since the first time. In fact, you've scarcely spoken a civil word for days and the wedding is supposed to be tomorrow.' She meant to be reasonable, but her voice sounded wounded, even to her. 'I thought we could be partners. I thought we could be friends.'

'I hope we can be friends,' said Joseph patiently, 'but just now I find it impossible. *Sensible.* That was one of the words you used about this arrangement of ours. *Bargain.* That was another. The only emotion you seem to have felt is embarrassment in the Kirk and fury with me - oh yes, you *did* ask me to leave you alone.' He paused. '*Sensible.* Is that what you really want? And do you really want to know why we don't have those friendly little chats?'

'Why? A friendly chat would be better than silence.'

'Because, you goose, I don't feel in the least bit *sensible* where you're concerned, so silence seems the best refuge.'

His voice was perfectly reasonable, so she hardly thought he meant it. It was ridiculous to think he might mean it, for actions spoke louder than words and his actions had all been confined to public places and meant to confuse their critics. 'You don't need to pretend to me here,' she said, biting her lip. 'There is no-one here to convince.'

Joseph rose from his chair and plucked the startled Alice from hers. Then he sat down again, bringing her onto his lap. 'Pretend, is it? Convince, is it? Keep still. You can't get up until we sort this out once and for all, Miss Campbell. I am tired of walking around with my hands in my pockets and my eyes on the ground and my tongue held firmly between my teeth. I am tired of your taking my arm in Mersey and walking six feet away from me on Glen Heather. So put your arms around my neck, and don't be so polite, and we'll see if we can't work this out.' He settled back in the chair with Alice held firmly against him. 'Now, what was all this about *pretending*? You cannot pretend to embrace. You cannot pretend to kiss. You most certainly cannot pretend when you're naked together in bed. Don't look so shocked.'

'I am not shocked,' she said valiantly.

'You are.' He gave her a little shake. 'Get your head out of the clouds, Alice Campbell. If you marry me there will be no *pretending* about it. It will be a real wedding tomorrow and a real wedding night and a real marriage to follow. This may not be your conventional love match, but I want you badly.'

Alice digested this and then turned to look at him incredulously. 'You sleep *naked*?'

'Why not? Do you think it indecent?'

That was unanswerable, so she extracted one hand and discovered that the white lock of hair felt just the same as the rest. She took it between her fingers and tugged gently. 'Do you think my son will have this too?'

'*Our* son. Probably,' said Joseph. 'But perhaps he'll just have black lamb's wool like you. In any case, he will be ugly; all babies are. And perhaps he will be a she. I wish you would forget this non-existent child and listen.'

'We are marrying to get a son.'

'*You* are marrying to get a son. Not me.'

'Then *why*?' asked Alice. 'You've never said *why*? Do you want a home? Security?'

'I could have a home without marriage. Security, too. I want something of my own, I think.'

'Then get yourself a dog,' said Alice.

'A dog won't do. It must be a lady and the lady must be Alice Campbell. I won't shock you by going into details, but the nights I've spent these last weeks trying to sleep and not imagine you lying pressed against me - no, keep still! Then I keep thinking of you shaking your hair loose in Isobel's hut - very erotic it is, to be hit by flying droplets, though you might not think so. I want to know what is under those clothes ...'

'You called my clothes deplorable.'

'Only because they cover you up. I want to see all of you and hold all of you. It will take me years to believe I have you to keep. It is an obsession with me - just as Glen Heather is with you.'

'But you told me - when I suggested you leave your wet clothes at Isobel's hut - that you might not be here in the spring!'

'You were the lady of Glen Heather and if you recall I had said some very harsh things. I thought they might fester, and you would change your mind about forgiving them and tell me to leave.'

'You were just as harsh in the office.'

'I proposed to you in anger. But after you accepted that all changed. Then you said you needed time to get used to the idea.'

'So I did,' she said tartly. 'At least a day. Instead, you have given me three weeks of sheer misery.'

'And you have given *me* three weeks of sheer dread.'

'That I wouldn't marry you?'

'That you *would* - and then regret it. Alice - there's a lot you don't know about me. Some of it I don't know about myself. You don't know who I am, and you don't know my ancestry.'

'I don't care for your ancestry,' said Alice crossly. 'You are you, whoever your grandparents were.'

'Yet *your* ancestry is so very important to you. Tell me something, Alice?'

'What?'

'Yes, *what*. What made you hit upon *me* for your proposition? Was it just because I was there?'

'My mother told me people would talk if I spent time alone with you on the mountain. I told her there was no risk of anything untoward, but she insisted they would talk.'

'So you decided to give them something to talk about.'

'Oh no. That would have been childish. It was really because of Reggie, I think.' Briefly and baldly, Alice told him of her experience in Launceston. 'He put his hands on me and it was like being touched by a slug. Kissing him was much worse. I was nearly ill - I would have been if I hadn't made him stop. I gave up my plan then. But it isn't horrible at all with you, so I thought I could face it. Have I made you angry?'

'Very,' said Joseph. 'As angry as when you made your preposterous proposal! And to me - of all people. Dear God, you didn't know the irony of it all! No *risk*!'

'You could have said yes or you could have said no.'

'You are taking a risk in being here right now,' said Joseph. 'And so am I.'

'Do you want me to go?'

'Not at all. I want you to stay.'

'You are being much nicer now,' said Alice thoughtfully.

'I could be a lot nicer still, and tomorrow I will be.' He kissed her cheek and then her willing mouth, stroking her breast through the prim blue blouse. Alice was enchanted, and ventured on a few explorations of her own, but Joseph stood up rather suddenly, spilling her from his lap and turning his back while he tucked his shirt into his waistband. After a few moments, he turned round, and looked at her grimly. '*No*, Miss Campbell! You are putting the cart before the horse. And don't you look so innocent. I know precisely what you want, and you are not getting it now.'

'If I do,' said Alice blushing, 'it's all your fault. You put things in my mind.'

'I would love to know what you mean by that but I am not going to ask. You are going back to the house and I am going to bed alone.'

'Can't I stay?' said Alice wistfully.

Joseph crossed the room in three strides and opened the door. 'Goodnight, Miss Campbell,' he said.

'Do you feel better now?' asked Alice. She was playing with fire, trying to convince herself that she was not making a dangerous mistake.

'No,' said Joseph. 'I feel terrible. What would make me feel better is the thought that you might one day be brought to view me as something other than a convenient male.'

CHAPTER 43

The wedding was a simple one, but Alice was touched when Joseph presented her with a bouquet of crimson heath and fern.

'How did you know?' she asked, smiling up at him so radiantly that he blinked and pretended to shield his face.

'How did I know what, Miss Campbell?'

'That crimson heath is the flower we all love best.'

'A lucky guess. I saw some on the mountain. Take care you don't make your fingers bleed.'

'It doesn't hurt if you hold it right,' said Alice.

Joseph claimed no close relations, and Mary had seized on that to avoid inviting her own extended family to the Kirk. She and Rosalind and Samuel attended, and so did Hannah and Arthur, Mr Bertram and the Llewellyns, but apart from these the only witnesses to the wedding were the curious few who had heard the banns and wished to satisfy themselves that the unequal union would really take place. The wedding breakfast was a cold snack provided by the Elders' ladies, for Mary and Rosalind were catching the train to Launceston, to stay awhile with Aunt Emily before returning in good time for Rosalind's own wedding. Alice was relieved; she and Joseph were to move into Glen Heather House and it would have been most uncomfortable with Rosalind there.

Isobel could not come to the Kirk, so Joseph suggested they should visit her on the way back to Glen Heather. Alice was distinctly nervous, for Isobel and Joseph had never met and she wanted them to like one another. At least Isobel knew the truth about their marriage, so there would be no need to parade their devotion. She said as much as they drove away from the Kirk and Joseph, remote and handsome in morning clothes, gave her an exasperated glance. 'You seemed devoted enough in the cottage last night, Mrs McKenzie,' he pointed out.

'That was not devotion,' said Alice with dignity. 'That was sheer - er -'

'Lust?' suggested Joseph. 'And why not? It makes a marriage so much more agreeable - or so I'm told.'

Alice could have hit him with her bouquet, but she folded her hands instead.

Jennie Christopher opened the door, and smiled her benediction. She also took Joseph's hat, told them Isobel was waiting, and took herself out to the garden while they entered the parlour. Isobel was very upright in her chair, her cane clasped between her hands. 'You've wed him then,' she remarked with satisfaction. 'I thought you'd met your match.'

Alice coughed. 'This is Joseph, Granny,' she said. 'Joseph - Isobel Galbraith, my grandmother Campbell.'

'I see you wore my gown, Alice,' said Isobel.

'It does not become me as it did you, Granny,' said Alice.

'No,' said Isobel. 'Clothes do little for you. Where did you find the gown?'

'In the attic, as you said.'

'I said - aye, so I did,' said Isobel, vexed. 'So I did - Joseph, you say? A fine name and a fine-looking laddie.'

Joseph bowed slightly over Isobel's hand, and her eyes twinkled with pleasure. 'I warned Alice about you, laddie,' she said in satisfied tones.

Alice bit her lip. 'Now, Granny -'

Joseph smiled at the bent old woman before him. 'How could you warn her against me when we'd never met, Mrs Galbraith? Have you the sight?'

'Not at all, but I know your type, young man, and I know the way she spoke of you. She said you were quiet and the quiet ones are dangerous. They think too much. That is a strange thing, your hair. Did it happen in France?'

'A freak of nature,' said Joseph, as he had said once before.

Isobel nodded. 'I have seen it before, you know - on a lady who came to Glen Heather many years ago.' She turned to Alice. 'Do you recall Jamie, child?'

Alice was looking a little disconcerted. 'No, Granny. Jamie went away before I was ever born.'

'Dear Jamie,' said Isobel again. 'Her name was Charlotte, you know. They were so in love, but they eloped, and the Law came searching.' She gave a reminiscent chuckle. '*I* sent the Law to the right-about, you may depend. It was rank foolishness to say Jamie had abducted the lassie.'

Joseph sighed. It appeared that his past was about to surface with a rush. Unless he could head the old lady off ... but he found he couldn't do it, after all. 'You were quite right, Mrs Galbraith,' he said quietly. 'Jamie Campbell did not abduct Charlotte - she went with him quite willingly, and would have married him if she could.'

Alice gaped at him, more ghost-like than ever in the ivory wedding gown. Her grandmother was right; the colour did nothing for her at all, and the crinoline made her look disproportionate. 'You're talking as if you know them,' she said in a taut voice.

'I never met Jamie Campbell,' said Joseph, 'but Charlotte was my grandmother.'

He saw that the old lady's hands were shaking, and her eyes were much too bright. Eyes like Alice's, so he touched her hand to comfort her.

'Charlotte,' said Isobel. 'And Jamie never married her! That was not well done of the laddie.'

'Don't blame young Campbell, Mrs Galbraith,' said Joseph. 'Grandma always said he would have married her if he could. They were caught, though, when they left the ship in Melbourne. Grandma's Uncle Frederick took her away, and when her lover tried to find her he was clapped up for abduction. The judge let him go, and he disappeared.' He laughed, not daring to look at Alice. 'It seems Uncle Frederick was a little hasty, because a few months later he found himself faced with the necessity of finding Grandma a husband anyway. Her Jamie was unavailable, so Uncle Frederick chose Jack McKenzie, a farmer from Wonthaggi.'

'Charlotte's grandchild!' said Isobel. 'Are you Jamie's too?'

Alice jumped up, almost tripping over the train of her wedding gown. 'How *can* he be?' she demanded roughly. 'How *can* he be? His name is McKenzie! Why - if he were Jamie's grandson he would be - he would be -' Her face was white and terrible, and Joseph's spirits fell. She was taking this very badly. He turned to Isobel, but the old lady was shaking her head.

'What would I be, then, Alice?' he asked. 'A remote connection of yours? Is that so terrible?'

'You don't understand!' cried Alice. 'You don't understand! Jamie Campbell was my grandfather's youngest brother - Joseph, our grandfathers were *brothers*!'

Joseph blinked. He had never thought the relationship as close as that. He had always supposed Jamie Campbell to be a cousin of the Glen Heather Campbells, for Charlotte had certainly never expected to live at Glen Heather.

'Why didn't you tell me?' cried Alice. 'Dear God, Joseph, why didn't you *tell* me?'

Now he felt a stirring of anger under the shock, and superimposed on these emotions, he felt shame that this ugly dispute was happening on their wedding day, before an old lady who should not be upset. 'Alice!' he snapped. 'Stop this!' A white bird which had been roosting in the corner ruffled its wings like a tombstone angel and hissed.

'Quiet, McCleod,' said Isobel Galbraith.

Joseph rose, and took Alice by the shoulders, pressing her down into a low chair. She looked up at him with pain-filled eyes. 'Listen,' he said more calmly. 'I didn't tell you when I first came to Glen Heather, because - frankly, because I didn't want to see your doubts. Think of it! There were you, the lady of Glen Heather, and here comes a shabby soldier daring to call you cousin! You would have thrown me out as an imposter! Or given me charity and sent me on my way.'

'Then why did you come at all?' she asked more quietly.

'I came because my sweetheart had jilted me,' said Joseph. 'Dorothy O'Riley, she was. I told her my story and she sent me off to the trenches and married another man behind my back. I decided I'd leave Tasmania, then - go right away.'

'I wish you had!' said Alice. 'I wish to *God* you had!'

'However,' said Joseph, 'I saw the advertisement in the newspaper and I thought I'd come and see Glen Heather, just for old time's sake. Grandma told so many stories - the house, the apple tree - even the bird McCleod that talked in Scotch. She told them to my father. She told him he was a connection of a fine old place in Tasmania. She meant to give him a pride in himself - to make up for the fact that Jack McKenzie could never be more than tolerant to a bastard stepson.'

'Yet he gave the laddie his name, this Jack McKenzie,' said Isobel Galbraith.

'So he did,' said Joseph. 'I believe Wonthaggi accepted my father at first, but after the other children came it was rather obvious ... they had tow-coloured hair and brown eyes. Someone chipped Jack about it, I understand, and he tried to save his face by ignoring the boy. Dad cut loose as soon as ever he could and took to the road as a shearer, but he always talked about Glen Heather when he was in his cups. Grandma's attempt to give him pride didn't work; it made him bitter instead. He used to talk about how he would go and spit in the faces of the rich kinsfolk who'd never offered him a helping hand.'

'We never heard from Jamie after he left us that day,' said Isobel.

Joseph sighed. 'So I discovered. I told my name to Alice here and she never blinked. It was obvious she'd not heard the old story before.'

'You might have told me then!' burst out Alice. 'Or did you plan to hurt us from the start?'

'I never meant to hurt you! I *never* did. I meant to satisfy my curiosity, that was all. I meant to stay a month and leave and never come back - but I got to like the place. And you.'

Tears were running freely down Alice's cheeks, splotching the wedding gown and hanging like dew drops of brine on the white heather brooch. 'You could have told me later. Before I made a fool of myself.'

'So I could. But by then you'd - er - ' Joseph glanced at Isobel in embarrassment.

'I asked him to give me a son,' said Alice angrily. 'Can you believe that, Granny? I asked *Jamie Campbell's grandson* to give me an heir for Glen Heather!'

'I was half in love with you already,' said Joseph, 'and I had some sort of stupid hope that you were fond of me -'

'I *never* would have married you if I'd known!' sobbed Alice. 'How could you do this to me?'

'What have I done to you? Deceived you a little - but what's a drop of shared blood? You wanted a Campbell baby, Alice - why should you care that the child will be a little more Campbell than you'd planned? A quarter more Campbell, as if it matters - and that from the wrong side of the blanket. Surely *that* doesn't bother you - that one of your precious Campbells sired a bastard? It happens in the best of families, or so I'm told. Good God - you were ready to have me do the same!'

'Can't you see? There was no need for us to marry at all,' said Alice with a sudden horrible calm. 'I married you to get an heir for Glen Heather and it was all for nothing. *You* own Glen Heather, Joseph - and you have done ever since my father died!'

There was a silence, broken only by Alice's sobbing breaths. Joseph stared at her, seeing his new-found life crumbling into dust. 'Alice, that cannot be true,' he said at last, with an appealing glance at Isobel. 'Your father owned Glen Heather, so obviously his grandson must be next in line. I am from another branch of the family.'

'Only if there are no older male descendants could a grandson inherit,' said Alice listlessly. 'And there is one, and it's you. Glen Heather is yours, and all my worry, all my work - all Mr Bertram's searching have been for nothing. When would you like me to leave?'

'Don't be so *stupid*,' said Joseph harshly. 'Even if what you say is so I wouldn't claim Glen Heather away from you. I *couldn't* if I wanted to.'

'I am only a woman. You are Jamie Campbell's grandson. A direct descendent of Auld Hector.'

'And I have no proof of that interesting fact at all. Grandma might have been romancing. Dad was definitely strange. Is there any insanity in the Campbell line?'

'Thrawn,' muttered Isobel. 'Thrawn as they come - obsessed, yes, but not insane, I think. I wonder what happened to Jamie?'

Joseph threw her an exasperated glance. 'Grandma never knew, but she always swore he must have died - otherwise he would have come back for her.' His mouth twisted. 'Which shows how romantic she really was. Mrs Galbraith - I think we should leave you now. And I hope you will accept my apologies for subjecting you to this unpleasant scene. Come, Alice.'

Alice gave him a glance of white-faced amazement. 'I'm going nowhere with you!'

'We are going home,' said Joseph heavily. 'You are my wife.'

'You go home,' said Alice. 'I am staying here.' She glared at him, and he thought how very ill she looked. He could insist - he could drag her out to the gig - but the idea was horrible. Joseph shook his head numbly, and went out of the cottage. The sweet-faced old housekeeper came out of the kitchen to hand him his hat, but he passed her without a word. Her smile wavered and she looked distressed, and Joseph pulled himself up with a jerk. His world had suffered an earthquake, but there was no need to be unkind. 'Thank you, Mrs Christopher,' he said with an effort.

Jennie put her hand on his arm. 'Mr Joseph? Is something wrong with Miss Alice?'

'Yes indeed,' said Joseph with a painful attempt at a smile. 'I have offended her deeply.'

'She'll come to you by and by,' said Jennie.

'When hell freezes over, perhaps,' said Joseph.

'She will come if she loves you,' said Jennie serenely.

'She doesn't love me,' said Joseph. 'She never pretended she did.'

Left alone with her grandmother, Alice raised a white and woeful face. 'Granny, what shall I do?' she asked, as plaintively as a child. And Alice had *never* been a plaintive child.

'You will do whatever you think is best,' said Isobel. 'That's what I always do. That's all I ever could do. To think of dear Jamie with a son, and he never knew!'

'But what if I make a mistake?' asked Alice.

'Then you must mend it.' And Isobel sighed, for some mistakes could not be mended. She knew Alice was looking to her for wisdom and comfort, but all she had to offer was age.

'You married once for convenience and once for love,' said Alice abruptly.

'I never did!' said Isobel, offended. 'I married twice for convenience. Once for John's and once for James' and both times for my own.'

'I see,' said Alice drearily. 'You didn't love them.'

'You cannot take a husband unless you make him a lover too,' observed Isobel. 'That's the convenience, you see. Give me my deedbox, Alice - I want to show you some of James' pictures.'

'*Now*?' said Alice.

'Now's the right time. You are a married woman now, so you won't be shocked.'

Alice fetched the deedbox and waited listlessly while her grandmother fumbled it open. She felt cold and hollow and very unhappy. Now she looked at it objectively, she couldn't quite see why she had been so distraught. She had married Joseph to become the mother of the Glen Heather heir. Now it seemed she was the wife of the heir instead. And if that could not be proved, she could be the mother anyway. Perhaps. Either way, she won the draw. 'Damn Glen Heather!' she said suddenly. 'It has caused me nothing but grief.'

Isobel ignored her. She was poring through some papers, sketches and paintings. 'Here is Jennie Christopher,' she said, 'and here is your father as a lad. This is McCleod - and these are all of me.'

Alice was not interested in pictures, but she took them politely - and blushed. 'Granny!' she said in dismay. 'You don't have any - er -'

Isobel twinkled at her. 'James liked painting bare ladies, and I was the only one I'd allow him to see. He always wanted what he shouldn't, James did, and he got me in the end - but he always kept on painting.' Her hands shook a little as she took out another sketch. 'This one was made the day James died,' she said. 'As you can see, he *always* liked bare ladies.' She gave Alice a sly, sideways glance. 'So did John, my dear. In my experience, most gentlemen do.'

'Granny, are you telling me to go to Joseph *and take my clothes off?*'

'I'm telling you nothing,' said Isobel. 'I never give advice. Do you want your husband or not?'

'I don't want a husband. I never did.'

'Do you want your man? Did you give him your word?'

'Granny -'

'Close the door as you leave, child. These autumn days are cold and the nights are colder - unless you have something to keep you warm.'

The gig was still in the yard, so it seemed that Joseph must have left on foot. Alice felt ridiculous driving a gig in her wedding gown, but she clucked up Blackwood and drove as fast as she dared. She had a nasty feeling she might be too late ... once before she had forestalled Joseph before he went through the door of the office - today she had let him leave Isobel's cottage without a protest. She must catch up with him now and see if anything could be salvaged from the marriage that had hardly begun.

She sighed as she considered Isobel's advice. No doubt it had worked for Isobel, but no modern woman would think of doing such a thing - it would be a betrayal of all that women had striven for since the end of the Victorian age. No longer frail flowers who needed a man to be head of their house and give them something to live for - Alice had proved that, had she not? She had known a husband would unnecessarily complicate her life. And she was right. She'd had a husband less than two hours and look what had happened already! But she was a woman of her word, and she had given her word and now she would keep it.

She overtook Joseph in the dusk, a hundred yards from the Glen Heather gate. 'Get in,' she said briefly.

'Orders, Alice?'

'A request. I made a fool of myself back there, so I am requesting your help in putting things right.'

Joseph looked up at her for a few seconds and she thought he was going to refuse. 'You look like a ghost in that gown, Alice,' he said.

'I feel like a ghost,' she said ruefully.

Joseph climbed up beside her and held his hat in his lap. He did not make any move to touch her.

Alice handed the pony and gig to a grinning Timothy at the stable and turned to Joseph. 'Come into the house and change your clothes. We shall feel more ourselves when we're in our proper clothes, I expect. Ivory satin and morning dress are not ... not ...' She lost the thread of what she was saying and fell silent, picking up her wide skirts and walking up the path to the house. 'Dear God, I feel like a tea-cosy! But come into the parlour,' she said, 'and make yourself at home. How foolish that sounds, for of course, you *are* at home. I have had your things fetched from the cottage and they are in my father's dressing room. Your dressing room, now, if you want it. If you decide to stay with me after my - unseemly outburst.'

'Alice, you are babbling,' said Joseph.

'I know,' said Alice sadly. Hoping for a sense of normality, she dressed in her old skirt and blouse, and emerged to find Joseph also back in his usual outfit. He was standing by the fireplace, looking up at the portraits. 'Auld Hector and Grannie Ness,' said Alice, and bit her lip. 'Our great grandparents, Joseph. These two are my Grandfather John and Granny. They were all painted by James Galbraith - Granny's second husband. And these two are my father and mother - studio photographs, as you can see.' She paused, but he was silent and she thought she couldn't blame him. 'If - if we decide to stay together we must have our portraits too. I would like to stay with you, Joseph. I was very, very foolish just now and I am sorry.'

'At least you came back,' said Joseph. 'But that begs the question - why will you stay with me? For yourself or for Glen Heather?'

'Damn Glen Heather,' said Alice wearily.

'You don't mean that, but I still have every intention of staying with you, Alice, so let's say no more about it.'

'I wish I could *think* no more about it.' She felt nervous and depressed, and she wanted comfort. 'Joseph,' she said desperately, 'do you remember what you said last night in the cottage? That you wanted me to stay? Why did you send me away?'

'I thought you might have your way with me and leave, and jilt me at the altar.'

'I would have had my way with you and stayed and married you today. And now I'd not be scared half to death of what I nearly did and what I have to do. I wish it was last night again. Oh dear - Dr Llewellyn would *not* approve of this if he knew.'

'Of what?'

'Of cousins marrying. He says it is unwise.'

'We are not so much related,' said Joseph. 'Never fear - they'll not cry incest on us.'

A bell rang from the dining room, and Joseph gave her a doubtful look.

'It's dinner time,' said Alice, but she was not very hungry. 'I have often wished Rosalind and Mother would not *talk* so at dinner,' she added when Maisie had cleared the covers, 'but you seem to have taken matters to the other extreme. I have said I am sorry. Why are you looking at me like that?'

'You look very tired, Alice,' said Joseph.

'I am. We should probably sit down and work out how we are going to do this. Shall we go to Mr Bertram or ...?'

'Alice, we have weeks to work out anything that needs working out. It's time we went to bed.'

'Are you asking me or ordering me?'

'I am making a suggestion, which is all I shall ever do.' He looked at her steadily and it was her gaze which dropped first.

It was strange, leading Joseph into the guestroom. Properly speaking, Mary should have moved out of the master bedroom, but Alice had hardly liked to suggest it to her. 'My own bed isn't big enough for two,' she said in explanation. 'I hope -'

'What do you hope?' asked Joseph curiously.

'Do you know, I have no idea!' said Alice. 'I suppose I hope you won't be disappointed.'

'Why should I be disappointed? You'll not rage and storm at me again.'

'No. I am entirely sensible now.' Alice took off her shoes. 'You might be disappointed when you see me without my deplorable clothes. I'm rather deplorable myself.' She pulled the pins out of her hair.

'I doubt that, really I do,' said Joseph. He moved over behind her, lifted her hair and kissed the back of her neck. With the sourness of his deceit and her violent reaction still between them, he expected her to move away, but though she stiffened at his touch she stood her ground. 'A woman of her word, is Alice McKenzie,' he murmured.

'I try to be,' she said in a hollow voice.

'Would you rather wait a while?' he asked. 'It has been a trying day.'

'No - go ahead. I - I want you to.' She turned her head to look at him and he saw uncertainty in her eyes.

He kissed her neck again; breathing in the warm scent of freshly washed hair, and then slipped his hands around to stroke her breasts through the blouse. She had liked that last night, he thought. Not all women liked the same caresses, and he supposed it was a matter of trial and error to discover the right way to pleasure a particular woman. He could hardly ask her what she would enjoy, for no respectable woman would have enough experience to know. He squeezed gently and she flinched, but whether he had hurt her or whether she was embarrassed or shrinking from his touch, he couldn't tell. He rather thought she was biting her lip, steeling herself for what was coming. Perhaps he should ask her after all.

'You've never had a man before,' he murmured into her hair.

'No. I told you that.'

'I've never had a wife before,' he said pensively.

'There's always a first time,' observed Alice.

'Yes indeed.' He slid his hands down her ribs to her waist and pulled the blouse gently away from her skirt. The skin underneath was warm, and he could feel the edge of some kind of bodice. 'What do you call this?' he asked, striving for a touch of humour. 'Is it a step-in?'

'No, it's a camisole,' said Alice.

'How does it unfasten?'

'With hooks and eyes. If you want me to take it off, I'll take it off, but don't pull!'

'Ouch,' said Joseph, dropping his hands. So much for that approach.

Alice eyed him uncertainly. 'I am sorry,' she said. 'I am so very sorry.'

'So am I. What's it to be, Alice? Shall I go back to the cottage? Or perhaps I should sleep in the dressing-room - for tonight, anyway.'

'No - don't go. I didn't mean to be rude, but the straps are too narrow - they were cutting into my shoulders.' As if to prove her words, she took off the blouse and turned her back to remove the camisole. 'There will be no more nonsense,' she said.

'Oh yes there will,' he said sternly, 'there will be a great deal of nonsense. I have my pride and I *will* not be treated as an - an inconvenience with whom you must bear for the sake of keeping your word.'

There *were* faint red marks on her shoulders and he bent to kiss them, sliding his hands around. He felt her heart rate beginning to pick up and rejoiced. That was one response which could not be faked. Despite what he had said to her the night before, he was well aware that embraces were not always what they seemed. Any harlot worth her salt knew how to make a man feel skilled - what even the best of them lacked was the ability to make a man feel loved. He was married to Alice, for her convenience and his pride, but if this were not to feel like a legal prostitution he must win some response beyond complaisance.

'What do you think you'd like?' he whispered, kissing her temple.

'To go to bed,' said Alice. 'It's cold.' She stepped away and out of her skirt and untied her petticoat, hesitated over the cami knickers and took them off as well before turning towards the bed.

Alice knew she was being stiff and impossible, but there didn't seem to be anything she could do about it. She wished Joseph had not sent her away the night before. She had wanted him then. Tonight, with the blessing of Kirk and society, the confrontation at Isobel's had come between them. No matter how much she told herself it did not matter that Joseph was of Jamie Campbell's line, she could only feel the hurt that she had not known, that she had gone on striving and worrying over something lost that Joseph had known forever. If she had asked him directly, would he have told her then? Probably, but why should she ever have asked?

Perhaps the revelation would make no practical difference, and she still would need a son, but tonight she could feel little but impatience to be done with it. Obviously, Joseph was still prepared to fulfil his part of the bargain. He would give her a son if he could, and help her keep Glen Heather. But she knew she must give him something in exchange, and he had said he wanted her. But why? Because she was Alice, or because she was the lady of Glen Heather? Times were changing, but a woman's property would still be popularly regarded as her husband's - despite what Joseph had said, was it really Glen Heather he wanted? As the father of her bastard child, he would have had no real rights. As an unproved grandson of Jamie Campbell he might have been an object of suspicion. But as her husband, he had many rights, including the right to her loyalty, her body - and her love.

If he *did* want Glen Heather, he was no worse than she, but at least she had been honest with him about her purpose. Forgetting her nakedness, she turned to catch him in a betraying expression - and froze.

Joseph was staring at her in lively astonishment. In her working clothes, Alice was a dowdy. In her Sunday best, she was smart and a little forbidding. In her grandmother's wedding gown she had been a sad and frightened ghost. But dressed in nothing at all, she was simply breath-taking, and he couldn't believe his luck.

'What is it?' she asked, turning back the quilt and he sensed that she, too, was striving for balance. 'Am I really so deplorable?'

'Deplorable! Alice McKenzie, you are the most beautiful thing I have ever seen.'

Something in his face must have convinced her he meant what he said, for a doubtful smile flickered. 'Well, well,' she said, 'perhaps Granny was right after all.'

Joseph wondered what she meant, but she was looking at him expectantly, so he took off his clothes and climbed into bed beside her. She *was* cold - he could feel the gooseflesh under his hands, but after a few moments he forgot the uncertainties of the day and revelled in his voyage of discovery.

Alice was a little shocked, the next morning, to recall how much she had enjoyed her husband's attentions after all. She had thought he would never kiss her as Reggie had, but he had done that and much more, and she had not only allowed him but had actively participated. At some point in the proceedings, she forgot the revelation that brought such grief and lost herself completely in his warmth and surety. And then she had gone to sleep.

It seemed strange, to be in bed with another person, and she lay for a while in silence, hardly daring to move in case she woke Joseph. She looked at his face, unguarded in sleep, and shivered, although she wasn't cold. How could she be cold when he was there beside her? His name might be McKenzie, and he might look like his long ago grandmother, but he was thrawn and proud and tenacious as the veriest Campbell of them all. Auld Hector would have been proud of Joseph, and so would Grannie Ness. Thrawn and proud - independent and loving. He could have taken her last night as a prize, he could have vented all his years of frustration on her. Instead, he had given her love and warmth and she realised now she had given the same things to him.

Joseph had said he thought her beautiful, and his hands and mouth had told her he hadn't lied. Now she realised that she found him beautiful as well. Beauty need not attract the eyes - it could come through the ears and fingertips, through a mingling of tongues and the taste of shared sweat and a lifetime spent together. James Galbraith had found Isobel beautiful at twenty-one, at forty and at fifty. No doubt if he had been still alive he would have considered her beautiful still.

So Isobel had been right - again.

If a lady took a husband for convenience, she must take him as a lover as well and be his lover in return. Anything else was unworthy of a lady - and of a Campbell.

Joseph might well give her a son, but that was in the future. For now she would forget their future and make their present as fine as she could. The years lay ahead, green as the flank of the mountain. Tears would fall like the flowing burns and sunlight sparkle on the brae. The thorns and stones would be there in life and so would the crimson heath.

Her husband moved restlessly, turning towards her, and she reached out in silence and settled him to her shoulder. Her breast touched his cheek and he sighed, nestling against it as a baby might. Alice drew in a long breath to ease the strange constriction that seemed to clench around her heart. Loving was going to be a painful thing; like the thorny heath it must be bravely grasped or let alone. A tear ran down her temple at the thought of what she might have missed - of what she had tried so hard to avoid, and Joseph opened his eyes.

He seemed a little surprised to find himself cheek to cheek with a bare breast - and why not? 'You've never woken like this before,' she observed.

'Never,' he agreed. 'Is this part of your bargain?'

Alice pushed him away and sat up abruptly. 'It is not,' she said. 'It was *no* part of my bargain to have you use me as a - a pillow! It was *no* part of my bargain to start loving you, either, but it looks like I'm stuck with both. Just as you're stuck with me, and Glen Heather, and McCleod, forever.'

Joseph looked up at her hopefully. 'Am I not such a complication as you feared, Alice?'

'You're worse. You're thrawn. You're sleekit. You're deplorable. And some of the things you did with me last night were ... *indescribable.* Well, Mr McKenzie? Have you nothing to say?'

'Plenty,' said Joseph, 'but more to do. I love you, Alice.'

'You see?' said Alice to the ceiling. 'Thrawn, as I said. Thrawn, just like all the Campbells. Thrawn, just like ... Joseph - what *do* you think you're trying to do?'

Joseph paused. 'Not trying. Doing. Do you want the polite term for it, Mrs McKenzie?'

'I have no use for polite terms,' said Alice coldly, but her smile was lighting the morning.

'Just as well,' said her husband, 'because, so far as I'm aware, there *isn't* one.'

ABOUT THE AUTHOR

Sally Odgers was born in Tasmania, where she grew up hearing tales of the early days. Some proved apocryphal, but they helped give her a love of a good story. Sally and her husband Darrel have two children and two grandchildren. They live with books, music and a lot of Jack Russells, an ancestor of whom inspired the Jack Russell: Dog Detective series. Sally also runs a small manuscript assessment and editing service.

More Great Releases from Satalyte Publishing

Langue [dot] doc 1305

Gillian Polack

LANGUE[DOT]DOC 1305

GILLIAN POLACK

There are people involved.
That's the first mistake.

Scientists were never meant to be part of history. Anything in the past is better studied from the present.

It's safer.

When a team of Australian scientists – and a lone historian – travel back to St-Guilhem-le-Désert in 1305 they discover being impartial, distant and objective just doesn't work when you're surrounded by the smells, dust and heat of a foreign land.

They're only human after all.

But by the time Artemisia is able to convince others that it's time to worry, it's already too late.

'Viscerally powerful, deeply felt, strongly written: Langue[dot]doc 1305 challenges reader expectations of time travel, of 'Grim-dark' and of mediaeval life and brings a haunting, authentic voice both to the past and to the struggles facing the present.'
~ Kari Sperring, author of Living With Ghosts

Available at all good book stores in
both paperback and ebook formats.

Printed in Australia
AUOC02n1114050515
267394AU00001B/1/P